Dead Men Don't Eat Lunch

This story is dedicated to my mother, Patricia Louise Gilson
(December 7th, 1926 – October 24th, 1999)
She never stopped believing

Geoffrey Gilson

Dead Men Don't Eat Lunch

....

Geoffrey Gilson

Geoffrey Gilson

DEAD MEN DON'T EAT LUNCH, Copyright © 2004 by Peter Geoffrey Gilson. All rights reserved. ISBN 978-1-304-87301-9. Printed in the United States of America. No part of this book may be used or reproduced in any manner whatsoever without written permission except in the case of brief quotations embodied in critical articles or reviews. E-mail: thatcherarmscorruption@gmail.com.

Dead Men Don't Eat Lunch

Acknowledgments

IF I TRIED to thank everyone who has helped to bring this work to fruition, I'd miss someone. And then I'd feel awful. You all know who you are. And you all know how I feel about you. Thank you.

There are three individuals, however, whom I will single out. And of the three, the first is the most important: my twin sister, Maggi. Then, there are my almost-ghostwriter, Simon Regan (now deceased), and Hugh's father, John Simmonds (also deceased).

There were many times I doubted myself. These three were always there to see me through. Primarily you, Maggi. If this book in any way defines me, it is because you showed me the way. I do not have the eloquence to do proper justice to the gratitude and love I truly feel. But, thank you.

Geoffrey Gilson
Chapel Hill, 2006

Geoffrey Gilson

Dead Men Don't Eat Lunch

Geoffrey Gilson

Dead Men Don't Eat Lunch

For now we see through a glass, darkly;
But then face to face: now I know in part;
But then shall I know even as also I am known.

Corinthians I, 13

Geoffrey Gilson

Dead Men Don't Eat Lunch

Prologue

IN NOVEMBER OF 1988, at the age of 32, living in the same small English town that I'd lived in all of my life, I considered myself to be a reasonably ordinary guy, going about a reasonably ordinary life.

I had met Hugh Simmonds as we fenced with each other on the local political scene in our mutual home town of Beaconsfield, Buckinghamshire. We became close friends, and set about our rise through the ranks of the British Conservative Party, then led by the redoubtable Margaret Thatcher.

We both shared the same ambition to become Members of Parliament, mine being a step or two behind Hugh's because of our nine year age difference. Hugh then managed to screw up a couple of opportunities in safe Conservative Parliamentary seats. So, while waiting for his third chance, he set up his own law practice in Beaconsfield, and I became his senior employee. Like I say, an ordinary guy, leading an ordinary life.

Then, that fateful November morning, I found myself staring down at Hugh's dead body, in the clearing of some local woods, and I couldn't for the life of me work out why he might have committed suicide. But, that's where weird only began to begin. Back at the law office, I discovered that some £5 million ($7.5 million) was missing from the firm's Clients' Account.

I was devastated by Hugh's death. Confused by the apparent theft. And concerned for his children, who were left with no suicide note. All of these would have been good reasons to want to know the truth behind Hugh's death. And indeed, they proved to be. Not least, my desire to find an answer for his children. But the primary reason I started poking around was much more prosaic – I needed to clear my name.

Society needed a scapegoat – who was alive. I fit the bill. My response was to ask questions. And that's when I was launched onto my rollercoaster adventure of international mystery and intrigue, an odyssey which has lasted 18 years so far. As innocuous as I thought my questions to be, they provoked a powerful response in very high places – all around the globe.

I was shot at, chased through the streets, warned off by the CIA, and threatened by Israeli and British Intelligence Officers. Two British Prime Ministers and a couple of US Presidents ran scared. Even the FBI lied to me. Blatantly. But not before I discovered that Hugh was a senior officer in and a contract assassin for MI6 (Britain's equivalent of the CIA); that he was mixed up with illegal arms deals with Iraq; that he laundered money for Mrs. T's wayward son, Mark – now Sir Mark; and…

But, I get ahead of myself. For the moment, let's just go back to the beginning…

Chapter 1

'SO. THAT'S WHAT a dead body looks like.'

I tried to think of something more sensitive to feel. But, I wasn't feeling very sensitive at all. In fact, I wasn't feeling very much of anything. My mind was completely numb. The only thing it could register was that I'd never seen a dead body before.

***

I'm just an ordinary guy. And it was just another very ordinary day. The Government should issue Health Warnings for 'ordinary' days that change the course of your life. Certainly, I would have appreciated an alarm bell or two on that seemingly inauspicious day, November 15th, 1988.

I collected the post, as I always did, at 8.15am from the Beaconsfield Post Office, and opened the law offices of Simmonds and Company at 8.30a.m. The proprietor, Hugh Simmonds, was not in, but this had become increasingly common since he started his own Wine Bar company, City Jeroboam Ltd., in 1986.

The staff of Simmonds and Company arrived at about 9.00am, followed closely by the Directors of City Jeroboam. There was a Board Meeting of City Jeroboam scheduled for that morning. Martin Pratt, a close friend of Hugh's and one of the Directors of City Jeroboam, came into my office shortly before 10.00am and asked if I knew where Hugh was. I replied, with a nod and a wink, that if he was this late he was probably visiting his mistress, Karen George.

Shortly after this conversation, Jill, the receptionist, rang through to say that she had a hoax caller on the telephone. She wanted me to deal with it. The caller said that he was a Police Constable and that the Police had found one of our shared company cars with a dead body in it. It appeared to be a case of suicide. At first, I was somewhat skeptical but, since he persisted, I agreed to meet him at the local woods where he said the car had been discovered.

I arrived at the spot and was directed to the scene by another Policeman. It was only as I got out of the car that I realized I'd never seen a dead body before. I had no idea what sort of grisly spectacle to expect. I mentioned this to the Police standing nearby. They were very understanding and explained that the body would simply look like someone had fallen asleep. I wasn't going to be in for a nasty shock. In this prediction, they would prove to be only half correct.

***

I entered the woods, coming across the small company car quite quickly. Perhaps too quickly. Looking back over my shoulder, I noticed that the car was sitting, all on its own, in a clearing, which, at a certain angle, could be seen quite clearly from the road. The thought swiftly passed through my mind that anyone wanting to commit suicide in this particular location would have had trouble with inquisitive passers-by.

That thought was quickly snuffed out by my first glimpse of the motionless body in the car. I couldn't see any facial features, but the clothes were the same ones that Hugh had been wearing the night before.

I've always heard that shock causes everything to slow down. At that moment, the world around me seemed to float along in silent slow motion. The birds may have been singing, but I didn't notice. All I could hear was the thumping of my own heart and the swish of my feet through the long, frost-covered grass.

I spent some minutes just circling the car at a distance, working up the courage to glance inside. Sunlight filtering through the gently swaying trees danced and bounced off the metal and glass. My breath formed little clouds in the crisp November air.

Finally, I strode up to the driver's side and crouched down using the door for support. Where the Policeman had been right was that Hugh simply looked as if he had fallen asleep. His head was leant back over the upright seat, his arms dangling gently between his legs. Save for the open mouth, and the half-closed and lifeless eyes, he could just have been having a nap.

I noticed a heavy book lying on the floor next to the accelerator pedal and a length of garden hose on the back seat.

That was when the shock hit me. I wanted to feel something. But I didn't know what, or where, or how. All I knew was that my very best friend was gone, and I couldn't for the life of me work out why.

The scene was lifeless. The air was still. His body was clay. And my mind was ice. Then, as I glanced once more at his immobile face, the whole frozen façade shattered like a dome of many-colored glass.

Dead Men Don't Eat Lunch

***

On the face of it, Hugh John Simmonds, CBE. was the epitome of Eighties' Thatcherite ambition. Forty years of age, tall, dark and handsome; a cross between Pierce Brosnan and Dan Ackroyd, on their good days. He was top heavy with charm and charisma, and used both shamelessly to fill his bed with a seemingly endless supply of conquests.

But life was not all play for Hugh. He balanced pleasure with a serious commitment to serve in Margaret Thatcher's Cabinet, before she concluded her time as Britain's most radical, right-wing Prime Minister.

For seventeen years, his life had been a calculated agenda, artfully designed to bring him to Parliament as a Conservative M.P. in early middle age. From a prep school background, at age 27, he had become a partner with Wedlake Bell, a small and exclusive firm of London solicitors.

The following year, he served as Mayor of Beaconsfield, his and my home town in the rural County of Buckinghamshire. He married Janet, the nearest thing to a childhood sweetheart that he could find. Small, slightly dumpy, with an elfin face and brunette hair, and an absolute wizard at organizing an office.

Hugh religiously paid his dues on the British equivalent of the political chicken circuit, putting in 17 hour days as he kissed babies, charmed old ladies and arranged for various local government departments to fix his constituents' sewers and potholes.

In the General Election of 1979, the Election which first brought Margaret Thatcher to power, he served the obligatory stint as a losing Conservative Party Parliamentary Candidate in a safe Labour seat. A grim and grimy seat called West Leeds. Hugh did, however, manage the distinction of achieving the largest swing to a Conservative Candidate in the entire North of England. No small success in Leeds, a decaying leftover from Britain's industrial greatness.

This put him in excellent stead to be awarded a safe seat, and indeed, he landed one of the five safest in 1983. True, he was then de-selected from South-West Cambridge because Janet opposed fox-hunting; the Cambridge Hunt being one of the oldest in Great Britain.

He then doubled his misfortune by being de-selected from another safe Conservative seat, South Warrington, in 1987. On this occasion, his illegitimate son was the stumbling block. But these were the Energetic Eighties. Cabinet Ministers had fathered children out of wedlock and became Foreign Secretary. Hugh's hiccups were no more than colorful episodes in his burgeoning biography. And a variety of different paths to political success lay just another hiccup away.

In 1988, he was still one of Thatcher's favorite speechwriters; the youngest ever recipient of the C.B.E. (one notch below Knighthood); and a sometime and hugely respected member of the Party's National Committee.

He had used his 'sabbatical' to establish his own law practice in Beaconsfield; he was developing City Jeroboam, a company that then owned five wine bars and a pub, and had a turnover of several million pounds; and in the previous six months, he had been negotiating a loan of £25 million ($37 million), with which to buy 100 pubs from Whitbread.

Wealth and political fame lay just around the corner. So why kill himself?

I had no time to consider the answer. I was fast approaching the outskirts of Beaconsfield, and had no idea to whom or how to bear the ill tidings. His mother seemed a good place to start.

***

Beaconsfield was typical of the stockbroker suburbs dotted in the Green Belt surrounding London. Overly large houses, in undersized plots. Lots of trees and pubs, virtually no racial mixing, and none of the urban problems prevalent just 30 miles away.

Beaconsfield had a rich history as an ancient market town, on the crossroads of two of England's oldest highways. It had a 700 year old street fair and an 'Old Town' that looked as if it had come straight out of a back lot from a Hollywood period movie.

'Dormitory' was the technical description used by the Census Bureau, but 'sleepy' is how Beaconsfield liked to think of itself. You went to work in London, you came home, shut the door and ignored the rest of the world.

Hugh's parents, John and Gwen Simmonds, lived in a comfortable manse on one of the sleepier cul-de-sacs, just a couple of streets away from Hugh. Their only son liked to affect an upper-crust south of England heritage, but Hugh's parents' rolling burr of an accent gave the game away. Both were non-fussy genteel folk, clearly hailing from solid north-of-England stock.

John Simmonds, whose short frame and sandy hair bore little physical resemblance to Hugh, was a self-made man. He had helped to develop the early radar, which protected Britain from the hordes of German bombers in the Second World War. He had established a string of small but successful civil engineering firms, and had served as President of the National Institute of Electrical Engineers. Hugh claimed that he had been offered but had refused a knighthood.

Gwen Simmonds, known to her friends as "Lyn," was a short, busy lady, with facial features that were a dead ringer for Hugh's, and later her first grand-daughter, Juliet. Lyn didn't spend too much time at home, which more often than not was empty, what with Hugh being the only child, and

Dead Men Don't Eat Lunch

John spending so much of his time staying over at his Gentleman's Club in London.

But she answered the door that morning, as I stood nervously in front of her, not knowing how to break the news. A couple of false starts, a quick outburst, and a half bottle of brandy later, and we were in the main sitting room, comforting each other with silence.

"I don't get it,' I blurted out, "why would he kill himself?" We'd already determined from his Harley Street doctor that he hadn't picked up a terminal nasty from his exotic sex life. "It can't have been about money; he had all that money he made trading Ferranti stock."

"What money?" came the gentle response. "The Ferranti stock was his father's, to be left to the grandchildren, Juliet and Tanya. Hugh didn't have a penny. In fact, he had to borrow £400,000 ($600,000) from his father just a couple of years ago."

Oops.

I needed to get back to the office. Fast. Lyn agreed to do the honors with Hugh's wife, Janet, and help to collect the kids from school. I wasn't one of Janet's favorites, and she needed someone she would feel comfortable sobbing against. I headed back to the looming disaster.

Before pulling out of the driveway, I paused for a moment, and risked one more glance back at the front door. Lyn stood there, dwarfed by the huge oak frame, hugging herself tightly. The bustling matron was long gone. All I saw now was a frail old lady, forcing a smile into her face, as the light slowly died in her eyes. Her only child was dead.

***

It didn't take long to confirm the worst. Waiting for me at the office was a representative from the Law Society, the national equivalent of a State Bar Association. Chap bore a distinct resemblance to Uriah Heep, all bone, gristle and six feet tall, with a few hairs greased over a balding pate.

Clients were complaining about not being able to get their money. Is there a problem, came Uriah's smarmy enquiry. Not unless a dead body constitutes a 'problem,' came the equally smart-ass response. Pleasantries aside, we quickly ascertained that the law firm's Clients' Account was shy about a million pounds, and that this had gone 'shy' in the past year and a half.

So, that was that. Bastard. He'd got bored with waiting for Parliament, blew a bunch of pocket change and scampered, leaving the rest of us to pick up the pieces. Not very nice, but actually, not all that surprising.

The rest of the day was a slow-motion swirl, fuelled by regular visits to the bottle of vodka one of the secretaries rescued for me. Curtains were pulled, curtains were opened. People came, people left. And the City

Geoffrey Gilson

Jeroboam Board stayed closeted in the conference room all day, wringing their hands in total, useless despair.

Even more clueless was Hugh's close buddy and sometime business partner, the aforementioned Martin Pratt. Hugh had a weakness when it came to extended families. Martin was a poster boy for fat and seedy, 30 going on 50. It was a toss-up as to which battle he'd lose first: the one with his waistline, or the one with his hairline. He quarantined himself in his small corner office, darting out from time to time, with the strangest expression on his face, before disappearing again, to get even more drunk than me.

I was left to comfort Hugh's mistress, Karen, who had burst into the office wailing, crying and bemoaning the fact that Hugh would not now be fulfilling his promise to move in with her and their 2 year old son, Paul. Hugh had begun an affair with Karen, who was one of England's leading show jumpers and horse trainers, after the loss of South-West Cambridge, in 1984. She too was small, a little dumpy, with an elfin face, but blond hair.

John Simmonds visited long enough to declare that there was nothing he could do. And then we played games with the curtains again. What the hell was the deal? I just didn't want the whole of Beaconsfield peering into a dead man's office.

At last, darkness fell. Everyone left. I was on my own. My twin sister, Maggi, arrived from London. She was visiting from Australia, helping to promote a play for a guy who wrote a couple of the episodes for the TV version of *Mission Impossible*.

Maggi is a little smaller than me, with a full figure, a boyish cut to her hair, John Lennon glasses, and a sweet, pixie face. That's how I always think of her, as a wood nymph, one of Peter Pan's mischievous pals.

She had never liked Hugh. She was repulsed by his cocksure chauvinism and his arrogant amiability. However, she had responded immediately to my telephoned plea for support, which was itself out of character for me. All my life, I had regarded myself as far too self-sufficient to need help of any kind, let alone emotional attention. Yet, here I was openly embracing it, and from Maggi of all people.

Notwithstanding the fact that we were twins, I had never considered us to be very much alike. We didn't look alike. And I could find little that we had in common, save for our birth date. She was artistic; I was a material cynic. She was definitely Venus; I was undoubtedly Mars. She was one in harmony with all the world's dimensions; while I was restless and unsatisfied, driven to experience all the world's glittering prizes. Bless her heart, she'd had good reason, on many occasions, to think of me as little more than a self-promoting poseur. And yet, she had dropped everything to come and be with me.

She sat down opposite me and encouraged me to talk. I was pretty

Dead Men Don't Eat Lunch

brusque. I didn't have the time. There was a mess to clean up. She insisted. Gently. Eventually, we got to the point. I couldn't escape the vision of Hugh driving past my apartment, on his way to those lonely woods, and not stopping and asking me to pick up the pieces, one last time.

"I mean, all I can see...he's in his car, going past the office, past my apartment...all alone. He didn't stop...he didn't come in and talk to me. He could have come in...and talked to me. What was so bad that he couldn't come in and talk to me...?"

I sucked in a long breath, and stared deep into my twin sister's eyes, as much to avoid her as to see her. I continued in a monotone made lifeless by my despair.

"He drove straight past me, and there was nothing I could do. He went to his death alone. I just see him dying so terribly alone..."

"Now, I understand," she said, so very softly I almost missed it.

I looked up. "What?"

"All the way here on the train, he was nagging me." Maggi was serious in her claim to have a psychic streak. "He kept saying, over and over, tell him it's ok, tell him I'm fine, he's not to worry."

My hands went limp in hers. "But, I wasn't there for him."

"Oh yes you were," was her immediate yet soft retort, "And he knows that. And whatever happens from now on, he'll be there for you. Always. For the rest of your life."

The day's self-control finally snapped. In the privacy of Hugh's personal office, in the safety of my twin sister's protective embrace, the emotional dam burst. I collapsed into her arms and cried. The confidence and arrogance were gone. In their place, the simple and honest anguish of a shattered human soul.

***

After what seemed an eternity, we separated. She went to make some coffee. With everyone else gone from the office, I wandered about, gently gathering files and records that I hadn't shared earlier with the Law Society. I'd had no cause to worry beforehand. Hugh was rich after all, right? But now, I wanted a more careful calculation of what had been going on the past year and a half.

The answer chilled me to my roots. There was some £5 million ($7.5 million) missing. There was no way Hugh had spent this over a year and a half. It would have amounted to throwing away £40,000 ($60,000) a week.

That's when I had a sudden vision of blinding clarity. It was the look on Martin's face. I had finally identified it. It wasn't shock, surprise or even anger. Those would have been understandable. It had been fear. Cold, naked, unreasoning fear.

Perhaps if at that point I had listened to the voice that was beginning to nag in my mind, I would have avoided what was to come. I would have continued with my ordinary life. But would I truly have wanted that?

Chapter 2

Hugh should have been an actor. Take away his stories of personal wealth, and what you were left with was a life that was one hell of an act. He was the 'almost' man; the 'not quite' guy.

He wasn't quite the gentleman. He had the tailored suits, the law firm, the fancy car, and membership in the Reform Club. But he was really from the wrong side of the tracks. His father was self-made, and maybe Hugh resented this. All of this. Both the fact that his father was a financial success, and the fact that he was cut from the wrong cloth for Hugh's ambitions.

It was as if Hugh was always trying to prove himself, but was never quite making the grade. His favorite trick was regularly snatching victory from the jaws of defeat, and then just as regularly, tossing it straight back into the slavering jaws.

He could talk himself out of any situation, but never saw the impossibility of the mess he was creating, a mess he normally left me to clean up. He was great at employing successful tactics, but could never grasp the larger, strategic picture.

Hugh believed he could do anything. He was ruthlessly ambitious, and wholly single-minded about achieving an objective, whatever the cost. This is why I'd been attracted to him. I had no political background to my family. He was going somewhere I wanted to be. And I was having my own success in his wake, in elections and in the Party, up to and including the national level.

He never thought twice about cutting corners. And maybe this was the problem. Maybe he'd grown restless at having spent 17 years with a political game plan, that was now on hold, but which in the meantime, had sidetracked him from emulating, or exceeding, his father's monetary success.

This then was the theory that quickly took hold with friend and foe alike, and which was splattered all over England's national press. Namely that Hugh, fabulously talented, but flawed young Conservative star, had emptied his firm's Clients' Account, in the single largest defalcation in the history of the Law Society, to finance some 'get-rich-quick' scheme, that then went wrong. Most everyone was agreed that he hadn't just spent the money; that there was some 'investment.'

That's where everyone else left it, but not me. They had an answer for his death: the missing money. But I didn't have an answer for the money going missing. I had no illusions about Hugh's character. No rosy-tinted spectacles for this boy. I knew better. And what I knew left two burning questions in my mind about the allegedly stolen money: why hadn't Hugh run away with it, and why had he thought he could get away with it in the first place?

***

Leaving aside his innate belief that he could accomplish absolutely anything, Hugh was not stupid. The bank accounts of sole practicing solicitors in England are rigorously controlled by the Law Society. Hugh would have known that there was no way that he could have hidden from them, and from his personal accountant, the fact that money had been removed from his sacrosanct Clients' account for his own personal use.

The crime is not failing to hide it, or being a little bit lax, the crime is taking even one red penny from that holy of holies, the Clients' Account. The crime would ultimately have been detected. It would have quickly been followed by disbarment and national disgrace.

Hugh's whole life, his career, his being, his very essence, was based upon perception. The perception that he was unassailable. Hugh would never have done anything to put that in jeopardy, unless he knew his back was covered. He would not have taken that very first red penny unless he was convinced, not only that he could put it back, but that he could do so without anyone ever raising a query. Hence my point: what could possibly have convinced Hugh that he would be able successfully to sidestep the Law Society?

Alright, something did go wrong. He was discovered, he did face universal opprobrium, and so, went the standard version, he took the cheap way out. Hmm. Wrong. I don't deny that Hugh could be cheap. But I knew enough about Hugh to know, beyond any doubt, that this would not have been his first choice of 'cheap way out.' He'd have flown the coop. Done a Ronnie Biggs. Gone to Argentina, got a local girl pregnant, and snubbed his nose at all and sundry.

But surely all the money was gone? Wrong. We knew it wasn't: months after Hugh's death, there was no sign of any of it. No companies wandering around, saying 'oops, we seem to have someone's investment.'

No receipts, no money trail, nothing. The money had simply disappeared. So, why hadn't Hugh disappeared with it?

In my mind, you needed an answer to these two questions to have a satisfactory explanation for Hugh's death. One hundred and one different theories were advanced, but not one of them came close to satisfying these two criteria. In the absence of satisfaction, and with access still to the office, I did some nosing around of my own.

The first thing I came across was the information that all the bad news had been dumped on Hugh on the same day. The Law Society had telephoned Hugh the day before his death to tell him they were coming that next day to see him. His bank, National Westminster Bank, had called that same Monday to tell him they were foreclosing on all his accounts the following day. And the Police announced that they had begun an investigation of their own that same Monday. What are the odds on such co-incidence?

Unless it wasn't co-incidence. I spoke at some length with one Bernard Goodchild, the Senior Manager in Beaconsfield for NatWest Bank. Seems that he and Hugh had been running a crooked scam for a year before Hugh's death to hide the recurring overdraft on Hugh's Clients' Account, an overdraft caused by Hugh's continuing rape of that Account.

The question wasn't whether or not Bernard should have known something was wrong. Of course he should, and did. There is no doubt in my mind that, had Hugh survived, both he and Bernard would have been occupying the same dock, on much the same criminal charges.

The question wasn't whether or not it was wise for Bernard to pull the plug, and foreclose on Hugh's Clients' Account with NatWest. Of course it was. Indeed, it would have been much more sensible for Bernard never to have wedged the plug into the hole in the first place – by conniving with Hugh to allow that Account to become so overdrawn in the previous year.

No. The real question was what was it that had inspired Bernard apparently to get the terminal willies on that specific day, at the same time as the Law Society and the Police? Had there been some universal protection for Hugh that on that particular day had been removed?

***

This was all wonderful fancy, guaranteed to cause intellectual indigestion, but was there anything circumstantial, within my own personal knowledge, that might give any credence to any of the fancies? And the answer came there, his health.

Hugh was in the bloom of vigor and fitness until May of 1988. Then, he fell mysteriously ill, with all the symptoms of what was then described as 'Yuppie Flu.' Simply put, a weakening of the Immune System, brought about by work-induced stress.

This condition progressively worsened, with moments of recession, up to the day of his death. We didn't worry too much about it because Hugh had us convinced that his Harley Street doctor, Dr. Richard Cooper, had it all under control. However, when I spoke to Richard from Lyn's house, on the day of Hugh's death, he denied having spoken to or seen Hugh for over a year before his death. Ok. No mystery there.

What, however, was strange was that, while Hugh was merrily emptying his Clients' Account, beginning in about April 1987, through to May of 1988, both he and his Immune System seemed to be gaily untroubled by all the repercussions that would befall him from the general direction of the Law Society, the Police, et al. Unless, he truly believed that there were to be no consequences, because he had this all-singing, all-dancing protective cover.

But what, you might say, if he had some sort of wonderful constitution that was simply able to put up with all manner of stress. Ok, but why then the sudden change in May 1988? Trust me. You had to be there. This wasn't a progressive wearing down. One day he was up, the next day it was the abyss, and there he stayed until he died.

This all suggests to me something big and powerful to keep him up all those months, and to keep some fairly big hounds at bay, followed by something equally mean and powerful to change the whole picture, push those dogs to one side and bring the pack of cards crashing down.

But again, I find myself straying into the world of evidentiary limbo. And in any event, it was all pretty much moot. Early on, the Law Society announced that they were appointing a leading firm of international fraud investigators, Carratu International, to track down the missing money. Everyone was confident that they would succeed in their task fairly quickly, we'd be presented with all of the answers, and the guessing games would be over.

***

So it was that I set about beginning the rest of my life. I had no intention of staying in Beaconsfield. The news of the defalcation was not yet widely known, but it would become so. I had had no part in the attendant crimes, but people are fickle, particularly in a small town, where you've dirtied your laundry in the steaming cauldron of local politics. Lynching had never been practiced in Beaconsfield, and I didn't want to be the first victim of a new tradition.

I had dual British and American citizenship, and so I put together plans for a new life in the Americas. I can't say that I felt particularly proud about this decision. I felt like I was running away from responsibilities. I was particularly torn at the thought of leaving behind Hugh's children, Juliet, Tanya and Paul. I had come to think of myself as their favorite Uncle. But I had to think of me also. Good line that last one. Only took me six months of therapy to learn to say it without breaking down.

The day came for my departure from Britain's shore. As luck would have it, I was scheduled to have lunch that day with John Simmonds. I had kept in touch with him since the day of Hugh's death. He'd had lots of questions. I'd answered them with brutal honesty. He'd stated repeatedly that he was grateful for this. Right. Kind of like being grateful to the surgeon. Oh thank you for the pain, doc. If I roll over, I think you'll find a spot you missed. I guessed he just wanted to say 'thank you' in his own, wonderfully old-fashioned style.

Lunch was nearly concluded when he leaned close and stated matter-of-factly that two gentlemen had come to see him privately, to tell him that Hugh had taken the money from his Clients' Account to help "get an agent out of a foreign country."

With enormous effort, I maintained a steady countenance, and asked if he felt these 'gentlemen' were credible. I was sure John could hear the pounding of my heart. He locked eyes with me. John was a gentle soul, but the fire in his eyes on this occasion was unmistakable. "Absolutely credible," came the stern reply, "but I'm bound not to reveal their identity or their occupation."

John is an experienced scientist. He was not given to flights of fancy or gullibility. Of course he was telling the truth. He was not the sort of person to do otherwise. He was relaying only that which had been told to him, without any contextual knowledge. What I knew and he did not, what I had omitted from all my guesswork to date, was that Hugh, while alive, had been a senior officer within MI6, Britain's equivalent of the CIA.

Geoffrey Gilson

Chapter 3

IT WAS A DULL and overcast Saturday, the sort for which Britain is famous, contrary to its reputation as a green and pleasant land. I had known Hugh just a few months, having met him at some worthy function or another in Beaconsfield in late 1975. He was just a Town Councilor then; I was still a lowly Youth Club leader.

We'd done lunch in one of the older hostelries in the historic part of Beaconsfield, and were now off on a meandering journey through the rural delights of western England. To be precise, the road signs stated that we were approaching the outskirts of Hereford, just a little to the east of the Welsh border.

Drizzle, another British specialty, was just beginning to spray as we pulled up to the doors of one more ancient drinking hole. "Wait here," Hugh commanded, "I'll be back in a minute." And a minute and a half later, he was back, with a small, wrapped package in his hand.

"You seem particularly uncurious," he stated, with an amused twinkle in his eye. I just shrugged, and returned my gaze to the vibrant but soaking wet landscape. I'd got used to episodes of strange goings-on when with Hugh. He made no secret of his involvement with British Intelligence. Seemed a little weird to me. Wasn't this all supposed to be shrouded in secrecy? Why tell me? His retort was always the same. I was his insurance; just in case something happened.

Eventually we stopped in a lay-by, on top of a spectacularly bleak and abandoned hill. We had been there no more than five minutes when an Army Land Rover pulled up behind us. Hugh again told me to stay put. He got out with the package.

He advanced slowly towards the Army vehicle. Three soldiers, in full camouflage got out, two with down-turned rifles. They took up positions on either side of the lay by, facing outward, scanning the surroundings. The third, clearly an Officer of some sort, met up with Hugh. They had a few moments of conversation. Then, just as Hugh was handing over the package, two extremely large and extremely noisy fighter aircraft came out of nowhere, and passed immediately overhead.

Hugh got back into the car, and we drove home. Not a word passed between us, save for one humorous aside from Hugh, "I love it when things go off according to plan."

I later learned that Hereford is the home base for the SAS, the Special Air Service, Britain's elite special forces unit, the one which had so dramatically rescued the hostages from the Iranian Embassy in 1981, on primetime national television.

***

I could fill a book with similar occurrences. So could other friends of Hugh's. Why did he tell us? Oh, I'm sure that some part of it had to do with this 'insurance' idea of his. But, the primary reason was that he wanted to impress upon us his vision of himself as the swashbuckling renaissance hero.

Hugh was attracted to the romance of espionage. Certainly, he was loud and brash and obnoxious; and ruthless and driven and ambitious, too. And I'm sure the intelligence services offered all manner of scope for those less attractive features of Hugh's character. But more than that, Hugh was an incurable romantic and dreamer.

Alexander was his hero. Arthur his passion. He devoured Tolkein and Asimov and Arthur C. Clarke. His dreams were the stuff of quest and conquest. Loyalty and honor. Passion and pride. If there were still a Big Game out there, and room for a latter day Lawrence of Arabia, he wanted a piece of it. I felt sure he believed that the best chance of finding it was with the clandestine services.

Hugh told me that he carried the Intelligence rank of Brigadier-General, and that he had, for a time, been attached to the Joint Intelligence Committee, the oversight body for all matters pertaining to Britain's intelligence services.

For certain, the Chairman of the Beaconsfield Conservative Association when Hugh first became active in local politics, in his early twenties, was one Colonel Ian Lapraik, a former Commandant of the SAS. Both of his political mentors, Sir Ronald Bell, the late Member of Parliament for Beaconsfield, and Enoch Powell, the former Conservative Cabinet Minister, had served in British Military Intelligence during the Second World War. And Hugh hung a Ceremonial Sword over his mantelpiece. Attached to it was the Scabbard Sling of the Black Watch, a secretive Army Regiment with close ties to the SAS.

In 1985, at the tender age of 37, Hugh was appointed the youngest-

Geoffrey Gilson

ever Commander of the Most Noble Order of the British Empire (CBE). The Order of the British Empire was created during the First World War in 1917 by George V. The King recognized the necessity for a new award of honor which could be more widely awarded, in recognition of the large numbers of people in the British Isles and other parts of the Empire who were helping the war effort both as combatants and as civilians on the home front. For the first time, women were included in a British Order of Chivalry, and it was decided that the Order should also include foreigners who had helped the British war effort.

From 1918 onwards there were Military and Civil Divisions, as George V also intended that after the war the Order should be used to reward services to the State, defined in a much wider sense to acknowledge distinguished service to the arts and sciences, public services outside the Civil Service and work with charitable and welfare organizations of all kinds. The Order of the British Empire is the Order of Chivalry of the British democracy. Valuable service is the only criterion for the award, and the Order is now used to reward service in a wide range of useful activities. Citizens from other countries may also receive an honorary award, for services rendered to the United Kingdom and its people. There are more than 100,000 living members of the Order throughout the world.

After some debate, St Paul's Cathedral was nominated by a special committee and approved by The Queen, as the Chapel of the Order. As the cathedral of England's capital city, it could accommodate services attended by very large congregations, and (in the words of one committee member) 'St Paul's symbolized the victory of the British spirit during the war of 1939-45 in that, although badly damaged and shaken, it survived the ordeal by battle in an almost miraculous way'.

A Chapel for the Order was subsequently built in the cathedral crypt (where Nelson, Wellington and Sir Christopher Wren are buried, amongst others) and its formal dedication in 1969 was attended by The Queen and The Duke of Edinburgh (Grand Master of the Order). Once every four years, approximately 2,000 members of the Order attend a service there to celebrate the Order. Many people who have been awarded an honor from overseas attend these services, and each person attending wears their award.

Ostensibly, Hugh was appointed his CBE in gratitude for his service to the Conservative Party. Indeed, he was recommended for a knighthood, but the then Chairman of the Conservative Party, one John Selwyn Gummer, found himself on the opposite side of the debate from Hugh about membership in the European Union, and so had downgraded the Honor. Most solely political Honors were specifically designated "for political service." Hugh's was described as "for political and public service."

On the evening of his Investiture, relaxing back at home with a tumbler of Scotch in hand, but still wearing his formal penguin suit, Hugh regaled his closest friends with every Seinfeldian detail of the day's events: his conversation with the Queen, the color of the drapes, the size of Buckingham Palace... Eventually, everyone but Janet and I had drifted away. Then, even Janet grew tired at the fifteenth recounting of the tale. She had, after all, been there as well.

When he was sure that Janet was in bed, he handed me the satin inlaid box holding the medal and supporting neck ribbon. I remember the pattern clearly. Grey silk ribbon, with salmon edging. Then, he lifted the satin inlay, to reveal a second ribbon. This one was the same pattern, but with a salmon stripe down the middle as well. I was later told by an expert on military decorations that this second ribbon was the ribbon for the military CBE. The first was the civilian equivalent.

Hugh told me that it was not usual for civilian officers in Intelligence to be honored. You can hardly have supposedly secret members of a government service wandering about town with a breast laden with hardware. However, in view of his civilian Honor, the powers that be had decided that it would be appropriate to take the opportunity to honor him with the military appointment to CBE as well.

After his chit-chat with the Queen, and while Janet was occupied elsewhere, Hugh had been taken to a private room within Buckingham Palace, and was there secretly appointed. He would not be allowed to wear the military ribbon in public, and would only be able to do so at discreet and vetted private military functions.

As luck would have it, the political region in which Hugh and I found ourselves playing politics was littered with safe Conservative Constituencies; oodles of retired and senior Army Officers, Conservative to a man; and a veritable shopping list of Army Bases, which delighted in holding regular Mess Days to salute all those retired and senior Army Officers. Hugh found himself suddenly invited to one Mess Day after another. Dutifully, he would dress with his civilian ribbon, and once at the Base in question, would change ribbons.

At one such celebration, and after much alcohol had disappeared, one lowly Officer leaned over and wondered loudly why a civilian snot like Hugh felt he had the right to sport a military ribbon. The retired General sitting next to Hugh calmly stated, with remarkable restraint, that the Officer had remained at such a lowly rank for so long because he was stupid enough to ask a question the answer to which was obvious, and to ask it of someone who was duty bound not to answer. The Officer went bright red, sat back and said nothing more for the entirety of dinner.

Of course, I could be fabricating all of this. But to what end? Equally, Hugh could have arranged all of it for my benefit, to impress me. Only problem is it would have required an enormous effort; Hugh was a busy guy; and I was singularly unimpressed by the whole charade anyway, a fact of which he was always and painfully aware. And it didn't account for the conversation John Simmonds had had with his two 'gentlemen.' I set about trying to put together a scenario that might adequately satisfy all the anomalies raised by the mysterious nature of Hugh's theft and death.

* * *

The most famous hostage crisis in the late Eighties was that involving Americans and Europeans being held by radical Shiite Muslims in Lebanon. The practice of taking hostages in the Middle East had begun with the Crusades, and had proved to be a source of trouble for the West up to and including Bush Jr.'s occupation of Iraq in 2003.

Israel, under its then Defense Minister Ariel Sharon, had invaded Lebanon in 1982 to clear out the PLO and its leader Yassir Arafat. The very same Arafat who, at the time of his death in 2004, was being laid to siege in the Gaza Strip by the very same Ariel Sharon who had by that time become Prime Minister of Israel.

Back in 1982, Sharon had let his Lebanese Christian militia pals, rabid enemies of all things Muslim, loose into the Muslim Palestinian refugee camps, where they had indiscriminately massacred men, women and children.

The West sent peacekeepers to break up the fighting. The problem was that nothing was black and white. It wasn't as simple as them and us. There weren't just good guys and bad guys. There were lots of different guys. There weren't just Christians, Muslims and Palestinians. There were loads of different factions of Christians, Muslims and Palestinians.

Very often, the different factions of the same religious or ethnic type hated each other more than they hated the other religious or ethnic types. The rule of survival was that your enemies' enemy was most probably your friend. And if you wanted to steer clear of trouble, you had always to be aware of the strangest alliances, constantly shifting across religious and ethnic divisions.

The intelligence of the incoming peacekeepers could not keep pace with the complexity of the situation on the ground. As a consequence, the peacekeepers found themselves being blown up or taken hostage by all sorts of different groupings of all sorts of different religious and ethnic types.

Indeed, this is a story that has been repeated in most of the areas the West has decided to perform peacekeeping or peacemaking duties since that time, whether in Somalia, Bosnia, Afghanistan, or Iraq.

Back in Lebanon, in the late Eighties, the most prevalent hostage-takers were the radical Shiite Muslims of Hezbollah, a newly-formed military and political organization, that had close ties to the radical Shiite Muslims of Ayatollah Khomeini in Iran. Indeed, it was those close ties that had given rise to the scandal known as 'Iran-Contra.'

The thinking had been triangular: Sell arms and military equipment to Iran. They desperately needed the same to fight off Iraq, which had invaded their country in 1980. Being oil rich, the radical Muslim Mullahs of Iran were prepared to pay well over market price for any and all military goodies. Use the profits to supply the Contras fighting the Communist Sandinistas in Nicaragua, and of course, to fatten those bank accounts in Switzerland and the Cayman Islands. Finally, use the goodwill generated with Iran to encourage them to persuade their allies in Lebanon to let the hostages go free.

Remember now, at this time, Britain's radical right-wing Prime Minister, Margaret Thatcher, and America's equally radical and right-wing president, Ronald Reagan, were both giving the same teleprompted 'get tough' message to the world's media: "we do not negotiate with terrorists."

The reality is that they were both negotiating like crazy, and willing to pay any price to avoid the same embarrassment Jimmy Carter had suffered with the 57 US hostages, held in the American Embassy, in the capital of Iran, from 1979 to 1981. They were particularly anxious to gain freedom for one William Buckley, the new CIA Head of Station in Lebanon.

Early on in the peacekeeping effort, in 1983 to be precise, the US Marine barracks had been blown up by one or other of the Lebanese Muslim militias, causing the death of 168 of America's finest. The same militia had also exploded a bomb outside the US Embassy in Beirut, killing among others at least eight serving officers of the CIA.

Buckley was head of the Special Operations Group, the paramilitary division of the CIA. He'd been stirring up trouble for a couple of years in Angola, a country which borders South Africa, and is rich in oil, diamonds and uranium. The CIA was supporting a nasty piece of work, called Jonas Savimbi, against the left-leaning FNLA (National Liberation Front of Angola).

Buckley was called back to Langley and given special responsibility to go to Lebanon, where he was to seek revenge for the deaths of the Marines and the CIA officers. He was to hunt down and kill as many Muslim militia members as possible. Unfortunately, the Lebanese Muslim militias in question had better intelligence than the West had bargained for, and Buckley was taken captive soon after arriving in Lebanon.

This case drew my attention for a number of reasons. First, it fit the bill of 'getting an agent out of a foreign country.' Secondly, it made me wonder whether one or more of the British hostages might not also be a British 'foreign agent.' Finally, Buckley was in cahoots with a renegade British spy-cum-mercenary, called Leslie Aspin.

Les Aspin, sometimes acting with his wilder brother, Michael, and sometimes not, was first a contract agent for British Intelligence. Later on, he defected to the United States, and acted under the direct authority of William Casey, Reagan's Director of the CIA.

Les had been up to all sorts of naughty no-no's in Angola with Buckley, and lately had been working as an 'adviser' for one of the Lebanese Christian factions, while smuggling arms to Iran as a night job. He was a perfect choice to help Buckley with his nasty activities in Lebanon. Problem was that one or other of the Lebanese Muslim militias found out about Buckley, and took him hostage.

Les then became lead contract agent in the efforts to find Buckley, negotiate for his release, or simply to break him free. Les was also the 'hard man' heading up the British Government's 'unofficial,' behind-the-scenes efforts to free British hostages.

The world believed that this task was, in fact, being undertaken 'officially' by Terry Waite, the Archbishop of Canterbury's special envoy to Lebanon. However, what the world and Terry – to his eventual cost – did not know was that the British Government was simply using Terry as a stooge, to provide cover for their secret 'shock-and-awe' operation. At the end of the day, Governments place far more faith in the barrel of a gun, than they do in prayer, holiness and a quick rendition of 'Kumbiya.'

Les is now dead, otherwise I'd have tried to make contact with him. His brother, Michael, served time in jail for fraud, although throughout his trial, he claimed that the money he had stolen had been taken to finance a deal to release hostages in Lebanon, an operation which had the full sanction of MI6 and the British Government.

The co-incidence between Michael Aspin's story and the rationale advanced to John Simmonds for Hugh's defalcation was intriguing. Indeed, there were a number of other matters which gave me cause to ponder the possible connections and similarities between the Aspin boys and Hugh.

For example, Les was formerly with the SAS. He owned a large house in Buckinghamshire, not far from Beaconsfield. One of his banks was the Barclays Bank branch in Stanhope House, Park Lane, London. Hugh did all of his City Jeroboam financing with the same bank branch.

The Aspins were heavily involved in gun-trading around the Mediterranean. The favorite triangle was: guns from Yugoslavia, Bulgaria or Czechoslovakia; deals done in Marbella, the jet set location on the south coast of Spain; and then, guns to Palestinian or Muslim militias in the Near or Middle East, by way of Marseilles, or some other port along the south coast of France.

Between 1986 and 1988, Hugh had a major client in Marbella: a timeshare operation called *Paradise*, whose two partners were Paul Prew-Smith and Victor di Gennaro. Paul came from a lot of textile money in the north of England, and had his own offices at 16 Pall Mall, London. His girlfriend at the time was the former Countess of Coventry. Victor was an

Dead Men Don't Eat Lunch

expatriate Italian. No-one knew much about where he'd come from, or where he eventually went. Hugh and I visited the south of Spain from time to time. Usually to do business. But also we spent a lot of time just wandering around the port area, looking at boats.

On one occasion, Hugh had remarked that one of the fancier motor yachts belonged to Robert Maxwell, the billionaire British publisher, who owned the London *Daily Mirror* and the *New York Post*, and ended up taking a fatal dive off the very same boat. I never stopped wondering how Hugh recognized the yacht. In the dark. From the other side of the harbor.

Large boats, the Mediterranean and the south of Spain were much in the British news at this point because of suspected gun-running, from Libya to the IRA, in Northern Ireland. Gibraltar had also figured. Gibraltar, the British colony, with its strategically vital location on the southern tip of Spain, is just a few minutes down the road from Marbella. There had been a huge row in the UK over news that a hit team from British Intelligence/SAS had killed a group of undercover IRA guys, who were doing who knows what in Gibraltar. Certainly, it seemed a strange place for Irish terrorists to be working on their tans. However, it is a well known 'secret' that MI6 have a huge training facility hidden beneath the Rock of Gibraltar.

Hugh had mentioned that he spent some time early in his Intelligence career undercover in Marseilles. Then, in about 1987, he and Martin spent a deal of time in Provence, the area just to the north of Marseilles, scouting possible small vineyards to buy. Finally, in the summer of 1988, a couple of months before his death, Hugh, his family and I had gone for a two week holiday in Cannes, just down the coast from Marseilles. It was obvious that he knew the area well, and had an especial fondness for the locality and its people.

The most interesting aspect of the Aspins was their role as contract agents. Every Intelligence agency has regular employees. When serving abroad, some are attached to their Embassies, but are generally given titles that bear no resemblance to their real work. Others operate free of the Embassy, but they are still bona fide employees of their Intelligence agency.

Then, there are contract agents. As the name suggests, they are offered jobs on a 'contract' basis. They are not full-time employees of the agency. When the job is over, they revert to their own full-time employment. Or they may perform the task alongside their usual employment, or use that employment as convenient cover.

This allows the agency in question to disavow any knowledge of the agent. Oops, no, we don't employ "X." Well, they don't. He is easily and legally deniable. Another way to make deniability easy is to hire people on the edge. After all, one is essentially asking them to lie, steal, cheat or kill. So, why not use people with shady backgrounds. They won't shy away from the job in hand, and it's easy afterwards to destroy their credibility, when it comes time to clean the laundry away.

In this particular regard, I have become fascinated over the past fifteen years by the apparent cross-over between civilian and military agencies, and legitimate and criminal enterprises. Again, Joe Ordinary thinks in terms of black and white, straight lines, honest compartmentalization. I think the truth is a lot murkier. I have come increasingly to believe that, when it comes to clandestine matters, governments leave it to others to do whatever is necessary, however it is necessary, and then just turn a blind eye.

I remember watching the television with Hugh when the SAS freed the hostages from the Iranian Embassy in 1981. As the black-clad and hooded SAS soldiers were leading the freed hostages to safety, a rogue cameraman followed an ill-kempt bloke, up to all sorts of strange behavior. He was wearing jeans, had long hair, and was darting from car to car looking underneath. "Oh dear," exclaimed Hugh, "we really shouldn't be seeing that."

Hugh explained later that the gentleman in question was with a 'civilian unit' of the SAS. And that would be...? Hrrmph, came the unexpected response, from the normally talkative Hugh. He did tell me that, during the Second World War, British Military Intelligence had begun a practice of forming *ad hoc* civilian units, that went out and hired whoever was appropriate for a particular job. Thus, if we wanted to steal some important designs from a factory in Occupied France, we went down to the East End of London, and hired a couple of safecrackers for the night. He left the rest to my imagination. An imagination that was now beginning to wonder if Hugh had been a senior member of a similar unit.

***

What of Hugh and his specific operation? After a deal of soul-searching, and what I would describe as rigorous intellectual analysis (others might call it a couple of bottles of ice-cold Frascati), I came up with the following ideas. Their primary attraction is that they do a better chance of beginning to square the anomalies of Hugh's theft and death than the rather half-hearted versions previously offered by the 'straights.'

Hugh was somehow involved in an operation to free a hostage in Lebanon. Part of his duties included making funds available, which he stole from his Clients' Account. The operation had the nod from the powers that be, which was why he felt he was protected. The funds would be replaced after the operation, either from profits from the operation, or by the same powers.

Something went wrong. Since the money was not replaced, one has to conclude that the 'something' interfered with the funds in some way. Either the very fact of it going wrong, or perhaps the fact that the funds were interfered with, which prevented the operation from happening, caused the powers to remove the protection, and leave Hugh to his own devices.

This hypothesis works. But only to a certain extent. A major question it poses is why did Hugh remain silent when it all went wrong? Why not leave some clue, at least as to where the money might be found? What in fact happened is that the silence left his family burdened with the most extreme stigma and financial cost.

I would say 'duty,' but it just doesn't feel right, in all the circumstances, and with everything I knew of Hugh's complicated character. I can only think that some sort of threat might have been made against one or other members of his family.

Hugh had made the art of his own survival a living extension of his own irrepressible arrogance. There was no situation he could not deal with. Every problem was merely a challenge. One swing of the sword, and any knot, however complicated, could be severed.

However, this dictum applied only to his own survival, not that of his family, his loved ones. Their care and concern came ahead of all else. Hugh was not all hardhead. He had a heart. He just kept it well hidden. Frankly, he was a psychological nightmare. A kaleidoscope of contradictions. A parody of paradoxes.

Loving and affectionate to friends, yet diabolically cruel to rivals. Desperate for love, yet the only true loner I'd ever met. Loud, brash and boorish in public, yet civilized and attentive in private. Always needing to be the centre of attention when in the company of an audience, yet solicitous and loyal when dealing with an individual's personal problems. Utterly convinced of his own invincibility, yet almost childish in his incomprehension of why things went wrong, as regularly they did. Charismatic and flamboyant, extravagant and petulant; yet kind and generous to a fault.

Hugh was also the most responsible father I had ever witnessed. If there was one matter more than any other that did not ring true, it was that he had left no suicide note. In particular, nothing for Juliet. At 11 years of age, she was the son he had always wanted. Serious, smart, his features, but with blond hair. Tanya, at age 8, had her grandfather's sandy hair and freckles, and her mother's infectious laugh. She was going to break a lot of hearts. Paul, aged 5, was all Karen in looks, and all Hugh with his attitude.

Hugh loved his children dearly. And he cared for them. And the two are not the same thing. Everything I understood about Hugh screamed at me that he would have found some way to tell his children what was going on. Mind you, there are days when I think I am the suicide note.

No-one just 'liked' Hugh. He did not inspire casual emotion. You either loved him or hated him, as Maggi had found out. And he returned the compliment four-fold. So, I had no difficulty believing that, faced with the possibility that his continued existence on this mortal coil would, of itself, have placed one single member of his extended family in harm's way – even for a single second – he would have chosen silent self-execution as the noble alternative.

Indeed, looking more closely at his health history at this time, his illness during the summer broke down into some interesting phases. He fell suddenly ill in May of 1988. Maybe this was when the major financial disaster occurred? He was bed-ridden for a month. Then, he picked up, and in the months July through September, he was almost frenzied with activity. Looking back, maybe he thought he had found a way to escape the trap? Martin Pratt told me that, during this time, Hugh was constantly discussing business schemes with him, to try to make money quickly. Then, in about October, Hugh seemed completely to give up. Was this when possible threats began?

At one stage, Hugh had left Janet to live with his mistress Karen. But he then returned to Janet, for the sake of his daughters. After this, he kept Karen somewhat at arms length. Yet, in the few months before his death, the steamy relationship with his steamy mistress was once more rekindled.

Janet lived in a large house, in the middle of a busy neighborhood, in premises heavily covered with burglar alarms and motion-operated lights. Indeed, the neighbors had complained more than once about the 'Hollywood Effect' every time Hugh and his family returned home. Karen, by contrast lived in a much smaller house, out in the middle of the country, her only protection a couple of teenage female horse-grooms.

After Hugh's death, Karen's mother, not Karen, told me that Hugh had told her in the week before his death that he was planning to move back in with Karen. Like Hugh's parents, neither Karen's mother or father are given to flights of fancy. Indeed, her father was a professor at a local university, and was held in some esteem by John Simmonds. Karen's parents expressed as much surprise as I that Hugh had told them this. Was Karen under threat?

***

More to the point, was I? Just as I was beginning to wonder why, in the light of all this MI6 revelation, no-one in a dirty raincoat had come asking questions at Simmonds and Company, I got a telephone call in America from a gentleman, with the unlikely name of 'Geoffrey Hughes,' who said he had traveled across the Atlantic "specially" to meet with me.

Dead Men Don't Eat Lunch

Chapter 4

MY SISTER, Susannah, is a few years younger than me, slim, blond and full of bounce. She'd married Gregg, a tall good-looking Midwestern boy, who loved to crack jokes, usually with other ladies. The divorce some years later was reasonably amicable. At the time, in 1988, they lived in a little fishing village called Little Compton, in Rhode Island.

Rhode Island is America's smallest state. Essentially, it's one vast inlet, with some land around the outer edges. Unlike the rest of picturesque New England, it's less clapboard houses and Pilgrims, and more heavy industry, smokestacks and Portuguese women, who bear a striking resemblance to Sylvester Stallone.

I was not unfamiliar with the area. My father's family hailed from some Mayflower Babes, twice over in fact. Indeed, uncanny as it was, and for no reason other than it's a small world, a bunch of our ancestors lay at rest in Little Compton's graveyard.

My father can trace his family back to kingdom come, and they were all Boston Brahmin medical, military or religious personnel. We have a U.S. Surgeon General tucked away somewhere. My Uncle Ben was an Orthopedic Surgeon and Captain in the U.S. Navy. Ben and his family still live in Newport, the only bright spot in Rhode Island: loads of old money, but a great big hole in the wall where the America's Cup used to be.

Indeed, Ben has a bit part in my saga. For a while, Maggi lived with him and his wife Sarah, in Newport. One day Maggi noticed a red telephone tucked away in the corner of Ben's office, a telephone clearly marked as being for security use. She wondered why a navy doctor would need a dedicated security telephone.

I was reminded of my sister Susannah's wedding to Gregg, held in Newport, in the autumn of 1987. Hugh and I had attended. At the reception afterwards, I noticed Hugh and Ben having an amiable conversation. All of a sudden, they stopped, looked at each other a little disconcerted and went their separate ways.

Hugh wandered over to me. "Interesting fellow, your uncle," he began, "I thought you told me he was a Navy doctor."

"He is," I replied, my mind elsewhere.

"Well, he's a bit more than that," Hugh chuckled. "We found ourselves having an interesting chat about submarines. Seems he's knows more about them than a simple doctor should. And I know more about them than a simple solicitor should."

My grandfather, Pappy, was a Bishop of Rhode Island. He'd inherited the position some time after the Reds took over China, and got rid of his day job in Shanghai.

My father, Charles Gilson, had been treading much the same path as the rest of the male family tree, until the Second World War came along. He flew B-29 bombers over Japan. After the war, he flew commercially for a while, married my mother in Okinawa, and set up shop in France and then in England, working the rest of his life for American Express, the people you can't leave home without.

In fact, my father's claim to fame is that he's the guy who introduced that version of the Green Card to the European side of the Atlantic, back in the Sixties. My father had a long and distinguished career with Amex, including a stint as their 'Ambassador' in Moscow, during the Olympic Games in 1980, which were sponsored by American Express.

My mother's background was much more prosaic. Czechoslovakian immigrants at the end of the Nineteenth Century; all horse thieves and drunkards. When they managed to get past the alcohol, a bunch of them established a tradition of scholarship and artistry. My mother's brother-in-law was a Professor at the University of Chicago; Maggi went to Oxford; and my elder sister, Liz, is doing her doctoral thesis at the University of North Carolina. My cousins, Patti and Monica, are variously actresses, story-tellers, dancers and authors. My contribution to this glamorous effort is this book, and a half a dozen pop songs that send six year old girls and their grandmothers into an underwear-throwing frenzy.

I was born on a U.S. Air Force Base in southern England. Hence, the dual citizenship. Forget Arnold Schwarzenegger and his growling Austrian vowels. The United States can now look forward to the day when it has its first President who speaks the language in its original form.

I did private elementary school, then the British equivalent of private prep school, although confusingly the English call that a Public School. I bypassed university. I wanted to get on with my life. I got involved with community affairs in my home town of Beaconsfield, and eventually met Hugh.

One of the more useful things that Amex did for us, in my formative years, was to pay for the family to have home leave to America every two years, no expense spared. Thus it was that I came to know New England so well, along with every large ocean liner doing the cross-Atlantic trip.

Later on, I did the same trip a couple of times with Hugh, but using Britain's very expensive supersonic airliner, Concorde. Of course, in hindsight, it begs the question, which one of his unsuspecting clients was paying for the airline tickets? Our last journey had been that one to Susannah's wedding, in Newport, in 1987, which is why I chose Rhode Island as my landing spot when I decided to move to America after Hugh's death.

However, just as nothing in my background had prepared me for a life of politics with Hugh, and its rather unwelcome aftermath, so nothing in that life had prepared me for what I was now convinced was to be my meeting with an MI6 assassin from England.

***

Gregg knew I was terrified, and offered, without my asking, to stay at home the day Geoffrey Hughes came visiting. They met outside the front door. Gregg was all business. "This is America, son. Don't know why you're here, but I'll be in the other chair." And so he was. All day. With a sledgehammer draped over his knees. Bless his heart.

In fact, Geoff was with us for two days. Notwithstanding the odd name, it turned out that he was perfectly kosher, the European Director for Carratu International, and the man in charge of the Simmonds investigation. He spent two days throwing names at me, to see what I could tell him about them. Time and again, I would make the point that I could tell him nothing without a context. At last, I tired of the game, and asked some questions of my own.

The upshot was that, after nearly six months of tracking leads, one of the world's leading fraud busters had found zilch. Notwithstanding their clean bill of health for me some months earlier, the powers that be, otherwise empty-handed, had now decided to turn the spotlight on the nearest available easy target, and that had turned out to be me.

"So, here I am thinking you're bringing the answer to me, and the answer you're bringing is, in fact, 'me'?"

Geoff, to give him his due, looked a little sheepish in response to that one. "Well," he stuttered, "the few leads we do have end up in Dallas, Atlanta and with a company in Atlanta, called Robinson-Humphries."

"Ah," I say, "and I have a brother in Dallas, another in Atlanta, and my father worked for forty years with American Express, of which Robinson-Humphries is a fully owned subsidiary?"

"Bingo."

Geoffrey Gilson

Oops.

Of course, I angrily pointed out to Geoff that if I had the money, I wouldn't be sitting penniless in a fishing village in New England, I'd be off in Argentina, looking for that gorgeous girl that Hugh didn't seem to want to run away to. In a fit of pique, I gave him my views on MI6. Not wise. Beforehand, he'd thought I was just a crook. Now, he thought I was a crazy crook.

It became very apparent that, the powers, having made the about face, were not slow to spread the ill news as quickly and as widely as they could. A friend faxed me a bunch of newspaper articles arising from the Coroner's Inquest into Hugh's death, and one national newspaper had been having a field day at my expense, and in my absence.

***

The Coroner's Inquest on Hugh had been held on March 20[th,] 1989. The verdict had been death by his own hand. It was on this occasion that the Law Society revealed for the first time the full extent of Hugh's defalcation. Interestingly enough, they didn't report it as £5 million ($7.5 million), but only as £3.8 million ($5.2 million). Why was someone not claiming their money?

Most of the articles were stodgy and boring. But one had headlines describing me as fleeing the country. The body of the article referred to the fact that I was refusing to return to the UK to answer questions. I telephoned the journalist, one Chris Hutchins, of the London *Today* tabloid. I was all piss and vinegar. Acidly, I asked him who his sources were. He told me that they were the Police and the Law Society.

I rang their representatives, and proceeded to have tart 'conversations,' which crammed as much Shakespeare vulgarity, as it was humanly possible to remember, into the time allowed to me by my phone card. Feeling much better, I then returned to Chris Hutchins to set the record straight.

I explained that their judiciously-placed red herring had all been a consequence of the fact that they'd been unable to turn up anything substantial. "So, do you have some theories of your own?" was the immediate come-back. Tabloid journalists may be the scum of the earth, but they can spot a story a mile off, with blinders on, and their heads shoved in a lead-encased toilet bowl. Chris knew he had gold dust when the pregnant silence dragged on for more than two seconds.

I really didn't want to make the same mistake, but this time with a national journalist, so I worked hard to keep my MI6 views to myself. Chris, however, proved to be psychic. And very gentle. Like a kick in the head from a Rodeo Bull is gentle. "Does it have anything to do with the D-Notice that was slapped against Hugh's story?"

You what?

Britain doesn't have a First Amendment. The media can print anything it likes, provided the Government likes it. Every media outlet has a civil servant from the Ministry of Defense on site. All articles have to be vetted by him. If he believes an article contains something that might endanger national security, he can yank it, or slap a D-Notice, a Defense Notice, on it.

Chris told me that a friend of his, a TV producer with the BBC, had told him that they had done a half hour segment on Hugh for *Newsnight*, the BBC's nightly, one-hour newsmagazine show. The segment had been D-Noticed. I told Chris to check with his source. If the source confirmed the D-Notice, and could give details, I'd think about talking to him.

About an hour later, Chris called me, in a very agitated state. A tabloid journalist gets ruffled about as often as an angel descends and goes on a shoplifting spree. Chris told me that the TV producer was now not only denying there was a D-Notice, he was even denying ever having spoken to Chris.

Some years later, I was told that the most serious level of D-Notice is called a Category A, D-Notice. This is the one they use when there's a War on, or a spy defects, or the Queen is photographed in bed with the President. It D-Notices the offending article, and then it D-Notices the D-Notice. Then it D-Notices the D-Noticer and then, just for good measure, it wipes all the fingerprints off the ashtrays. My source told me that the Hugh D-Notice had to have been Category A.

So. We were now definitely out of the realm of Frascati-induced speculation. Kansas had been left a long way behind. There was definitely something going on. Something being hidden. And it was up to me to find out what it was, because somebody had me firmly in their sights as the next fall-guy. I needed to get information, any way that I could. And I needed to get it fast.

***

One of Susannah's friends from work suggested going to a medium friend of hers. What did I have to lose? His name was Bill. He was not what I was expecting. He looked more like a lumberjack than a wizard, although he did have a pony tail and a long wispy goatee.

His tiny office was hung with Buddha Bells, and laced with incense, and we went through the card-shuffling, mumbling routine for a few minutes. Then, he settled down, and the most amazing things poured out of his mouth. Tightly clasping a chunk of clear crystal, his eyes closed shut, he gave me a complete rundown on Hugh, his family, his career, everything. I gave him nothing but a photograph, and here he was giving me chapter and verse, down to the names of all of Hugh's children, and the kind of wines he used to like. It was eerie, and I was fairly freaked. But not as freaked as Bill was about to be.

I thanked him for all of this, but mentioned that I wanted some specific information about what Hugh might have been up to just before his death. I made no mention of the circumstances surrounding his death. Bill said, somewhat confused, for the first time that afternoon, that he was drawing a blank. Could I give him a clue? I uttered just one word. MI6.

Bill's eyes flew open, he shot back in his chair, clutching his stomach and bending over violently. I was quite worried. After a moment, he sat up slowly, gasping for breath. He made it quite clear the session was over. I asked him if he could tell me anything. He stated firmly that he did not want to talk about what he had experienced. He did not want to go there. I coaxed him gently.

After a few minutes, he calmed down. He agreed only to tell me what he had sensed for that first moment, but refused to try to divine anything further. He said the instant that I mentioned my word (he would not repeat it), he had seen a whole episode in one flash, followed by a searing pain in his stomach.

All Bill was prepared to tell me was that, before his death, Hugh had been doing something for MI6. Bill had no idea what or who MI6 was. Someone close to Hugh had double-crossed him, causing what he was doing to fall apart. Bill had then seen two men of Mediterranean or Middle Eastern extraction attack Hugh in a field. And the searing pain was something Bill said mediums experienced when viewing a violent death.

In his opinion, Hugh had been murdered, and Bill wanted nothing further to do with either me or Hugh.

***

Hugh had never told me he borrowed money from his father. Not surprising. He'd told me he was independently wealthy; independent from what was happening with the law firm, that is. If I'd thought he was strapped, I might have looked too closely at what was going on with the firm's finances in 1988.

Looking back, I know now that Lyn was probably right. In about 1985, Hugh had massively tightened the old belt, and downgraded all his spending. At the time he'd told me it was to give the new law firm, Simmonds and Company, a chance to get on its feet.

One of the primary items that was downgraded was Hugh's car. He went from big Rover sedan to little BMW run-around. However, by 1987, the big spending ways were back with a bang, and we had reverted to huge, dark green, BMW sports coupe, Mark "M," with all the bells and whistles. Once more, one has to wonder whether it was Hugh or one of his clients who was paying for the new found luxuries.

Martin, Hugh and I had gone out into the countryside, one rainy Saturday lunchtime, for a long, lazy and very 'heavy' afternoon meal. At an old but welcoming hostelry. I remember the trip back very well. One of the Men's Wimbledon tennis semi-finals was on the radio. I believe Boris Becker was making mincemeat of some unfortunate sod. Hugh was on the car phone to Janet when there was this loud bang on the car door next to me.

Martin was driving. Being Britain, that meant that he was in the right-hand front seat. Hugh was in the left-hand seat. I was in the back seat, on my own. We were driving in the overtaking lane of a six lane Motorway, what the Americans would call an Interstate.

We immediately began to plane on the wet surface. We rotated ever so lightly and crashed in to the barrier on the right. We bounced across three lanes and hit the barrier on the left. This was the point at which I threw off my spectacles, and went face down on the back seat.

I remember Hugh calmly telling Janet on the telephone, "oh dear, we seem to be having an accident." I was left wondering who had left the film canister marked "My Life" on empty, because the only damn thing flashing past my eyes was a crap load of lint from the seat I was crushing myself into.

We careened back across three lanes and hit the right-hand barrier one more time. We never rolled, although I was waiting for it. We then spun one more time across the three lanes, and came to a rest in the emergency lane on the left.

We were able to exit the car only by crawling through broken windows. A ton of Germany's best engineering was now scrap metal. Martin swore then, and to this day, that the car started planing all on its own, that he never touched the brakes to begin with, and that when he did, there was nothing.

I had completely forgotten this incident until that moment with Bill the medium. I went home to Susannah and Greg's. I said nothing. I left them to listen to the tape of the session with Bill, and went upstairs to lie down.

When I came down, Gregg was booking airline tickets. Gregg and Susannah are another two not easily given to flights of fancy, yet they were convinced of two things listening to that tape: there were questions that needed to be answered, and the answers lay in Old England, not New England. It was also about this time that we all started experiencing weird echoes and clicks on the telephone.

Geoffrey Gilson

Chapter 5

GREGG AND I had some time to kill on the way to Providence Airport, so we stopped off at the home of another medium, called Joe. We took the view that a second opinion wouldn't hurt. We got almost the same reaction as the first time around, but this time with a few extra surprises.

The session began simply enough. A horoscope, some Tarot cards, your grandmother misses you. Plus, something about my being on a Journey or a Quest; and that when I was finished, I would be the most powerful Tarot, the Emperor, gifted with all of the Mystical Mysteries of Life. Cool. Would I be able to trade them in for a new model Mercedes? No response.

Instead, I gave Hugh's name to Joe. But, I was careful to give him no other clues. At first. Again, we danced around for a while. Holding my breath, I then mentioned the money that Hugh was alleged to have stolen, and the fact that Hugh was supposed to have committed suicide. As with Bill, the reaction was instantaneous: Joe fell over backwards, holding onto his solar plexus.

Joe looked very upset. He paced up and down the room for a while. Then he sat down again, shut his eyes and concentrated hard. For the longest time, he seemed to be doing nothing. Every so often, he would nod his head, or shake it, and mutter something, like "yes," "mm hmm," or rather more sharply, "I don't want to see that."

Finally, Joe looked up: "Hugh and I have agreed a way forward," he said, "he was involved with some organization. Some sort of Security Bureau, called M6, or MIT, or MI6? Well, the missing money had something to do with that. Now, I don't want to get mixed up with that. You may have noticed that some of what Hugh was showing scared the crap out of me. He has agreed to continue, and to edit out the stuff I do not want to see."

Once mediums get into their trance or channeling mode, they tend to talk in short, staccato bursts, as they try to pass on immediately what it is they are sensing. As we carried on, Joe shifted into this form of communication.

"First thing. Hugh did not commit suicide. He was murdered. Quite brutally. I got lots of pain. I saw guns. Men from the Middle East. I can't tell you what he was involved in. Correction I can. I just don't want to know. But, I can tell you something about the missing money.

It's not missing. That is to say, it's still out there. Waiting to be found. It was converted into jewels, maybe diamonds, for easier transportation. I'm also getting what I think is a Bank Account number. Or a safe deposit box number. Possibly Swiss. I can't see the numbers clearly, although the first two numbers appear to be a 9 and a 0.

Now the scene has completely changed. I'm being told it still has to do with the money. Perhaps, a hidden clue. I'm seeing a church. A white church. On top, there's a cross. But not an ordinary cross. The ends of the crosses are splayed. Like a Maltese Cross. I'm getting a name for the church. Either St. Peter's or St. Paul's. You're possibly outside the church. I'm seeing a gravestone. A statue. One arm is pointing at a hidden clue. There are roses all around.

It seems that there's a clue in the church. Or near the church. And the church is near one of those red telephone kiosks they have in England. There's a picture. An icon. Maybe a plaque of some sort. On the wall. There's writing on it. I can't see it, but I'm told that it will mean something to you when you see it. There is a clue. Something in writing. Behind whatever it is. A document possibly. That document contains the answer to the missing money. It is the 'key.'

Now I'm seeing another document. I don't think it's the same one. There's something wrong with it. I think I may be seeing a computer. I know this is a strange question. But is there something wrong with Hugh's Estate? I think I'm seeing the Will. The Will is important in some way."

***

The day before he died, Hugh redrafted his Will, amidst much show and fanfare. As was usually the case, I checked all of the typing while he was out of the office. The most important distinction between the old and the new Wills was the inclusion in the new one of specific arrangements for his funeral. Those arrangements were full of the most obvious mistakes.

Hugh had apparently included an instruction to read Corinthians I, Chapter 11 from the 'Good News' Bible, when all his best friends knew that Hugh would only ever read from the St. James' Version. He wanted a passage read from "Lord of the Rings," the section just before the Rohan appear at Helm's Deep. Yet, he had misspelled Gandalf as Gadoulf.

The remainder of the changes were not mistaken as such, merely a little tacky. Like having us sing the "Battle Hymn of the Republic." Why on earth would an Englishman have us sing an American Civil War anthem?

Naturally I changed all of the mistakes, and had the new Will re-typed. However, when he returned to the office, Hugh not only put all the mistakes back in, he specifically instructed the secretary in question to tell me that he'd made her do it.

A signed and witnessed copy of the 'new' Will was never located. I had concluded that the whole process had been some sort of exercise in 'leaving me a message.' Perhaps there was more to the 'message' than I realized?

This last point was somewhat underscored by the fact that, in the 'new' Will, Hugh had changed his executors from Peter Smith and Philip de Nahlik to his father and Neil Relph. We will come across these characters later on in the book. At this point, the relevance is that Smith and de Nahlik, who were supposed to be two of Hugh's closest friends, turned tail and ran as soon as Hugh died. Meanwhile, Hugh's father and Neil Relph have remained true, through thick and thin.

***

"I'm getting a name." Joe was totally oblivious of my momentary reverie. "Reggie. Does that mean anything to you? You're supposed to show a document to him. I can't tell whether it's the will, or the document from the church. But when you show this document to Reggie, he will know what it means. And he will be able to help you.

Now I'm with a girl called Karen, at her house. I'm not sure if I'm confusing the church scene with this scene. I'm seeing a photograph of a son. Paul. In a frame. Maybe there's something behind a photograph of Paul. But I'm not sure if I'm not messing this up with the clue in the church.

I say that because now I'm being shown a stone wall. There's a clue in the stone wall. 'A key in the wall.' There seem to be 'keys' all over the place. I'm back to the photograph. Something behind the photograph. Writing. A symbol. There's a telephone book. Near the photograph. Either there's a clue in the telephone book. Or the telephone book is near the photograph with the clue. And the clue and the 'key' both lead to the money.

Oh dear. Karen. She's in trouble. Ouch.

With this last point, Joe doubled over in pain again.

"Ok. I just felt a major pain in my solar plexus again. Karen is in immediate physical danger. And she doesn't know it. There are people watching her. Plus, somebody is pretending to be her friend, but isn't. They're looking for clues too. I keep getting this insistent message: she's in a lot of trouble. The name 'David' keeps popping into my head.

Hugh's kind of going. No. He's trying to say one last thing. I think I've got it. No. He's gone. He's been cut off. I get the strong feeling it was against his will."

Joe explained that sometimes a connection will be broken off by spiritual guides at 'the other end,' because they feel someone at this end may be learning stuff it wasn't in their best interests to hear. At that precise moment, Joe stopped dead, apparently deep in thought, or trance, whatever. Then he looked at me, somewhat ominously. "That second pain I experienced earlier," he said, "I'm not sure now if it was in reference to Karen, or to you."

Joe took the view that I was about to get mixed up in a very dangerous situation. He warned me to be careful. "Beware the double-headed eagle," he added cryptically, "and his gun." Finally, he told me to be on the lookout for a gentleman called 'Joe Bath,' who would help us in our quest.

***

Our plane touched down in Belgium in the late afternoon. As we made our way up an escalator, after our dealings at the immigration desk, I looked back, and noticed a nondescript man emerge from a door behind the desk, walk over and collect our papers, before disappearing back through the door.

We walked to the nearby railway station, to catch the subway to the ferry, which was to take us across the English Channel. The station was a typical Old European mock-Renaissance monstrosity, all chandeliers and huge staircases, with enormous balustrades. At the top of the staircase leading to the subway was a man, standing around, doing nothing, with a newspaper tucked under his arm.

Nothing wrong with that. Except that when we got down to the subway and turned around, there he was, about twenty paces away. Gregg and I looked at each other, went back upstairs, passing Newspaper Guy on the way, and waited up top. Sure enough, Newspaper Guy followed us, and renewed his perch at the head of the staircase. We shrugged, and went downstairs again. Whereupon, the routine was repeated. Without shame.

From that moment on, and for the next couple of months, there was clear evidence of being followed almost all the time, either on foot or by car.

***

We arrived in Dover, on the south coast of England, after dark. We immediately hired a car, and made our way to a small village near to where Karen lived. I knew there to be a church there named for St. Peter.

It was nearly midnight as Gregg and I found ourselves rummaging around the gravestones, looking for something remotely white, with the illumination provided by our brand-new military flashlights. We'd been doing this for about half-an-hour, when almost by telepathic synchronization, we both stopped at the same time.

We looked at each other, very sheepishly, the light from our torches glistening on the sweat dropping from our faces. It was, after all, a muggy night in the middle of June. We coughed. We smiled. I fancy we both blushed, but you couldn't tell. We then burst out laughing. You could tell the same thought was going through both our minds, 'just what are we doing?' Then, the laughing stopped, and we looked at each other one more time. No smiles this time. I shrugged, and we got back to the furious rummaging.

***

Karen lived in a house that had been converted into one dwelling from a row of three, small town cottages. It was situated on the side of a wooded valley, deep in the countryside, about twenty miles from Beaconsfield. A hedged driveway led from the road in the middle of the valley all the way to the front door. One way in, and one way out. A perfect trap. No wonder Hugh had been worried.

Gregg and I spent the whole morning carefully reconnoitering the valley. We came across two cars, parked by the side of roads, with clear views of Karen's house. When we approached, the cars drove away. Finally, at midday, we suited up. We weren't sure what all this medium-speak meant, and it's not easy to get hold of guns in England, so we'd bought some helmets, flak jackets and baseball bats.

We went charging up the driveway in our van, ready for anything. We jumped out of the van, not unlike something you might see on one of those "Extreme Makeover" shows, and banged furiously on Karen's front door.

Word to the wise, if you care for the opportunity to have children later in life, do not call unexpectedly on a lady who trains half ton horses for a living, wearing get-up that would frighten Dracula out of his coffin. Half-an-hour later, when most of the swellings on my body were beginning to simmer down, I tried to explain why we were there.

To her credit, when she managed to stop the shouting, and then got the hysterical laughter under control, she did spend the rest of the evening helping us to find the alleged clues. Without any success. Gregg went back to our motel. I stayed the night as a guest at Karen's house. I felt I ought to make some effort to mend broken bridges, and I was still concerned about the cars we had seen apparently watching the house.

***

Dead Men Don't Eat Lunch

Next morning, I woke up bright and early. Or rather, Paul, now five, woke up bright, and then proceeded to wake up the rest of the household, very early. We met up in the kitchen. We had always been a little wary of each other. I never forced an introduction with young children. I took the view they would do whatever they wanted to do, whenever they wanted to do it. And he was his father's surly son.

On this occasion, however, and without a word, he dragged me into his playroom-studio. He wished to show me his portfolio. Karen stage whispered to me that he didn't normally let anyone see his pictures. I was honored. Paul just threw her a dirty look. And loudly shut the door.

I was taken by hand around the gallery, the walls of which were covered with his handiwork. I got off to a bad start by guessing that one particular ball of spaghetti was an elephant. "No stupid," came the immediate admonishment, "that's a horse." Oh, of course. How silly. And the legs are where? For which I received another dose of the trademark Simmonds' glare.

By the time we got to his rendition of Concorde, my spectacles, clearly redundant, had long since been consigned to my inside pocket. My eyes ached, and my head throbbed, but I was beginning to get the hang of it.

Ah yes, Concorde, and the wings are here? I gamely pointed at two seemingly similar blobs at opposite ends of the piece of paper. Yes. He was most impressed. I was now ready to be treated as his equal. He gazed at me expectantly.

When I did nothing, he grabbed some paper, some scissors, a crayon or two, and a roll of sticky tape and shoved them into my hands. Suddenly I remembered my camera in the other room. I took him into the dining room, and stood him against the wall. I then constructed a montage around him with the artist's tools he had given me. As a final flourish for this living sculpture, I posed him with arms folded, and took several snapshots.

Karen came in, and had a screaming fit. Something about expecting this from a five year old, but not an adult. Well really, I was an artist. I didn't need to take this sort of abuse. Paul just stood there beaming at his new-found friend. Someone else made Mummy angry by destroying her home. He made me sit next to him at the breakfast table.

At about this time, Karen's new beau dropped in for coffee. Paul, thinking he might be on a roll, plonked some of his pictures in front of the poor, unsuspecting sod. He feigned interest in the scribblings, poked at one, and wondered what it was. Paul gave him a look of withering disgust, and glanced at me. I leaned over. "Oh that would be Concorde," I affected, "see there are the wings, there's the wheels, and that's the pilot."

The chap stared at the picture again, but to no avail. He looked up hopelessly, and then shot an apologetic grin at Paul, who would have none of it. He just glared at the beau, and without breaking eye contact, reached over and gently patted me on the arm. I don't think the beau ever returned.

As she was driving me back to the motel, Karen mentioned that she had received a telephone call from Philip de Nahlik that morning warning her that I was in England. Philip was another seedy-looking friend of Hugh, tall and thin, with a disappearing neck, and a heavily pockmarked face. His only claim to fame was that he came from a long line of Polish Papal Counts.

I had told no-one I was traveling to England. Except my twin sister, Maggi. On the telephone. It was definitely time to be getting a move on. Gregg and I had churches to visit.

***

Gregg was used to living in a country that had not experienced anything much older than the American Revolution, some 200 years earlier. He was fascinated by Norman arches, dating back nine centuries. I had never experienced so many churches dedicated to just two saints, in such a small area. Our combined Magical Mystery Tour and Treasure Hunt dragged on into its second week, seemingly without end.

There was continuing evidence that we were being followed. The troubling thing was that we would engage in all sorts of automotive gymnastics to lose the cars behind us, and more often that not, it appeared that we had been successful. Yet every morning, there'd be a new car waiting for us.

One time, we double-backed and gave chase halfway to London, reaching speeds of 120 miles an hour on the Motorway. However, the other guy's car was more powerful than ours, and we lost him in a huge spaghetti junction.

As we came out from one particularly spectacular St. Peter's, we spotted the ubiquitous sentinel, with folded newspaper, on the other side of the road. Gregg had had enough, and ran towards him. However, before Gregg could grab the surprised watcher, a car pulled up, dragged the guy in, and sped off.

***

At last, we found ourselves outside another church in the charming village of Tring. I forget how many churches we had scoured up to this point. In fact, I can't swear if this one was St. Peter or St. Paul. I just knew it was going to be the last one.

We gave it the once-over in the afternoon. There was one promising plaque at the front of the church, on the left. Hugh and I were both fans of irony, and this plaque was dedicated to the local branch of the Pratt family.

That night, as we looked out the window, we could see the church

Dead Men Don't Eat Lunch

lit up by huge spotlights. The old stone shone brilliantly white. We felt it was a good omen.

The next morning, we marched into the church, full of bravado. Only to be met by the massed ranks of the local Mother's Union preparing the flowers for the Sunday services. Previously, our cover for having a peek under wall plaques was that we were taking a rubbing of the plaque, for research purposes. However, the other churches had always been empty. We were going to need something a little more clandestine if there was going to be an audience.

We hustled out to the car to see what we could find. A tarpaulin, some rope, a crowbar and glue; a hammer, a screwdriver, and a flashlight or two. Good. That should do it. We headed back towards the church. And stopped. Looked at each other. And I went back, and got the shovel out of the boot. Just for good measure. Now, we were ready for anything the old ladies had for us.

I held the tarpaulin up with my right hand, and tried to lever the plaque with the screwdriver. No movement. Gregg was holding the tarpaulin with his left hand, and the plaque with his right. He let go of the tarpaulin. But that exposed us. So, I tried to hold the tarpaulin up with both hands, with the screwdriver now in my mouth. Gregg attempted to lever the plaque with the crowbar, but almost pushed me off balance. I went to grab him. He lunged for the plaque, but let go of the crowbar. And the screwdriver…

Imagine if you will a stone church crowded with the faithful on a Sunday. Organ music plays gently in the background, overlaid by the gentle murmuring of the throng. Every so often a baby cries, or there's a sudden rush of strangled coughing. Yet. When that one poor individual at the back drops his missal, you can hear it in every corner of the church.

Take away the dulling effect of the crowd. Remove the organ. Dispense with the murmuring, the baby and the strangled coughing. Leave only silence. And replace it all, not with a gently-bound missal, but a collection of workman's utensils that would make a dozen plumbers proud, all striking stone at the same time, and you have some idea of the echoing roar that stopped the entire Mother's Union in their tracks.

Gregg and I counted to ten. Then, we both peered out from underneath the tarpaulin. The old ladies were staring at us. We stared at them. Then at each other. As one, we began hacking, wheezing and coughing. I glanced at the old ladies. Made waving motions at imaginary dust, and hacked some more. The old dears looked at us knowingly, and returned to the flowers.

I glared at Gregg. "What happened," I hissed.

"Dunno," came the equally irritated retort, "but how are we going to replace the plaque?"

"Plaque," I said, confused, "what do you mean?" Then realization dawned. Slowly. I glanced down at the floor. There, nestled on top of the pile of tools was the pride and joy of fourteen generations of the Pratt Family of Tring.

As one, we both lunged for the Plaque. Inevitably, we went through a Stooges' routine with lots of upping and downing, and hitting each other with various angular parts of the anatomy, before we had the Plaque safely hidden back under the tarpaulin. At which point, I saw the piece of paper that had been lying behind the Plaque, and which had fallen onto the floor at the same time.

I looked around. No-one was watching. Gingerly, I reached down, palmed the piece of paper, and slid it into my side pocket.

Then, Gregg and I returned to the Tarpaulin Ballet, complete with another gutsy round of hacking, wheezing and coughing, this time to cover the sounds of screwdriver, hammer and glue-gun, as Pratt Pride was restored, in all its glory, to its rightful mounting on the wall.

Once in the car, and with the doors safely locked, I peeled open the dusty, brown parchment. In fevered anticipation, I read the opening sentences. It was a program for an Antiques Fair, held at the Parish Church we had just left – an Antiques Fair held in 1947.

***

To be fair, when we'd begun the Treasure Hunt, we'd known it would probably be more Monty Python than Discovery Channel. But, we'd got caught up in it. If you stare at clouds long enough, you genuinely begin to believe that it is you, and not the elements, that are making them move. And we'd been through such a rollercoaster of emotions in the previous two weeks, that we had truly started to believe that we might find the answer to all the riddles. And some diamonds, to boot.

Gregg took it worse than I did, but we both got equally drunk at the dinner table that evening, as we dueled to see who could come up with the more appropriate form of torture for the next medium that we met. Somebody heard us. As we staggered out of the dining room, we caught sight of a bulletin board, with the newly-posted schedule of events for the coming weekend. It seemed that our hotel would be hosting a convention of the paranormal for the next two days.

We spent the two days being thoroughly bored, and falling ever deeper into the depression brought on by anti-climax. Until we happened across a small table, in a dark corner of the convention hall, a small table belonging to a palm reader called "Joe."

Gregg kindly volunteered me for the honors. We went through all the back-patting nonsense about love lines and business success; grandmothers and pets who still loved me. Gregg and I played along, as we both searched high and low for some evidence of "Joe's" last name. There was nothing.

By this time, "Joe" had moved onto telling me that I was in England to write a book. Perhaps too brusquely, I countered that I was doing no such thing. He insisted that, even if I did not know it, that is, in fact, what I was here to do.

It may have been lack of sleep, or boredom, or the accumulation of the previous two weeks of emotional rollercoaster, but I decided just to cut to the chase, and asked, a little testily, what his last name was. I was not in the least surprised when he replied "Smith." Well, so much for mediums.

We paid him and were about to leave, when, on an off-chance, I turned and asked him where he lived. "Oh," he responded pleasantly, "I'm not from around here. I live in Bath. And by the way, I think you're both in a spot of danger. Bye now."

I'll say this for astrologers and the like. They may be a bit flaky, but they know how to turn a profit. Gregg and I cleared £300 ($450) in about as many seconds, stocking up on crystals, incense and just about every herb known to ward off ghouls, ghosts and goblins. We then barricaded ourselves in the bedroom for the night.

Gregg wedged his bed against the door, and went to sleep with a baseball bat in one hand, and a particularly large crystal in the other. I opted for incense under the pillow, and some concoction of foul-smelling herbs scattered around the bedsheets.

We both tossed and turned all night long. But insomnia must have some advantages because, during the night, I had a brainwave. Jogged by my remembering a name Joe had conjured up in our session in Providence.

Hugh had had a partner-in-crime in his Intelligence adventures, and I knew where to find him. He went by the unlikely name of Reginald von Zugbach de Sugg, and, bearing in mind his name, he was to be found in the even more unlikely city of Glasgow, Scotland.

Geoffrey Gilson

Chapter 6

IN THE FIFTIES, the Americans helped to bring the Shah of Iran to power, to give them an ally to protect the Persian Gulf, and all the tankers bringing their precious cargo from the Gulf oil fields to the gas guzzlers of Detroit.

By the end of the Seventies, the original Shah had been succeeded by his son, who was still protecting the Gulf, denying his countrymen democracy and basic human rights, and maintaining an expensive military, full of toys sold to him by the British and the Americans.

An important point to remember is that Iranians do not regard themselves as Arabs. Iranians are the heirs to the Persian Empire, which ruled their then known world for hundreds of years before Alexander, the Romans or Christianity. To them, Arabs were and are nothing more than desert-wandering, homeless hoboes, who got lucky because they were sitting on liquid gold.

Remember the dictum about 'your enemies' enemies are your friends.' Well, during the time of the two Shahs, Iran hated Arabs almost as much as the Israelis. As a consequence, the Iranians and the Israelis found themselves close, if somewhat covert, allies.

At the end of the Seventies, the people of Iran had had enough. Led by their radical Islamic mullahs, their spiritual leader, Ayatollah Khomeini, and a rag-tag bunch of students, later known as the Revolutionary Guards, the Shah was ousted, and Khomeini put in his place.

Almost immediately, Iran's neighbor, Iraq, an Arab nation, led by the ubiquitous Saddam Hussein, who was never able to keep his hands out of other peoples' pockets, decided to take advantage of the turmoil, and invade Iran, to grab some of its richest oil-bearing land.

What followed was one of the ugliest blood fests between two countries in the history of a region whose blood fests make Tennessee blood feuds look like a playground romp. No quarter was given. The fight took itself all over the Gulf. The West became worried about the safety of its oil supplies, and so began armed naval patrols up and down the Gulf.

In July of 1988, the USS Vincennes accidentally shot down an Iranian airliner, mistakenly thinking it was an Iranian military aircraft about to launch an attack. The then Iranian President, one Hashemi Rafsanjani (who made a surprising comeback as the 'moderate' candidate in the Iranian Presidential Election of 2005) met with one Ahmed Jibril, and paid him $10 million to blow up an American airliner.

Ahmed Jibril was the leader of the Popular Front for the Liberation of Palestine/General Command, a particularly militant Islamic Palestinian group, which was still headquartered in the Bekaa Valley, in East Lebanon. From that position, he took regular potshots at both the Israelis, who were occupying West Lebanon and its capital, Beirut, and their allies, the Lebanese Christian militias. He also did roaring business trading in the drugs which were grown with abandon in the Bekaa Valley.

Jibril was close not only to the Iranians, but also to the Syrians, who then occupied East Lebanon. Jibril enlisted the aid of one Monzer al-Kassar, a Syrian arms broker, who was helping the Iranians illegally to buy military hardware to fight the Iraqis. Both Iraq and Iran had been placed under a military sales embargo by the United Nations.

Al-Kassar was also using his connections to assist the West in negotiating the release of their hostages from the Lebanese Muslim militias in Lebanon. Part of those efforts by the West included opening back channels into the West for those Lebanese Muslim militias and their Muslim Palestinian allies to pipeline their Bekaa-grown drugs into the West.

This backdoor pipeline was operated by DEA and CIA agents using their luggage to smuggle the drugs into Europe and America. The baggage was never searched, because the agents had diplomatic immunity.

In this way, in October of 1988, a suitcase bearing not drugs, but a bomb, was brought onto flight Pan Am 103 by one of a number of DEA and CIA agents traveling home on that flight. The suitcase began on a connecting flight out of Malta, and joined 103 in Frankfurt.

The bomb exploded over Lockerbie, Scotland during the night. Everyone on board was killed, and the wreckage fell onto the village of Lockerbie, killing several more unsuspecting Scots.

The British domestic security service, known as MI5, was instantly made aware of the import of what had happened and how. For one full day, before the emergency and rescue services were allowed to search the village of Lockerbie and the surrounding fields, which were littered with wreckage and bodies, the whole area was sealed off to all but teams of DEA, CIA and MI5 agents.

All of these agents were looking for the bomb-carrying suitcase, to remove the evidence that it was a suitcase belonging to a DEA agent. The suitcase was eventually found by one enterprising MI5 officer, high in a tree. When the final inventory was published, it indicated that there was, indeed, one suitcase missing.

This tragic episode had an even sadder twist in its tail. Those investigating the Lockerbie bombing originally tracked the trail as far as al-Kassar. At which point they discovered the extent to which the West had been in partnership with al-Kassar in the whole arms-for-hostages and Iran-Contra dealings.

And so, the story suddenly changed. The focus shifted. The perpetrators became two lowly agents in the employ of Libyan Intelligence. There is, indeed, some evidence that the Libyans, and their leader, Muhammar al-Gadhafi, were involved. They remained unhappy with the Americans for Reagan's bombing of their capital in 1986. However, they were never more than supporting actors in the Lockerbie saga.

This fact was somewhat underlined at the self-important kangaroo court that the international community later staged at The Hague in the Netherlands. The two agents had finally been handed over by Gadhafi, and were put on trial in a specially-convened Scottish Tribunal, held at the World Court, in order to assuage Libyan sensitivities. One of the two agents was acquitted, and the other agent, who was found guilty, immediately filed an appeal.

No-one cared. The subterfuge had worked. The Syrians were let off the hook, and they later backed President George Bush the Father in his invasion of their longstanding enemy, Saddam Hussein's Iraq, in 1991. The nature of the West's interaction with al-Kassar and his buddies in Syrian Intelligence was covered up. And after paying several billion dollars to the relatives of the Lockerbie victims in 2004, Gadhafi was welcomed back into the international community, and its never-ending flow of aid dollars, by the Labour Prime Minister of Great Britain, Tony Blair.

Ever since John Simmonds told me about Hugh taking his clients' money to "get an agent out of a foreign country," I had been keeping my eyes open for any and all unusual events occurring between about May and December 1988 that might have had a possible connection. As a potential candidate, Lockerbie seemed to fit the bill.

***

Gregg and I arrived in Glasgow, Scotland on a Friday. A more depressing city you can not imagine. All goth and grime. It was as I imagined some of the worst Soviet cities must have looked. We made a bee-line for the Public Library, to try to find a home address for Hugh's intelligence buddy.

After some difficulty, we succeeded. The difficulty was to be expected. We'd been looking under 'Sugg,' and there he was under 'Zugbach' all the time. The first thing I noticed was that he lived in the town of Dumfries, which was barely a stone's throw from Lockerbie. I had difficulty shaking from my mind the image of Reggie, disheveled from being woken early in the morning, rummaging around a Scottish field, and coming across a suitcase full of drugs, high up in a lonely tree.

Further research indicated that Dr. Reginald von Zugbach de Sugg had once been a British Army Major, but at the time was a Professor in Management Studies at the University of Glasgow. Reggie (which was how I remembered Hugh had always referred to him) had published a book, called "Power and Prestige in the British Army." The book was critical of management structures within the services, and it had aroused the interest of senior officers in the French Army.

Reggie's home address was deserted. A neighbor told us that Reggie and his wife were getting divorced and that they had both moved out in December. Rats. We'd have to wait until Monday, and try to catch him at the University.

We had time to kill, and almost got killed by a roving band of drunk Glaswegians. We were saved by my brother-in-law's timely impersonation of Crocodile Dundee. Although in this case, the 12-inch knife he produced like magic was hidden in his cowboy boot. I have yet to work out how he got it through airport security.

***

Bright and early Monday morning, I telephoned Reggie at the University. He had no idea who I was, but agreed to have lunch with me at the Glasgow Royal Automobile Club. He met me mid-day at my hotel, and we walked the few streets to the Club.

Notwithstanding the Teutonic name, Reggie bore all the hallmarks of a classic British military officer. Just watch any period movie about the British Empire in India, and you have Reggie in your mind's eye. Six foot tall, cropped hair, ramrod back, the arrogant stain of Empire still evident on his hard, upturned face.

We set off at a clip for the RAC. Reggie didn't look at me, just fired questions. Who was I? Why was I here? Why did I want to see him? Had Hugh been murdered? This last one stopped me. Reggie carried on a few more paces, before noticing that I was no longer in step with him.

"Why the last question?" I asked, matching Reggie's hardness with my own.

Reggie came back, and leaned down into my face. "I don't yet know who you are, but I knew Hugh. And he was not the type to take his own life." He hesitated for a second. "But if he did, he was under some mighty duress."

We circled each other for a few moments. "I'm here because I'm trying to make sense of his death," I offered as a challenge.

"But, how can I help?" he responded, warily.

"By confirming he was in British Intelligence," was my quick retort.

"How could I do that?" Reggie now had a half smile on his face.

"By confirming that you are," a smile advancing over my face as well.

With this, Reggie thrust his hands into his pockets, and wandered over to me, slowly. He whispered gently into my ear, "Problem is, laddie, if I am, the Official Secrets Act requires that I deny it; and if I'm not, then I have to deny it. Try something else."

And so the games began.

***

I merrily responded to Reggie's invitation by regaling him, throughout lunch, with all of the anecdotes Hugh had told me of their daring-do, while the two of them were in Czechoslovakia together. That had been in 1968, the year in which the Soviets had invaded that poor, repressed country, in order to re-impose Stalinist-style Communism.

The one I liked the best was the one where Reggie and Hugh had been captured in a barn. Reggie had been shot in the back. While the Soviet guards were doing something particularly nasty and painful to Reggie's fingernails, the only pleasure he had given them was when he finally screamed, "shit that hurts!"

Reggie had feigned indifference for going on an hour by this point. But with this last story, he put down his fork, studiously wiped his mouth with his linen handkerchief, and, mustering a thousand years of combined Teutonic and British pride, archly pronounced that, being a gentleman, he never screamed. Thank you. "And the word I used was 'ouch,'" he concluded, with an aristocratic sniff.

He then got up from the table, and motioned me to follow. We entered the Men's Toilet. Reggie locked the door, checked the window, and ran a couple of the faucets, I assumed to deter any listening devices. How exciting. Just like the movies. Yawn.

Reggie looked thoroughly amused. "It seems Hugh was a little indiscreet."

"Not really," I rejoined, "It served its purpose. No-one else believes me; but I know enough to be here engaging you."

"Hmm. Maybe." He looked at the floor for a few minutes, obviously deep in thought. It's a good thing that all the other RAC members

Dead Men Don't Eat Lunch

were constipated. Finally, he looked up. "Ok. I can tell you this much, but no more: I was in a military branch of British Intelligence, and Hugh was in a civilian equivalent."

At lust a nugget. A tiny crack. I was ecstatic. So much so that I found myself babbling about all sorts of nonsense. Ending with the declaration that this probably explained why I had been followed all the way to Glasgow by what was clearly a very professional outfit.

Suddenly I was aware that, except for the echo of my own voice, there was no other sound in the bathroom. I glanced over at Reggie. His face had turned white, and he was muttering to himself. The aristocratic sneer had disappeared. "…damn, I thought I'd got rid of them, but you've brought them back…" This last comment was directed at me, and the hard stare was back in his eyes.

He grabbed my arm, unlocked the door, and shuffled me towards the Club entrance. "Look," he barked, "if you value your life, you will do exactly as I say." And with that, we were into the sunlight, and onto a chase scene that was more bizarre and twisted than anything Ang Lee ever could have devised.

***

As we crossed the road in military two-step, he whispered harshly in my ear, "stay to my side, don't look up, they may not recognize you." We maintained the brisk pace all the way to the car in the parking lot, with Reggie giving me a running commentary:

"You were right. They're out in force. One on the corner over there. One on the other side of the road. No, don't look," he hissed. "I wonder if they're after you or me? Oh very clever…one behind us dressed as a police-woman…"

Once in his car, he told me to lock my door, and then locked his own. We made our way slowly across the parking lot, Reggie glancing in every direction. He stopped briefly at the exit. "Roll down your window," he commanded, "and just stare obviously at that man standing on the corner, over there on the left."

Hey, what did I know? I did as Reggie suggested. The man, apparently on cue, turned away. At which point, Reggie swung the car violently to the right, tires squealing. We would have sped off down the road, if we hadn't been stopped by the traffic lights. Not the way it happens in the cinema, at all. A car tucked in behind us. "Damn," came Reggie's muttered oath.

The lights changed. And we entered a realm of fantasy driving, not to be found on the daytime menu of your average downtown driving school. My heart was pretty much firmly lodged in my mouth. Indeed, this time a whole series of scenes did flash before my eyes. But they weren't about me. They were about Hugh.

***

It was the British General Election of 1979. Hugh was the Conservative Parliamentary Candidate in that safe Labour seat of West Leeds. One of Margaret Thatcher's closest lieutenants, Airey Neave, was assassinated by an IRA bomb, which had been positioned underneath his car. It was generally known that Neave had been in British Military Intelligence during the Second World War. In fact, he was something of a hero, having been imprisoned in Colditz, Germany's top-security prison castle.

The day after Neave's assassination, a nondescript little man appeared at our campaign headquarters. He spoke to Hugh in urgent whispers, and then disappeared for an hour or two with my brother Jon, who was helping out by being Hugh's campaign driver.

Later that night, Jon, unable to contain himself any more, revealed to me that he had spent the afternoon with this guy, who did not offer his name, learning all sorts of driving tricks with Hugh's Rover sedan.

How to perform a 180 degree emergency-brake turn. How to judge and navigate sharp corners, without braking. And best of all, how to know which parts of the car were least vulnerable to being hit.

"Why?" I asked Jon, already guessing at the answer.

"So that I know which parts of the car I can use to ram other cars, if we're in a trap," he exclaimed, the look of a happy five-year old plastered all over his beaming face.

Some years later, in the Eighties, when Thatcher was Prime Minister, another of her close aides, Ian Gow, was assassinated in a similar car bombing. This was followed by a rash of IRA assassinations, including that of the British Ambassador to Eire (Southern Ireland), and Lord Mountbatten, the Queen's cousin, and a Field Marshal in the British Army.

I remember standing by Hugh as he gazed sadly at the television set, recording the funeral of Lord Mountbatten. Softly, as if I was not there, he murmured that the IRA had good sources because they were killing off all the former British Intelligence desk officers for Northern Ireland.

That was some years before the Good Friday Peace Accord, brokered by a combination of Northern Irish Catholic and Protestant politicians, and midwifed by Bill Clinton, John Major and Tony Blair. Before the Accord, the Seventies and Eighties had been a time of regular IRA bombing campaigns on the UK mainland.

The first IRA bomb, aimed at civilians in Great Britain, had been planted in the Seventies, at the Old Bailey, in London. The Old Bailey is England's premier criminal court. A bomb scare was telephoned into the central desk. All the courts were immediately emptied onto the street fronting the building. Some moments later, the massive bomb exploded. But outside, not inside the building, catching innocent bystanders, who thought they had reached safety. Hugh had been at the Old Bailey that day, and was standing outside when the bomb exploded. He was unscratched, save for some temporary hearing loss.

As the years passed by, the British public became much more safety-conscious, decades before the American public had to go through the same routine, in response to 9/11 and the threat from radical Muslim militias. Police were alerted to suspicious packages left on trains; overparked cars were blown up with controlled explosions.

This was how I had known, instantly, that the subway bombs, in London, in 2005, had been the work of suicide bombers. The British public had become far too aware of terrorist threats to allow five separate bombs to sit around unquestioned. Those bombs had to have been introduced in a fashion that would have gone unnoticed, and then been detonated by people in close proximity.

Some years after the first IRA bombing campaign in London, Hugh found himself dining one evening with a friend, at an exclusive restaurant in London, called *Wilton's*. Suddenly, there was a crash of glass, and a heavy object came tumbling in through the shattered window. Hugh was quick to react. He upended the heavy table at which he and the friend were sitting, seized his friend, and took cover behind the table.

His friend had been a little faster. As Hugh was reaching for him, so he too grabbed the open and expensive bottle of claret they had been drinking, and hit the floor, cushioning the precious bottle with his body. The IRA bomb exploded a second later.

Again, both Hugh and his friend were unhurt, but, as Hugh recounted cryptically some years later, there weren't two many 'civilians' who found themselves in the midst of two IRA bombings. I still wonder whether or not Hugh's initials are carved somewhere on that Northern Ireland desk. I wasn't doing much wondering at the time, though. I was more focused on Reggie's exotic driving skills.

***

Reggie had us circling blocks. Dodging through parking lots. In and out of driveways. Stopping. Starting. Doubling back. Down one street. Up another. Until we found ourselves trapped in a dead end.

We reversed hurriedly, the engine screaming, the gears grinding. At the last moment, Reggie swung the car around in a perfect 180 degree emergency brake turn, just missing the car that had been on our tail. "Yup," I thought to myself, "that's how Jon did it." A couple of Middle-Eastern looking swarthies leaned out the windows, cursing and spitting, and waving hand-guns at us.

Reggie was into his groove now. We went the wrong way down one-way streets. Turned right, while signaling left. Slowed down; speeded up. In and out; roundabout. And found ourselves back in another dead end.

I glanced at Reggie. He smiled wanly. "It really doesn't happen like this in the movies," was his weak explanation, as he crunched us into another body-slamming 180 degree turn, and almost slammed into the body of the car that was still behind us. The swarthies didn't bother to threaten us this time; instead, they mocked us with catcalls and whistles, as we squeezed past them in abject humiliation.

Whereupon, the Keystone Chase continued. Much more bobbing and weaving. A lot more geography of Greater Glasgow. Ducking and diving. Running stop signs. Up, down, all around town. And then, the knock-out punch. A third dead end.

Reggie gently lowered his forehead onto the driving wheel, and let out a long sigh. He checked his mirror, and grunted. Gathering what remained of his shattered pride, he asked me, with studied politeness, if I would signal out the window to the car that had been chasing us, "and see if they'd be so good as to back up, and let us out."

I waited a second for the punchline. When none came, I rolled down my window, leaned out and waved vaguely at the car behind us. It was all the swarthies could do not to shoot themselves by mistake, they were laughing so hard.

But they quickly got into the act. While the driver, tears of mirth rolling down his cheeks, carefully backed his car out of the way, to let us pass, his partner went through an elaborate charade of guiding us out of the dead end, using the automatic weapon in his right hand and the handgun in his left like a couple of airport batons.

Halfway through the process, a third car pulled up with a screech of tires. Out of this vehicle spilled a rogue's gallery of angry thugs, all yelling and screaming and waving a veritable safari of guns at us. It was becoming quite the cocktail party.

The scene from *Smokey and the Bandit* resumed for a further twenty minutes of stomach-churning nonsense, until Reggie lost all of the pursuers. Either that, or they simply gave up because they decided they'd had enough amusement for one wet, Scottish afternoon.

Reggie pulled into the parking lot of a rather seedy apartment complex. As we entered, Reggie rummaged around behind a small cupboard by the front door, extracted a six-shooter, and tucked it into his coat pocket. As he was doing this, I couldn't help but notice the gold signet ring on his left pinky finger. Engraved as it was with the crest of a double-headed eagle.

Dead Men Don't Eat Lunch

***

I know I should have been terrified, but I wasn't. I found myself unusually calm, with everything happening around me in a kind of warm slow motion. I sat in a chair in the corner of his living room, and just watched Reggie with detached bemusement.

He was making a telephone call. Didn't say very much. Just a couple of words. Then hung up. Finally, he turned to me. The confident air was gone. However I might have been feeling, Reggie was clearly now a very agitated man.

He sat down on the edge of a sofa, nervous and twitchy, and the words came tumbling out of his mouth. Hugh and he had not met accidentally. The implication was that he had had something to do with Hugh's original recruitment. Reggie confirmed that he had been with Hugh in Czechoslovakia in 1968. He even confirmed the "ouch" story, though he embellished it somewhat.

I got the feeling Reggie was trying to convince me of something, but I couldn't work out what or why. Frankly, he'd had me at "ouch."

Nevertheless, Reggie continued unchecked. He stated that Hugh had been involved in some "interesting bits and pieces" before his death. Reggie did not believe that Hugh was a crook. And he repeated that he did not hold with the line that Hugh had committed suicide. "Not with all we've been through," was his heartfelt explanation.

Reggie mentioned that he'd been threatened in a local telephone call, made to his then home, in Dumfries, in October 1988. The message had been picked up by his answering machine. The chilling message had stated, matter-of-factly, that "we are going to get you, Doctor." He had handed the tape over to the Police. I could check.

Both Reggie and his wife had received continuing telephone calls, always threatening. His house had been broken into, on a number of occasions. So had his car. Papers had been taken. His mail had been interfered with.

Although Reggie did not discuss his wife, he did say that, since the end of 1988, he'd had to move from apartment to apartment, in order to keep his night-time location a secret. Every evening, he'd go through the same rigmarole I'd just experienced in his car, just to get home safely. No-one would bother him during the day, in the open. That would invite unwanted attention. No. The cloak and dagger routine was reserved for the dark hours, away from public gaze.

"But they're in the open today," I countered.

He looked at me darkly. "Yes," he spat, "and you brought them with you. I thought they'd lost interest in me last April. Now, I can't work out whether they want me, or you."

Reggie held my gaze for a second longer, and then dropped his head in his hands. He explained that he'd been in fear of his life since before Hugh had died. That's why he'd been hiding out. "God," he cried out, flinging his arm around the tiny room, "you think I choose to live like this?"

I asked him why he thought he was in danger. His stumbling response wasn't very convincing. There were things he was not prepared to tell me. He began chopping and changing his routine, one minute alluding to the things in which Hugh had become involved, the next, affecting ignorance of anything and everything.

I asked him who he thought was causing all the trouble – MI6 [Britain's foreign intelligence service] or MI5? For the first time, he laughed out loud. "Neither," he exclaimed, with genuine amusement, "whoever they are, they're far too sophisticated for British Intelligence."

He paused for a second. Then continued. "Look. I'd like you to see me and my new girlfriend, later this afternoon. Say about 5.30.p.m?"

I wondered why.

"I want you to repeat everything to her," he reasoned, "about Hugh, about the missing money, about your suspicions. I want her to hear it from someone else. I want some insurance. Ok?"

I shrugged my shoulders. Why not? How much further could I descend into Wonderland?

After this, Reggie went silent. Then, he made another abbreviated telephone call. This time, he did more listening than talking. By the time he hung up, his facial expression had hardened. "Right," he said coldly, "time to go."

He reached into a desk drawer, and pulled out a passport. Tucked it into another pocket of his coat. I asked him where he was going: "Away for a while." What about the meeting with your girlfriend? "Cancelled," came his taut reply.

We went back to the car. There was a man standing by the entrance to the parking lot, watching us. We got into the car, locked the doors, and drove past the man, without looking at him. As we pulled into the street, a new car slipped in behind us. And so the circus act began again.

There was no further conversation between Reggie and me. He concentrated on his alarming driving regime. Finally, we approached a multi-story car park. As we sped into the basement, he shouted more instructions at me. "When I say 'jump'," he ordered, "you get out fast."

We swerved around a couple of pillars, and then as we came up to a dark corner, he yelled at me to jump. I flung open the door, and launched myself out. The car was still moving, and I staggered for a few steps. But I quickly steadied myself, and then looked back at Reggie's car.

He had brought the car to a halt, and was leaning across the passenger seat. Aiming his six-shooter at me. Without thinking, I threw

Dead Men Don't Eat Lunch

myself towards a half-open door, nestled in the dark corner, about five feet away. The last thing I heard, as I disappeared through the welcoming doorway, was the sound of two ear-splitting explosions behind me.

Geoffrey Gilson

Chapter 7

As SOON AS I'd known I was traveling to England, I'd telephoned Maggi, who was back in Australia. Calling her for help was becoming something of a routine now.

I'd originally intended for her to accompany me to the UK. Gregg quite reasonably had pointed out that, if I was facing half as much trouble as common sense suggested I might be, leave alone the input from all the ghosties and ghoulies, I would probably need more than a five-foot slip of a girl covering my back. So, Gregg came with me and held a baseball bat, while Maggi stayed behind in Rhode Island and held the fort.

After listening to the tape of the medium session, Maggi had insisted on working out a security regime to give her and Susannah some sort of heads up if we got into trouble. Gregg and I would telephone Rhode Island every afternoon at 4.00 p.m. precisely, British time. Up to my meeting with Reggie, we'd kept to the system religiously for the two weeks we'd been in England.

I practically ran back to the hotel after Reggie 'dropped' me off. I burst into the hotel room, and danced a jig around the room. I was too high on adrenaline to be scared. I told Gregg about the meeting in detail. And then I did it twice more for good measure. When finally I calmed down, and one of us remembered to look at a clock, it read 5.00 p.m.

My sisters are neither one of them tall. They make up for this with attitude. They took it in turns to excoriate us, employing the full range of Shakespearean English. Gregg and I took turns in holding the telephone at arms length, occasionally getting close enough to utter a grunt of apology.

When finally the girls had run out of steam, Maggi told me about her own session with Bill. They had dabbled in a bit of Previous Life Regression, or whatever the heck they call it. Apparently, Maggi and I had been lovers back in ancient Greece. I had walked in on her embracing a male friend of hers in total innocence, I'd got the wrong impression, and in a stupid fit of jealousy, I'd committed suicide.

Bill had told Maggi that the purpose of my current incarnation was to learn trust. And that somehow, the triangle between Hugh, me and her was to be instrumental in this. Ok. I could get into this. I wondered if Hugh might have been the 'male friend' in the previous life? And if, in some fashion, his suicide in this lifetime was a subconscious 'gift' of atonement, and a token of what trust meant?

I could tell an entire phone line away that Maggi wasn't sure if I was taking the piss or not. In any event, for reasons of which she was not quite certain, she had thought this information might be useful to me.

We then engaged in a protracted kiss-and-make-up routine, and offered mutual apologies for losing our respective tempers. After hanging up the phone, I noticed that Gregg was looking a tad somber. He'd been a good companion, but it was time for him to return home. The Treasure Hunt had been a hoot, a cross between Monty Python and Benny Hill, but he was not cut out for the cloak-and-dagger nonsense. He was tired and he missed his wife.

Fortunately, his wife had another good deed she could throw my way. A childhood friend of hers, Rissa, had offered to let me stay with her in London as long as I needed. On my way to take up that offer, I dropped Gregg off at Heathrow Airport.

I was having so much fun, I'd quite forgotten it was my birthday. Rissa took me out for dinner, and treated me to my first taste of civilization in two weeks. I have a feeling now the treat might have been intended to include more, but at the time I was way too much the self-absorbed idiot. I crashed and slept like a baby in the spare room.

In any event, I needed all the sleep I could get. Before leaving Glasgow, I'd arranged a meeting for the following day with the Law Society and Carratu International. They'd had no idea I was in England, and had sounded quite nervous.

***

The Law Society, headquartered in Chancery Lane, finds itself surrounded by the gothic spires and turrets of London's ancient High Court. Perhaps inspired by surroundings that date back to the Middle Ages, my meeting with the Law Society turned out to be something akin to the Spanish Inquisition. There were six of them, including Geoff Hughes, on one side of a conference table, and me on the other. Geoff had a tape recorder on the table in front of him. I had one hidden in my jacket pocket.

It proved to be a singularly frustrating get together, the reason for which was established with the first exchange: "Why are you here?" asked the Law Society's head honcho, who did not introduce himself.

"Well," I replied, "I've always liked England in the summer; the cool climate, the languid afternoons, the sound of leather against willow at a village cricket game..."

"No Mr. Gilson," the no-name interrupted curtly, "why did you want to see us?"

"Oh," I feigned surprise, "to clear my name. But, more to the point, to find out why you were the ones who decided to start dragging it through the mud? You told me I was in the clear."

"Yes. Well. We've determined in the last few months that Simmonds must have had help," was the short reply, "And it was decided that you were the most obvious candidate."

After that, they pretty much clammed up. They quite openly took the view that the only reason I was there was to throw them off my trail. "But here I am, do your worst," I countered. To no avail. They were convinced I was trying to pull something clever. If they only knew.

I hammered away for an hour. I was riding a confident streak after my episode with Reggie. I had nothing to lose.

They did admit that they had recovered no money. After some baiting, they grudgingly confessed that, in fact, they hadn't actually traced any of the missing money. They had no clue as to why only £3.8 million ($5.6 million) of the £5 million ($7.5 million) missing had been claimed.

I was beginning to see why they were turning the spotlight on me. They had run out of alternatives. In some exasperation, I finally wondered aloud why on earth they were even bothering to spend time with me that morning.

In equal frustration, a little weasel of a desk clerk, John Bateman, suddenly piped up from the back: "Because we think you know where the £10 million ($15 million) came from."

Except for the quite audible sound of leather shoe impacting on Bateman's exposed ankle, you could have heard a pin drop in that room.

"Come again," I said. "I thought we'd just established that you hadn't traced any money?"

Silence.

"And now we're talking about some £10 million extra?"

Another pregnant pause, broken by the no-name head honcho. He cleared his throat noisily: "We appear to have found some £10 million that does not belong to any of Simmonds' clients. We wondered if you had any ideas...?"

I'd had enough for one morning. I gave them Reggie's telephone number, and suggested, my voice icy with sarcasm, that they give him a call. As I was leaving, I noticed out of the corner of my eye Geoff Hughes, looking quite amused. He signaled me to have a word with him.

I had mentioned in the meeting about my being followed. Geoff wanted to take up a hidden vantage point in the parking lot before I made a move for my car. I obliged, waited a few, and then drove off, quite obviously being followed by a fake taxi.

A couple of days later, I telephoned Geoff and asked him if he had seen the taxi. "Oh yes, the taxi," he answered softly, "and the other two cars as well."

In Geoff's opinion, I was being tailed by what he described as a classic three-car tandem formation. I asked him to define what he meant by 'classic.' He hung up. Geoff was no pen-pushing desk jockey. His first career had been as a Senior Inspector with Her Majesty's Customs and Excise.

***

On which note, my next port of call was a Senior Inspector with Her Majesty's Police Constabulary. I was in no mood to be trifled with. If I was going so openly to be held in suspicion, I might as well tackle the accusers head on. Specifically, I met with a Detective Inspector Lambert and a Detective Sergeant Brown. Another inconclusive conversation followed.

The Police had already cottoned to the fact that Hugh appeared to have been messing around with more than just his clients' money. Lambert said that they too were now openly looking for an accomplice. However, he didn't seem to be making any real effort to find one. Except for continually asking me if I was yet ready to tell him where the missing money was. He almost visibly yawned when I suggested that he might find the answers with British Intelligence.

Lambert did, however, confirm that I was being followed. Not by them, he hastened to add, with a heartless chuckle. But by a car that followed me into the Police parking lot. An officer had been dispatched to talk to the driver, but he'd driven away before they could catch him. The Police in England aren't much into "Cops"-style T.V. chases.

I gave Lambert a list of license plate numbers for the cars that had been following Gregg and me. A few weeks later, Lambert informed me that two of the plates were "odd." One belonged to a firm of private investigators in Surrey; the other to a company that "doesn't exist." When asked to explain what that meant, he wouldn't say any more. He sounded somewhat embarrassed.

Not half as embarrassed as when he had to admit that the tape-recording of our initial interview didn't exist because his recording machine hadn't functioned.

This might have had something to do with the phantom Detective Sergeant Brown. Nick Brown, as he'd been introduced to me, had contributed nothing during my interview with Lambert. When I called the

Police Station the first time to speak with Lambert about the tape-recording, I'd been told Lambert was not in the Station. When I asked for his assistant, Sergeant Brown, I'd been told that they'd never had a Sergeant Brown in the Station.

MI5 is the domestic counterpart to Britain's foreign intelligence service, MI6. However, it should not be confused with America's FBI, which is a national law enforcement agency, as well as a spy-catching operation. MI5 can only go after foreign spies. It has no 'every-day' law enforcement capacity. It can not arrest or even question criminal suspects. For this to be done, it has to get its officers to 'pretend' to be Police Officers, so that they can sit in and listen while real Police Officers question suspects. As has been proven time and again by investigative journalists, the tell-tale sign of such MI5 'sit-ins' is their subsequent 'disappearance' when enquiries became a little too intrusive.

Curious. If I was so far off base with my enquiries, why was MI5 interested in me? As a lark, I contacted Geoff Hughes, and asked if I could have a copy of the tape-recording Carratu made of our meeting at the Law Society: "Um, funny thing, Geoff," he told me, "but that tape-recording's been lost…"

***

Rissa had been the perfect hostess, even attempting to take an interest in what I was doing. I don't think, however, she believed a word of it. So it was with enormous surprise that she flung open the door that evening to tell me breathlessly that Reggie had called and would be calling later: "Oh my goodness, Geoff, he exists; he really exists."

Chapter 8

"It's A GOOD THING you're a fast runner, and I'm a lover of mankind." I'll say this for Reggie, he certainly knew how to start a conversation in style.

"So, what was the parking lot all about," I asked, my calm voice belying my frantic heart, which was tapping a merry tattoo on my ribs.

"I had my orders," Reggie replied. Those orders were to kill me. Not because someone knew what I was doing, but because no-one knew what I was doing. Better safe than sorry. But Reggie had doubts. He wanted now to play a double game. Pretend to be getting information from me, while actually trying to find out what was going on.

"I'll be in touch," was his last comment before hanging up. I'd had no time to get a home telephone number, or come to think of it, quiz him as to how he'd found out Rissa's telephone number.

***

Well, that was somewhat shorter a conversation than I had hoped. Time for a quick review: no diamonds; no Gregg; Reggie's on 'walkabout;' the Law Society and the Police were on hold, plus they were taking the view I had no right to be poking my nose into all of this. What was a chap to do?

I came up with the bright idea that maybe I should be poking my nose with a little more depth and breadth. So, while waiting on Reggie, I decided to spend my time and my money making the rounds of as many of Hugh's friends and acquaintances as I could to see what they might know. Another Treasure Hunt, only this time it wasn't diamonds I was looking for, but rather, more 'nuggets' of information.

***

Geoffrey Gilson

I must have given Karen the telephone number to my rented cellphone. She called me, all breathless. She'd been to see her medium, 'Cheryl.' I feared I might be starting a trend. Cheryl told Karen that Hugh had a plan, and would have sorted things out. But he hadn't had enough time. He'd been betrayed by one man.

In the same breath, Karen mentioned that Hugh had had a major bust up with David Pembroke in the summer of 1988. She added that David had been spending a lot of time at her house since Hugh's death, all friendly, but asking a bunch of strange questions.

David Pembroke was a shady East End lad made good; a middle-aged Cockney ferret in a stockbroker suit. London's East End is a tough environment. It makes Queens or Brooklyn feel like a Sunday stroll through Peoria. It was here that David had made his first fortune, publishing newspapers. One of his primary customers had been the *Daily Mirror*.

Then he'd decided to head for greener pastures: namely Beaconsfield, and the lush opportunities offered by residential development. Not surprisingly, the well-heeled locals had not taken kindly to this parvenu yahoo, trampling all over their chrysanthemums, in his haste to build tacky new sub-divisions.

So he'd hired Hugh as his personal guide. To help him negotiate the maze of local planning regulations. And the wiles of elected officials. Who wielded their restrictions like so many suburban chastity belts. Hugh, with his mouth, his arrogance, and his local government background, proved too much of a match. The successes flowed. As did the money. And in the ensuing years, Pembroke had become a mainstay of Hugh's bottom line. Until, it would seem, the summer of 1988.

***

I spoke with Karen while on my way to see Hugh's former receptionist, Jill: tall, leggy, blond and as sweet as an iced glass of cranberry juice, on a hot summer's afternoon.

Jill reminded me of one of Hugh's Italian clients, one Alberto Sabbatino. Although Alberto's primary source of income had been a jewelry importing business, based in London, he was in fact a member of the British 'branch' of the Mafia, with extensive interests in Bournemouth, Britain's equivalent of Atlantic City, New Jersey.

Alberto had a mistress. The Mafia apparently have strict rules about mistresses. Particularly concerning money. Alberto wanted to bend the rules. He needed a discrete lawyer, with balls, who was not connected to the Mob in any way. Hugh fit the bill.

According to Jill, Hugh and Alberto had had pretty much of a rollercoaster working relationship in 1988. At the beginning of 1988, Alberto was really anxious to see Hugh. About some information Alberto needed for his Accountant. Hugh had stalled.

Then came springtime, and Alberto was Hugh's best pal. Always took his telephone calls. Met with him on a regular basis. Went out to lunch at Beaconsfield's best Italian restaurant. Finally, during the summer months of 1988, Hugh had avoided Alberto like the plague.

I remembered an episode from the day Hugh had died, one I had completely forgotten. Jill had come into my office, and shut the door. She acted very shifty. She told me that, in the week before he died, Hugh had told her that, in the event anything happened to him, she should tell me to contact Alberto, who would explain everything.

Hugh was dead. I knew nothing. So, I had called Alberto. He was effusive in both his surprise and his condolences. But, he hadn't the first clue what I was talking about. Sorry. Goodbye.

Jill was very concerned for me. Bless her heart. She gave me a long hug as I got up to leave. Bless her everything else. When I began to feel things stirring, I gently pried us apart, and made my farewells. To her and her husband.

***

I should never have given Karen my telephone number. I was now being subjected to a running commentary of her thought processes. She rang me this time to tell me about Bob Pickard, one of the two Directors of Sensonics Ltd., a former client firm of Hugh's.

Karen had been to a 1988 Christmas Party with an on again-off again boyfriend called "Nick," who had an interest in polo ponies. Bob Pickard had been at the same party. They lived only a few minutes away from each other.

During the evening, Nick had come up to her and said that he'd just had the most extraordinary conversation with Bob, who told him that Hugh had been a Brigadier-General in MI6, and that he'd taken his clients' money to pay some ransom.

What the heck, I thought. Let's go and talk to the Sensonics boys.

***

Sensonics Limited was a smallish electronics firm in Amersham, a town some seven miles from Beaconsfield, and a stone's throw or two from the wooded beauty spot where Hugh's body had been discovered.

I never did learn how Hugh had come to know the two directors of Sensonics, Bob Pickard and Horst Rauter. But he got to know them well enough that, in the mid-Eighties, they asked him to handle the multi-million dollar buyout of their company by a large German firm.

Part of the sale process required that Hugh hold the sale proceeds in his Clients' Account for a while. Not surprisingly, most of it disappeared in Hugh's defalcation, and indeed, that had been the primary cause of the Law Society getting involved. Apparently.

In all of the circumstances, Horst Rauter proved to be a remarkably courteous host when he agreed to see me. Horst looks like Robbie Coltrane's twin brother, only with a better haircut. You will remember that Robbie plays the giant, Hagrid, who looks after the monsters in the *Harry Potter* movies.

Horst had little to offer. He spent most of our lunch meeting alternating between bemoaning the loss of his good friend, Hugh, and cursing him for his betrayal. He did, however, tell me that Sensonics had one contract with the British Ministry of Defense: it was to develop a small electronic device that could be attached in a particular pattern to the hulls of submarines, and would then give the submarine the sonic signature of a humpback whale. He also mentioned that his family came from a region now in East Germany, and they had a bunch of bank accounts in East Berlin.

Tentatively, I raised the subject of Bob Pickard. Horst had had little to do with him since Sensonics had been sold. He'd always found Bob a strange fish. Bob knew things other people did not know. Bob had warned Horst that Hugh was skint, months before Hugh's death. Somehow, Bob had managed to get all of his money out of Hugh. Something no other client had achieved. Indeed, the last payment by Hugh to Bob had caused the permanent overdraft on Hugh's Clients' Account which had been the ostensible reason for NatWest's foreclosure. What hold had Bob had over Hugh to force him to take this terminal step?

Horst told me of a recent conversation he'd had with Bob, when Bob had told him that I was back in the country. Bob knew all about my adventures with Gregg, and told Horst that we had "ransacked" Karen's house, while being dressed "to hijack." Finally, Bob had said that Hugh had had £5 million ($7.5 million) on him, either on the day of his death or the day before. Hugh was heavily involved in drug-trafficking. And that he'd been in the woods, where he was found dead, not to commit suicide, but for an early morning and clandestine rendezvous. How did Bob know all this? What were his sources? What was the money for? If the money was for the 'operation,' what had happened to the money and to the 'operation.' I drew little comfort from the fact that Bob lived only a few minutes from the woods where Hugh had been found. And he would not return my telephone calls.

***

Dead Men Don't Eat Lunch

I had more luck with Horst's Accountant, Neil Relph. Neil was the classic success story of Margaret Thatcher's attempts in the Eighties to turn Great Britain into an enterprise economy like America's: a country which had its own Dream, to which every Ordinary Joe could aspire through hard work and dedication. Neil hadn't been to the best schools, but he'd earned his college degree, studied to be an accountant, found a working balance between charm and sweat, and was now next in line to be Senior Partner of Rouse and Company, Beaconsfield's largest firm of Chartered Accountants.

He was also a friend of mine, and a dedicated buddy of Hugh's. We found an out-of-the way pub to have a quiet lunch together. Even before our orders were taken, Neil was telling me about his young son. How he had a rare spinal disease that was terminal without expensive surgery. Hugh had found a surgeon, and made the introductions. Upon learning that there was no way Neil could afford the procedure, Hugh had paid for the whole operation. Leaving aside the unspoken concern that we had now had no idea precisely whose money Hugh might have used, Neil had been Hugh's to command from that point on.

Neil had suspected that Hugh was stealing. Neil was not only Sensonic's accountant, he was Hugh's too. And Neil did regular business with the branch of NatWest where they both banked. Hugh had not allowed Neil near his law firm's accounts for two years. Then, when Neil started hearing rumors from Horst and from Bernard Goodchild, Manager of NatWest, he knew something was wrong.

Neil tried on three separate occasions to persuade Hugh to let him into his law firm's office. All Neil wanted to do was to help. Finally, in the week before Hugh died, Neil telephoned Hugh late at night at home. He had pleaded with Hugh. Neil knew that at least £1 million was missing. It would take him 24 hours to get the books up to date. They could then get a loan from Hugh's father, and negotiate with the Law Society. Hugh had been gentle but firm. He was not going to get Neil into trouble. That was all he would say. Neil sobbed quietly at the lunch table. He was one of the very few true friends that Hugh had had. I hoped Hugh realized that before he died.

Neil then raised the first suggestion that I'd heard of potential political involvement or protection at a high level. He said that it had not been Bernard Goodchild's idea to foreclose on Hugh's bank accounts, and on that particular day. The instruction had come directly from the Office of the Chairman of National Westminster, Lord Boardman, who had served as a Treasury Minister in a former Conservative Government, and had been Joint Treasurer of the Conservative Party in the early Eighties.

Boardman had to resign as Chairman of NatWest in 1989 because of a scandal involving what was then a large British company called Blue Arrow plc. NatWest's stockbroking subdivision had been involved in all sorts of illegal activity with regards to a huge share issue for Blue Arrow in 1987. Martha Stewart and Enron did not invent stock and accounting fraud in the Second Stock Boom in the Nineties. They'd learned their skills from all those who cut their teeth doing the same things in the First Stock Boom in the Eighties.

At this point, I turned to lighter matters, and regaled Neil with stories from Gregg's and my Treasure Hunt for the diamonds and the hidden clues. Neil was all ears. He was also by now well into his cups. Not to be outdone, he leaned over and told me conspiratorially that Karen had been seeing a medium as well. I knew this, I told him. Undeterred, he stated that she had told him that her medium had told her that there was a document hidden in or near a church. Up a lane with high hedges. And that the document "told everything." Including where the money was. "And," he added with a gentle slur, pulling closer, and treating me to a full blast of brandy fumes, "I know where that church is."

We grabbed a bottle for the road, and bundled into Neil's car. We headed for another little village near Beaconsfield called Hedgerley, where, interestingly enough, Martin Pratt had his home. Well into the spirit of the moment, on all sorts of levels, Neil accepted my instruction on the finer points of evading possible tails. We needn't have bothered. Anyone following us would have had no problem with the two drunk clowns in the car ahead. "Ok sir," I could hear them communicating to control, "they've just taken five minutes to turn left, while their signal is indicating right. Crafty that. We might have missed it…"

We didn't care. We were Masters of the Universe that afternoon. It mattered not that the rest of the world simply saw Jerry Lewis retreads. Eventually we found Hedgerley. And the church. Parked the car in the duck pond. And staggered up the path to the church – a path bordered by high, unkempt hedgerows.

The church was locked. Par for the course. But this did not stop us investigating every gravestone. Every wall. Every nook. Every cranny. And every single promising mole hill. Finally, Neil jumped up on the other side of the graveyard, waving frantically. I dashed over. 'Dash,' of course, including two trips and a cartwheel over gravestones that the alcohol in my system had hidden from my eyes.

"Look," he cried triumphantly. I stared at a gravestone in the name of someone called 'Smith.' "So what?" I cried, wondering vaguely why both Neil and his twin felt this was important. "Shhh," he hushed savagely, at no-one in particular, "it could be an alias."

"But Neil" I responded, common sense finally breaking into a corner of my befuddled mind, "this 'Smith' guy died fifty years before Hugh was born." Neil gave me a withering look of disdain, gathered around him what dignity the grass-stains on his suit trousers would allow, and waded back through the pond to the car. I followed quietly, the hang-over already beginning to pound against my skull.

***

Bob Pickard was not the only strange fish Hugh had known. Another was Oliver Hill. He was a South African businessman. At least he had been until he illegally shipped his entire chemical plant, and all of his wealth, out of South Africa during the years of Apartheid in the Eighties.

Oliver could have spent the rest of his years living the life of leisure with the millions he'd got away with. But he was a man of action and purpose. And besides, he had a fully-stocked chemical plant sitting on a ship in harbor.

So, he hit on the idea of building an explosives factory in Northern Ireland. Bearing in mind the two decades of open warfare that province has suffered between its Catholics and its Protestants, this struck me as being about as sane as wanting to build one in Baghdad.

Nevertheless, Oliver was serious, and he was joined in that seriousness by Hugh and Martin Pratt. Which made me wonder once more about those 'powers-that-be' lurking behind Hugh. In any event, Hugh's death brought the guillotine down on this particular venture. But I still thought it might be worthwhile paying Oliver a visit.

Oliver lived in unashamed opulence in a large townhouse on fashionable Eaton Square, in Belgravia, London, just a notch or two up from Fifth Avenue in New York. He himself is not an imposing man to look at. Small and rotund, with a small amount of black hair slicked over his glowing pate; his ruddy face all flesh and the good life. The image was rounded out by a very limp handshake.

Yet the appearance belied the sharpness of the mind behind his dark darting eyes. He gave away nothing in a conversation, which very quickly ground to a natural halt. His only substantive contribution was the observation that he could not understand why Hugh had stolen his clients' money. "It doesn't make sense," he said. "I made millions getting money out of South Africa. I invited Hugh to join me. More than once. He refused. Because it was less than wholly legal. And then he goes and does what he did…"

***

I received an urgent telephone call from Geoff Hughes of Carratu. He wanted to see me. This time I met with him at his firm's plush offices in Surrey. He said he had some papers he wished to show me. Before this, I reported to him on all the matters that had come my way. I noticed in passing that there was no tape-recorder this time.

I can't say as he seemed all that interested in what I was telling him, but he listened courteously. Geoff then explained that he was reasonably excited because the Law Society, for the first time, had actually given him some papers of Hugh's to look at. Clearly my silence caused some sort of reaction in him because he felt the need to explain further.

Until this moment, Geoff's investigation had been given no access whatsoever to Hugh's papers. Their trace of the missing money had relied solely on the Law Society passing along information, and leaving Carratu to make of it what they could. This didn't strike me as very efficient. I wondered what the Law Society might be hiding. Judging from the look on Geoff's face, I imagined he might have been thinking much the same thing.

Anyway, with great ceremony, Geoff took me through the few scraps that he had, and asked me for my input. With absolutely no context to each of the lonely pieces of paper, there was, needless to say, little that I could offer.

Somewhat disappointed, Geoff moved on. Paul Carratu, the son of the owner of his company, Vincent Carratu, had been looking at Simmonds and Company's computers, yet had come up with nothing. Did I have any ideas? Yes. Ask Martin Pratt for the passwords. He was Hugh's business partner.

This led to a bit of a wing-ding between Geoff and me. He accused me of being deliberately obstructive. I countered by saying the whole investigation was designed to be obstructive, rather than constructive. "What you need to be doing," I explained, "is not looking at 'what,' but rather at 'who,' and the right 'who' at that."

It was, and still is, my position that, in order to find out what happened to the missing money, you have to recreate Hugh's activities in 1987 and 1988. The best way to do that is to put the five people, who knew what he was doing 98% of the time in those two years, in the same room, with a team of investigators, and our personal and business diaries for those two years.

Those five people are: Martin Pratt, Philip de Nahlik (Hugh's closet friend, best man, one of the former directors of City Jeroboam and one of the two individuals who revoked their Executorship of Hugh's Estate), Janet, Karen and me. If the team of investigators is any good, they'd have a day-by-day calendar for Hugh within a week. Geoff did not respond. He merely changed the subject. Went back to throwing names at me.

None was of any interest, until he got to Stephen Hiseman. He was a dicky one. He had been one of the original Directors of City Jeroboam, until he and Hugh fell out, had a big Boardroom battle, and Hugh had bought him out. Hiseman was a youngish man. Disappeared to Greece without two pennies to rub together. Then turned up a few years later, a rich man. There had been rumors of drugs, arms-dealing and connections to "an Arab-owned bank."

With that, Geoff calmed down. He explained that it was the general consensus that too much secrecy could hamper an investigation. At the same time, too much openness could undermine it. He would pass on my suggestions for looking at 'who' as well as 'what' to the Law Society.

On which note, I asked if anyone had yet contacted Reggie. No. The British Government? No. Had any money yet been recovered? No. Any more traced? No. Don't you think it might be a good idea, in all the circumstances, to pursue every avenue? Um. It was as much movement as I could hope for in one session with bureaucracy.

***

By this time, I was well in need of a pick-me-up, and so I traveled to Beaconsfield to see my friend Jules. She is a little older than me, and looks surprisingly like Maggi – similar height and build, high cheekbones, and the same pixie face with short black hair.

Jules claims descent from Badouin I of Jerusalem, the French Knight placed on that throne as a consequence of the First and only successful Crusade at the end of the 11th Century. She is an actress, and is the voice behind Britain's phone-in speaking clock. She is also gifted with healing powers.

I was chatting away about all that had happened since we last saw each other at Hugh's funeral, when she came over all strange. "This doesn't normally happen to me," she said, "but I seem to be getting a message from Hugh." Blimey, what was it with this guy? He was proving to be busier on the etheric cellphone since he'd died than he'd ever been on the real thing when he was alive.

Jules apologized. She had never liked Hugh: she found him to be both a bore and a boor – another characteristic she had in common with my twin sister. Jules explained that she was probably picking up Hugh's signal because they had formed a psychic link the evening she had tried to ameliorate Hugh's fibrosis.

I was getting used to mediums, and the staccato fashion in which they interpreted what they saw. Jules said she was getting all sorts of confusing pictures: a rose bowl. With flowers in it. In a churchyard. In a corner between the church and a porch. There was a wooden structure nearby. And the flowers were on top of a stone slab. Which was "off the ground."

Then we moved to the Caribbean. The southern part. Trinidad? After that, the southern coast of Spain or France. Jules mentioned Andorra. "The money is there."

Geoffrey Gilson

The name of a church was coming through. St. Joseph's. Follow the signs. Remove the grass. Lift a sewage plate. [Oh my sainted mother. Was it too much to ask that these diversions be made pleasant, just once? I mean, why not throw in some rats and snakes, for good measure?] Inside there will be flowers, a rose bowl and a book. And the document telling all.

Jules became very excited. I tried to tell her that we'd been through all this before. Frankly, I'd had quite enough of looting churches, exhuming graveyards and generally defiling heavenly places of worship. Somebody somewhere was keeping score, and I'd already earned at least three and a half excommunications. But Jules was not to be thwarted in her desire to 'help' me.

However, bless her heart, she did feel it was only fair to wait for her fiancé, Duncan, to get home, so that he could also take part in the adventure. Oh joy. Let's invite the whole neighborhood, and let them all share in my further humiliation.

Upon reflection, however, I decided this might be an excellent idea. To wait for Duncan that is. He was an old family friend, and came from sensible Scottish stock. Cooler heads would prevail, and we'd spend a pleasant evening over a glass of wine in front of the TV. I could not have been more wrong. No sooner had Duncan walked in the door, than Jules explained everything in a hurried 30 seconds, and Duncan was herding us back out into his still warm car.

Duncan MacDougal is the spitting image of Hugh Grant: same height, same build, same constantly perplexed expression; even the same sounding voice, only with wavier hair. He had been a friend of my family's since our schooldays, and had dated two of my three sisters. At the same time. Which had caused his one and only contretemps with my mother. Duncan is also a very accomplished musician.

Ah well, in for a penny, in for a pound. I threw myself into this 'treasure hunt' with the same vigor as all the others. I suggested we began with St. Joseph's Hospital, the nun-run establishment where most of Beaconsfield's babies are born. Being as there were nuns, there would also be oodles of statues, crosses, chapels and roses, and a ton of wooden structures.

We bustled into the reception area. Without really knowing what we were going to do next. A nun approached. Could she help us? Jules and I as one immediately turned to Duncan. Who, without missing a beat, said that a good friend of his had passed away in the hospital the previous week, and he wondered if we could spend a few minutes alone in the hospital chapel? I swear he shed a tear. We were all going to hell. And I was head of the queue, because I was turning all of my friends into liars.

The nun dutifully led us to the chapel. Unlocked it. Let us in. and closed the door behind us. "Right," said Duncan, all the man in charge, "I reckon we've got five minutes. Split up. And strip search." Jules checked behind the Stations of the Cross. I waylaid the altar. And Duncan concentrated on the wooden pews.

At four minutes and thirty seconds, with nothing found, Duncan called a halt. We scrambled to the front pew, and adopted our best Sunday School praying postures. Just in time for the nun to return. We made a great production of bowing, scraping, genuflecting and crossing ourselves repeatedly. And then followed behind the nun as she led us out.

Duncan re-engaged his deeply pious face for the farewell. "Thank you…Mother…Sister…Ma'am." And we fled. Discretion became the better part of valor, and we retreated to Duncan and Jules' home for an après-ski drink or two. Having recovered from his reincarnation as Indiana Jones, Duncan turned to more earthly matters.

Duncan had long been friends with one of Hugh's former partner's at Wedlake Bell, Richard Andersen. The word from Richard was that 'London' was saying the Conservative Party (also known for short as "the Tories") were stifling everything.

The Fraud Squad had been set on Hugh, and then, almost as quickly had been removed. The Tories. The media had eschewed all interest in the issue. The Tories. There was a connection with the British Army on the Rhine; something to do with a ransom. The Law Society had been interested; and then had halted that part of their investigation. The Tories.

Duncan shared his musical passion with another solicitor from Beaconsfield, Chris Waldron, who was one half of a partnership, the other half being Ian Wetherell. Ian's grapevine had turned up information that 'someone' had ratted on Hugh, and that £3 million had turned up in Ireland and America, as a consequence of some drug-running by Hugh.

Jules' last contribution was to give me the name of a 'good' medium in London. She felt that since Hugh was 'coming on' so strong whenever he had the chance to communicate with me, I should take advantage of it. What did I have to lose? Other than my sanity.

***

Michael Colmer was an older gentleman, in the bloom of middle age. Tall, aristocratic and charming to a fault. He lived in a small apartment on the rooftops of London, in genteel and comfortable poverty. He had once been a journalist for the London *Financial Times*, but had given that all up for a life of spirituality and calm.

He was voyant in all his senses: seeing, hearing and smelling. He did not, thank goodness, go in for all the crystal-sniffing, trance-like processes that I'd been subjected to before. He was just normal English gentry, and we spent a lot of the time, during the warm-up moments, simply chatting about cricket scores.

Michael began by doing a series of 'readings' for me. Horoscope. Tarot Cards. And some delightful little buggers called 'Angel Cards.' All this, while waiting for Hugh to come on board. Michael exclaimed, with some delight, that I had the astrological sign Leo in four of my planets. "This is good?" I asked. Oh yes. I would be a musician. But not just any musician. Mick Jagger and Paul McCartney, to Michael's certain knowledge, each had Leo in two planets. Beethoven had Leo in three. But with four, I was a certified musical genius. I thought of my drum kit, and the handful of pop songs I'd been trying to write for a decade, and smiled weakly.

At that time, Jupiter was entering a lot of my planets. There was this continual sexual connotation to much of the astrological language. I was never sure whether to be uncomfortable, or just laugh. To myself, of course. In any event, Jupiter would remain with me for twelve years of good fortune. In particular, I was to expect big changes and opportunities in August or September of the current year, being 1989.

Hugh then 'arrived.' I had told Michael nothing about Hugh, except for his name and his date of birth. Immediately, Michael told me he was getting confusing messages about the reason for Hugh's death. After that, we got into the usual mode of staccato interpretation. Could it have been his health? Cancer? A "John" friend figured. There was definitely some sort of pressure involved with his death. Maybe he had an inordinate fear of illness?

Whatever it was, Hugh was apparently relieved to be dead. He had "freed" me. He was like a pig in muck. He'd met a lot of old friends. Some of them mutual to the two of us. For some reason, a "Scottish local gent" was important.

Michael carried on in much the same vein for a while longer. When he came to a convenient resting moment, I decided to give him a little nudge. I showed him an article from the London *Times* giving all the lurid details of Hugh's life, defalcation and alleged suicide. This had much the same effect as it had on Bill and David: Michael leapt back in his chair, clutching his stomach. We adjourned for a coffee break.

Unlike the other two mediums, Michael was prepared to continue, not least because he was intrigued at how clear and strong the signal was from Hugh. "This is someone," Michael explained, "who definitely has something to say. I've never come across this before."

And continue, Michael did. In his own peculiar style. For the most part, he would sit there, gently rocking, with his eyes closed, softly spitting out half phrases. Then, when he reached what he deemed to be a juicy part, he would lean forward and offer some earnest commentary. His days as a journalist were clearly not that long forgotten:

Hugh was proud. Many reincarnations. Three tranches of money. Suicide not connected with financial problems. One of Hugh's clients used his departure to pull a fast one. There were verbal arguments. Golf or Gulf. One client used Hugh's departure to sling mud, or get out of a sticky situation. "He who protests too much." One who has most to hide. Pursue that avenue. Uncover mystery. That will turn up a large chunk of the missing money.

Hugh was not guilty of any malpractice, malfeasance or re-direction of clients' funds. Matter of personal pride and honor. Adamant. I was not far from uncovering a major fraud. The 'author' lives near Buckinghamshire. Hugh's spiritual guide was saying that I was hovering on the brink of a major discovery. Somebody took advantage of Hugh's departure to do some hasty paperwork. Creative accounting.

Michael said he was getting names of people who could be suspect. A McKinney, McKay, MacNeil, McHenry. Something like that. I should know them. Vaguely. Through the law practice. Also, John, Stephen, David. If I stuck at it, I would find all the 'hidden' money.

I gave Michael the name 'Reggie.' Michael leapt back again. Clutching his solar plexus. I should handle Reggie with care. Keep my distance. Professional association with Hugh. He'd kept Reggie at arm's length. Slight element of fear from Reggie about Hugh. Fearful of animal. I'd be ok. I could handle it. Michael asked me if the name Williams, Wilkins or Wilkinson meant anything to me? Michael was getting the name "Liddell." Maybe "George Liddell"?

Michael then asked if I was certain it was Hugh's handwriting on the Clients' Account checks or instruments of withdrawal? Did Hugh know the money was disappearing? I was to check this out. Hugh felt something of a victim.

Ransom: Persian Gulf connection. Luncheon at Golf Club? Middle East connection. Terry Waite connection. Maybe Hugh was acting as an adviser? Check his passport. All the money was "out there," waiting to be recovered. Swiss bank account. There was a Swiss check floating around somewhere. Find out who'd signed it. Offshore accounts. Isle of Man. Hugh had made an elementary mistake. Slipped up dealing with funds. Dates on the checks stubs. Compare them with office diary and passport.

If I sat sit tight for two or three months [it was currently July of 1989], everything would be revealed to me. Michael said that he knew I wanted to speed things up. But if I did, I would become privy to information that Hugh was telling him it would be dangerous for me to possess.

I was causing embarrassment to someone at Stag Place, near Victoria, London. [The central offices for the Law Society Complaints Bureau and its Compensation Fund were, at that time, in Stag Place. These were the Law Society guys I'd been dealing with so far.] No, Michael continued, not the Law Society. Something completely different. Something was about to be uncovered that would answer much. Dealing on a very high level. A senior branch of the British security services.

If I continued with my investigation, I would be asked to sign the Official Secrets Act. I was making some "higher-ups" very uncomfortable. Jupiter – step where angels don't tread. No doom or gloom. No direct violence. Something important would break in two to three weeks.

Hugh then broke off. And Michael and I had a cigarette. There really are some very strange similarities between aspects of astrology and sex. I found it all quite fascinating. I returned to dinner with Rissa, who had exciting news on two fronts: Reggie had called again, and we were about to baby-sit a wolf.

Chapter 9

It WAS JUST another ordinary day. And right there should have been my first warning. I padded from Rissa's spare bedroom into the kitchen, yawning and scratching my boxer shorts. Rissa had already left for work, so it didn't matter too much how little I wore, or what I did with it.

I was rummaging around in one of the cupboards, looking for a glass, when I heard this low growl behind me. I looked around, and there was this bundle of fur, laid out between the kitchen and the walk-through living room. I immediately went into the coo and cuddle routine, and then it stood up.

Rissa had asked me the night before if I liked dogs. Of course, dogs and children, my favorite. She had agreed to look after a friend's dog for a month. When I got up in the morning, I should introduce myself, and everything would be fine.

I'd forgotten the introduction part. This dog was obviously a stickler for the common courtesies. And Rissa hadn't mentioned that the dog was a fully-grown Irish Wolfhound. Now standing five feet tall. With three inch long teeth and a drooling snarl. Which were separated from my future married life by nothing more than a skimpy piece of silk bearing the motto, "I'm not Irish, so you can kiss me anywhere.'

I tried to stare him down. Wrong decision. The teeth moved closer. Ok. Go into the subservient pose. Stand still. Worse. The teeth were now a foot away. He had me backed into a corner near to the front door. I spent an hour gauging how much flesh I might lose trying to slip out the front door. And, more to the point, from which of the most tender parts of my body.

Finally, as the puddle of doggie drool expanded to meet my bare feet, I decided I'd had enough. I made silent prayer to all manner of heavenly saints, and dashed through the front door, as Rover's teeth grazed my departing behind.

I stood there, in the shared hallway with the upstairs apartment, sweating and shaking, when I heard this Emma Thompson voice behind me: "Can I help you," she said, in that posh, nasal whine, "we couldn't help but notice the screaming and shouting. I was beyond coherence. She led me gently upstairs, and served me hot tea.

Rissa was all apologies, but it was too late for Rabid Teeth and me. First impressions count. As I had not said 'hello,' Rover was now convinced I was a burglar. It didn't matter how many times Rissa patted my head in his presence. Fortunately, Maggi had some friends nearby, Magda and Christian Webb. They had agreed to take over Rissa's chaperoning functions. Unfortunately, I had to leave before Reggie called back. But not before I got another invite from Geoff Hughes.

***

We were back to having a tape-recorder on the table. I never was sure whether there was any tape in it or not. Within minutes of my arriving, Geoff whipped out photocopies of Hugh's old black Filofax, much like a Matador producing his Cape with enormous flourish. What did I think of them marbles?

The first thing I noticed was that the copies represented about one third of what I remembered as being the rich thickness of Hugh's overflowing Filofax. That beast had been a walking Bible. I recalled Janet telling me that Martin had said that he'd 'recovered' the Mysteriously Mobile Filofax, and given it to the Law Society. About two weeks after Hugh's death.

Geoff asked me to work my way through the copies, and comment on the names written down. "The handwriting shows someone who is successful," I began deadpan, "but I see trouble brewing. Could suicide be on the horizon?" Geoff was very proud of the fact that he had, at last, got the Law Society to start looking at the 'who's,' and he was not amused by my making light of this accomplishment. I apologized, and got on with the task in hand.

"R. Harrison": the patriarch of the Harrison family, whose family-owned business print all of England's postage stamps, in High Wycombe, a light industrial town, some seven miles from Beaconsfield.

"Bhudrhani": a partner of an Indian client of Hugh's, Damon Ray. Bhudrahani was based in Atlanta, Georgia, where he had money invested in the downtown Hilton Hotel, built in the mid-Eighties. Most of the money had been invested by Robinson-Humphries.

"Tony Brown": blank.

"Shotokan": blank.

"Spec. Services Cl.": other than the fact that it sounded obviously fishy, blank.

"The Church of the Immaculate Party": this is a family publication; we don't want to go there.

"P. Cundell": Hugh's racing horse trainer.

"Peter Hodson": his racing bookie.

"Clive Holmes": now we're getting interesting. A bona fide crook. Former owner of Tudorbury Group, a financial services group, that was accused of all sorts of criminal improprieties in the First Stock Market Boom in the Eighties. I never could work out why Hugh, in 1988, went into business with Holmes, starting a national glossy magazine for accountants, called *The Associate*. It did nothing but lose thousands of pounds. Holmes had a lavish lifestyle, including a string of expensive racehorses, which he stabled just down the road from Karen.

"T. Scott Coleman": blank.

"Neil Spekeman": a 'businessman,' who was based in Hong Kong. He had a peripatetic partner called Barry Thorpe, whom Hugh had known since Young Conservative days. Barry's claim to fame was that, according to Hugh, by the age of 30, Barry had already made and lost a couple of fortunes. Hugh had been talking 'business' with Neil and Barry starting in about 1987, but I had no idea what sort of 'business.'

"Harry Cohen": blank.

"Tony Roche": blank.

"Martin Walters": Martin Walters had been Hugh's rival in the Young Conservatives. They became working colleagues once they graduated to senior Conservative stuff. Martin was a stockbroker with the small London firm of Schaverien & Co. This company handled the private share issue for City Jeroboam.

"Brian Smith": a former CEO of Rank Xerox in the UK, and Hugh's Vice Chairman at City Jeroboam.

"Alan Preen": the entrepreneur who, in 1988, was brokering the purchase by Hugh and Brian of 100 tenanted pubs from Whitbread for £25 million ($38 million). Whitbread is one of Great Britain's largest breweries.

"Nick Snook": small time arms dealer, who lived in Beaconsfield, and occasionally hung out with the Young Conservatives, when I was their Chairman.

"Stuart Thorn": a member of the Thorn family, as in Thorn-EMI, one of the largest electronic companies in the world. The Thorn family had originally hailed from Switzerland. Stuart was, not surprisingly, a wealthy young trust fund baby. Messed around with Hugh as friend, client and stockbroker. Stuart specialized in small unlisted rights issues. Shortly before Hugh's death, Stuart had moved to Colorado.

"Musa": interesting; Middle East twang to that name, but blank.

"Grenville Trust": Oh dear, oh dear, oh dear. I'd almost completely forgotten about these people. When I had my meeting with Uriah Heep from the Law Society, on the day of Hugh's death, I'd telephoned all of Hugh's bankers to find out what was the immediate financial picture. That had included NatWest, who had been Hugh's primary bankers for over a decade; and Lloyds Bank, which he had used almost solely for *Paradise*, the timeshare operation in Spain. Then there had been Grenville Trust. At the time, Grenville Trust was a small, exclusive banking outfit, with offices in London, and connections with the small island tax haven of Jersey, located in the English Channel, just off the coast of northern France. Hugh had opened accounts with Grenville early in 1988, and had been doing an increasing amount of business with them throughout the year. They had been the only bank to refuse to talk to me. I still do not know if Geoff had more luck with them than me.

"Leverhulme Trust": Geoff got quite animated with this name. But it meant absolutely nothing to me. Years later, I did some internet research on it. All I could find was that it was a private foundation, which financed all sorts of fascinating 'good works,' including a restoration of the birthplace of Jesus.

This represented Geoff's best shot at looking at 'who.' "I thought I'd suggested it should be the 'right' who?" I said, perhaps a little too sarcastically. Any chance of the sit-down with the five of us and our diaries? No. Contacted Reggie yet? No. The Government? No. Found any more money? Geoff fought back on this one, and told me I would have to speak to the new Administrators of Hugh's Estate. "Geoff," I responded, "do you ever feel that someone's jerking your chain?"

***

The Law Society had covered all of their bases. They had appointed their own solicitors as Administrators of Hugh's Estate. A firm by the name of Charles Russell, out of Hale Court, in Lincoln's Inn, London. Between them and Carratu, the Law Society had monopolized all the information on Hugh's financial affairs.

I checked with the Probate Division of the High Court in London, where Hugh's Will was registered. A signed copy of Hugh's re-drafted Will had never been found. So, the original one had precedence. The two named Executors, Peter Smith and Philip de Nahlik, had revoked their positions as Executors within days of Hugh's death. This left the Estate adrift, and Janet pretty much adrift too. Peter and Philip had been Hugh's closest friends until his death. To my knowledge, Janet never heard from them again.

The Probate Division records indicated that Hugh had left bona fide assets of some £1.6 million ($2.4 million). Not bad for a 40 year old, who had dedicated the major part of his adult life to the 'non-profit' pursuit of politics. It was also something of a dose of cold water for those who kept referring to Hugh as 'failed.'

Problem was that the Law Society, as was their right, had claimed against the Estate for the £2.7 million ($4 million) they had already had to pay out to Hugh's former clients in compensation. This had technically bankrupted the Estate, leaving Hugh's family penniless. It was only John Simmonds' unfailing generosity and loyalty which saved Janet and Karen, their houses, and their children's childhoods.

As soon as the Law Society made claim against the rudderless Estate, they were entitled to appoint their own Administrators of the Estate, and this they had done. Technically, it is not the Law Society or their investigators (in this case, Carratu International) which recovers money. Technically, the Estate's new Administrators 'decide' to hire the Law Society's investigators, who hand over all the information they have gathered about the whereabouts of any money and assets, bona fide or otherwise. It is then the Estate's Administrators, on behalf of the Estate's creditors, who take the action necessary to recover any money, and dispose of the assets.

Taking up Geoff's suggestion, I went to have a rather useless meeting with Patrick Russell, one of the appointed Administrators, and a Partner of Charles Russell. We had an initial spat about his responsibilities. He took the view he was beholden only to the Law Society. I reminded him that, regardless of who had appointed him, he was now responsible to all of the Estate's creditors, and that included me.

Once we had cleaned the testosterone off the walls, Patrick became a little more forthcoming. But only a little. The Estate had only been able to liquidate or recover only £100,000 ($150,000) of assets or missing money. But, I exclaimed, the Estate's Administrators had themselves reported to the Probate Division that Hugh had left £1.6 million ($2.4 million) of legitimate assets. Patrick's only response to that was to stutter that Carratu were on the trail of property on the other side of the Atlantic, and the Estate remained hopeful. I'd heard more likely promises from Presidential prospects in the Iowa caucuses.

But I thought I'd push Patrick a little harder on the property angle. I think he felt a tad embarrassed, because he revealed more than he probably ought to have done. A condominium had been located in Florida. There was some sort of shopping center 'investment' on the West Coast, maybe California or Colorado. And a hint of something exotic in the Caribbean.

I was reminded of a trip that Martin Pratt and Hugh had taken to America in 1985. The primary purpose had been to accompany Martin, who is an accomplished chemical engineer, to a NASA conference in California. All military brass and champagne. Martin was presenting a paper on bio-systems in the Space Shuttle. However, the trip was rounded off with a visit to Florida, and a quickie cruise through the Caribbean.

Geoffrey Gilson

One consequence of the Estate's continuing failure to recover money or assets, with which to repay the Law Society the £2.7 million ($4 million) it had paid out to Hugh's clients, was that, for the first time in its history, the Law Society had to institute a special, once-off "Simmonds Levy" on each and every solicitor in England and Wales.

***

I really didn't want to meet with Martin Pratt, but his name kept popping up. I met with him at his home, "Three Pins," which was squeezed in next to a pub on Hedgerley's postcard-perfect village high street. The get-together was courteous, if a little strained. It was impossible for my list of questions not to sound like a cross-examination in a criminal trial.

Martin's take on everything was that Hugh had stolen the money long before 1987 and 1988, and that it had simply taken this long for everything to catch up. Otherwise, like Sergeant Schultz from *Hogan's Heroes*, he knew nothing. Of course, he said this. He had to. Otherwise, he'd have been admitting that he was slap bang in the middle of all that Hugh was doing illegally. Because, as he kept boasting, he was the business partner closest to Hugh in 1987 and 1988.

However, Martin's assertion that he knew nothing was somewhat undermined both by the Mysteriously Mobile Filofax, and by the quite separate Saga of the Mysteriously Moving Manila Folder. On the day of Hugh's death, when I had made my calculation that Hugh had stolen some £5 million ($7.5 million) my primary source of information had been that Manila Folder.

I had found it, centered quite prominently and all alone, on the front of Hugh's desk. It had contained, much to my surprise, since I was seeing them for the first time, written and telephoned demands from all those clients who were, at that time, awaiting money that Hugh no longer possessed.

As I'd held the Folder, I'd recalled seeing it the day before, without knowing what it had contained. Mind you, there would have been no reason for me to have known. Why on earth would I have known what was in a Folder sitting on Martin's desk?

In support of his wayward hypothesis that Hugh had stolen the missing money long before 1987, Martin made reference to a couple of Trust Funds that Hugh, as their Executor, had 'inherited' from Wedlake Bell, when Hugh and Wedlake Bell had gone their separate ways in 1980. Apparently, the Law Society had found those Trusts to be empty after Hugh's death, and Wedlake Bell had had to pay up about £1 million ($1.5 million) to the Law Society's Compensation Fund. It made no impression on Martin when I asked if there was any evidence that Hugh had emptied those Trusts before 1987. Martin simply refused to acknowledge the question. I had no doubt

Dead Men Don't Eat Lunch

that Hugh had stripped the Trusts clean. But, he could just as easily have done so in 1988.

Martin knew of no 'safe house' from which Hugh could have been arranging financial matters separate to Simmonds and Company. He had not been with Hugh the day before he died, except to go with Hugh to collect the small office Mini from the service garage. This was the car in which Hugh's body had been found the following day. Martin finally admitted also to having accompanied Hugh to a Garden Center after collecting the Mini.

As a final point, Martin was adamant that he'd had nothing to do with British Intelligence, and believed I was simply fabricating Hugh's escapades. On my way out, Martin mentioned that he now had a new job with British Petroleum. He would not give me a business card, but I espied a few on the table by the front door. The address was Stag Place, Victoria.

***

On my way back to London, quite by chance, I stopped off at Hugh's and my favorite haberdashers in Beaconsfield, part-owned by a nice chap called Stuart. For some reason, Stuart was all nods and winks, and 'come and talk to me in the corner.' I obliged.

"A policeman friend of mine came to see me," he said *sotto vocce*, "said if I was to see you, to pass on this message." Why on earth would I be likely to see Stuart? In any event, Stuart explained that this un-named policeman was aware that I thought David Pembroke was somehow involved in Hugh's shenanigans. "The message is: wrong construction company; wrong end of town."

The only construction company at the other end of town was Michael Shanley Construction. I knew Michael to be friendly with both Hugh and Martin, but I was not aware of his having any business dealings with Hugh. I did, however, do a bit of legwork, and discovered that he was heavily financed by an Arab bank, the name of which no-one would reveal.

Notwithstanding all sorts of exotic threats, Stuart would not give me the policeman's name. Nor would he expand on the rather unlikely circumstances of his coming by this 'message.' It was just another curious incident in what was already becoming a very curious affair.

***

On my way out of Beaconsfield, I telephoned Neil Relph. I relayed to him Martin's information about the Trusts, and his opinion that Hugh had been stealing for years. Neil was spitting mad. He was nothing if not a true professional.

Neil had been personally responsible for auditing the Clients'

Geoffrey Gilson

Accounts for Hugh's firm each and every year of its existence, with the exception of 1987 and 1988, when Hugh had refused to allow him near his books. That covered all clients, including any Trust Funds.

Furthermore, Neil was bound by his profession's regulations, and those laid down by the Law Society, to account for each and every penny of each and every client. No margin of error was allowed. Any theft from the Clients' Accounts of Simmonds and Company could only have occurred in 1987 or 1988.

Neil had two tidbits of information for me. Janet had received in the mail a check drawn on a Swiss bank account for several hundred pounds. He wasn't sure which bank, but he thought it might be the Swiss Bank Corporation. He had no idea who had signed the check. All he knew was that Janet had given it to her new solicitor, David Platt of Beaconsfield, to give to the Law Society.

The other news flash was that David Pembroke was going bankrupt for about £12 million ($18 million). Neil and I had discussed the 'spare' cash that Carratu was discovering alongside the money stolen from Hugh's clients. We had agreed it would be sensible to keep an eye open for people suddenly finding themselves short a bob or two.

***

In the same context, I read about an interesting company called Eagle Trust. This company had just gone bust as well, with some £13.7 million ($21 million) unaccounted for. The Government's Department of Trade and Industry, and the Metropolitan Police's Serious Fraud Office were investigating the involvement of the Swiss Banking Corporation.

Savory Miln, the stockbroking subsidiary of the Swiss Banking Corporation, had been paid a total of £10 million ($15 million) in fees for handling an unsuccessful £21 million ($30 million) share issue by Eagle Trust in 1987. And the boys in blue wanted to know what was going on.

Eagle Trust described itself as an investment holding company. The companies it owned included: Samuelson (film services); Walter Somers (engineering); Pavis (plumbing equipment); John Sydney (bathroom accessories); and Trio Containers (waste disposal).

***

The following day was a slow one. So, I decided to pay a visit to Stag Place, and see what was there that was proving to be of such interest to everyone. I stood in the middle of a drab and dreary concrete square, slowly rotating, as I tried to find some aesthetic beauty in the sheer horror of four ugly slabs that represented the worst of British office design from the

Dead Men Don't Eat Lunch

Sixties.

Sure enough, there was a BP company, and all sorts of other oil-connected companies, which might have provided a home for Martin's chemical engineering skills. But I was really hoping for something a little more obvious and helpful. James-Bond-Find-A-Spy-And-Your-Missing-Clients'-Money Plc would have made my day a bit brighter and this book a lot shorter. As it was, I reduced to writing down all the names, in the hope that they might prove useful later on:

Portland House

Sun Alliance Insurance Group
American Airlines/Sabre
H&G Engineering
British Offshore Engineering Technology Ltd.
Earl and Wright, Consulting Engineers
Monk Dunstone Associates
American Express – UK Travel Related Services
Crown Prosecution Services
Solicitors' Complaints Bureau
Booker plc
SAECS Ltd. – The Conference Secretariat
Sabic Marketing Europe Ltd.
Oil Companies International Marine Forum
British Petroleum – Miller Development
G and J of the UK prima
Best
Blue Circle Industries Plc

Glen House

Career Care Group Ltd.
Real Time Insurance Systems Ltd.
Commission for the New Towns
Datasolve Ltd.
Stora Cell Ltd.
Short Brothers plc
Rowbotham Tankships Ltd.
Jack L. Israel Group plc
Anthony Worham Ltd.
John Martin Foods Ltd.
G.C. Williams and Company Ltd.

Geoffrey Gilson

Tobacco Advisory Council
Saintseal Travel Ltd.
Cusdens Ltd.

Short Bothers were a firm of aircraft manufacturers, based in Northern Ireland.

16 Palace Street

Armand Hammer Productions Ltd.
The Occidental Petroleum Corporation

Armand Hammer was the original, larger-than-life, American oil tycoon. He loved to rub shoulders with the rich and famous, and was a great supporter and chum of Prince Charles and Margaret Thatcher. Gordon Reece, Margaret Thatcher's favorite image consultant, did consulting work for Hammer. And between 1983 and 1989, so too did Cecil Parkinson, another one of Thatcher's primary political lieutenants.

Hammer's companies had played a major role in developing Britain's oil fields. Hammer himself was well known for playing both sides of the fence: his companies provided a front for CIA activity, while Hammer did deals with all manner of dictators on the Communist side of the Iron Curtain.

Indeed, double-dealing was and remains the very essence of good intelligence gathering. Hugh explained this to me on one occasion. No-one gathers very much useful information by being on the outside, looking in, not even with modern electronic intelligence devices. You have to be on the inside. And those you are with, those you are spying on, have truly to believe you are one of them. So, all of the best spies are double agents. And the very best are triple agents.

A good spy starts off with some information provided to him by his own spy service. Some of the information is good, the rest is rubbish. He then 'allows' himself to be turned by the enemy spy service. They think he is now working for them. He 'proves' this by providing them with information.

However, he is only useful if he goes on providing information. So, the enemy spy service has to ask him to 'stay in place' in his original spy service. The enemy spy service also knows that he is only 'safe' if he reports back to his original spy service that he has been turned, but he is still 'true' to his original spy service, and will try his hardest to get good information from the enemy spy service. The latter play along by providing him with a mixture of good and bad information.

Effectively, the spy now has two masters, and only he knows which is his 'true' master. This schizophrenia is obviously very stressful. A lot of even good agents don't last too long. Add to this the fact that neither of his masters really trust him, and his life expectancy is not something he can consider to be very long. Pensions are not something he spends a lot of time thinking about.

Which is why the best are triple agents. The only insurance is to have a third master. Themselves. And to tuck away running money and documents somewhere safe. Along with the best of the information, to be released to the wrong party in the event of death.

At one lunch in 1979, Hugh went all somber on me, and asked if I would ever consider giving everything up and moving to Moscow. If he did, would I? It was at that lunch that he mentioned that the conventional wisdom of a very few was that Kim Philby, the most notorious of Britain's Communist moles, was in fact a double agent.

I wasn't entirely certain how this would work, since he wouldn't be able to relay information back to England. "Oh no," said Hugh, "in his case, it wouldn't work like that. He would burrow himself deep into the highest levels of the KGB, and feed them crap about British Intelligence. Its philosophies, its policies and procedures, its agents and moles in the Communist world. He would feed the Russkies garbage, and they would believe him because he had given up everything when he defected. The net result would be that he would cripple the Russians in their approach to British Intelligence for years to come."

Eland House

The British Government's Overseas Development Administration

New Scotland Yard

The Metropolitan Police Headquarters [and Special Branch, and so, maybe MI5?]

***

On which subject, I met again with Geoff Hughes. But on this occasion, I was the one who requested the meeting. My first order of business was to report the Swiss check that Janet had received. Geoff knew nothing about it. He was very excited. But I never heard about it again.

Next, I asked him about the Trust Funds issue. This opened an interesting can of worms. Geoff noted the protestations of Neil Relph and Rouse and Company, but indicated that Carratu had come across three instances of 'foul play,' which suggested criminal intent by Hugh long before 1987:

1. Sometime in the middle Seventies, Hugh and Martin Walters had had their wrists slapped over a marginally illegal share transaction originating out of Hong Kong. Money had been returned, and everything had been hushed up by Wedlake Bell.

2. After Hugh had left Wedlake Bell in 1980, it had been discovered that Hugh, while installing Wedlake Bell's new computer system, had created a series of dummy Clients' Accounts, into which certain bona fide clients were depositing funds. It was clear that Hugh had had access to those funds, without the prior knowledge of Wedlake Bell.

3. There had been two or three Trust Funds that Hugh had continued to administer, after 1980. Those Trust Funds were now empty. [One of the Trust Funds had been for a member of the Drummond family. The Drummonds were a Scottish clan of long repute. They had established one of Scotland's oldest banks, Drummond Bank, which had close ties to the Royal Bank of Scotland. Hugh had acted as lawyer for a number of the Drummonds' personally.]

My response to this was immediate and harsh:-

A. No-one was denying that Hugh was a crook. That was now undeniable.

B. It mattered not what he had done with Wedlake Bell. What we were all trying to determine currently was what had happened to the money from Simmonds and Company. And when that money had been stolen. Unless, the Law Society was suggesting criminality on the part of Rouse and Company [which the Law Society later hastened to point out that it was not], then it was clear that that money could only have been stolen in 1987 and 1988.

C. What this information did make clear was that there were serious questions that needed to be asked of Wedlake Bell. For, in 1980, when Wedlake Bell had allowed Hugh Simmonds to leave them, and set up a new law practice with a bunch of their clients, and Wedlake Bell had said nothing to the Law Society or to the Police about his alleged criminal behavior, they had knowingly launched on an unsuspecting public a crook, who would later rape the public for some £5 million ($7.5 million). The Police were looking for accomplices. Why weren't they mounting a prosecution of Wedlake Bell and its partners?

For the first time, Geoff was struck dumb. He went bright red. I couldn't tell whether it was from embarrassment or bottled-up anger. All he could stutter was, "frankly I have a 101 questions I'd like to ask of Wedlake Bell, but I'm not being allowed to." And with this extraordinary declaration of impotence, we moved onto another subject.

Geoff had two more names on which he wanted my input: he had come across a Simmonds and company check made out to "P. Gillinsky." I think Geoff thought the similarity to my own name (P. Geoffrey Gilson) a little too co-incidental. I too was amused, but none the wiser.

He had also turned up an alias that Hugh was using, "Perlberger." Perhaps "John Perberger." I hadn't a clue, but I couldn't resist wondering aloud if this wasn't the sort of thing that you'd find a spy using. I think Geoff had had enough of me for one day, and he wouldn't rise to the bait.

***

As I drove away, I got to thinking about Wedlake Bell. Did they also have some sort of protection, as I believed Hugh may have had for his 'operation'? Was the source the same, and were the reasons the same? Had Wedlake Bell been a 'cover' for Hugh during his years with them? They had one or two interesting connections.

The Senior Partner of the firm, when Hugh had joined, was a crusty old patrician, by the name of Harry Ellis. Harry didn't take a lot of bull. He took to Hugh instantly. So much so that he asked Hugh to be one of the named Executors in his Will. Apparently, there were special responsibilities that went with the job. Harry was a named Executor for the solicitor who, in turn, had been the named Executor for the solicitor who acted for the Duke of Windsor.

In 1936, the then newly-crowned King Edward VIII had abdicated the throne, in order to marry his American love, Wallis Simpson. The King's constitutional advisers had told him that under no circumstances could he marry Wallis as King because she was a divorcee. As Head of the Protestant Church of England, the King could not yet condone divorce. We were many years away from Charles and Diana. The King had been told he would have to make a choice.

The decision to abdicate threw the Royal Family and the upper reaches of the British body politic into a panic. The problem is that every new King or Queen not only inherits the title, they also inherit a huge fortune in land and holdings, and centuries of secret knowledge, which could cause untold damage if it was to find its way into the wrong hands. Edward VIII had already inherited all of this. No-one could force him to un-inherit it. All the Family could do was to negotiate with him.

It was a delicate balancing act. On the one hand, you could ask nicely, he could say 'no,' and you were no further forward. On the other, you could be 'mean,' force a deal out of him, leaving him bitter and near penniless, when he might go and spill all the beans. As it was, the newly-designated King, Edward's brother and about to be George VI, and his advisers took the 'mean' route. Edward was effectively exiled, with just enough money to live in reasonable comfort, with a new title, the Duke of Windsor, and a new job, as Governor of Bermuda.

According to Harry Ellis, the treatment of Edward VIII had been brutal. Never underestimate the Royal Family when it comes to protecting its own. A feature that would be re-visited when it came to Diana, Princess of Wales, many years later. Before he had been allowed to become a named Executor, Harry Ellis had been sworn to keep secret all the information that was divulged in the Estate he would be Administering, including all the details of the deal done under the Abdication, and a not insignificant amount of the 'secret knowledge.' Apparently, Hugh had had to engage in a similar sworn declaration. It made me wonder if Hugh had been chosen because of his 'second career,' and if Wedlake Bell made a habit of harboring 'sensitive' individuals.

***

I returned to Michael Colmer for some spiritual sustenance. He was having fun. He'd never had such a clear connection. He felt like a telephone exchange. And our sessions were more exhilarating than a James Bond movie.

Michael had prepared an astrological chart for Hugh on the day of his death. The extraordinary thing was that the chart indicated that Hugh should have been in a very positive frame of mind. It was not compatible with suicide. The whole thing was an enigma.

At this point, Hugh joined us. He told Michael that I'd caused a flurry in the dovecot. Expect a visit soon. On the Intelligence question. Hugh was advising me to soft-pedal this aspect. If I continued to push, I might cause embarrassment to someone in the Security Services, and "they might not like it."

Revolver. Desk drawer. Top right. Manila envelope. *On Her Majesty's Service* logo on envelope. Regulation desk. Modesty panel. Panel with paper clips. Drawer underneath. Desk locked. Envelope: 15 inches by 12 inches. Weapon loaded. Six bullets. Spillage on blotting paper or envelope. Sheaf of papers.

Short barrel. Ridged grip. Hugh had gun at his head. Literally. Diary. Summoned to Whitehall. Stag Place, Victoria has a security connection. There had been an Invitation to Hugh. Or, there would be one for me.

Envelope open. Five documents. Letter-size paper. IBM-typed. Heavy quality. Paper-clipped. Water-marked. Clipped to lined paper. *Her Majesty's Stationery Office* watermark. Government. Notes taken. Then typed. Going through inquiries. Made notes. Someone typed up.

It wasn't embezzlement. My theory was closer to the mark. Ransom. I wasn't to push too far, too soon. I was being followed. Thought of suicide put in Hugh's mind by someone else. Not of own volition. If became known, would cause more than a flurry.

Hugh was telling Michael that he had spoken to an elderly woman the week before he died. His mother, or the mother of someone close. Whoever it was, they were puzzled by the reason for his approach.

There were links to the Government. I was to examine the most recent Cabinet Reshuffle. See who had benefited.

At this point, we took a coffee break, and discussed the recent game of Government musical chairs to try and come up with some names to throw at Hugh after the intermission. The year was 1989. We were almost exactly a year away from the night of the bloody knives, when the Conservative Party, for the first time in its history, dumped a sitting Prime Minister, Margaret Thatcher.

It is customary in the summer for the Prime Minister to review the Cabinet and make changes. Get rid of deadwood, reward cronies and bring on younger talent. The only difference this summer was the extraordinary extent to which Thatcher overhauled her Government, root and branch.

She'd been in power for a decade, and she pretty much wiped out the Old Guard, who'd been with her since the start, and replaced them with a new team of rising stars. Who, in time-honored fashion, returned the favor a year later by doing the Julius Caesar on her.

The new boys to 'benefit' included John Major, who was promoted to Foreign Secretary, and was effectively earmarked as her eventual successor. Chris Patten to Environment: he later became a highly successful Chairman of the Conservative Party, the last Governor of Hong Kong and a European Commissioner. Norman Lamont to Treasury: he was the hugely unpopular Treasury guy, who after being dumped by Major for incompetence, hounded Major over the issue of Europe until the Conservatives lost power in 1997.

I had met Chris Patten once, in the mid-Eighties. He was Member of Parliament (MP) for Bath. He was due to speak at a political meeting that Hugh was chairing in a small town called Salisbury, in Wiltshire. Salisbury is famous for its beautifully preserved cathedral. Patten, who in 2004 was elected Chancellor of the University of Oxford, was always more rumpled scholar than wily politician. So it was that, with an hour to spare and decked out in the traditionally British duffle coat, Chris gave Hugh and me a guided tour of the more esoteric delights of Salisbury Cathedral.

In 1983, John Major was still a lowly MP, lost in the horde of Conservative wannabes vying for the attention of Margaret Thatcher. Yet he still had the grace and personal touch that would become his hallmark when Prime Minister. South-West Cambridgeshire sits right next door to Huntingdon, which was Major's Parliamentary Constituency. When Hugh hit his political troubles with the Cambridge hunting folk in 1983, John was one of the first on the telephone to offer advice and support.

As true to form in death as in life, Hugh couldn't let a political discussion go by in which he was not involved. He came back online with Michael: "Hugh wants you to look at Cecil Parkinson and Malcolm Rifkind."

Cecil Parkinson was a living Greek tragedy all on his own. He had been Thatcher's original golden boy. The man destined to continue her revolution into the next Millennium. He was promoted fast through the ranks of Government, and held all in the palm of his hand in 1983, after he had orchestrated Maggie's re-election in a landslide.

Then, in actions reminiscent of Hugh years later, he threw all the glittering prizes away with the toss of a hand. Or some other bodily appendage. It was revealed that he had had an illegitimate child a couple of years earlier. The lady in question was no 'lady,' and was turning over all the ugly details to whichever tabloid would pay.

Cecil resigned in some disgrace, and set about getting his affairs in order. For the next few years, he pretty much lived in the political wilderness. Ironically, one of those who remained close to him was Hugh. Perhaps, they sensed a kindred spirit in each other? Hugh had first formed a friendship with Cecil when the latter was Chairman of the Party, earlier in the Eighties, and Hugh had been serving on the Party's National Board of Finance.

In the 1989 reshuffle, Thatcher returned her favorite to the Cabinet, out of personal loyalty more than anything else. In political terms, it was an empty gesture. Cecil had no political capital remaining, and Thatcher had transferred her political 'affections' to new boy, John Major.

As for Hugh's reference to Malcolm Rifkind, I had no clue. Rifkind had joined the Cabinet in an earlier reshuffle. As the youngest member of the Cabinet, he was definitely a rising star. Indeed, he would later become Minister of Defense, and then Foreign Secretary.

At the time of the 1989 reshuffle, Rifkind was already Secretary of State for Scotland, having replaced George Younger in that position. George Younger had been moved to Defense. The reshuffle left Younger, who was one of the Old Guard, with nothing but a gold watch. Almost immediately, he was ennobled, becoming Lord Younger, whereupon he was instantly offered the job of Chairman of the Royal Bank of Scotland.

This seemed to clear politics out of the ether, and we resumed: "Geoffers," sighed Michael, "go away for three months. By then, you will have your revelation. There is nothing you can do in the meantime. There will be a deal. The families will be made financially secure. Janet will be given the proof. For insurance. Public vindication. In part.

The document in the desk is a record. The person is agonizing. He's a convenient scapegoat. If you push too hard, he may go over the edge. The office is in a tower block. Stag Place. New Scotland Yard. Some sort of security force." And with that final utterance, Michael's eyelids fluttered shut, and he resumed his staccato delivery.

Powerful link with US Embassy. My making contact would force person to disclose file. Let them decide in their own time. Gulf connection. US link. Wealthy, expatriate clients of Hugh's.

Not a regular church-goer. Remembrance service. Connections with high-level Anglican. Terry Waite. Ransom with US help. Almost reached success. Money back into system. No questions asked. Went wrong. Couldn't admit publicly. Went quietly. No Russian links…

At that point, Michael, Hugh, whoever, ground to a halt. And we all returned to our respective 'homes.'

***

I was in desperate need of some light relief. I went and had a drink or three with Philip Brewster, who had been the office's all round support staff, and latterly, Hugh's driver. Philip had a lot in common with Brad Pitt, and like Brad, he had a lot to keep the girls happy: great eyes, great smile and apparently some extra punch below the belt.

Philip had started driving Hugh around in 1986, after Hugh picked up an unpublicized DUI. I asked Philip if he could remember driving Hugh anywhere interesting. After a couple of false starts, limited to dropping Hugh off in Victoria a lot, he finally came up with one memorable excursion.

In 1987, Hugh had joined Bob Pickard for lunch at Langan's Brasserie, a London restaurant part owned by the actor Michael Caine. When Hugh returned to the car, it was clear that he was full of the joys of spring. And not a little alcohol. He told Philip, with a nod and a wink, that Bob wanted him to meet someone who needed to buy arms. A deal worth some £300,000 ($450,000) to Hugh as a middleman.

On and off, Philip had got quite friendly with Martin, particularly since Hugh's death. He laughed out loud when I told him that Martin had denied any knowledge of Hugh's involvement with MI6. Apparently, Philip had seen Martin only a few days before. Martin had mentioned his meeting with me, and had told Philip a very different story.

Martin confirmed having seen the military ribbon to Hugh's C.B.E. He told Philip that the sword in Hugh's living room had been a sword of the Guards Regiment. And Martin recalled having been approached in University by a recruiter for British Intelligence.

Before Philip joined Simmonds and Company, Martin had occasionally driven Hugh to London. Dropped him off at an address near Piccadilly. Hugh would mumble something about it being "his turn as duty officer." Martin would then collect him at 10 o'clock the next morning.

Martin also stated that Hugh had done a lot of traveling in Eastern Europe. When Hugh was in his late teens or early twenties. Martin knew this because he had surreptitiously peeked at Hugh's old passport one day.

***

On the subject of light relief, when I returned to the Jebb household that evening, I was met by the message that Reggie had tracked me down, and would be calling later that evening. Magda and Christian were both as excited as Rissa had become. The spirit of adventure was really quite infectious.

Dead Men Don't Eat Lunch

Chapter 10

I HAD KIDDED my twin sister Maggi relentlessly about the upper-crust accent she had brought back with her from the University of Oxford, England's centuries old and premier institution of higher learning. I had to keep reminding myself not to do the same with Magda and Christian Webb.

The two girls were attractive and charming products of England's venerable landed gentry. Easy with money, easy with their charm, and easy with their generosity. For which I was most grateful. They never charged me a penny for the months I overstayed my welcome with them. Ever so occasionally, I would attempt to repay their kindness with a bottle of wine to accompany dinner.

They, and Rissa before them, provided me with a welcome oasis of stability, as I dealt daily with the frustrations and possible danger of the investigation I was pursuing into Hugh's activities. There were only two moments of slightly unsettling irony.

The first was not so much irony as simple irritation with those ever-meddling 'powers.' It was late summer. I had been in England for several months now. I was circling what the English call a roundabout on my way through Fulham, a section of West London, when the car behind me caught my attention. It had been behind me for some time.

Almost from habit, I mentally noted the license plate number. When I got back to the Jebb's that evening, I checked through the voluminous notes of all the other plates I had noticed. There it was. Two months to the day, the same car had pulled in behind Gregg and me on one of our trips through Beaconsfield.

I remembered it because we'd had to engage in all sorts of games to get rid of the car. Including circling the roundabout in the historic section of Beaconsfield five times before the car's driver realized he'd been 'made.' Someone was sure dishing out a lot of money just to keep me under tabs.

Geoffrey Gilson

The fully ironic moment occurred as I was browsing through the Jebb's books one lazy afternoon. Other's might call it nosing, but since it was in their living room-cum-library, 'browsing' sounds much more congenial. I came across a biography of Guy Liddell. It turns out he was a former Deputy Director of MI5, and one of its original founders, during the Second World War. He was also a Great Uncle of the two Jebb girls, with whom I was staying.

In fact, the whole episode turned into a double irony, since I spoke with Reggie that evening while sitting in the same room. Staring at the biography of Guy Liddell.

***

Reggie adopted what was becoming a normal approach with me on the telephone. All cagey and melodramatic. I was never certain if this was an act to impress me, or whether he was half as scared as he made out.

He indicated that he was not prepared to say too much on an open telephone line. And at first, he didn't want to confirm too much of anything, either. On this occasion, I took the lead in asking questions, since so little had been achieved in our previous telephone conversation.

Reggie claimed not to have any idea who was following me. Or him. He did not believe it was anyone 'official.' He believed that Hugh had become involved in something 'non-kosher' in the lead-up to his death. Reggie was pretty certain he knew the broad outlines, but he was not being upfront in sharing it with me.

I pushed Reggie to tell me who had recruited Hugh. He went all enigmatic on me. Whether this was because it was him, or he did not want to name names on the telephone, I couldn't tell. Certainly, there was ample opportunity for recruitment to have been by way of the Army.

On the outskirts of Beaconsfield is a large Army Base, called 'Wilton Park.' It is one of the worst kept secrets in Beaconsfield that the seemingly innocuous Base is, in fact, the home of the Army's Languages School, which trains the Army's spies. Wilton Park also houses the huge underground bunker, which would have been used by the Government if the nuclear bombs had begun to fall.

Reggie finally admitted that he had indeed "invited Hugh to the party," and that the year 1968 was important. All I could think of was that this was the year in which the troubles in Northern Ireland began heating up again, and the year in which the Soviets had invaded Czechoslovakia.

Reggie said that he wanted to help me, but that it depended on the risk. He felt that the matter might never be resolved, and he did not want to attract too much attention to himself in a useless cause. He became very agitated when I wondered if he and Hugh had fallen out. "Why, who's suggesting that we did?"

On a flier, I asked if there was a branch of the security services in Stag Place. Reggie became the model of concern. His response was immediate: "Yes. How did you find out? That's supposed to be top secret. Do not go anywhere near there. You are not unknown."

I pushed my luck a bit more. I asked if Occidental Petroleum had links with the CIA. Reggie's response was esoteric, to say the least. "Yes, and with the Knights of Malta." I wondered who on earth they were. Reggie recommended, *sotto vocce*, that I would only understand the context for everything that had occurred if I read two books: *Holy Blood, Holy Grail* and its sequel, *The Messianic Legacy*.

I was becoming a tad frustrated by this game of allusion and illusion. I got to the point. Open telephone or not, I set out the scenario I had worked out, concerning the Lebanese hostages. Right down to the part about Government 'protection,' and the double-cross preventing Hugh from putting the money back. I added a few bits and pieces from Michael's sessions, just to test out Michael's prowess.

Again, the reaction was instantaneous. "How do you know this?" Reggie hissed. "Who are you? You're so very close." A pause. "You have no idea how close. Look, you're in no danger at the moment. But if you keep on messing around, you're going to start pissing off someone. My advice to you is to go home." Then without warning, Reggie hung up. Scared, or pissed off?

***

Well, on a scale of 1 to 10, I called that a near-certain 9 that my homegrown, medium-inspired, Lebanese scenario was pretty much on the button. I felt relieved finally to have some sort of confirmation from someone other than "Dead Man Talking."

As a consequence, I felt it time to do a little more in-depth research of the whole sorry Iran-Contra/Lebanese hostage saga. Partly to understand it better. Partly to see if I could find anyone that looked like it might be Hugh, even if using an alias. And partly to see if I could find any context into which Hugh might have fit.

I failed miserably on the last two points. But I did succeed in beginning to understand the saga in a way that I hadn't before. And in a way I was pretty certain Joe Ordinary still didn't.

My primary realization was that the entire Reagan-Bush adventure had begun long before the Dream Team was even elected in 1980, and with a hostage crisis that preceded the drama that later unfolded in Lebanon in the Eighties.

Jimmy Carter's Presidency was crippled in its waning years by its perceived impotence in the face of the capture by Khomeini's Iranian Revolutionary Guards of 57 American hostages in the US Embassy in 1979. Carter had tried everything to secure the release of his countrymen, including an ill-fated rescue attempt in the middle of election year, 1980.

The Republicans were convinced that Carter would pull an 'October Surprise,' securing the hostages' release just in time for the goodwill to sweep Carter to a second term. There were too many in the military and, in particular, in the CIA, which had been devastated by Carter's wholesale assault on their Operations Directorate, who wanted to do all they could to prevent Carter's re-election. JFK déjà vu, all over again.

A plot was hatched. The initial core consisted of ex-CIA officer Miles Copeland (whose primary public claim to fame was that he was the father of Stewart Copeland, drummer for the British supergroup, *The Police*); William Casey, ex-CIA and close friend of the new Republican Presidential Candidate, Ronald Reagan; and Robert McFarlane, a former Marine Colonel, senior aide to Texas Republican Senator, John Tower, and later, one of the chosen fall guys for the Iran-Contra debacle.

Part of the deal struck between Reagan and George Bush Sr., which allowed the latter so graciously to accept the Vice Presidential nomination, was Reagan's agreement that, as Vice President, Bush would have *de facto* control over all sensitive foreign relations matters. For which read 'covert operations.' Bush wasn't waiting for Election Day. There was work to be done immediately, and he very quickly linked up with Casey's mob.

There was even assistance from inside Carter's administration. Donald Gregg was a member of Carter's National Security Council. He was later accused of leaking the Democrat's Debate Briefing Book to the Reagan team, allowing Reagan to best Carter in the first, and ultimately deciding, Presidential Debate. He also regularly briefed Bush and Casey on Carter's moves in regards to Khomeini and the hostages, in the months leading up to the Presidential Election.

All of these machinations culminated in a hugely secret meeting in Paris, on October 12th, 1980, just under a month before the US Presidential Election. In attendance were Bush, Casey (soon to be the next Director of the CIA), McFarlane, Gregg, Robert Gates (who became Director under President Bush Senior) and one George Cave. Cave had been officially purged from the CIA in 1977, as part of Carter's cleansing of the CIA. However, he remained 'unofficially' active until 1989.

The Americans were in Paris to meet with a delegation of Iranians, led by a man called Karrubi, who was there as the personal envoy of the then Iranian President, Hojjat El-Islam Ali Akbar Hashemi Rafsanjani. A Devil's Deal was struck that day: In exchange for $52 million in cash; the unfreezing of Iranian assets in America; and guarantees of arms sales to Iran (which sales were desperately needed to stave off Iraq, which had invaded Iran earlier in 1980), the Iranians personally guaranteed to Bush and his team that they would delay the release of the American hostages until after the Presidential Election. Thus, it was that Bush supplanted any possible Carter 'October Surprise' with one of his own.

Bush and his team were flown to Paris in a BAC-11 owned by King Khaled of Saudi Arabia, and piloted by one Heinrich Rupp, a former employee of the Saudi national airline. Arrangements were made through Four Seasons Travel, an alleged front company for the CIA.

No records of the airplane, or its flight plan, were ever logged on the Federal Aviation Administration computer database. However, there was one overlooked piece of paper evidence: a manual card index containing details of the airplane and its flight plan. This card index was filed away with other FAA archives in the Alfred P. Murrah Federal Building in Oklahoma City, which building was destroyed by a truck bomb in 1995.

Meanwhile, Reagan and Bush were elected in 1980. Reagan kept his word and put Bush in charge of covert operations. Bush kept his word, and began the flow of arms to the Iranians. McFarlane became Reagan's National Security Adviser. Casey became the Director of the CIA. Gregg became Bush's National Security Adviser, while Bush was Vice President. Carter returned to Plains, Georgia. And Miles Copeland continued listening to his son's pop records.

To be fair to the Republicans, Carter bust his own gut in the autumn of 1980, trying to do a Dirty Deal to get the hostages released before the Presidential Election. His problem was that he chose the wrong partners. Which was pretty much a metaphor for his whole Presidency, bless his heart.

Carter made contact with the Hashemi brothers: Cyrus, Jamshid and Reza. Frankly, they had more in common with the Three Stooges than high-level clandestine operators. You have to say this for the Republicans: they now how to pick their crooks.

The Hashemi brothers, who lived in the West, claimed to be cousins of the Iranian President. Whether true or not, they had no other clout with the Iranians, and certainly had no connections to Khomeini and his Revolutionary Guards. However, the Hashemis had no qualms about trading on their new-found influence in the White House, to sell small quantities of military equipment to the Iranians, and make a few bucks for themselves on the side.

As a result of all of the misdeeds of the CIA, up to and including the Vietnam War, Congress created oversight Committees for the CIA's merry band of warriors at the end of the Seventies. Quite aside from the secret sale of arms to Iran, which was banned by international law, there were all sorts of other covert actions that Vice President Bush wanted to instigate, that he simply did not want to have Congress knowing about. So, he had to find ways to get things done outside of the CIA and 'normal channels.'

The first thing Bush had Reagan do was set up, under top-secret National Security Decision Directive NSDD #3, a new intelligence organization, under Bush's control, with the specific purpose of waging covert wars. This organization was known as the Special Situation Group/Standing Crisis Pre-Planning Group (SSG/CPPG). Congress had no control over this group. After the assassination attempt on Reagan's life in 1981, neither did Ronald Reagan. For the next decade and a bit, America had a former head of its national intelligence agency running its covert foreign policy. In the middle Eighties, the American foreign policy establishment freaked when the Russians countered by appointing the head of the KGB as their President.

George Bush Senior (known affectionately as "Poppy") was appointed Director of the CIA in December 1975. But evidence suggests that he may have had connections with them long before that date. There is substantive speculation that George Bush was active with the CIA in Texas in the Sixties. And that he was involved in the embarrassing Bay of Pigs invasion of Cuba, which caused the CIA to fall out of favor with President Kennedy. Later, J. Edgar Hoover, the then Director of the FBI, is reputed to have given a formal briefing to a George Bush "of the CIA" on the Cuban exiles' response to the Kennedy assassination, which occurred while Poppy was active in Texas.

Even though Bush Sr. now had his own organization to circumvent Congressional oversight, he still thought it wise to engage in the illegal arming of the militant Muslims in Iran using surrogates. The Israelis, led by the right-wing Likud Party and its die-hard Prime Minister Menachem Begin, were happy to oblige. Indeed, the Israelis had helped to organize Bush's 'October Surprise' in Paris. Begin had never forgiven Carter for embarrassing him with his Camp David Peace Accords with Egypt. All Begin required in return was that Shimon Peres, the Foreign Minister in his Coalition Government, and Leader of the left-wing Labor Party, be excluded from all activity involving arms sales. And the lucrative profits. Shared by Likud, the CIA and the non-CIA Americans – or ex-CIA Americans, as in the case of Vice President Bush.

The Israelis supplied Iran with American military hardware they had previously bought. The Americans then re-supplied the Israelis from NATO stockpiles in Europe. Everything was fine until a Palestinian terrorist group assassinated the Israeli Ambassador to the UK, Shlomo Argov, on the streets of London. Israel invaded Lebanon in 1982, to clean out the Palestinians from that country. The 'cleansing' took a nasty turn in the Palestinian refugee camps in Beirut. Western peacekeepers arrived. Muslim militias blew up the US Embassy, the Marines' barracks, and a couple of other Embassies. The US retaliated with William Buckley. And the Muslim militias started taking hostages. Somebody noticed that the same Muslim militias were being openly backed by Iran, and got the bright idea of using the arms sales as a bargaining chip to release the hostages in Lebanon.

Meanwhile, Congress had stopped the CIA funding of the Contras' attempts to overthrow the leftist Sandinista Government in Nicaragua. So Bush had had to find some other way of financing the Contras. He did this through SSG/CPPG, using the enormous profits from the arms sales to Iran, among some other rather creative sources of money. And so the ugly triangle of Iran-Contra was established. Indeed, when the Dirty Deal was done to exclude Syria from blame for the Lockerbie bombing, it was done specifically to cover the backside of Bush Sr. Who later entertained al-Kassar, the Syrian kingpin at the Middle Eastern corner of the triangle, as an honored VIP in Washington.

As the Eighties progressed, this triangle expanded to include other covert operations around the world, all of which needed to be conducted out of sight of the Congressional Oversight Committees. This, in turn, required off-the-books funding, however strange or illegal. It has now been conclusively proven that a channel was established by the CIA to allow drug-running into Los Angeles, the profits being used to support the Contra's. Ships were needed for transporting weapons; tame banks were set up to launder money; every conceivable aspect of logistics was considered and provided for. Bush's SSG/CPPG became a huge global business, and was known variously as either 'The Enterprise' or 'Octopus.'

Pretty much everyone now knows of the involvement of Oliver North with the arms sales to Iran. Some may even know of the extent to which he occupied himself with the funding and arming of the Contras. But not too many are aware of his hands-on role with respect to the hostages in Lebanon. And not just the US hostages.

North had close contacts with both Les Aspin, who was the British intelligence operative who was at the sharp end of the efforts to secure the release of British hostages, and Terry Waite, who was the Archbishop of Canterbury's special envoy, and was pretty much a public relations front man.

Waite became a figure of some controversy. Eventually, he became a hostage himself. There are those who believe he should be canonized for his sacrifice. There are others who suggest he brought it upon himself, and that he very nearly jeopardized the whole effort to release the British hostages.

Waite was an amateur playing a very dangerous game. A game which may more properly have been left to the 'professionals.' He believed that he could achieve the right outcome by being an honest broker. With the emphasis on 'honest.'

He met with everyone – militias, Governments, CIA, North,

whoever – without necessarily understanding the impression of collaboration he was creating. It is suggested that, with the intention only of being seen to be the 'honest' broker, he may have revealed too much to the Muslim militias.

Those same militias, fearing that he might be doing the same about them in his meetings with North and the CIA, may have decided that the safest thing to do was simply to keep Waite out of the picture. And use him as a bargaining chip, by playing on the sensitivities of the great British public.

***

Armed with all of this new information, I now felt fully equipped to have a productive conversation with Reggie, if only he would overcome his sulk and contact me. And if only I could keep him on the telephone long enough. We began a cat and mouse game that lasted through the month of August 1989.

I telephoned every day, both at his home and at the University. I left messages on his answering machine and with his assistants. I heard nothing, or his staff would say that he was "popping in from time to time." It was most frustrating. As the month progressed, it also became quite worrying. I wondered if he might be in serious trouble.

Finally, Reggie called late one evening. He said he was in Germany, "helping to test a new weapon." Sometimes, I felt that Reggie, like Hugh, was trying desperately to impress me with all this cloak and dagger. The problem is, it made as little impression on me as it had with Hugh. I had a single item on my agenda: finding the truth.

On this occasion, Reggie was very abrupt. He seemed a little distracted. "I've got problems," he explained, " 'Friends' are causing me problems," he added cryptically. "I left the country two days ago…hang on…I'll call you back." He hung up.

I wondered if he was just messing me about. A few minutes later, he called again. He had just begun to talk again when there was an electronic sound on the line. "What was that?" he asked sharply. "This is your cellular, right? Blast. I'll call you back on the regular line. They've picked us up on your cellular. Too easy." The phone went dead again. James Bond never had it this difficult.

A few minutes later, Reggie was back. "Right. We've got one and a half minutes. That's how long it takes to trace. Then, we'll switch back to your cellular. And so on." Blimey, it was like a high school science project. Reggie claimed he had tried to send me something, but the chemistry hadn't worked. His life was worth nothing now. Mine even less. He would try to meet with me in London.

Dead Men Don't Eat Lunch

I asked him baldly what his intentions were with regards to me. He hesitated for a second: "To give you information, without breaking the law. I will send you something. But because of events, there are certain people who do not want some 'snot-nose' snooping around." I flushed with embarrassment at the compliment. "So steer clear of dark alleys," he concluded, ominously, "particularly around Leicester Square." He might just as well have given me detailed directions. Talk about your red rag to the bull.

***

Leicester Square is one of those wonderful melting pots you seem only to find in the heart of truly vibrant cities. It is the spot where all of London's movie premieres are staged. Yet, in 1989 certainly, it was also the gathering place for a sizable section of London's homeless people.

I arrived early the following morning, cheap throwaway camera in hand, eager to see what I could find. It didn't take me long. There, on the northern side was The Swiss Centre, home to all manner of Swiss chocolate and fancy lederhosen, in the ground floor tourist shop, and to the Swiss Bank Corporation, in its upper levels. Co-incidence was becoming a daily part of my routine.

As I made my way through the dark alleys around the exterior of the building, I noticed that the office area was singularly impenetrable, even for a bank. As I was aimlessly wandering along, peering up at the top of the building, I bumped into a man walking fast in the opposite direction.

I recognized him, but could not remember a name. He clearly recognized me also, but said nothing. Just brushed past me and disappeared into The Swiss Centre. After a few minutes standing still, scratching my head, I recalled that I'd seen the man with Hugh at Wedlake Bell years before, but I still could not grasp a name.

By the time I'd completed my circumnavigation, I found another man waiting for me. With the ever-ready but unread newspaper. I was bored. I decided to have some fun. Strolled around the Square, just to make sure that he was following me, and that he was staying close. Then, when we hit an open patch, I turned abruptly, and began to snap away with the camera.

This was clearly something they'd not covered in spy school. The poor chap went all Peter Sellers on me. First one way. Then the other. Doffed his hat. Went bright red. And stalked off in the direction of The Swiss Center. At which point, I noticed that I'd picked up two more gentlemen with ever-present yet unread newspapers.

***

Geoffrey Gilson

In the meantime, life carried on. In ways which did not seem immediately to be of concern to me, but which would come back later to visit me. In mid-August, there were two explosions at a small hotel in West London. The story put out, after a couple of days, by the Anti-Terrorist Squad of the Metropolitan Police, was that a small band of Lebanese Muslim radicals, intending to attack Salman Rushdie, had blown themselves up by mistake. Salman Rushdie was a well-known immigrant British author, who had had *fatwah* declared on him by Ayatollah Khomeini for writing a book that Khomeini claimed was heretical.

***

Since I wasn't having much luck finding answers 'on the ground,' I tried my luck in the 'ether' again. Michael told me that Reggie was indeed under a lot of stress. The document he wanted to send to me was the 'Stag Place' document. Either literally, or Reggie wanted to impart to me the essence of the information in that document. I needed to stop pushing him. Let him find his own way, in his own time. Again, Michael gave me the prediction that "all would be revealed" at the end of September.

At this point in our session, for no apparent reason, Michael started talking about computers and floppy disks. Then, he stopped and laughed. In an earlier session, I had told him all about the Magical Mystery Tour of England's churches. It now seemed that Michael's American counterparts had possibly misinterpreted all of the signs about a plaque. The flat icon, on a wall, with information behind it was, in all probability, a computer.

Hugh was telling Michael that he had left much of the financial information about his 'operation' on a series of floppy disks. They were to be found at Karen's home. And the disks were disguised as those containing Equine Bloodstock Agency data. I can't say that this immediately leapt to the top of my list of priorities, but I made a mental note.

I was getting more than a little frustrated. I'd tried bluntness with Reggie. Maybe it would work with a ghost. I wondered aloud if the missing money was recoverable. Michael said the floppy disks had bank account numbers on them. There was a Swiss bank account, number: 90 030 5250.

I raised the 'rumor,' which had been passed onto me by a Producer with the BBC, that Hugh had donated large sums of money to the Conservative Party, in return for a safe Parliamentary seat. Michael dismissed this as gossip. However, I forced the issue. I asked if there was, perhaps, a more surreptitious deal, whereby Hugh would 'place' some money 'somewhere,' and then miraculously, the Party would 'reward' him with a seat. Michael became very serious. "These are dirty waters. Where angels fear to tread."

Then, we made another esoteric detour: "Did Hugh ever have any connection with the Olympic Games? I'm getting a scene of Germany and the Olympic Games. And something to do with Reggie again. Now I'm getting an image of the Knights of Malta. Or the Knights of St. John. One or the other. That strange cross. With the splayed ends."

We took a coffee break. When we resumed, Michael mentioned that it normally takes new spirits about a year to settle down before they can be of any 'use.' However, Hugh was so anxious to help out, that he was undergoing 'intensive training.' "Oh," I rejoined sarcastically, "nice to see that death has introduced a welcome note of humility into his make-up."

A deathly hush fell over the small room. I looked up. Michael sat stock still, his face all ashen. "Well Geoffers," he said with a clipped voice, "you've gone and upset him now."

"You what?' came my startled response.

"You've been rude." Michael explained, absolutely deadpan. "He has nothing more to say today."

"A ghost, throwing a pissy fit?"

"Even spirits have feelings."

I tried apologizing. There I was, begging for forgiveness, from a bunch of dust motes, floating in the still air. But all to no avail. He was gone. I had truly left Kansas far behind.

***

That evening, I got well and truly drunk. I'd had more than my fill of obstruction and delay. And every day I felt more like a nursemaid in a scene from "One Flew Over The Cuckoo's Nest." The following morning, while in the depths of a searing hangover, I had a brainstorm. Maybe if Reggie had a 'document' of mine, he would find it easier to talk to me on the telephone.

I spent the day crafting a letter for Reggie. I set out everything I thought I knew, and then everything I knew I thought. And then for good measure, I put in a list of questions about the things I thought I thought. Reward was swift. At the end of September, Reggie finally opened up. Just as Michael, Hugh, whoever, had predicted.

Geoffrey Gilson

Chapter 11

IN ENGLAND, when two roads cross each other, it's called a "crossroads." Where five or more roads come together at any point, that junction in known as a "circus." Where one or the other has a small island in its center, around which vehicles must travel in a single direction, in order to ease the flow of traffic, that island is known as a 'roundabout.'

Beaconsfield's downtown district is huddled around a small circus, right next to the railway line that leads to London, an hour's train ride away. The south side of this circus is dominated by a three story brick edifice, built just under a hundred years ago.

The ground floor is made up of a row of shops. The *faux* two-floor turrets at either corner are occupied by offices. In between the two turrets, and on top of the row of shops, are two tiers of apartments, fronted by a heavy stone balcony. The apartments are accessed by a grand stairway, which splits the whole structure into two. The overall effect is that of a badly-designed, mock-Tudor castle.

Simmonds and Company had been tenants of the left-hand turret for the best part of the Eighties. Looming large as it did over the small downtown circus, Hugh was able to sit in his office in this turret, and survey the busy scene in the district below. Not unlike some feudal warlord. Which was appropriate, given the fact that this is how many of the town's residents had come to think of him.

In the year before his death, I had bought the apartment immediately next to Simmonds and Company. My front door was a foot away from the office's backdoor. Two feet further on was one of the windows to Hugh's office. At the time, the purchase had seemed a fine idea. It was the next best thing to having someone 'sleep over the shop.' In September of 1989, it was about to become a major bugbear.

By this time, I had long since outstayed my welcome at Magda and Christian's, although the two girls were far too well bred ever to say anything. In any other circumstance, I'd have packed my bags and returned to Rhode Island, but I'd caught the psychic 'bug.' I was now as convinced as Michael that there would be some 'revelation' at the end of September, and I did not want to miss it.

Having run out of other options, I had nowhere else to turn but to the empty apartment I still owned in the middle of Beaconsfield. The problem was that, as visible as the turret was, and as notorious as it had become once the extent of Hugh's larceny became known, so it made it almost impossible for me to slip back unnoticed into my next-door apartment.

Like the proverbial thief in the night, I slunk into town well after dark, and took refuge secretly in my little eyrie. However, the secret was out the moment I had to venture forth for supplies. I understood how lepers must have felt in the Middle Ages. No-one actually stoned me, but I could feel their hot eyes boring into my back.

Some threw discretion to the wind. One doctor who had helped my younger sister and brother into the world, and who had been our family healer and jester for as long as I'd been sentient, cut me dead one day as I greeted him in the street. I simply reminded myself of my purpose, grit my teeth and looked for real friends where I could find them.

***

In which spirit, I went to see Michael. There were no preliminaries. Hugh was immediately present. And we got straight down to business. The last session was forgiven and forgotten. Michael was proving to be quite consistent: the timeline to the 'revelation' had remained constant; and it was now almost upon us.

The powers-that-be had been meeting in Stag Place. They had been made aware of my letter to Reggie. If I'd have pushed earlier in the summer, they might have had 'bumped me off' as an irritant. Now, they were minded to allow certain information to come my way. Enigmatically, Michael suggested that the source might be indirect. It might well be through Janet.

Hugh meanwhile had been 'promoted' to a heavenly team trying to bring resolution to the hostage crisis in Lebanon. Michael glared at me for a moment, daring me to end the session with another mistimed wise-crack. I stifled myself manfully.

One team was influencing the American efforts; Hugh's group was focused on the British. "Who are much more involved than the general public realize." The Americans, apparently, were leaning very heavily on the British to help resolve the hostage crisis any way they could.

Hugh's operation, while he had been alive, had not been a one-man deal. There had been three people involved. One an Arab. He had been the turncoat. Hugh had been responsible for the money. The Arab had caused the money to disappear. Hugh hadn't been able to turn to anyone for help because everyone had thought he was the one who had turned. Plus, he had been considered expendable.

Michael admonished me for not contacting Karen about the disk. Hugh was adamant that information was left on disks in her possession. I replied that I'd made a fool of myself the last time I was 'encouraged' to visit Karen by a medium. I was in no hurry for a repeat performance.

Michael went quiet for a while. Then he laughed out loud. Apparently, Hugh had an explanation. As he always had done when alive. Bill shouldn't have been able to contact me at all. Hugh's spirit was so strong that he'd broken through to Bill and Joe before he'd transformed sufficiently to communicate sensible information. What those two mediums had received was garbled information. I was no more convinced by Hugh dead than I was when he was alive. But I gave him marks for creativity. I promised to find Karen.

At that point, Michael became quite excited. He told me that he was getting a very clear message that Reggie would start talking that evening. Everything would be revealed. Then, Hugh tried to jump the gun by giving Michael a name. Without success. Others apparently intervened.

"How extraordinary," Michael exclaimed, "I've never had this happen before. Hugh's spiritual guides have yanked Hugh away. He was about to give me information they regarded as too sensitive for you. And they've literally cut him off."

***

The primary reason for my returning to Beaconsfield in September 1989 had been that I was running out of money. That meant no more rental car and no more rental telephone. Contacting Reggie, or anyone else for that matter, meant using the nearest public telephone. When it came to Reggie, I settled on the old red telephone kiosk behind the railway station a couple of minutes walk from downtown Beaconsfield.

On my way home from Michael that afternoon, I had stopped and bought a small microphone for my tape-recorder. It wasn't sophisticated enough actually to attach to the telephone earpiece. So, I had to engage in an acrobatic exercise, balancing the microphone between the earpiece and my ear.

Often this would prevent my being able to hear Reggie, so I'd have to plead deafness, and ask him to repeat himself. On other occasions, when a train came into the station, I'd lose Reggie altogether, or the microphone would swing loose. Not for the first time in this adventure, I had cause to wonder if real-life spies had half this much trouble. However, the upshot was that I had a full transcript of that evening's conversation, and all the other evenings of enlightenment that followed.

Geoffrey: "Did you get my letter?"

Reggie: "Yes. What can I say? I think you're on very dangerous ground."

Geoffrey: "Because I'm close to the truth?"

Reggie: "Yes. And because you're still in England. Can I direct your reading?"

Geoffrey: "Yes."

Reggie: "Go to the last chapter of *The Messianic Legacy*."

Geoffrey: "All I can find is the Knights of Malta."

Reggie: "Got it in one."

Geoffrey: "So, it's not British Intelligence; it's the Knights of Malta?"

Reggie: "I'm not saying that. I'm saying no-one is acting alone.'

Geoffrey: "So, it's British Intelligence-ish?"

Reggie: "Ish."

Geoffrey: "Knights of Malta-ish?'

Reggie: "Ish. But not alone."

Geoffrey: "Ish?"

Reggie: "Ish."

Geoffrey: "CIA-ish?"

Reggie: There was a pregnant pause. "Beautifully said on

Geoffrey Gilson

my telephone. Well done."

Geoffrey: I persevered. "Ish?"

Reggie: "Ish."

Geoffrey: "Ish." It felt like we were in a mosque. I almost began to chant. "Ok. So, Hugh takes the money, which, from various sources, I gather to be about £5 million [$7.5 million]..."

Reggie: "...£15 million [$22.5 million]..." Well, he fell neatly into that trap.

Geoffrey: "£15 million. Ok. In 1987 and 1988. Probably more 1988."

Reggie: "From May 1987." He was giving away a lot, wasn't he?

Geoffrey: "Doesn't spend it. Stashes it. Hides it. We know he's hidden it, because the combined forces of the Law Society and the Police can't find it."

Reggie: "No. The combined forces of the Law Society, and one or two other unnamed institutions, can't find it."

Geoffrey: "So. We're in November 1988. Something's gone wrong. Why doesn't he put the money back, or run away? Why does he kill himself?"

Reggie: "I don't believe that Hugh killed himself. I believe that Hugh went out to that location, wherever it was, to meet somebody, and I believe they killed him."

Geoffrey: "Why can't we just stop messing about? Why can't you just tell me?"

Reggie: "It's not as simple as that. I'm a soldier. I signed things. And they may be taping this."

Geoffrey: "Tell me something."

Reggie: Long pause, broken only by the occasional sigh.

"Look. I believe that what he was doing ran counter to what some other people were doing. And I believe that he was taken out accordingly. Or that some other people wanted it done."

Geoffrey: "There were two things going on?"

Reggie: "There were lots of things going on. The problem is that you're seeing it through a very simplistic lens. How does it go? Try seeing it through 'a glass darkly.' You're assuming that all of the parties are working together to the same end. Not the case. Today some parties may be working together; tomorrow against each other; the day after they're friends again. If you want to name names, for the time we're talking about, I would see two groupings. I would see America, in the form of the CIA. I would see Mossad and they working together. And I would see the Knights of Malta with them. On the other side of the fence, there is another grouping. There are two Protestant versions of that organization. I'd investigate the Knights of St. John and the Knights of Lazerus. Then, other institutions of a British and German origin.. I believe they are in opposing camps."

Geoffrey: "What can I do?"

Reggie: "I believe Hugh was…when you came to see me in Glasgow, I didn't know. But now…my contact with Hugh had been quiet for a long time. I believe that he was involved in something quasi-official. That money was being used for that purpose. It was not stashed away for personal gain. There was some 'higher purpose.'"

Geoffrey: "What was going to happen at the end of the day? Was he going to be paid back?"

Reggie: "I don't know…I can only…look…I've got to be cautious…" He sounded genuinely nervous. "…I mean my advice is to…Counsel's Opinion is to fuck you off…I wouldn't walk down any dark alleys if I were you…"

Geoffrey: "…you mean like around The Swiss Centre, in Leicester Square?"

Reggie: "…you know what 'wet operations' are? Well, that's where one of the London centers is..."

Geoffrey: "Can you tell me anything else?"

Geoffrey Gilson

Reggie: "Well, I hadn't quite finished actually. There are two sides to this, and I believe Hugh got caught up in the middle. I think in a general sense your scenario was probably right. But my contact with that part of the world stopped in February. When I had a warning not to go on a trip I was planning to take. A friend of mine, called David Heald, who is well known about the world of economics. Gave a lecture in Pakistan fairly recently. He is well known in the Islamic world. His advice to me was not to go to Beirut. Got similar messages when I started poking around on your behalf. Was told to steer clear of Buckley, and stay the hell away from Waite. The view on him is that he can rot in hell. I believe that Hugh was involved in some plan, much along lines we've discussed. He was the lynchpin of the whole thing. As you've suggested. And he was taken out because of it. By people who didn't want it to happen. Now that's a slightly different picture to the one you're painting.

Geoffrey: "Ok. That makes a lot more sense."

Reggie: "Have you read any of those books yet?"

Geoffrey: "Some." Um. The Introduction.

Reggie: "I'm going to draw your attention to a particular passage. In the hardback version [of *The Messianic Legacy*], it's on page 190. Hugh was not a Freemason. Therefore, he missed a lot of things. Chapter 8. Twenty pages in. The paragraph begins: 'Initial inquiries were undertaken by an Englishwoman...' Then, there's a sentence that starts: 'One journalist...' Read that, and take note. I don't think you can prove anything. I'd be hard put to know where to start."

Geoffrey: "Do British Intelligence know about it?"

Reggie: "Yes."

Geoffrey: "But they can't find the money."

Reggie: "At this stage, I think the money's irrelevant. It's merely a means to an end. Without the money, there's no action. Without Hugh, there's no action. One or the other."

Geoffrey: "Ok, you have lost me."

Reggie: "Look. Hugh was involved in something. Other people didn't want it to happen. It doesn't happen if either Hugh disappears or the money disappears. Someone with Hugh was a crook, or worse. And made one or the other happen."

Geoffrey: "Do you know who?"

Reggie: "I'm not sure it's not you." Said in a dead quiet voice.

Geoffrey: "Oh. And I'm looking for the money?"

Reggie: "No. You know where it is." The chit chat was definitely over. A much harder voice had taken its place.

Geoffrey: "But…if I know where it is, why would I be wandering all over England?"

Reggie: "Because you didn't know where I was. And I might know something."

Geoffrey: "Fair enough."

Reggie: "You remember that afternoon in Glasgow? I was taught to be cautious. I made a telephone call. I was given instructions. My military record shows an interesting background. I was a marksman with a pistol, until 1969. Then, I was made a 'bare pass.' To…er…hide me. It became useful. We weren't sure you weren't there to eradicate me."

Geoffrey: "So British Intelligence knows about me?"

Reggie: "Oh, you figure pretty high on one or two lists. Europe's not a very safe place for you at the moment."

Geoffrey: "But why? Why would anyone consider me a threat?"

Reggie: "It's not so much who you are. As what you're doing. You fly in from nowhere. No-one knows who you are. And you're poking around places no-one wants anyone poking around. And then, you come looking for me. Anyway, I've got to go. Watch yourself, mate."

For the first time in this whole saga, I was truly scared. I didn't leave the well-lit telephone kiosk for at least fifteen minutes. I then quick marched all the way back to my apartment. It was only a few minutes walk, but it was the longest 'few minutes' of my life. I kept glancing over my shoulder. And nearly freaked when I dropped my key at the front door.

I locked the door, piled a month's worth of trash against it, and wedged a broomstick under the door handle. I grabbed a bottle of wine, and disappeared into a closet. In the comforting darkness, I got well and truly drunk and cried myself to sleep. All I cared about, at that point, was getting someone to help me help three small kids. As for all the cloak and dagger stuff, on that particular evening, I was convinced I was not cut out for any of the rest of it.

***

When I'd originally left for America at the beginning of 1989, I'd put my apartment on the market, and had switched off the electricity. Without money, I was unable to reverse the process. So along with everything else, I had no light, no heat and no hot water. Ever resourceful, I spent the next few days hiding out in my lair, and working on a routine to cope with my poverty. I felt like Rowan Atkinson in "Mr. Bean."

Winter was underway. I still had a mattress and a duvet, which I'd left in the apartment when I'd moved to America. But no bed, sheets or pillows. I'd wake up, making little spiral freeze clouds with my breath. Every morning was a struggle to convince myself that I really did want to leave the warmth of the goose down. The shortest time on record for this exercise was fifteen minutes.

I'd dash to the bathroom, to perform my morning ablutions, singing at the top of my voice. There was no radio, and the singing took my mind off the cold. It also took the neighbor's minds off whatever they were doing, usually evidenced by loud thumping on the walls.

The previous night's clothes line would be removed from over the bathtub, which I'd fill with freezing cold water. It's a strange phenomenon. However cold the ambient temperature, it tends not to be as cold as water from a pipe. So, although entering the bathtub would be accompanied by much screaming and cussing, along with more in tempo thumping from the neighbors, getting out was a gas. The apartment would always seem quite warm by comparison.

No matter how many times I did it, the sensation always struck me anew. For the few minutes that the warm sensation lasted, I felt quite exhilarated. And usually got dressed to more loud singing. And even louder thumping.

With nothing else to do but wait for Reggie's continued 'revelations,' I used what little money I had left to buy reading material, which kept me occupied for most of the day. I'd eat out of cans, and drink water. As night drew in, and the light faded, I'd pull the apartment's one chair closer and closer to the window, and the streetlight outside. In the evenings, I'd stay warm by adding more layers of clothes, and downing a bottle of 'El Cheapo' from the nearby liquor store.

Since the first letter to Reggie had made him so loquacious, I took the view that a second could do no harm. I was beginning to find myself increasingly guided by intuition, inspiration, call it what you will. I set out all the different ways Reggie might be able to help me, and made a list of all the potential candidates for the individual who had double-crossed Hugh.

***

A series of abbreviated, late-night conversations with Reggie followed. The second letter proved most useful. According to Reggie, Hugh's 'construction friend' was just a simple crook, who had been and was still trying to muscle in on the money. However, Reggie did confirm that two of Hugh's close friends were also operatives with British Intelligence. And that one of his closest was a Knight of Malta.

The Sovereign Military Hospitaller Order of St. John of Jerusalem of Rhodes and of Malta, commonly known as the Order of Malta, traces its origins to Jerusalem where, before the First Crusade (1099), it was founded by its first rector, Blessed Gerard (died 1120) when the Holy City was recovered by the Christians.

It is the fourth oldest religious order of Christendom, preceded only by the Basilians, the Augustinians and the Benedictines. Blessed Gerard founded a hospice-infirmary for pilgrims in Jerusalem, and that facility and an adjoining Church were dedicated to St. John the Baptist and ministered by a religious confraternity. By a Bull of February 15th, 1113, Pope Paschal II approved the institution of the Hospital and placed it under the protection of the Holy See.

By 1126, the Order underwent a transformation that was to mark its identity through succeeding centuries: the need of armed protection for the sick and the pilgrims and later for the defense of the Christian States in the Levant against Muslim attacks, induced the confraternity of the Hospital to assume military-chivalric functions in addition to its religious-hospitaller tasks. The Order constructed great fortresses at vulnerable points in the Kingdom of Jerusalem and launched its own military campaigns in the defense of Christendom. The Order became the first Western standing army and the first organization of chivalry. It expanded its network of hospices for service to and defense of pilgrims along important routes of travel.

The upper classes of the Order are fastidiously aristocratic and must be able to display a family coat-of-arms dating back at least 300 years in unbroken succession from father to son. The friend of Hugh's that Reggie had said was a Knight of Malta was also an hereditary Polish Papal Count, and had been married in the distinctively round Temple Church, in Lincoln's Inn, London. This was the same district in London where Wedlake Bell had had its offices for many years.

The Temple, now a cluster of buildings housing London's legal community, and to be found just a stone's throw or two away from the Law Society, used to belong to the Knights Templar, the fabled warrior-monks, whose Order also was formed immediately prior to the First Crusade, and whose armed members accompanied pilgrims on their holy journeys to Jerusalem. One only had to walk among the soot-laden castellations and time-weathered cobbles of The Temple to feel the very essence of ancient knights doing battle in shining armor, their white tunics emblazoned with the distinctive, long red cross.

The Vatican had excommunicated the Knights Templar in the late 14th Century, for heretical beliefs they had allegedly picked up in the Middle East. Following the excommunication, their power and their lands had been taken over by the Knights of Malta and the Knights of St. John. Only senior affiliates of those two Orders had an automatic right of service in the Temple Church.

Whether as a sequitur or not, Reggie then asked if I knew an "Andrei Lowenoff Rostovsky." A fellow Knight of Lazerus, and a longtime officer for British Intelligence. Used the code name "Russell." Meant diddley-squat to me. Frankly, I was becoming thoroughly confused by all these Teutonic and Slavic-sounding people parading around as British spies.

Somewhat cryptically, Reggie sent me greetings from a colleague who knew me, but did not wish to be revealed at that time. I really was making some people quite jumpy. He wished only to be identified as "Charlotte."

Apparently, this was a Square in Glasgow, which at that time was regularly frequented by the local yuppies and preppies, or as they are known in Great Britain, the 'Sloanes' and the 'Hooray Henry's.' In her time, Princess Diana had been the Queen of the Sloanes in London.

Reggie's information was that Hugh had at least £3 million on him at the time of his death. And more stashed away elsewhere. British Intelligence had not the slightest interest in knowing the details of Hugh's operation, nor what had gone wrong. Their interest was singular: contrary to what Reggie had told me in our last conversation, British Intelligence were now keen to know where the money was. Join the queue. But why on earth would British Intelligence be so interested in what I understood, at best, to be no more than £15 million? Were they that hard up? Reggie would not or could not enlighten me.

Reggie did however startle me with his assertion that he had been told that Hugh had been killed by the Mafia, working on instructions from the CIA. The reason for Reggie's continuing fear was that he believed that the CIA were now after him. And possibly me. His immediate preoccupation was with further investigations. And with getting rid of the mortal threat. Communication with me would continue to be spotty, at best. But he promised that he would try.

***

I was not completely alone and trapped in Beaconsfield. I stayed in regular contact with Maggi, who with magnificent effort, was holding together my fast-dwindling financial affairs in America. Duncan and Jules took care of me every Saturday. In return for helping them to build a pond, they fed me and allowed me use of their hot water. Big mistake. It always took me the best part of the following week to get used to the arctic water in my apartment again.

Then there was Janet and her kids. I re-established contact by just turning up on their doorstep. It turned out to be quite convenient. In the year before Hugh's death, Janet had achieved election to a couple of levels of the local government, and she needed a babysitter every other Thursday evening. I re-acquainted myself with Juliet and Tanya, we all ate Chinese and Janet did her municipal duties. By unspoken compact, I never mentioned any part of my quest.

Tanya's birthday fell in this period. I had no money, so I came up with the bright idea of composing a song for her. The two children had known of my pop yearnings while Hugh had been alive. And Tanya had come up with a couple of lines of quite passable white rap. Chris Waldron kindly volunteered his small recording studio, and we spent a pleasant afternoon laying down Tanya's birthday track.

Chris Waldron, or "Waldo" as he is known to his friends, is a great big teddy bear of a man, with a twinkle in his eye and a chuckle always lurking in his throat. His voice is a rich, gravelly baritone, all hale and heart: Johnny Cash alive and well in the English burbs. Although I fancied I could write pop songs, Chris didn't fancy them at all. But he was all for the nobility of the cause, and gently warbled his way through my concoction without a murmur of complaint.

For reasons that I could never understand, Juliet and Tanya always insisted that I 'help out' at their parties. I use the quotes advisedly. It seemed to me that all I did was drink wine, admonish the little tykes on a regular basis, and run the end-of-party bingo session. But they and their friends appeared to enjoy it. And Tanya loved her song. Into which Chris and I had interwoven the couple of lines of rap, as originally sung by Tanya. Thirty or so white, suburban, nine year olds, lip-synching to an English rap ditty, sung by a Seventies' rock and roller. Ah yes. These were the moments that made the noble quest worthwhile.

***

And the noble quest was about to take a dramatic turn. It was the fall of 1989. Momentous events were shaking the very foundations of the global political structure that had existed since the end of the Second World War. And Reggie was involved at the sharp end. In East Germany.

Dead Men Don't Eat Lunch

Chapter 12

RONALD REAGAN rode to power in 1980, vowing to bring down the "Evil Empire." Not too many people believed he meant it. But his Secretary of Defense, Caspar Weinberger did. Bill Casey, his director of the CIA believed him also. As did George Bush, the new Vice President, and soon-to-be proud owner of his very own covert intelligence organization, the SSG/CPPG.

Reagan put into play a new Doctrine that soon bore his name. Every President since the Second World War had satisfied themselves only with containing Communism. Reagan wanted to roll it back. And he was determined to do so by engaging the Soviet Empire at every level, and in every region.

He instigated a massive arms build-up, daring the Soviet Union and its satellites in Eastern Europe to bankrupt themselves trying to keep pace. He exacerbated the economic squeeze by ending the policy of easy credit to those wishing to do business with Russia.

Through Bush and his SSG/CPPG, Reagan supported covert military actions specifically designed to wear down the Communist military machine on as many different fronts as possible. The gloves were off. Holding actions were a thing of the past. It was time to kill Communists. Do to them what they had done to the Americans in Vietnam.

Covert wars were waged in Nicaragua, Angola and elsewhere. In particular, a billion dollars a year was poured into the mujahideen in Afghanistan in the successful effort to drive the Russian 40th Army out of that occupied country.

Indeed, it was the radical Muslims the CIA supported in that effort, taken together with the radical Muslims inspired by activities in Lebanon and on the West Bank of Israel, that directly gave rise to the individuals and organizations who lead the Islamic Jihad against the West today. Whether in Baghdad, London or New York.

Geoffrey Gilson

By the mid-Eighties, the Russkies had had enough. They brought to power Mikhail Gorbachev, whose remit was to get the Americans off their backs. He tried. But it was too late. The steps he took would eventually backfire against the whole Communist edifice.

Matters finally came to a head in Poland, the homeland of the first non-Italian Pope for centuries. The Poles take their Catholic religion seriously. And their Nationalism. And they had hated the Russians through all of their various occupations of Poland, including the Communist one in the 20th Century.

In 1981, inspired by the visit of the new Polish Pope, John Paul I, or as the Poles still knew him, Karol Wojtyla, the Poles established a free trade union/political party called *Solidarity*. This entity sought to challenge the monopoly of the Communist Party. Such challenge in the past would automatically have triggered the Soviet Army, massed on Poland's border, to invade and crush the insurrection.

Indeed, throughout the Eighties, a cat-and-mouse game was played between *Solidarity* and the Soviet leaders, with the Polish Communist Government playing a very nervous referee. Then, with the ascension of Gorbachev, as General-Secretary of the Communist Party in the Soviet Union, the signals from Moscow seemed to change. Or rather, they stopped.

For the first time in generations, the Polish Government was apparently being left on its own to do what it saw fit. Step by careful step, looking over their shoulders with anxious anticipation, the Poles went through the process of legalizing *Solidarity*.

Eventually, in the Fall of 1989, the Polish Government announced that it would be holding partially-free Parliamentary elections in 1990, and that it would be allowing *Solidarity* to take part. It was a foregone conclusion that *Solidarity*, under the direction of its charismatic leader Lech Walesa, would win those Elections, and bring to an end the dominant role of Communism in Polish affairs.

Everyone around the world held their breath, waiting on Moscow. But Gorbachev did nothing. And with that, the floodgates opened. Hungary declared that it too would be holding Elections. Czechoslovakia opened its borders to the thousands of East Germans who finally sensed freedom. And East Germany, under enormous pressure, tore down the Berlin Wall. All in the space of a few months.

No-one, not even Reggie and his pals, had foreseen the collapse of Communism happening that fast. The *Velvet Revolution* staggered the world with its speed, and, for the most part, its lack of bloodshed. "We thought maybe 1991, 1992," exclaimed an overjoyed Reggie, "but not this soon."

***

Dead Men Don't Eat Lunch

Reggie had gone 'missing' for a couple of weeks again, but then, in November, it was all I could do to keep him off the telephone. He had been operating day and night out of a base "a few minutes away from Templehof," an airport near West Berlin, deep in the heart of what was then still Communist East Germany. (Quite separately, I discovered that, in Berlin, MI6 regularly used as a base of operations the otherwise empty Olympic Stadium, which Hitler had built for the 1936 Berlin Olympics.)

Reggie had been taking large amounts of money clandestinely into East Germany for the CIA. "All is forgotten and forgiven with respect to Lebanon," Reggie explained. Whatever trouble Reggie had been in was now gone. His enemies had become his friends. He had a talent: he could speak German in whatever dialect his new friends fancied.

Reggie had also been given new and completely different information in respect of Hugh's activities. Lebanon scenario had been a smokescreen, used to deflect Reggie before he became one of the 'chosen few.' In fact, Hugh had been laundering large amounts of money into Bulgaria and Yugoslavia. For whom, Reggie would not or could not say. However, according to Reggie, Hugh had made at least two visits himself to Bulgaria and Yugoslavia within the ten month period before his death.

This money was to be used either to bump someone off, or to buy them out. Whatever or whoever it was, 'others' had not been in favor of the operation. Steps were taken either to deny Hugh access to the money, threaten him, or kill him. What remained the same was that the villains were unchanged. They were still the Mafia, acting on behalf of the CIA.

This complete change of direction was more than I could handle after only one bottle of wine. I threw something of a wobbly at Reggie over the telephone. He was impervious. He kept jabbering away about seeing friends of his from Lazerus and British Intelligence on the TV News, parading around the streets of the former East Berlin, rejoicing at the fall of the Wall.

"I keep telling you, dear boy," he laughed, "you've got to read those two books. It's the only way you'll understand what's happening. We're about to win a war we've been waging for a thousand years." I knew I wasn't all that good at history, but it was my impression that Eastern Europe had been under the Communist yoke for only fifty years.

***

Holy Blood, Holy Grail sets out 'evidence' for the existence of a clandestine group called the 'Priory of Sion,' which has abrogated to itself the duty to protect the bloodline of Jesus. *The Messianic Legacy* is the sequel, which establishes the covert role the Priory plays in world affairs today.

Geoffrey Gilson

Both books were written in the Eighties by a trio of journalists commissioned by the BBC to investigate some interesting discoveries in the South of France, and the books form the 'research' basis for the wildly successful fictional work, *The Da Vinci Code*.

The premise behind the books is that Jesus was, indeed, the King of the Jews. He was the blood heir to King David. The Bible stories of him being a poor carpenter were an allegory, kind of like saying Prince Charles is a painter. It's something he did. It's not who he was.

Jesus was concerned with ridding his homeland of the Roman occupiers, and to replace the upstart King Herod, but he needed to play his cards cunningly. He adopted a multi-pronged approach. On one, very discreet level, he made arrangements with his other Jewish aristocratic friends; he married Mary Magdalene; had children; and had a Royal Bloodline ready to assume the newly-vacant Jewish throne, based, once again, in the ancient Temple of Solomon.

On another level, he forged careful bonds with the radical Zealot movement, whose adherents were recognized by their fad for dying their hair orange, hence Judas Iscariot (the latter name referring to the color of his hair).

But Jesus was not just about the material. An important part of his being was his spiritual side. He was a Rabbi, whose brand of Jewish teaching was set apart from the traditional Jewish beliefs. Jesus followed the views of the Essene tribe, views which today would broadly be described as Gnostic, or occultist, or to be more modern, 'New Age.'

His disciples, who were indeed peasants and fishermen, knew nothing of Jesus as royal heir, or aristocratic schemer. They simply knew him as the radical Rabbi, who gave the Sermon on the Mount, which was a much more simplistic version of his true beliefs. When the Pharisees and the Romans called Jesus' bluff and crucified him, these same disciples set out to ensure that this heritage of Jesus, the Christianity that they understood, became the only 'true' heritage of Jesus Christ.

Over those early centuries, the die was cast. The disciples recast their version of Christianity in a form that borrowed much from Roman religions, so that it would eventually become the one religion adopted by the entire Roman Empire. As such, it no longer operated out of Jerusalem, but rather made Rome its new home for its new leader, the Vicar of Christ, the Pope.

Meanwhile, Mary Magdalene and her children fled to the South of France. Just as the true teachings and origins of Jesus had been clandestine in his heyday in Israel, so too the job of protecting his bloodline and their legacy became a project of long-term and covert scheming.

For a thousand years, the two powerbases, the one in Rome, the other in France, struggled clandestinely over the legacy of Jesus.

Dead Men Don't Eat Lunch

Compromise was almost reached. With the bloodline married into the powerful Merovingian Kingdom in France, a deal was brokered to create a new Europe-wide Holy Roman Empire. The Pope would recognize the Emperor as the true heir of Jesus, and in return, the Emperor would support the Pope as the undisputed leader of 'his' church. The deal broke down in acrimony, both sides blaming the other.

At the end of the 11th Century, a group of knights close to the bloodline formed the Priory of Sion, named after a hill (Mount Sion) near Solomon's Temple, Jerusalem. This entity, wishing to remain in the shadows, then established a more public organization, which it called the "Knights Templar." The latter organized and led the First Crusade. Jerusalem was retaken from the Muslims for 'Christianity.' The then heir to Jesus was named Badouin I of Jerusalem. Victory was short-lived. Jerusalem fell after only a few years, never to be retaken by any of the subsequent Crusades.

These bloody escapades did have one long-lasting legacy though. They were the catalyst that transformed the Islamic religion into a warring jihad against all things European and Western. In the minds of many modern Muslims, the West's continued 'rape' of their countries, latterly in the name of oil or 'democracy,' has merely been a continuation of the tradition of invasion and occupation established by the Crusades.

After coming so close to success with the Crusades, the Priory dug in for the long haul, and took the view that their aim might no longer be as simple as putting the heir of David back on the Israeli throne. Indeed, there had been no real 'Jewish' Israel since the Romans drove all the Jews out in 70 A.D.

Jews had scattered to the four corners of the world. Some plotted to re-establish their old country. Others took the view that they would rather find success in their adopted countries. Others still took the view that the latter was the road to achieving the former. Whatever their outlook, all became known by the collective title, the 'Jewish Diaspora.'

The Priory took its lead from the Diaspora: it sought many paths to power, just as Jesus had done in Israel. It tried marriage into royal houses, and today many European Royal Families, including that of Great Britain, lay some claim to be descended from the House of David. The last Great House to be so favored was the that of the Hapsburgs, whose Empire, until the first World War, included much of Eastern Europe, Italy, Bulgaria and Yugoslavia.

The Priory continued to strengthen the Knights Templar, who, in the Middle Ages, were one of the most powerful entities in Europe. The Pope eventually excommunicated them, and their lands were taken over by a variety of fraternal orders, including the Knights of Malta, the Knights of St. John, the Teutonic Knights and the Knights of Christ. The splayed red cross of the latter became a regular sight on the sails of explorers. It is said that the expeditions of Christopher Columbus were financed by the Knights of Christ.

The Knights Templar were 'reborn' spiritually, and were then indoctrinated with the alleged 'true' beliefs and practices of Jesus, which beliefs and practices necessarily had to be held secret from the prying eyes of the Roman Church and its Inquisition. When the Templars were forcibly disbanded, those occultic secrets found their way into new organizations: the Rosicrucians, the Illuminati and eventually, the various degrees of Freemasonry.

The Priory also invested much effort attempting to influence political developments behind the scenes. The Knights Templars were the first bankers in Europe, and there is still much Priory/Masonic influence in major banking circles around the world.

The Founding Fathers were much inspired by Masonic ideals, and the symbology of the latter's secret occultic beliefs is redolent in American institutions. For example, the All-Seeing Eye on the back of the One Dollar Bill.

Much effort is today expended on the unification of Europe. A Hapsburg was the European Union's first Ambassador to Hungary after the Communists had been removed from power. Otto von Hapsburg, reputedly the current heir to Jesus, was present in the capital of Slovenia the day it declared independence from Yugoslavia.

As Europe and its colonies spread across the globe, not least with the British Empire, so too have the secret agendas of the Priory. It would be overly simplistic to talk of one Jewish-Masonic New World Order. There are today many competing factions in and around the Priory. And there are as many different versions of that New World Order.

The Roman Church, and its Protestant offshoots, have fought hard for two thousand years to destroy the Priory and all its various facets and channels. The notion of Satan, and occultist worship as evil, was promulgated by the Roman Church, in order to demonize the gentle beliefs of true Gnostics.

The persecution of the Jews has been unremitting. Little heed has been paid to the difference between Jews, the Jewish Diaspora and the Judeo-Christian Priory of Sion. Until recently, Freemasonry was banned by the Catholic Church.

The ultimate ambition of all of the machinations of the Priory has been to 'reveal' the truth behind the Priory. And to do so in a cultural, religious and political environment, which the Priory already 'controls,' all be it covertly. Hence the need for a 'New World Order.'

The eventual revelation awaits what the Priory regards as the right moment. In the meantime, partial revelation is engaged in on an ongoing basis. Usually using the medium of culture and entertainment as a subliminal 'educational' tool.

Much of the cultural explosion of the Renaissance used the secret behind the Priory as its inspiration. As did *The Da Vinci Code*. And in the same vein, in the last few years, there have been a welter of movies dealing either with the battle between the 'Church' and occultist powers, or with Masonic theme. It was no accident that the remake of *The Omen*, which chronicles the fictional coming of the Anti-Christ, was released a couple of weeks after the movie release of *The Da Vinci Code*. The Roman Church has made a cottage industry our of portraying the blood heir of Jesus as the fictional Anti-Christ.

However, not all of the action takes place on the Big Screen or on the Big Stage. It is visible in every High Street. There are Masonic Lodges in almost every town. And churches the length and breadth of America are today engaged in a relentless rearguard effort to prevent the infiltration into their congregation of what they describe as New Age Charismatics.

Most 'organized' Christianity draws its lifeblood from the creed that one can only enter heaven by joining a church and being 'saved.' Christian Charismatics say that the true path to heaven lies in personal enlightenment. In other words, they are Gnostics, who believe that Jesus was one of the greatest Gnostics. And they are the local foot soldiers of the Priory of Sion.

***

I was minding my own business one dark and chilly evening, in early December of 1989. As usual, I had taken up a post by the window nearest to the streetlight, and was quietly imbibing a warming glass of red wine. As the wine took effect, the thoughts swirling around my head gently coalesced into a picture of Reggie, dressed as a warlock, muttering incantations on a lonely hillside in Scotland.

My reverie was broken by the sound of furious thumping on my front door. For the first time, I experienced what it meant when they say 'your heart is in your mouth.' Either that, or I'd just swallowed the cork. I peered carefully out of the window. It was nothing more harmful than Martin Pratt. Who had suddenly become very talkative.

We went to a nearby pub, where Martin poured forth. It turned out that he had been sacked earlier that day by City Jeroboam, and he wanted someone's shoulder to cry on. That, at least, was the reason he gave. But I think he had other matters he wanted to get off his chest, since he talked about nothing other than Hugh.

Martin now confided that he had known all along that Hugh was in MI6. However, he still clung to his claim that he knew nothing of what Hugh had been involved in before his death. Martin did, however, have much to say about Philip de Nahlik, the friend of his and Hugh's who was the Polish Papal Count.

Philip was apparently always talking to Hugh about the Knights of Malta and Freemasonry: "Philip wanted Hugh to join all sorts of secret societies." Martin's last comment, as he staggered to his car, was that I should stay away from Philip, "he's more dangerous than he seems."

***

Until the 19th Century, the Vatican was not only a great religious authority, it was also a sovereign power, holding sway over a large territory in Italy, known as the Papal States. After the Italian national revolution in 1870, the Pope was stripped of his lands and was reduced to being the "Prisoner of the Vatican." Perhaps to compensate for the loss of his earthly kingdom, Pope Pius IX (1846-1878) convoked Vatican Council I, with the purpose of promulgating his hold over his 'subjects' through the doctrine of papal infallibility.

For his role in delivering the Italian nation into the bloody hands of Mussolini, Pope Pius XI (1922-1939) received the equivalent of $80 million, and restoration of the Papacy's temporal sovereignty in Vatican City, under the terms of the Lateran Treaty of 1929. Pius and his successors would exploit this treaty to create a Vatican Bank, also known as the Institute of Religious Works (IOR). This bank was effectively beyond the reach of any regulation by secular authorities, and was thus uniquely suited to the work of tax evasion and money laundering.

In 1968, Pope Paul VI found himself in a quandary. The Italian Government had just abolished the Vatican's tax exemption for income from Italian investments. Fearing embarrassment at the public disclosure of the enormity of its financial portfolio, Paul decided that the best course of action would be to find some clandestine way to remove the domestic assets overseas.

He turned to a shady banking character called Michele Sindona, and his sidekick, Roberto Calvi, who would later become known as "God's Banker." Sindona's spectacular rise from veritable rags to control of a vast international banking empire was partially due to the support of his patrons in the Mafia, and in P2, a secret Masonic society controlled by one Lucio Gelli.

The P2 Lodge (*Propaganda Due*) was founded in 1877 to provide for provincial Freemasons. It became a secret lodge in 1970 to recruit men of right-wing persuasion to prevent a Communist takeover. It was allegedly disbanded after a major scandal in the Seventies, but it still wields enormous influence in Italian government circles and even in the Vatican.

Dead Men Don't Eat Lunch

Like Sindona, Roberto Calvi had also managed to achieve banking success on the backs of his Mafia and P2 friends. He took a small regional bank, *Banco Ambrosiano*, and turned it into Italy's largest private bank.

Pope Paul did not pay too much attention to what was being done in his name, so long as the Vatican's assets were being successfully liquidated overseas. Which was just as well. The bottom line is that all sorts of commingling of funds was taking place between Vatican money, Mafia funds, A*mbrosiano* offshore accounts and shell companies all over the Caribbean. And necessarily, a large percentage was simply being creamed off the top.

The whole sorry mess finally ended in disaster in the early Eighties: Pope Paul's successor, John Paul I, apparently uncovered the criminality and would have exposed it, along with a list of Freemason Cardinals, if he hadn't turned up dead in his bed a matter of days after being elected Pope.

In 1978, a report by the Bank of Italy on *Ambrosiano* concluded that several billion lire had been exported illegally. In May of 1981, Roberto Calvi was arrested, found guilty of fraud and sentenced to four year's imprisonment, but was released pending an appeal.

Then on June 17th, 1982, Calvi was found hanging from scaffolding beneath Blackfriars Bridge in central London, with bricks in his pockets and $15,000 on his person. Days later, it was discovered that some $1.3 billion was missing from *Ambrosiano*. The Coroner's Inquiry determined that Calvi's death was suicide.

Although the Vatican Bank denied legal responsibility for the 'hole' in *Ambrosiano's* finances, it did acknowledge "moral involvement," and paid $241 million to creditors. *Ambrosiano* was eventually re-constituted with funds being invested by the Bank of Italy and the *Banca Nazionale del Lavoro* (BNL).

On March 23rd, 1986, Michele Sindona was poisoned to death in the Italian jail in which he was serving time for ordering the death of Giorgio Ambrosioli.

In an interesting twist to the story, the British police re-opened their investigation into Calvi's death in 1998, after a second Coroner's Inquiry declared that Calvi's death was not suicide. On the basis of the conclusions of the Police, Italian prosecutors in 2004 announced that they would be prosecuting four known members of the Mafia for the murder of Roberto Calvi.

In their report, the prosecutors stated that they believed that Calvi was murdered by British elements of the Sicilian Mafia and their mainland Italian cousins, the Camorra, as punishment for pocketing money they had asked him to launder through *Ambrosiano*. Perhaps not surprisingly, the amount allegedly pocketed was the same as the $1.3 billion that had gone missing.

Geoffrey Gilson

It is said that the assassination attempts on President Reagan and Pope John Paul II, both in 1981, created a special bond between these two veteran anti-Communists. Both pledged to help each other in any way that they could to roll back Communism in Eastern Europe. Some years after the scandal with Calvi and *Ambrosiano* had died down, Calvi's briefcase turned up in the Vatican. Containing all of the details of the Vatican's secret channeling of CIA funds to *Solidarity* through *Ambrosiano*, and by way of the Knights of Malta.

Chapter 13

"THERE ARE ALL SORTS of interesting people, with all sorts of interesting agendas, running around Eastern Europe, trying to recreate it in their own image," declared Reggie. "It's not just what you're reading in the newspapers."

Reggie was adamant that my concerns and interests were now lost. Hugh was history. As was I. At one point, I was proving useful "to one or two organizations of a Christian bent." My investigations, while irksome to some, were seen as a boon to others, precisely because they were an irritation to their enemies. But the dramatic change of events had rendered me insignificant.

I tried my hardest to figure out who might once have been 'friends,' and who, 'enemies.' Plus, what they might be now. But it was all to no avail. When he wasn't talking to me in parables, Reggie might just as well have been speaking in tongues. A typically cryptic comment was his declaration that "all the forces of Christendom had been allied against 'The Bear' [Russia]. And it wasn't even against 'The Bear.' Because they were on our side, too."

I couldn't even pretend to understand. But I attempted valiantly to swing the conversation back to me and to Hugh. Reggie was more animated than he had ever been. And was equally dismissive. No-one cared. All the focus was now on Eastern Europe. And the Priory of Sion, and its attendant Fraternal Orders, including the Knights of Lazerus, were right in the thick of it. Slugging it out with the 'secular' intelligence agencies of the West and East, and with each other.

"We've been preparing for this battle for a thousand years," Reggie exclaimed, "and this time, we're going to be victorious." Knights of Malta were organizing in Hungary. Reggie had not only been carrying money into the East for the CIA. He had been in Dresden, East Germany the week before using US Dollars to free half a dozen Knights of Lazerus from jail.

Geoffrey Gilson

I could make no further impression on Reggie. Like a man transformed, he stated that he had undergone a "spiritual rebirth" in the previous week, and that there was now no turning back for him. I concluded I was wasting my time.

"Remember the warning you were given about the double-headed eagle," Reggie asked, "well, the eagle on my ring is from a different branch, but the same 'family' as Otto von Hapsburg. That's what it's all about at the moment. This is no longer about Hugh, or me, or you. It's about major changes in the world political balance. On levels you can only begin to imagine. Read those two books. Hugh missed a lot because he was not a Freemason. And you're missing the bigger picture, as well."

Reggie had one more personal warning for me before he hung up for the last time: stay away from Philip de Nahlik. This was the close friend of Hugh's, whom Reggie had identified as being both British Intelligence and a Knight of Malta, "although his primary allegiance is to the latter, and the two loyalties have now probably come into conflict."

***

I was lost in thought as I climbed the stone stairs to the darkened balcony fronting my apartment, and I did not immediately see the two figures huddled by my front door. They were dressed in Police garb and as I drew near, I noticed that they were, in fact, looking at what had previously been the window to Hugh's office. It was open.

I paid the two apparent Policemen no heed, until one stopped me as I was about to enter my apartment. "You used to work here, didn't you, Mr. Gilson?" I had not given him my name. I had served on the City Council for four years. Beaconsfield is a small town. And I did not recognize him, or his mate. Plus, I had told no Policeman I had returned to Beaconsfield. I tried to hurry on past.

The Policeman made to stop me again. "Can you tell us why this window is open? We couldn't help but notice it from the street." The balustrade to the balcony was too high for the window to be seen from the street. And it was too dark to see anything anyway. I had no idea what these two had been up to, or what they wanted to do. I only knew that, at that moment, I was going to find myself in my apartment. Which I did. A few moments later. After a bit of pushing.

I spent a good deal of the night shaking. As soon as it was light, I checked the window to Hugh's office. Whoever my two visitors had been, they had not seen fit to close the window. I never saw or heard from them again. Nor any other Policeman legitimately following up on mysterious open windows.

Dead Men Don't Eat Lunch

***

I was done. I was tired. I was cold. And Reggie was not going to give me anything more. It was time to return to America. I began my round of farewells. Neil Relph was first on the list. He had another interesting nugget from Carratu: a nameless client reported that Hugh had shown him a briefcase one day, stuffed with cash. Hugh was apparently taking the cash to Geneva, "to consummate a deal."

***

I had been attempting to talk with Hugh's mistress, Karen, for months, without success. With wonderful timing, she turned up on my doorstep, and whisked me off for an Indian dinner. I might have wished that it was more. But it wasn't.

She spent most of the evening going all weepy on me. She hadn't returned my calls, because she was scared of all the crap I was getting into. When she calmed down, I tried to find a way to raise the issue of Hugh's computer disks. I was expecting something of a bad reaction, bearing in mind the last time Gregg and I had turned her house upside down.

However, as soon as I mentioned Bloodstock Agencies, her mouth hit the floor. She and Hugh had been seriously contemplating setting one up, and yes, she did have a bunch of disks that Hugh had given her. But she couldn't for the life of her think of where they were. The last time she'd seen them, Paul had been playing with them. Even Laurel and Hardy had it easier than this.

Karen promised to go straight home and look for them. A couple of days later, I telephoned her from a public booth. She had found them. She would bring them to me. And I've never heard from her again.

***

I had a last visit with Geoff Hughes. He was courteous as always. He reported that the Police had stopped looking for an accomplice. They were certain it was me, and would be delighted whenever I felt fit to let them know where the money was. As would Geoff, the Law Society and the Estate.

The tally for recovered money and assets remained a paltry £100,000 ($150,000). I gave Geoff a long letter re-iterating my belief that the best hope for recovery still lay with either twisting the arms of his closest friends or prodding British Intelligence. I continued to get the impression that he believed he might actually be doing both simply by talking with me.

Geoffrey Gilson

Definitely the weirdest 'investigation' I'd ever encountered.

Geoff did break down a little and confirmed Neil's story about the cash in the briefcase. He had not, however, been able to establish whether or not Hugh had actually traveled to Switzerland. Although, there was evidence he had made trips to Europe in the year before his death. Yugoslavia or Bulgaria, I wondered aloud? Geoff went shifty on me. No-one had been able to find Hugh's passport.

As I was leaving, Geoff came over to shake my hand. He held on a little longer than normal. "I shouldn't say this, but you're a decent guy," he said, ever so softly. "I might have got further without interference from the Law Society. You're not so wrong. It will all come out. Just not in the timeframe you might wish." He would say no more. But he wished me well. And that was that.

***

Geoff had told me that a journalist from the London *Independent* magazine, one Suzie McKenzie, had been trying to contact me. Suzie met with me in a pub in Beaconsfield. She was a blonde bombshell, obviously out to prove that she was more than just a pretty face. Although this didn't stop her wearing the smallest and tightest black leather mini-skirt I've ever seen painted on someone's backside.

We dueled for a couple of hours, each of us trying to tap the other for information. It became obvious that she had been fully briefed by the Law Society. Certainly, she was giving up more than Geoff Hughes ever had. But only with difficulty. What she wanted from me was sleazy gossip, to spice the meat she'd already been given. I did not oblige. All I was prepared to offer were hints about MI6 involvement.

We both finally got bored. She ended up writing an airhead piece that faithfully followed the approved line: Hugh was a simple provincial lawyer, who got sticky fingers, and got caught. She had the last laugh with me, bless her heart. She reported my MI6 ramblings, but wholly in the context of my being a starstruck nutcase.

No hard feelings, though. I'd had a pleasant evening with her. She drove me home in the rain. And she did me the courtesy of laughing at my 'missing money' story: a week earlier, I had been in the same pub with Jules and Duncan. It was my turn to buy a round. Phil the Barkeep, who was none too happy at my presence anyway, served the drinks, and told me it would be £3.50. I made a great show of patting my pockets, looked up and wondered if Phil had change for £5 million. He didn't laugh. Suzie did.

***

Dead Men Don't Eat Lunch

  I gathered my last letter to Reggie, and the tapes of the ensuing conversations, and hightailed it to London, to see Michael one last time. He was in fine fettle. As were Hugh and his spiritual guides. They had nothing to offer on the saga itself. I was told that what I held in my hand was the 'revelation' I had been promised. My plans for returning to America were, according to all and sundry, timely, to say the least.

  Michael took the opportunity to introduce me to my three spiritual guides. They were all, apparently, senior figures form America's political past, and had signed on to help me with the American end of my quest. In that regard, Michael predicted that my journey would lead to an important political figure in Texas, and a bank with Italian connections.

  Before I left, he gave me one more Tarot reading, and in a manner strangely reminiscent of Bill from Rhode Island, he told me that I represented a combination of the Fool and the Wizard. I was on a Quest for Knowledge. That I would achieve the Powers and Mystical Wisdom of the Wizard. But, as was my nature, I would cloak it always with the Humor of the Fool. Although, Michael pointed out sternly, the Fool is not always just about Jest. He too is a Quester. Always traveling. Always searching. Much like Don Quixote. Hmm. Change that from a Mercedes to a Bentley.

***

  My last duty before leaving Great Britain was to say 'good-bye' to Janet, Juliet and Tanya. They were understandably upset at having to do the tearful farewell again. No words were spoken about Hugh. We hugged, we cried, and I returned to Rhode Island.

***

  It was the depth of winter, and conditions seemed to be little different from those inside my apartment in Beaconsfield. The only difference was that the ground in Rhode Island was covered with three feet of snow. But at least I had the luxury of enjoying hot showers morning, noon and night.

  Maggi had performed miracles in holding my finances together in my absence. I tried to find employment, to get myself back on my feet as soon as possible. However, New Englanders while famous for their poetic scenery and warm hospitality towards tourists, are none too happy about foreigners trying to steal their jobs. After six months, I had run out of luck, and my bank account had run out of money.

  But not before I had taken the opportunity to contact every media outlet I could track down in Great Britain, in a vain attempt to rustle up interest in my discoveries about Hugh. I kept it simple. The press release I used focused on Reggie's second scenario, with a little embellishment of my own.

I told the media that Hugh had been working for persons unknown, but with the knowledge of British Intelligence, to launder money into Yugoslavia and Bulgaria, to help foment the 'velvet revolution' in those countries. The CIA had become unhappy, either with Hugh or his 'masters,' and had had him bumped off, via the good offices of their Mafia buddies.

I sparked interest from only two quarters. The first came by way of a telephone call from a Paul Halloran, claiming to work as a journalist for *Private Eye*, a well-known satirical and investigative journal in Great Britain. The conversation was as strange as it was short. Halloran evinced no interest in Hugh, British Intelligence or the CIA. He was concerned solely with determining if I knew where the money was, and if he could be my exclusive media contact when I found it. When I asked him why, he hung up.

The other interested party was the CIA, which introduced itself to me almost as soon as I returned to England. This I did when my money finally ran out in America, because England, at that time, remained the only country in the world where I knew how to survive when broke.

Chapter 14

WHEN THE BRITISH lost their Colonies in America, they set out to expand their Empire in the rest of the World. By the end of the Nineteenth Century, there were British Colonies on all the Continents of the Globe. From the blazing sands of the Sahara, to the freezing desert of Antarctica; from the opium dens of China, to the denizens of the Indian Sub-Continent, the Union Jack held sway.

The British genuinely believed that they were sharing their largesse with 'the heathen.' They brought with them their own religion, the Church of England, a Protestant version of the Roman Christianity, and left behind democratic systems based on their own Houses of Parliament. It never occurred to the British that those they wished to 'civilize' felt that they were already quite civilized enough. On the whole, the British proved to be as sensitive to the indigenous peoples of the other lands they conquered as they had been to the original Natives of the American Continent.

It is an interesting notion that 'Americans' are held morally responsible for the vicious treatment of America's Indians, and for the importation of slaves from West Africa. It is a fact that the people who initiated these inhuman practices were the British. They became 'American' only later. It is one of the less endearing traits of the British that they make Pontius Pilate look like a saint when it comes to washing their hands of the sins of their forebears.

On the subject of another interesting notion, namely the fact that history continues to repeat itself, Mikhail Gorbachev made an astute observation on the dangers of trying to impose civilization on the already civilized. Mikhail Gorbachev was the last Soviet President, being made redundant by the ascension of Boris Yeltsin to the Russian Presidency in 1991. After the Second Gulf War in 2003, Gorbachev warned the West about a 'crusade' to impose democracy in the Middle East. Gorbachev reminded people that his own country had undertaken a similar and utterly disastrous crusade, back in the Twentieth Century, to export Communism to the rest of the world, genuinely believing that mankind would benefit from that Soviet largesse.

Whether by choice or not, the Brits finally got the message about the unpopularity of 'Empire,' and began the process of granting independence to its member countries. However, even in this, the British managed only to leave chaos in their wake. They paid virtually no attention at all to ethnic sensibilities when carving up former Colonies into new national units. Borders merrily wandered in and out of tribal territories, with no thought given to the consequences of forcing sworn enemies to occupy the same country. It is the case today that almost every global hotspot of the past century can trace its origins to the mindless cartographers of the World's last great Empire: among them, southern Africa; India and Pakistan; Afghanistan; the Middle East; and South-East Asia.

As one last gesture of goodwill, the British gave to all the inhabitants of its former Colonies the right to British citizenship. Again, seeming generosity got the better of good sense. Beginning in the 1950's, the members of what was then known as the British Commonwealth cashed in on the promise. They started to emigrate to Great Britain, an island which, with a squeeze, can fit into the State of Georgia.

By the Eighties, the flow had become a flood. Primarily, the immigrants have been from West Africa, the Caribbean, and Pakistan and India. They have brought with them their cultures, their foods, and their religions, and these have had the effect of slowly changing Britain's identity. The national dish is no longer fish and chips. It is curry. One can find a mosque and a Hindu temple in almost every large town. However, even though immigrants from the same countries have tended to group together in the same areas, there has, on the whole, been a conscious effort to become a part of their new nation. Everyone in Great Britain describes themselves as 'British.' There is no ethnic qualification such as 'African-British.'

Although the original reason for their journey was mostly economic, for many the relative freedoms afforded by British democracy and openness have allowed others either to import or to develop within Great Britain a political identity, which is sometimes frowned upon in their country of origin, and often finds itself at odds with the British mainstream. For example, in both Gulf Wars, it was not uncommon to find representatives of the British Muslim community siding with Iraq.

On occasion, this 'identity' has moved beyond the merely political. When Osama bin Laden's communication equipment was captured in Afghanistan, it was discovered that the majority of his contacts had been with telephone numbers in Great Britain. A number of the hijackers responsible for 9/11 had spent time in British mosques. The Shoe Bomber was a British citizen. Cat Stevens is now famous not only for his songs, but also for being refused entry into the United States for his alleged ties to Islamic terrorist groups. And the London Bombings of 2005 were not launched from foreign soil by Middle Eastern terrorists, but were executed by British citizens born of Pakistani immigrant parents – parents who, to all intents and purposes, were happily pursuing what they would describe as the 'British Dream.'

Perhaps most disturbing for me, since it struck so close to home, was the information, widely trumpeted around the world, concerning the Muslim British citizens allegedly involved in the plot in August 2006, to hijack a whole bunch of airliners, traveling from the UK to the US. The theory was that they were going for a repeat of 9-11. What shook me was the fact that many of the alleged plotters were arrested in High Wycombe, Buckinghamshire, a town of some 50,000 people, barely five miles away from Beaconsfield. A town where I had gone to school. Where I had sung myself hoarse at my first pop concert. An unassuming market town. With no blighted industry. No inner city. No race riots.

What on earth was happening in Great Britain that was so terrible that it could persuade young, suburban British men to adopt a cause half a world away, and to use that cause to turn violent against their families and neighbors? What was, and still is, so very wrong in the Middle East that it could so inspire young, suburban British Muslims – most of whom had never even been to the region that so moved them – what could move them sufficiently that they were prepared to sacrifice their lives for that cause?

We can go on sending other young, suburban men and women to the Middle East, to fight wars, ostensibly to protect our freedoms. But until we try to find answers to these questions, I fear that all that's going to happen is that we're going to go on welcoming back those same young men and women, in body bags, at the very same airports from which their brothers were allegedly planning to leave, in order to make their deadly statements in the United States.

Many people, particularly Americans, labor under the mistaken belief that the majority of Arabs and their brethren from the Middle East are a bunch of semi-literate diaper-heads, stumbling around the desert, eating sheep's eyes. The truth is that the area between the Rivers Tigris and Euphrates had civilization while Britons were wearing nothing but wolf skins and blue paint. Many Arab scientists hold doctorates from the best American and British Universities. And both Iraqi and Iranian Air Force Pilots were regular attendees at the Wilton Park Languages School.

There is a legend popular among immigrants that you leave London's Heathrow Airport by heading out westwards on the M4 motorway, traveling as far as your money will allow. The richest make it as far as the west coast and Wales. The middle classes reach the Silicon Alley and relative rural beauty of Swindon and Reading. The unluckiest, however, barely have time to hiccup before falling over and landing in Slough, which sits at the end of Heathrow's flight path.

The BritCom, "The Office," which won two US Emmys in 2003, was based in Slough. Frankly, the TV show did it too much justice. Slough is a light industrial town, which makes 'bland' sound exciting. John Betjeman, a former British Poet Laureate, wrote a sonnet during the Second World War which began, "Come friendly bombs and fall on Slough." He was being kind.

However dull it might be though, I knew Slough well, for it lay just a few miles south of Beaconsfield. And, in 1990, I did not want to return to my home town of Beaconsfield. The experience of six months earlier was not one I wished to repeat. And besides, this time I wanted to stay out of peoples' hair, and generally remain incognito. I felt that Hugh's various families had been sufficiently disturbed by me last time around.

The single greatest attraction of Great Britain to me at that time was its socialistic Welfare State – great Conservative that I am! I had accommodation, paid for by the state, within days of my arriving in Slough. Mind you, we were talking about what the English call a 'bedsit.' For fans of Rowan Atkinson, and his creation "Mr. Bean,' that's what he lives in.

The landlord, in my case an incomprehensible Pakistani called "Ahmed," divided a townhouse into several one room 'efficiencies.' Each unit had the basic bedroom furniture, with its own metered heating and lighting, and sometimes a small washing and cooking area. There was then a common kitchen, dining area, bathroom and toilet.

Ahmed was almost always in trouble with the local housing authorities. This was not surprising, given the fact that he insisted on saving money by doing all the construction and repair work himself. Ahmed was no 'Extreme Makeover.' The back door and windows in the kitchen and bathroom were mere holes, without the inconvenience of frames, door or glass. The common areas were filthy, and none of the appliances worked. I disinfected my room before moving in, and continued to disinfect the bathroom every time I used it. Suddenly the cold apartment in Beaconsfield (which had eventually sold at a loss earlier in the year) became a fond memory.

Being as I was now most definitely at the bottom of the food chain, I pretty much put my life on the line every time I set foot in another part of the house. Shouts, screams and other noises, that still defy human description, were the norm. My upstairs neighbor spent one evening with me and his knife, trying to convince me he was Gandhi. I avoided a beating from another only by persuading him that I was undercover MI6. It's amazing what effect drugs will have. Once again, I felt I had joined Alice in her Wonderland.

More fun lay in store every time I braved the outside world. I

Dead Men Don't Eat Lunch

quickly discovered that my bedsit lay next to a street, which was popularly known, in our part of this ghetto, as the 'Green Line,' and which separated the Pakistani and the Indian enclaves. I was pretty much the only white man as far as the eye could see.

My understanding of racism had, until this moment, been strictly black and white. We didn't understand them, and they all hated us, not least because we reminded them of the redcoats from their Empirical past. Slough was a quick introduction to the many shades of human 'black,' and the fact that, generally speaking, they hate each other more than they hate us.

I developed a good friendship with a Punjabi from northern India. His name was Michael. We went drinking together. But, when it came time to go home, he would leave me at the end of the street. The rules were absolute: Pakistani's did not enter the Indian enclave, and Indians stayed well away from the Pakistani enclave. And I lived slap bang in the middle of the Pakistani enclave.

Once, a Pakistani had strayed into the Indian enclave. He had been shot in the eye with a shotgun. I never saw a West Indian or African because they are hated by both Pakistani and Indian alike. The upside was that I could go wherever I wished because they all thought of me as an oddity, being the only white guy in the neighborhood.

As soon as the rat droppings were cleared away, and I had fortified the door to my bedsit, I went looking for my Unemployment Benefit. For which I was immediately eligible, such being the generosity of Britain's Welfare State.

Americans sometimes wonder why British pop music has been so innovative since the Sixties. The answer is the Welfare State, which really came into its own during that decade, when the Socialists were in power. American musicians are forced to work for a living, while developing their music. Their music has to pay almost immediately. As a consequence, it has to have more mainstream appeal. British wannabe musicians are freed from commercial constraint. Many 'draw the dole,' and have the time and space to create a sound which doesn't automatically have to make money.

As generous as the Welfare State was, the money wasn't enough to keep me alive. Whenever I'm in doubt and out of funds, I resort to selling advertising space. I hopped on the train to London, and had a job lying for a living later that same afternoon. Ironically, it was just around the corner from Michael the Medium.

***

We sold advertising space in a circle, in an open office environment. Essentially, we had a desk, a telephone and a stack of directories. We telephoned companies worldwide, aiming to speak with

Geoffrey Gilson

Presidents or CEO's. We sold pages in a non-existent trade annual, at $5,000 a pop. When we had enough sold, an editorial team downstairs would concoct the trade annual, we'd shove the artwork in, send it to the advertisers and move onto the next group of industry suckers. A host of media industry executives will now reach for their notepads and pen letters of outrage to my publisher, explaining that this sort of behavior is not the norm in the business of selling advertising space. Don't be fooled. Yes, it is.

I made it past the first week of fire-walking only because I got drunk one morning, and managed to persuade the South African Chamber of Commerce that President Bush and Margaret Thatcher were about to lift economic sanctions on South Africa, and my trade journal would be the first opportunity their member industries had had to advertise to the international community in over a decade. I hit the motherlode. We couldn't beat them off with an M-1 tank. In general, however, success for rookies was as scarce as a six-pack at an AA meeting. As a consequence, we tended to have about a 100% turnover of staff every 10 days or so.

At the beginning of my second week, our group was joined by an African-American guy who called himself Roy Thomas. He was in his late twenties. Every lunchtime, we'd all go out to a local hostelry, and mess about while wolfing down food as quickly as possible. Bit by bit, Roy let his story slip. Always in my presence: first, he'd been in the Navy; then he'd been in the SEALs (the US Navy's elite special forces unit); finally, he'd been attached to the CIA. This last one caused my ears to perk up. I got him alone, walking back to the Subway one evening. Told him I wouldn't mind having a chat with him sometime. Alone. Socially. He suggested his house that coming Sunday afternoon.

Roy rented an old Victorian townhouse, just a few streets over from Magda and Christian. He lived there with his wife and two-year old daughter. He had just left the Navy, and was taking a year or two to see something of Europe. We spent about an hour that Sunday afternoon chatting and drinking a couple of glasses of wine. He showed me pictures of his family, and we played with his daughter for a while. Then, his wife discreetly left us alone.

I got straight to the point. I wondered what he could tell me about his service with the CIA. Roy was very professional. He said that he could not tell me much. He said that his primary attachment had been with the Navy and the SEAL's, but that he had performed some work for the CIA as a 'Watcher.' Which occupation is exactly what it suggests. The CIA contracts thousands of individuals, on a part-time basis, as and when they are needed, to watch people and places, and report back. Roy was not allowed to tell me, or anyone else, who or what he had been watching.

I ran the "I've got a friend" line, and then, without mentioning names, proceeded to tell him all about Hugh and Reggie. My theme was that

Dead Men Don't Eat Lunch

this friend had information that might embarrass the CIA, and that he was interested in meeting with someone from the CIA to discuss the information. How did one go about meeting the CIA, without getting shot? I asked Roy.

Again, Roy was very professional, and did what in cricketing terms is known as 'keeping a straight bat.' He would not give anything away. We danced around. I could give him the information. No, my friend would rather do it direct. Well, the CIA doesn't just 'have meetings.' They probably knew the information already. Highly unlikely. Well, don't worry about it, the CIA has thousands of Watchers; my friend was probably already being watched; if the CIA really did feel that they were about to be embarrassed, they would find a way to get a message to my friend, to warn him off. At which point, the best thing my friend could do would be to listen to the warning.

It became quite clear that either Roy did not believe me, or that he was too wise in bureaucratic ways to be of any use to me. We looked at some more photographs, chatted about my relatives in America, and after a suitably courteous interval, I made to leave. Roy silently accompanied me to the front door. As I stood on the doorstep, he gently pulled the door behind me, and tapped my shoulder. I turned.

"Ah, Geoff," he began softly, "you know I said I was a Watcher? Past tense?"

"Yes," I answered, completely unsuspecting.

"Well, I'm still very active," Roy continued, "and the message for you is this: if you know what's good for you, stop with your investigations…bye now." And with that, he shut the front door.

We never saw Roy again. And I saw my advertising sales firm for only a couple more days. Personal safety was one concern. The other was that I can only lie for a living for about a month before my conscience gets in the way.

I made some arrangements, and found that I could survive without a job for about eight months. I used the time, and some of the money, to buy and read a whole host of books. I had decided that it was necessary to do some in-depth research, to get a better idea of what had been going on in the Eighties. Of course, it never occurred to me actually to heed Roy's advice. I did try to contact Reggie to warn him, but he had disappeared again.

***

Life was not all drudge. I had discovered an oasis of delight in Slough's social desert. It was called the *Landmark Café and Bar*. It was straight out of Casablanca. All potted palms, wicker chairs, large mirrors and atmosphere. It was owned and operated by John McEnery and his father. John was a few years younger than me. Bit of a rugby lad, without the rugby. Six foot tall, lots of laughs, lots of beer, and dirty stories about the girls.

Geoffrey Gilson

I would hang out every lunch and evening, and in time, became their best regular. Many was the afternoon I'd spend making notes in a book, while gently working my way through a bottle or two. It was here that I met Mike the Indian. He was a low-budget con man. But he made me laugh, and I had a tendency to like loveable rogues.

I had learned to play American pool in a Biker's Bar in Rhode Island. My tutor had been a leather-clad gent, by the name of Troy. He was good guy underneath. In fact he invited us to a party at his friends' house. It was easy to find. The double row of Harley Davidsons gave it away. Along with the sound beating a group of the boys were giving to some other gang member, who'd strayed onto the wrong turf by mistake. No-one had mentioned dress code. So, with our Hawaiian shirts and Ocean Pacific Bermudas, Gregg and I were the one spot of color amongst the black-on-black leather couture. We survived and left in one piece. I think this had a lot to do with our merrily giving out fictitious telephone numbers to some awfully large guys with tattoos, who insisted on calling us 'girlfriend.'

Troy was a great teacher, not least because he was brutal. Once, just once, I potted the black ball on the break, which as any pool player knows meant I'd won the game without Troy ever taking a shot. He was gracious in his congratulations. And then told me that if I ever did it again, he'd break my legs. Bar Rules. Troy's amended Bar Rules. There was a pub across the road from the *Landmark* called the *Rose and Crown*. In the backroom, was a smaller version of a pool table, ruled over by a drunk Welshman called "Smitty." He too had his own Bar Rules. Which, like Troy, he made up as he went along.

Frightening figures were not the province only of Bikers' Bars in America. Case in point was "Robbo." Well, that's what I'll call him, because it rhymes with 'yobbo,' which is a term generally used about English soccer hooligans. Robbo looked the part: cropped hair, beer belly and a scowl for face decoration. And when he opened his mouth, it was clear that he was pure-bred Northern Ireland Protestant, or 'Prod,' as he was fond of boasting.

When Robbo got in his cups, which was most every time his lips touched a pint glass, he'd go through the same routine. This began with showing me his bullet wounds, and ended with a foul-mouthed, twenty minute rant about every bad thing emanating from the 'Papists' back home, who'd forced him to flee to Slough. I thought it best never to mention my own Catholic upbringing. And wise also never to ask too much about the actual circumstances of his departure from Northern Ireland.

Robbo was a daily wake up call about the price one pays for living in a free society. That nutcases are given full rein to say whatever they want, go wherever they want, and pretty much do whatever they want. Martin McGuiness, the Deputy Chief of the Provisional IRA, got it right when he said that, whereas a free society had to be on guard against terrorists 24 x 7, night and day, 360 degrees in every direction, all a terrorist had to do was get lucky once.

In Great Britain, we've learned that lesson. The hard way. When the IRA stopped bombing the military targets, and turned their attention to 'soft' targets. Pubs at lunchtime, parks on a summer's afternoon, and Army recruiting offices in lonely strip malls. No briefcase goes unnoticed, if it stands untended for too long in a bank. And a car that has gone uncollected for 24 hours is reported to the Police. America has yet to learn this lesson.

And so. It was into this merry circus that Maggi descended a few months after I arrived. I couldn't work out if she had become bored with America, or just wanted to be around to make sure I was ok. That was her way, and I was beginning to be quite grateful for it. In any event, she was going through a bad patch in her life. In her own quest for the meaning of life, she had sort of lost touch with how to stay afloat in the material world. We struck a deal: in return for my teaching her some of the ways I'd learned to cut corners with bureaucracy, she would draw on her own spiritual research and beliefs to introduce me to the occultist tradition that was at the heart of the Priory of Sion and its attendant branches.

***

As far as I could work out the belief system was as simple as it was ancient. Long before there was Jesus Christ, there was an inherent, mystical belief that man could have a personal relationship with God. With all the noise and clatter of modern life, we had lost touch, with God, nature and ourselves. All we needed to do was stand still for a moment, put aside the fears of the material world, and we would re-discover the existence of God in everything around us, and the mystical powers inherent in all of us.

These were the essential beliefs of Jesus, and were not consonant with the mainstream Judaism of his age. That is why he had so much trouble with the Pharisees. There is some suggestion that Lazerus was not actually raised from the dead, but rather that metaphorically he was released from matters material, and with the aid of Jesus as teacher, was reborn with a new and more spiritual outlook.

Mysticism, or 'the occult,' or 'New Age,' whichever description best suits your prejudice, also believes that through this personal relationship with God, we come closer to God; we are literally made in his image because we are all on a path to become one with him. Or her. Jesus was so far along this path that it was fair to describe him as a son of God.

There is no evidence to suggest that Jesus ever attempted to establish a church around his beliefs. They weren't his, in any event. He was merely passing them on. It was his disciples who founded the church – in their own ironic reflection of the alleged resurrection of their departed teacher.

The early decades were difficult for this new 'christian' following: the Romans were increasingly crushing all things Jewish. Survival was rendered possible only by adapting the nascent church to Roman beliefs, and by making the church itself indispensable as an institution.

It was as a consequence of these necessities that the Roman Church of Christ abandoned the concept of a personal relationship with God, and in its place substituted the notion that God could only be found through Jesus, and more especially through the strictures of the Roman Church. In order to emphasize the point, the Roman Church invented Satan, who is not to be found in any teachings before 2,000 years ago. It drove home the point that salvation from Satan could only be found within the Roman Church.

There was no room for other religions. No room for other belief systems. The Roman Church knew it was setting itself up for confrontation, covert or overt, with the protectors of the bloodline and teachings of Jesus. There was no room for competition of any sort. It had to justify itself, and its limited and limiting teachings, as the sole legacy of Jesus Christ, on every level, and as the only legitimate pathway to heaven.

Of course, reality is wildly different. There is much still about the Roman Church and its various branches that holds true with the original occultist teachings of Jesus. At the end of the day, the Church is an institution which venerates a great teacher and mystic, and that is why so many who hold occultist beliefs also find themselves able to go to their local Church on Sunday. Indeed, there are many within the Roman Church who describe themselves as 'Christian Mystics.' They have found their own path to God. For them, God is inclusive. It is the Church which has made itself exclusive.

And so it is that the Roman Church, for the past 2,000 years, has staggered under the belief that it must demonize, exclude or excommunicate anything and everyone that it sees as a threat, including any who hold and preach occultist beliefs, and all Judeo-Christian-Masonic institutions and entities which are or may be associated with the bloodline and occultist teachings of Jesus.

Jews have been persecuted; gypsies have been slaughtered; Freemasons have been excommunicated; and today, in small hamlets in north Georgia, preachers spend their afternoons warning teenagers about the Satanic 'nonsense' inherent in the beliefs of the New Age, not because its adherents are truly followers of a Dark Tradition, but because they threaten the spiritual and financial hegemony of the preacher's Church.

I have three sisters who have differing spiritual beliefs. Yet I am of the opinion that they have all chosen mystical paths, that bring them closer to God, and that they are to be commended for taking those same belief-systems and employing them to social good for those around them. Neither they nor I attack each other because our belief systems are different. Not one of us says that our own belief system is the only true path. That is a nonsense. It is a device used by the leaders of organized religion to manipulate their members in an ongoing attempt to win a geopolitical struggle with the adherents of the Priory of Sion.

***

All of this esoteric research left me quite thirsty for a session with my old friend Michael Colmer. Hugh, however, was off with his 'team,' and was not available to talk. Michael made it clear that the next major revelation to be inspired 'from the other side' would occur when "the last Israeli hostage is released from Lebanon." At that time, an important 'nugget' of information would come my way, and it would be enough for me to complete the book.

In the meantime, Michael did indicate that he had a surprising prediction to share with me. But it didn't concern me and my sage. It had to do with dramatic events in the Conservative Party. I'm bound to say I was still somewhat the cynic when it came to Michael's predictions, even though he'd proven himself useful in my sparring with Reggie. So, it came as something of a shock that, on this occasion, Michael was spot on.

Geoffrey Gilson

Chapter 15

IT WAS ONLY at the beginning of the last Century (the 20th Century) that the Socialists in Great Britain organized themselves into a political party. For years, they were unable to break through the stranglehold held by the Conservative and the Liberal Parties (respectively equivalent, at that time, to the modern Republican and Democratic Parties in the United States).

The Labour Party, as the Socialists styled themselves, briefly had a grip on the reins of power in 1928, but they only achieved office for a full Parliamentary term when they defeated Winston Churchill in the General Election of 1945 The Labour Prime Minister, Clement Atlee, like his counterpart in America, President Truman, was left the gruesome task of finishing off the Second World War.

Atlee was no fanatic left-winger. That side of the Labour Party didn't rear its ugly head until the Socialists were elected for the third time in their history in 1964. I have a tenuous connection to Clement Atlee. One of his grandchildren was my first girlfriend in Beaconsfield. She later went on to become Mayor of Beaconsfield in 1995, a feat I had always longed to achieve.

The Labour Party made up for lost time in the Swinging Sixties. Under the guise of modernizing Great Britain, they nationalized all the major industries; spread the power of trade unionism; and merrily threw money into every crackpot educational and health scheme they could find.

It had been eons since the Tories had been out of government. They were determined not to lose any time in regaining what they regarded as their rightful place running the country. At what was supposed to be a secret meeting of the Party's top strategists one weekend in the late Sixties, the Party drafted what would become the most radical Manifesto the Party had ever seen.

On paper, it epitomized what would later become associated with

Dead Men Don't Eat Lunch

Margaret Thatcher. However, the Leader of the Conservative Party at that time was a brash young metrocrat called Edward Heath. After that weekend, he was also known as "Selsdon Man," named for the Selsdon Park Hotel, in which the meeting had been held.

In an unexpected turn of events, the Labour Prime Minister, Harold Wilson, and his Party, were defeated in the General Election of 1970. It is possible that the victory also caught the new Prime Minister, Edward Heath, by surprise. Barely two years into his Administration, he threw the Selsdon Plan out the window, and proceeded to implement policies that seemed little different from his Socialist predecessor.

One policy in particular became closely associated with what the rank and file of the Party saw as the treachery of its Leader: the move to join the European Economic Community. Edward Heath fostered a deep split in his Party, between those who wanted to make Europe into a United States, and those who believed in a Europe of close co-operation between firmly separate Nation States.

The division was not confined to the Conservative Party. The Labour Party was equally split. With the Tories, the right-wing preached that the country, which had once ruled the largest empire the World had ever seen, should not cede one ounce of sovereignty to those who had proven so inferior in two World Wars. The left-wing of the Labour Party were concerned that any United Europe would be dominated by capitalists. The two wings found themselves strange bedfellows in the years to come on this issue; one which has continued to bedevil the leaderships of both Parties up to and including the present day.

In 1972, there was open rebellion within the ranks of Conservative Parliamentarians. Ministers resigned. Ordinary Members made clear to the Leadership that they would not support the Conservative Government on votes which pursued a socialistic agenda, or sought to take Great Britain down a path towards a Federal Europe.

Two of the leaders of the Conservative Rebellion were Enoch Powell, a former Conservative Cabinet Minister, and Ronald Bell, the then Member of Parliament for Beaconsfield. I would come to know Ronald Bell quite well, when later I served for seven years as the Chairman of the Beaconsfield Young Conservatives, and as a Vice Chairman of the Senior Conservative Association. Small of stature, his right-wing views and quiet manner belied his sharp mind and quick wit. In 1972, however, his protégé was the then Chairman of the YC's, one Hugh Simmonds.

Edward Heath reacted brutally to the challenge of his underlings. Secretly, he instructed the Conservative Central Office to run heavyweight candidates against each of the rebelling Parliamentarians during the process that, in England, was the equivalent of a primary. In Beaconsfield, the young and dashing Michael Heseltine was given the task of 'deselecting' Ronald

Geoffrey Gilson

Bell.

These fights quickly became *causes celebre*, although the tactics used nowhere near matched the perceived majesty of the purpose. And in this regard, Hugh established himself as king. No stone was left unturned in Hugh's efforts to save Ronald Bell his Parliamentary seat. New members were bussed into meetings; headquarters and safes were broken into; and all manner of negative stories were spread, wherever they would do the most damage. Ronald Bell defeated Michael Heseltine, and Hugh made a name for himself as a right-wing 'dirty tricks' meister *par excellence*.

Hugh lost no time in building on his new-found Party fame. While establishing an elective record in local politics in Beaconsfield, he also set up camp on the national scene. This was a heyday for groups on the right-wing. The choice was bleak: a Conservative Prime Minister, who thought he was a Socialist, or the Labour Party, which had moved even further to the left, and now thought it was the Communist Party. There were many on the right who genuinely believed they were now fighting for the very soul of Britain's continued independence and freedom. Hugh became heavily involved in most of the right-wing groups organizing against socialism and Communism (at home and abroad), and against Europe. Some of these were quite 'safe,' while others were way out on the fringe.

Hugh even created a few of his own. The most successful was the Selsdon Group, a pointed reference to Edward Heath's now forgotten nickname. Hugh was the founding Treasurer of this Group, which established itself as the primary guardian of right-wing philosophy in the Conservative Party throughout the Seventies and Eighties. It was to a private meeting of Selsdon Group leaders that Margaret Thatcher first announced her intention to challenge Edward Heath for the Leadership of the Conservative Party in 1975, after the Tories lost the two General Elections held in 1974. It was also from this Group, that Thatcher drew early inspiration for her speeches, from Hugh, and from the likes of John O'Sullivan and Frank Johnson, well-known writers for the London *Daily Telegraph*.

Notwithstanding Edward Heath's disastrous policies, the Tory Party has always placed a premium on loyalty. Leaders chose to leave; they were not forced. And if it became necessary, finally, to 'bend' a Leader's ear, it was done quietly, by the 'Grey Men.' It was still considered heresy openly to challenge the sitting Leader. But this is what Margaret Thatcher did in 1975, and she faced an uphill battle. It was for this reason that she relied so heavily on groups, like those with which Hugh was involved, to provide her with the logistics necessary to challenge the Conservative Central Office powerbase, which was still under the control of Edward Heath. As would happen to her fifteen years later, Heath made a poor showing in the first round of voting, and resigned, leaving the path clear for Thatcher's victory in the second round.

Victory in a vote did not guarantee the love and respect of the masses. Thatcher still had much to prove in the years leading up to the next General Election in 1979. And the right-wing organizations that had brought her to power had battles of their own to fight in her support. First on the list was the European Referendum of 1975. Harold Wilson had returned as Labour Prime Minister, and in order to appease the left-wing in his own Government ranks, he had agreed to allow the British public to vote on continued membership of the European Economic Community, by way of a National Referendum.

Britain's political parties realigned for the Referendum. With his growing reputation as a political organizer and public speaker, Hugh was invited to join the National Committee of the "No" organization, campaigning against Europe. He found himself alongside the likes of Enoch Powell, Michael Foot (later Leader of the Labour Party) and Tony Benn (a long-serving Labour Cabinet Minister). The Committee to rescue Britain's sovereignty also saw one or two other interesting affiliations, represented at least symbolically by the presence of an Organizing Secretary who had been awarded the Military Cross with three bars (Britain's third highest military decoration).

The "Yes" vote prevailed. And this set the stage for much healing within the Conservative Party. The 'real' enemy, after all, as sensible heads kept repeating, was the Communist-inspired Labour Government. Public spending was running out of control. Eventually, the public purse would run dry, and the Labour Government would have to go cap-in-hand, like some Third World banana republic, to the International Monetary Fund, to bail out the country. Industry was being nationalized wholesale, and rendered bankrupt through inefficient state management. And the Trade Unions were given powers that turned collective bargaining into blackmail. Those industries that struggled to stay in private hands ground to a halt because of the excessive wage demands of their Trade Union members; demands that had to be met, and which then massively stoked the fires of rampant inflation. The Tories knew they had to get their act together, and fast, if they were to win the next Election, and turn the tide.

However, the Party had suffered egregiously as a consequence of the bruising battle over Europe. A major effort would be needed to heal the wounds and move on. The Party turned to Hugh, who recognized that this was his chance to enter the mainstream of the Party. I was with him as he toiled day and night to rally the rag-tag bunch of Tory individuals and organizations who had fought valiantly against Europe. The message was simple: that fight is over; it's time to join forces, defeat the Socialists and win the upcoming General and European Elections. As far as the latter was concerned, it didn't matter whether you liked the European Institution or not, if there were elective positions up for grabs, they needed to be filled with Conservative trousers.

The focal point for all this effort was a private meeting of the Party's Central Council, and a heavily stage-managed 'debate' on the issue of Europe and its Elections. This debate was held in mid-1978. Hugh was slated to give the keynote speech. He and I worked on it for two weeks. The idea was that every major anti-Europe individual and organization would then take the podium and give their support to the consensus language that Hugh and I had crafted. Douglas Hurd, the leading Conservative Pro-European, and the man chosen by Thatcher to expound the Party's views on Europe publicly, would then offer a gracious closing speech. The device, although Soviet-like in its organization, was a complete success. Wounds closed, the Party pulled together, the Tories won all of the British seats up for grabs in the European Elections, and the peace that Simmonds and Hurd had negotiated on Europe lasted until Margaret Thatcher was deposed as Prime Minister and Leader of the Conservative Party, in 1990.

The Party had already managed to find consensus on other issues, and had produced a document, *The Right Approach*, which, although not as dramatic as the original Manifesto of the Selsdon Man, was nevertheless gripping enough to garner my attention. I had discovered local affairs in 1972, when I attended a meeting of the Beaconsfield Community Association, and won a motion to allow sixteen year olds to be members. They invited me to join the Executive Committee. I took over their Public Relations, and never turned back.

In 1976, it was time to decide my direction in national politics. The Labour Party had produced what was intended to be the background platform for their eventual Election Manifesto. It was more radical than the Communist Party program. It called for state control or supervision of every aspect of industrial life and social welfare in the country. *The Right Approach*, on the other hand, engaged in few polemics. It merely stated that it was time for the pendulum to swing in the other direction. I can't say that I became a rabid Tory; I just agreed with what needed to be done at that time.

And the timing was good. I met up with Hugh just as he was gently extricating himself from the right-wing loonies, and was preparing to fight his obligatory safe Labour Parliamentary seat in West Leeds. My alignment may have been pragmatic, but the public generally were hungry for a Conservative victory. On the streets of Leeds, we were constantly approached by former working-class Socialists who were disgusted that their own Party had turned its back on its social democratic roots. They would be voting for "Maggie" in droves, and they became her equivalent of Reagan's Democrats.

The Tories won the General Election of 1979 overwhelmingly. Hugh lost West Leeds, but achieved the largest swing to the Conservatives in any seat in the north of England. I won my own election in Beaconsfield. I had parlayed my own track record in community affairs, together with my newfound position as Chairman of the Beaconsfield Young Conservatives, into a candidacy for the Beaconsfield Town Council. At the age of 22, I was now on my own path in elective politics.

Nationally, the Conservative Government lost no time in undoing the worst of the Labour Party. It took a whole term, but the Tories got inflation under control. They restored public finances, such that we were repaying the national debt by the end of the first term. Taxes were slashed. And an aggressive policy of denationalization was put in place. There was much early resistance from the neo-socialist Heath supporters, but Thatcher easily undid them with the disdain for which she later became notorious. She took to referring to them as "wets.' And then simply ignored them. Shame and humiliation did the rest of the work.

Hugh spread himself far and wide throughout the Party, in an attempt to find a safe Parliamentary seat for the next General Election. He became Chairman of a Regional Committee of the Party, so that he could sit on the National Union Executive Committee. This was the national organizing committee of what was known as the voluntary wing of the Party. Basically, the retired Colonels, their bustling wives, and whippersnappers like me, who got the vote out at Election time, and ran tea parties in between. Hugh was approached by a few on the NUEC in an effort by them to groom him for its future Chairmanship. He wasn't interested. His sights were firmly set on Parliament.

In this regard, he thought it wise to ingratiate himself with Conservative Central Office, then under the Chairmanship of Cecil Parkinson. CCO represents the hired help or professionals within the Party, from the Constituency Agents up to the National Directors. Hugh became one of the Honorary Legal Consultants to CCO, and advised on everything from privacy matters regarding membership lists, to tax consequences of seat redistribution. Again, there were some who thought Hugh would make an excellent Chairman of CCO, once he had a seat in Parliament, and became part of Maggie's Government. He was young, dashing, intelligent, articulate and easily straddled the voluntary, professional and Parliamentary branches of the Party.

No-one for a moment doubted he would easily pick up a safe seat. It was just a matter of time. When his mentor, Ronald Bell, died in 1982, Hugh came close to inheriting his home town seat. But he'd made a few too many enemies on his own turf while climbing the greasy pole, and at the final selection meeting, a few bad checks were cashed in. Finally, he was selected for South-west Cambridgeshire in 1983, only to lose it a couple of months before the General Election. Again, no-one saw it as much of a setback. Indeed, he received a wealth of good press nationally, and Maggie herself invited him to join her on her Campaign Bus, as a show of personal support. In her later memoirs, Hugh can be seen in the photograph of her Campaign stop in Newbury, Berkshire, just down the road from Slough.

Aided in part by her victory in the Falklands War, and with a resurgent economy, Margaret Thatcher won the 1983 General Election in a landslide. She took the opportunity to remake her Government in her own image, and set in motion one of the most radical agendas, designed to turn Great Britain permanently into an 'enterprise economy.'

Capital taxation was overhauled, making Britain one of the most business-friendly countries in the world. Both nationalized and public utility companies were put up for privatization. Plans were set in motion for transforming the country into a property-owning democracy. Thatcher took the view that responsibility and ownership went hand-in-hand. Public housing was practically given away to sitting tenants. Shares in denationalized industries and utilities were offered to every citizen. Professions were deregulated to increase competition and improve service. The Stock Market was set free, and Britain enjoyed its most significant stock boom since the Twenties.

I exited my first episode in elective politics in 1983. I had spent my four years on the Council acting pretty much like Dan Quayle on steroids: utterly clueless; my only consistency being the extent to which I managed to piss off both my fellow Councilors and the electorate. The latter duly voted with their feet come re-election time, and that was the end of my short Council career.

Hugh turned his attention to assisting with the finances of the Conservative Party. He became one of the eleven Regional Treasurers, and a member also of the Party's National Board of Finance, under the Chairmanship of the Party's then National Treasurer, Alistair (later Lord) McAlpine. Hugh's reasons were not completely altruistic. One of his jobs was to tour rich (i.e. safe) constituencies, imploring the local big-wigs to up their contributions to the Party nationally.

Fund-raising, like charity, begins at home. With my hands now idle, other than my continuing YC Chairmanship, I set out to help Hugh institute some changes in financial practice in the Beaconsfield Constituency itself. Beaconsfield was one of the first to introduce a computer-based membership and recruiting system. We were years away from Windows. The operating system was still M-DOS and I became reasonably familiar with changing the field sizes, to incorporate Hugh's latest whims. This caused me later to become somewhat confused about all the fuss generated over Y2K. You just changed a 2-digit field to a 4-digit field. But, I'm running ahead of myself.

Hugh concentrated on policy. I got down in the trenches, and went collecting door-to-door, in an effort to demonstrate how to up the ante face-to-face. I never did understand the fuss about President Clinton selling favors for cash. When you were the Party in Government, that's what you did. I got a £10,000 ($15,000) corporate donation out of one Liberal Democrat voter on a balmy Saturday afternoon, not because he'd switched Parties, but because he was promised 15 minutes with the Chancellor of the Exchequer (equivalent to the US Treasury Secretary). Alone. Unrecorded. In the privacy of the tiny town-house headquarters, of some remote Tory constituency, tucked away in the nether-boondocks.

As immoral as this all seems now, at the time, we believed we were the 'young turks' of *Maggie's Revolution*. We felt we could do anything, with impunity. Just as there were 'Masters of the Universe' on Wall Street and the London Stock Exchange, so we and our buddies were the political equivalent, raising money wherever and however we could. Hugh and I got so good at the double act, that we were invited to join a National Campaigning Unit, whose members would travel around the country, teaching constituency activist how to recruit members, raise money and get good publicity at the local level.

Beginning in the Eighties, and moving into the Nineties, Beaconsfield developed a reputation as a focal point for the finances of the Conservative Party. The Beaconsfield Constituency Association became one of the most consistent fund-raisers, not only for itself, but also for the National Party, and for nearby but less well-off Associations, like that of Slough, just to the south of Beaconsfield. Hugh served on the Conservative's National Board of Finance, and was later succeeded by our mutual friend, John Strafford, who was Chairman of the Beaconsfield Association when Hugh was a Vice President and I was a Vice Chairman. Peter Smith, close friend of Hugh's and another Vice President of the Association, was Senior Partner of the London Accountancy firm of Coopers Lybrand, and was associated with the Audit of the Party's National Accounts. Finally, the new Member of Parliament for Beaconsfield, Tim Smith, was appointed a Vice Chairman of the National Party, with special responsibility for Finance, in 1992.

The Annual Conservative Conference offered Hugh a candy store of opportunities to schmooze with those he wanted to have pick him, and those with whom he hoped soon to be partying in Government. Fun and games aside, the important thing at these Conferences, which are no different to American Political Conventions, was not to listen to platform debates, but was to take part in them. All Party debates are heavily stage-managed. Inclusion involves a long process of vetting, which can take months, and makes the American Primary season look like a kindergarten field trip.

The trick, however, is not just to get chosen once, but to perform so well that you enter an upward-moving conveyor belt of elitism, like the various Degrees of Masonry. First time around, you have to do the six-month vetting. If you do well, then next time round, it's just a single chat and an 'ok.' If you do well again, then on the following occasion, you can pick your own debate. Do well again, and they start asking if you want to speak that year. I spoke twice, and with my second speech, on economic affairs, in the early Eighties, I managed to upstage the Chancellor of the Exchequer, who received less coverage than I, in *The Times* report the following day. In my way, I had arrived. But it was nothing compared to the exalted level that Hugh had achieved, as I was to discover one drunken lunchtime in the mid-Eighties.

Hugh was considered to be one of the Party's experts on Race Relations. I think this is because he'd dated a couple of Caribbean girls. In a momentary lapse of judgment, the otherwise sage Chairman of that year's Conference had decided to engage in some real democracy, and invite an ordinary member to take part in the debate. Unvetted. As chance would have it, the speaker was an un-reconstructed Neanderthal, who made the Ku Klux Klan sound like a ladies' knitting circle. Repatriation was too good for the immigrants. Better just to put them up against a wall and shoot them.

Unlike American National Political Conventions, prime time for Party Conferences in Great Britain is during the young mother watching hour of 11.00am to 12.00pm. We were right in the middle of this. The first Hugh and I knew about it was when we were ordering our seventh Campari and Soda, in a bar, tucked away at the far end of the Convention Centre.

All of a sudden, a phalanx of Central Office heavies surrounded Hugh's chair, exchanged his Campari for a cup of steaming coffee, lifted him bodily out of the chair, and dragged him out the door. In the background, over the loudspeaker, I vaguely heard the Chairman announcing, "...and following Miss Snodgrass, Hugh Simmonds of the National Union Executive Committee."

I caught up with Hugh, who had at last managed to get his feet moving at something approximating the speed of his forward propulsion. Those holding up the left half of his body were variously adjusting his tie, wiping his face and combing his hair. Or was it wiping his hair, combing his tie and adjusting his face? No matter. It was all to no avail. Hugh was past being presentable in even the dingiest bikers' bar.

On his right, an anxious-looking techno-nerd was doing his best to brief Hugh on the Neanderthal, the Party's line on the required response, and the nascent concern that, unless something was done fast, the Conference Hall might well, by nightfall, resemble one of the more grisly scenes from the movie *Zulu*. For all the signs of life evident in Hugh's eyes, the nerd would have achieved better results speaking Sanskrit backwards.

One final flick of the comb, and Hugh was hurled bodily into the Hall in the general direction of the podium. Where he proceeded to give, chapter and verse, a lucid and well-received exposition of the Party's true platform on Race Relations. Carving up the Neanderthal in the process, and thereby saving the day, and making the world a safer place for Party, Queen, and Country, Uncle Tom Cobbley and all. Upon exiting the Hall, Hugh fell into the arms of the waiting heavies, who dragged him back to the bar, dumped in his chair, and gave him back his half-finished Campari and Soda. Whereupon he woke up.

Hugh was not only the Big Man on Campus, putting on a public show in the Conference Halls, he was also a trusted troubleshooter, helping the National Party in its more secretive Back Corridors. For all this, and more, Hugh was honored in 1985, at he age of 37, with being appointed a Commander of the Most Noble Order of the British Empire (CBE). One notch below Knighthood (KBE, as in 'Sir Hugh'). Of more interest to him was that he was selected for another safe seat. This time South Warrington. Which he lost six months before the General Election of 1987. I remember the evening well. I recall how devastated he looked as he received the telephone call. To this day, I fancy I saw not only disappointment, but also a flicker of fear. I wonder if he thought that his becoming a Member of Parliament might have saved him from his eventual fate.

A year before the General Election of 1987, the Conservative Party had looked exhausted; physically drained and devoid of ideas. Then, Norman (now Lord) Tebbit took a hold of the Party as its new Chairman. He devised a whole new agenda, focusing on a continuation of denationalization and privatization, buttressed by a slew of social and educational reforms. The Tories swept to a third consecutive victory.

It was probably just as well that this effectively marked an end to Hugh's and my immediate national ambitions in the Conservative Party. We were neither of us particularly right-wing when it came to social issues. Indeed, humor aside, Hugh had actually gained his knowledge of Race Relations as one of the advocates at the Scarman Judicial Inquiry into Britain's race riots in 1981. All of the other advocates had been supporters of either the Liberal or the Labour Parties.

In 1986, I had indicated to the organizers of that year's Party Conference that I wished to speak in the Law and Order debate. I wanted to state to the Party faithful that, as we were now the Natural Party of Government, we Conservatives had a duty to look after everyone. That included those immigrants in inner cities who were more scared of the Police than the criminals, because of the illegal practices of the Police. I was finally called to a private meeting with the Chairman of the Conference and with Douglas Hurd, now Lord Hurd , who, at the time, was the British Home Secretary (equivalent to a combination of the US Interior Secretary and the US Attorney-General). They told me that, although they agreed with everything I said, they could not call me to the podium to express my views, because afterwards, they would not be able to guarantee my safety from that same podium.

Geoffrey Gilson

I stuck my toe one more time in the waters of Beaconsfield elective politics, this time as both Council candidate and campaign manager. The voters were far too smart to fall for me a second time, but I did manage to help Hugh's wife, Janet, get elected. As I write this book, seventeen years later, Janet is still faithfully serving her constituents in Beaconsfield and Holtspur. I have nothing but admiration for the dignified manner in which she has borne all that life has thrown at her, and has managed regardless to steer a steady course for herself and her two daughters, Juliet and Tanya.

I had one more political foray before Hugh died. But on this occasion, I was dabbling in the politics of my second homeland, the United States. For my sins, I took a shine to Michael Dukakis in 1988. I began to use the office fax to send talking points to his speechwriting team in Massachusetts. Much to Hugh's chagrin. No one was more surprised than me, when, in the debate on foreign policy, Dukakis used one of my submitted answers, word for word.

On the day after his defeat, I received a telephone call in the office from Susan Thomases, later Chief of Staff to Hillary Clinton, when she was First Lady, but who, at that time, was taking care of Gubernatorial matters in the State of Massachusetts, while Governor Dukakis was waging his Presidential campaign. Susan rang to say that Dukakis had received my fax of condolence, and had been so moved by my sentiments and choice of prose that he had instructed her to thank me, and to have the fax pinned on every noticeboard in his headquarters. Hugh couldn't contain himself. While roundly criticizing me for not supporting the Republican candidate, he took great delight in showing all his clients my original fax to Dukakis.

Michael Colmer's prediction in September of 1990 had been that, within three months, the Tories would undergo a major change, and that Maggie Thatcher would be replaced as Prime Minister by either John Major or Michael Heseltine. The latter had served in Thatcher's Cabinet, first as Secretary of State for the Environment, and later, as Minister of Defense. He had resigned in 1995 over a spat to do with the ownership of Britain's helicopter industry.

Throughout her time in office, Margaret Thatcher trod softly around the subject of Europe. She did not want a divided Party on her hands, as it had been with Edward Heath. She would sound loud and strident on safe subjects, like getting Europe to refund monies which she claimed Britain had been overcharged by the wayward European bureaucracy. However, year by year, she also allowed herself to be persuaded to adopt positions that brought Britain closer and closer to a future with a Federal Europe. For reasons known best to her, she finally picked the fall of 1990 to explode. She'd had enough. So far, and no further. She got up at a European meeting in Bruges and simply ranted: "No, no, no."

The ardent Pro-Europeans had their revenge, but at a terrible cost.

Dead Men Don't Eat Lunch

Led by Michael Heseltine, they deposed Margaret Thatcher as Prime Minister. She was replaced by her chosen one, John Major. However, the peace on Europe within the Party was destroyed. The ensuing open warfare would lead to Major's eventual defeat in 1997. And was one of the primary factors preventing the Tories from coming up with a coherent platform with which to challenge the political hegemony of Blair and his New Labour Party after 1997.

Margaret Thatcher's time as Prime Minister is still regarded by the British with mixed feelings. No-one doubts that she set in motion a radical new direction in Government. But the jury is still out on the price that had to be paid. As is so often the case, she is respected more abroad than she is at home. Many Americans remember with fondness her closeness to President Reagan. They also recall how she gave backbone to President Bush (the Senior) when he faltered in August 1990 about declaring that Saddam would be forcefully removed from Kuwait if it proved necessary.

A delegation from the Labour Party and Britain's socialist Trade Union movement was one of the first groups to be received by Lech Walesa after his *Solidarity* was elected into office in 1990. The leader of the British delegation droned on and on about matters he thought would be of assistance to a neophyte politician and brother trade union leader. Finally, Walesa lost patience, and asked the British group to tell him all about Margaret Thatcher. The Brits were dumbstruck. Why would Walesa want to know about that right-wing harridan. Walesa's response was iconic and ironic, "why do you Westerners always assume that we're socialists because we're trade unionists? We just spent 50 years getting rid of socialism. Now, tell me about her privatization plans…"

The resignation of Margaret Thatcher was the passing of an era for many besides myself. But there were those who derived more pleasure from it than me. Top of the list were my socialist sister, and my new drinking buddy, Mark Saunders. Mark was at that time a lowly photographer and journalist for the *Slough Express*, but he was about to invite me to join him on a journey that would lead to his becoming the most notorious of all of Princess Diana's paparazzi.

Geoffrey Gilson

Chapter 16

S<small>LOUGH IS A CITY</small> with an identity crisis. It's a pimple of industrial blandness, surrounded by the lush verdance of rural England, at the end of a couple of runways, belonging to the largest airport in the world. Yet, the greatest dichotomy is experienced by taking a 15 minute walk outside the city's southern limits. Away from the Green Line and the racial wars; the warehouses and the gas tanks; the row upon row of crumbling slums; take a stroll past a couple of bus stops, turn left and there are the playing fields of Eton, the school attended by Britain's royal heirs. You could not find a greater contrast. Unless you cross the small bridge at the end of Eton's High Street, when you find yourself face to face with Windsor Castle. I was living in Queen Elizabeth's back yard.

In some strange way, that Autumn of 1990, after Margaret Thatcher left the office of Prime Minister, it was as if Slough was a reflection of the whole nation, which was just then beginning to suffer its own identity crisis. It seemed that everywhere one looked great institutions of state were falling apart. What was worse than the seeming degradation was the fact that every time something went wrong, a journalist or photographer was nearby, waiting to record the humiliation. Reading the newspaper each day, I began to feel like the upstairs lodger, unable to keep out the sound of the dysfunctional family fighting downstairs once again.

At first, it was the Royal Family. For a decade, since the marriage of Charles and Diana in 1981, the nation had basked in glory as the children of its Queen met beautiful consorts and led charmed lives. Then, towards the end of the decade, it all turned into the worst Joan Collins soap opera. By the time I arrived in Slough in 1992, the nearby Windsor family was in turmoil. Anne and Peter had already separated; the Yorks were arguing; and Charles and Diana were rumored to be following suit. And every gasp and grimace was being captured by the paparazzi.

I first met Mark Saunders late one evening at the *Landmark*. The

Dead Men Don't Eat Lunch

Duke and Duchess of York had built a huge and rather grotesque mansion a few miles from Slough. It had been christened *South York* by the horde of paparazzi who clamored at its front gates, waiting to catch a snapshot of the Royal breakup. Mark was taking his own recess from standing duty. He had pretty much figured himself cursed with a career at the local newspaper level, until fortune smiled and offered him a couple of failing Royal marriages on his local beat. Mark felt that he ought to have a significant advantage over the imported national and international paparazzi because he'd been born, bred and made his living in Slough.

If Kevin Bacon had an English cousin, much the same age, but a little chubbier in the face, and with a South London accent, he'd be Mark Saunders. I had a thing about befriending rogues, and Mark was about as caddish as they came. He treated women like carpets. But since I wasn't his girlfriend, I got along with him well enough. And he was anything but predictable. The only certain thing about him was that he had much the same effect on Maggi as Hugh had done. She despised them both.

Whether you found him charming or not in social company, once he picked up a camera or a notebook, he became the worst tabloid nightmare. On one occasion, an Indian gang had kidnapped a Pakistani fellow. He was gone a few days. Before he turned up. At home. Or more specifically, his head turned up. In the family mailbox. Mark was assigned to talk to the grieving widow. His first question, in a room full of the widow's relatives, and in full earshot, was to ask her to describe what her deceased husband's head had looked like. Mark was bodily thrown out. But he had his story. And no sense of shame whatsoever.

Mark and I would meet at the *Landmark* from time to time. Have a few drinks. Sometimes play some pool at the *Rose and Crown*. We even got together, on a couple of occasions, and played music with some other band members. But Mark's prevailing interest was in getting his foot in the door with one or more of the tabloids. And that meant taking the greatest possible advantage of the Royals' mini-series of miseries.

On one occasion, he burst into the *Landmark*, at lunchtime, and buttonholed me at my favorite table in the back corner. He had some inside information from one of the staff at *South York* that Fergie was definitely moving out. But he had no way of finding out when she was going, or where. We mulled it over, until the alcoholic fumes interfered with all conscious thought. At which precise point, either he or I, we forget which, had a brainwave. Mark knew all the Estate Agents in town. It was a reasonable bet that one of them would be selling the place Fergie would be buying. Mark shot out the door. And the next day, one of the national tabloids had a full color photo of Fergie's new thatched cottage on its front cover. I never did discover whether or not it was actually her cottage. But it was a cottage. And that's the essence of tabloid journalism.

Geoffrey Gilson

Another time, Mark had two tickets to the Cartier International Polo Competition at the Windsor Castle. The Royal Family always attended, and Mark took the view he might pick up something. Besides, he wanted me to see what it was all about. Somewhat sheepishly, I took along my camera. There was a little white cottage, with a fence around it, off to one side of the Polo Grounds. This was the Royal Pavilion. Alongside it was a roped-in area. This was where the photographers were allowed to gather.

Mark and I began by getting thoroughly stewed in the Hospitality Tent. Then, since it was a bright, sunny day, we meandered out to join the other photographers. We all lined up quietly along the rope, cameras up and pointing at either the rear, the front or the upstairs balcony. All of us motionless. This is what you did. You just stood there, like a marionette, waiting for the right head to appear. Mark had told me that you didn't need to be a great photographer to be a paparazzi, you just needed to be patient, fearless and lucky. So, I stood there, with the others, like a statue, trying hard not to laugh.

I've always had pretty good peripheral vision. I tend to know what's going on around me. So, I became aware that there was some sort of commotion. A car pulling up. Journalists disappearing. Some returning. People bowing and scraping at the front of the Pavilion. And then at the rear. For some reason, my mind said to me, "look where no-one else is looking." So, I pointed my camera up at the first floor balcony, and snapped one shot. Of the Queen smiling down at my camera. Mark had also told me that all Royals are trained never to look at cameramen. It's undignified. And the resulting pictures are worth about ten times more.

My single camera click sounded like a cannon-shot in the preternatural silence. Every head turned my way. A hissing began, not unlike one of those scenes with Indiana Jones and all his snakes:

"You got her smiling, didn't you?"
"She was looking at you, wasn't she?"
"I'll buy the picture."
"I'll buy the camera."
"I'll pay double. In cash. Right now."

I backed off into the Hospitality Tent, where Mark was doubled-over with laughter. I liked my camera. No, I did not want to sell the film. No, I was not a tease. And no, I was not a Communist. I stuck to my guns, even when the bidding reached ridiculous sums in the five figures. Mark was amused because he had achieved his purpose: I had been introduced to the money that was there for the making.

Mark was convinced that this was only the beginning. That the real fun would occur when Charles and Diana split up. At this point, there was little evidence of what would later become one of the most public divorces of all time. But there were one or two tell-tale signs. And some circumstances that caused me to take pause.

For example, late in 1991, a national tabloid ran the story that it had managed to tape a cellphone conversation between Charles and his lover Camilla. Everyone concentrated on the details, which were relatively juicy. What not everyone noticed was that another tabloid took issue, saying that the first tabloid had stolen its story. Investigations were undertaken.

What was discovered was that the two newspapers, in totally separate weeks, had apparently taped, over the open air, the same conversation. The separate tapes were examined by an expert. There was no doubt that the conversations were identical; that the two people were definitely Charles and Camilla; and that the nature of the tapings suggested that both newspapers had taped a recording, not an original conversation. So, who was bugging the Royals; who was broadcasting the conversation; and why was this 'someone' so intent on embarrassing the Royals in the media?

Mark asked me more than once if I wanted to join him in his quest to be a paparazzi. To be honest, fun as he was in social company, I thought he was more talk than trousers, and I had other fish to fry. Specifically, since money was running low, I was looking to get back into some sort of legal work. This proved to be more difficult that I had originally imagined. The name of Simmonds had carried far and wide. With perfect timing, just as I was about to contact the Law Society to berate them about their lack of progress, and its continuing deleterious effect upon me, who should telephone, but Geoff Hughes. He had finished his investigation on behalf of Carratu, and he had things to tell me.

***

As it turned out, he didn't have all that much to tell me, but what he did was fairly explosive. The Law Society had brought the investigation to a halt. The total monies recovered by the Estate had topped off at £166,000 ($250,000). Yet, evidence had been uncovered suggesting that Hugh had been laundering money for at least 100 'entities.'

This did not surprise me. When Hugh had been with Wedlake Bell, money laundering had been Hugh's specialty. But, back in the days of socialistic Britain, when top tax rates ran at 80% and rising, this sort of laundering was still legal, and it went by the more sanitized description of 'Money Management and Tax Assistance.' I remember a huge chart on Hugh's office wall, showing all the interconnecting lines between Jersey, the Isle of Man, Switzerland, Lichtenstein, Luxembourg, Hong Kong, Liberia and the Cayman Islands, to mention but a few.

Geoff became more coy when I asked for details of names and quantities of money. He was prepared to confirm that no-one had had less than £30,000 ($45,000) laundered. I responded by stating that no-one was going to follow me for over a month in England for £30,000. Geoff slipped, and replied that they might for a few million. I did some quick mental math, and declared that we could be talking about a total of anything from £30 million ($45 million) to £100 million ($150 million). Geoff did not reply. The meeting was over. He wished me well. And left.

Geoff did mention that the Law Society were in receipt of Carratu's final reports, but that they were unlikely to be released. I devised a ploy. I sought legal Counsel's Opinion, and drafted a lawsuit against Hugh's Estate (i.e. the Law Society) for damages. My novel argument was that a special trust existed between a Solicitor and his senior staff. That trust was recognized by clients and other employers alike. Hugh had broken that trust by stealing clients' money. I had been rendered unemployable by that breach.

One of the monopolies that Maggie Thatcher never broke up was that of the legal profession. Not surprising since she was a lawyer herself. The Law Society has omnipotent powers over the practice of law by Solicitors. It trains them; gives them their practicing certificates; oversees their finances; acts as their trade union; and when they've been naughty, performs all the functions of a kangaroo court, acting as judge, jury and executioner. This is not where it ends, however. The Law Society is also the organization which administers Legal Aid.

In my impecunious state, I found myself in the unusual position of applying to the Law Society for Legal Aid with which to sue the Law Society. They responded with the evenhandedness that I would have expected. They refused me. They knew very well that the first item of Discovery in any Trial would be the entirety of the folder from Carratu. Yet, their double-dealing did not go un-noticed. I appealed. And won. I had spent a week with Maggi practicing my hour-long speech to the Independent Appeal Tribunal. They didn't give me a chance even to get out my notes. Almost as soon as I walked in the door and sat down, the Chairman declared that he'd never read such a load of…nonsense as the reasons given by the Law Society for refusing me Legal Aid. Appeal allowed.

Unfortunately, that was as close as I ever got to seeing the Carratu reports. I had become involved with a consortium applying for one of the new Commercial Radio Station licenses, then being offered in public auction, pursuant to the Tories' deregulation of the State Broadcasting monopoly. I expected to be the focus of some local public attention in Slough, and did not want to mess up our chances. It was a difficult choice. Rendered more poignant by the fact that the first business of the investors I attracted to our bid was to ditch me for their own candidate as Managing Director. At least the exercise had offered me an opportunity to spend some time with Maggi. Life was not treating her well, and I did what I could to provide her with a moment or two of enjoyable diversion.

Dead Men Don't Eat Lunch

***

Maggi would come and visit on weekends. I'd wine and dine her around the delights of Bland Land. On one occasion, we spent an afternoon at a carnival in sight of Windsor Castle. On another, we spent a very drunken evening at a wedding reception, to which Mike the Indian had invited us.

An Indian wedding is an experience from which it takes something approaching a week to recover. The men wear simple western suits. But the women are bedecked in the most elegant and colorful of saris. It is considered bad form to wear the same sari twice, and some are so intricately made and so delicately interwoven with gold thread that they can cost upwards of £5,000 ($7,500) a piece.

One arrives at mid-day. Mike and his family are Punjabi, and in the strict caste system of India, this ranks them fairly high. So, even though Maggi and I were pretty much the only white people in attendance, since we were with Mike's party, we were treated with some respect. There is no food to begin with. Only alcohol. We start with scotch. When those bottles are gone, we move onto kegs of beer. After that, we all sit down at long tables in the wedding hall, where we find neatly arranged centerpieces consisting of more bottles of vodka and gin. It is only after those have been disposed of that the food arrives. Just in time to soak up the alcohol already in the stomach, and make room for the bottles of wine now making their way around the tables.

For anyone who can see as far as their watch, we are now approaching 6 o'clock in the evening. Time for the young couple to get married. A moment of great ceremony in any western church, but met with utter debauchery in our wedding hall. The service is perfunctory, because everyone is bursting to get onto the dance floor. No western disco here. Oh no. The curtains on the stage part, to reveal a giant of an Indian, with the largest conga drum I've even seen strapped around his person. The band behind him strike up what Mike tells me is *Bhangra*. It is hugely rhythmic, and Maggi and I are soon caught up dancing what can only be described as a cross between that Greek jigging thing and Michael Jackson. Although I have little recollection of it, I am apparently an enormous hit, and am christened with an Indian nickname that approximates to "Legs."

Maggi missed her own friends, most of whom she had not seen since she first left for Australia ten years earlier. At the beginning of 1991, she held a party for them at a friend's house in London. I had little to do with the preparation, but I had agreed to help her with the hosting. She was very nervous. And then somewhat disappointed with what she felt was a poor turnout. I tried to explain that ten years was a long time, and two weeks rather short notice to give to people, who probably now had children and needed babysitters. My political and marketing background told me that the 15% response she'd had to her 'cold canvass' was actually remarkably good. I don't think she believed me, and she went to bed a little despondent.

I consoled myself by watching Oliver Reed make a fool of himself on an after-midnight chat show. Oliver Reed was a tremendously impressive British stage and screen actor from the Seventies. Did a lot of stuff opposite people like Glenda Jackson. And played 'Porthos,' in the remake version of *The Three Musketeers* which stars Michael York, who also plays Mike Myers' boss in the *Austin Powers* movies. Sadly, by 1991, Reed had succumbed almost entirely to the attractions of the bottle.

The chat show was a novel concept. A group of about eight people sat on sofas, in an informal circle, and discussed a particular topic. The show was live and unscripted, and was held after midnight so that it did not offend the young ones with its subject matter or language. Unfortunately, someone had also decided that it would loosen tongues if alcohol were available to the participants. Suffice it to say that Reed's tongue got altogether too loose, and ended up burrowed down the throat of one of the participating women, who happened to be a declared and proud lesbian. I watched in delighted horror as some poor schmuck of a TV producer saw his career going down the toilet.

I couldn't stand it anymore and went upstairs to wake Maggi. I thought that this, at least, would raise her spirits. However, by the time we got back downstairs, the program had been cut short. Its stead, we were being treated to the opening stages of *Desert Storm*, or as it is now known, the First Gulf War, in order to distinguish 'Poppy' Bush's war against Iraq from the Second Gulf War waged against Iraq by his son, in 2003.

Iraq had originally invaded Iran in 1980 to gain more oil reserves and some beachfront property. Iraq did not have sufficient sea access to the Persian Gulf. When that war ended inconclusively for Iraq in 1988, Iraq looked elsewhere. Saddam Hussein believed that the Americans gave him the green light in 1990, and so in August of that year, he invaded Kuwait. Margaret Thatcher, who was visiting President Bush the First at that time, put some steel in his spine, and together they announced that they would send Saddam packing. And here we were, Maggi and I, at 1 o'clock in the morning, watching that promise being fulfilled.

Stage One, as we armchair experts all now know, is massive bombing of military targets. This was the first war in which bunker-blasters with their own cameras were used. And the powers that be had decided to entertain us with live pictures of Saddam's military installations being blown to smithereens. The objective was obviously to blind any criticism with the joy of pyrotechnics. Judging from the reaction of Maggi, my ardently socialist sister, the calculation had been correct:

"Oh, this is shocking," she exclaimed, " imperialist America…ooh, did you see that...once again oppressing a poor country...that explosion was amazing, do you think they'll show it again...in the Third World...oh come on, that was a squib, where are the big ones?...just to protect their oil supplies...is it over?..."

What was interesting was how little the actors were to change from the First to the Second performance of the Gulf War. In the first showing, we had Bush the Father; Cheney as Secretary of Defense; and Colin Powell as Chief of Staff. By the second showing, it had become Bush the son; Cheney as his Vice President; and Powell as Secretary of State.

What was also intriguing were the stories that were beginning to emerge of the huge and illegal effort that had been undertaken by the West in the Eighties to provide Iraq with the very military hardware and technology with which it was now killing the West's young soldiers. Apparently, the arms industries of the West had merrily played both sides in the Iran-Iraq War, as Arab killed Persian, and vice versa, by the hundreds of thousands. Hardly a move designed to inspire already disenchanted Islamic radicals to view the West with any more respect.

***

As a consequence of my chat with Geoff Hughes, I was now on the lookout for entities showing financial holes in the significant millions, and situations where money-laundering talents were required. Both started popping up like snowdrops in springtime, and many with intriguing links to the matters I was investigating.. To be fair, the first financial 'hole' had appeared sometime before. I just hadn't noticed it.

In the run-up to the General Election of 1987, the Conservative Party had declared itself to be flush with cash. However, within a year or so, it stated that it had a deficit of some £30 million ($45 million), and was only staying afloat by using extensive overdraft facilities with the Royal Bank of Scotland, its primary banker. Then, by the early Nineties, the deficit had miraculously disappeared. I wondered where the money had come from in the first place; where it had all gone to; and then how it had managed to be replaced in such short order. I also wondered about the extent to which those matters with which Hugh had been involved might have had something to do with it.

***

1991 was not only the year of the First Gulf War, it was also the year that marked the beginning of the violent dissolution of Yugoslavia. When Reggie had made his comments about Bulgaria and Yugoslavia, I had laughed. At that time, in 1989, Bulgaria was the most strident of the

Communist nations, and Yugoslavia was an island of peace and moderation on the eastern flank of the Mediterranean. Now, barely a few years later, Bulgarian Communism was a thing of the past – indeed today, the Bulgarian royal heir has foresworn his heritage, and occupies the office of Prime Minister instead. Yugoslavia was a more complicated prospect.

Yugoslavia was a loosely knit confederation of very different countries, which had been held together since the end of the Second World War less by Communism and more by the personal magnetism of its wartime resistance leader, Marshal Tito. When Tito died, there were those who said it would only be a matter of time before the confederation split up. For some years, a shared leadership had staved off that fateful day, but then in 1991, the northern-most Republic, Slovenia, declared independence. Terrible war ensued, with the majority Serbs seeking to prevent the secession of the component parts of the greater Yugoslavia.

When the war with Slovenia finally ended, the next Republic to the south, Croatia, decided it was its turn. And the bloodshed renewed. It is strange how the mind can play tricks. And how history is never so much fact, as it is the political view of the victor. During the Second World War, the Western Allies found common cause with the Communist Tito and his Serbs, because they opposed the Nazis and their fascist allies in Croatia. Fifty years later, the Croats were the heroes and the Serbs were being demonized by the West. Yet, atrocities had been committed by all ethnic groups in Yugoslavia in the Second World War, as they had been in earlier years. Memories died hard in this part of the world, and the new fighting was to be marked with ethnic revenge every bit as horrific as the sins perpetrated by the Nazis.

As 1991 progressed, I found that every story I investigated had a strange twist. As the violence in Yugoslavia unfolded, there were unconfirmed yet persistent reports in the British press of Serbian money making its way illegally into the Conservative Party's coffers, in an effort to influence Government policy. Was this the sort of measure the Tories were using to make up their financial shortfall?

***

In October of 1990, one of Britain's brightest corporate stars, a company called Polly Peck, surprisingly went into the British equivalent of US Chapter 11 bankruptcy. No-one had seen it coming. Soon enough it became clear that millions of pounds were missing. The former head of the firm, Asil Nadir, fled to northern Cyprus, where he'd been born, shortly after it was announced that he faced 66 charges of theft amounting to £34 million ($47 million).

Nadir was safe in northern Cyprus, because Great Britain had no extradition treaty with the unrecognized northern half of the divided country.

Dead Men Don't Eat Lunch

Not so lucky was the Conservative Party. A veritable soap opera played out in Britain's tabloids over the ensuing weeks, as it became clear how close Nadir was to the Leadership of the Party. Hundreds of thousands of pounds in contributions from Nadir and Polly Peck were revealed. The scandal was so far reaching that the then Conservative Minister of State for Northern Ireland, Michael Mates, a close lieutenant of Michael Heseltine, resigned over his links to Nadir.

These developments marked the beginning of the years of Tory 'sleaze,' which phenomenon would be central to the public's eventual loss of faith in the Conservative Government. Yet, even though these episodes proved to be visceral and fascinating, in terms of the amounts of money involved, they proved to be mere appetizers for what was to come later in 1991. Great Britain was about to become center stage to a couple of scandals that between them would represent financial 'holes' totaling in the billions. And Hugh had connections to both scandals.

Geoffrey Gilson

Chapter 17

I GUESS ONE of the reasons I wanted to spend as much time 'entertaining' Maggi as I did was that I felt so grateful for all she had been doing for me. She had merely to sense a need in me, and she was there to help. Now that she was having problems of her own, I had the opportunity to return the favor, and help to lift her spirits. At the same time, I was aware that, when we had been younger, I hadn't spent that much time with her, twin to twin. I generally preferred to play on my own. In part this may have been a defense mechanism to the on-again off-again absence of my parents, my mother in her struggle with alcohol, and my father on his trips for American Express.

My father joined Amex in the Fifties, and found himself initially in Verdun, France, where my elder sister, Liz, and brother, Chris, were born. And where all sorts of strange French nicknames for 'toilet issues' entered my lexicon. Never to leave. The family then moved to Beaconsfield, where my mother gave birth to the remaining four of us: Maggi, me, Jon and Susannah, in order. My father occupied himself on the banking side of Amex business. Then, in 1962, we spent a year living in Westfield, New Jersey, while my father was trained in New York for a new project in Europe.

I remember little about Westfield, other than the fact that I 'failed' first grade at Lincoln Elementary School because I couldn't 'paste.' I could read, I could add up, but I lacked sufficient dexterity to paste two square pieces of paper together evenly. My mother always delighted in this story. Even managed to tell it to the Headmaster of my Catholic Boarding School in England the day she dropped me off for the first time. At the age of 13, an incredibly awkward time, when the impression of one's peers is oh so important. Bless her heart. The other memory I have of Westfield is my first crush. I was six and she was five. She was the younger sister of my best friend Tommy, and her name was Cathy.

We returned to England, and to Beaconsfield, in 1963. My father's assignment was to introduce the American Express card to all points east of the Atlantic Ocean: to Europe, the Middle East and Africa. Yes, you read right. He was the one responsible. I'm really quite proud of his achievement. However, not surprisingly, the project kept him traveling five days out of seven; sometimes the full seven. I missed out on the joys of the father-son exploration of issues such as fishing, soccer matches and, of course, the delicate matter of the opposite sex, and what to do with them. I entered the fantasies of my own mind, and played them out in whatever surroundings I could find. And we found ourselves in a pretty lavish environment to begin with.

On our last excursion in Beaconsfield, my parents had befriended the local Lord of the Manor, Lord Burnham, and his wife, on the cocktail circuit. Now, in 1963, we found ourselves living out of a hotel due to the paucity of local real estate large enough to accommodate all of us. Burnham's forebear had made his fortune when, as the commoner Edward Lawson, he had founded the London *Daily Telegraph*, which became and remains a fervent advocate of the Conservative Party. With status came the need for a country home, and so Lawson bought Beaconsfield's manor house, a mansion a mile out of town called Hall Barn. Shortly thereafter, Lawson was ennobled. The title "Beaconsfield" had already been taken fifty years earlier by one of Britain's most famous Prime Ministers, Benjamin Disraeli, who had also lived near my home town. There is a convention about these matters, and so Lawson named himself after a nearby village, Burnham.

At the time my parents met the Burnhams, times were not going too well financially for them. The Burnhams couldn't afford the upkeep of the main house, and so lived in a smaller house on the edge of the expansive property. Hall Barn itself was empty. The Burnhams offered to rent the top floor to my parents. And so, for the next six years, I found myself living in the next best thing to the lap of luxury. I took to it instantly, and have never really got over it. The grounds to Hall Barn had been designed by a famous French landscaper, Le Notre, in the 18th Century – indeed, the same gentleman created the gardens of the French chateau, used as Teabing's Estate, in the movie version of *The Da Vinci Code*. There was a huge formal lake, and acres of faux rolling hills, and specially laid out woods, called "The Grove." One entered the woods by a small, castellated stone gazebo, where one instantly came upon a privet maze. The rest of this enchanted forest consisted of huge trees with straight trunks, and a thick undergrowth of rhododendrons and azaleas, the combination all leading to a ravine and a rushing stream. I spent many hours in that stream. Building dams. Forever battling the forest demons. On the side of the friendly elves. And rescuing Wendy and the Lost Boys several times every day.

The Burnhams made money where they could, and this quite

regularly involved renting out Hall Barn. Usually this was for use by film companies, shooting at the nearby Pinewood Studios. Most recently, the mansion was used in the highly successful movie, "Gosford Park." The Burnhams and my parents had agreed terms about the use of the grounds. We were given full rein over those areas to the left of the lake, and those on the right were to be left alone for the use of those hiring Hall Barn. On one occasion, we were told that the lower floors were going to be leased out to important guests of Her Majesty's Government. There was a deal of secrecy surrounding the visit, but we did manage to glean the information that the primary guest was the brother of the then Sultan of a place on the Persian Gulf called Abu Dhabi.

There was much excitement as we watched a convoy of limousines pull up to the front door, and unload a bevy of Middle Eastern potentates, and what appeared to be the entirety of this man's harem. The men were wearing robes, and the women were completely covered in black, except for their eyes. They stayed for a couple of weeks during that hot summer in the mid-Sixties. We were very careful to abide by the rules governing use of the grounds, and spent most of our school holidays in the small swimming pool my father had erected in front of the entrance to "The Grove." One afternoon, as we approached the pool, we noticed that someone else's children were already enjoying the delights of our cool water. We quickly realized that it was the children of the visiting Middle Easterners.

The eldest boy was a few years older than me, and was none too friendly. We were equally undiplomatic, and chased them off. A few days after the party left, we read in the newspaper that the Sultan's brother had returned to Abu Dhabi, where, with considerable assistance form the British, he had deposed his brother, and become the ruling Sheikh of Abu Dhabi. Apparently, Sheikh Zayeed had been in Great Britain to finalize plans with his British partners, whose only interest was to have their own puppet controlling the vast oil reserves present under the sands of Abu Dhabi. In order further to strengthen their control of as much oil as possible, the British then sponsored Zayeed in his ambition to control a confederation of the other small emirates surrounding his lands. The confederation became known as the United Arab Emirates, (UAE), and they were important partners of the West in both the First and the Second Gulf Wars. The children at our swimming pool were indeed Zayeed's children, and the older boy was his eldest son. I had pissed off the heir to a fortune worth several billions of dollars. Story of my life.

***

The actual progeny of the Bank of Credit and Commerce International is a little uncertain. It depends on who is telling the story. And what are the affiliations and agendas of the person telling the story. There is no such thing as an objective writer. Some say it was the personal brainchild of a Pakistani banker called Agha Hasan Abedi, who ultimately sought the patronage and financial support of Sheikh Zayeed of the UAE in order to establish the world's first global Muslim bank. Others say that British Intelligence used their puppet Zayeed as a front to set up a conduit for transferring their money undetected around the world. The rest was mere cover.

Whatever the case, after its initial foundation in Pakistan in 1972, BCCI grew quickly, and operated on two quite separate levels. On one level, it was what it claimed to be: a bank where Muslims in all participating countries could safely deposit their money with an institution whose traditions were the same as theirs. In particular, Muslim expatriates found it useful when wiring money to their families back home. In this latter regard, BCCI established a firm footing in England, and ultimately registered itself in Great Britain, where it fell under the supervision of the then Government-controlled Bank of England.

Such friendly supervision, whether a consequence of chance or design, proved most convenient with regards to the second and more clandestine function of BCCI, that of money-launderer for MI6. BCCI's usefulness developed quickly, and it soon became the center of a network, used not only by MI6, but also by the CIA and by Bush's SSG/CPPG. Since these bodies were themselves doing business with all manner of criminals, drug-traffickers and crooked money-launderers, the network became, in short order, a vast, international, underground, trading exchange.

Intelligence agencies, organized crime and terrorist groups could feed into the network, or feed off it. All you needed was something to trade with and some thing to trade for – hostages for arms; money for guns; drugs for political influence – and the network and its friendly bank, BCCI, would set up the trade, provide you with the finance and even the ship to transport it. BCCI was nicknamed the Bank of Crooks and Cocaine International. I have come across no name for the wider network, and so have christened it InTerNet – the International Terror Network. When, at the end of the Eighties, so much evidence of other nefarious activities was 'cleaned away,' InTerNet remained. It still served a purpose. And besides, its activities had become self-generating.

BCCI was not so lucky. The charade began to fall apart in 1988, after it was indicted in Miami for drug-running and money-laundering. BCCI's auditors, Price Waterhouse, engaged in a massive exercise in deception, trying to fool banking authorities in both the US and the UK that everything was fine, but eventually, even the Bank of England had to open its eyes, and shut down BCCI in 1991. Thousands of small Muslim depositors, in Britain and around the world, lost their money. When eventually the cobwebs of duplicity were brushed aside, it was discovered that there was a huge hole at the centre of BCCI's finances, amounting to several billions of dollars.

Notwithstanding the charges that the Democratic Candidate for the Presidency in 2004 did nothing while in the Senate for twenty years, Sen. John Kerry was in fact at the forefront of efforts to investigate the activities of BCCI. It was the scrutiny of his Senate Foreign Relations Sub-Committee on Terrorism, Narcotics and International Operations that uncovered links between BCCI, Manuel Noriega and the laundering of drug profits by the one for the other through Panama, and which led, in part, to the indictment of BCCI in Miami in 1988. And it was the invasion of Panama by the senior President Bush, and the subsequent imprisonment in a US prison of Noriega, that conveniently covered up the fact that Noriega's criminal activities were his share of the partnership between the CIA, Bush and Noriega in their assistance of the Contras. There was more than just bad politics between Sen. Kerry and the junior President Bush in 2004.

Partly in an attempt to stave off unwelcome probing by the likes of Sen. Kerry, BCCI had made a practice of 'fostering' close relationships with figures of political influence. One of the closest was with the pre-eminent lobbying firm of Kissinger Associates. At that time, Kissinger Associates had five partners: President Nixon and President Ford's former Secretary of State, Henry Kissinger, whom I'd met once in the Concorde lounge at Heathrow Airport; Daddy Bush's National Security Adviser, Brent Scowcroft; Bush's former Secretary of State, Lawrence Eagleburger; international economist, Alan Stoga; and investment banker, T. Jefferson Cunningham, III.

The dramatic collapse of BCCI was all over the front pages of the British press in 1991. Most of the attention at that time was focused on the terrible hardship imposed on the thousands of Muslims who had lost their money. But details were already emerging of the illegal activities of the Bank, not least the evidence that the Bank had been used by companies in the US and the UK to finance illicit sales of military technology to Saddam Hussein and Iraq in the Eighties. One immediate consequence of the collapse of BCCI, bearing in mind its importance to InTerNet, was that I kept an eye out for other banks, whether associated with BCCI or not, that might be candidates for having shared its clandestine functions, or might now be ready to step into its shoes.

Quite separately, and purely on a hunch, I telephoned Geoff Hughes, and asked him if Hugh had had a bank account with BCCI. After a deal of huffing and puffing, Geoff confirmed that Carratu had uncovered evidence of an account with BCCI, at their Park Lane branch. This reminded me of a strange episode I'd experienced with Hugh back in about 1985.

Dead Men Don't Eat Lunch

***

The tree-lined boulevard of Park Lane, a name which will be well known to players of the English version of *Monopoly* (the American equivalent is Park Place), represents a one-mile stretch of some of the most luxurious accommodations in all of London. It is marked at its northern end by the huge faux-triumphal Marble Arch, and at its southern end by a group of posh hotels, including the Dorchester and the Intercontinental, favorite haunts for rich, visiting Americans and international fashion shows. The remainder of the gently snaking thoroughfare is made up of grand and gracious Victorian townhouses, most of which have now been converted to offices, with only a few still serving their original function as homes to the fabulously wealthy.

The Park Lane branch of BCCI used to be on the corner of Park Lane and Piccadilly, opposite Marble Arch. Almost diametrically across from this corner were storefronts for the Iranian National Airline and the Melli Bank of Iran, the latter of which figured prominently in the arms transfers to Iran in the Contra debacle. A pedestrian subway opens out just south of Marble Arch, leading into a large concourse one level down from the street. You can see into the opening to the concourse from Park Lane, but you can only enter the concourse from the pedestrian subway, which has its entrance north of Marble Arch.

On a glorious summer's afternoon in 1985, Hugh and I drove to this part of London, parked the car, and went for a stroll. Hugh was strangely silent, checking over his shoulder from time to time. I had long since got used to these esoteric pass-times. We entered the subway, cautiously. When we arrived at the concourse, Hugh checked all around the upper level. I wasn't certain what he could have been looking for. All I could see was blue sky.

He then left me there, with strict instructions to remain until he returned, however long that took. I was as ready as the next guy for a prank, but even this was too weird for me. Yet, Hugh became quite intense. It was imperative, for reasons he could not explain, that I stay in the center of the concourse until he got back. Since it appeared to matter so much, I agreed. An hour passed. Nothing happened. Another hour passed slowly by. Finally, Hugh emerged from the subway, once again looking around cautiously. His only concern was that I had not moved. When I'd convinced him that I hadn't, we went home.

Hugh never explained what had been the purpose of the excursion. Indeed, he never discussed it. Yet, even at the time, I had the sense that he had been engaged in some transaction that he did not wish me to witness, while wanting to impress upon me the location. I also had the distinct feeling that someone had been watching me from the street above.

Geoffrey Gilson

Park Lane forms the western side to the 'Mayfair Square Mile' of London that not only contains some of the most expensive real estate in London, but which is also redolent with mystery and intrigue. Many of the clandestine adventures of the Eighties took place in this oasis of elegant decadence, along with one or two moments in Hugh's life also. MI5 used to have their headquarters buried on one of its backstreets. At an exclusive gaming club on Curzon Street, in the late Seventies, Hugh played bridge at International level with, among others, Iain McLeod, who, until he died, had been tipped as a future Conservative Prime Minister. The American Embassy, with its modern exterior and fortress-like moat, stands guard over Grosvenor Square, buried deep in the heart of the 'Mayfair Square Mile.'

***

I didn't have enough money to put a telephone in my bedsit, and besides, living in a slum, it wasn't wise to draw attention to the fact that one might have more than food stamps in one's back pocket. I made all of my outgoing telephone calls courtesy of John and the *Landmark*. I had given that telephone number to no-one. So, it was with some surprise that I arrived one lunchtime to be told that someone had called for me.

The caller was one Sushma Puri, who, when I returned the call, claimed to be an Associate Producer with *This Week*, a well-known documentary program on *Thames Television*, London's leading commercial television station. She had heard of my investigation, and told me that her Producer was interested in doing a slot in an upcoming show. I didn't want to ask how she knew, and she didn't bother to explain. We agreed to meet in London.

I recognized the front entrance to the *Thames Television* building from the credits they ran at the beginning of their evening news' programs. Sushma was a slip of an Asian girl, with pretty features and long dark hair. She seemed to be much the same age as me, in her thirties. I was a shade bemused when we didn't go to a conference room or a private office. Here she was, supposedly the Associate Producer of the station's flagship news magazine, and we ended up perched on a desk, in a tiny cubicle, lost in a vast ocean of open-floor office space. I couldn't even find a plaque with her name, and I wasn't convinced that this was where she normally resided.

Without any chit-chat, she asked to listen to the tapes of my conversations with Reggie. I had prepared some clippings of the more exciting stretches, while leaving out the details. If there was to be a documentary, I wanted to have some control over eventual content. Small I may be; stupid I'm not. She quickly lost interest in the edited version. I indicated that there wouldn't be time to listen to all six hours of the total tapes. She wondered if she could have a copy for her Producer. Which led me to wonder where he was, since we were supposed to be meeting him.

Sushma then completely changed tack, and began grilling me about my knowledge of Hugh and the 'missing' money. What had been his schedule; foreign visits; bank accounts; spending patterns. I desperately wanted a major media outlet to take an interest in my investigation. But Sushma was making me feel uncomfortable. Once again, I felt that I was talking to someone who had an unhealthy interest only in the 'missing' money. I think Sushma sensed my jitters. She brought the 'interview' to an end, mumbled something about needing to talk to her Producer, and directed me back to the front entrance. I never heard from Sushma again. Indeed, I telephoned *Thames Television* a couple of times, and they seemed completely unable to locate her.

In the entire BCCI affair, no entity was more mysterious and yet more central to the bank's eventual collapse and criminality than Capcom, a London and Chicago-based commodities futures firm, which operated between 1984 and 1988. Capcom is vital to understanding BCCI because BCCI's top management and most important Saudi shareholders were involved with the firm. Moreover, Capcom moved huge amounts of money, billions of dollars, which passed through the futures markets in a largely anonymous fashion.

Capcom was created by the former head of BCCI's Treasury Department, a young Pakistani protégé of BCCI's founder, called Ziauddin Ali Akbar. The company was staffed primarily by former BCCI bankers, and the major investors were almost exclusively Saudi and were largely controlled by Sheikh A R Khalil, the then chief of Saudi Intelligence. Capcom numbered among its financial advisers and auditors Price Waterhouse, National Westminster Bank, and American Express.

Along with the original Treasury Department of BCCI, Capcom was one of the single largest sources of the eventual financial 'hole' associated with BCCI. Capcom proved to be a convenient financial conduit both for siphoning off assets from BCCI, and for laundering billions of dollars from the Middle East to the US, and to safe havens around the world. It was while I was studying up on Capcom, some months after my ostensible episode with *Thames Television*, that I came across the information that Akbar had had a close female associate called Sushma Puri.

***

In October of 1991, the famed American investigative author Seymour Hersh published a book exposing Israel's program to build a nuclear bomb. From a British perspective, the most sensational aspects of the book were those allegations by a former Israeli spy that Robert Maxwell, billionaire owner of the London *Daily Mirror* and Labour Party stalwart, had been for many years a critical agent in the service of Mossad.

The Israeli spy was one Ari Ben-Menashe, who was to become a figure of some controversy in matters relating to the Eighties and Nineties. He had been arrested in the US in 1989 for conspiring to sell military aircraft to Iran. At first, Israel disavowed all knowledge of him. However, he was later acquitted of all charges when the Israeli Ministry of Defense had to fess up that Ari's allegations that he was a spy acting on instruction from the Israeli Government were, in fact, quite true.

In many ways, the story of Robert Maxwell was more the stuff of the American Dream than something one associates with the stuffy upper crust of Great Britain's class-ridden society. This might account for the perverse pleasure he so often gained shocking that society with his vainglorious behavior. Maxwell was born a Jew in Czechoslovakia, and fled that country after the Nazi invasion in 1939. Most of his family was killed in the holocaust. Like so many other Central European refugees, he was attracted to Great Britain, where he enlisted in the fight against Hitler and his hordes. He rose to the rank of Captain in the British Army, where he served with some distinction in their Military Intelligence.

After the Second World War, Maxwell stayed on in his adopted country, changed his name, and set about making his fortune. With trademark energy and ebullience, he soon owned a controlling share in Pergamon Press, which he built into a successful publishing house, specializing in trade journals and technical and scientific books. Based partly on that success, Maxwell won a seat in Parliament, serving as a Labour M.P. from 1964 to 1970. Even after his electoral defeat, he continued to be one of the Labour Party's leading benefactors. Through the Seventies, and into the Eighties, he focused on massively expanding his publishing empire on both sides of the Atlantic, increasingly using the financial tool which came to define the later corporate scandals of the Eighties, the leveraged buyout. In this way, Maxwell gained control of the left-leaning *Daily Mirror*, Macmillan (a large US publisher) and *The New York Daily News*.

Seymour Hersh's book told how Israel became a secret nuclear power, recounting Israel's clandestine mission, from the building of the Dimona reactor site in the remote Negev desert during the late Fifties, to the establishment by the late Seventies of a nuclear capability that targeted and threatened the Soviet Union. Ben-Menashe's contribution was to state that Maxwell had been a spy for Mossad, as well as the British, almost from the time he had landed on English soil. Through Maxwell's extensive global contacts, and particularly relying upon the friendships he had forged with the Communist dictators of Eastern Europe, the Israelis had used Maxwell for a number of important secret missions.

In reference to the subject matter of his book, Hersh alleged that Maxwell had conspired with the Mossad to kidnap Mordechai Vanunu, the

Dead Men Don't Eat Lunch

Israeli technician who broke the story of the Dimona reactor to the London *Sunday Times* in 1986. Vanunu was lured to Rome, where, apparently under the supervision of Ben-Menashe, he was then abducted and taken back to Israel, where he was put on trial and then imprisoned for espionage. Vanunu was released in 2003, after 16 years in prison, but is free only on the basis of the strictest parole conditions, which include not talking with any media.

Ben-Menashe also revealed that Maxwell, together with the Foreign Editor of the *Daily Mirror*, Nicholas Davies, arranged to buy arms for Iran as part of the Contra-Hostage triangle. The arms-buying had been effected through a company called The Ora Group, a company registered in London, and of which Ben-Menashe and Davies were both Directors.

The always dapper Davies had a special fondness for the game of polo, the ponies for which proved to be a hobby too expensive for the salary of a tabloid journalist. Even so, Davies denied all the allegations. However, he came unstuck when his then-girlfriend confirmed much of what Ben-Menashe had been saying about Davies. He lost his job, and for some time was out of work, until he hit on the notion of writing books about all the then-developing Royal scandals, for a well-known publishing outfit called Blake Publishing. The books proved to be a success, and Davies' first best-seller included the information, on its front sheet, that the solicitors acting for him in the matter of copyright were none other than Wedlake Bell.

Maxwell's *Daily Mirror*, along with the *Sunday Times*, lost no time in savaging the credibility of Ben-Menashe in their respective newspapers. However, just a few weeks after the original revelations in Hersh's book, Robert Maxwell's huge naked body was found floating face up in the chilly Atlantic waters off the Canary Islands, near the south coast of Spain. Twenty-four hours earlier, the crew of Maxwell's yacht, which had set sail from Gibraltar a few days beforehand, reported the flamboyant publisher missing. The autopsy ruled out death by drowning, due to the absence of water in Maxwell's lungs, and settled on heart failure.

Maxwell's body was flown to Jerusalem for burial in November 1991, on the historic Mount of Olives, the resting place for Israel's most revered heroes. The burial service had all the trappings of a state occasion, attended by the country's Government and Opposition leaders. No fewer than six serving and former heads of the Israeli intelligence community listened as the serving Prime Minister, Yitzhak Shamir, eulogized: "He has done more for Israel than can today be said."

Those who stood among the mourners that day included a man dressed in a somber black suit and shirt, relieved only at the throat by his Roman collar. Born into a Lebanese Christian family, he was a wraithlike figure, barely five feet tall and weighing a little over a hundred pounds. However, Father Ibrahim was no ordinary priest. He worked for the Vatican's Secretariat of State, it's official Foreign Office. His discreet presence at the funeral was not so much to mark the earthly passing of Robert Maxwell, but to acknowledge the still-secret ties developing between the Holy See and Israel, in their respective clandestine global struggles. You make your friends where you have to in order to achieve your goals.

Meanwhile, the publishing empire that Maxwell left behind was coming unraveled. The hallmark of the corporate scandals that attended the stock market boom of the Eighties was the leveraged buyout. This was a fancy term for a company borrowing money way in excess of its actual value, in order to effect a merger or acquisition, and using the shares of the new company as collateral. This worked fine until the global economic recession of the early Nineties played havoc with share prices.

Unscrupulous corporate tycoons, like Maxwell and Asil Nadir, attempted to overcome the problem by stealing money from their companies' coffers, and then buying their own shares, thus artificially supporting the share price. When that failed, Maxwell took a swim, and Nadir fled to northern Cyprus. In Maxwell's case, it was quickly discovered that his company's auditors, Coopers Lybrand, had again been asleep on the job, and had allowed Maxwell to empty his pension funds of billions of pounds, potentially leaving hundreds of employees without their retirement funds.

The corporate scandals of the 21st Century, for instance those of Enron and WorldCom, were just more of the same. The stock boom of the Nineties was followed by a bust. Companies couldn't afford to allow their share prices to fall. Corporate executives and favored investors did not want to let their stock options or their investments diminish. So, company accountants cooked the books, thus falsifying profit margins. When this failed, the individuals concerned broke the law, sold their shares ahead of bad news, using inside information, and then, like Martha Stewart, took extended vacations courtesy of the federal prison program.

***

In 1992, my younger brother, Jon, called from Atlanta to invite me to come and help market his computer software company. It didn't take me long to accept. I had, once again, come to the end of my finances. Notwithstanding its blandness, Slough had proven to be a good home, and I was sad to leave it. However, as was happening with increasing frequency, I was about to find myself traveling to exactly the right place, at exactly the right time. Revelations aplenty awaited me on the other side of the Atlantic, not least about the illegal arming of Iraq by the US and the UK.

Dead Men Don't Eat Lunch

Chapter 18

CO-INCIDENCE IS THE BEDROCK of conspiracy. But it is sometimes a less than trustworthy bedfellow. Not all juxtaposition is proof positive of clandestine partnership. I was to discover many situations evidencing both sides of this argument while in Atlanta.

My brother Jon had his own small computer software company, which specialized in designing and maintaining software to assist banks with the processing of customers' checks. When I arrived in 1992, he had just a couple of contracts up and running. One was with the First American Bank of New York. Jon had recently won this contract in competition with Perot Systems. The same Perot who, at that time, was running as a third party candidate for the Presidency, against Bill Clinton and the incumbent President Bush Senior. Ross Perot had previously owned Electronic Data Systems (EDS), a huge data processing outfit, operating out of Dallas, where Jon had once worked for the Dallas Federal Reserve, and my elder brother Chris and his family still lived.

In the late Seventies, BCCI had decided it wanted to stretch its wings across the Atlantic. It was able to operate in the United States, but it could not own branches, and therefore could not collect the all important deposits. BCCI's 'Rob Peter-Pay Paul' style of banking required new and ever-larger pastures to harvest when it came to other peoples' money. Perhaps the American banking authorities already knew something about BCCI that the Bank of England was not at that time sharing, because the British Government needed to keep BCCI alive for its own clandestine purposes. Whatever the reason, BCCI was refused permission to open branches in America.

Not to be thwarted, BCCI simply resorted to subterfuge. It employed front men to broker secret deals to obtain controlling shares in already-established banks, and thus garner deposits by the back door. Through the offices of Clark Clifford, a powerhouse of the Democratic

Party, and his partner Robert Altman, BCCI thus became the secret owner of First American Bank of New York. When BCCI began to unravel in the late Eighties, this illegal arrangement was uncovered. Clifford and Altman stood trial in the Nineties for their fraud. Altman's lawyer was one Robert Fiske. The same Fiske was later tapped as first candidate to be the Special Prosecutor into the Clintons' associations with Whitewater.

Before First American, BCCI had targeted the much smaller National Bank of Georgia, owned at that time by Bert Lance, who had been Jimmy Carter's primary political lieutenant while Governor of Georgia, and in his successful campaign for the Presidency in 1976. The broker for BCCI on this occasion was Jackson Stephens, a multi-millionaire from Arkansas. Lance operated out of Atlanta, just down the road from where I was about to live, near my brother.

Jackson Stephens is a member of that interesting cast of characters that one finds regularly re-appearing at the interface between the Presidency, the CIA, and large amounts of 'dirty' money. He and his brother headed a mini-empire in Arkansas that included banks and a sizeable computer software company called Systematics, a firm with which Jon found himself competing from time to time. Stephens financially supported the Presidential campaigns of Jimmy Carter in 1976 and 1980, before switching his allegiance to Bush the Father in 1988 and 1992, at which time one of his banks opened a line of credit of some $3.5 million for the local boy, Bill Clinton, then still Governor of Arkansas. Later, through his ownership of the Worthen Bank, Stephens donated heavily to the Presidential campaigns of Bush the Son.

In the mid-Nineties, I wrote to the newly-elected Speaker of the House of Representatives, Newt Gingrich, who was the Congressman for the District in Georgia in which I lived. Indeed, before becoming a Congressman, Gingrich had taught Economics at the University of West Georgia, in Carrollton, where I spent about six months in 1996, hanging out with some friends. The purpose of my letter to Gingrich was the potential conflict of interest I saw in having Fiske, someone who had indirectly acted for BCCI, investigate Clinton, an indirect recipient of BCCI's largesse. I never got a response. I never saw anything in the press. But, with little fanfare, a couple of months later, Fiske was replaced by Kenneth Starr. Perhaps, Gingrich had already noticed the connection?

In addition to its 'normal' business, Systematics performed contracts for the CIA and for the National Security Agency (NSA), the American agency responsible for all electronic spying, from telephone taps to satellite imagery. Stephens also owns Alltel, one of the largest telephone companies in America. On one occasion, in the Eighties, Systematics designed software to be used by banks to control electronic transfers of money around the globe. What purchasers did not know was that the software had a variety of 'trapdoors.' These allowed NSA and the CIA to track movements of other peoples' money, and to allow them to piggy-back their own fund transfers. In 2006, there was something of a fuss in the US media about revelations that the administration of Bush Junior was monitoring global bank movements, in order to keep an eye on terrorist finances – as if this was something new.

All contracts for Systematics were handled by the Rose Law Firm trio of Webster Hubbell, Hillary Rodham Clinton (Bill's wife, and now junior Senator for New York), and Vince Foster, who became President Clinton's in-house Legal Counsel. Clinton and Foster represented Systematics in Stephens' financing of the BCCI takeover of First American. Hillary became self-taught in intellectual property, an important consideration for a software company. And Stephens picked up some interesting software from one Earl "Cash" Brian, a former member of Ronald Reagan's administration when he was Governor of California.

In 1983, the Stephens brothers had acquired controlling interest in Arkansas' largest bank holding company, Worthen Banking Corporation. Another major shareholder in Worthen was Mochtar Riady, a billionaire Indonesian banker, who was head of the huge Lippo Group and was closely connected to President Suharto. Jackson Stephens met Riady in 1976, when Riady wanted to buy into an American bank.

Two years later, Riady and Stephens Inc. set up a joint venture, Stephens Finance Ltd., in Hong Kong, to write letters of credit. Later, in 1983, Stephens and Riady bought Seng Heng Bank in Macao, and in 1984, they bought the Hong Kong Chinese Bank. Riady also controlled the Bank of Trade in San Francisco. Hong Kong was then the banking center for the heroin trade, just as Manuel Noriega and BCCI had made Panama the banking center for the cocaine trade.

Riady and Lippo were at the center of one of the many fund-raising scandals in which the Democrats became embroiled in the Presidential campaign in 1996. Potentially illegal donations found their way into the Clinton coffers through Mochtar's son, James, who was then a resident of Arkansas; a major investor in his own right in Worthen Bank; and an over-the-border neighbor and business acquaintance of the then Governor of Texas, George Bush Junior, and Mark Thatcher, son of the former British Prime Minister, Lady Thatcher, and at that time a resident of Dallas.

There are some who say that this interface between Presidencies, the CIA and 'dirty' money is no accident. That it has existed ever since the CIA was established after the Second World War. Many take the view that control of the office of Presidency has always been the foremost ambition of the CIA, so that it might, in turn, possess the primary lever over the conduct of America's foreign policy, both overt and covert.

Indeed, it is salutary to observe what has happened to those

Geoffrey Gilson

Presidents who have sought to clip the CIA's wings. Everyone is by now familiar with the charges that the CIA were behind the assassination of President Kennedy in 1963, because he intended to 're-organize' the CIA in his second term. Jimmy Carter achieved what Kennedy had threatened: namely, the virtual dismantling of the CIA's covert operations capability. Carter's reward was to be thwarted in his bid for re-election by the Bush and CIA-engineered "October Surprise."

Certainly, it is interesting to note the re-appearance of the same CIA personnel at the heart of sensitive operations in different US Presidencies. So it is that we find those involved with Air America, the illegal war effort in Laos in the late Sixties, turning up in the Contra Wars in the Eighties; and again in Central Africa, in the Nineties and 21st Century, in the various struggles over precious minerals, in that sad, almost forgotten corner of the Darkest Continent.

Howard Hunt, one of Nixon's 'plumbers,' caught red-handed at Watergate in 1972, was reputedly one of the 'tramps' arrested, and then later released, in Dallas, after the assassination of Kennedy. Felix Rodriguez, a specialist in killing techniques, and the alleged gunman on the 'grassy knoll,' reported regularly on his Contra operations to Donald Gregg, Bush's Chief of Staff while he was Vice President and head of the SSG/CPPG.

Bill Clinton's close friend and Hillary's law partner, Webster Hubbell, through a mutual friend Sam Hall and one Barry Seal, negotiated the use of a small airfield, in Mena, western Arkansas, by the CIA, in its efforts in support of the Contras in the Eighties, when Clinton was Governor of Arkansas. Weapons were flown south, and drugs and money were conveyed back. The deal struck with the CIA was allegedly that, in return for having free rein over a chunk of Arkansas, the CIA would support Clinton in his later candidacy for President. Clinton had seen too many Democratic Presidents fall foul of the CIA, and did not want to repeat the process.

There are those who say that the CIA seeks sway over US foreign policy to counteract the clandestine machinations of the Priory of Sion and its offshoots, of which there are many. It has been a long time since the Roman Church has had only to contend with a single adversary. The Priory has separate strands which differ over the importance they attach either to the Judeo-Christian spiritual aspects of the organization, to the Judeo-Masonic rituals or to the restoration of the royal bloodline of Christ. Indeed, some adherents have became totally secular in their outlook, abandoning all pretence at being Jewish, Christian or Masonic. They like the idea of global unity and control, without the 'religious-royal-masonic' trappings. Chief among them is a group which Reggie liked regularly to call the 'Anglo-American Contingent.'

These secular sects have split into left and right-wing groupings. The 'left' have always preached the same message: a New World Order, under a unifying, secular, globalist umbrella. They have given rise to all manner of politico-economic groups, from private organizations like the Council on Foreign Relations, the Bilderburg Group and the Davos Economic Forum, to Governmental bodies such as the United Nations and the European Union. More often than not, the same individuals are found to be involved, the Rockefellers being a favorite of the conspiracy theorists.

Right-wing groups, while employing much of the same language, are less concerned about peaceful unity, particularly if it involves 'uniting' with the left-wing organizations. It is normal to find the right-wing parading under the banner of white supremacy. Hitler's Nazi's were well aware of the Priory, and made it a cornerstone of their reign of terror to wipe out the Jewish population, in the hope that this would eliminate what it perceived as a Jewish conspiracy to rule the world.

The various white militant groups gaining popularity in the US and elsewhere around the world still make the same mistake of confusing the Judeo-Christian-Masonic origins of the secular New World Order (NWO) movements with the aims of the Jews and their Diaspora. Certainly the Jews and the modern state of Israel have their own political agendas, which they feel free to pursue around the world. However, those agendas owe nothing to the New World Order.

This does not stop white militant groups from spreading their poisonous brew of racism and anti-Semitism, mixed with amusing and regular warnings about black helicopters of the United Nation's stormtroopers, leading the invasion of sovereign US territory. Sadly, even the relatively tamer versions of right-wing Christianity in the US delight in their depictions of secular and non-secular globalists as the forces of Satan, led inevitably by the Anti-Christ himself. Many say that the latter is, in fact, merely an invention of the Roman Church, designed to demonize the royal bloodline of Christ.

There is reason to believe that Allen Dulles, the first Director of the CIA, while performing clandestine work in Switzerland during the Second World War, came fully into contact with the covert aspirations of the various elements of the Priory. It is interesting to note that the original founders of the CIA, including Dulles, referred to themselves as the 'Knights Templar.' Some say that the primary intention of the CIA and its political supporters is to supplant the notion of a New World Order, where power is shared with others on the globe, with a *Pax Americana*, which if not actually an American empire, is a world where America calls the tune.

One secret society that has gained recent prominence, and which was established in the 1820's to ready potential American leaders in their fight to protect US interests against the globalists, is the *Skull and Bones Society* of Yale University. A trend that some have noticed in the late Nineties and the early part of the 21st Century is that the various protagonists potentially involved in this covert global struggle have been becoming more active. Three of the candidates in the Presidential Election of 2004 were members of the *Skulls*: Bush Junior, Sen. Kerry, and Gov. Dean of Vermont. President Clinton also attended Yale.

Neither membership of the "Skulls" nor his previous Directorship of the CIA could save Bush the Father. He lost his bid for re-election to Bill Clinton, shortly after my arrival in the United States in 1992. One of the reasons for Bush's defeat was a scandal then brewing, as happenstance would have it, down the road in Atlanta. It served to re-direct my attention to the evidence that had been accumulating, since Bush had thrown Saddam out of Kuwait the previous year, that his administration and his SSG/CPPG group had been actively involved in arming the very country they had just defeated in war – Iraq.

***

Saddam Hussein came to power in Iraq in the early Seventies. One of his first priorities was to use the profits from Iraq's oil wells to build up his armed services. Saddam needed a strong military to maintain control over the fractious factions within his own country, to intimidate the neighboring Arab nations, and to keep Israel at bay.

At first, Saddam was content merely to buy a ready-made arsenal from the Soviet Union, which had been supplying all of the Arab nations, in order to maintain a balance of terror with the American-armed Israelis. However, after the Yom Kippur War of 1974, fought between the Israelis and the Arabs, when Israel came close to launching its nuclear bombers, Saddam decided he needed to diversify his sources, and also to extend the focus of his purchasing.

The Soviet Union had taken to using its position as sole source of supply as a lever to 'encourage' client countries like Iraq to follow its line on foreign policy. Saddam was less concerned about having an independent view on world affairs as he was determined to have a military machine that was under no-one's control but his own. First, he sought merely to buy weapons from France as well as the Soviet Union. However, in 1981, the Israelis bombed his Osirisk nuclear reactor, which was just beginning to produce plutonium for Iraq's nascent attempts to build an Arab nuclear bomb. At this point, Saddam set out in earnest to create an indigenous military industry for Iraq, not only producing basic weaponry, such as artillery and shells, but also making available a nuclear, biological and chemical warfare capability.

Saddam put in motion a global effort to purchase the component parts for his wide-ranging military effort. The concept was not merely to buy the tools necessary to build weapons, but also to become the owner of

Dead Men Don't Eat Lunch

foreign companies engaged in this industry, so that the blueprints for their machine-tooling could be exported back to Iraq. Saddam was determined to have an Iraq-based military industry that would ultimately be immune to interference from other countries, whether by military action or economic sanction.

The man put in charge of Iraq's covert and worldwide military-purchasing effort was Hussein Kamil, Saddam's son-in-law and the head of his Intelligence Service. It was primarily from Kamil that the West and the United Nations learned of the full capability of Saddam's Weapons of Mass Destruction, when Kamil defected to the West in the Nineties. Back in the Eighties, Kamil's first order of business was to purchase front companies, and find tame banks, behind which Iraq could hide its true intentions.

There were few countries that did not hop on the illegal Iraqi bandwagon, particularly those from Western Europe. However, much of Kamil's trawling was done in the United States, and it was here that, alongside BCCI, he found his other greatest banking asset. The young and brash Christopher Drogoul became Manager of the new Atlanta branch of the Italian Government-owned bank, *Banca Nazionale del Lavoro*, in 1984. Between then and 1989, when it was finally seized by the FBI, he was suckered into illegally lending Iraq some $5 billion, all of which was used to buy illicit military technology. Almost all of the loans were underwritten by Government export credit guarantees. Thus eventually, the entire tab was picked up by the American taxpayer.

Government export credit guarantees are the same the world over. A company wishes to sell a product to a foreign country with a less than stellar financial history. First, the country places an order for the product. The company then issues an invoice. Before the product is shipped, and in the case of military hardware, the company has to obtain an export license and an end-user certificate, confirming that the military product is not going to a no-no foreign country. This is pretty easy to circumnavigate.

During the Eighties, when billions of dollars of illegal military business was regularly being done with Iran and Iraq, the favorite scam was for a US company to buy a UK company, and produce an export license and an end-user certificate for the UK subsidiary. Once there, the product disappeared, and later turned up in either Iran or Iraq. When it was UK companies doing the selling, the process was reversed, with fake export licenses and end-user certificates being produced for the US partner.

The next step in the process is to get a commercial bank to underwrite the transaction. They will only do this if the Government agrees in turn to bail out the loan if anything goes wrong. The product is then shipped to the foreign country, the commercial bank pays the totality of the purchase price to the company, and it then turn its attention to bringing in the monthly installments on the loan from the foreign country.

Geoffrey Gilson

More often than not, and this was particularly true with Iran and Iraq, the foreign country defaults on the loan, and the commercial bank looks to the government to bail out the loan, landing the American taxpayer with the bill. This is how the US Government finally caught up with Christopher Drogoul and BNL.

By the time I got to Atlanta in 1992, the scandal was already hitting the press, because the US Government was trying to plea bargain a deal with Drogoul, in order to keep the 'real' BNL story out of the media. Namely, that the US Government had been actively supporting the Iraqi attempt to build its own military machine, and had been fully aware of the activities of the Atlanta branch of BNL. The US District Court Judge in Atlanta, Marvin Shoob, tried his hardest to blow the lid on the deal, but he was no match for the full weight of the US Government, even with newly-elected Democrat, Bill Clinton, at its helm.

BNL turned out to be another international bank with interesting political connections. Once again, Kissinger Associates was to the fore. BNL was a client of Kissinger Associates, which throughout the Eighties used its close connections with the Reagan and Bush administrations to help BNL in Atlanta to obtain export licenses for the military technology it was helping Iraq illegally purchase. During the same period, Henry Kissinger served on the BNL International Advisory Board.

Before joining the administration of Bush Senior in 1988 as Deputy Secretary of State, and later acting Secretary of State, Lawrence Eagleburger served as President of Kissinger Associates. In that capacity, Eagleburger was also a Board member of Ljubljanksa Bank, a Yugoslav bank with substantial ties to BNL, in the period leading up to the implosion of the Yugoslav nation. After his service with Bush Senior, Eagleburger joined the Board of Houston-based Halliburton, Inc., when Dick Cheney was its CEO. Halliburton became the center of controversy in the 2004 Presidential Election, amid allegations of financial impropriety during Cheney's tenure, and claims of cronyism with the award of lucrative contracts in the rebuilding effort in Iraq after the Second Gulf War.

It was not enough for Hussein Kamil to provide his father-in-law with nuclear, biological and chemical weapons. To be of any use, Saddam needed the capacity to deliver these weapons to the enemy. From the other side of the Atlantic, came the news that Kamil had been searching the UK for such delivery systems.

In 1991, the UK Customs Service discovered that Walter Somers, a British engineering firm, was trying to export pieces of a huge artillery gun to Iraq. The gun, which was nicknamed the "Supergun," was being constructed under the auspices of Iraq's secret Project Babylon, led by a brilliant Canadian scientist called Gerald Bull. For many years, Bull had been at the forefront of artillery design, but had fallen on hard times, when he was caught performing illicit work for the apartheid regime of South Africa, which was at that time the subject of international economic and military sanctions.

Iraq desperately needed artillery superiority over Iran, which was throwing millions of its fanatical soldiers at Iraq's eastern border in the war between the two countries, which had been started by Iraq in 1980, but which it was losing. Bull agreed to upgrade the Iraqi's artillery and extend the range of their SCUD-B missiles, in return for funds to develop his "Supergun." Bull kept his word, and the new artillery which the Iraqis brought into use at the end of the Eighties proved so successful that the Iranians finally agreed to a ceasefire in June 1988. The UK Customs Service discovery brought the "Supergun" project to an end, and led to several convictions for illegal arms-trading for Bull's partners in Great Britain. Bull escaped prison time because his company and he were based in Belgium. But in March 1990, he was shot to death with five bullets in the back of his neck, after answering the door to his apartment in Brussels.

More fortunate were the Directors of another British company called Matrix Churchill. This company was a machine tool manufacturer which had been purchased in 1987 by an Iraqi-controlled company, TMG Engineering. This company, in turn, was owned by a larger Iraqi company, Technology and Development Group Ltd., which was one of Kamil's primary fronts for buying into companies with technology required for Iraq's military industry.

In the late Eighties, two significant contracts were placed with Matrix Churchill. The first contract came from Industrias Cardoen of Chile, and was to supply Iraq with machine tools to manufacture fuses for shells. The second contract was placed directly by Iraq's NASSR Establishment for Mechanical Industries for a project code-named "ABA." Under the terms of the agreement, Matrix Churchill was to provide NASSR with machine tools to construct multi-launcher rocket systems. The British government granted export licenses for both of these contracts on the basis that the materials were for civil use, as the applications had specified.

In the spring of 1990, West German Intelligence informed the British Government that Matrix Churchill machine tools were being illicitly diverted to Iraqi military programs. Soon after learning of these reported breaches of British export control regulations, Britain's Department of Trade and Industry and UK Customs began their investigations of Matrix Churchill.

Those inquiries confirmed that the two contracts, both of which had been financed by BNL in Atlanta, had indeed circumvented British export guidelines. As a consequence, the Directors of Matrix Churchill were charged and stood trial. However, the whole pack of cards came tumbling down when the nature of the relationship between Matrix Churchill and the

Geoffrey Gilson

British Government was revealed.

Paul Henderson, the Managing Director of Matrix Churchill, was a contract agent for MI6, with a specific brief to report on illicit exports to Iraq. And, as a consequence, the British Government had known all along about the activities of Matrix Churchill. The Judge dismissed the charges with the famous comment that he was damned if he was going to send to prison individuals who were acting on orders from their Government.

To the surprise of most informed observers, Prime Minister John Major reacted with speed and almost unseemly propriety. He immediately ordered a Judicial Commission, headed by Lord Justice Scott, to examine the whole issue of the sale of potentially dual-use technology to Iraq, to determine whether it had been used for military purposes, and whether or not the Government had been aware of this fact.

The British media were not used to a politician prepared to search for the truth. Particularly when it seemed obvious that the truth would prove to be so unpalatable to the politician seeking it. As soon as the Commission was announced, journalists and authors fell all over themselves in their eagerness to present the wealth of evidence apparently confirming not only the British Government's awareness of illegal arms sales to Iraq, but its open encouragement of those sales.

After Iraq invaded Iran in 1980, the international community had imposed military sanctions against both countries, forbidding anyone from selling any hardware that would significantly alter the offensive balance between the two nations. The world took the view that this definition offered such wide latitude for interpretation that illicit sales to both countries began almost immediately.

Head of the queue were American companies and those from Western Europe, while their respective politicians did what they could to make the job easier. To their credit, the politicians at least paid lip service to the idea of balance. At first, the Iraqis held the upper hand. For this, and a host of other reasons, including the hostages in Lebanon and the "October Surprise," Governments favored export licenses for Iran.

Around about 1984, luck had begun to favor the Iranians. Saddam had not achieved success with his intended quick punch. The Iranians had rallied, and were now pouring footsoldiers of Islam into the battlefields by the thousand. The Iraqis simply did not have enough weapons to kill them all. Plus, the Iranians were not proving as co-operative in Lebanon as the West had hoped. Accordingly, the political 'tilt' was altered to lean in favor of Iraq.

Notwithstanding her calls to stand firm against terrorists and their allies, Britain's then Prime Minister, Margaret Thatcher, and her Government were not to be left out of the pig's trough developing in the Persian Gulf. The Ministry of Defense actively encouraged British defense contractors to enter the fray, while Ministers from the Department of Trade and Industry held unofficial seminars, where they told arms dealers how to complete applications for export licenses in a manner that would circumvent the very regulations they were supposed to be enforcing.

After 1987, the United States and Great Britain increased the 'tilt' towards Iraq. Iran had proven useless in Lebanon; the need to honor the "October Surprise" had run its course; and both countries were, at that time, importing more of their oil from Iraq than ever before. Besides, Saddam was proving to be a reasonably 'tame' dictator, and both Governments took the view that a firm hand was required in the Persian Gulf to keep the Iranians and others under control. This new policy continued after the ceasefire in the Iran-Iraq War, declared in the summer of 1988. Indeed, it was still in place when Saddam invaded Kuwait in August of 1990. British soldiers returned home from the First Gulf War bearing photographs of artillery shells captured from the Iraqi Republican Guards, and bearing the imprint of British Government-owned weapons factories.

The London *Sunday Times* went a step further, actually suggesting in a series of explosive articles that high-ranking members of the British Conservative Party and Government made money off the illicit arms sales. The thrust of the allegations was that, during the Thatcher years, a group of defense contractors, businessmen, City bankers, senior civil servants, intelligence officers and high-ranking Conservative politicians had conspired to organize huge arms deals, both legal and illegal, with the covert connivance of Thatcher's Government, and in pursuit of Thatcher's private foreign policy agenda. The group, which was nicknamed the *Savoy Mafia*, in honor of its regular meetings at London's Savoy Hotel, included a host of well-known names, perhaps the best-known being those of Thatcher's husband and son, Denis and Mark Thatcher.

In return for expediting the arms deals and promoting Margaret Thatcher's hidden foreign policy agenda, the members of the *Savoy Mafia* pocketed very generous commission payments. Specifically, members were alleged by the *Sunday Times* to have earned a secret $360 million commission for brokering a $35 billion agreement (known as *Al Yamamah I*) in 1985 to supply British jet fighters, naval mine-hunters and ammunition to Saudi Arabia, over the ensuing 10 years.

Almost of more interest to the media than the suggestion of Government corruption were the details of Mark Thatcher's involvement. For years, the British press and public had wondered how on earth this acknowledged dimwit had managed to turn himself into a millionaire. After a series of embarrassing episodes in and around Europe, Mark had been bundled off to Dallas, Texas, there to sell Lotus sports cars for a company called British Auctions, whose Chairman was a member of the *Savoy Mafia*, and was also a personal friend of Mark's dad, Denis. Miraculously, in the mid-Eighties, Mark became filthy rich, and married one of Dallas's socialite princesses.

Now, sources close to the *Al Yamamah I* deal were saying that Mark's cut of the commissions was $18 million. The *Sunday Times* stated that this was the money he had used to set up home and business in Texas. In addition, the respected newspaper suggested that the Scott Commission into arm sales to Iraq threatened to implicate Mark as an alleged middleman who could secure arms deals at a drop of his family name.

A follow-up investigation by the *Sunday Times* then alleged that Mark was being investigated by US Customs as part of an inquiry into the illegal export of military equipment to Iraq and Libya. Agents were to examine two Texas companies in which he had a holding. Aida Perez, an intelligence agent in the US Customs enforcement department in Florida, said officers were looking at allegations linking Mark to arms deals. The inquiry centered on Grantham, Mark's holding company in Houston, and Ameristar, a jet refueling company in Dallas, in which he had an interest. However, one of the primary problems experienced by all those wishing to nail Mark Thatcher, as the media at the time were the first to acknowledge, was that no-one could find a money trail.

***

New light was about to be shed on this subject, and a host of other scandals from the Eighties, with the much-anticipated publication of Ari Ben-Menashe's book, *Profits of War*. To paraphrase a leading reviewer, if half of Ben-Menashe's claims were true, then the massed ranks of the world's media had been well and truly caught with their pants down, while missing most of what had really been happening in that crucial decade.

Dead Men Don't Eat Lunch

Chapter 19

When I was six, my primary school teacher was a battleaxe by the name of Miss Sully. She had a stern face, a pudding waist and never wore make up. I believe she kept the local drapers in business for many years, with her purchase of the material she used to make her sailcloth dresses. It seemed to me that she went out of her way to find fault with every aspect of my behavior. Certainly, I spent more time in detention than anyone else in my grade.

According to my mother, she ran into Miss Sully one day on the streets of Beaconsfield, many years later. Almost the first words out of Miss Sully's mouth were an enquiry about me. My mother gave her a brief, but factual account of my toings and froings. But, apparently, Miss Sully was not satisfied. "Ah Peter," she sighed (I only began to use my middle name, Geoffrey, after I was 21).

In my wanderings around the world, since those balmy days of prep school, one of the more poignant features of human frailty that I have discovered is the love-hate relationship between older, spinster school teachers, and the naughtier of their young male flock. I do not believe for one moment that there is anything sexual to it. I think, rather, it is a secret longing for that scallywag of a son, with which they feel certain they would have been blessed, if only they could have enticed the right man into their grasp.

And so Miss Sully had sighed, a misty look in her eyes, and a half smile playing on her lips, "Ah Peter," she had said, sighing once more, "he had an answer for everything. The rest of us had to be content with either black or white. But Peter, oh Peter, he always saw grey."

I'm bound to say the passing years now fail me. For as hard as I tried to follow Reggie's advice, and broaden the way I looked at world events, I could still only see black and white. Over and over he had insisted that I needed to see grey, in order to understand what Hugh had been involved with. However, notwithstanding Miss Sully's backhanded testimonial, I still had problems understanding that the world of intelligence was not simply about 'them and us'; but instead involved many different shades in between. That is, until I began to read about Israeli Intelligence.

***

The modern state of Israel is a tiny sliver of land that has existed since the Second World War solely due to the efficiency of its armed forces. In war after war, the country has prevailed over neighbors, who seemed to want nothing more than to drive the Jewish people as far into the Mediterranean as they would go. In no small part, the military owed its success to the excellent performance of the nation's intelligence services. And they, in turn, lived and died by a code of silence that made the Mafia's *omerta* look like a friendship ritual between first graders.

So it was with no small sense of outrage that Israelis awoke in October 1991 to read that a renegade member of Mossad, one Viktor Ostrovsky, had spilled the beans on some of its more exotic training practices and escapades in his book, *By Way of Deception*. While there was considerable public and press interest in the book, at least outside of Israel, it was nothing compared to the reaction that met his second book a few years later.

The essence of this second book, *The Other Side of Deception*, was that the first book, and indeed the very suggestion that Ostrovsky was renegade, was merely a device to undermine dangerous right-wing elements in Israeli Intelligence by exposing their activities. Apparently, there was a continuing struggle within the various factions of Israeli Intelligence. Broadly speaking, the left-wing, openly in support of Israel's Labour Party, and with whom Ostrovsky claimed allegiance, took the view that clandestine work, on behalf of the state, should know some codes of behavior, and should pretty much be restricted to Israel and the lands of its immediate enemies.

The right-wing faction, which allied itself with the then-governing Likud Party of Prime Minister Menachem Begin, and later, his successors Yitzhak Shamir and Ariel Sharon, took the rather more aggressive stance that, in the fight for Israel's survival, all bets were off, and that Israeli Intelligence could and should do whatever necessary, wherever necessary. If this meant assassinations and faked attacks by militant Palestinians, then so be it. If Israelis needed to interfere covertly with the political balance in other, supposedly 'friendly,' countries, in order to engender the right level of support for Israeli ambitions, then this should be done with gusto. The left-wing faction felt that the right-wing group could no longer be controlled from within Mossad alone, and this had led to the subterfuge with Ostrovsky.

Dead Men Don't Eat Lunch

All of this was so much gentle appetizer for Ben-Menashe's book. Notwithstanding his protestations to the contrary, page after page seemed to be an unapologetic chronicle of some of the more outrageous schemes of the right-wing faction of Israeli Intelligence.

Both Ben-Menashe and Ostrovsky claimed they were now telling their stories because both, in their fashion, had been dumped by their former faction leaders. Ben-Menashe claimed to be pissed that his former bosses had taken so long to come to his aid, while he rotted in an American jail, sharing space with a bull redneck, who insisted on calling him "girlfriend." Meanwhile, Ostrovsky was upset because the leader of his left-wing faction, who went by the code-name "Ephraim," had, apparently, found a new boyfriend, and no longer returned Ostrovsky's telephone calls. One can not help but wonder whether or not these two protest too much. Ostrovsky had already run one successful disinformation campaign with his first book. Could it be that Ostrovsky and Ben-Menashe were now partners in another, more elaborate intelligence scam? As Reggie was fond of saying: "Once a boy scout, always a boy scout."

Certainly, Ben-Menashe had many detractors when it came to his personal credibility and the allegations in his book. He was labeled a professional liar, a man who always found himself at the center of every major intelligence triumph. *Newsweek's* national security correspondent, John Barry, said on CNN: "Ben-Menashe is a fabricator...If you were talking about the American Civil War, he would tell you he was the guy who planned Lee's campaign."

It never ceases to amaze me that otherwise intelligent people seem to assume that intelligence services hire angels. They don't. Spying is about being a crook. And crooks are who they hire. Besides, when one looks a little closer, one finds that so many of those in the media who attack Ben-Menashe are the ones who missed out on the true events of the Eighties, and they're just sore. The fact remains that whatever may be the truth about Ben-Menashe, he is still sought out by governments and intelligence services the world over. And Rafi Eitan, Mossad's former Deputy Director of Operations, has gone on record as confirming the bulk of the content of Ben-Menashe's book.

The central controversy of Ben-Menashe's book was its total rewrite of the script for the Iran-Contra and, at the time, still-developing Iraqgate scandals. Whatever may have been his true value to the Contra operation, North is described by Ben-Menashe as a sideshow to the real event on the Iran end of the debacle. Worse than being merely irrelevant, it is Ben-Menashe's contention that North was set up as a stooge to attract attention away from the serious arms deliveries to Iran, which were occurring elsewhere.

The "October Surprise" set the scene for the effort illegally to supply Iran with the military technology it needed to push back the Iraqi invasion after 1980. From 1980 to 1984, this exercise was undertaken, in the main, by the right-wing faction in Israeli Intelligence. Bush Sr. and his SSG/CPPG needed to keep this process at arm's length, so as not to trigger Congressional oversight. And since the right-wing Likud Party, under Menachem Begin, was at that time in control of Israel's Coalition Government, the left-wing group in Israeli Intelligence was frozen out of sharing the spoils. And riches there were aplenty.

Ben-Menashe was one of six individuals on Israel's top secret Joint Committee on Israel-Iran Relations, who spent their time traveling the world, buying up weapons wherever they could find them, shunting them through front companies, like The Ora Group with Nick Davies, and selling them to the Iranians at grossly inflated prices. It was not long before greed overcame common sense, and beginning in about 1984, Bush and his mob began arranging for their own parallel supply-line to Iran. The combined effort was called the "Blue Pipeline," after the Danish shipping company that was used. All in all, Ben-Menashe reckons that, by the end of the Iran-Iraq War in 1988, the illegal sales to Iran had been worth some $82 billion in total.

That level of sales created huge profits, which needed to be laundered cleanly and then hidden somewhere safe from prying eyes. Enter Robert Maxwell. Ben-Menashe and company used Maxwell's publishing firms and his contacts with the leadership in Eastern Europe to launder the profits into secret bank accounts on the other side of the Iron Curtain. At their peak, separate funds for the Israelis and the Americans each contained revolving totals of some $600 million. This was exactly the sort of operation I had been looking for. Money-laundering is a skilled business, and I had seen nothing in either Maxwell or Ben-Menashe's CV's to suggest they knew the first thing about laundering money. Unlike Hugh.

By 1985, and under the terms of Israel's Coalition partnership, the leader of the left-wing Labour Party, Shimon Peres, became Prime Minister of Israel. Almost the first item on his agenda was a demand for a piece of the Iranian arms' pie. A close associate of his, Amiram Nir, made contact with Robert McFarlane, Reagan's first National Security Adviser, and Oliver North. Ben-Menashe and his team made as if to co-operate, while keeping the 'newbies' as far away from the real action as possible. In the end, North and company managed to ship a grand total of 1,000 TOW missiles to Iran, for the kingly sum of $1 billion. Not only that, but the missiles were useless to the Iranians since they still had Israeli Defense Force logo's all over them.

North got pissed, and played stool pigeon on some of Ben-Menashe's colleagues, then passing through New York. They were jailed. Ben-Menashe responded in 1987 by spilling the beans on North and his outfit to a newspaper in Lebanon. Partly this was malice. Partly it was a 'smokescreen' ploy. Congress was getting itchy. Enquiries were being made.

Dead Men Don't Eat Lunch

Ben-Menashe and his colleagues took the view that, by offering up a juicy tidbit in North, Congress would be so preoccupied that they would look no further. Ben-Menashe proved to be right.

No-one really knows why Congress didn't push harder. Perhaps both Democrats and Republicans supported the ambitions of Bush's secret agendas? Perhaps Democrats were cowed by Reagan's popularity? Perhaps no-one wanted to see another President impeached so soon after Nixon? Or perhaps Ben-Menashe and his cohorts simply outsmarted them? Whatever the case, North and his comrades took the fall, yet were later either pardoned or had their convictions overturned on Appeal. And the media did nothing, except call Ben-Menashe a liar for revealing what they had all missed while it was happening.

Ben-Menashe was sacked for his disloyalty to the competing 'left-wing' Israeli-American arms pipeline to Iran. However, even the limited disclosures in Congress about North's Iranian adventures pretty much brought all pipeline business to Iran to an end in 1987. Just in time for the Iraqis to get the upper hand with Gerald Bull's improved artillery, and bring about the ceasefire in the Iran-Iraq War in the summer of 1988. Ben-Menashe was immediately recalled for higher duties, as the Counter-Terrorism Adviser to Yitzhak Shamir, the new right-wing Likud Prime Minister.

Top of Shamir's agenda was the need to plug the separate, but equally covert, arms pipeline to Iraq, which had picked up pace in 1987, as the US and the UK became more reliant on Iraq's oil. Ben-Menashe's new role as Shamir's 'bully boy' saw him traveling to the US, the UK, and Europe. Ben-Menashe's book even describes a scene where he is in the office of Carlos Cardoen in Chile, warning him to 'back off,' at which point Cardoen dramatically introduces Ben-Menashe to his new chum and partner, Mark Thatcher. Ben-Menashe takes the view that the introduction was staged to convince him that Cardoen believed he had enough friends in high places to be unafraid of Ben-Menashe.

Ben-Menashe claims also to have met with Gerald Bull, shortly before he was murdered. Bull also feigned indifference, but he turned up a few days later with five bullets in the back of his head. Ben-Menashe does little to dispel the notion that he was somehow responsible. Ben-Menashe seems to play a double game. On the one hand, he appears to be spilling beans of substance. Yet whenever sense dictates Mossad involvement in a situation where the connection might rebound badly on Israeli Intelligence, Ben-Menashe performs somersaults trying to convince the public there never was any Israeli involvement.

Maxwell took advantage of the slush funds in Eastern Europe to expand his business empire. He took out bank loans, which were underwritten by loan guarantees, permitted by Yitzhak Shamir, with the blessing of Bush Senior, on the basis that any default in the loans would be covered by the money in the slush funds.

In 1989, an operation was compromised when it was leaked that Israel was negotiating with the PLO for the release of soldiers in Lebanon. Ben-Menashe was again blamed for the leak. Sensing another round of doom and gloom, Ben-Menashe, who was one of only a few signatories to the Israeli slush fund, began to move the money around, while making a fair proportion of it disappear altogether. This had the effect of undermining Maxwell's loan guarantees, and Shamir was furious with Ben-Menashe.

Soon after, Ben-Menashe lost his 'protection.' He found himself in jail, set up by the CIA, disowned by his employer and abandoned by his wife. However, he may have had the last laugh. When it came time to hand over the slush fund money, Maxwell returned most of the Likud money, but he cut the Americans out of their share, being some $780 million. Shortly afterwards, Maxwell took his last swim off the Canary Islands. Ben-Menashe is quick to put the blame for Maxwell's death on the CIA. Yet Ben-Menashe's 'rival' Ostrovsky, and others with interests closer to the left-wing in Israel, paint a different picture.

They say that, in September of 1991, the vultures were circling Maxwell and his shambolic financial affairs. Parliament was threatening to investigate, and the media was only being held at bay by Britain's draconian libel laws and a bevy of high-priced lawyers. Maxwell begged for more monetary assistance from the Israelis. When they balked, he threatened to expose the secret meeting he had hosted earlier in the year on his yacht between the Head of Mossad and Vladimir Kryuchkov, the Head of the KGB.

At the meeting, Kryuchkov had discussed his plans to stage a coup against the sitting Soviet President, Mikhail Gorbachev. Mossad had promised to use its influence with the United States and key European countries to recognize the new regime in Moscow. In return, Kryuchkov would arrange for all Soviet Jews to be released and sent to Israel. The discussion came to nothing. But the coup was staged. And failed. Revelation of the secret meeting would seriously harm Israel's credibility with the existing Russian regime, and with the United States.

Maxwell received a call from the Israeli Embassy in Madrid. He was asked to come to Spain the following day, where according to Ostrovsky, "his caller promised that things would be worked out so there was no need [for Maxwell] to panic." Maxwell was told to fly to Gibraltar, just down the road from Marbella, and to board his luxury yacht, the *Lady Ghislaine*. He was to order the crew to set sail for the Canary Islands, "and wait there for a message." The message was delivered by a Mossad hit team of two assassins, one of whom injected a bubble of air into Maxwell's neck via his jugular vein. It took just a few moments for Maxwell to die, whereupon his still warm body was stripped and then dumped overboard.

Notwithstanding their occasional disagreement over Mossad's responsibility for particularly controversial deaths, Ostrovsky and Ben-Menashe were agreed on one thing in their respective books: in the Eighties, the right-wing in Israeli Intelligence, egged on by its political masters, had ploughed a scorched earth path around the world, laying waste to Israel's perceived enemies with assassination and dirty deed. One of the truly disturbing features of Ben-Menashe's revelations, not in his own book, but as a source in another bestseller (*Abu Nidal: A Gun for Hire*, Patrick Seale), was the implication that the 'dirty deeds' might have included faking terrorist incidents in order to whip up a frenzy of support for punitive action.

Abu Nidal, born Sabri al-Banna, was always regarded as one of the more vicious of the Palestinian terrorists. His organization was responsible for a series of violent acts in Rome, Vienna, Istanbul and London. Nidal's name was linked to the Lockerbie bombing, and he gave the order for the assassination in London of Israel's Ambassador, Shlomo Argov, whose killing was used as the pretext for Ariel Sharon's invasion of Lebanon in 1982.

Not all of Nidal's killings were ideological. He was for many years a hired gun for a variety of clients, including Iraq and Libya. Nidal had a close relationship with Saddam Hussein for many years, killing many of Iraq's enemies around the world. The relationship lasted until 1983, when Nidal took the view that Saddam had become too cozy with the West in his desire for financial and military help in his war against Iran.

This then was the public face of Abu Nidal, the most extreme of Arab Palestine's militant champions. Yet, Ben-Menashe and others suggest that the truth was more complex. That Nidal was, at the very least, a quadruple agent, bought and paid for variously by Mossad, MI6 and the KGB, all the while continuing to parade as the purist of Palestinian idealists. The implication was that Nidal was everyone's favorite playtoy; a dangerous weapon, used as a last resort for work that had to remain beyond the undeniable.

Primarily, Mossad used Nidal to blunt the military efforts of the Palestinians. The thinking was that by staging particularly controversial terrorist incidents in Europe, the public would turn against the Palestinian cause, and formerly wavering European Governments would line up behind Israel's aggressive stance. The British and the Russians had their own agendas.

The British tricked Nidal into providing them with voluminous information on the activities of all the Palestinian groupings. In this task, the British required the help of another notorious Middle Eastern criminal, one Monzer al-Kassar, whose name regularly appeared as a part player in most of the unseemly dramas in the Middle East in the Eighties. Like Nidal, al-

Kassar had many masters, including the British. But his primary allegiance had always been to Syria, the land of his birth.

By the Eighties, al-Kassar and his brothers operated as the East Mediterranean 'franchise' of InTerNet: they were the central exchange for the region's terrorist, arms and drug networks. They had close ties to BCCI, along with their own banking network, which they offered as a service to any that would do business with them. And everyone did. If you needed help in the Middle East freeing hostages, buying guns, placing a bomb, or simply obtaining drugs and laundering the profits to another part of the world, Monzer al-Kassar was your man. Clients included the CIA and their British contract agent, Les Aspin.

MI6 approached al-Kassar at the end of the Seventies in his capacity as the "Banker for the PLO." He was enrolled in a plan to convince all of the Palestinian terrorist groups to place their funds with the Park Lane branch of BCCI, in London. He began with Nidal, who soon was in on the deal. The two then joined forces, and had tremendous success with the other PLO factions. Eventually, the British were able to monitor the greater part of the Palestinians' financial activity, giving them a heads-up on future terrorist incidents.

However, on the face of it, this advantage provided little by way of warning for the Lockerbie bombing, a proportion of the finance for which apparently came from Nidal's BCCI account in Park Lane. Certain authors have suggested that, in order to hide the existence of the British monitoring process, it was necessary both to allow certain terrorist attacks, and to keep the exercise a secret from the Israelis.

The history of intelligence activity around the world is replete with instances of such double-dealing treachery. Mossad recruiters were past masters at pretending to be something they were not, in order to enlist support from those who would otherwise run screaming from the suggestion that they help the Israelis.

The Brits hired themselves out to do the CIA's dirty work in Lebanon in the Eighties, when the latter were seeking retribution for the bombing by Muslim militants of the American Embassy and the US Marine barracks. The CIA, forbidden by Presidential Decree from engaging in assassination, used the British to take out some of the nastier of the militant Muslim leaders.

The British have long proven themselves not to be less than overly squeamish. There is now a wealth of evidence that, during the troubles in Northern Ireland, British Intelligence regularly fed Protestant groups with the information they needed to target Catholic assassinations.

One paragraph in particular caught my attention in Ben-Menashe's book. In it he described how a Mossad hit team had traveled to Europe in November of 1988, where they had worked their way through a list of assassination targets. The list had earlier been compiled by a secret meeting of Mossad, and consisted of those involved in arranging arms deals for Iraq, or others who handled the financing and the subsequent laundering of profits.

In a moment of what seemed to me at the time to be inspiration, I wrote to Ben-Menashe, wondering if Hugh had been on the list. It wasn't so much the timing that had given me cause to ponder; it was Ben-Menashe's statement that the hit squads had been made up of Palestinians, hired buy a Mafia Don, who was in the pay of Mossad. I couldn't help but think of Reggie, and his allegations about who might have killed Hugh.

***

John Major, while Prime Minister of Great Britain from 1990 to 1997, was often thought of as a Jimmy Carter-like figure: decent, but ineffectual. The reality was quite different. Both before and after his unexpected Election victory in 1992, Major had a deal of political success. While struggling to repair Britain's economy after the global recession of the early Nineties, Major sought to extend Thatcher's social and industrial reforms. At the same time, he wanted to improve the lot of those requiring a safety net by making public services more responsive to their 'consumers.' Major's Government was the living embodiment of the kinder, gentler society preached on the other side of the Atlantic by Bush Senior.

Major successfully guided almost all of his agenda through a boisterous Parliament, and established a personal reputation for decency and honesty. The economy was put back on track, and by the time of his Election defeat in 1997, the country was in robust good health. Major's problems lay not with his political program, but rather with those in his own Party, who seemed hell bent on undermining all the good work he was doing on their behalf. The period 1992-1997 represented a period of considerable shame for the Conservative Party. The years were marked by one sleazy scandal after another, and open rebellion by the right-wing against what they regarded as Major's 'moderate' sell-out.

The scandals began with David Mellor, one of Major's closest political lieutenants and a leading Cabinet Minister. Mellor looked, acted and talked like a lead character from one of the *Revenge of the Nerds* movie. Unkempt and uncoordinated, with spectacles and a gap-toothed grin, he was always gushing about this new arts program or that particularly interesting piece of broadcasting legislation. Yet, like his heroes in the movie, his mind never strayed far from the subject of endless sexual gratification. And this was the beginning of his undoing.

In July of 1992, just after Major's success at the polls, *The People* tabloid newspaper revealed that it had been part of a sting operation to catch

Geoffrey Gilson

Mellor red-handed with his hot-blooded mistress, Antonia de Sancha, a struggling actress. The newspaper spared no detail in its account of Mellor's activities, including the fact that Mellor enjoyed wearing the uniform of his favorite soccer club while engaged in his carnal pleasures.

Other newspapers jumped on the bandwagon, and the revelations about Mellor's personal life were quickly followed by more serious allegations about his business and social connections. In August of 1990, Mellor enjoyed a free holiday in the south of France as the guest of the daughter of a leading official of the PLO. On another occasion, a holiday was paid for by Sheikh Zayeed of Abu Dhabi. Mellor had already achieved international headlines when, in the full glare of nearby television cameras, he had publicly berated a couple of Israeli soldiers for allegedly ill-treating a Palestinian woman. Mellor was, at the time, on an official visit to the occupied territories of Israel as a British Foreign Office Minister.

Mellor eventually cut his losses and resigned from Major's Government. But not before two interesting pieces of information came to light. The first was that Antonia de Sancha had originally been introduced to Mellor by a friend of his, Paul Halloran of *Private Eye*. And the second was that the intermediary, who had assisted *The People* in setting up Antonia in the love tryst where the newspaper had its cameras and microphones hidden, was reported as having close links with Israeli Intelligence.

***

Mohammed al-Fayed is now best known around the world as the father of Egyptian playboy Dodi Fayed, who courted Diana, Princess of Wales, in her final days. However, al-Fayed had been for many years a figure of some controversy in Great Britain. His story of peasant Egyptian to Anglophile riches is as amazing a journey as that of Robert Maxwell. And it has many similarities.

Mohammed Fayed was born the son of a schoolteacher, in a small town outside of Alexandria, in Egypt. Even at an early age, Fayed demonstrated the drive and ambition that would later bring him so much success. Along with a flawed judgment that would lead to a number of embarrassing debacles. So it was that Fayed found himself associated with Saudi businessman, Adnan Khashoggi, with whom he made his first fortune selling arms.

Fayed proved successful enough to establish his own shipping company in Egypt. However, money was not enough. Fayed desired status also. He had grown up admiring the British who ruled Egypt at that time. Fayed wanted nothing more than to be accepted into the inner circles of the British aristocracy. He dreamed that one day he might be able to join their ranks.

Dead Men Don't Eat Lunch

He set about attempting to achieve that ambition by moving to Great Britain in 1974. Immediately, he aped the dress and mannerisms of the English upper-crust. He added the honorific 'al-' to his name, and found appointment to the Board of Lonrho, London-based company, then on its way to becoming a financial powerhouse in the Third World. Although on the face of it, this latter move seemed to al-Fayed a sensible attempt to impress the financial elite in the City of London, Lonrho, like Khashoggi, had something of a checkered reputation.

Tiny Rowland, the Chairman of Lonrho, was another rags to riches story, a crude businessman, with few moral scruples. The primary business of Lonrho was with Africa, and in particular, with the exploitation of its wealth of raw materials, from diamonds to oil. Africa was then, as it still is today, a hotbed of tribal enmity. Tiny Rowland did what was necessary to gain 'safe passage' to the raw materials he desired. Whether this meant offering bribes, illegally shipping arms, or providing much sought after British mercenaries for personal protection.

It was in this latter regard that William Buckley of the CIA and his ex-SAS British chum, Les Aspin, found themselves fighting the left-wing FNLA in Angola in the Seventies. The reason was less ideology and more the oil, diamonds and uranium to be found under the ground. For his part, Tiny Rowland was accused of breaking international sanctions and doing business with Libya and the apartheid regime of Rhodesia. Specifically, Lonrho had been running arms to these two countries.

Rhodesia, which became Zimbabwe after its independence in the Eighties, had been made an international pariah, after its white government declared 'illegal' independence from Great Britain in the mid-Sixties, without the approval of its masters. The Labour Government of Harold Wilson had insisted that 'legal' independence would only be granted to Rhodesia if its new Constitution allowed for majority rule by blacks. The whites-only Rhodesian government of Ian Smith balked, threw out the British, and continued to deny the vote to its black population.

Rhodesia, along with South Africa, became a cause celebre for Conservative Party right-wingers in the late Sixties and early Seventies. The argument they used in support of both countries was not dissimilar to the one run by the southern States in the American War between the States: it was not a question of the rights of the blacks; it was about honoring the integrity of a sovereign nation or state.

The Tory right-wing said that Britain had no right to interfere with the self-determination of another country. Every nation had the right to choose its own form of government, and run its economy the way it saw fit. None were more eloquent in this regard than a very young Hugh Simmonds, who received a standing ovation at his first Party Conference, when he delivered a speech supporting the sale of British warships to South Africa.

Geoffrey Gilson

There was uproar in Great Britain when the allegations of Lonrho's illegal sanctions-busting on the African continent came to light in the early Seventies. It caused major embarrassment to the Conservative Government of Edward Heath, who described Rowland and Lonrho as the "unacceptable face of capitalism."

In the mid-Eighties, Rowland bought 29.9% of the shares of the luxury department store, Harrods, and made a bid to purchase a controlling share of the store. The Conservative Government of Margaret Thatcher was less than happy at the thought of a scoundrel like Rowland at the helm of one of Britain's most cherished and venerable institutions. The bid was referred to the Monopolies Commission, in the hope that someone more palatable would come forward and buy Harrods, while Rowland's bid wallowed in bureaucracy.

Al-Fayed spotted his chance. In the course of his dealings with Khashoggi, al-Fayed had developed a network of contacts around the world, including the Sultan of Brunei, the ruler of an oil-rich kingdom to the north of Indonesia. In 1984, al-Fayed approached Rowland with a proposal. Rowland should 'temporarily' sell his Harrods shares to al-Fayed, who would then make a bid for Harrods, that would appear on the surface to be Lonrho-'free.' Once successful, al-Fayed would then sell the shares back to Rowland.

Al-Fayed convinced both Rowland and the British Government that the money he was using to buy Harrods, valued at something just under $615 million, was his own, and that his wealth had derived from his family's shipping and cotton empire, founded on the banks of the River Nile. The truth was that the money was being spotted by the Sultan of Brunei.

Rowland had only agreed to sell his shares to al-Fayed, believing that the latter would not have enough funds to buy a controlling share. However, barely a few hours after selling his 29.9% stake in Harrods to al-Fayed, Rowland learned of the true source of al-Fayed's money, and realized that he'd been conned. Four months later, the British Government, still believing al-Fayed's lies as to the source of his funds, agreed to allow al-Fayed to purchase control of Harrods.

Rowland was furious, and began a decade-long feud with al-Fayed that only ended with Rowland's eventual death. Rowland owned his own British Sunday newspaper, the much-respected *Observer*. The accusations made by Rowland about al-Fayed's lies became so vocal that, in a strange twist of irony, Thatcher's Government was finally forced to mount an investigation of al-Fayed's bid for Harrods through the same Monopolies Commission that had thwarted Rowland's bid.

The inquiry eventually reported that al-Fayed had indeed lied to the British Government about his background and his wealth. For reasons that were not immediately apparent, little by way of punitive action was exacted against al-Fayed by the British Government. However, in one matter dear to his heart, al-Fayed was about to be stymied as a consequence of the fall-out. From that moment on, the Conservative Government would deny his repeated requests for British citizenship. The gentleman primarily responsible for this refusal was the Right Honorable Michael Howard, QC, MP, the Conservative Home Secretary at the time. [The Home Secretary is, roughly speaking, equivalent to a combination of the Attorney General and the Interior Secretary in the United States.] Howard became Leader of the Conservative Party in 2003.

Al-Fayed believed he had more than paid the price of entry into the upper echelons of Britain's overly stratified society. He invited the 'great and the good,' including the Countess Spencer, stepmother of the Princess of Wales, to join the Board of Harrods. He donated generously to all the favorite Royal charities, including the Great Ormond Street Hospital for Children, which was close to Diana's heart, and was itself the recipient of all royalties emanating from the rights to "Peter Pan." Al-Fayed wore the right clothes, ate the right food and attended the Queen's garden parties at Buckingham Palace. He was convinced that ennoblement, and the honorific title 'Lord al-Fayed,' was within his grasp. Just as soon as he became a British citizen.

Now that ambition was dashed. Al-Fayed blamed the right-wing Government of Margaret Thatcher, and later that of John Major. He swore publicly that he would do all within his power to bring the Tories to electoral defeat in 1997. Al-Fayed leaked to *The Guardian*, Britain's leading left-wing 'quality' newspaper, the information that, during the inquiry by the Monopolies Commission into his bid for Harrods, he had secretly bribed several Conservative Members of Parliament to ask questions in his support in Parliament.

The ensuing uproar became known as the "Cash-for-Questions" scandal, and it rocked the Government of John Major. Two Government Ministers were among those accused. One was Tim Smith, the unfortunate Member of Parliament for Beaconsfield, who with dignity and distinction immediately made the correct decision, and resigned from the Government. His local Constituency Association behaved with less grace, and later 'invited' him to resign his seat. The other Government minister was Neil Hamilton, and he was a whole different kettle of fish.

Hamilton was first elected to Parliament in 1983, and served as MP for the Tatton constituency. Hugh had been the leading candidate for that seat, until he withdrew his name upon being selected for the much-safer seat of South-West Cambridgeshire. That, however, was not the first time that Hamilton and Hugh had come into contact with each other. Both had cut their teeth in many of the same right-wing fringe organizations in the late Seventies. But not all the same organizations. In the early Eighties, the BBC ran a program accusing Hamilton and a close buddy, Gerald Howarth, later a Conservative Defense Minister, of associating with neo-Nazi groups. The two sued for libel. One of the first to render them advice had been their old friend, Hugh Simmonds.

Hamilton was no gentleman. He did not resign immediately. He added to John Major's embarrassment by sticking it out for three long weeks. Finally, Hamilton was forced into a closed-door session with the his own Conservative Government's Chief Parliamentary Whip. Only then, did he finally agree to do the right thing, and resign. However, Hamilton did not go quietly.

His friends in the right-wing pressure group, No Turning Back, a phrase which had been a favorite war-cry of Margaret Thatcher, helped Hamilton to compose a stinging 'resignation' letter to John Major. The usual practice, whatever the circumstances, is for both resigning Minister and Prime Minister to exchange friendly and congratulatory missives.

Hamilton then announced his intention to sue *The Guardian* for libel. This court case garnered much media attention, right up to the moment it was due to go to trial, when Hamilton engaged in an embarrassing climb down, and dropped the action. Hamilton later sued al-Fayed for libel in 1999, but he lost the trial and the subsequent appeal. Hamilton had, in the Conservative electoral defeat of 1997, already lost his safe seat to a well-known BBC War Correspondent, Martin Bell, who stood as an Independent. In 2001, unable to pay legal fees and costs amounting to some £3 million, Hamilton was forced to declare bankruptcy.

Hamilton and his well-heeled friends on the right of the Party always maintained his innocence, and they weren't shy in being vocal about the fact. This kept the issue in the eye of the general public. The unwelcome media coverage that was generated was a serious thorn in Major's side, and helped severely to derail the Conservative Election Campaign in the run-up to 1997, contributing to the Party's worst electoral defeat in 150 years.

The protestations of Hamilton and his right-wing buddies might be dismissed as so much sour grapes were it not for the work of two journalists and their web-site, *GuardianLies.com*. In well-researched detail, this web-site makes the claim that the "Cash-for-Questions" affair was an invention of al-Fayed and *The Guardian*, created as a consequence of their rabid desire to see John Major removed from power.

The one surprising element of the allegations on *GuardianLies.com* is the suggestion that this conspiracy was hatched with the connivance of the London *Daily Telegraph*, a newspaper noted for its support of right-wing Tories in general, and Margaret Thatcher in particular, both before and after her ouster as Prime Minister. Why would a bastion of the right-wing be involved in such a crude attempt to remove John Major?

Dead Men Don't Eat Lunch

***

This was just the beginning of the 'sleaze' factor, which was to do so much damage to the reputation of the Conservative Government in the years leading up to the General Election of 1997. There were the two-a-penny Ministerial resignations due to peccadilloes with underage girls and research assistants. Then there were one or two more exotic departures. One Minister waved an axe at motorway campaigners. Another called the Germans "warmongers" and the French "collaborators." The resignations which garnered most press attention, however, were those that related to homosexual affairs.

Quite aside from prurient self-interest, these latter stories proved to be so newsworthy because of the suggestions of homosexual networking in the corridors of power in the British Establishment. British public schools are known to be hotbeds of early teenage homosexual experimentation. They are also the training ground for most of the British Establishment. Many do not lose their taste for the 'forbidden fruit,' even as their careers progress and marriages are entered into.

There has been much talk of an upper-class homosexual network, that is as secret and as binding as the most stringent Masonic sect, and which draws its 'membership' from the Tory elite, the upper reaches of the Civil Service and the Military, and senior officers of the Intelligence Services. Private gatherings are held at Conservative Party Conferences. Members of Parliament share information about where to hire themselves a 'bit of rough.' And it is alleged that one Conservative Cabinet Minister achieved his promotion only at the insistence of another Minister, who had been his lover at Eton.

One of the Conservative Members of Parliament who resigned his seat in 1994, after allegations of a homosexual relationship with a 20 year old student, was a good friend of Hugh's. Michael Brown and Hugh had fought the good fight side by side on the right-wing fringe of the Conservative Party in the Seventies. However, unlike Hugh, Michael Brown saw no reason to compromise either his views or his behavior to appear more palatable to the Conservative mainstream.

For many, the lasting impression of Brown will be of a slight figure advancing alone on the ranks of a Trade Union mob, protesting at a Party Conference in the Eighties. The Police did nothing to intervene, as Brown strode up and down the front-line, heckling and harassing the screaming crowd, not unlike Mel Gibson in *Braveheart*. The working-class of Great Britain, like the rural rednecks of America, admire attitude and courage. They quickly warmed to the task of answering Brown's challenges, but with increasing good humor. Eventually, Brown returned to the Conference Hall, his face split by smiles, and the cheers and applause of his philosophical

Geoffrey Gilson

opposites ringing out behind him.

***

John Major's trouble lay not only with the 'sleazy' behavior of some of his Government Ministers. The right-wing of his Party in Parliament had been in almost open rebellion since the removal of Margaret Thatcher as Prime Minister in 1990. The ostensible reason had been the breakdown of the peace negotiated over the issue of Europe back in the late Seventies by Hugh and others.

Margaret Thatcher's outburst over Europe, along with her ensuing ouster, proved to be a rallying cry for those on the right-wing of the Party. After her resignation, a slew of groups was formed, with names such as "No Turning Back" and "Conservative Way Forward." They set themselves up as the self-appointed guardians of Thatcherism, and in particular, open advocates of a newly-vocal opposition to membership of the European Union, a stance which earned its adherents the label 'Eurosceptics.'

The right-wing rebellion against John Major notched up its virulent opposition a gear or two after the unexpected Conservative election victory of 1992. Right-wing Conservative MP's had anticipated a Tory defeat, and the opportunity to choose a new, more right-wing leader. Indeed, there were some openly calling for a return to a Thatcher leadership. They were disappointed at what they saw as a lost opportunity. However, they quickly recognized the advantage that had been presented to them with the slimness of Major's winning Parliamentary majority, which had been reduced to 20.

From that point on, it seemed that, every week, the right-wing in Parliament was handing embarrassing defeats to John Major, on a host of issues, including Europe. John Major was a decent and humane Prime Minister. This proved to be a red flag to the neanderthals of the right, for whom any display of sensitivity and intelligence branded Major as a throw-back to the 'wetness' of Edward Heath.

The right-wing appeared to care nothing for the damage they inflicted on the Party's reputation with their rebellions. It got so bad that, in 1995, a former right-wing Cabinet Minister, John Redwood, challenged Major for the leadership. For a period, it looked as if the Conservative Government would implode with the second ouster of a sitting Prime Minister in less than five years. Major prevailed, but the rebellions and 'sleaze' had a permanent effect on the Conservative Party's image.

Some on the right, disappointed at the failure to remove Major from within the Conservative Party, turned their attention to efforts to achieve the same result from outside. Sir James Goldsmith, a billionaire owner of a chain of grocery stores, and a firm supporter of Margaret Thatcher, together with Alistair McAlpine, former Treasurer of the Conservative Party in the

Dead Men Don't Eat Lunch

Eighties, formed the Referendum Movement. The name was drawn from the growing demands on the right for the Government to hold a National Referendum to allow the British public to vote on whether to join the European Monetary Union, an important component of full membership of the European Union.

The attacks from the Referendum Movement added to the pressure on Major. In 1997, the Movement became the Referendum Party, and selected its own Parliamentary Candidates to stand in opposition to official Conservative Candidates in the General Election. As a consequence, a number of well-known Conservative MP's, who were in close fights, lost their seats, including David Mellor.

***

I had served with the Conservative Party for a decade. One of the primary tenets of this, the oldest Political Party in the world, was the absolute loyalty one showed to one's leaders at all time. Any differences that there may have been were always dealt with behind the scenes, with dignity and grace. This open warfare in the ranks was both ugly and self-defeating. I did not understand it.

These thoughts, however, were dramatically brought to a halt when I returned to my apartment in Atlanta one sultry summer's evening in 1993. There on my answering machine was the voice of Ari Ben-Menashe. He was in the New York offices of his publisher, and needed to speak to me as a matter of urgency. He knew the name 'Hugh Simmonds.'

Geoffrey Gilson

Chapter 20

I'VE ALWAYS BEEN NERVOUS around girls. I don't have a clue what to say to them. Of course, it never occurs to me that they're part of the same species, and have the same thoughts running through their heads. My Indian friend, Mike, tried to help me one evening in England.

He met me at the railway station in Slough, armed only with a clipboard and his ever-present smile. He wasted no time in his self-appointed role as my personal pick-up-line tutor. He began the night's seminar into the esoteric rituals of chatting up women by introducing himself to the only other person waiting at the station. A young lady – on the other side of the tracks. Literally.

I don't know whether it was charm or simple belligerence, but after the shouting was over, he had her telephone number, and an invitation to dinner the following evening. As it began, so it continued. And by the time we returned home, some four hours later, after a rapid tour of London's hotter nightspots, Mike had seventeen names and numbers on his clipboard. Lest I thought it all a game of chance, he contacted me the following day to announce that seven of them had confirmed their dinner dates.

Mike was adamant that it was all a case of confidence in oneself, rather than any unique potion of schmooze and clever language. I had improved over the ensuing few years, and as I returned to my apartment in Atlanta, that summer's evening in 1993, I was expecting just such a confirmation from a pretty girl I had spoken with a few days earlier.

However, the voice on the answering machine was that of a man. A high-pitched but gentle voice, with a sing-song cadence. It was Ari Ben-Menashe, and he wanted to speak with me immediately. So, I rang him back. As near immediately as I could. I could hear my heart beating in my ears I was so nervous. Ben-Menashe wasted little time with small talk. And I wasted little time turning on my tape-recorder:

Dead Men Don't Eat Lunch

Ben-Menashe: "After I saw your letter this weekend, I got very interested. I was with my publishers in upstate New York. We were sifting through all the letters. We called you from there. That was my first call. About your friend. I already spoke to Kevin Robinson. He was the Matrix Churchill lawyer. He represents me in the UK I spoke to some friends there. What we already came up with is that he [Hugh] was somehow connected to GEC (UK) [General Electric Company (UK): Great Britain's largest privately-owned engineering company; manufacturers of everything from warships to nuclear power stations; not to be confused with the American company of the same name]. GEC is nothing new. I testified to the [Parliamentary] Select Committee on Defense in London. The whole thing with GEC and [Gerald] Bull and the motors for the SCUD[-B] missiles came out. And your friend seems to be on some list of people who died as a result of their connection to those guys."

Geoffrey: "Are you saying that from your own knowledge, or from your belief?"

B-M: "We came up with these facts after I saw your letter."

G: "Who is we?"

B-M: "Me and the lawyer who represents me in the UK with respect to the Scott Inquiry. Kevin Robinson. He's the same lawyer that represented Matrix Churchill. When I put through your letter, he found the name on a list.

G: "On what list?"

B-M: "People connected with GEC that died. I don't want to go into details on the telephone."

G: "Are you prepared to help me?"

B-M: "Yes. I was very interested in the letter. Of course, before I commit myself totally, I'd like to look into it some more. There is a possibility that I will be in London either this weekend or the beginning of next week. As you said at the beginning of your letter, you are not a madman. Your friend's name was on this list. I wanted first to hear you out. If you don't mind, I do have some friends in the Labour Party. One person I'm going to talk to about this, because he has been investigating it, is a fellow called George Foulkes. He's a Spokesman for Defense. I have my reasons why this is a very interesting case. Let's see what I can come up with. I will probably call you next week."

I got spectacularly drunk that night. In fact, I stayed over at my brother's house, just to make sure I didn't do something stupid, like trying to get into a car. After a welter of near misses, I seemed to have something resembling a near hit on my hands.

***

Ben-Menashe got back to me somewhat sooner than he expected – just two days later. He left a message asking me to call him, and saying that he would like to meet me. I returned his call almost immediately. And again, the conversation was recorded:

B-M: "Is there a chance of getting together in Montreal next week?"

G: "Yes."

B-M: "I will be away for the first part of the week. Then, I'll be back for the weekend. I'll call you from wherever I am on Tuesday to finalize the details. Let me just tell you a little bit about what happened. I know a number of lawyers in Britain. Your friend is known. Most of them are convinced...let me give you a scenario: Guy has a Clients' Account with £5 million [$7.5 million]. He has a lot of expenses. He has a girlfriend. He runs off with the money. He's caught. Instead of facing the music, he commits suicide. Possible scenario?"

G: "Yes. Lots of problems..."

B-M: "But, that's what first comes to mind?"

G: "Yes."

B-M: "The guy is not an unknown person. In certain circles, they knew who he was. And he did live the high life. He liked traveling. But, it still doesn't add up. He was involved with a group of people who were exporting GEC motors from the UK to Iraq. That we have established already. I have spoken to somebody who knew about this involvement. Just wanted to make sure. The dates fit. Everything fits."

G: "Is this information you're going to make available to the Scott Inquiry?"

B-M: "About the Scott Inquiry. You understand that they don't have *sub-poena* powers?"

G: "Yes."

B-M: "They have powers to invite people. And they are now on a break. I have been invited officially. This goes back to the Matrix Churchill case. That's Matrix Churchill in Ohio [USA]. The people there knew me from the past. Their lawyers asked me for a copy of the pre-publication draft of my book. They then used it in their Defense [of the criminal charges in the UK against Matrix Churchill]. They didn't name it, but they used the book as the framework for the Defense. They got a few people in. And then they won the case. Lord Justice Scott knows all about this. The same lawyers that defended [Paul] Henderson are representing me. Including Geoffrey Robertson, Q.C. So, he [Scott]knows all about this. He wasn't too happy to open up the subject of Mark Thatcher. But his hand was forced. Then Mrs. [sic] Thatcher was invited to testify too. But, they might limit the scope because we have given written things about GEC and other stuff. The lawyer did a lot of work. What happened was your friend's name popped up, as soon as I mentioned it, on the GEC list. That's why I got interested. Various people will know about that bit. But again, it's going to be very hard because there was a Police Inquiry that said that the guy was bad and committed suicide. Now, usually bad guys don't commit suicide. I'm sure he was a bad guy – so was I."

G: "That's been my point exactly. If he was so 'bad,' why didn't he do a runner?"

B-M: "I have a favor to ask. Is there any way of getting in touch with the girlfriend – and not the wife?"

G: "Yes."

B-M: "Do you know where she is?"

G: "Yes."

B-M: "Is there a way of speaking to her?"

G: "If she will speak. She's a very frightened girl."

B-M: "Does the wife have money? Does she work?"

G: "She works. The girlfriend trains show-jumping horses."

B-M: "Is she on the dole [Unemployment Benefit]? What?"

G: "No. Neither of them do that. In so far as they are short of money, they are looked after by Hugh's father."

B-M: "Why am I asking these questions? Is there any trace of the £5 million [47.5 million] anywhere?"

G: "The answer to that is 'yes; and the Law Society have it'. The Law Society is sitting on it, and not telling anyone what they've found."

B-M: "How much?"

G: "I don't know. But, what I do know is that, in the course of their investigations, they discovered that Hugh had been laundering money for other people..."

B-M: "Yeah. Ok."

G: "...from 1984 on. Anything between £3 million [$4.5 million] and £100 million [$150 million]."

B-M: "Does the name Guy Lucas ring a bell? He's a lawyer in England. He's indicted right now. He was working with a couple of Indian businessmen that were working on arms sales to Iran. Indian brothers in business together in London. Now there's a civil lawsuit against them because they were involved with BCCI. The lawyer is indicted for laundering money. His name jumps up with your friend's name."

G: "I've heard of the name, but I'm not aware that Hugh knew him. You obviously know more about these matters than I do.

Dead Men Don't Eat Lunch

Do you have a definitive answer as to what was Hugh's fate, or do you just have some interesting circumstances?"

B-M: "I don't have any definitive answers yet, but we probably could get to it. But I need more information. I will know what his fate was. I will know that. If I end up thinking he just committed suicide, I'll tell you that. But it seems strange. The guy was involved with a person that was selling motors to Iraq for the SCUD missiles. They replaced the motors...the SCUD motors...the Russian ones...with GEC motors to make their range longer. The project was being co-ordinated by Gerald Bull. He's now dead. But, some of his assistants are still alive. One of them is extremely angry at the British Government because he was arrested for a while. A fellow called Dr. Cowley. He knows a bit about this stuff. Then, there was a lawyer who was dealing with the money transactions that knows your friend. An English lawyer that I spoke to."

G: "I don't know what his [Hugh's] involvement was, but I would think that he would have had some involvement with money transactions. That was his specialty when he was a tax lawyer in the Seventies. When we had a Labour Government. He designed complicated tax avoidance schemes. Now, of course, they're pretty irrelevant because the tax structure is much more lenient. As I pointed out to the Law Society's investigators, nowadays you only launder money if the money itself is illicit. They agreed. Which means that all the money Hugh was laundering was illicit."

B-M: "Quite. You aren't hiding money from the tax authorities. You're hiding it because its source is funny. Anyway, the GEC connection is very strong. There's one more comment: you don't gas yourself in a car; it's very nasty. Would you gas yourself in a car?"

G: "No. Only people who have no imagination do it that way. I couldn't sit there knowing what was happening to me. I'd get a bottle of Scotch, a few bottles of sleeping pills, a couple of my favorite videos, and do it that way."

Ben-Menashe and I then made arrangements for a meeting in Montreal. And that was the end of our first conversation. Frankly, I was too numb from input overload to know how I felt.

***

Geoffrey Gilson

Montreal is a cold city. Even in balmy September. But it's not the city that lacks warmth. It's the people. The French as a species are renowned for their rudeness. And their cousins in Montreal live up to the reputation. They seem to delight in torturing visitors by firing French at them. Only giving up when the poor victims turn red in the face from frustration.

The city itself is pleasant enough. Particularly the Historic District, down by the river. All French bunting, cobblestones and horse-drawn buggies, full of gaping tourists. Ben-Menashe owned a smart townhouse a block away from the District, and I took a taxi there straight from the airport.

Both Ben-Menashe and his wife Haya were out when I arrived late afternoon, but Ben-Menashe's mother was visiting from Israel. She was small, with prominent Semitic facial features. And she was the first friendly person I'd met since crossing the border into French Canada.

Ben-Menashe and Haya returned in the early evening, and immediately swept me away to a nearby Indian restaurant. I got the impression there were things Ari did not want to talk about in front of his mother. We sat in a quiet, candle-lit corner of the restaurant. And like all good spies, Ben-Menashe chose a seat facing the rest of the room, and with easy access to a nearby exit. Except most spies do not have a pretty wife hanging on their arm.

Ben-Menashe was small and round, and for all the world, looked like Jason Alexander, the tubby guy from the TV comedy series, *Seinfeld*. But with a head full of wavy, black hair. His voice never seemed louder than a murmured whisper, and rose and fell like a snatch of New Age music. He seemed utterly harmless. But then I remembered Hugh telling me that the best agents are those whose seeming blandness allows them to lull their opponents into a false sense of security.

Haya was petite and pretty, and in many ways, reminded me of Julia Louis-Dreyfuss, also from *Seinfeld*. I had Jerry's whiny voice and mop of curly hair. If the waiter had looked like Kramer, we'd have had the whole cast gathered around that table, in a small Indian restaurant in Montreal.

I should have been nervous. In fact, at first I was expecting to be clobbered over the head, and dragged off to some warehouse on the river, there to be interrogated until the last breath left my body. But, it was a little difficult to be scared sitting opposite 'George' and 'Ellen.' Particularly since Ben-Menashe's 'George' had such a delightfully impish sense of humor.

The scene was made that much more surreal when the conversation turned to serious matters. There we were chatting about life, death and international arms sales as casually as the *Seinfeld* ensemble would talk about a clogged toilet, while having breakfast in the neighborhood diner.

At first, Ben-Menashe stuck to peripheral issues. I think he was feeling me out. However, one or two interesting things did crop up:

He mentioned that he had been in England, and that he had asked around about Hugh, to find out how well known he was. Ted Heath [former Conservative British Prime Minister] had indicated that he knew him, but had only bad things to say. Something along the lines of: "I knew that shit would always end like that." Heath had never forgiven Hugh for the fight over Ronald Bell, and his strident stance against a Federal Europe. I was intrigued that Ben-Menashe had managed to discover this nuance of Hugh's standing within the upper reaches of the Conservative Party.

Ben-Menashe mused at length, and with no apparent purpose, about the activities of the Conservative Government in general. How under Thatcher, and now Major, it seemed continually to be following a pro-Arab, anti-Israel line. Ben-Menashe "and others" were worried about where this might all lead. In particular, they were concerned about who might succeed Major as figures of power in the Conservative Party and Government.

The subject of David Mellor [John Major's chief political ally] arose. After a bout or two of conversational aerobics, Ben-Menashe admitted that Mellor had been set up in an Israeli-sponsored sting. Mellor was considered to be much too close to the Palestinians, and the Israelis were terrified that he might become the next Conservative Prime Minister. Besides, Ari added with a wink, Paul Halloran was way upset that Mellor had cut him out of a lucrative arms deal.

These last utterances tempered my earlier favorable impression of the political savvy of Ben-Menashe and his friends. Anyone who knew anything about British politics at that time knew that Mellor was a clown, a lightweight. He'd struck lucky by backing Major early in his ambition to be Leader of the Conservative Party. But Mellor had about as much chance of being Prime Minister as the Devil had of taking up permanent residence in a shady suburb of Heaven.

Ari and his friends apparently saw Hugh in much the same light as Mellor: a fast-riser in the Party, and someone who was not unduly friendly towards the Israelis. Ben-Menashe also stated that it was well-known that Hugh was close to Thatcher. In many different ways, Ben-Menashe added, enigmatically.

At this point, Ben-Menashe abruptly changed subjects. He mentioned that Hugh was on good terms with Nick Davies, and claimed that Hugh, Davies and Robert Maxwell [late billionaire British publisher] met regularly in Maxwell's office atop the *Daily Mirror* headquarters in High Holborn. Apropos of nothing at all, Ben-Menashe further confirmed that the CIA had killed Maxwell. It would not be the last time that Ben-Menashe adopted a position that seemed designed to protect Israeli interests.

I confess I was beginning to like Ari. He was a charming host, a friendly chap, and had an attractive wife gracing the space beside him. What was not to like? Besides, I have an affinity for rogues. And Ari was clearly one of those. However, for all his entertainment value, I had no reason to trust Ari further than I could throw him. And so I took much of what he was saying with a massive grain of salt.

In particular, I remained intrigued by Ari's clandestine support of Israel's point of view. Sure, Ari would regularly criticize Israel. He would state with finality that there would never be peace in the Middle East, because Israel did not want peace, it wanted victory. And yet, Ari was careful always to deflect the more serious charges about Israel's covert activities away from its Intelligence Services – his former employers. And thus it was the CIA, not Mossad, that had killed Maxwell.

Then again. Just when a listener might believe that Ari had over-reached credulity, he would softly toss away a morsel of information that had about it an uncanny ring of truth. Little scraps that could only be known by someone who was truly connected.

Hugh was not a great TV watcher. He liked to read, and preferred that his children did the same. However, I hate to read, and would rather that someone else spoon feed me my input. Preferably inconsequential mush. So it was that I found myself one evening with Hugh's kids, watching a program, where the host guided us around a fancy room, and we had to guess to whom it belonged.

The room on this occasion was a vast office, in chrome, grey and black. Money and hi-tech screamed from every surface. From the electronic window blinds, to the thick shag on the floor. From the bank of TV screens arrayed behind the desk, to the multitude of expensive communication toys lined up around the edges of the same desk.

Hugh had been in another part of his home. Halfway through the program, he wandered in, fixed himself a scotch, glanced at the TV screen and, on his way out, stated casually, "oh, that's Robert Maxwell's office." I couldn't for the life of me think what Hugh would be doing with a staunch supporter of the Labour Party. Clearly, arms-dealing and money-laundering easily crossed political boundaries.

Ari offered no further information about the relationship between Maxwell and Hugh. At least not on this occasion. In fact, we were just about done for the evening. On his way to driving me to a nearby hotel, however, Ari did mention that Hugh's girlfriend knew all about his arms-dealing activities.

***

Bright and early the following morning, I caught a taxi to Ari's townhouse. Haya and Ari's mother had gone shopping, leaving us alone to talk further. The townhouse itself was expensive and elegant. Obviously, Ari had done well from his clandestine endeavors in the Eighties. However, for all its luxury, Ari's home felt unlived in: white leather furniture and chrome tables, but no homely knick-knacks or family photos.

Again, Ari wasted no time in getting down to business. He dove straight in on the subject of Mark Thatcher. Ari told me that he and "others" had been trying to nail Mark Thatcher for some time for his involvement in arms sales to Iraq. The impression I gained was that they were less interested in Mark than his Mother. All that they had lacked was proof, in the form of the money trail. And I had, unwittingly, supplied that.

Examination by Ari and the "others" of Hugh's activities and interests, even an admittedly cursory one, had revealed that he was a business partner of Mark Thatcher's; that the business was arms sales to Iraq; and that Hugh was responsible for laundering the proceeds back to Thatcher in Texas. Ari and his "friends" had been in possession of Hugh's name for some time (a list, once again, was mentioned; I did not find out whether it was the same one or not), but they had not considered pursuing a possible connection until I turned up on the scene with my information.

I was curious as to who "others" and "friends" were. I raised this with Ari. I said that, on the one hand, I found it difficult to believe that it could be the Israelis, after they left him to rot in an American jail for a year. Yet, on the other hand, the agenda he seemed to be pursuing bore all the hallmarks of one the right-wingers in Israeli Intelligence might want a 'rogue stooge' to pursue, if they were so inclined. Indeed, exactly the sort of shenanigans Ostrovsky had been drafted by the left-wing, as their 'loose cannon,' to thwart.

Ari's retort was a model of enigma. With a wry smile, he said, "'They' got pissed off at me because my revelations [about Bush Senior and his SSG/CPPG] removed their ability to blackmail Bush. I'm trying to make 'them' less pissed off at me." He was, however, still unwilling to be drawn on the identity of 'they' or 'them.'

We quickly returned to the subject of Hugh and money. Ari alleged that, in addition to sending the arms sales' proceeds to Texas, Hugh had also sent the money stolen from his Clients' Account. The money had gone by a roundabout route, which included a Trust Account in Jersey, some lawyer in Bermuda, and another lawyer by the name of Rebecca Parsons. She resided either in Reading, England or in Dallas, Texas. Ari was fuzzy on this point. But he was crystal clear about the fact that Rebecca had had an affair with Hugh.

Rebecca had also acted for Mark Thatcher, and was known to his sister, Carol. Ari didn't say what happened to the affair, but he did say that, at one point, Hugh had tried to get his money back from Rebecca and she had refused to return it. This, Ari claimed, somewhat confusing me, may have been why Hugh had committed suicide.

In the middle of his presentation, Ari was called away to the telephone. When he came back, he looked rather baffled. "Do you know someone called Peter Smith?" he asked.

"Why yes," I responded, unsuspecting. "He was a good friend of Hugh's, and one of the Trustees of his Will – before he revoked. Why do you ask?"

"Can you think of any reason why he would have just rung me, and told me not to speak with you, because you are a crook? Come to think of it, can you think of any reason why he would have my telephone number, and how he would know that I am talking to you?"

I was equally baffled, and told Ari so. Then, a thought struck me. I shared it with Ari. Peter was, in the Eighties, a Senior Partner with Coopers and Lybrand. One of his assignments was to oversee the Annual Audit of the Conservative Party's national accounts. Could that have anything to do with it? "He sounded quite scared", was Ari's only reply. Curiouser and curiouser.

After this intervention, Ari seemed rather agitated, and he quite quickly brought the session to an end. He said he would need more time to make further inquiries, and asked if I would, in the meantime, suspend my own investigation so that we would not be stepping on each other's toes. As he bade me farewell at the front door, Ari, looking quite distracted, mumbled something about being in touch within a couple of weeks to report on progress.

***

I left Ari's townhouse and Montreal with my head spinning from the new directions then appearing in my investigation. Whether as a renegade, or acting as a deep 'sleeper' for Israeli Intelligence, Ari's allegations about interference in Britain's political affairs were startling, to say the least. Little did I realize that I was about to be startled even more by the unlikeliest of Ghosts from my own mis-spent Past. Apparently, Mossad wasn't the only intelligence service messing about in Britain's political waters.

Chapter 21

By THE AUTUMN OF 1993, I hadn't had a proper vacation in something like six years. I was pondering this sad fact when who should telephone me but my old buddy in crime, Mark Saunders. He didn't mess around with much small talk. Got straight to the point. Would I like to join him for ten days of sun-drenched bacchanalia in Palm Beach, Florida?

"What's the catch?" was my suspicious response. Mark said he had something he had to talk to me about, which he couldn't share over the telephone. What the heck. No-one needed to break my arm twice to persuade me that I wanted sun, fun – and alcohol. I made my excuses with my brother, and caught the next flight to South Florida.

The flavor of the expedition was established when Mark picked me up from the airport in a rented Cadillac convertible. The mood, however, was almost immediately spoiled when Mark panicked as we drove through a less than salubrious neighborhood. Mark was convinced we were about to be attacked by a mob of rioters.

There is nothing quite so undignified as two Englishmen driving along at 60 miles an hour, trying to raise an automatic convertible roof at the same time. As is my wont, a wholly inappropriate song title leapt into my mind: something about "Hood in the Hood."

After this excitement, we did what would become our anthem for the next ten days – we adjourned to a nearby bar. Mark was in no mood to get down to business, and I was none too ready to push him. Certainly not after a glass or six of frozen white wine. Instead, Mark took me on a tour of Palm Beach.

A small island, off the East Coast of South Florida, Palm Beach was established as a playground for the seriously rich at the beginning of the last Century, by one Henry Flagler, an oil and railroad magnate. The money is generally old, although troubled times make for strange bedfellows, and in recent years, the bluebloods and blue rinses allowed Donald Trump to buy one of the larger houses, and convert it into a Country Club.

Although you have to be rich to live on the island, you only have to pretend to be wealthy to be able to play in the clubs and shops along Ocean Drive. With our English accents, Mark and I did a passing good impression of grace and flavor, as we floated hither and thither on our regularly-refueled liquid cushion.

Life became a blur of sun and sea, bronzed limbs – and alcohol. A passing glimpse of Mediterranean-style villas, high security fences and white sand. And then back to loud nights; bright lights; dark, salty smells - and yet more alcohol.

Autumn is the start of the Palm Beach 'season.' While the rest of America heads towards wintry cold, South Florida averages daily temperatures in the seventies. Many of the famous local bars only open during this 'season.' And Mark insisted on taking me one evening to the most famous – the "Au" Bar. This is the Bar that was made famous as the spot where Ted Kennedy's nephew picked up the girl he was later acquitted of raping.

I couldn't work out what the fuss was about. The place appeared to be smaller than my apartment. It was so dark that I'm surprised the nephew even knew who he was picking up. And the whole place smelt like his Uncle Ted's underwear. The effect was made even more cramped by a huge U-shaped bar, occupying half of the middle of the room, and the fact that the beautiful people were packed like sardines.

Mark abandoned me about three rows back from the bar, with the instruction to get all the drinks we would need in that one visit. I found myself surrounded by tall, luscious women, not one of whom seemed the slightest bit interested in the midget in the whites, with the horny smile plastered all over his face.

Until. All of a sudden. They were interested. First, the dark-skinned beauty, on my left, nudged me gently, smiled down at me and asked how I was doing. I say 'asked.' I mean yelled. As in, the music was way too loud to do anything but either yell or mouth. And we weren't that intimate just yet.

I grinned foolishly, and screamed something unintelligible, which she condescended to find extremely amusing. Then, her statuesque blond twin, on my right, moved slightly in front of me, leaned down, and whispered something husky and fragrant into my ear, and all over my face. Again, I say 'husky.' For all I could hear, she could have been reciting the entirety of the United States Constitution, in a gravelly Long Island drawl. But tell that to the effect it was having on my trousers.

I had been trying gamely for many minutes to catch the attention of one of the fast-moving bartenders. With no luck. I had grabbed a couple of paper napkins and was about to give an amateurish rendition of naval flag signaling, when two of the blighters suddenly appeared in front of me, like magnets around a chunk of iron.

It was as if the seas parted. I found an immediate path to the bar, the girls firmly attached to my sides. The music itself seemed to dim, since I heard the bartenders perfectly. Almost in unison , they wondered what I would like, with two of the largest smiles I've seen this side of a Neiman Marcus 99% Off Sale.

It was at about this moment that intelligence caught up with innate arrogance, and I realized that I hadn't suddenly become Brad Pitt. I looked around, and there, at the other end of the bar, was Mark, in fits of laughter, talking to yet another bartender.

I gently pried myself loose from the obviously welcome attention, and made my way over to Mark, accepting, as I went, all the further indications of warm welcome yet to come. Once by his side, and maintaining a dignified smile, I wondered crisply what was going on. "Oh nothing," was Mark's retort, "just that I dropped the gentle hint that you were Princess Diana's second cousin, the Duke of Marlow, and you really would appreciate being left alone…"

I got angry. I got quiet. He looked at me expectantly. I looked back blankly. I shrugged my shoulders. Then I straightened them. And finally, I loudly ordered the hovering bartender to get me another glass of wine, in my best British upper-crust. I raised my glass to the room. There was a smattering of applause, and I headed back to the twins.

***

It was only as I awoke the following morning that I realized we were not staying in a grand hotel. Rather we were ensconced in a very seedy motel, the name of which is long forgotten; itself in a very seedy part of West Palm Beach. The latter is the town that Flagler built on the mainland of Florida, opposite the island of Palm Beach, where he and his buddies hid their servants and workers.

The motel was a one-story affair. Three wings of fading pink stucco and brick arches, wrapped around a small swimming pool of brackish-green water. The steaming smell of rot came either from the water, or from the not-too-clean bed linen. Or perhaps, from the elderly live-in residents, who spent most of their days sitting in front of their motel rooms, in various stages of undress and dirty underwear.

I lay fully-clothed on top of my lumpy bed. I cracked open an eyelid, and rubbed away the night's crust. Mark was hunched over a makeshift desk, sorting out some papers. Without turning around, he stated way too loudly that it was time to get up. "Today's the day you earn your keep," he declared happily.

Geoffrey Gilson

I grabbed a shower, and threw on some rough, cool clothes. We made our way to a deserted part of one of the municipal beaches. Once there, Mark reached into his briefcase, and withdrew a couple of sheets of paper, "What do you make of them?" he wondered, warily.

The sheets were covered with a typed transcript of what appeared to be a private conversation between Princess Diana and Prince Charles. Underneath each line of typing were regularly-spaced groups of six numbers. My head became very clear, very quickly. I affected nonchalance, and handed them back. "I dunno," I muttered, "what do you think?"

Mark looked at me for a couple of seconds, and then sighed. "Here's the deal, mate," he began. Apparently, Mark had been having some luck with his Royal Paparazzi stint since I'd last seen him. He'd moved up in the world, and was now regularly supplying national tabloids with both photographs and stories. He'd become quite friendly with one James Whittaker, who was the Royal Correspondent of the *Daily Mirror*, and was one of Diana's favorites.

The transcript Mark had shown me was, indeed, of a conversation between the Princess and Prince, at their country home, Highbury Grove. Without saying how he had come across the transcript, Mark gave me copies of the front page articles that *The People*, a sister tabloid of the *Mirror*, had run in January of 1993. It was the usual faked shock-and-horror drivel about 'oh my God, the Government are bugging the Royals.'

But I scanned the articles more carefully, looking for the tell-tale nuggets. I hadn't been doing the 'investigation thing' for nigh on six years for naught. As I scanned, I spoke my thoughts out loud, in no particular order.

I told Mark that the alleged bugging bore all the hallmarks of being the work of an intelligence agency. However, I added, that did not necessarily mean that the agency was a British one, or, if it was, that it was operating at the behest of the British Government. 'British Intelligence' did not automatically mean 'British Government.'

British Intelligence was founded at the beginning of the Twentieth Century as a past-time for well-bred gentlemen. Those blue-bloods believed their first loyalty was to the Crown, and not necessarily to the elected Government. "Which," I mused gently, "makes this sort of behavior all the more strange."

Little half-pictures began to form in my mind. The articles said that the Government had denied that MI5 or GCHQ (the English equivalent of America's NSA – its electronic intelligence gathering entity) had eavesdropped on any Royals. The transcripts had been rescued from DI (Discarded Intelligence) at GCHQ. And the transcripts themselves were highly damaging to the Princess, and none too flattering of the Prince.

Dead Men Don't Eat Lunch

The whole world had been made privy to Diana's inner feelings, as a consequence of the bestselling book by Andrew Morton (*Diana: Her True Story*). The scenario that had been painted was of a tender, misled young girl, cruelly abandoned by an older and overbearing cad, who spent his time running around with a former girlfriend., who had the face of an undernourished horse. The transcripts, in contrast, portrayed the Prince as a decent soul, trying his best to care for the children, in the face of a screaming bitch, who cared only for herself.

I put the articles to one side, and drank deeply from a now warm can of Coke that had been scrunched into the sand next to where I was sitting. I gazed out over the clear, still blue sea, and spent some time watching a pelican go through its endless ritual of hover and dive, hover and dive. Without, of course, catching any fish. It seemed to me that the sea teased us both, with the faintest trace of fishy odor. Far away, a cruise ship let out a joyous 'whoop' on its horn, as it disappeared slowly over the horizon.

Without looking at Mark, I invited him to tell me exactly how he had come across the transcripts. Mark paused, and after a second or two, let out a long sigh. He had been 'cultivating' an Intelligence source, whom he called "Peter."

"And how did you come across this source?" I asked.

"Actually," Mark replied, "he rang me." It was my turn to sigh, but I did so inwardly, being careful that my facial expression did not change.

Anyway, Mark continued, this source and he had been talking for a couple of months, when a meeting was arranged, and the source gave Mark the transcripts. There were now only four copies in existence, outside of the Intelligence Services: one with the Editor of *The People*; one with James Whittaker; one with Mark; and…um…one that Mark was instructed to give to me. I looked over at Mark sharply. He blushed. Opened his briefcase, and gave me my copy.

"Where," I asked, "was the meeting?"

"Washington, D.C.," Mark responded.

"So," I continued, "how did you know that the transcripts came from GCHQ?"

"Because that's where "Peter" said they came from." Mark explained that it was Peter's job to shred DI, but that he had specially saved this transcript.

"Did you pay him?" I asked.

"No."

"Why not?"

"Because he didn't want money. "

"Then, what did he want?"

Again a pause. Again a sigh.

British Intelligence, explained Mark, had become personally involved in the feud between the Prince and the Princess. Sides had been taken. Both sides engaged in activity to undermine the other side's pet Royal.

"There was none of this in your articles," I snapped. "All you say is that MI5 regularly bug the Royal residences as a security precaution. So that they have early warning of any unfriendly intrusion."

"Quite," said Mark, "that's why I came to see you." I had told Mark all about my investigation, and he had thought that I might be able to help his newspaper with a problem they were having.

"Which is."

"We think "Peter" may be a plant."

I turned around very slowly, and stared Mark full in the face, "You think?" He had the good grace to go bright red.

I took it from the top. First, the numbers were not what the newspaper had described them as being. They were not code for identifying speech patterns. They were standard Transatlantic Six-Group Intelligence Encoding – what I had been told was the preferred code of the NSA.

Secondly, there had been since 1949 an agreement between British and American Intelligence Services, called the UKUSA Treaty. It allowed both Intelligence Services to circumvent their own countries' restrictions on domestic bugging.

The NSA bugged Britain, from listening posts on US Air Force Bases; sent the product back to America in encoded form; and then released it to the Brits on American soil. And the Brits did the same in reverse with GCHQ, using listening facilities in Canada. This was, of course, before the advent of communications satellites.

The British Government had been telling the truth when it said that GCHQ and MI5 had not been eavesdropping on the Royals. It had been the Americans. And George Bush the Second was telling the truth when, in 2006, he said that the US Government did not listen to American citizens. The British did it for them. And in all probability, the NSA were correct when, later in 2006, they denied bugging the Princess of Wales' cellphone on the day of her death. It had probably been either the French or the Israelis.

But the question journalists should have been asking, I said to Mark acidly, was not why an Intelligence Service (either British Intelligence, or some other agency acting as its surrogate) would be bugging the Royals; but rather, why they were recording the conversations; and then releasing them to the media? The upshot of all of this 'revelation' was that the Royals were, slowly but surely, dying the death of a thousand embarrassing cuts. What would British Intelligence have to gain from embarrassing its own Royal Family?

Mark was speechless. A little more gently, I asked him what Peter was doing in Washington. Mark sheepishly responded that he was actually an Intelligence Officer attached to the British Embassy there

"So, he wasn't anything to do with GCHQ?"

"No."

It was my turn, once again, to sigh. But this time, quite openly.

I wondered aloud if anyone had thought to confirm "Peter's" output?

"Oh yes," came Mark's excited reply, "we have another source called "David"."

"And how did you come across David?" I asked, knowing the answer even before it was given.

"Oh, "Peter" suggested him…" Mark's voice trailed off.

Mark wanted me to speak with Peter and confirm his *bona fides*. I had no problem with talking to a purported Intelligence Officer. I just wasn't keen on Mark's script. He wanted me to pretend to be an Intelligence Officer myself, and glean information on the buddy-buddy principle. I knew I didn't have much credibility, but I was not about to render into tatters what little I did have on such a hare-brained scheme. I told Mark as much.

Instead, I offered to put "Peter" in a situation where he would have to establish his own *bona fides*. Plus, give a little leg up to my own investigation. I would ask "Peter" to provide me with information about Hugh's Intelligence activities. Under the brutal terms of Britain's Official Secrets Act, "Peter" would be exposing himself to a considerable prison sentence by complying with my request. But he would also establish irredeemable good faith with Mark's newspapers. On the other hand, if "Peter" refused even to try, he would in all probability expose himself as a stooge.

Mark was not convinced. He wondered where the story would be. Again I sighed. And again I tried. I ran Mark through the last couple of years of my investigation, and set out what I believed I had discovered to be a pattern, linking all the troubles then besetting various public institutions in Great Britain.

***

As part of my investigation, I had come across information describing how certain Intelligence Services, in particular Britain's and America's, were well versed in Destabilization Techniques, which they used when combating insurgencies.

If you wanted to impose order in a situation that was unfriendly to you, first you undermined the processes and institutions from which the 'unfriendly' people drew strength. Then, in the ensuing confusion, you imposed your own 'order.'

America had used the techniques to great effect in destroying the village structure in Vietnam. They had moved whole villages to new compounds, where the residents were less susceptible to the ministrations of their village leaders and the Viet Cong.

On the face of it, there did not seem to be any pattern to the troubles then befalling the Royal Family, the British Government and the Church of England, until one noticed that the sources of the 'trouble' were almost always the same: right-wing Tories; British Intelligence; or right-wing newspapers. And that they all had one thing in common: they loved Margaret Thatcher. And that the 'troubles' had only begun in earnest when Mrs. T had been uprooted unceremoniously from 10 Downing Street.

Britain is a country that is wide open to Destabilization Techniques. It has no Constitution, no Rules as such. All the processes of public life and government are, for the most part, operated on the basis of understandings and agreements: 'Gentlemen's Rules,' in effect. These 'Conventions,' as they are more properly known, only continue to work if those Public Institutions which are privy to their understanding and operation continue to maintain the confidence and trust of the people over whom they hold sway.

So, in Britain, you don't need anything approaching a Revolution or a massive Covert Psychological Operation to undermine written Constitutions and embedded Judiciaries. You just need to embarrass a few people, who represent the leading Public Institutions.

I reminded Mark of what had been happening to the Royal Family over the previous few years. John Major's Government was fast becoming a laughing stock. And the Anglican Church was just beginning its path towards irreparable schism over the emotional issues of women priests and homosexuality.

Most of the 'dirt' had first been published in newspapers belonging either to Rupert Murdoch or to Conrad (now Lord) Black. Neither were native Brits: the first, a dispossessed Australian, who took American citizenship so that he could buy US TV stations; the other, a dispossessed Canadian, who had taken British citizenship so that he could garner a Peerage (in which ambition, he had proven more successful than fellow media cowboys Maxwell and al-Fayed). Murdoch and Black also had in common the fact that they competed heavily for the title of 'Media Baron Most Loved By Margaret Thatcher.'

Murdoch is the better known of the two. He has a media empire that spans three continents, and includes all manner of newspapers in Australia; *Fox* and the *New York Post* in America; and satellite television and newspapers in England, the latter including the stately London *Times*, and the somewhat more trashy *Sun* daily tabloid. Murdoch's right-leaning *Fox*

Dead Men Don't Eat Lunch

TV network, slavishly adores all things Bush, while the first stories about Bill Clinton and Gennifer Flowers appeared in the *New York Post*, back in 1992.

Conrad Black's media vehicle, Hollinger International, has been embroiled in controversy in recent years. Black had to resign as Chairman at the end of 2004, accused by shareholders of milking some $70 million for the personal use of himself and other Board Members. Before this turn of events, however, Black had built up Hollinger into one of the globe's most successful media holding companies.

Hollinger still dominates the Canadian market. And in 1992, Black, a confirmed Anglophile like Maxwell and al-Fayed, bought London's venerable and right-leaning *Daily Telegraph*. Over the years, Black had shown himself an avid supporter of Israel, where Hollinger continues to own the *Jerusalem Post*, the *Jerusalem Report*, the *Shaar Lamatchil*, *This Week in Israel*, the *Student Post* and the *Christian Jerusalem Post.* Hollinger has strong links to the US in the form of its major investment in the *Chicago-Sun Times*, and in the person of Henry Kissinger, who is a Board Member.

The millionaire Barclay Brothers of London stepped in to take over the helm of the Hollinger Empire when Black finally jumped ship. The only major experience the Barclays had previously had in media was with the ill-fated *European*, which they bought in 1992 from the Receivers of the equally ill-fated Maxwell Estate.

Between them, the *Daily Telegraph*, the *Times* and the *Sun* had fallen over themselves to chronicle the misfortunes of the Royals, John Major and the Anglican Brethren. Right-wing Conservatives MP's, and their allies in other newly-formed political pressure groups, had delighted in causing as much pain as possible to John Major. Well-known Tories were at the forefront of moves by the conservative Anglo-Catholic faction in the Church of England to foment a split over sex and gender. And Mark had just spent the best part of a day's drinking time explaining how British Intelligence were embarrassing the Royal Family. While all of this was going on, even *The Economist*, that most staid and understated of Britain's weekly journals, ran an article wondering if moves were afoot to bring Margaret Thatcher back to power.

I wondered disingenuously whether Mark had heard anything in Britain's journalistic community about patterns such as these? Mark was all at sea. Or maybe he was just looking at the sea. Or possibly trying to spell it. In any event, he had no time for my ruminations. I believe he was upset I wouldn't play the fool for him with "Peter." And he still wanted to know where the story was…

Sighing was becoming a regular part of our communication now. We both took five, and looked achingly at the same pelican, wondering painfully if we might somehow find all of our answers in its fruitless fish-diving. Then, soundlessly, we gathered our belongings and agreed to spend the rest of the holiday just drinking and partying. I poured myself onto a plane a few days later. In hindsight, I think I got the better part of the bargain.

***

Back in Atlanta, I resumed the excursions to my favorite watering hole. But the starting time for drinking was beginning to crawl out of the dark depths of the middle evening, and into the dangerous light of the early afternoon.

Van Gogh's was a safe haven. Whatever the trouble at work or in my personal life or with the investigation, I had only to enter the plush paneled interior of this luxurious restaurant and bar, and all my cares just slipped away.

On a day shortly after my adventures with Ari and Mark, I arrived at *Van Gogh's* somewhat later than was becoming normal for me – at about 7.00pm. I had had only one glass of wine all day. I sat at the bar chatting to the bartender Patrick, and worked my way through another two. As I was drinking, I loudly announced, to myself as much as to anyone else, that I would be leaving after the second drink. Definitely.

Without much effort, Patrick persuaded me into a third. I clearly remember drinking about two sips. I clearly remember the level of the wine in the glass. I clearly remember being unaffected because, in that way that drunks have of adapting their speech so as not to sound drunk, I knew I was not consciously having to change my speech pattern.

At this point, Patrick and his boss, Chris, take over the story. Patrick suddenly noticed that I was not talking any more. He turned around, to find me collapsed on the bar top, my face white as a sheet. He called Chris from the back, and Chris and a waiter bundled me into a car, and took me to the Emergency Room.

Chris later told me that he was convinced I was on drugs, because he and Patrick knew enough about my drinking habits to know for sure that I had not passed out from alcohol. In fact, Patrick repeatedly said that I was way too chatty to be drunk. Apparently I then said something half-way intelligent in response to one of Chris's enquiries, because he decided not to take me into the hospital, but instead, to ask a mutual friend, Tom, to take me home.

I was conscious of leaning against the balustrade outside the door to my first floor apartment. I saw Tom, shortly before I passed out again. Either I passed out after I hit the concrete balcony, or the other way around. Whatever the case, I ended up being taken to the Hospital by Tom after all.

Dead Men Don't Eat Lunch

Tom kindly stuck around. I know this, because he was the first person I saw in the Emergency Room when I woke up. I was later told that this was about 9.00p.m. The next thing I saw was a needle advancing towards my eye. I yelled out. However scared I might have been, it was nothing compared to the reaction of the female Doctor upon being assailed with my wail.

The good Doctor assured me that she was only stitching up my eyebrow, and that, no, I would not be needing an anesthetic. I think I detected a note of sarcasm in her voice when she explained that I had quite enough pain killer in me already.

Either then or later, I can't remember which, I was told that my Blood Alcohol level was 0.38, which any serious drinker will know is pretty high. The legal limit is 0.08. And after about 0.40, they start pulling out the paperwork to register you as clinically dead. The lady Doctor kept bringing in people to see me. She explained that this was because the medical staff had never seen a 0.38 before, let alone one who was conscious – and coherent.

Tom drove me home at about 11.30pm. At which point, my internal biological meters started doing all sorts of weird things. They were insistent that, as always, I needed to be drunk before I could go to sleep. But, I remonstrated verbally and loudly, I'd just been declared near dead from alcohol. How much more did I need? We don't care, they shot back; you're sober, so get drunk. Which I did, by imbibing another bottle and a half of really shoddy white wine.

As I lay on the floor in my sun room, my face an inch from my favorite Ficus tree, I gently wondered what the good lady doctor would make of all this. What would my blood be registering now? And who on earth could be telephoning me this late in the evening?

Geoffrey Gilson

Chapter 22

I LEARNED ADVANCED survival skills at an early age. My mother was an alcoholic, and my father was an absentee father, for most of my formative middle years. This was not normal.

As a good friend put it to me, when you go to school and are told that the sky being blue is 'normal,' and then you go home, and are told that the sky is red, you draw into yourself, and develop survival mechanisms to defend against the abnormal, and to make yourself feel safe. I developed the mother of all survival mechanisms.

I would play on my own, and build fantasy worlds, the better to keep reality at bay. I would talk to myself. Loudly. To keep my own thoughts at bay. I became obsessively tidy. I still am. Ask anyone who has lived with me. A good room-mate, Geer, had a girlfriend who did not believe I could be more obsessive-compulsive than him.

I arrived home to find them grinning stupidly on the couch. I thought I had caught them *in flagrante*. Until I hit the bathroom. According to Geer, he counted the seconds out loud until I burst out of the bathroom. "What's the matter?" was his innocent question. "Oh very funny," I replied, "so who's idea was it to move my glasses, turn my toothbrush upside down, and leave my toilet roll hanging one sheet down? Huh?" Geer was in fits of laughter. His girlfriend sat there with her mouth hanging open.

But this was tame stuff compared to the task of managing the wider world, so that it could not hurt me. And so that I would not have to deal with my feelings. I learned to manipulate, to cheat, to lie, to steal; to break all of the rules, all of the time; to do whatever it took to create around me a safe barrier, that presented to the world only the façade I wished it to see.

And I wanted the world to see me as a clown and a hero. As someone who was both stoic and fun; caring, yet serious. The good guy. The nice guy. The angel. That sweet boy. Yet, I knew within myself that this was entirely at odds with the demons that lurked within, ready to strike in order to survive.

Curiously, many of these survival traits have proved quite useful, in a positive way, in the various occupations that I've pursued. With my heightened sensitivity to my social environment, and my innate 'tidiness,' I am able quickly to get to the height of most situations presented to me. Whether it's a business problem, a legal matter, a political scandal or an acting role. Indeed, it is this same craving for 'tidiness' which has fuelled my investigation into Hugh's death.

My 'skills' at manipulation and control allow me quite expeditiously to find a solution or understanding, even if it means 'bending' the rules. And then, I have little problem with presentation: be it spin from a political platform, an address before an administrative judge, a marketing seminar, or the role of Uncle Max in *The Sound of Music*. And again, this 'talent' for seeing or creating 'patterns' has been of inestimable assistance in the writing of this book. But. However much 'good' may have come from my dysfunction, it has always been accompanied by the 'bad.'

My father, who did not talk to me for a decade, says that I have always lied. Always. My whole life. He is right. I battle every day to try and stop. But reality is so full of fear. My kid brother, the same Jon with whom also I do not now speak, once said that I believed the world owed me a living. He too was right. The world does owe me a living. Lighten up. It was a joke. But seriously, I fight against this feeling every single day as well. Like any addiction, it can only be taken one day at a time.

When I finally achieved drinking age, I discovered the joy of alcohol. It allowed me respite from the battle in my psyche; the dichotomy between my angelic exterior, and the turbulent interior. Somehow, this construct stayed in place for the best part of twenty five years. Until the Summer of 1994.

I don't remember what was the final trigger. I know things were not going well with my brother's company, and that there was the real possibility that I would have to start all over again, at something else. And then, one day, the thought was there, sitting like a cancer in my mind: I really couldn't face starting over again. I'd just as soon end this life; and get on with the next incarnation as soon as possible. Thank you very much.

Later I was told this was a 'nervous breakdown.' Oh, you think? Quickly it developed into 'chronic alcoholism.' No-one ever defined for me the distinction between being an ordinary drunk and a chronic drunk. I took the view that the threshold for me was waking up one morning, fully dressed, underneath my bed, cuddling an empty bottle of Scotch. With my first thought being that I would enjoy a crisp *Sancerre* from the Loire Valley with my breakfast of scrambled eggs and hurl.

Geoffrey Gilson

My brother Jon was wonderful. We talked about Rehab. We discussed it with my mother. We all three decided that the best plan was for me to go to Michigan, where my mother lived; do Rehab at a very good local clinic; and then do post-Rehab with her. She no longer drank.

Jon would cover for me within the company. More than that, and for reasons I will never understand, he essentially agreed to allow me a leave of absence over the Summer, to have one last, long drunk before cleaning up.

And drunk I got. And long it lasted. Usually through most of each night. Once or twice I tried to get clean on my own, only to come face to face with the suicidal thoughts. And back to the bottle I went.

Most of my time was engaged quite uselessly, but pleasantly, in the local *Hooters*. To this day, I will not hear a word against a *Hooters* girl. They looked after me. They fed me. And they drove me around. They kept me alive. And I owe them my life.

There were many, but in particular, I will never forget Dawn, Nicky, Melita, Stacey, Angel, Brandy, and Courtney. The first and last were both of Cherokee descent. Someone, somewhere once said that you marry a girl who looks like your mother. Both my mother and my twin sister had Slavic high cheekbones, dark skin and dark hair, looks which in many ways duplicate the features of Native Americans. Go figure.

In any event, there were many wild adventures, which I'm sorry to say will have to form the basis of another book. Yet, however awful it got, and however unruly I became, there was always one of the girls there to make sure I did not hurt myself, and to ensure I got home safely.

They threw a party for me on the day before I left. I spent that evening with my brother, just to be sure I did not go missing. The next day, as Jon drove me to the airport, I was scared stiff of what was to come. For one brief moment, however, the terror was placed on hold as we drove past the neon sign, outside *Hooters*, wishing me luck. The girls had put it up last thing the previous night, to be sure that I would see it first thing in the morning.

***

The person who had been telephoning me late on the night I had apparently registered 0.38 blood-alcohol level was none other than Ari. I found this out when I telephoned him from my mother's, to let him know I was in a new town. Even through the alcoholic haze, I had become worried that "a couple of weeks" had become a couple of months. I taped the conversation. Which was just as well, because it made no more sense to me then, than it does now, reading it nine years later:

Dead Men Don't Eat Lunch

    B-M: "Your friend is being checked. And something may be coming out. I was in your homeland after I saw you. A lot of people are interested in your friend. Raised quite a bit of interest. Let's see what we can come up with. From the point of view of your friend, your trip was probably the best thing that you did. It started off a whole...thing. And we shall see what happens. But, what's interesting about it is that one person I talked to right away turned off. As soon as he heard his name, he didn't want to deal with it. He warned me off. Well known person. [Pause] Very, very well known person. [Pause]"

    G: [Goodness, was Ari scared? Because he sounded almost incoherent. Or was it just another Ari act? I decided to affect boredom, and see what happened.] "Well. I shall look forward to your telling me what you can, when you can."

    B-M: "You're still around?"

    G: "Yes." [Short and sweet]

    B-M: "Good. I hope you'll be around for the next month or two. There will be a lot of this coming out." [Pause]

    G: [Yawn] "Well. Let me know what happens."

    B-M: "Definitely. On your behalf, I stirred a lot of shit."

    G: "Well. Keep in touch." [Look. If you've got something to say, then spit it out.]

    B-M: "I will. I'll not contact you for a while. I'll call in about a week or so."

Yeah right. Just like last time. I wouldn't be lighting any candles.

***

Grand Rapids, Michigan is the 'Slough' of America. It's the same sort of armpit, only with a little less character, and a lot more skyscrapers. Just as cold and featureless was my Rehab Clinic, sitting as it did atop a concrete block of a hospital, one floor up from the psychiatric wing.

In almost surreal contrast, the first thing you notice after a couple of days of detox is the laughter. It's not that anything funny is happening. It's just that everyone is enjoying their first few days without a hangover.

But then, without skipping a beat, the emotional hangover kicks in. You start to recall what you've been hiding from all your life. Naively, I thought I was addressing my fears quite openly. But actually, my manipulative side was simply kicking into another gear. I spent the first week casually telling everyone what they wanted to hear, so that the real me lay safely hidden.

In the second week, I was taken down a very long hall to a small room with a group therapy leader called David. All I knew was that some of the other patients had warned me that only the 'difficult' patients were assigned to David. Difficult? Who was difficult? I was a lamb.

So, I sat in the room with David. And the other ten or so people in the therapy group. And I waited. And I waited. And I waited. And I waited. Finally, after one and a half weeks, I exploded. "When the fuck is someone going to talk to me!" David looked around, and with a voice dripping with honey, he purred, "Oh Geoffrey, welcome at last to the group. What would you like to say?"

I was struck dumb. No-one. Not one single person in the forty some years of my existence had ever out-maneuvered me. And it only got worse. Every single day was torture. David was forever one, and sometimes two steps ahead of me. It was unnerving. But he did, at last, get me to look at myself. And what I saw frightened me. For the first time in my life. Because I saw nothing.

And that's when the group folded their emotional arms around me, and began the slow and agonizing process of piecing me together. A process in which my mother played a huge part. She was the family member who visited me on the day set aside for my family. She stood small, frail and alone in front of the group, and bared her soul in order to save her son. I have not been blessed with a sufficiency of verbal grace even to begin to describe the bravery I saw displayed that day in her show of love for me.

Baby steps. All is baby steps. But by the time I left, David, my mother and the group had laid the foundations. They had convinced me that I was 'nice,' and that 'nice' was ok. Seemingly a small victory. But huge for someone who for forty years had seen only a vacuum.

***

Needless to say, Ari did not call back in "a week or so." However, one way or another, I kept tabs on Ari through to the end of 1994, once I was out of Rehab. He reported to me that a private investigator, associated with one of his lawyers in England, was looking into Hugh's financial affairs.

Dead Men Don't Eat Lunch

Somehow, Ari had laid his hands on a copy of the Carratu Report. Ari hoped that the investigator would be able to turn up hard evidence of the link between Hugh and Mark Thatcher.

***

There were one or two emotional issues that Rehab had not been able to address. And for these, I had a series of sessions with a psychiatrist recommended to me by David. It all came down to survival. I was a survivor. Apparently, a pretty good example of one. But, as my psychiatrist pointed, the defense mechanisms we employ to survive do not provide us with the appropriate social skills to function normally in the real world. The choice was now mine: did I want to go on living in the past, or did I want to move on? If I chose to live in the real world, then I would need to find a reason to want to peel away the defense mechanisms that I had erected in order to survive. If I didn't, then I would never fit in. Sounded like pretty good Dr. Phil to me.

***

At the end of 1994, Ari invited me to Montreal once more. He said he had proof to give me. Though I was skeptical, Ari promised me that I would come away with substantive evidence. So, I went.

This time, there were no champagne suppers in his townhouse. We met in my small hotel room. And Ari never took off his raincoat. It was all very John Le Carre. Ari told me that his investigator was a former MI6 officer. My, but there seemed to be a lot of those around.

This investigator had spent the previous year following leads. He had spoken with Hugh's wife and mistress. He had found a proportion of the missing money. He believed he could recover it. Hurrah. I'm all for a quick round of applause. Why is Ari giving me the man's resume? Because the investigator wants $500,000 before he is prepared to continue. Good for him. So? What does this have to do with me? Well, do you have $500,000?

After I picked myself up off the floor and wiped away the tears of mirth, I told Ari to stop being so stupid. Of course I didn't have that kind of money. I told Ari to tell his investigator to try the Law Society. I felt certain they'd be delighted to negotiate a finder's fee.

In any event, I didn't have any interest in the missing money. I never did have. I couldn't understand why everyone was so preoccupied with a couple of million pounds. Including Ari, and his investigator. I just want to know what had happened to Hugh. On which subject, I asked Ari please to produce the hard evidence he'd promised me.

Geoffrey Gilson

Well, Ari ummed and ahhed, and shuffled his feet some. And then he shuffled his feet some more. But eventually, overcoming his disappointment at the failed shakedown, Ari did offer me something. Granted, it had to be taken with a pinch of salt. But the problem with Ari is that, in amongst the trash, there was always a nugget of something truthful. That's why Governments and Intelligence Services went on talking to him.

Ari stated that, in the two years before his death, Hugh had transferred at least $12 million, from bank accounts under his control in England, through a bank account in the tax haven of Jersey, to bank accounts under the control of Mark Thatcher in Houston, Texas. This was the 'seed money' for Mark's fortune, the phenomenon no-one had been able to explain. This is what Ari and his friends had been able to piece together when I brought my information to them.

At some stage of the process, Simmonds had become greedy. He wanted more money. Either he asked for it, or he just took it. Whatever, his associates had become unhappy with him and they had killed him. It did not escape my notice that Ari's story about Hugh's death had changed again.

Having just gone through the psychological wringer myself, I allowed myself to take a mental step backwards, and give Ari the once over. Ari was quite clearly having a few battles with his own demons. Just when you thought he was nothing but a con man, he would come up with something that was too close to the truth to be invented. Ari had no way of knowing that I knew that Hugh had had access to the Jersey bank account of a dead client.

Ari seemed torn within. He obviously knew stuff, but seemed under 'orders' not to give too much away. He was like a young, restless stallion, albeit a rather chubby one, champing at the bit. He appeared so desperate to be seen to be at the center of everything. Sly, little personal quips that could only mean that he had been 'there.' And yet, at the same time, he seemed to realize that too much admission might indict his intelligence masters. And so, he would immediately distance himself and them from any unseemly action. Like Hugh's death?

Instant dichotomy. Time and again. Unless, of course, this was the impression Ari wanted to create. To stay one step ahead. The master of manipulation. A science I understood only to well. The ultimate intelligence practitioner? Or a seedy con man? Or both? Grey, Geoffrey, grey. Always remember, it's grey.

I decided to indulge in a bit of game-playing myself. I mentioned that Ari had always indicated that his knowledge of Hugh's activities had been obtained third hand. Ari smiled sweetly, as if in agreement. "Yet," I continued, "I know that you knew Hugh personally." Ari's smile froze on his face.

Dead Men Don't Eat Lunch

"And how would you know that?" he asked, his voice ever so gently beginning to freeze over. Oops. Maybe just a little too much of a push. Sphincter muscle began working overtime. Ah well, I'd started, so I'd finish.

"Since you were in business with Nick Davies [the Ora Group]," I stated, with a casualness that redefined the expression 'forced,' "and since you have already admitted that Davies was well-known to Hugh, it follows that you must have met Hugh when he was alive."

The steel in Ari's eyes softened slightly from cold blue to a warmer…silverish…sort of…look…I wasn't the slightest bit interested in his eyes. Sod the Philip Marlowe. I was concentrating on just one thing: exactly how many bones could I possibly save jumping from a window on the sixteenth floor?

"Ah yes," purred Ari, after what seemed an eternity, "but he wasn't using his real name."

Oh really? My sphincter snapped shut. Any chance you could give me his alias? Ari shot me a glance that had me counting the hotel's floors again, and I backed off. Ari made to leave, but not before announcing that Scott was due to report very soon, and that his Report would deal with Hugh. All I had to do was wait. Well, that was a piece of information that was worth the change of trousers. I let Ari leave without getting close enough to shake hands… or be strangled.

***

Recovering from addiction, a process which never ends, involves an element of spirituality. One is told that one has to hand one's life over to a higher power, preferably God. Between the joy of sobriety, the warm and fuzzies that therapy had left, and my own innate survival instincts, somehow that last part kind of slipped by me.

I felt quite superior about the whole business because of my own research into matters spiritual and occultic. God? Yes, of course, something created everything. Heaven? Why not? After all, I'd been talking to a dead person the past five years. Handing over to a Higher Power? Well, I don't know about handing over, but both Maggi and Michael have told me that I have Spiritual Guides. Is it ok if I talk to them?

Beyond that, I can't say that I was particularly attracted to any form of organized religion. My own research had given me the strong impression that, as with me, an awful lot of unnecessary 'bad' accompanied the 'good,' and I felt I could do a lot better on my own. Besides, even in recovery I have a problem with authority, and someone telling me what are the rules. If I'm going to have a relationship with God, I'd prefer it to be a direct one. I don't think I need an intermediary.

Geoffrey Gilson

***

Ari seemed to work on a different timeclock to the rest of the world. His promised "very soon" turned into weeks. Then months. I tried to stay in touch with him on the telephone from my mother's, where I was indeed working in the proverbial basement. I felt quite the Trekkie. But even when I did get hold of Ari, he wavered between inscrutable and downright unfathomable.

First, he hinted that the investigator might now be willing to share some of his findings with me without my having to pay anything. Then not. Something might be about to happen. Then not. Hugh would definitely be in Scott's Report. Then not. It was a good thing that I had the opportunity to watch my mother knitting in the evening, to keep pace with all the suspense and excitement.

On one occasion, from the safety of my mother's bathroom, hiding in the shower, with the door closed, I tied to push the outside of the envelope with Ari again. I wondered out loud why Ari was still alive. He was in a good mood, and the sing-song voice was in full mode. "Oh," he trilled, "I have a few friends still in high places. A lot of people were happy with what I did about Maxwell."

"So, did your hit teams bump off Hugh off in 1988?" I ventured bravely, the bathtub loofer held menacingly at the ready. This drew only a hearty laugh from Ari, along with the enigmatic comment, "you don't always need to bump someone off to stop them; sometimes all you need to do is stop their bank accounts."

Just once, just one blessed time, I would like to hear real fear from this accursed gnome. He was like Barney the purple dinosaur. No matter what happened – rain, snow, force 5 hurricane – there was always time for one more smiling rendition of "I love you," followed by that excruciating group hug, and lots of chuckles…

I think it's time for my medication again…the drool is splattering the typewriter.

***

Maggi telephoned from England to tell me that she had read an article in a British newspaper that suggested that Conservative Ministers might at one time have held shares in Grantham, one of Mark's corporate vehicles in Texas, and the recipient of some of the arms money that had been channeled to him.

Of course, there was no way of knowing whether the shareholdings had been instigated simply by a desire to be in Ma Thatcher's good books, or whether there was a more serious implication. I'm bound to say I couldn't help but be reminded of Peter Smith's telephone call to Ari in Montreal.

A little later, I had an opportunity to speak with Geoffrey Hughes on the telephone. If I thought Ari was inscrutable, Geoffrey was the Grandmaster of the Honorable Order of Inscrutable Nods and Winks. He absolutely refused to come out and say anything definitive.

However, after about half an hour of gouging, it seemed that he was willing to admit, in his own way, that he had come across evidence of Iraq and Mark Thatcher; although he was only prepared to describe the latter as a "politically-attached individual in the southern United States; someone you [Geoff Gilson] would have come across...." You ask simple questions, and all you get is double-speak. Lord, save me from the English Language.

The upshot of this conversation was that the Carratu Report should have mention of Iraq and Thatcher. Maybe this was why the Law Society had been so reluctant to make it public? Suddenly life seemed a lot simpler. Hah. All I had to do to bust the investigation wide open was to get a hold of the Carratu Report. So, this would become the focus of my efforts. I was ready and raring to go. Enough of the shackles of recovery.

***

I also felt that I was more than ready to get back to Atlanta, and start putting my new-found sobriety into effect with Jon's company, and, more importantly, with the girls down at *Hooters*. I was convinced they were going to be in for a shock. But this time, the laugh was on me. The shock was going to be all mine.

Everyone warned me about returning to the scene of my ultimate stress-out. Everyone warned me off emotional attachments in my first year of recovery. Again, too much stress. Did I listen? Did I heck. I was Master of my own tiny little Universe.

I imploded. Was it a second nervous breakdown, or a continuation of the first one? Who cares? I went into what I have now been told was total 'disassociation.' I was completely aware of what I was doing. I just had no understanding of the consequences. I got the '2 + 2' part, but there was no longer any 'equals 4.'

Again, for all the good it was worth then, I am now told that, when faced with stress, I become slightly sociopathic. I strike out to protect myself, and have little concept or concern about what damage I might be inflicting. And I caused plenty of damage. Primarily to my kid brother, Jon.

Of all the ugly things that an addict can do to another person, I did all of them, and worse, to Jon. After all that he had endured for me over the previous year, I did terrible things to him. I say 'we' do not talk. It is not 'we' who do not talk. It is 'he' who does not talk. And I do not blame him.

Geoffrey Gilson

Finally, one chilly January morning, Jon caught up with me, and to add insult to injury, I ran. I discovered a safe place, and dove straight back into the bottle. A week later, I found myself in the driving seat of a rented car, a bottle of scotch in one hand and three vials of sleeping tablets in the other. It was 9.00p.m. in the evening, on a Wednesday, in the parking lot of a *Wendy's*.

Three things stopped me from emptying both hands: I wasn't going to let my mother outlive her son; I wasn't going to leave my twin sister to face alone the material world she detested so much…and I hadn't yet had sex with Courtney. I still haven't had sex with Courtney. But now she has a chance to find me. Oh. And my ma and sister were quite happy about my decision, too.

I had 35 cents left to my name. I called a friend. He said he had been expecting my call. I borrowed $200 from him. And for the next two years, without any hesitation, he and his family helped me once again to put my life back together. But not before, on February 15th, 1996, the British Government finally published the Scott Report. There was now another reason to stay alive.

By the by, did I mention that, upon returning to Atlanta, I learned that, for no reason anyone could determine, my bank account had been closed, and it had become impossible since then to re-open it?

Chapter 23

I HAD COME to the picturesque hamlet of Clayton, in Rabun County, primarily to heal. I didn't need to do the Rehab work again. I'd finally got the point. I just needed to recover, and then discover myself. Merely a life time's work.

I couldn't have picked a better spot. Nestled as it is in the foothills of the North Georgia Smoky Mountains, it is no accident that Rabun County is regarded as one of America's fastest-rising resort and retirement communities. It is also the place where James Dickey wrote his masterpiece *Deliverance*. The film was made nearby, too. Signed pictures of Burt Reynolds abound in the local hostelries.

The scenery is still the same. Wild, untamed peaks and soft velvet ridges, covered in great swathes of maple and pine. A cool, green paradise of forest, lake and hidden, cloud-hung cove; of air like champagne, of bubbling creeks and lush rhododendron; and furious waterfalls crashing over massive granite scars.

Hovering cloud and rising mist combine with the Southern sunshine and torrential rainfall to produce one of the world's truly natural temperate rain forests. The Cherokee called it "The Land of Mist;" the white man preferred the more prosaic "Blue Ridge Mountains," after the deep aquamarine revealed as the condensation swirled around the forested slopes.

Some things have changed since the days of "Deliverance," though. Main Street has given way to The Strip, the nickname given to the new four-lane highway bludgeoning its way through the valley situated below what is now known as Historic Clayton. The Strip may know little of the region's history as the one-time frontier of the recently-independent United Colonies, but it is no stranger to the mores of modern America. It is dotted with the requisite icons of fast-eating and convenience shopping.

Canoes can still be seen around the town. But now they're made of fiber-glass, not wood. And they're usually to be found on the roof of luxury sports utilities, bearing tags from Florida, rather than Atlanta. The chances are that the boy with the banjo sold off his Daddy's hillside farm for development a long time ago. You're as likely to bump into a high-class subdivision as a tin shack in the surrounding countryside.

No reason to fear backwoodsmen with rampant libido's when you go for a leisurely paddle down the now tame Chattahoochee River. And the natives are much more friendly. Sometimes too friendly. The fierce rivalry among the personnel of the local volunteer emergency services can sometimes leave the occasional 911-caller feeling they're in the middle of one of Custer's last Great Cavalry Charges.

Other than that, Clayton is pretty much the same as it's always been. The maple leaves blaze in the autumn. The dogwoods and azaleas do the honors in the spring. In summer, the blistering sun, tempered during the day by the cool, sweet-smelling mountain air, is finally put to rest by the late afternoon thunderstorms. The girls are all "purdy," and the menfolk still woo them with soft country love songs. The Confederacy never died, and the term "redneck" is still regarded as a compliment.

Truly no better place to settle life's deepest problems. And that's exactly what I needed. Because the demons swirling in my head made Hamlet look like a stumbling novice.

***

The problem was, I couldn't get past the guilt. Maggi spent many hours on the telephone with me, trying to convince me that everyone deserved to be forgiven. Over and over and over. However many mistakes they made.

The trouble was I didn't feel that I was ready yet to forgive myself for what I'd done to Jon. I remember, even now, the kid brother who always had my back. With whom I got my first scrapes and bruises. But Maggi insisted. And slowly but surely the message got through. I found that I could walk outside my small efficiency apartment, raise my eyes and finally feel worthy of soaking in the beauty all around me.

My apartment was part of a small wooden building, situated half-way up the steep western side of a cozy, little valley. A valley surrounded by tall oak and maple, the leaves gently swishing, the sun-dappled shadows hiding all manner of lush shrub and skittering wildlife.

I had a clear view across the valley to gently-rounded hills on the other side, all covered in trees, like so much rumpled green velvet. Although I could see The Strip in the valley below, we were far enough away that all I could hear were the gentle sounds of nature.

One of the best features of my new accommodation was the large flat concrete pan in front, for which I developed an instant fondness. I spent long periods pacing up and down, taking the sun, listening to music on my Walkman and allowing thoughts to tumble helter-skelter through my mind.

***

The Scott Report was a whitewash. In blinding contrast to all of the testimony, Scott had concluded that there had been no illegal arms sales to Iraq from the UK. More to the point, there was no mention of Hugh, Mark Thatcher or any deal involving GEC engines and SCUD-B missiles. So much for my waiting three years at Ari's behest.

Ok. Strike One. So, I tried the other report: the Carratu Report. First stop was the near invisible Ari. He bleated about how upset he was with the Scott Report. But it didn't ring true. He sounded a little nervous. I asked him if I could have a copy of his Carratu Report, and he became as skittish as the local wildlife. Muttered and spluttered, and finally hung up. The bottom line was he probably never had a copy.

I tracked down Geoff Hughes, who had left the employ of Carratu, although he insisted that had nothing to do with Hugh's investigation. He didn't sound nervous. He sounded terrified. He didn't have a copy of the Carratu Report. He claimed he had been asked to return his Notes. He couldn't remember a thing. Who was I? Who was he? Good-bye.

I'm being a tad unkind. Geoff did at least take the time to say, on the record, that his investigation was not so definitive (through no fault of his own) that he could totally rule out the possibility of my allegations concerning Iraq having some basis in fact. Geoff always did have a strangle-hold on syntax.

The bottom line with Geoff was that he did not recall telling me anything about Iraq and Mark Thatcher in 1995. Nor would he now. But. His investigation was brought to an abrupt halt by the Law Society when his inquiries hit Atlanta. So, he could not say that his investigation had been "complete."

Next, the Administrators of Hugh's Estate: they were rude, obnoxious and unhelpful. No way would they ever let me see the Carratu Report. Last gasp, the Law Society: they were pleasant, eager...and unhelpful. Another 'no' to my request to see the Carratu Report. They did, however, produce a letter stating that there were strong suggestions that Hugh had engaged in money-laundering activities and export fraud in North America and Africa.

Fine. Strike Two. I tried Reggie one more time. He was sober, but still pretty scared about the whole situation. He affected boredom, and said he was not prepared to talk about Hugh's Intelligence activities any more. Reggie did, however, let slip that British Intelligence had never really been interested in finding out why Hugh had died; they were solely concerned with finding the money. What was it with that money?

Before leaving the subject, Reggie did muse for a moment. "You know," he said softly, as he did when he thought he was passing on something of import, "instead of looking at the Eighties, you might look at the Seventies. Everyone from the Eighties has been 'got at.' The doors have been closed. Go back to when it all began. To the people he was with then."

Reggie then enthusiastically changed the subject, becoming much more animated when I told him where I was, and that I hoped to form a band to play my music. "Oh really," he chirped, if a plummy upper-class accent can actually chirp. "The Land of the Banjo," he exclaimed. Suddenly, there was silence on the line, until I heard perfect bluegrass being plucked ever so furiously in the background.

After a few minutes, a breathless Reggie came back on the line to tell me that he'd trained on the mandolin; but he'd picked up the banjo, since they involved essentially the same techniques; and could he possibly be in the band? He promised to wear his kilt. I'm in the middle of a serious investigation, which is fast falling apart, and I'm surrounded by nutcases. I sighed. And I promised.

Then, somehow, we got onto the subject of the movie version of the story. Again, I was back in *Alice in Wonderland*. Like one of that book's stranger characters, Reggie became quite the pompous marionette. He was very proud of his Equity card, and he wanted to be sure that I would use his full and proper stage name. Sniff.

I was almost impressed, until he broke down, and wondered excitedly if he could be played by Roger Moore? I left him with the threat that he'd be played by Stephen Fry unless he became more co-operative. I felt sure that Seymour Hersh never had to put up with this. Nor John Pilger.

And so. Strike Three. I'd been convinced the past three years, that when Ari's imposed waiting period was over, one or other of these leads would provide the final key to unraveling the mystery. And now I was empty-handed. Ever the optimist, Maggi told me that I should use the hiatus to start writing the book. But I wanted to sulk for a while first.

The wonderful thing about 'healing' is that you're allowed to give vent to your feelings, and pretend that you're an adult, all at the same time. That's the whole point. Feeling. And I was doing a lot of that. Couldn't stop crying all the time. I found myself feeling not only my own pain, but the pain of everyone else around me. And I couldn't block it out. Still can't. Maggi says it's all about experiencing stuff that I've simply been able to avoid the past forty-odd years.

***

I knew from past experience that something would eventually turn up to re-start my 'investigation. So, the sulking did not last too long. In the interim, I took Maggi's advice, and began to write furiously.

On a particularly slow Sunday morning, I was penning the section dealing with Michael Colmer's prediction from 1990, that the next major revelation "to be inspired 'from the other side' would occur when 'the last Israeli hostage is released from Lebanon.'"

Literally, as I finished that Chapter, I looked over at the Sunday paper, and read that the last known 'living' Israeli hostages at that time were being released by Lebanese Muslim Militias, in a prisoner exchange with the Israeli Government. The article mentioned that the deal made no reference to Ron Arad.

Ron Arad, an Israeli pilot captured in Lebanon in 1986, remains a figure of controversy in Israel to this day. There are many, including his daughter, who insist that he is still imprisoned in Tehran, where he ended up after being passed from the Amal Muslim Militia in Western Lebanon, to Hezbollah, and then to the Iranian Government.

Leaving aside the obvious tragedy represented by the uncertainty of his fate, I wondered whether or not the 'terms' of Michael's prediction had been met. I wasn't holding my breath. But. I lie. I was holding my breath.

***

And when I wasn't turning blue in the face from lack of oxygen, I took the opportunity to meet my neighbors. This was new for me. Part of making myself feel safe the 'old way' was to erect barriers, not to reach over them. And so, I came to know the 'redneck,' the essential human character of the American working class.

They are primarily of Irish and Scottish stock, and were drawn initially to the Appalachian Mountain range, that huge backbone of Eastern America, by the similarity in countryside to their homelands. From there, over time, they moved westward, and into the large cities, primarily in the North. The term 'redneck' derives from their pale skin, which the sun turns bright red on the neck, when they spend long hours laboring outdoors. The pale skin is usually freckled, and the hair generally a sandy color.

I spent seven years in the caring embrace of the mountain folk of Rabun County. I spent long hours reading about their origins, and many a night wondering how best to write about their uniqueness, and their contribution to the American Spirit – and to the revival of mine. In the end, I found an old passage, tucked away at the back of a second-hand bookstore, that expressed it far better than I could ever hope to emulate. I confess I did not take note of the author's name. But I offer him my apologies for the adaptations I have made to his original writing:

Geoffrey Gilson

"They express simple truths, simply expressed, and loyally adhered to. The topics, the language, the bias. The lazy, highland profanity, emanating a secret, delicious hilarity. And not limited just to the male gender. I found myself 'loafering' on that verandah with as many women talking this way as with men.

Those who have not experienced the people and the way of life call its proponents 'white trash.' They are not. They are proud, independent, naturally intelligent people. Unsullied by the corruptions of narrow-thinking education. Honest in thought, forthright in action. Quick to temper, but loyal as a watchdog.

They know where they stand, and they know, in the way that only the truly confident peasant, tied to the land and at peace with his empathy with his environment, can know, that the rest of the world stands behind him. Sometimes, a long way behind him. For the very traits that are their strength are sometimes also their weakness. On occasion, your average redneck can be a right royal 'independent' pain in the ass.

A fierceness born of the many privations they have suffered over the centuries. From the moment they had to carve a livelihood out of the living forest when they were America's first wild frontier – the wild South coming a good ways before the wild West.

The Southern mountain man helped to keep alive the spirit of freedom, independence and democracy during the Second Revolutionary War with Great Britain at the beginning of the Nineteenth Century, and protected the Union from many of the mesmerizing excesses of the New Englanders at a time when the flower of Virginia's Founding Fathers were in their waning years.

It was this same resolve to protect the original precepts of the Founding Fathers that led the South to secede prior to the Civil War. It is a prevalent misconception that it was all about slavery. That is an historically incorrect prerogative which is always the exclusive domain of the victor in any war – the right to re-write the history books.

Of course slavery was abhorrent. Just as racial prejudice is. Of course, the real abhorrence is the fact the Founding Fathers did not have the guts to deal with it when they originally wrote the Constitution. They knew it was a battle that was being put off until another day.

No. Secession and the War were about the rights of States versus the omniscient and not-so-benign power of central government – be it the recently-departed British one, or the newly-installed one in the American capitol.

Unfortunately, the South has only itself to blame. The privations of Reconstruction have created a veneer of unseemly prejudice against all that the victors stood for and in favor of any and all irrelevant symbols that appear to stand for what they lost. Hence the ridiculous infatuation with the

Dead Men Don't Eat Lunch

Confederate Flag.

Why it's a shame is that the veneer masks a mentality which is at once admirable and impressive, honest and consistent. It is that more profound mentality that gave rise to the War, not the War which gave rise to the mentality. That which outsiders take for the Southern mentality is merely the unfortunate veneer. However, it's a little difficult to see deep down when one's vision is continually being clouded by multitudinous waving of the Stars and Bars.

The history books say the South lost the War. But indeed, they won the argument. For today, the Federal Government treads very warily when seeking to interfere with State rights. The Union can be grateful for the fact that the gritty Southerners believed in themselves and their principles so much that they were prepared to fight to the bitter end for both. Those principles were and are the foundation of this Union.

We should be grateful to the South for reminding us of their importance. We should be grateful in the knowledge that we mess with them at our peril, and the peril of the Union. And every Southern man has the right to stand by the Stars and Stripes with honor, for he fought and lost over the principles for which that flag stands. It's a shame that too many Southerners don't take off their sheets long enough to understand that fact.

If he did, he would remember that the South is America. It was the Southern Coastal States as much as those of New England which fought Britain in the two Revolutionary Wars, which provided the authors for the Bill of Rights and the Constitution, which provided America with its early and some of its best Presidents. A walk through the historic ports of Savannah, Charleston, Jamestown and Annapolis leaves one as charged with a sense of the early struggles of this nation as similar walks through Boston and Concord.

Rural southern music is an attitude, a withdrawal into myths and an early agrarian dream about the promise of a new republic. And regardless of its vague quality, its false sense of romance, its restructuring of the reality of our history, it is nevertheless as true to someone listening to the Grand Ole Opry as his grandfather's story, which the grandfather had heard from his father....."

***

I put down my pen, and rubbed my eyes. Always stop when you have a little more left in you. That way you'll have a place to start in the morning. Hemingway used to say that. Though I think it had more to do with finding an excuse to start drinking at five o'clock in the afternoon than with literary finesse. Whatever. I could associate with either reason.

Geoffrey Gilson

I left my apartment and wandered lazily to the edge of the concrete pan and stood there, my hands in my pockets, soaking up the early evening ambience. It was high summer, and the air retained a shimmering memory of its earlier heat; the sickly-sweet smell of pine sap still warm in my nostrils. My mind, already tired, was swiftly coaxed into a numbing, humming trance.

My gaze drew itself slowly upwards; so that it met the slowly emerging moonface, smiling and glowing a vibrant orange in silent tribute to the dimming sunset. My thoughts, unconnected and disconnected by the easy rhythm of the evening, drifted nowhere and everywhere.

The air, cool and soothing on my skin, was alive with the furious chatter of crickets. The piney woods, lit up like Christmas trees with winking firebugs, reflected the preternatural brilliance of the stars carpeting the Southern night sky.

My solitude was interrupted by Clint, a precocious 17 year old High School student, who lived next door with his mother. He'd been working up the nerve to ask me what my book was about. Lazily, I gave him the 30 second version. His immediate response: "Well, did the Police ever catch the guy who took the money from Hugh, and did that person kill him?"

I was slow from the evening's heat. I asked Clint to explain, without taking too much notice. "Well, you told me this Hugh character stole £5 million ($7.5 million) over two years, didn't spend it and turns up dead. So, someone stole the money from him, which is why he didn't run away with it, and the guy who did it probably killed him to shut him up."

Something snapped in my head. I've never been able to work out whether it's called a brainstorm or a brainwave. Whatever it was, it took me away from Clint, and back into my apartment to grab my pad and pen.

Inadvertently or no, Clint had awoken me to something so simple and so obvious that I had difficulty understanding why I had not seen it at any time in the previous eight years. Possibly because I too was simple and obvious? So much for the frantically 'tidy' mind, and the overarching powers of calculation.

We knew that Hugh had died in order to stop his using the stolen money for his operation. But. As Clint had pointed out, if Hugh was dead, why was the money still out there? Why had it not, in fact, been stolen?

Perhaps the 'bad guys' had not known about the money? But, sure they did. That's why everyone and his uncle were bent over backwards looking for it. Unless. Unless, we were talking about two different pots of money.

We had already come across much larger caches of missing money. Caches of a size that would make it worthwhile for the likes of British Intelligence and Ari Ben-Menashe to spend their time looking for them.

What if it was these caches that formed the basis of Hugh's

operation, and what if it was these same caches that everyone was looking for? Not Hugh's stolen money. What if, in fact, no-one knew anything about Hugh's stolen money?

What if Hugh had only started stealing his Clients' money in 1987, to use as a 'Runaway Fund,' because something was going horribly wrong with the operation? And what if he had simply piggy-backed this stolen money on top of the larger caches of cash he was already laundering?

This would explain why the Law Society had come across larger amounts of money in the same bank accounts as the stolen money. It would also explain why they had then shut down the Carratu investigation with such unseemly haste. It would further explain why those people, whose larger caches were missing, could do nothing to recover them: they had no idea, when Hugh died, that their money was all mixed up with other money, which would then become the subject of a Law Society investigation. No wonder they spent so much of their remaining funds putting me under surveillance. But man, were they going to be disappointed.

After a deal of thinking, I came up with some new twists for my rolling scenario: Hugh had become involved in something that was much larger, and possibly much 'uglier,' than I had previously imagined. This would have been about 1984. Whether 'official,' 'quasi-official,' or utterly rogue, this 'something' at least garnered Hugh some sort of 'protection,' which was what had kept the Law Society off his back. At least, at first.

Something went wrong – very possibly the fact that Hugh was caught creaming off the top. He needed a way out. In January 1987, I was with Hugh when he learned that he had again been de-selected from a safe Conservative Parliamentary seat. We were on our own in his office, and I remember the scene vividly, because it was the first – and only- time I had ever seen fear in Hugh's eyes.

In the early days of the British and then the American Intelligence Services, most of the recruits were selected from the ranks of 'Gentlemen.' This was true across the rest of Europe, and into Russia also. Intelligence was a 'Game' for Gentlemen, and the Game was played according to 'Gentlemen's Rules.' You didn't shoot people in the back. You didn't take out your counterpart when they were on home soil. If you had an 'asset,' who then achieved high political office, you backed off.

Could it have been that, aside from simple political ambition, Hugh had seen the possibility of election to Parliament in 1987 as his best way of avoiding the fallout from the mess he had got into with his covert 'something'? Did he believe that in some way the 'Gentlemen's Rules' would apply to him once he was seen as a potential Government Minister? And could it have been that when the door to that exit strategy was closed, that he devised another? Involving the stealing of his Clients' money to create a 'Runaway Fund'?

If so, Hugh was certainly in good spirits from the moment he began the stealing in April 1987, all the way through until the early part of the Summer of 1988. Had something changed? And if so, what?

What if Hugh's innate greed had caused him simply to put too many fingers into too many pies? What if he had spent the better part of 1987 and 1988, with his glib tongue and his gilded sense of invincibility, simply promising everyone everything, while delivering nothing, in a vain attempt to keep everyone happy, while he continued with his exit plans?

What if, by the beginning of the Summer of 1988, too many of the parties had simply become too pissed with waiting for so long? Or perhaps, one or more had discovered the exit plans, and realized that Hugh had no intention of honoring anything? What if Hugh's attempts at making himself indispensable had only had the effect of finally convincing certain parties just how 'dispensable' he truly was? Maybe the pressure was increased? Maybe a bank account or two suddenly became unavailable?

The possibilities are endless. What is certain is the fact that, at the beginning of the Summer of 1988, Hugh suddenly changed from Mr. Happy-Go-Lucky to a very stressed and very unwell individual. Also, according to Martin Pratt, he also became frantic about earning money. Large amounts. Any way that he could. This was the period when Hugh began to speculate furiously on the shares of Ferranti, a British defense electronics giant. Did he have some 'inside' information that allowed him to earn large sums on the daily fluctuations in the share price?

Then, at the end of the Summer of 1988, and again, with equal suddenness, Hugh just lost heart and hope. The furious activity ceased. He calmed down. It was as if he had become resigned to his fate. Maybe the Summer had been unsuccessful? Maybe the threats had been re-directed from Hugh to his extended family, and he realized that the only way he could protect them was to 'go' – and to go quietly, so as to avoid retribution against that extended family? Maybe the 'protection' had been removed? Maybe that was why the Law Society, the Police and National Westminster Bank all took their action against him on exactly the same day? Maybe there was a little persuasion? Maybe someone, somewhere was simply 'cleaning house'?

***

All of which left me looking for that 'something larger and uglier' that could have been Hugh's operation. Which process, in turn, left me gently wondering if I'd stepped way over the edge, and far out into the abyss of unreality. Until I heard from Ari, who, for once, actually had something to add that was both startling...and helpful.

Dead Men Don't Eat Lunch

Chapter 24

I HAD FOUND MYSELF doing of lot of 'loafering' of late, in Rabun County. I had convinced myself it was a part of the process of healing. However, rather than sitting on a porch, I spent my 'loafering' time wandering around Clayton, looking at the scenery and watching people.

For the first time in as long as I could remember, I enjoyed the simple pleasure of enjoyment. John Lennon said: life is what happens while you are busy making other plans. I wanted to stop 'being busy,' and start living. Maggi called it 'playing,' and she said that one could never spend enough time playing.

Once, I was in the car park of a supermarket, and this kind lady came up to me and asked if I was ok. I told her I was fine. Then I wondered why she had had asked. She said it was because I had spent the past ten minutes, standing in the middle of the 'road,' staring at one of the surrounding mountains. But why not? It was, after all, a spectacular mountain. Almost Tolkeinesque in its shape. As were so many of the surrounding mountains.

The Blue Ridge Mountains are truly ancient. They are the mere remnants of a range that once rivaled the majesty of the Himalayas. All that is left now are the barest of worn nubs. But their sparkling granite slabs hold mysteries and secrets going back to the beginning of time.

The area is said to be a region of 'divine intervention.' The Cherokee claimed that the nearby Tallulah Gorge was once occupied by the 'Little People,' and even now, mainstream Churches and Artistic Organizations build secluded retreats, tucked away in forgotten valleys.

So, as I walked, I stopped often, and simply soaked up the beauty around me. Always there were clusters of lush green, cone-shaped mountains, poised like so many gentle waves ready to wash down lazily on top of me.

I was captivated by the deep, swimming-pool blue skies.

Geoffrey Gilson

Intoxicated by the sweet, sharp smell of pine. The days of summer were slow and lazy. Thunderheads gathered in the afternoon. The pyrotechnics in some of the lone cumuli flashed and dazzled like silent fireworks displays. The air was always thick with the smell of ozone at the end of the day.

After the late-afternoon downpours, everything closed in. Dark, brooding clouds lowered themselves onto hillsides hung heavy with bending, drenched tress. The humid, unmoving air was now fat with the pungent, sickly aroma of rotting woodland humus. Smoke curled up from chimneys, and mixed with the mist rising off the mountains; looking for all the world like long, wispy tendrils of fairy gossamer.

The savage beauty, combined with the stark tranquility, had me feeling fully alive. My senses were heightened. And I felt reborn. I was more aware of my own beauty; and truly felt, rather than saw, the beauty all around me. I began to understand and experience all the mysteries life had to offer. And for the first time in my life, I began truly to understand what it meant to be close to God.

The universe has been around for some 13 billion years. And in this incarnation, I will live no more than about 80 years. There are currently some 6 billion people on this planet – and we are just one of many possible inhabited planets.

In the greater scheme of things, I am, on the one hand infinitesimally insignificant. A pin prick in the advance of time. Yet. After years of study, by some of the greatest brains in robotics, no-one can actually duplicate the way I walk across a room. And there never has been, nor will there ever be anyone exactly the same as me. I am unique. I am special. I am infinitely irrelevant, yet infinitely spectacular, and both at the same time.

It now seems clear to me that my purpose is not to achieve any specific accomplishment in my life. What possible ambition of any significance can anyone realize in just 80 years? That's the beauty of the shortness of our life-span.

Rather my purpose is, precisely as Maggi said, to get off the tread mill. To turn my back on the rush of society. To jump off. To halt. To reach out to life. And to enjoy. To play. To place greater moment in the journey, than in the destination. Particularly when the journey seems regularly to include telephone calls from Ari Ben-Menashe.

***

For once, bless his heart, it was indeed Ari that called me. And all excited he was too. He telephoned all friendly and helpful. He was anxious to share with me the relevance of the prosecution, by the US Attorney's Office in Philadelphia, of a man called Clyde Ivy.

Apparently, this guy had been the right-hand man of one James

Dead Men Don't Eat Lunch

Guerin, founder of International Signal and Control (ISC), a rather shady defense electronics company in America, and sanctions-buster to the likes of South Africa and Iraq.

Guerin might have stayed in the shadows had it not been for his company's high profile merger with prestigious UK defense electronics company, Ferranti, in the Eighties. It wasn't the merger that attracted so much attention, as the spectacular collapse at the end of the Eighties, when it was found that ISC had only managed to pull off the merger with promise of a $1 billion contract with Pakistan, which contract never existed.

The ensuing financial hole killed off the newly-merged entity, but Guerin was never convicted of fraud. Instead, he pleaded guilty to a completely different charge: that of illegally supplying arms to apartheid South Africa. Not, however, before he had received loud support from a distinguished pillar of the US Intelligence community.

In December 1993, President Clinton nominated Admiral Bobby Ray Inman to be Secretary of Defense. Inman served in a series of senior Intelligence positions, including Director of Naval Intelligence (1974-76), Vice Director of the Defense Intelligence Agency (1976-77), Director of the National Security Agency (1977-81) and Deputy Director of the Central Intelligence Agency (1981-1982).

In the early Eighties, Inman, then a private businessman, was named to the shadow board of ISC. These boards are required for US defense companies, wholly or partly owned by foreigners, and are supposed to guarantee that no US secrets get into foreign hands.

In April 1992, prior to Guerin's sentencing, Inman wrote to the Judge that between 1975 and 1978 Guerin "voluntarily provided the US government with information obtained during his foreign travels which was of substantial value, particular that related to the potential proliferation of nuclear weapons."

Several of the other defendants in the ISC case (including Clyde Ivy) claimed the US government knew of their sales to South Africa, and that they provided information on South Africa's defense, including its nuclear weapons program. Guerin was sentenced to 15 years in jail. He could have received up to 61 years. In January 1994, Inman withdrew his nomination for Secretary of Defense.

Once Guerin was in jail, all the goodies on ISC came spilling out. It was a company that found itself at the interface of a whole bunch of illegal arms networks, selling military technology to the likes not only of South Africa, but also Iraq and Iran. In the main, the defense electronic technology sold related to ballistic missiles, and ISC was found to have close links with Gerald Bull, Carlos Cardoen, BNL, Christopher Drogoul, BCCI, MI6 and the CIA.

Clyde Ivy was one of six other defendants indicted along with

Geoffrey Gilson

Guerin for their illegal sales to South Africa. The long-delayed case had finally come to trial in Philadelphia. Ari was calling me to tell me that Ivy's specialty was rocket science, and that he was part of the same extended group as Hugh.

And what 'extended group' would that be?

The group around Margaret Thatcher which sold arms to Iraq and a few other nefarious destinations, and then channeled kickbacks and profits to her and others in senior positions in the Conservative Party and Government.

Ari had by now become something of a master of the unsubstantiated tease. And I had become somewhat irritated. I affected boredom. Ari, however, was really quite insistent. He had evidence, and was prepared to provide it to me to help with my book. However, he did not want to entrust it to the mail or to the telephone. So, he wanted me to come back to Montreal.

Not a chance, I responded. I didn't have any money. Instead, I invited Ari to come visit me. For reasons I did not find wholly surprising, he did not feel safe crossing the border into the US. Oh well. End of conversation.

***

I stomped around my apartment and the concrete pan for the best part of a day, yelling at myself. And thoroughly scaring the natives. There was zero chance anyone around there was going to attempt funny stuff with me in the backwoods. They were way too terrified of what I might do to them. But the best part of Rabun County is that crazy passes for pretty normal. Most of the time.

Without a doubt, Ari was the most infuriating part of my investigation to date. So much that made sense. From a person interested only in cents. And yet accompanied, always, by so much drivel. Then I stopped my pacing. And mentally hit myself. Enough of the ranting. Find some proof. Anything. Just one morsel to give me a tiny bit of comfort about Ari's allegations. I had another brain spasm.

I called Directory Inquiries, and miraculously, obtained the telephone number for Christopher Drogoul in Atlanta. Christopher was the very definition of helpfulness. He recalled the name Simmonds, but not the exact context. Chris could, however, clearly remember the Atlanta BNL Branch issuing a Letter of Credit to the Central Bank of Iraq in favor of GEC for a considerable sum of money. He thought maybe about $28 million, but he couldn't swear to that.

Chris' memory was also a little vague as to whether it was for engines or spare parts. But he believed it was to do with rockets of some sort. No matter. His lawyer in New York, Robert Simels, had all of the paperwork. Chris would call him, and have him root out the Letter of Credit.

I went one better, and called Robert Simels myself. Robert was the model of New York charm and grace. Unfortunately, all of the papers for the trial were in about 70 packing cases in the firm's warehouse. But hey. For a modest fee, he could get one of his assistants to rummage through them, to find the offending documentation.

The funny thing was, Robert continued, since the FBI had pretty thoroughly cleaned out the entirety of Chris' and BNL's offices in Atlanta, for his Defense, Robert had had to obtain all of his documentation from the US Attorney's Office, by way of Public Discovery. Robert also felt that he could remember the GEC deal. Which meant that he had to have read about it from those Discovered documents. Which, in turn, meant that the information should be in the Public Domain.

I was so dumbstruck that I decided to take a breather by collecting my mail. Maggi had sent me another article from England. Huge allegations, all over the front page of the most recent London *Sunday Times*, about the Iranian Hashemi brothers and Margaret Thatcher. One of Cyrus Hashemi's older brothers, Jamshid, was being charged in Great Britain with fraud over a non-existent commodity deal. Jamshid was attempting to use what was becoming a common defense in the Nineties – namely, that the Government knew all about it. Yet, with Jamshid, there was a suspicious ring of truth. Hence, the *Sunday Times* article.

Jamshid, like his brothers, had a long history of involvement with both the CIA and MI6, infiltrating Iranian circles, and using the cover of illegal arms deals to filter useful information back to his Intelligence masters on both sides of the Atlantic. Indeed, in the end, Jamshid was convicted, but Judge Andrew Collins granted Jamshid leniency, because of the "valuable information" he had given British Intelligence.

But this wasn't what had caught everyone's attention. It was Jamshid's allegation that, in the Eighties, he and his brothers had paid the Conservative Party some $120,000 to have a meeting with Margaret Thatcher, then still the Prime Minister. The thing of it was that the Party weren't denying the money, and Thatcher wasn't denying the meeting. They were merely denying the connection, and were strenuously refuting any allegation that illicit arms deals were discussed at the private meeting. Once again, we were clearly a long distance away from Kansas.

I walked slowly back up the path to my apartment. Didn't notice the beauty, or pay much attention to the chattering of anything, except the voices in my head. I read and re-read the article. And ran through in my mind the conversations I'd had with Drogoul and Simels. Maybe, on this occasion, Ari had spoken sooth. Maybe Hugh was doing something with Iraq, and possibly with rockets/ But, was it all a rogue operation? Or was it at the behest of Margaret Thatcher, as Ari was intimating? For, I was holding in my hands the possibility that there were dirty dealings at the very heart of the Conservative Party. Were they and Hugh connected?

I ate a large slice of humble pie. And called Ari. Many times. He would not answer, nor did he return my calls. Finally, I lost my temper, and left a false message. I stated that my source in British Intelligence was pissed with Ari's suggestion that Hugh's 'friends,' and by implication, British Intelligence, might have had anything to do with Hugh's death. My source had proof that, indeed, it was the Israelis, and very likely Ari himself, who were responsible for Hugh's death. Would Ari care to comment?

Of course, as soon as I put down the telephone, I remembered the hotel room in Montreal. So, I locked the door, shut the curtains, and waited by the telephone, with my Mickey Mouse table lamp firmly in my grasp. I did not have long to wait. Ari rang, in a cold fury. "I do not," he hissed, "I do not respond to threats."

"But Ari," I ventured cautiously, "apparently you do."

There was a pause, followed by the slightest of chuckles. The ice, although not broken, had cracked a little. I explained what had happened, and offered a moment or two of groveling apology. He was still sulking with me for hanging up on him. God, we were like a couple of quarrelling lovers from a really bad American soap opera. But he did offer a piece of useful advice. At least, I thought it might be useful. It certainly had the advantage of being different. Again.

"Look more closely at the Eighties," he said, "Where you're getting it wrong is that you're still thinking it was about Intelligence Operations and Politics. It wasn't. It was about money. It was all about money. Arms and money. Everyone was making money. Me. The Israelis. The British. The Americans. Everyone. Look at the money."

And that was that. Except that he wanted to state quite clearly that the Israelis would not have killed Hugh. "We would not have killed someone like that." Ari was adamant on that point. Repeated it over and over. What was that comment about protesting too much? Then he put a little stinger in the tail, "You should be turning your attention to Hugh's friends in British Intelligence: they killed him when Hugh got greedy.'

Hello. What's this? Life imitating art? I fake a 'row' between British and Israeli Intelligence over Hugh's death, just to lever information. Only to discover that I may have stumbled across a real falling out? Interesting that Reggie never mentioned any of this. And anyway, why would British and Israeli Intelligence be at odds about anything? They were generally the staunchest of allies. Or, was this some more of Reggie's 'grey'? Had a friend become an enemy over a temporary or regional conflict?

Whatever the case, it was way too much for me on a warm and sunny day, in the mystical environs of Rabun County. So instead, I turned my attention to other advice given to me separately by Reggie and Ari, and I had me a good look at the machinations of both the Seventies and the Eighties.

***

Great Britain had not known a foreign conqueror since 1066, when William of Normandy took a holiday on Britain's southern coast, decided he liked it, and began a Royal Succession, which essentially has continued to this day. Unlike Julius Caesar, our Will came, saw, conquered – and stayed.

For all the history lessons about the *Magna Carta*, rights won and lost, seeds of democracy, the Mother of all Parliaments and an Empire that knew no setting sun. For all the boasts of Albion bringing freedom to the oppressed natives of the world – while taking one or two of them off to the American Colonies, to experience a whole new form of oppression. For all of this, and a host of other sins, too many to mention, it remains the fact that Britain does not have, and never has had, its own written Constitution.

But then, it never felt that it had any particular need to protect itself. Abroad, it had its Empire, its Navy and those splendid men in their 'who-needs-camo' Red Outfits. At home, it had the Great Public Institutions of the Establishment, its Gentlemen's Clubs, and in case anyone got too frisky, it simply confused them with five days of Cricket.

That is, until Socialism and Communism reared their ugly heads. I grew up in England in the Fifties, Sixties and Seventies. We lived with the very real certainty that the Soviet's Red Army could sweep through Eastern Europe to the Rhine in three days. And that a hiccup and a sneeze later, it would be where Hitler had been in 1940 – peering at us from the other side of the English Channel.

A fictional book along these very lines, and called *Third World War*, became a bestseller in Britain in the late Seventies. It was penned by General Sir John Hackett, who had commanded the 4th Parachute Brigade at Arnhem, during the Battle of the Bulge, in the Second World War. Hackett's military career culminated with him as both Commander of the Northern Army Group of NATO, and Commander-in-Chief of the British Army on the Rhine; he was also Principal of King's College, London.

As if this scenario was not bad enough, the previously 'cuddly' Labour Party then took a decided turn to the Left, and became seriously Socialist in the Sixties. This was a time of Kennedy and Luther King in the States. Shooting on the Kent State campus. Riots on the streets of Paris. And revolution in Czechoslovakia. Harold Wilson led the Labour Party to power in the Sixties on the bandwagon of change, reform and modernization. But hidden behind the friendly façade was the uglier specter of the Totalitarian Left.

Geoffrey Gilson

At least, that is what the Ruling Classes saw. And, after all, they had been blessed with the task of protecting Blighty from the savage abroad and the savage at home. Remember. No Constitution. No Rules. It was down to the Ruling Classes and their new hangers on, the *parvenu*. And they were not adapting too well to the changes of the Twentieth Century.

Anyone who watched the British television series *Upstairs Downstairs*, or saw the more recent movie *Gosford Park*, will have a glimmer of an understanding of what this might have meant in the Sixties and Seventies. Before then, everyone 'knew their place.' No-one reached above their station. Provided everyone abided by that 'Convention,' all would stay put, and all would be well. But the Socialists and the Communists threatened radical change. And the Ruling Classes had no Constitution, no Rules to fall back on. So they fell back on themselves.

It began with the Troubles in Northern Ireland at the end of the Sixties. Things quickly got out of hand with the IRA. So, the British Government slipped in MI6 and the SAS, to do the dirty on them. The problem was, that the Government was a bunch of left-wingers, even when it became Ted Heath's Conservative Government in 1970. And they were all a bit squeamish about the Dirty War being fought in Northern Ireland. So, political backing was kind of like political backing for the veterans returning from Vietnam at the same time. Non-existent.

And the Intelligence people in Northern Ireland, who were, after all, for the most part Gentlemen, didn't take to it too well. And they took certain matters into their own hands. They began to use the skills they had been honing 'over there,' 'over here.' As it were. PsyOps personnel commenced one or two dirty maneuverings against British politicians on the mainland. Not to get the wrong impression, mind; it was only to ensure that the Northern Ireland activities had the 'proper' political support. That's all it was. Honest. Nothing more. At least, not at first.

Yet, one or two Intelligence Officers broke ranks and told a different story. They spoke of rogue right-wing Officers gone barmy. Actively pursuing right-wing agendas against any politician or leading figure who had leftish views. Former Senior MI5 Officer Peter Wright, made famous by his book *Spycatcher*, and even more famous by the unsuccessful attempts of Margaret Thatcher to suppress it, alluded to these illegal activities.

A lesser known case was that of Colin Wallace. Colin had been an Information Officer in Northern Ireland, but his specialty had been PsyOps. Misinformation and disinformation against the IRA. But he found that some of the work was also being directed against politicians. He complained. So, he was dismissed. He exposed. So, he was set up with a conviction for the murder of his wife.

Closer examination of the Wallace case found yet another insidious network in operation in Great Britain. That of the Freemasons. Masonry came to the fore in Great Britain in the Eighteenth Century. By all accounts, Freemasonry was the result of superimposing the secret rituals of the Knights Templar onto the equally secret shenanigans of London's Masons' Guilds. Which would account for all the spooky imagery about Solomon's Temple.

What most of its proponents, even today, do not realize is that there are dozens of Degrees of 'Membership,' way higher than the Three your High Street merchants play with. And those higher Degrees lead directly back to the Priory of Sion. Freemasons are, indeed, merely the footsoldiers of *The Da Vinci Code*. The icons relating to Solomon's Temple are not emblematic or allegoric. They are real. They exist because Freemasonry represents the lower rungs of the movement to bring back to temporal and spiritual power the heir to the line of David and Jesus.

More to the point, what has been documented is the political and religious leaning of Freemasonry against established authority, and in support of the 'rights of man.' Freemasons believe that authority comes only from God. And that one should pay little heed to figures who to choose to intercede between the individual and God. Indeed, one should remove them.

And so, the precursors of Freemasonry found themselves supporting the anti-Pope feelings that led to Protestantism in Europe. While Freemasons themselves helped to foment the Revolutions in France and the Americas. Against oppressive monarchies. Masonic and Occultic icons are redolent in the Foundation of the early United States. Even today, senior Freemasons tend towards supporting the more secular versions of Globalism and the New World Order, rather than those that are more entangled in the Royal Heritage of Jesus.

At the ground level, what all of this meant for Colin Wallace was that he got nowhere, because both the people he was trying to investigate (Intelligence Officers) and those he was trying to get to do the investigating (Police Officers) were members of the same secret network of Freemasons. And Wallace wasn't a Freemason. He was on the outside, looking in.

Oh, by the by, if you are not a Freemason, you may not pick up on all of the secret hand signals and hand shakes. But look out for political leaders, or even your local grocer, using expressions that include words or phrases like "on the level," "it's all square," "the architect of this or that," and "I was taught to be cautious." There's a chance they are being used as mere harmless construction metaphors. But the fact is they represent common Masonic terminology, and in all probability, they are being employed to convey recognition. All good spooky stuff, eh?

In the late Sixties, Hugh was in his early twenties, and had recently graduated from Merchant Taylor's School. Not quite Eton, but very swank anyway. According to Hugh and Reggie, this was the time that Hugh had been 'recruited,' and had then spent time in Czechoslovakia, and perhaps, on the seafront at Marseilles.

Hugh's father told me that it was his understanding that Hugh worked at a *Radio Shack*, in West London, at this time. Indeed, Hugh had shown me a house that he rented during this period, in the Kensington part of West London. But, was this ruse merely a cover for Hugh's real activities? According to Hugh, he was a part of the real *Austin Powers* set: Intelligence work by day, and Swinging London by night. Czechoslovakia during the week, and parties on the French Riviera at the weekend, with Mick Jagger and Bianca. Meanwhile, I was still at school. And all I wanted to be was a farmer.

And so, we moved into the Seventies. Edward Heath pretty much became a Socialist, and then Harold Wilson returned to power. But this time, there were other people at work behind Wilson. The Trade Unions, themselves seen as hotbeds of the coming Totalitarian Left, were in control, and were given extraordinary powers by Wilson's Government. Then, in 1976, the Labour Party printed its Annual Program, which was intended to form the basis of its Manifesto in the forthcoming General Election. It pretty much laid the groundwork for transforming Great Britain into a Communist junkie.

Ugly right-wing talk began a-brewing in the Gentlemen's Clubs of London, in particular the Reform Club, the location for the filming of *Around The World In Eighty Days*, and a favorite haunt of senior Intelligence Officers. In the same Gaming Club that Hugh frequented in Curzon Street, in the 'Mayfair Square Mile,' Lord Lucan (later made famous when he murdered his children's nanny) preached to his friends about the better aspects of *Mein Kamf*.

The remnants of the pro-Hitler gentry from the Second World War silently joined forces with the organizing talents of the New Right, and created new entities, ostensibly to 'protect' Great Britain from socialism and communism: parapolitical, far-right groups, like the *Freedom Association* of Norris McWhirter, who is better known for founding the *Guinness Book of Records* with his twin brother, Ross McWhirter, who was later killed by the IRA. Along with the parapolitical came the paramilitary. David Stirling, formerly a senior officer in the SAS, formed his own private army, *GB75*.

Even the mainstream Conservative Party, in the form of its right-leaning faction, the *Monday Club*, got into the action. Stalwarts such as Enoch Powell, and its Deputy Chairman, George Kennedy Young, a former Deputy Chief of MI6. Something needed to be done to protect Great Britain from the leftist threat. And with backs to the wall, it could not be left to the well-cushioned denizens in Parliament.

Paramilitary groups were set up. Extra-legal activity was condoned in the Intelligence Services. Intelligence Officers freely offered their views and advice at Monday Club meetings. The frenzy eventually settled down into three lines of approach:

1) Strenuous organizing activity on the right of the Conservative Party, to re-align it more aggressively against Socialism - and Europe: the lovers of Blighty no more wanted to be run by Frogs and Spics than they did by Cossacks. In this case it was more a case of hating foreigners *per se*, rather than hating their politics.

It still is. Norris McWhirter was, until his death, a Patron of the United Kingdom Independence Party (UKIP), which came to fame in 2004, when it came from nowhere, to win almost half the number of seats in the European Elections as the Conservative Party. The primary political goal of UKIP is to withdraw the United Kingdom from the European Union.

UKIP is seen as part of the new populist right-wing movement in Great Britain, which has begun to emerge since the accession of Tony Blair's New Labour Government. As a rule of thumb, this movement adheres to what has become known as the *Cabbie Manifesto*, a loose collection of intolerant, muscle-flexing, nationalistic rantings. Not unlike the views attributed to *NASCAR Man* in the US.

2) Aggressive moves by neo-political groups like the Freedom Association actively to confront what they perceived as the first shots being fired in the War Against The Socialists. This found its greatest expression in the Watling Street Siege. When the Fleet Street Barons attempted to break the stranglehold of the print unions on the British Press.

Day after day, Trade Unionists battled on the streets, outside the new Press headquarters in the East End of London, with representatives from the Freedom Association, and other right-wing parapolitical and paramilitary groups. Meanwhile, those same organizations distributed care packages to the families of those workers who crossed the picket lines. The Barons won. The Fleet Street monopoly was broken.

This was a forerunner of the two Miners Strikes' in the Eighties, when Margaret Thatcher took on the Unions and won. Those two Strikes, and their failure, pretty much spelled the end of Trade Union power in Great Britain, a step Thatcher and others regarded as essential in preventing the return of Socialism to Great Britain.

3) Equally insistent, but more discreet, assistance from right-wing elements in the Intelligence Services: advice; a continuation of the already-commenced psychological operations; and other more direct action.

In respect of the last and the first, it was no accident that Margaret Thatcher, the newly-crowned darling of the Tory right found herself surrounded in her ascent by many with Intelligence connections: Airey Neave and Ian Gow, to name two. And it was seen as no accident by those on the right that those two were singled out as early victims of IRA assassinations. In the Seventies, the right-wing truly believed itself to be at war with International Socialist Terror. Every bit as much as the UK and the US now perceive themselves to be at War on Terror. And this attitude infused everything that Margaret Thatcher did in her march to power, and then her exercise of it.

If you want to be better informed about the sorts of personalities and organizations involved in all of this activity in the Seventies, look no further than the coalition brought together to fight for the 'No' vote in the European Referendum of 1975. You will find among their number certain leading left-wingers, including Michael Foot, Tony Benn and Hugh Scanlon, a leading Trade Unionist of the time. As a consequence of the fact that even his own regarded Benn as something of a wayward lunatic, he found himself, for the most part, addressing meetings in Wales and the West Country, where the sheep and their shaggers formed the largest component of the otherwise sleeping audiences.

Funny thing about the left-wing. Sure, they were worried about Europe too. They no more wanted foreign Capitalists running Great Britain than the right wanted foreign Socialists. But their effectiveness against the right-wing coalition of paramilitaries and Intelligence personnel, whom they ought to have been exposing, was always undermined by their being in bed with most of them. Whether it was for money or patriotism, or misguided two-way information exchange, the Intelligence Services generally found that their best informants were left-wing politicians, trade unionist and journalists.

Further evidence of the shenanigans of the 'loony right,' and its allies in high places and backstreet alleys, in the Seventies, can be found in a splendid book, called *Smear!: Wilson and the Secret State*, by Stephen Dorril and Robin Ramsay. A couple of excerpts of interest:

***

"Beyond the [Conservative] Parliamentary Party, the revolt centered round the Monday Club, inheritor of a long tradition of right-wing groups primarily concerned with the [British] Empire. The Monday Club had been formed in 1961 by a group of imperial-minded Tories concerned by Conservative Party policies towards Britain's remaining colonies. It acquired the immediate patronage of Lord Salisbury, the leading Tory peer. Though its initial impetus was opposition to [Conservative Prime Minister, Harold] Macmillan's policy towards Africa, it soon became the focus of a variety of right-wing tendencies within the Party unhappy at the perceived

continuing drift towards the center. As well as the old imperialist right, the traditionalist conservatives and the economic liberal right, there was what might best be called the nationalist strand which overlapped with both the other tendencies. The nationalists focused on the issue of the growing population of Afro-Caribbean, African and Asian people from the British Commonwealth in Britain, and sought to use it to create a populist political cause and a means of unifying the right. The central figure in this was George Kennedy Young, who retired as Deputy Chief of MI6 in 1961 and joined the merchant bankers Kleinwort Benson. In 1975, based on intelligence sources and information from his contacts in the anti-fascist movement, [Labour Prime Minister, Harold] Wilson identified Young as one of the 'plotters' against himself and his Government.

Young was introduced into the Monday Club by Tory MP John Biggs-Davidson in 1967. The Tory Party began shifting to the right that year, a move largely triggered by the Race Relations Act, Tory opposition to which was led by Monday Clubber Ronald Bell MP [for Beaconsfield]. Bell was also a leading member of the then secret '92 Group' on the right of the Conservative Parliamentary Party. Young's name first surfaced in the media as one of the signatories to a 1967 appeal for funds to meet the legal costs of four members of the Racial Preservation Society charged with inciting racial hatred. On joining the Monday Club, Young set up an 'Action Fund,' 'for action throughout the country,' using it to hire young, right-wing staff for the Club's HQ, placing his own cadres on key committees.

In 1969, the Monday Club published Young's pamphlet 'Who Goes Home?', in which he advocated repatriation of the black and Asian populations of this country. The Club's founder-member, Paul Bristol, resigned when he saw the draft of the pamphlet, which was 'even more extreme than the published version.' Young's destructive course through the Club begins here.

The Club subdivided into subject-based committees and sub-committees, with considerable autonomy. In 1970, the sub-committee on subversion organized a conference on the theme at which the principal speaker was General Giovanni di Lorenzo, a deputy in the Italian Parliament for the neo-fascist party, MSI, and former head of the Italian secret service SIFAR. [In 1964, Di Lorenzo attempted to seize power in Italy through a presidential-type coup.] Young had served in Italy at the end of the [Second World] War and became a specialist in Italian fascist police methods in combating subversives. He retained a life-long interest in re-establishing a Special Operations Executive-type organization to fight communism. Di Lorenzo had been heavily involved in the 'Strategy of Tension' in Italy during the late Sixties and early Seventies and was a leading member of the 'Gladio' network, revealed in late 1990 to have been set up by the CIA to combat communist subversion within Europe. Others in

Geoffrey Gilson

attendance included former ex-FBI agent at the United States Embassy in London, Charles Lyon, who was the London contact for the Robert Maheu Agency which had close links with the CIA and, allegedly, with British Intelligence. Also there were Sir Robert Thompson, the British counter-insurgency expert who made his name in the campaign in Malaya, and Ian Grieg, a Monday Club founder and Chair of the subversion sub-committee. It may be no coincidence that in 1970 a 'covert group' called the Resistance and Psychological Operations Committee (RPOC) was set up in Britain very much on the lines of the 'Gladio' network. It is said to have had links with the Ministry of Defense, the SAS and the Foreign Office's propaganda unit, the Information Research Department.

In 1971 the Monday Club began discreet but open collaboration with the extreme right outside of the Tory Party. The impetus came from the Club's immigration committee, set up in 1971 at Young's suggestion. Young sat on the new committee, which also included Gerald Howarth, at that time also a member of the Society of Individual Freedom (SIF); Bee Carthew, a former member of the Special Operations Executive [and a suspected continuing officer of British Intelligence]; and three MPs, including Ronald Bell. The chairman Geoffrey Baber, a 26-year-old Conservative councilor in Kensington, was an ally of Young and a director of his Action Fund. Baber was also an assistant to Donald Johnson MP at the right-wing publishers, Johnson Publications, one of the few regular advertisers in 'Monday World,' the Club's magazine. Johnson was a member of the Society for Individual Freedom, President of the Monday Club's Croydon branch, and a friend of Edward Martell and Henry Kerby MP. All were ex-Liberals who had been directors of Martell's National Fellowship, a forerunner of the Monday Club.

Young's campaign within the Monday Club climaxed in 1973 with his challenge for the Chair of the Club. This led to a fierce faction fight between Young's supporters and those of Jonathan Guinness [of the Book and Beer family], the incumbent Chair. A rancorous campaign ran, in public, through March and April. The subtext of the campaign was collaboration with groups like the National Front. However, Young's personal agenda was nothing less than ridding the Tory Party of Edward Heath. That year, Bee Carthew, an ally of Young's on the Monday Club Executive, had her flat burgled and various papers stolen.

The Young 'slate' included Bee Carthew, who was Meetings Secretary, and Harvey Proctor, Assistant Director of the Club, who stood for Editor of the Club's journal. [Proctor had to resign as Conservative MP for Billericay in 1987, after pleading guilty to charges of 'gross indecency,' with a couple of 'rent boys' he had hired for sex. The following year, with financial backing from former colleagues, including Michael Heseltine and Jeffrey Archer, the author, he opened two shops selling luxury shirts. In

Dead Men Don't Eat Lunch

1992, Proctor and Neil Hamilton, then a Government Minister, were assaulted by two men on a 'gay bashing expedition.' Hamilton's nose was broken in the attack in Proctor's shop in Richmond-on-Thames. In 2000, Proctor's stores were forced into liquidation after legal action by H.M. Customs over an unpaid VAT bill.]

Young was defeated and resigned immediately, as did Ronald Bell MP and Young's protégé, Geoffrey Baber. Bee Carthew was expelled and later worked with John Tyndall in the National Front. As many as 150 other members were expelled or threatened with expulsion in the purge which followed Young's defeat.

With all this bad publicity, the Club became a virtual pariah within the Parliamentary Party. Most of the MPs resigned, those whose primary interest was in economics resurfacing in other new groups. One such was the Selsdon Group, the organizing secretary of which was Anthony Van der Elst, who had been employed by Ronald Bell MP, on the recommendation of Young, in the offices of the Halt Immigration Now Campaign, which was run by Young. [The founding Treasurer of the Selsdon Group was Hugh. Tony Van der Elst gave the Eulogy at Hugh's funeral service.] A number of Tory MPs, including Nicholas Ridley (SIF member) and Richard Body, switched their allegiance to the Selsdon Group. Richard Body MP was Chair of the Economic Radicals, a 'small, unpublicized group of MPs, Tory candidates and academics' which met regularly in the House of Commons. Body had been in the Monday Club, had stood for Chair in 1972, but had left over the Club's 'wog-bashing image and obsession with darkest Africa.' John Biffen was also a member.

These groups continued the laissez-faire economic tradition which had been kept alive in the Tory Party by groups like the Institute for Economic Affairs and the free-trade, free-market remnants of the pre-War Liberal Party, most spectacularly represented by Edward Martell's organizations, such as the Freedom Group. Although none of these ventures had much success at the time in changing Tory Party policy, they are the antecedents of the mid-1970s groups like Ross McWhirter's Current Affairs Press and Self Help, and the National Association for Freedom. The core supporters and ideas of what became known as 'Thatcherism' can be traced back to these groups, and, in particular, the Selsdon Group.'

***

"Midway between the two [General] Elections of 1974 occurred what became known as the 'private armies' episode. Its origins lie in the [yet another!] 1972 Miners' Strike and subsequent rumblings of discontent within the British Military which found their way into the columns of 'The Times' that year. In late 1973 two complimentary movements began: one

Geoffrey Gilson

was press speculation about the possibility of some kind of military coup, which began with Patrick Cosgrave in the 'Spectator' in December 1973 and continued later in 1974; the other was the formation of voluntary organizations led by former military and intelligence personnel.

'Unison' was created in 1973 after a group led by George Kennedy Young tried and failed to take over the Royal Society of St. George, which one of this group described to the authors as a 'patriotic organization that wasn't doing anything.'

According to that 'Times' story 'Unison' had 'an inner committee including City bankers, businessmen and barristers,' of whom only Young, Ross McWhirter, General Sir Walter Walker, Admiral Ian Hogg and Colonel Robert Butler have been identified. Hogg and Young were friends of the late Sir Maurice Oldfield, with whom Young had worked in MI6 when Oldfield was its Chief. Young and McWhirter were the key members. Both had been active in the Society for Individual Freedom and the Monday Club and McWhirter was chairman of the 1971 Hain Prosecution Fund that raised [$30,000] to mount the SIF-sponsored private prosecution of Young Liberal Peter Hain [later, a Cabinet Minister in Tony Blair's New Labour Government] for his role in the campaign against the UK tour by the South African rugby team. Former MI6 officer, and friend of Oldfield and Young, Anthony Cavendish, was identified to one of the authors as a 'Unison' member but denies being a full member, admitting merely to attending a handful of meetings.

Sir Walter Walker was recruited by Young on the strength of a letter of introduction from the late Field Marshal Sir Gerald Templer ('Templer of Malaya'), and Colonel Butler volunteered his services. Though over 70 at the time, Templer was Lord Lieutenant of Greater London, the Queen's representative, and, formally at any rate, in charge of contingency planning – preparations for civil defense and civil disasters – for the area. After active service in counter-insurgency campaigns in Malaya and Borneo, Walker finished his career as NATO Commander-in-Chief Allied Forces Northern Command, 1969-1972. After retiring from the Army in 1972 Walker became one of the siren voices warning of the 'Communist Threat' to Britain and had given talks on this issue to, among others, the Monday Club and the World Anti-Communist League. For Young 'et al' a newly retired NATO Commander-in-Chief was a major coup and, whether Young intended it or not, Walter Walker became the public focus of attention."

***

"[Journalist] Chapman Pincher's account of his contacts with the Tory Party before and after the February [1974] election [when Edward Heath's Government was defeated by Harold Wilson] gives an important *glimpse into the networking between the state, the Tory Party and sections of the media. Pincher openly describes his role as an adjunct to the campaign: 'What was required of me in the main was that I should make use in the 'Daily Express' of material in my possession so that other papers would be encouraged to do likewise.' Another glimpse of this network was given to journalist Hugh Young. Later in 1974, Young met a former 'respected politician in the Heath Cabinet.' This 'prince among the wets' intended to stay in politics, he told Young, to get rid of Wilson, whose Government was full of 'Muscovites.' He had seen the files while in Government – on [Barbara] Castle, Foot, Benn and [Denis, now Lord] Healey. (Labour Cabinet members were refused access to their own files, let alone those on their opponents.) As Young was entering the politician's home, another man was leaving, casually described to Young as 'the chap who kept me informed on these things when I was in Government.' This is what the novelist John Le Carre, who as David Cornwell served in MI5 and MI6 in the 1950s and early 1960's, referred to as 'the natural intimacy between the secret services and the Conservative Party.' If a Labour Government was elected, Le Carre said, 'the secret services would be cuddling up with the Conservative Party-in-exile day and night.'"*

***

Hugh, at this time, had re-appeared in Beaconsfield, and had become interested in politics. He quickly advanced from the local scene to open rebellion against Edward Heath. And from there, to glory, at a national level, within the newly-active right-wing of the Conservative Party. In this latter regard, he had been taken under the wing of both Enoch Powell and Ronald Bell. Both had served with British Military Intelligence, and Ronald had subsequently qualified as a Barrister.

Shortly after these two mentorships began, Hugh suddenly developed an interest in the Law. He obtained an 'outside' degree with the University of London, in History; was articled at Wedlake Bell; and was invited to become one of that firm's partners almost as soon as he qualified as a Solicitor in 1974. I have always wondered whether this spate of activity on Hugh's behalf was part of 'someone' creating a 'jacket' for him. Meanwhile, I had left school. I now wanted to be an actor.

Harold Wilson's successor as Labour Prime Minister, James (now 'Lord') Callaghan, was required by Convention to call a General Election by 1979. In the run-up to that time, Thatcher's poll figures were off the wall. Labour Party members, who yearned for the days when Labour was still 'safe,' were defecting left, right and center. Thatcher could almost smell the lavender from the toilets at 10 Downing Street. She began to clean up her act, and to distance herself from the more overt loonies, who had brought her this far.

Hugh did much the same thing, in preparation for fighting the Leeds West constituency. He patiently kissed good-bye to all his former friends in the Monday Club. I wasn't kissing anybody. I was only just beginning to learn how to spell P-O-L-I-T-I-C-S.

We now know that, upon her accession, Thatcher immediately set in motion a radical agenda to transform Great Britain into an 'Enterprise Economy;' an agenda that was pursued, in more moderate form, by both of her successors, John Major and Tony Blair, even though they claimed different political persuasion.

We are also aware that Thatcher's government was aggressive in pursuing legal arms deals, particularly those available among the oil-rich Arab states. And there is some evidence of former *Monday Club* members, from the Seventies, being involved in illegal sales of arms to Iran and Iraq, in the Eighties. But nothing hard and fast about grand conspiracies between them and the Thatcher Government. At least, not at that stage of my investigation.

One of the more prominent former *Monday Club* members to hit the press was Gerald James, who was also reputedly involved with the *Savoy Mafia*, through his Chairmanship of Astra Holdings. Astra was one of Britain's leading arms suppliers in the Eighties, until it came under heavy Government investigation for alleged illegal arms sales.

Astra owned BMARC, which was accused of being deeply engaged in the supply of military technology to Iraq (and, with admirable lack of bias, to Iran, also). Astra had also bought PRB, a Belgium gunpowder manufacturer, from Societe Generale Belgique, one of the largest companies in the world. Either Societe or PRB, in turn, had a stake in Space Research Corporation, the corporate vehicle of Gerald Bull.

One interesting byline about Astra was that, just before its ignominious collapse, Alan Clark, then Minister of Defense, was avidly buying up shares in the company, and was doing it through the stock brokerage firm of Schaverien & Co.

At the time of his death in 1999, after complications involving a brain tumor, Alan Clark was MP for Kensington and Chelsea, which, situated on the border of the 'Mayfair Square Mile' in London, is Britain's safest Conservative Parliamentary seat. The local Conservative Association prides itself on choosing leading Conservative characters to represent it. Before Clark, they had Nick Scott, who, although a close friend of Clark's, was firmly on the opposite end of the political spectrum.

As a confirmed left-wing Tory, Scott was considered a fast-riser when Heath was Prime Minister, but was confined to the backbenches when Thatcher assumed power. Clark, on the other hand, as a populist right-winger, saw regular service in Thatcher's Governments, either in the Ministry of Defense, which helped to arrange arms sales, or in the Department of Trade, which issued the Export Licenses, and approved the Export Credit Guarantees, for those same arms deals.

In the Eighties, Clark came into a lot of money. His story was that he had inherited this money from his father, Kenneth (Lord) Clark, the author of the highly successful bestseller, *Civilization*, which had been made into an equally well-rated series of TV documentaries. However, rumors persisted that Clark made a regular habit of holding illicit seminars in his Ministry, where prospective arms dealers were tutored in how to get around the arms export oversight legislation. The corollary was that the latter was not unconnected with the sudden increase in Clark's wealth.

One thing that Scott and Clark had in common was their reputation as unabashed libertines. Clark is probably best known for his series of wild Diaries, which caused a sensation with their expose of Clark's sexual adventures among the hunting and sherry set in Great Britain. One famous episode in particular had Clark cuckolding a South African judge. Not only with the Judge's wife. At Clark's castle. But also with his two daughters. At Clark's castle. On the same weekend.

After Clark's death, his Parliamentary seat was 'inherited' by Michael Portillo, a former Conservative Secretary of State for Defense under John Major. Portillo had lost his own Parliamentary seat in the 1997 Tory election defeat. Upon his return to Parliament in 2001, Portillo was seen as the front runner in the Election for Leadership of the Conservative Party, following the resignation of then-Leader William Hague. Portillo campaigned on a platform of radical Party reform and a greater emphasis on public service. However, he was defeated, partly as a result of the intervention of Margaret (now 'Lady') Thatcher, who indicated that she did not now support him, and partly as a consequence of his earlier revelations of having had homosexual adventures before he was married.

Portillo resigned as Kensington's MP at the General Election in 2005, when Tony Blair's New Labour won again, but this time, with a greatly-reduced Parliamentary majority of 60. Portillo was succeeded by Sir Malcolm Rifkind, another former Conservative Minister, who had lost his own seat in Blair's electoral landslide of 1997. Like Portillo, Rifkind was seen as a future Leader of the Conservative Party, having succeeded Portillo as Secretary of Defense in 1992, and having then gone on to serve as Foreign Secretary under John Major. Unfortunately, Rifkind's hopes of such higher office were dashed by the slick campaign of young, Blair-alike candidate David Cameron, in the Conservative Leadership Election that followed the General Election of 2005.

After his Parliamentary loss in 1997, Rifkind was appointed Knight Commander of the Most Noble Order of St. Michael and St. George, in gratitude for his service to the foreign affairs of Great Britain. This Order was instituted on April 27th 1818 by the Prince Regent (later George IV), and it was intended to commemorate the placing of the Ionian Islands under British protection; originally it was intended for distinguished citizens of the islands, and also of Malta. At first, the Order was conferred upon those holding high position and commands in the Mediterranean; the islands there, acquired as a result of the Napoleonic Wars, were at that time very strategically placed and thus of importance to Britain.

Towards the end of the Nineteenth Century, due to the expansion of the British Empire, the Order was then extended to those who had given distinguished service in the Dominions and Colonies, as well as in foreign affairs generally. Today, the Order is awarded to men and women who have held, or will hold, high office, or who render extraordinary or important non-military service in a foreign country. It can also be conferred for important or loyal service in relation to Foreign and Commonwealth affairs.

The Order consists of the Sovereign, a Grand Master (currently The Duke of Kent), and includes three classes: 125 Knights and Dames Grand Cross (GCMG), 375 Knights and Dames Commander (KCMG and DCMG), and 1750 Companions (CMG). Members of the Royal Family may be appointed as Extra Knights and Dames Grand Cross. Foreigners can be appointed as honorary members.

His Royal Highness, Prince Edward, Duke of Kent, Grand Master of the Order, is brother to Prince Michael of Kent, and is a cousin to the Queen. As well as holding various other British and foreign Orders and decorations, the Duke of Kent is a Knight of the Garter, Britain's oldest and most senior Chivalric Order, and is also Grand Master of the United Grand Lodge of English Freemasons.

The motto of the order of St. Michael and St. George is *Auspicium melioris aevi* ('Token of a better age'). The banners of arms of the Knights and Dames Grand Cross are hung in the Chapel of the Order, which is in St Paul's Cathedral. Unique to this Order is the arrangement under which the enameled metal plates of the complete armorial achievement of all three classes are placed in the seats of the Chapel.

The Star and Badge of the Order feature the cross of St. George, the Order's motto, and a representation of the archangel St. Michael holding in his right hand a flaming sword and trampling upon Satan. The collar of the Order is composed alternately of the lions of England royally crowned and of white enameled Maltese crosses, and of the cyphers SM (St. Michael) and SG (St. George); the center of the collar consists of two winged lions each holding a book and seven arrows, surmounted by an imperial crown. The composition of the collar is therefore a reminder of the origins of the Order.

In Great Britain, there has never been any irrefutable 'proof' to the charges of illegal arms dealing and political profiteering by Governments or its senior members in the Eighties or Nineties, either in spite of or perhaps because of Major's Scott Inquiry. In contrast, just about every other major Government, in what used to be Western Europe in the Seventies, Eighties and Nineties, has since been tarnished with all manner of scandals relating to arms, kickbacks and illicit political profiteering.

The man whose place in history should have been cemented by his unifying of Germany in 1990, Helmut Kohl, has seen his legacy left in tatters after allegations of political corruption. Kohl, and his right-wing Christian Democratic subordinates, illegally accepted millions of dollars for political campaigning from wealthy individuals and businesses in the Eighties. Much of that money was lodged in personal accounts in Switzerland, and may have been used in private business deals.

In France, the conviction of Alain Juppe did little to enhance the image of his political patron Jacques Chirac, himself implicated in more than one corruption case, primarily arising from his stint as Mayor of Paris in the Eighties. Chirac enjoyed immunity from prosecution as a result of a decision in December 2000 to grant him that perk by a Commission he himself appointed.

Before Chirac, Socialist President Francois Mitterand helped assure the re-election of Helmut Kohl with tens of millions of francs. Mitterand's fellow socialist Edith Cresson's nepotistic ways led to the mass resignation of the European Commission in 1999. Cresson was also caught up in the Elf scandal in the early 1990s, being paid over three million francs ($1 million) by Elf – the French oil multinational.

A spin off from Mitterand's help for Kohl's re-election campaign was a favorable deal for Elf to buy the Leuna oil refinery in the former East Germany. During the second period of Mitterand's presidency (1988-1995), Elf's senior managers stripped out over 305 million euros ($400 million). The company was rotten right through. Of 37 officials accused, 30 were convicted.

Elf was created by the late French Nationalist heart-throb, Charles De Gaulle, in 1963. Intimately linked to structures of government in France and its former colonies, it played a king-making role in Africa from the start. It has been described as "a parallel Oil Ministry." Elf was also involved in the sale of six frigates to Taiwan under the second Mitterand presidency, which deal included the payment of 780 million euros ($1 billion) in illicit commissions...or 'bribes,' as we understand them. Foreign Minister Roland Dumas was convicted in that particular scam in 2001.

Elf offered Europe-wide welfare for top politicians. Not only did the company help finance Kohl's election campaigning but also that of Felipe Gonzalez, former Spanish Prime Minister. Inside France itself, it emerged during legal proceedings against Elf that Mitterand struck a deal with Elf's chief so as to spread its political funds more equally among the rival political parties. Before, Elf had favored only the Gaullists. Judicial examination of the Leuna refinery deal elicited this memorable saying from one of the accused, Alfred Sirven: "Lobbying without cash – that doesn't exist."

Mitterand's son, Jean-Christophe, who served as his African Strategy Adviser from 1989-1992, was implicated in 2000 in alleged illegal arms sales to Angola. Jacques Mitterand, brother of Francois, while not publicly connected to any of his brother's scandals, held senior ranks in the French Military, and was also Grand Master of the French Order of the Grand Orient Masons.

Indeed, Francois Mitterand was assiduous during his Presidency in successfully promoting French appointments to head organs working for European unity, touted by some as the 'regional goal' of the secular ambition for a New World Order. So it was that Jacques Delors, who was appointed Minister of Economy and Finance in Mitterand's first Government, became President of the European Commission in 1985. And Jacques Attali, a former Special Adviser to Mitterand, helped to found the European Bank for Reconstruction and Development, and served as its first President from 1991 to 1993.

The so-called 'secular ambition' of the various New World Order movements finds itself at odds with the aims of the royalist/religious strands within the Priory of Sion, who also want a united Europe, but for more than just political reasons.

The Priory has spent centuries promoting European unity, through war, royal marriage and political manipulation, so that the heir to the Jesus bloodline might have a suitable temporal and geographical base from which to exercise his or her royalist/religious leadership. The nearest the Priory came to such an ambition was first with the Merovingian dynasty, and then with the Holy Roman Empire, and finally, with the Stuart bloodline of Scotland.

Indeed, it was precisely to thwart the European machinations of both the Godless 'secular ambition' and the Priory that a German theological purist, Josef Ratzinger, was elected Pope Benedict XVI, in succession to John Paul II.

And on the subject of Italian skullduggery and Vatican maneuverings, and getting back to the list of senior European politicians who came a-cropper as a result of wrongdoing in the Eighties, the P2 Scandal finally caught up with former Italian Prime Minister and pillar of post-war Italy, Giuilo Andreotti. No-one truly believes his acquittal in 1999 on charges arising out of his alleged long-standing links with the Mafia. After all, the trial itself was held in the Italian Mafia's very own backyard – in Sicily.

When Bettino Craxi, another Italian Prime Minister, died in Tunisia in January 2000, he was on the run from Italian justice. Craxi had led the center-left coalition that ruled Italy during the 1980s. His Government was itself a political mafia that was exposed after the arrest of a leading Socialist politician in Milan on corruption charges. Craxi had been sentenced to 27 years when he fled the country.

Silvio Berlusconi, along with many other leaders of the Italian business and political right, attended Craxi's funeral. Berlusconi, a Prime Minister himself, and worth around 10 billion euros, developed his own problems, ending up being accused of tax fraud, bribing judges and false accounting. However, his parliamentary majority enabled him to pass a Bill granting him immunity so long as he remained Prime Minister.

Even though that Bill was eventually ruled unconstitutional, and the trial was ordered to proceed, Berlusconi has wriggled out of numerous minor investigations since his election in May 2001. However, this trial promises to be an incomparably more severe and high profile test for Italian justice. It comes when the multi-billion dollar Parmalat scandal has laid bare Europe's business and financial culture, just as Enron did in the US.

So. I looked around the world of the Eighties. And everywhere my gaze fell, I saw evidence of the 'Enterprise Eighties.' Rules being bent and broken. Money being made; money being moved and laundered; and money going missing, in huge amounts.

I saw the illegal 'Enterprise' of Vice President Bush's SSG/CPPG. I saw western country after western country merrily engaging in illegal arms sales to embargoed countries. I saw government ministers happily stuffing their pockets with backhanders. I saw intelligence agencies jumping onto the same bandwagon, and going into business for themselves. Bank accounts, with illegal arms profits, tucked away in Arab banks or Communist nations. Other banks, and savings and loans, being raped for billions. Companies collapsing, as their recalcitrant officers fled into exile with stolen pension funds.

But. I did not see one shred of hard evidence linking any of this, beyond reasonable doubt, to Margaret Thatcher, her Conservative Government, her Ministers, her son, or her Party. At least, not at that point of my investigation. Maybe it was because no-one could find the money trail. Whatever the reason, all I knew, Ari notwithstanding, was that I had only circumstantial evidence linking Margaret Thatcher and her ilk to serious corruption.

To be sure, Thatcher and her successors promoted an 'Enterprise' culture, in which anything and everything was acceptable, as far as making money was concerned. Rules didn't matter. All that mattered was not getting caught. I knew about that culture. I was a part of it.

To be sure, this culture led to Britain's very own stock market crashes and financial scandals in the Eighties and the Nineties. To be sure, it led to giant holes in companies' finances, in corporate collapse after corporate collapse. To be sure, it involved some rather exotic fundraising practices in the Tory Party. And to some equally exotic sexual practices among certain Conservative MPs, the exposure of which led to the 'Sleaze Factor,' in the run-up to the Tories' eventual electoral collapse in 1997. But, there was not a smidgeon of iron-clad proof about the Conservative Government or Party profiteering from any of this rule-breaking enterprise. Not yet, anyway. Except for circumstantial evidence, and Ari's say-so.

To be sure, Thatcher came to power on the backs of some pretty grim characters. And again, it is a matter of public record that Thatcher, upon becoming Prime Minister, dramatically increased the budgets of the various Intelligence Services, and pretty much gave them a free hand to do what they wanted in Northern Ireland, and in pursuit of the defeat of Communism abroad.

What is also well known is that, even when Prime Minister, Thatcher exhibited a continuing fondness for close advisers with close links to the Security Services: Airey Neave and Ian Gow have already been mentioned. Sometimes that fondness was for operations and operators of a slightly more clandestine nature. I quote from an article by Richard Norton-Taylor in the London *Guardian* of May 12th, 1990:

"A group of former intelligence officers attempted in the early years of Mrs. Thatcher's leadership to set up a secret cell – with access to arms – to undertake clandestine operations abroad, 'The Guardian' has learned.

Those behind the scheme included a former Foreign Office minister, and George Kennedy Young, former deputy head of MI6. The idea received enthusiastic support from Airey Neave, Mrs. Thatcher's close adviser who was killed by a terrorist attack in 1979.

It was suggested at the time of the Falklands conflict that it could be used inside Argentina, supplying arms to Argentineans opposed to the ruling junta.

Mrs. Thatcher is said to have backed the idea initially but dropped it as too risky after the attack by the French secret service on the Greenpeace ship, 'Rainbow Warrior.'"

But again, I came across no evidence of Britain's Intelligence Services breaking any rules. Nothing to suggest they went into business for themselves in the Eighties. No proof of illegal arms-dealing or money-making. Again, not at that time. In fact, all those 'grim' intelligence-related supporters of Thatcher from the Seventies had became remarkably invisible in the Eighties. At least, at that point in the story. All I was left with was circumstantial 'shadow' – and Ari's say-so.

And what of Hugh? To be sure after the debacle of 1983, he

dedicated himself to pursuing different paths. And most of them had to do with making money – either for himself, or for the Party. By this time, I was at his side, and together, we made merry hay with political fund-raising, the 'Clinton Way,' all through the middle Eighties.

There is no doubt that Hugh was well-considered in the Party. His service on the Conservative Board of Finance and his C.B.E. are a testament to that. A small anecdote, but I recall Hugh dancing with Margaret Thatcher at one of her first Conservative Conferences. Afterwards, Hugh told me that she'd grabbed him with the words, "for God's sakes, Hugh, let me dance with someone young and good-looking for a change."

I remember a curious exchange with Peter Walker. Curious, because Walker and Hugh seemed to be quite friendly. Whereas I had been led to believe that they had fought tooth and nails on most of the political issues in the early Seventies, when Walker had served as a very young Cabinet Minister in Heath's ill-fated Government.

Peter Walker was anathema to Margaret Thatcher, but she respected him as an effective political operator. She invited him to serve in her Cabinet, but only at the cost of persistent humiliation. Walker, for his own part, even though perceived by all as a leading 'wet' from Heath's days, confounded everyone by hanging on in Thatcher's Cabinet with gritty determination. Even though he hated her politics and her treatment of him. It was if he had some higher purpose on his agenda that allowed him to bear all of the rest.

Anyway, Walker was holding forth to a group of admirers at a Conservative Conference, a group which included Hugh and me. He was remembering his glory days as a senior Heathite. He was on an important Trade Mission to the Soviet Union. Quite by accident, Walker discovered that the senior British Embassy official, his Civil Servant and he had all attended the same small private school, tucked away in the hedgerows of England, somewhere utterly insignificant.

Walker knew that the Mission was going nowhere, so he decided to have some fun. From that day, until the Mission's completion, all three wore the same Old School tie. As the days progressed, Walker could sense that his Soviet counterparts and their minions were paying less and less attention to the business at hand, and more and more attention to the ties.

Eventually, at the post-Mission *après ski*, which, in good Soviet tradition, was well-fueled with vodka, the Soviet Trade Minister leant over to Walker. "So, Petrovitch," he breathed heavily, "tell me about the ties."

Walker, more than ready for the killer punch, breathed back, equally heavily, "Well Sergei, you know Eton?"

"Yah."

"And you know how they say 'the leaders of Britain are forged on the playing fields of Eton?"

"Oh yah."

"Well, no more," Walker declared, waving his tie at the entranced Soviet, "now it's our school..."

Walker swore that half the room emptied, as Soviet minions ran off to research the three Brits' school, and begin the lengthy process of infiltrating its poor unsuspecting faculty.

Moving along, I knew that Hugh was an operative in MI6. But was he senior? Hugh had told me about the Battle of the Bulge, and the near-disaster that befell the 4th Parachute Regiment at Arnhem. All because the senior military planners would not listen to the lowly Intelligence Officer, who was attached to their unit, but who seriously under-ranked them. The Intelligence Officer continued to insist that the insignificant blobs dotting the area where they planned to drop the Regiment were, in fact, camouflaged German tanks.

From that moment on, all Intelligence Officers, including those in their 'civilian equivalent,' all of whom are also military officers (the "MI" in MI6 and MI5 stands for Military Intelligence), are always appointed to a level that outranks whatever situation they find themselves in. Hugh told me that he bore the rank of Brigadier General.

The Conservative Party were aware of Hugh's Intelligence credentials. In 1985, the IRA came close to wiping out the entirety of Thatcher's Governing Cabinet, with a well-placed bomb in the Grand Hotel, in Brighton, during the annual Conservative Conference.

Five people were killed and 34 injured. The blast wiped out Margaret Thatcher's bathroom, minutes after she exited it. The casualties to her Government involved individuals who, after this length of time, probably mean nothing to the reader.

Imagine an Islamic bomb taking out Bush's hotel at a Republican Convention. Imagine it killing his Chief of Staff, and the wife of the Republican Majority Leader in the Senate. Imagine the seriously injured including Donald Rumsfeld and his wife. Imagine Bush's reaction. Imagine Thatcher's in 1985. And then wonder why she gave free rein to her Intelligence Agencies in Northern Ireland.

A statement at the time, from the IRA, said, "Today we were unlucky, but remember: we only have to be lucky once; you will have to be lucky always." That statement is attributed to Martin McGuiness, who was reputed at the time to be the Deputy Chief of the Provisional IRA.

Later on, McGuiness became the Deputy Leader of Sinn Fein, and was closely involved in the Northern Ireland Peace Process. In 2007, he was appointed Deputy First Minister in the new power-sharing administration in Northern Ireland.

McGinnis's statement has become a credo for all terrorist groups, and is a testament to the adage that today's terrorists are tomorrow's statesmen. Along with the fact that, in 1999, the bomber convicted of the Brighton outrage was released under the Good Friday Peace Agreement.

I had been in the Bar of the Grand Hotel barely three hours before the bomb exploded. The sound of the explosion woke me up, just in time for me clearly to hear the masonry crack, and collapse on top of the unfortunate residents below. Hugh awoke in the Hotel immediately next door to the Grand.

He told me that he ran out into the street, where the dust still billowed. Cabinet Ministers and Senior Party Officials staggered onto the seafront boardwalk, and then onto the darkened beach. Anything to get away from the cloying debris in the air.

Hugh headed for the beach, his eyes scanning the pitch black sea in front. He found an Official he knew intimately. "Get them off the beach," he hissed, waving hysterically at the sea. "If I were IRA, I'd have a man out there right now, in a dinghy, with rocket grenades." The Official was all business. Within minutes, Police vans arrived, and herded the objecting Ministers off to destinations unknown, until the scene became more secure.

To be sure, Hugh had well-honed money-laundering skills, from his days with Wedlake Bell. And I know from Karen George that someone approached Hugh to do something dangerous in 1984. I know that, at that time, Hugh was hurting for money, and was also hurting from political 'failure.' He was ripe for doing something bold to get to the next level in one leap. And he was none too squeamish about 'breaking the rules.'

To be sure, if what Ari was saying about Margaret Thatcher was true, then undoubtedly Hugh was 'there or thereabouts.' He was in an excellent position, with the right connections, the right talents, and the right 'rule-breaking' attitude to do 'dirty deeds' for Thatcher. Whether it be arranging dirty arms deals, laundering illegal profits, looking after her son, whatever.

But. At that point off the investigation, I still had no proof about misdeeds involving Margaret Thatcher. And I had nothing definitive about Hugh's dirty dealings, in so far as they might have been on the lady Thatcher's behalf. I had nothing clear-cut, at that stage, to persuade me that Hugh was other than a 'rogue operator.' Save for the albeit reasonably persuasive, yet circumstantial, evidence of his proximity to Margaret Thatcher. And Ari's say-so.

And so it was that I found myself troubled. And in the new-found tranquility of the North Georgia mountains, I did what was becoming a regular past-time of mine, particularly when stress reared its ugly head. I went a-loafering. But Ari had decided it was time to pester me. Again. He simply would not leave me alone. He insisted on knowing what progress I was making. And in the midst of this harassment, I received another startling jolt. But this time, it didn't come from Ari. It emanated from his wife, of all

Geoffrey Gilson

people

Chapter 25

I FOUND MYSELF BACK in my favorite place at the corner of the concrete pan. It was the end of another furiously hot day. I was tired from writing, and sitting in the same posture all day long. I stretched languidly, and looked out past the billowing tree shapes at the edge of the bluff, silhouetted as they were against the warm blue wash of the twilight sky.

My eyes caressed the soft recesses of the valley's gathering darkness, the plump velvet roundness of the rambling hills rising on the other side. The acid smell of burning concrete rose up and enveloped my senses like a blanket. While the slowly descending night air became filled with the sound of night insects, cursing and chattering. I was woken from my reverie by a friendly yelp behind me.

I turned around. Billy was the quintessential redneck. As always, and even at the most sweltering of times, he was decked out in camouflage trousers and a black T-shirt; the latter emblazoned with some complicated, psychedelic design incorporating the Confederate Flag and a bevy of unclad biker girls.

His head was bereft of hair, save for a Marine-style, blond buzz-cut on top, and a painstakingly-trimmed moustache curling around the corners of his mouth. His eyes were a sharp blue, and held mine in a steely gaze as if challenging me to some endless death struggle.

"Whassup Geoff?" he drawled drunkenly, but with good nature. Before waiting for a response, he invited me to go loafering with his friends the following day. Visions of "Deliverance" were instantly dismissed from my overactive mind, and I accepted. "Be up at dawn then," Billy slurred, as he turned back to his apartment, "I'm driving." It didn't seem to matter that Billy didn't have a driver's license. Not too many guys in the mountains do.

Sure enough, Billy's Camaro was revving up as the first rays of dawn hit the lower reaches of my bed. I threw on some clothes, and ran outside. Billy's car had once been painted red. Now, it was red from the rust. I hopped in, and we sped off down the side of the valley.

We burned rubber around all manner of confusing roads and tracks. I instantly lost all sense of where we were. Perhaps sensing my confusion, Billy looked over at me and winked. "You're not the only one," he chuckled, "they say there's more'n one Fed buried around these parts…"

The sky was immense over our heads, and the mountains were blue and sharp in the sunlight. Pieces of cloud hung in the pines on the far peaks. Soon enough, we slowed down, but only long enough for Billy to swing into a narrow lane that disappeared behind a heavily-wooded spur.

Here the scenery closed in alarmingly. The slopes came down to the very edge of the road. And the dense forest was not far behind. Overhanging branches clawed at the top and sides of the car as we whisked by.

The ground dipped and yawed like a choppy sea. But this had no measurable effect on Billy. Who was pretty much driving blind as the sun was almost completely obscured, and his headlights didn't work.

On and on we went, lurching and jouncing through a landscape that looked undiscovered even by the original Cherokees. Tulip trees, a hundred and twenty feet tall, rose like high, thin columns on every side, mixed in with hickories, oaks, ash, maple and ironwood. These are some of the oldest mountains in the world; and there are more species of trees cloaking their contours than there are in the whole continent of Europe.

Every so often, the solid curtain of trees would give way to a small clearing, hacked out of the living landscape. There, holding its own against the looming presence of mountain and forest, would stand an ole-timey homestead of poplar logs. A quick flash of dark, weathered timbers, misshapen by time and the elements. A rusty-red roof, more holes than cover. A rickety old verandah, and moss-covered smokestack. And then the woods would swallow us up again.

Billy was hooting and hollering now. Yelling about the good ol' days, back when the roads were dirt, and the cops were dirtier. When his father used to do moonshine runs into Tennessee for Ol' Poke. Who ran an unlicensed bar and whorehouse right next door to the County High School. And who got an unwelcome haircut one day, when an unruly customer shot him point blank in the forehead with a Colt 45.

Eventually, the death-run came to an end, as we entered an oasis of tranquility drawn from the very depths of nostalgia and memory. The trees parted and gave way to a small, open valley. The tarmacadum road seemed almost immediately to become a dusty dirt track, two deep ruts indicating the direction we should take.

The valley, or 'holler' as its known in these parts, was crammed with the clutter and scraps of long-time human habitation. Every spare inch was in use; however untidily. Thrown-together, cinder and wooden shacks sat side-by-side with farmyard pens. Dogs were in kennels, goats on the loose or tied up to the occasional worn-out flowering shrub. Unpainted picket fences wandered aimlessly, more for decorative purpose than utilitarian. Chopped wood was heaped in piles at nonsensical intervals around the dell.

There was a small cluster of fruit trees, or what I took to be fruit trees, gamely fighting age and dust in their annual struggle to produce a harvest. And scattered around the dwellings were small patches of maize and corn, pea and bean, cucumber and squash; all the necessities of an essentially self-supporting community. The air was busy with the sound of insects, as flies fought with mosquitoes to gain access to my exposed skin.

We headed for one of the larger homes, situated up against the edge of the forest so that the tall trees offered some respite from the searing sun. Bill parked his now-steaming car alongside a couple pick-ups. And we both got out to meet the welcoming committee.

First up was a living rendition of an oversized dwarf straight out of Snow White. Small and rotund, with a pot belly, dimpled cheeks and a round red nose. His sandy hair gave away his Scottish heritage. His name was Jesse. And there was constant merriment in his voice and a twinkle in his eye.

"Golly Jesus," he squealed, "you let that maniac drive you?" This was followed by a wild cackle of laughter. For some reason, he already knew who I was. Billy must have told him. Jesse introduced me to a rag-tag collection of men, women and children. With a wink, he carefully removed the can of beer that one of the young un's had squeezed into my hand. Billy had apparently told him everything about me. In a curious way, I was charmed.

We all settled, in various stages of repose, on a variety of seating furniture, situated around the verandah. And we then proceeded to loafer. Which, on that particular day, meant drinking and laughing. Followed by more drinking and laughing. Interrupted by occasional drinking and laughing.

I listened in awe to the symphony of their cross-conversations. Aware once again how distinctive is the dialectic music that mountain folk create. They love to fill their mouth with words. Let them roll and tumble like pebbles in a bubbling brook. Serenade each other with sing-song vowels. And fence like gladiators with consonants as harsh and as angular as the granite peaks.

The accent is pure Dolly Parton. And like the actress, it has its many moods. At times, a genteel burr, as soft and seducing as a humming-bird's wings. But when roused and raucous, a hard-edged squawk so abrasive it can cut through steel.

Geoffrey Gilson

For these people, conversing is not simply about communication; it's about painting a picture with words. They begin sentences not knowing where they will end. They mix metaphors, and split infinitives. They change tense from sentence to sentence, with nary a breath drawn from one swallowed word to the next. They mutter and mumble, gargle and garble, and altogether butcher what the rest of us treasure as the finer aspects of the English Language. But by the time they've finished, they've woven a tapestry so rich and so clear, and spun a spell so hypnotic and entrancing, it's enough to put even Shakespeare to shame.

All of a sudden, I found myself surrounded by lusty young lads, still sporting the odd garment of Confederate Grey. Wrestling with each other, while the girls in their sun-bleached frocks hollered and whistled; whooped with delight as their favorite beau was thrown to the ground with a resounding thump.

Dogs barked, and cocks crowed. The pigs in their lean-to pens snuffled in the dirt for non-existent delicacies. A mangy old goat, pegged to the side of a shack, strained to reach a thread-bare sheet left hanging too low from one of the washing-lines.

The sun, playing in the gently-swaying trees, created a mesmerizing pattern of dappled light and shadow on the ground before me. The heavy-sweet stench of farmyard manure rose up and gently clung to the back of my nostrils. A cry rang out behind me. "Come on dopehead, wake up!" I turned to see Hugh, standing in the doorway, hammering a dinner triangle with all his might.

At that moment, I woke with a start to find Jesse standing above me rattling his car keys against an empty beer can. "Yurrrrp. Geoff's a natural loafer," came his triumphant shout. Along the verandah, my blushing embarrassment was met with hearty guffaws and vigorously-slapped thighs. But there was no hint of malice. Rather, they were hailing the induction into their ranks of a worthy newcomer.

Shadows had drawn long. And they crawled up the hillsides, to meet the darkening sky, as night fell. Jesse expressed himself unhappy with my descriptive narrative. He preferred a simile describing the night sky spitting darkness like tobacco juice, so that it drooled slowly down the mountain slopes. I promised that I'd mention his input.

On the way home, Billy's driving was just as wild. As was his yammering. This time, he was giving me chapter and verse of the anti-Semitic doctrine of the White Christian Church and the Knights of the Ku Klux Klan. How they were the last line of defense against the Jewish-Masonic Conspiracy, the United Nations, and the Federal Reserve's black helicopters. I decided to have a little fun with him.

We stood side by side on the darkened concrete pan, as I explained about the 2,000 year struggle between the Roman Christian Church and the

Dead Men Don't Eat Lunch

Priory of Sion. How all of the various Judeo-Masonic Conspiracies flowed from the Priory, at one time or another. That there was more than one. That some were religious, and some royal, and others merely secular. But, how they all had in common one thing: the fact that they, and the Roman Church, were based upon the teachings of Christ. Who was a Jew. So, both the Conspiracies and the Christian Church were Jewish. Including the White Christian Church. And, indeed, the KKK, which is simply based upon those Chivalric Orders that had their origin with the Knights Templar.

Bill staggered to bed, now more confused than drunk. I didn't feel too guilty. I knew that he'd remember none of it the following morning. I hung about a few minutes, soaking up the ambience of late night. I pushed out my face. Looked around the bluff and the valley. And then up into the night sky, where wisps of spectral cloud sped silently across the moon, like ghostly whispers. I stared for a long time at the bright, white full moon, as if hoping to find mystical answers skipping down its translucent moonbeams. The night sounds began again. But all else was silent. Rabun County was asleep.

***

I had spent the years, 1993-1996, doing little to rock the boat primarily so as not to get in the way of Ari. But I was also conscious that I wanted to get my 'preliminary' research and investigation completed before I 'tipped off' those closer to the action as to my intentions.

In all the circumstances, I took the view that I'd pretty much exhausted anything that would pass as 'preliminary,' and, following my experience with Christopher Drogoul, decided it was now time to talk to a few more 'horses' mouths.' However, the approaches would have to be effected quickly and in a group, so as to prevent anyone from comparing stories.

First, I thought it wise to wolf down another huge helping of humble pie, and go and talk to Ari again. I knew that the immediate chances of my flying up to Montreal were zero. So, instead, I craft a questionnaire. It really was time to get some sort of verification for all that he had been telling me.

When I telephoned him to get a fax number, he exuded charm and helpfulness. But, he was very nervous about transmitting any information to me other than face to face. He did not trust the security of anything electronic or postal. He certainly didn't want to discuss my questions through the telephone. He was very agitated at the thought that I might let a name or two slip. As a compromise, he agreed to let me give him a 'preview' of one of the more innocuous questions.

Totally at random, I chose one asking for the name of the lawyer he mentioned in one of our earlier chats, in 1993. The lawyer he claimed had handled money transactions for those selling arms to Iraq, and had known Hugh and what he was up to. From his explosive reaction, you'd have thought that I'd asked for a night alone with Ari's wife. Which, of course, would have been very nice. But. Ari had a conniption. In fact, he had a whole litter of them.

He wanted to help me, he hissed dramatically. He understood I needed verification. But. He had to be very careful, he continued in his stage whisper, as if whispering was going to confuse a hi-tech bugging device. This was all very sensitive. There was only a very small group of people involved in all of this. No more than 40. If Ari was inadvertent in the way he described a source, it would immediately be apparent to the 'others' who'd been talking. It wasn't just a simple case of his giving me a name...wheeze...gasp...

I was very impressed with the performance. I gave him an 8 out of 10, a bouquet of fresh roses, and a series of free lessons with Sir John Gielgud. But what on earth was so important about this lawyer?

Before I could say anything, however, all was overwhelmed by the sound of scraping and scratching on the telephone. And then Haya was on the line. She sounded very angry. She wanted to know why I was trying to get her husband into danger.

I mumbled something utterly useless and forgettable, all the while wondering what it was that Hugh could possibly have been in involved with that had a decent woman thinking I could be a source of danger to her husband. Someone who had been a senior officer in one of the most feared intelligence agencies in the world.

I expected games with Ari, but Haya was a straighter shooter. Along with being cute, she was genuine and honest. And, on this particular day, very scared. It was a reaction I was to get used to over the ensuing months and years. Three were some more scraping sounds on the telephone, and Ari's honey-coated purr returned. He seemed to have recovered his poise.

In much calmer mode, Ari explained that the lawyer in question acted for a number of people in senior positions in the Conservative Party. It was through him that Ari had discovered much of what it was he knew about the connections between Hugh, Iraq and the Tories. This lawyer, in turn, had obtained his information from his clients.

Ari said that he would need to make a couple of telephone calls to determine if it would be possible for him to give me the sort of information I wanted. He would then call me back. To my surprise, on this occasion, he did.

Ari confirmed that he could make the verifying information available to me, but that he was not prepared to speak through the telephone, or to put anything in writing at that stage. In the absence of a face-to-face, he promised that, once I had a publisher, he would meet with me and the publisher.

It sounded a little like Ari wanting to be the center of attention again. But I was still mindful of Haya, so I shrugged my shoulders and thanked him. And then felt freed to continue with my own inquiries.

***

I sent out a whole bunch of faxes, to the likes of the US President, the UK Prime Minister, the Chairman of the Conservative Party, Lord Justice Scott and Lord Prior, the Chairman of GEC (UK).

In one form or another, I made the allegation that Hugh and Mark Thatcher had been selling arms to Iraq; that one deal was for GEC (UK) engines, to extend the range of Iraq's SCUD-B missiles; and that Hugh had been laundering profits, kickbacks or both back to Mark Thatcher and senior officials of the Conservative Party and Government.

At the same time, since I couldn't get up to New York to see Robert Simels, I began the process of trying to obtain evidence of the BNL Letter of Credit from every Federal Department I could think of. Which turned out, co-incidentally, to be every Department in the telephone book.

It was difficult to dignify this process with the expression 'shoestring investigation.' It was more of a 'sandal.' Just one of them. And the left one at that. I felt like one man and his dog, without the dog.

***

I dug out the *Sunday Times* articles on Mark Thatcher, and made contact with Keith Praeger, a Senior Agent with the US Customs in Miami, Florida. Hell yeah, said Keith, they were still interested in Mark Thatcher. And yes, they'd be interested in any information that I could give them. The one thing they'd always been missing was the money trail. How soon could I let them have some leads?

I confess I became a little cagey. I didn't want law enforcement officers trampling all over my sources until I'd finished with them. I explained this to Keith, who fully understood. He's be waiting, just as soon as I was ready. In the meantime, I gave him Hugh's name, and the details of his theft and death, so that he had something to check out. See if he could find out something all on his own.

***

I spoke with Paul Carratu, son of Vincent Carratu, and the new boss of Carratu International. A man also with an inveterate need to talk. Vincent had been in charge at the time of Hugh's death, and Paul had been assigned to search all of the computer databases at Simmonds and Company. He seemed amused that I was calling him. He remembered me perfectly.

Most of what he said was strictly off-the-record, but the gist of it was that Geoff's on-the-record comment was considerably less than half the story. Paul remained convinced that the unsatisfactory outcome of the Carratu investigation was deliberately stage-managed by third parties.

He was less surprised by the outcome than the fact that his Company had been hired in the first place. It was clear that the investigation was not intended to get anywhere serious. Every time it got close, the Oversight Committee of the Law Society stepped in, and sent Carratu off in a new direction.

I did some research, and discovered that the Vice Chairman of the so-called 'Oversight Committee' was a solicitor who worked in a town just seven miles from Beaconsfield, and who loathed Hugh. And that one of the other members had an OBE.

Upon contacting the appropriate civil servant in Whitehall, I was told that there was no citation given for the OBE in question (like for instance, 'meritorious service in cleaning lavatories'). Reggie had previously told me that, when you come across an honor with no citation, it is usually indicative of Military Intelligence.

Think about it. Lawyers have this whole 'confidence' thing going for them. "Dear boy, let's talk about this in confidence; off the record, can you pull a few strings for me...?" And lawyers are everywhere: private corporations, charities, government departments – they all have lawyers. And politicians? Heck, half of them are lawyers. You couldn't have a more efficient 'secret' network than lawyers. And here was an investigation being conducted by the Mothers' Union of all lawyers. If there was anything that had ever been susceptible to a few nods and winks from lawyers doing the shifty, it had to have been the investigation into Hugh's missing money.

***

Lord Prior of GEC (UK) is the first to respond to my fax. Lord Prior was a Cabinet Minister under Margaret Thatcher between 1979 and 1983. His letter exemplifies the unparalleled contribution the Conservative Party has made to the art of dissemble in the past 200 years.

In my mind's eye, I could clearly see Prior dictating the letter. First, he shifted his weight gingerly to the left butt cheek, and very carefully remembered to forget everything; without actually denying anything. Then, he carefully shifted all of that weight to his right butt cheek, and threw in a little personal memento; just to show that he was sending a signal, so that the judge would be a tad more lenient during the sentencing phase of the corruption trial.

And so it was that he stated categorically and definitively, for all the world clearly to hear that…he found it difficult to believe that there was any foundation to my allegations. I, in turn, still find it difficult to believe that the Chairman of Britain's largest, privately-owned engineering company admitted to not knowing, beyond all doubt, whether or not some $28million of his company's products had been sold illegally to an embargoed country.

An embargoed country that had just fought a military engagement with the Chairman's own country. In which, allegedly, the products might have been used to extend the range of missiles, at least one of which had been fired upon and had ostensibly killed civilians in the State of Israel. But then, perhaps I'm losing my sense of objectivity.

Prior's one saving grace, and given the context, it was almost comic, was that he ended his brief letter remembering that he had met with Hugh on a couple of occasions. Would that have been at the Sedgwick-upon-Thames Annual Ladies Knit 'n Barbeque? Or would that have been when you, Hugh and the lads from the "Dispatch" were loading the warheads onto the flatbed?

***

Keith Praeger had been busy. He had a couple of 'friends,' from "former occupations," who were attached to the American Embassy, in the "Mayfair Square Mile" of London. These 'friends' had checked out Hugh. Keith was happy to report that he was now definitely interested.

He was eager to know if I had anything more he could get his teeth into? What the heck. I'd hit rock bottom with the Law Society. Keith was Law Enforcement after all. He knew how to be careful. I gave him chapter and verse on the Carratu investigation. Keith said he would look into it immediately.

***

The Chairman of the Conservative Party, Dr. Brian Mawhinney MP, chickened out. He got his Communications Director to hedge and fudge for him. The Director wrote to me and said that the Chairman had no comment to make regarding Hugh John Simmonds.

Back in 1989, during our very awkward drink together, Philip Dumville, the Conservative Constituency Agent for Beaconsfield, had told me that a constituent from Beaconsfield had accused the Conservative Party of accepting millions of pounds from Hugh in an attempt, by him, to buy a safe Conservative seat.

Geoffrey Gilson

The then Chairman had fallen over himself to make public a letter categorically denying this charge. Although he did admit that Hugh had donated some $30,000 a year, each of the three years he had served on the Conservative Board of Finance.

Comments by the leadership of the Conservative Party, regarding the Hashemi allegations, warranted the front page of the *Sunday Times*, so determined were those leaders to ensure that not one scrap of mud should stay stuck to their Party in the run-up to the General Election.

And yet, here I was accusing that same Party of receiving kickbacks from an illegal arms deal with a country with which their Government had just gone to war. And the only raise I could get from one of the most formidable political spin machines in the world was "no comment"?

I thought of the Emperor Nero playing his fiddle while Rome burned to the ground. I thought of another individual with a penchant for dressing in white and gold, Michael Jackson, who had sung songs from the top of a van, outside the courthouse where he was facing charges for child molestation. I wondered if there was a depth of guilt, beyond which public denial is deemed useless, and only self-denial can fill the void?

***

While pondering this, I heard again from Keith Praeger. Good news. A friend (another one) in the (London) Metropolitan Police Fraud Squad had an 'in' at the Law Society (wonderful things networks), and he was going to use it to try and obtain a copy of the Carratu Report. Praeger told me that he would then effectively 'take over' the unfinished investigation of Hugh's financial affairs.

***

I received a bashful example of 'oops-was-I-there?' from the Secretary to Sir Richard Scott's Inquiry. I had written asking if there had been any submissions, besides mine, relating to GEC (UK); deals for rocket engines; Hugh Simmonds; Ari-Ben-Menashe; or Mark Thatcher.

The Secretary's reply stated only that there had been no other submissions about Simmonds. The other names seemed, oops, to have slipped his mind. And he stated, oops, that he was relying only on his memory.

I wrote back, commending him, oops, on his excellent memory, which appeared, oops, to have instant command of what had been some 80,000 documents that had been submitted. I then wondered if he would like now, oops, to perform a slightly more, oops, scientific search of the, oops, computerized indices. I never heard back. Oops.

***

John Simmonds wrote to tell me that Geoffrey Hughes had told him that Carratu had discovered that Hugh owed a large sum of money to an arms dealer; that the arms dealer had never made a claim against the Law Society; and that the arms dealer had stated that Hugh had expert knowledge of a handgun in general use by the British Security Services.

John added that he had spoken further with Karen George, who was now prepared to state that Hugh had been involved in a complicated arms deal at the time of his death. On behalf of Margaret Thatcher. I ignored the vicious little voice on my shoulder that hissed that it might have saved me some eight years of blindly careening around the world, if I had been given this snippet by Karen at the beginning of the exercise. When she had been egging me on to get to the truth.

***

I immediately dashed off a letter to the Law Society, letting them know that I was now in possession of this information, and wondering how they felt able in their last missive to me to say: "The [Carratu] Report does not cover the issues you raise or touch on the allegations you have put to me both verbally or in writing [regarding Hugh's involvement with the Intelligence Services, and with arms sales]. I understand that you have several theories about Hugh Simmonds' activities, but I have to tell you that none of these are in anyway substantiated by the Carratu investigation."

***

I made my own contact with Keith Praeger, from whom I had not heard in a while. He was sorry all over the place. The fact is that his hands were tied. There was loads he'd like to do, provided he wasn't seen to be doing anything.

It genuinely was not his fault. Reading between the lines, it would seem that Aida Perez kind of jumped the gun back in 1994, when she had said the house was going to fall in on Mark Thatcher. I gathered that Mark's lawyers pretty much brought the house down on US Customs in Miami instead.

As a consequence, we had a vicious circle: Keith couldn't be seen officially to be doing anything with potential connections to Thatcher, unless he had iron-clad evidence. Which he couldn't get without being seen officially to be doing something with potential connections to Thatcher.

Geoffrey Gilson

All he could do was cheer me on from the sidelines. Just as soon as I had the whole jigsaw puzzle, he'd be delighted to issue a warrant for Mark T. I felt genuinely sorry for Keith. Politics can be a bum rap. I wish I'd been able to get him that puzzle before he retired a couple of years later. I hope he's marlin fishing now, and naming every single one that doesn't get away, "Mark."

***

I had a telephone conversation with the Press Officer of the Law Society. Her response to my letter about Hugh and the elusive arms dealer was to stonewall. Something about the alleged arms dealer not being in the file in front of her. I suggested that she might want to protect her own back, and get it in writing from her superiors that what was in her file was, in fact, everything that had been found. She was just doing her job, and we had quite a playful conversation.

***

Which put me in the mood for getting playful with someone else. What the heck? I telephoned Mark Thatcher's lawyers in America, and came up with some cock and bull story about Mark and Hugh. How Hugh had left me a letter telling me to get in touch with Mark. It almost worked. I got as far as Mark's Executive Assistant, before someone – Mark? – smelled a rat. But Hugh's name had rung some sort of bell.

***

I had been looking forward to speaking with Peter Smith, for a long time. He had been one of Hugh's closest friends. Peter's wife, Cherry, and Janet had been tea and gossip buddies for years and years. They'd shared the bonding experience of child-birth and child-rearing together.

When Hugh died, and the Winnie-the-Pooh hit the fan, I was comforted in the knowledge that one of the Executors of Hugh's Will was Peter. Until he revoked. Which was ok, because he'd told Hugh's father that he could do more for Janet and her family outside of the Estate. Which was also ok, because Peter was a senior chartered accountant, and he was ideally placed to help Janet negotiate the financial minefield that her life, and that of her children, had just become. Until Janet told me that she'd never heard from Peter again.

I was put through to Peter's office almost immediately. Interesting, bearing in mind that Peter had now achieved the exalted status of Chairman of Coopers & Lybrand UK, one of the then Big Four accounting firms in

Dead Men Don't Eat Lunch

London. At first, he was charming. I was not. I got straight down to business.

I asked him why he had told Ari not to speak to me because I was a crook? Without missing a beat, Peter said that he did not know the man, had never met him, and had never spoken to him.

I was impressed, but a little voice nagged at the back of my mind. But too quietly for me to hear. I pressed on. With admirable insouciance of my own, I thanked him, and promised that his denial would be repeated without alteration in the book.

Peter's façade cracked ever so slightly. There was the hint of a stutter, before he regained his composure. But why, he wondered, would I even want to include any quote from Ari (interesting, he didn't fluff the name), if he didn't know him? I didn't need to include a denial if the conversation had never occurred. The little, nagging voice was getting louder.

Gosh, I said, hoping the sarcasm dripped, what to do, what to do? I sighed. I'm sorry, I continued, it appeared I had two different versions. Ah well. It seemed only fair to include both.

Peter's charm had now gone completely. In a voice that did a much better job of dripping acid, than mine had done with irony, he suggested that I have a lawyer read my book before it was published. I thanked him. And Peter hung up. The little voice had finally become a loud yell, and was all of a sudden very clear.

Peter was a man who should have been as secure as any man alive could hope to be. He was, at that time, the Chairman of the largest firm of chartered accountants in Great Britain. He was intimately involved in the merger negotiations, which married Coopers & Lybrand to Price Waterhouse. Together, they would become PricewaterhouseCoopers, the largest financial services company in the world. Peter would hold the position of Senior Partner in PricewaterhouseCoopers UK. He would later ascend to the Chairmanship of PricewaterhouseCoopers International, becoming one of the most distinguished and respected icons in his profession, in the world.

Peter was a man who should have become comfortable within the corridors of power. He served on the UK Commission for Corporate Governance, the President's Committee of the Confederation of British Industry (equivalent to the US Chamber of Commerce), and the Governing Council of the Institute of Chartered Accountants of England and Wales.

Peter knew me personally from our days serving together in the Beaconsfield Constituency Conservative Association. So, with self-confidence overflowing, having taken the time to catch up with an old friend, why hadn't he just chuckled, and joshed me gently about, perhaps, getting some psychiatric help?

Maybe he was caught off-guard by suggestions he regarded as

being whacko? Hmm. I don't think so. Trust me, this is not a man easily found with his trousers hanging around his ankles. And if such were to happen, he would have the presence of mind never to allow anything so ordinary as a blush to pass over his features.

Ok then. Maybe he did take the accusations seriously, and reacted in a manner that was not only appropriate, but also probably very sensible? I might be prepared to buy this, if it were not the fact that there was none of what I would expect to be the normal follow-through.

Since that conversation, I have gone to great lengths to give Peter every opportunity to take legal action against me; to test whether or not he takes my allegations seriously. I have written to his lawyers; set out in minute detail anything and everything I could possibly think of that might be libelous; and have given them an address in England with which to serve me with a lawsuit for libel. I have heard nothing in response.

Could it be that Peter has simply concluded that I am harmless, my claims are so much nonsense, and that they and I can have little effect upon him? Let's examine that possibility a little more closely.

Ii is the case that, as of 2006, Peter has moved on to even greener pastures, with no sense that he is carrying any baggage that I might be able to expose. He is a Non-Executive Director of N.M. Rothschild and Sons Ltd, the leading London merchant bankers, and a favorite target of theorists waxing lyrical about Jewish Diaspora's and Masonic Conspiracies. Oops. Would that be me?

Peter serves with some interesting other Non-Executive Directors. There is Lord Guthrie, a Freeman of the City of London and a Knight of Malta. Peter Birch, a Professor of Economics. Sir Graham Hearne, of Enterprise Oil. Gerald Rosenfeld, an investment banker. And until 2002, Lord Wakeham, a one-time Cabinet favorite of Margaret Thatcher, and whose wife tragically was murdered in the Brighton Bombing.

Best of all is Sir Clive Whitmore. Clive was once the top Civil Servant in the UK Government's Home Office, the Department with responsibility for MI5. He has been appointed to the UK Security Commission by Tony Blair. And also serves as a Non-Executive Director of Racal Electronics, the defense electronics company. Truly, a selection of Non-Executive Directors amply representing the City, the Intelligence Services, the Defense Establishment and the Tory Party.

Peter is also a Non-Executive Director of Equitable Life Assurance, one of Britain's premier insurance companies, where he serves on their Audit Committee. I trust he is acquitting himself in that role with somewhat more propriety and legality than he did while overseeing the Audit of the Tories' corrupt National Accounts. In addition, at the end of 2005, Peter became Chairman of Savill's, one of the largest property services companies in the world.

Dead Men Don't Eat Lunch

Notwithstanding his abandonment of Hugh's family, Peter still affects an altruistic streak, and currently occupies the post of Treasurer of the Institute of Chartered Accountants of England and Wales. Peter was only a little older than Hugh, and clearly he harbors some further ambitions.

I am reminded of the early Seventies, when Peter and Hugh began their political careers together in the Beaconsfield Young Conservatives, Peter's Treasurer to Hugh's Chairman. They formed a dinner club, called the Tamworth Society. All of the members had a gameplan for achieving political success, and each member shared theirs with the other Society members.

Hugh had told me that Peter's was different to everyone else's. Peter had stated that it was his intention first to achieve success as an accountant, and then to gain status with public service that was not overtly political. He anticipated working his way up the Honors' 'ladder,' through a Knighthood to eventual Peerage. He then expected to be invited to join a Conservative Cabinet, holding one of the senior financial posts, when he was still in his fifties or sixties. As Lord Smith.

In many respects, Peter's gameplan seems to be on track. Except that, to date, he has not received so much as a lowly British Empire Medal. Now, this might have something to do with the file that resides in the Ceremonial Department of the Cabinet Office. A file that I passed onto them.

This file includes allegations that Peter, as part of the Coopers & Lybrand team, which audited the Conservative Party's National Accounts in the Eighties, was well aware of illegal financial activity in those Accounts, and acted to cover up that activity, in contravention of his professional responsibilities as a chartered accountant.

Now, it may well be that the powers-that-be at the center of the British Establishment have their own reasons for not wanting to bestow honour upon a man, who, in any other circumstance, would seem eminently deserving of at least a Knighthood by now. But I don't think so. I believe their only reason is my file; the information it contains; and that fact that those 'powers' know it to be true.

I believe that Peter threatened me with a lawyer during our telephone conversation, because he was surprised I had discovered as much as I had. I believe he never followed through with his threat, even though this book now exists, because he knew that the truth contained in that file would come spilling out during a libel trial.

And that is where the situation will remain, in perpetuity: Peter will never receive an honour. I have permanently destroyed his pathway to high government office. He ought to be suing the pants off me. But he won't. Ever. And if you wanted even the smallest scrap of circumstantial evidence that the official version of Simmond's death is not the real version of events, that's a good a place to start as any.

Geoffrey Gilson

Don't take my word for it. Savills is in the telephone directory. Ask Peter Smith if he denies the allegations I have made against him. He won't. Ask him if he intends to sue me for libel. He will side-step the question.

Why have I spent so much time and effort on one individual? Because that one individual was the one individual who had the best chance of helping Hugh's families to negotiate the financial and emotional minefield that Hugh left for them. Peter had the opportunity and the skills. He was in an ideal position. And he had the moral responsibility, as one of the Executors of Hugh's Estate.

Peter abandoned that responsibility, because he perceived that association with Hugh and his families might upset his oh-so-precious pathway to high government office. You don't need me to point out the irony that, due to the abandonment of that responsibility, and with a nudge or two from me, that pathway has now disappeared, in any event. The bar is set higher for someone who places himself so firmly in the public eye. And I have lowered that bar on Peter.

***

Next, I heard from Bill. As in Clinton. We Southern Boys have to stick together. Ok, not from Bill exactly. His Correspondence Department. Alright, maybe that machine that signs twenty letters at a time. In any event, Bill said that he'd handed my letter to the National Security Council to sit on…I'm sorry…to investigate. An investigation which is still underway, two electoral cycles, and another generation of Bush Presidencies later. I've left instructions in my Will for someone to chase Jeb's grandson.

***

More fun was to be had with the British Prime Minister, who at that time, was still John Major. Back in 1993, I had sent a letter to Major asking him if he'd be prepared to confirm if Hugh had been attached to any branch of the British Intelligence Services.

Major's Principal Private Secretary (or PPS), one Alex Allan, had written back to me personally to say that it was the Government's policy "neither to confirm nor to deny matters pertaining to national security and the intelligence services." Standard line, but I was intrigued by having heard from Allan personally.

The British Prime Minister's PPS is a curious animal. There really is no equivalent in American politics, where all of the White House staff are now political appointees. The PPS is a Civil Servant, albeit the most senior Civil Servant attached to the Prime Minister. The PM's PPS is almost always promoted to the most senior offices in the Civil Service or Foreign Service, like, for example, the Head of the Domestic Civil Service – a step above what Sir Clive Whitmore was.

I guess the nearest American equivalent to the PPS would be Bush's Karl Rove, or Clinton's George Stephanopoulos. So, imagine writing to the President about your concern over the UFO's hovering over your house every day, and a personal letter from Karl Rove pops into your letter box a few days later. My letter to Major, followed by a personal response from Allan was that significant.

Hmm. I almost got it, but not quite. Let me try that a different way. There is one huge difference between a 'Rove' and the PM's PPS. The latter is always what the position suggests: a Civil 'Servant.' The PM's PPS does not do his own bidding. He does not have his own correspondence. He is the factotum of the Prime Minister. He does what the Prime Minister says. And he only does what the Prime Minister says. He does not do anything off his own bat. So, when Allan wrote to me, it was only after Major had personally read my letter, and had then personally instructed his PPS to write to me. That's the point. I had definitely ruffled feathers.

And not just once, but twice. Because I wrote back to Allan, to pursue an additional point, and he replied to me again. Personally, saying that he had nothing further to add. Which, in Civil Servant-speak, meant that the Prime Minister had nothing further to add. But hang on, it got better.

At the end of 1996, I sent Major the same fax that I sent to everyone else, with exactly the same allegations about Hugh, Iraq and kickbacks to the Tories. Once more, Allan wrote back to me. Oh heck, by this time we have to be on first name terms. He's probably written me more letters than he's received Valentines. So. Once more, 'Alex' wrote back to me.

On this occasion, he referred me back to his first letter of 1993. Oh what fun. We were now at the coy stage of our relationship. I dug out the first letter, and noted that, essentially, all it did was refer to national security and the intelligence services. So, tongue-in-cheek, I sent another letter to Alex, asking him if this meant that he could not comment about my allegations because of their national security implications? I also wondered if he had a particular yen for Chopin and Chinese take-out, on a moonlit evening?

Alex was already taken. For he replied almost immediately, saying he had nothing further to add. Again. Zounds. And gnashing of teeth. Rending of cloth. Rejected.

But I was not done. Oh no. I sent off a further missive. To be honest, I can't remember what it said, but I was having way too much fun, giving PM and PPS regular doses of PMS with my TNT. But then the fun stopped. For I got a telephone call. From a Woman.

Now, to be honest, I do not believe that I ever put my telephone number on any of the faxes that I sent. But then again, we were talking about the Prime Minister of Great Britain. In any event, this Woman told me that she was John Major's personal Correspondence Secretary, and would I be so good as not to bother nice Mr. Major and his PPS any more.

Well, first thing is, she sounded like John Major's Tea Lady, not his Correspondence Secretary. But, you will be glad to know that I resisted the temptation to ask for a couple of lumps and some milk in mine. Thank you.

Second thing is, this was now becoming serious. Fun and games aside, I'd had a quick word with Reggie. He told me that this sort of thing just didn't happen. There were hordes of good-looking girls, who did nothing all day long but write standard nonsense replies to nutjobs like me. He knew this, because he used to work with the Ministry of Defense in London, and he spent most of his day chatting up their Nutjob Girls. Clearly, I was onto something.

So. I told the Woman that I was recording the conversation and would she mind she'd just said. And she did. She gave her name. She confirmed that she repeating what spoke with the authority of both the Prime Minister of Great Britain and his Principal Private Secretary, and they didn't wish to be bothered by me any more.

It was the Peter Smith syndrome all over again; and again, I was confused. If there was no truth to anything that I was saying, why not just deny it? If what I was claiming was so far off in the realm of deluded fantasy, why perform all of these bureaucratic somersaults, just to avoid saying so?

Unless it was and it still remains the case that a Prime Minister, who has staked his claim to a place in history on the purity of his image as 'Honest John,' could not and would not be seen to deny something he knew to be true; he knew to be devastating; and which he believed might one day come back to haunt him, and stain history's perception of him?

Then again, I might simply have been on a sugar-high.

***

I took the view it was time to talk to the 'serious' press; by which I meant Britain's fearless cadre of intrepid investigative journalists. Hurrah for the cavalry. The good news was that I kept hearing the same refrain: what we've been missing is the money trail to Mark Thatcher and the Conservative Party. The bad news was that none of them actually wanted to do any work in helping to nail it down definitively.

I worked my way through every single well-known media sleuth in Great Britain. You can dress a newspaper up in a fancy broadsheet, but at heart, they are still all Tabloid Trash. In almost every instance, they either wanted the instant story, over the phone, like yesterday. Or they wanted me to bundle up all my stuff, and express it to them (at my expense), so that they could then regurgitate it, rapid fire, over their own by-line.

I didn't mind the end-product being over their by-line. I just wanted to be sure that they reported the story in a credible rather than a sensational fashion. And for that to happen, I wanted joint input. Not a chance. Cheerio. Bless his heart, and I know he won't take offence, but I expected this sort of treatment from the likes of Mark Saunders; but not from the 'quality' newspapers.

At last, I came across Richard Norton-Taylor of *The Guardian*. He had been suggested to me by Max Clifford, one of Britain's leading publicists, and the source for many of the sleaze allegations against the Tory Government of John Major. Max had suffered an unhappy experience at the hands of Britain's National Health Service, and blamed the Conservative Government for the spending cuts it had imposed on the Health Service.

I explained to Richard what I saw as the essential conundrum of timing at that particular moment. John Major's Government had been reduced to a Parliamentary Majority of One. All it would take would be one Conservative MP to abstain or not side with the Government, and the Government would fall.

While I believed my story to be one that would make copy, and while I wanted the product to be handled with care and sensitivity, I also wanted us not to miss the opportunity at hand. There was a chance for Richard to be the journalist who broke the story that brought down a Government. And I would have wonderful exposure, both to unearth currently invisible information, and to promote sales of the ensuing book. Heck yes, I'm an opportunist. Whatever it takes to get satisfaction for Janet, Karen and their kids.

The alternative would be to let the story slip to the other side of the forthcoming General Election. When either the Tories would have a safer majority. Or New Labour would be in power. In either eventuality, there wouldn't be a Conservative Government ripe for the plucking.

Richard seemed to be very sincere. Along with being a nice guy. I took the plunge, swallowed my fears, and sent him a folder, with the highlights of what I had uncovered to date. When I spoke further with Richard, he appeared to be genuinely interested. Until he just stopped taking my calls. I never have found out why. I couldn't help but think of the earlier BBC D-Notice.

***

There was another avenue to bringing down the Conservative Government, and that was the Opposition New Labour Party. I sent a briefing about my exchanges with John Major and Alex Allan to George Foulkes M.P., who was, at that time, New Labour's Frontbench Spokesman on Overseas Aid, and who was also still their point man on Iraq.

I telephoned George's Parliamentary Assistant, Nick, about a couple of weeks later to be told that Foulkes was so excited that he hadn't even bothered to wait to talk to me before Tabling a Question for John Major at Prime Minister's Question Time.

Anyone who is an aficionado of C-Span, particularly at 9.00p.m., on a Sunday evening, will know that Prime Minister's Question time is the half-hour period, staged twice a week, when Members of Parliament have the opportunity to ask any question they like of the Prime Minister, while he is in the House of Commons.

I waited and I waited, eagerly scanning the newspapers and the Internet, but I read of no Question being Tabled. I tried telephoning Nick, but my calls were no longer being returned. Then, after the Christmas Holiday, I received a letter from George. I think that would be a "Dear Geoff" letter.

George wrote to tell me that he had spent the whole of the Holiday Season agonizing over my information, and had decided, reluctantly, that the Labour Party really didn't want to soil their hands or rock any boats with my allegations so close to a General Election.

I think his actual language was a tad more politically correct than that, but that was the upshot. Along with the very definite implication that the decision had been a group one. From higher up. But, to be fair, not in so many words. George was, after all, a politician. And a Scottish one at that.

No matter. The British General Election of 1997 was now upon us. And a good many boats were about to be severely rocked. A number of individuals, with close links to my investigation, would be left with seriously soiled hands. And the matters with which they were going to be soiled would be directly connected to the death of Diana, Princess of Wales.

Dead Men Don't Eat Lunch

Chapter 26

My ODYSSEY INTO MATTERS spiritual had brought me, for reasons I couldn't begin to fathom, to studying pre-Christian religions, and those of Great Britain in particular. These religions are often referred to collectively as Paganism, or the 'Old Ways,' although, ironically, they bear much in common with what are now termed 'New Age' beliefs.

The age-old Pagan principles of an individual relationship with the spiritual (as opposed to one requiring the assistance of a 'go-between'); reverence for Nature; recognition of many divinities; and insistence on the importance of the Goddess (usually the Moon Goddess), the female divine principle, as well as the God, the male divine principle; are found throughout the world. In the indigenous religions of Europe, those of the ancient Celts, the Greeks, and the Romans, and in modern religions, such as Hinduism and Shinto, the Pagan outlook can be found.

I came across Paganism because of its growing popularity – and the increasing prevalence of Pagan web-sites on the Internet. If one was to believe in such things, the fact that I am a Cancer, the horoscopic sign governed by the Moon, might also have had something to do with my attraction to Paganism.

But I was also impressed by the respect its adherents displayed for the ways of Nature, leading them not only to use natural medicines, and to exercise ecological awareness, but also to see the Earth itself as a living organism, the goddess Gaia. I could hardly fall in love with the beauty and spirituality of a place like Rabun County, and not be moved by basic beliefs such as these.

I turned my own attention to a number of the different forms of Paganism, including Druidry and the Dianic Movement. But I also knew of Maggi's interest in Shamanism. She had long talks with me about her interest in developing a form of Shamanism that could be practiced in an urban environment. Her central theme was that of the "Urban Totem."

Geoffrey Gilson

Almost all belief systems use some form of icon or symbology to help to inspire them in their worship. Whether it was the totems of Native Americans, the Crucifix in the Christian Church, or the crystals of New Agers. As I understood what Maggi was saying, beauty can be found everywhere, even in the shape of the man-made artifacts of the modern urban landscape. The trick to helping those lost in the urban rush to finding some inner peace is to allow them to use those artifacts as a substitute for the more 'natural' or 'spiritual' icons of the past.

Druidry, one of the primary religions that preceded Christianity in Great Britain, draws its inspiration from Celtic traditions. Druidry stresses the mystery of poetic inspiration, and explores healing, divination and sacred mythology.

Women's spirituality is one of the most dynamic forces in modern Paganism. And one of the best known women's traditions is the Dianic Movement, named after the Goddess Diana, also known as the Moon Goddess, the Goddess of Hunting and the "Lady of the Beasts."

Women's traditions have an especially powerful vision of the Earth as the Goddess, and are deeply involved with caring for the Earth, and protecting it from the excesses of modern civilization.

Most peoples' experience of the British Pagan tradition is in the myth surrounding Arthur, the Knights of the Round Table, and the Holy Grail. Arthur and Camelot are most often portrayed as the champions of Christian purity against the evils of the witch Morgan Le Fay, and her wicked son, Mordred.

An alternative view has Paganism as a tolerant religion, that welcomed accommodation with the views of the new Christian Tradition. Morgan Le Fay and Mordred were merely seeking to protect their own Tradition against a monotheistic religion, which gave the impression not only of insisting upon one God, but also upon only one religion. Indeed, one of the most attractive features of Paganism is its genuine tolerance for other beliefs and religions.

Of course, those who may have read the books recommended by Reggie will know that the guardians of the Priory of Sion believe that much of the myth surrounding Arthur and the Holy Grail is in fact an allegory for the hidden bloodline of Christ.

An interesting 'interface' between Paganism and Christianity is that many of the Christian Holidays and Myths, such as Christmas and Easter, have their origin in Pagan Legends. It has been suggested that the one was superimposed upon the other to make Christianity more palatable to its newly-converted adherents, in the early centuries after the death of Jesus.

Superimposition occurs even in modern times, as is to be found in the practice of "Santeria," one strain of which is more popularly known as VooDoo. The Pagan religion of West Africa was brought to the United

Dead Men Don't Eat Lunch

States and the Caribbean Islands initially by the slaves. The Plantation overlords forbad its practice. And so, the slaves simply substituted the Christian Saints for their multiple gods, and continued their worship unscathed.

Way back in 1991, my initial foray into studying the occult had been an exercise in trying better to understand the spiritual element of the matters I was investigating. Since then, I had undergone a not-so-subtle 'conversion,' which affected my continuing investigation, my interaction with the players and my life generally.

***

After eighteen years in power in Great Britain, the Conservative Party was massively defeated in the General Election of 1997. The majority of Tony Blair's New Labour over the crest-fallen Tories (about 167 MPs) was almost the same number of Conservative MPs left in total in the House of Commons.

I spent the day on the hot, concrete pan, outside my apartment, in tears. And most of the time, I did not even know why. Maggi had telephoned, jubilant. She had always been a dedicated Socialist. I allowed her the moment. After all, she had waited since 1977 to celebrate. And back in the bad old days of bad old Geoff, I had never been precisely gracious when the Tories had thrashed her Party.

But, she wondered at my sadness. She thought I'd be delighted to see them suffer for what it had appeared they might have done to Hugh. I saw that. But. It was the end of an era.

I had been a proud part of 'Maggie's Revolution.' So had Hugh. A few bad turns in the road wouldn't change that. And I still felt that there was so much yet to be done. But even that didn't feel like the source of my despondency.

After all, many of my views had changed dramatically. It's always difficult attempting to effect change you believe in, when you have to do it in four-year bites, and in between Parliamentary Elections. Eggs are going to be broken. Badly.

But, for example, what we did to the miners, in the name of taming the trade unions, was appalling. We ripped the living soul out of mining community after mining community. For no reason other than to make an example of the Miner's Union. And to send a message to all socialist trade unionists that they would get the same treatment if they stood in the way of our trade union reform. There is no economic 'truth,' or vision of tomorrow, which can ever vindicate such brutality. I will feel ashamed for my, albeit small, part in that process for the rest of my life.

So why the grief? As the day wore on, I realized it was less sorrow and more anger. I was angry that they were gone. I was angry that they hadn't stuck around long enough for me to stick it to them. I was angry that they had left me behind. I was angry that he had left me behind. What? I was angry that he had left us all behind.

Well, that was the first time I'd had that thought. For forty years, I had remained emotionally numb, either as a consequence of conscious suppression or the application of liberal doses of alcohol. It was amazing how an extended period of sobriety and spiritual reflection could so totally unleash unknown and unrealized inner feelings.

I spent the best part of an hour on the telephone with Maggi. For the first time in nine years, I truly grieved. And then, I got angry. With white hot, scorching anger. The bastard. What possible right did he have, with three young children, getting involved in something he must have known to be dangerous?

The miserable, unspeakable, selfish bastard. Was material advantage of such importance to him that it was enough to strap a millstone of stigma and financial desperation around his two families, for the best part of his children's growing years? And then when the going got rough, was his dramatic exit truly the best answer for all those he left behind – left behind to pick up his pieces, and face his music? Oh yes, I got angry.

So, why did I continue with the investigation; and then, the book? Was I still trying to clear my name? Was it all about finding the truth for Hugh's children? Was it just pig-headed stubbornness? Curiosity? Obsession? Financial reward? Or simply that I wanted to finish something I'd begun? To be honest, as I sit here typing, I no longer have a clear answer. I hope I do when the story is completed. But will it ever truly be over? I'm guessing I'll know when I get there.

In the meantime, I know only this, whether or not his children and their families ever choose to acknowledge me, I will not abandon them the way their father abandoned us. That in itself may have to serve as the only justification I will ever experience for this stage of my adventure through life.

***

However, back in Clayton, in the summer of 1997, all was not total unhappiness. Things were suddenly beginning to look up for my story.

Even in his moment of crowning glory, with the tatters of the formerly invincible Conservative Government lying at his feet, the warrior al-Fayed was not satisfied. He was recorded hither and thither, through any media outlet that would listen to him, promising to continue with his revelations of 'sleaze,' until the Tories were fully ground into the dust.

Of particular interest to me was al-Fayed's assertion that those revelations would include a complete rundown on all of the Tories' illicit arms deals in the Eighties. As a famous British TV cop of yesteryear was fond of saying: "'ello, 'ello, 'ello; what do we 'ave 'ere?"

***

Now, as with Ari's allegations, I might have been prepared to ignore such apparent nonsense were it not for the fact that al-Fayed's claims found almost immediate corroboration from within the Conservative Party itself.

On the very evening of their Election defeat, a damning statement was read from the steps of the Conservative headquarters by someone claiming to be a representative of the Tory Reform Group (TRG). This pressure group had become the resting ground of the left-wingers and 'wets' in the Tory ranks, during Thatcher's triumphant right-wing reign.

Indeed, Thatcher was once seen at a Conservative Conference, storming up to the petrified young Chairman of TRG, all handbag and harridan. "What exactly, young man," she bellowed, "what exactly is it that you want to 'reform,' anyway?" The poor man was too stunned to respond, and without a backward glance, she swept onto other 'shock and awe' engagements.

The TRG statement warned that any serious lurch to the right in the Party, resulting from the Election defeat, would be met with a detailed exposition of what the right got up to in the Eighties with respect to illicit arms sales. And there we were, back doing the "'ello, 'ello, 'ello" dance once again.

Finally, Tim Yeo, a former left-leaning Conservative Minister, announced that he was going to write a book about those alleged arms transgressions. He was later bought off by the new Leader of the Conservative Party, William Hague, with the Agriculture portfolio in his Shadow Cabinet.

Yeo remained in the Shadow Cabinet, under the two right-wing successors to Hague, right up to the General Election of 2005. I'm sure that Tim and Hugh would have found much in common on the subject of untrammeled ambition.

***

I believe it is never too soon to take advantage of an opportunity. And so I wrote to George Foulkes, who had been appointed to serve in the New Labour Government, as Minister for International Development. Perhaps he might be less shy about helping now that he was on the 'inside'?

I asked George if he could have a look-see, and perhaps send me whatever he could find, lying around in Whitehall's voluminous archives, about Hugh's activities.

George went all squeaky-new bureaucrat on me, and wrote to me, telling me pompously that he had handed my request over to the Foreign and Commonwealth Office, who had told him they would look into it. George was clearly becoming very comfortable with the notion that he was all grown up now, and could wear long trousers, and tie up his own shoelaces.

***

A couple of months after the Election, the subject of Tories and illicit arms business hit the front pages again. Former Conservative rising star Jonathan Aitken met a sticky end when it was proven that he had lied in a libel action he brought against *The Guardian* newspaper.

The newspaper had alleged that, in 1993, while serving as Minister for Defense Procurement, Aitken had had his hotel bill in Paris paid for by Said Ayas, a well-known bagman for the Saudi Arabian royal family in its arms purchases.

Aitken had been swearing up hill and down dale that his wife had paid the bill. Until *The Guardian* had proven that his wife was in Switzerland at the time. Big oops. Huge. Major league. End of political career. Divorce. Penury. And time in prison for perjury.

Aitken was an urbane, right-wing, Tory charmer. Not unlike Hugh. In fact, the two looked a lot alike. Aitken had finally made it into Government in 1992, when John Major made him Minister for Defense Procurement – for which read, 'Defense Sales.'

The story was that Margaret Thatcher had refused Jonathan office for years because he'd dumped Mark's twin sister, Carol, in less than pleasant circumstances. If you've ever seen a picture of Carol, the only surprising thing is that Jonathan had ever dated her in the first place. Perhaps Jonathan was trying a little too hard to ingratiate himself?

Now, Jonathan came to office with an enormous amount of baggage. He was reputed to have made his money as a partner in the asset management company of one Wafic Said. Wafic was another of those Middle Eastern cowboy businessmen, who loved the English lifestyle.

The thing of it was that, to all intents and purposes, the only assets that Wafic and Jonny managed were the commissions, backhanders and kickbacks earned by them on behalf of the various members of the Saudi Royal Family.

Saudi Arabia is one big feudal candy store. It is all owned, lock, stock and barrel, by the Royal Family. And there's a lot of them. The bin Laden family (Osama too) are distant cousins. That's where he got all his money.

Dead Men Don't Eat Lunch

The country is divided between all the family members. Both on an activity basis and on a geographical basis. So Prince Fred, Second Cousin to the Ayatollah Harry and his wife, the Sultaness Germaine, might get the southern Province of Ali-Babadom, and the sardine fishing industry. What happens then is that every single time there is any sort of governmental financial transaction (generally a construction or supplies contract) involving one or t'other, Prince Fred gets a kickback.

But, there is no way that Prince Fred can be seen to be soiling his hands with such filthy lucre. Heavens no. So. He has a 'bagman.' Two of them in fact. One, from the country originating the services; and the other working out of the Middle East. Got to help the local brothers.

Now, Jonny and Wafic were respectively the British and the Middle Eastern 'bagmen' for the biggest 'bananas' on the fruit tree. Oh yes. And Said Ayas was the Middle Eastern 'bagman' for the Saudi Minister of Defense.

Take a trip back with me, on the magic carpet of history, to the dark days of the Carter Presidency. His Director of CIA, Admiral Stansfield Turner, is ripping the guts out of the covert wing of the Intelligence Services. The big men of the CIA are worried. And the sheep are terrified. Something has to be done.

Some bright spark from Analysis comes up with an idea. Produce a fake Presidential Briefing. Convince Carter that the Soviet Union is going to run out of oil in the middle of the Eighties. And that they will then almost certainly invade the Middle East, beginning on the East, and working their way round to the rich pickings of Saudi Arabia. Kind of what George Bush is doing. But going in the other direction. Carter falls for it. Has a shrieking fit. And immediately demands that Congress agree huge arms sale packages to Saudi Arabia.

Then we have the *October Surprise*, and Grand Pop comes to power. The CIA admits, oops, it made a mistake. Grand Pop nods, winks, chuckles and gets shot. And Bush Senior takes over Foreign Policy.

For all sorts of reasons, including the fact that Congress finally decides it doesn't like them, the US sales to Saudi Arabia wither a bit in the early Eighties. At which point, enter the British, who pick up the slack. And effectively become the personal supplier of arms to the richest Royal Family the world has ever known. And these playboys want some expensive toys.

So. When we say that Jonny and Wafic were acting as 'bagmen' for British arms sales to Saudi Arabia from the Eighties on, we mean that they were making absolutely obscene amounts of money, for their principals and for themselves. And for others. For both were intimately involved with the *Savoy Mafia*. Why on earth shouldn't the British companies and individuals responsible for the arms sales also share in the candy?

It is believed that Wafic and Jonny were major brokers in the initial

Geoffrey Gilson

Al Yamamah deal. The way it worked was this: the deal was a 'rolling contract.' The parties (the British and Saudi Governments, and the Brokers) agreed an overall figure for the deal. *Al Yamamah I* was $35 billion. They then agreed an amount for each year. *Al Yamamah I* was planned to 'roll' for ten years.

Each year, the Saudis would produce a shopping list of what they wanted British Santa to bring them at Christmas. British Defense Contractors would then submit bids to the British Government, and 'Santa' would award contracts accordingly.

When the services, goods, guns, missiles, ships, whatever, were subsequently supplied, the Saudi Government would pay money over to the British Government. The British Government banks with the Bank of England. The major chunk of the money would go into a visible Bank of England account, and would then be disbursed by the Government to the appropriate defense contractors.

Meanwhile, there was a less visible Bank of England account, into which commissions would be deposited, on an accruing basis. On average, that Bank account has been accruing at the rate of $300 million a year, every year, since 1985. It was the job of Wafic and Jonny then to carve up those commissions among their Saudi principals, the 'other' British people, the *Savoy Mafia* and themselves. For more information on *Al Yamamah*, go to:

http://cryptome.org/soil/soiled-dove2.htm
http://www.guardian.co.uk/saudi/story/0,11599,1014975,00.html
http://www.corpwatch.org/article.php?id=9008

Wafic was a great chum of Denis and Mark Thatcher. Apparently, there is a famous picture of Margaret and Denis in a 'family' shot with Bush Senior and Barbara, at their luxury condo in Houston. Margaret and Denis bought a unit in the same complex, at Bush's suggestion. The Thatchers were in Texas visiting Mark, Diane and the kids, and they are in the photo too. As is Wafic, and his ravishing young wife.

So. Why would John Major ask a crook to join his Government? Maybe it was all just co-incidence? Maybe it was co-incidence that Jonny was close to the Saudi Royal Family, and had a history of doing shady arms deals with them? Maybe it was co-incidence that, less than a year after being appointed Minister for Defense Procurement/Sales, Jonny pulled off a negotiating coup with his Saudi buddies, signing them up for *Al Yamamah II*? And maybe it was mere co-incidence that, at much the same time, the Conservative Party's Election overdraft of some $30 million simply disappeared?

Whatever the case, no sooner had the applause subsided than Jonny found himself rewarded with appointment to the position of Chief Secretary to the Treasury, a place at the Cabinet Table, and the general assumption that he was now Major's successor-in-place.

Dead Men Don't Eat Lunch

The allegations about the hotel bill surfaced in the Guardian in 1995, with the information being supplied by none other than Mohammed al-Fayed – who just happened to own the hotel in question, the Ritz, in Paris.

At the time, Jonny did what everyone concurred was the honorable thing: he resigned his Government post, and vowed to fight to the bitter end to restore his reputation. Which fight had just ended with egg being liberally smeared all over his face.

However, while everyone and his Auntie were busy falling over themselves with delight at the fall of yet another Tory icon, no-one seemed to be paying the slightest attention to what I believed was the truly important question: just what was Jonny, the Minister for Defense Procurement, doing meeting with Said Ayas; a meeting which Jonny himself deemed so suspicious that he had to lie about its circumstances?

It didn't seem to cross anyone else's mind that Jonny was most probably discussing with his co-'bagman' how exactly they were going to carve up the commissions from *Al Yamamah II* – details so obviously 'delicate' that they required discussion away from any official ballyhoo. I mean. Why on earth would Jonny rule himself out of the illicit largesse just because he'd become a Government Minister? But then again, most of the media also missed the fact that Jonny's partner in crime, Wafic Said, had his own room in the Ritz that same weekend.

The libel laws in Great Britain are draconian, and are heavily weighted in favor of the entity allegedly libeled. A particularly nasty device, used to much effect against less than well-off defendants, is a clever little item known as 'aggravated damages.'

Once a Libel Writ has been issued, if further alleged libel takes place, punitive damages can be levied for the further aggravation. This device is supposed to stop retaliation by the libeler against the poor, as a 'punishment' for issuing the Writ. However, over the years, it has become a favorite instrument of the rich and guilty, in their usually successful attempts to muzzle honest accusation. Bet Michael Jackson wishes he lived in England.

It occurred to me that the reason Richard Norton-Taylor did not pursue my story is that, since it dealt with matters already the subject of Jonny's Libel Writ, his editors may have been worried about aggravated damages.

Al-Fayed was, of course, beside himself with joy. Not only had the offending event occurred in his hotel, but he had been able to get *The Guardian* story going in the first place, with his invaluable inside information about Jonny's meeting.

More than that. Al-Fayed had then been able to apply the *coup de grace* personally. For it was he who had supplied the trial with the Ritz Hotel fax that had proven that Jonny's wife was in Switzerland, and not in Paris.

Geoffrey Gilson

Tubby little Fayed bobbed and weaved around London, in merriment and mirth, rubbing his hands in glee, just like Danny de Vito as The Penguin in *Batman Returns*.

Along with the bobbing, and just before the weaving, al-Fayed was also trumpeting to the press that he would now hammer the nail well and truly into the coffin of the Conservative Party with total exposure of the Tories' remaining dirty dealings with respect to *Al Yamamah*. I put two and two together, and came up with five, as regularly I do, and wondered whether he was in a position to do this because those dealings had also occurred in the Ritz Hotel?

I wrote a letter to al-Fayed, setting out my reasoning, and asking him if he'd happened to come across Hugh in his Hotel, up to no good. Not really expecting al-Fayed to respond, I got a little 'familiar' in the letter, and commended him on his courage in speaking out so boldly about arms merchants, who probably wouldn't be too happy at his threats to expose them, along with right-wing Tories.

Less than a month later, in the middle of the night of August 31st, 1997, his son, Dodi, was killed in mysterious circumstances, in a car crash in Paris, as he was traveling from the Ritz Hotel, back to his apartment, with his girlfriend. The girlfriend was Diana, Princess of Wales.

***

There is apparently an old saying in the Middle East, where retribution and feuds are more common place than on the loneliest hilltops of Tennessee: if you want to hurt someone, then hurt the one they love. And if there is a message to be conveyed, then send it with as much of an exclamation point as possible.

The only major nation not to suffer regular hostage-taking in Lebanon in the Eighties was the Soviet Union. This is because, when the first two Russians were kidnapped, the KGB went out, found a couple of foot-soldiers of the Islamic Militia responsible, and delivered them to the doors of the Militia's headquarters, bound and tied, with their balls in their mouths. The two hostages were freed within the hour. No more were ever taken.

There could have been no more poignant an exclamation point for Mohammed al-Fayed than the death of Diana. It proved to him the utter ruthlessness of those conveying the message. They were simply unmoved by the enormity of any 'collateral damage.'

To this day, Mohammed al-Fayed has uttered not a single word more about arms deals, arms merchants, arms middlemen, the Ritz Hotel or the Conservative Party.

Dead Men Don't Eat Lunch

***

The Lebanese hostage-takers got involved in a game where they thought they had established the rules. Only to come across people who played by different rules. Or no rules.

Mohammed al-Fayed interfered in a game, where he did not understand the rules. Or he knew them, and then broke them. Or again, he incurred the wrath of people, who, ultimately, were prepared, shamelessly, to toss the rule book aside.

I believe that Hugh Simmonds arrogantly and recklessly became involved in a game whose rules he thought he could bend. Or he thought he could con other people into thinking he was abiding by them, when in fact, he was breaking them. And those people, at the end of the day, just didn't give a fig what the heck Hugh was doing about any rules, in any event. They just wanted their money.

Ari was right. Everything changed in the Eighties. Money became 'King.' Everything became subordinate to money. As it still is. And money is power. People don't like having their power taken away. They will do whatever they have to do to protect it. And, at the end of the day, they won't allow rules to get in the way.

***

All of which said, of course, still left me, at the time, without a shred of hard evidence to suggest that the fatal crash that had killed the Princess of Wales was anything other than a tragic accident. But, without going over all the ground that has been well trampled *ad nauseam* by others, there were one or two interesting links to my investigation.

[The Report of the Investigation by Lord Stevens and the Metropolitan Police into the death of Diana was released on December 14th, 2006. I have chosen not to change my book in response. On the one hand, I think my commentary is still relevant, and indeed almost prescient, bearing in mind it was written without the aid of a staff of 15 and a budget of some $7 million. On the other hand, we are all of us, including Lord Stevens, engaging in conjecture. The fact remains that no-one, who witnessed the incident, who is still alive, and who has any recall, has come forward to offer their irrefutable testimony as to what happened in that tunnel. For the record, Lord Stevens is a Knight of St. John.]

A couple of weeks after the crash, the Police in Paris reported that a third test on the blood alcohol level of Dodi's chauffeur, the now infamous Henri Paul, indicated that he had had three times the legal amount of alcohol in his blood. There were significant traces of Prozac (an anti-depressant well-known to recovering alcoholics), and another prescription drug, neither of which should have been taken with alcohol. Al-Fayed's lawyer made a statement admitting that Paul should not have been driving his son's car.

In the final analysis, both the law enforcement agencies in France and the world's media, rather strangely supported by al-Fayed, took the general line that the crash was the result of a chauffeur who was out of it on a cocktail of alcohol and prescription drugs. Furthermore, much was made of the fact that witnesses had noticed, in the months preceding the crash, that Henri Paul had been making a habit of drinking excessively.

First point. Al-Fayed had failed in his desperate desire to become a part of the British Aristocracy. But Diana represented his best chance of becoming something even better – a British Royal. If Diana married Dodi, Mohammed would be step-grandfather to the future King of England.

It was no accident that Diana met Dodi. In a very literal sense, al-Fayed moved the Mountain to Mohammed. He went out of his way to ingratiate himself with the British upper crust by first buying their favorite shopping place, Harrods, and then making it even more 'elegant' than it had been. Well, depending on what you regard as good taste, that is.

As part of this exercise, al-Fayed had invited the new wife of the Earl of Spencer, Diana's stepmother, and also the daughter of Britain's leading romance novelist, Dame Barbara Cartland, to join the Board of Harrods. That is how Diana first met Dodi.

Mohammed al-Fayed was more than aware of Diana's longstanding run-in with the paparazzi, and went out of his way to ensure that, whenever she was with Dodi, she was fully 'protected.' This was one of the reasons that Diana enjoyed her time with the Fayeds – she had space and solitude.

Mohammed took his role of self-appointed protector very seriously. All the evidence is that he hired only the very best personnel to act as chauffeurs and bodyguards for his son and the Princess. The cream of Executive Protection specialists. Individuals trained by Governments to protect world leaders, and remove them from harm's way, at a moment's warning. They knew how to bodyguard, and they knew how to drive fast and safely.

Indeed, Trevor Rees-Jones, the British bodyguard in the front passenger seat of the car in the crash, had served time with both the British Parachute Regiment and the Royal Protection Squad. Even though Henri Paul may not have had similar elite training, there is simply no way al-Fayed would have endangered either his son or his meal ticket by entrusting them to the driving of someone he knew to be a drunk.

Second point. In Clayton, I had a neighbor who was a recovering alcoholic. He wasn't doing too well at it. Drank more than he 'recovered.' Of course, I spent time with him. Helped in what little ways that I could.

He told me about his favorite trick. He got an unending supply of Prozac from the local doctors, who thought they were helping him. He would then mix this with liberal doses of vodka. He would develop an immediate and very intense 'high.' Not surprising. The drug removed the depression and the inhibition. The alcohol then exacerbated the good feeling. The only 'downside' was that, after half an hour, he would black out. Every time. Without fail.

There is no indication from any of the video tapes of Henri Paul in the short time he was in the Ritz Hotel, before leaving with Dodi and Diana in the Mercedes, that he was on any sort of 'high.' And let me tell you, when I say 'high,' I mean my neighbor was bouncing off the walls. He couldn't have stopped it, even if he'd wanted too.

Plus, if Henri Paul was on both Prozac and alcohol, as is being suggested, and he had done this before, as is also being suggested, either he would have known what the effect would be, or one of his co-workers in the Hotel would have witnessed it happening to him. I couldn't prove anything one way or the other. I wasn't even sure I could articulate to myself what I was driving at. Other than the fact that my experience told me the accusations about drugs and drink just didn't ring true.

***

Meanwhile, all was not well in British Intelligence. People were resigning. People were talking. About all sorts of shady goings-on. In both MI5 and MI6. We had one David Shayler, from MI5. And Richard Tomlinson, from MI6.

Now, it's a huge no-no for British Government employees, in sensitive parts of the bureaucracy, to talk about their work in public. It breaches the Official Secrets Act, which all 'sensitive' employees have to sign when they are first hired. Hence, Reggie's initial reluctance to talk to me. Until someone decided it might be useful to have him talk to me.

Shayler became the more celebrated 'whistle-blower,' because he did a runner to France, and then held court with the press for some years. Eventually, he returned to Great Britain, did a little prison time, and disappeared into the countryside.

Tomlinson did his 'thing' the other way round. He served prison time first. And then published his expose. Which was a deal more explosive than anything Shayler had said. In particular, Tomlinson had some interesting input on Diana's crash.

Tomlinson agreed with Shayler that the core of British Intelligence had become rotten, beginning in the Eighties. But he went one further. He went on record to say that British Intelligence actively engaged in assassinations around the world. Among other startling accusations, he insisted that the circumstances of Diana and Dodi's death bore a remarkable resemblance to a plan MI6 had been working on to 'take out' Slobodan

Geoffrey Gilson

Milosevic of Serbia, in 1992.

Tomlinson also confirmed that the Ritz in Paris had had a reputation as a 'safe haven' for arms deals and secret meetings between competing intelligence agencies, ever since the Second World War.

That last point got me thinking. Surely, al-Fayed would have known this when he bought the place? Indeed, maybe it's why he was so interested in it. Al-Fayed had a background in illicit arms dealing with Adnan Khashoggi. He would have been deemed an 'acceptable' owner by its 'shady' patrons. So long as he continued the tradition of confidentiality.

What I was wondering was what those same patrons might have thought when al-Fayed was reported all over the British press, promising to betray those very confidences he might have been expected to maintain?

Tomlinson also raised the suggestion that Henri Paul was a paid informant for a number of intelligence agencies, including MI6. This would make sense. Your average intelligence agency would probably think nothing of playing both ends against the middle. Demanding 'confidentiality' from the owner, and then bribing the staff, to spy on the other guys.

It was, therefore, no surprise that, later in 1997, it was reported that one of Paul's bank accounts had been found to have had about $150,000 tucked into it shortly before the crash. Mind you, wasn't it Ari that had mentioned that bank accounts could be played with?

Tomlinson also revealed that Paris had been awash with British agents the weekend of the crash; agents that included the Director of the Security Service, MI5.

But the information which caught my attention most acutely was that relating to 'Mickey Finn's.' I have to be honest, my notes indicate that this information came from Tomlinson's allegations, but I can not swear to that fact. I wrote to Tomlinson, but he never responded.

In any event, the information which I scribbled down, because it fascinated me so much, was that there are knock-out drugs, which agents slip into drinks. That of itself is not so surprising. What stunned me was the claim that one of the primary features of the drugs is that they also raise blood-alcohol readings to incredible levels, for very short periods of time. The consequence is that immediate testing suggests that the black-out is the result merely of alcohol. So, no further tests are conducted; tests which might otherwise find traces of the drugs.

While I could see the implications for the accusations being made about Henri Paul, I must confess that my thoughts did not linger long with him. Rather, they drifted back to my own experience in *Van Gogh's* in the Autumn of 1993.

***

Dead Men Don't Eat Lunch

At about this time, the rather rustic computer that I was using in Clayton had a fatal spasm. I took it down the hill to the one computer service store in the whole of Rabun County. It was owned by a fifty-something Egyptian expatriate, by the name of Rezzac. Co-incidence is an extraordinary animal, that will leap up, and bite you in the soft, nether regions the very moment you stop paying attention.

Rezzac had been born and raised in the same small town in Egypt as Mohammed Fayed. Mattria, between Alexandria and Port Said, close to the Suez Canal. According to Rezzac, Mohammed was well in with the local British Forces, which, it being the Fifties, were still stationed in Egypt, along with the French. Mohammed was known by all to be a regular smuggler of hashish from Israel into Egypt. Which suggests that his was a name most probably also known to the Israelis.

Rezzac said that Mohammed also "did some kind of dirty work for British Military Intelligence. He was 'looked after' by them." In 1956, the British, the French and the Israelis got up to all sorts of 'dirty work' in Egypt, when they launched military action, in an attempt to topple the nationalistic leader of Egypt, Gamel Nasser, and wrest back control of the Suez Canal from him.

The whole sorry adventure came to a messy end when the Americans pulled the plug, refusing to condone the military action. This led to what is known in British history books as "The Suez Crisis." The Conservative Prime Minister at the time was forced to resign. It also effectively spelled the end of the British Empire as a serious global contender.

Just to back track a bit, it is now known that, in the years before 1956, the Israelis themselves were undertaking some 'dirty work' of their own in Egypt. During a three-week period in July 1954, several terrorist bombs were set off: at the United States Information Agency offices in Cairo and Alexandria, at a British-owned theater, and at the central post office in Cairo.

An attempt to firebomb a cinema in Alexandria failed when the bomb went off in the pocket of one of the perpetrators. That, in turn, led to the discovery that the terrorists were not anti-Western Egyptians, but were instead Israeli spies, bent on souring the warming relationship between Egypt and the United States, in what came to be known as the *Lavon Affair*. Little wonder that, two years later, the Americans stuck it back to the Israelis, and their British and French partners.

Let's assume that British Military Intelligence had established in Egypt a network of people, like Mohammed Fayed, whom they 'looked after.' What happened to them when the British were forced to leave after 1956? The British could hardly hand them over to the Egyptian authorities. They would have been excoriated as 'collaborators' and spies, and no potential asset would ever trust British Intelligence again. The French were out of the question, because they were being forced to leave as well. But. You don't just let a good network go to waste. It's way too valuable. So, you find a 'friend' somewhere to hand it to. Who else was left? Doesn't sense suggest that the only remaining option was the Israelis?

Is it beyond the realm of fantasy to suggest that this network, including Mohammed, was handed over, lock, stock and barrel, to Israeli Intelligence? An intelligence service which might already have been well acquainted with some of its members? Say, the ones smuggling hashish from Israel into Egypt? Maybe the Israelis had been 'running' them for some time, in collaboration with the British and the French, while they, the Israelis, were up to all their other 'dirty work' in Egypt?

If one sees this conjecture through to the end, it is entirely conceivable that Mohammed Fayed simply got caught up in the Israeli net. It would have been way too easy to use blackmail to keep him ensnared. In fact, the more he became involved with illicit Arab arms deals, the more valuable he would have become to the Israelis.

Shift forward to the Eighties. There is much suggestion that al-Fayed (as he had now decided to call himself) was heavily involved, throughout the early Eighties, in the illicit arms trade with Iran, out of London. Well, who wasn't? Then came the famous 'tilt' by the West, and by Bush and Thatcher in particular, towards Iraq. And the Israelis got pissed. In 1987, Ari was dispatched by Yitzhak Shamir to do whatever was necessary to put a plug in the arms pipeline to Iraq.

I had already heard from Ari that this included targeting right-wing Tories, both in Government and on the rise (Mellor and Simmonds), who might have had a pro-Arab leaning, and who might also have been centrally involved in the pipeline to Iraq.

Now, who else at that time was taking aim at right-wing Tories? None other than Mohammed al-Fayed, who had declared himself dedicated to exposing the shenanigans of the Tory right-wing, and who had already claimed the individual scalps of Aitken and Hamilton, along with the defeat of Major's Government.

Was this mere co-incidence, or was it that al-Fayed continued to be an 'asset' of Israeli Intelligence, under specific orders from Ari, at the end of the Eighties and the beginning of the Nineties, to upend any and all right-wing Tories, particularly those engaged in the illicit sale of military technology to Iraq?

***

Let's take another look at the "Cash-for-Questions" scandal, which al-Fayed instigated, when he began bribing Conservative MPs in about 1987.

Dead Men Don't Eat Lunch

Most of the MPs targeted were either influential or right-wing or both. All except for one. Tim Smith.

Tim was a charming young man. A former Chartered Accountant. But he was not an MP of influence. At the time, he held no Government Office. And he was not right-wing. Far from it. He had been a leading light of the Tory Reform Group. Tim had only one qualification as a target, in the context of my allegations: he was the Member of Parliament for Beaconsfield. He was my Member of Parliament.

So. Why would al-Fayed mistake Tim for an MP of influence, or a right-winger? What if it was not he that had made the mistake, but another party with an established record of political naivety? My mind made an immediate bee-line for Ari and 'his friends,' who had concluded that David Mellor, far from being the strutting clown that all knew him to be (bless his heart), might actually be a future Conservative Prime Minister.

Now, Ari would have known that Beaconsfield had a reputation for being an 'overt' financial powerhouse for the Conservative Party. All you had to do was get one of the handbooks for the annual Conservative Conference to see that, year after year, the Beaconsfield Constituency was one of the top money-makers for the Party. Add to that the known fact that one of its Vice Presidents was a member of the Conservative Board of Finance, while another Vice President had a senior role in the Auditing of the National Party's Accounts.

We also know, from Ari himself, that Hugh's name was on one list of people, who were associated with arms sales to Iraq, and on another list of people, who were involved with Mark Thatcher and his money. Even if Ari and his "friends" ostensibly did not make the connection until I arrived on the scene.

What if Ari just assumed that the Conservative Member of Parliament for the constituency, in which all of this Conservative activity, both overt and cover, originated, obviously either knew about it or, indeed, was heavily involved? Then, it would be perfectly reasonable for him to consider that Conservative MP a prime target for 'destabilization.'

Let's not be too hard on Ari. After all, to some extent, the Conservative Party itself made the same mistake. They looked at Beaconsfield, saw that it was this financial powerhouse, and just assumed, like Ari, that Tim must in some way have been responsible. That's why, in 1992, before Tim's exposure over "Cash-for-Questions," John Major made Tim a Vice Chairman of the Party in charge of Finance and Fund-raising. A position Tim did not hold for very long, precisely because he'd had nothing to do with making Beaconsfield a financial mainstay of the Conservative Party, and because this fact became painfully apparent rather quickly.

It is also rather telling that the period of time during which Hugh was stealing his Clients' money coincided precisely with the period of time during which al-Fayed's money passed to Tim. Is it possible that the two were connected? Was al-Fayed setting up one Beaconsfield target, Tim, identified incorrectly by al-Fayed's 'controller,' Ari, as a dangerous right-winger; while Ari was applying pressure to one of his own Beaconsfield 'assets,' Hugh, because Ari thought he had the makings of a future, right-wing Conservative leader?

All of this said, I would add that I always liked Tim Smith. With the possible exception of John Major, you will not find a more decent man who has served as a Conservative Member of Parliament. I do not think he did anything dishonest. I think that he made a genuine mistake. He forgot to inform the right Committee at the right time about monies that he'd received from a lobbyist. And then, in shining contrast to that parliamentary spiv, Neil Hamilton, and with no thought for his own welfare, Tim rushed to do the decent thing, hoping to spare his Party and his Prime Minister any embarrassment.

I had already left Beaconsfield when the brown stuff hit the fan. I wish I had been there. For Tim was not well treated by his Constituency Association. Along with all of the other Rules and Conventions that were waylaid in the Eighties, the notion of loyalty seems to have been a casualty also. Tim had always shown his Association the utmost loyalty, in often difficult circumstances, when his personal political views ran counter to the majority opinion of that Association. It would have been nice if the courtesy had been returned.

Tim is no longer the Member of Parliament for Beaconsfield. Wherever you are, Tim, I wish you well. For what little it is worth, know this: for all that Hugh and I thought your political views sucked big wind, we would have stood by you. You were a good friend. Enjoy your new life. And say hello to your wife. She was a corker, too.

***

All this talk of "Cash-for-Questions" had me thinking again about the *Guardianlies.com* web-site. They had made great play of the fact that *The Guardian* (left-wing) and the *Daily Telegraph* (right-wing) were, in fact, 'in bed together' because they jointly owned the printing company that produces both newspapers.

The implication from the web-site was that *The Guardian* and al-Fayed were natural partners, because they both, for obvious and seemingly overt reasons, wanted to target a Conservative Government and its right-wingers. And that they then both suborned Conrad Black and the *Daily Telegraph*, using the printing set-up as a lever.

I think the web-site may have it the wrong way round. Perhaps it was Ari who enrolled al-Fayed? And perhaps it was Conrad Black, an unashamed cheerleader for the State of Israel, who enrolled *The Guardian*?

***

Here's an interesting thought. If there are still Israelis and their 'assets' out there looking to knobble right-wing Tories with links to Beaconsfield, maybe they should look no further than the current Conservative Shadow Secretary of State for Defense, Dr. Liam Fox MP.

Liam came a close third in the 2005 Conservative Party Leadership Election, and many consider him to be the Conservative Leader-in-waiting if new-boy David Cameron should slip up.

Liam first did his obligatory stint, standing for an unwinnable Parliamentary seat, in Scotland. He then moved south, to Beaconsfield., where he practiced medicine, one of his first patients being Hugh's daughter, Tanya.

Liam served with Hugh on the Beaconsfield Town Conservative Committee, while looking for his safe Conservative seat in England. Even now, a heart-beat away from the top of the greasy political pole, Liam lists in his biographical details his continuing membership of Beaconsfield's Conservative Political Discussion Group.

After publishing this book, I was contacted indirectly by Phillip Dumville, the Conservative Agent for the Beaconsfield Parliamentary Constituency at the time of Hugh's death. He wanted to let me know that the doctor who had signed Hugh's Death Certificate was none other than our Liam.

Mind you, it is highly unlikely that Liam ever will be 'knobbled' by the Israelis – because they already have him in the bag. Like his neo-con buddies in the US, Liam proudly boasts that he is a huge fan of all things Israeli.

***

Mohammed al-Fayed did not raise himself up from a lowly Egyptian township to being within a sneeze of British Royalty by imploding every time misfortune reared its ugly head. And so, before anyone had even had time to ask who had sneezed, al-Fayed was pumping up his own disinformation campaign about the death of his son and the Princess of Wales.

And a clever one it has been too. He has taken many of the elements, which it has been difficult to disown, and has then woven them into a fraudulent package, that totally deflects attention from his potential role in the death of the "Peoples' Princess."

There has been accusation after accusation from al-Fayed about the

Geoffrey Gilson

insensitivity of the Royal Family. Angry finger-pointing every time a Tomlinson comes out with more allegations about British Intelligence involvement. The cumulative implication has been that his son and his girlfriend were assassinated by British Intelligence, or agents of the Royal Family, or both.

To be sure, the current crop of British Royals makes the "Married With Children" mob look like the Brady Bunch on tranquilizers. And sometimes, they make Howard Stern look like a poster boy for political correctness. But that is a far cry from planning to kill Diana, because she was about to marry a Muslim.

Have you looked at Britain recently? There's been regular immigration from the Asian sub-continent for the best part of the last fifty years. There's a mosque in every reasonably sized city. Heck, there was one down the end of my road in Slough. The national dish is no longer fish and chips; it's curry.

This Royal Family is nothing if not 100% aware of a public relations opportunity when it jumps up and slaps them up the backside of the head. In many ways, Diana was perceived as being harmless. She was no longer going to be Queen. So, who cared if she was a Muslim? In fact, if it had the effect of showing the extended Royal Family to be a better reflection of the 'New' England, then so much the better.

Of course, and slipping off on a tangent, there is something of a downside to this broadening of the social, religious and cultural base of Great Britain. Particularly, when it is added to the fact that Britain is, in many ways, one of the most 'open' societies in the Western World.

It is a country which it is relatively easy to enter. It has open borders to Europe, and pretty much open skies with America. Plus, take a look at a map. If you want to enter the country illegally...well, it's a bloody island, for pete's sake.

Once you're in the country, you have full freedom of movement. At the time of writing this book, there are still no picture ID's, although Blair's New Labour Government is trying hard to introduce them. The British are more opposed to invasion of privacy even than the Americans.

Britain is now a tax haven for corporate finance. London is Europe's primary financial center. If you want to raise money, or move it, legally or illegally, London is the place. Add to this the fact that Britain is also a country that takes freedom of speech more seriously than the Americans, and you have, unfortunately, a country where the climate is ripe for abuse by militants and terrorists. None more so than Muslim militants and terrorists.

Many of those arrested in connection with 9-11 spent time in one or other of Britain's mosques. Some of the flight training took place there. The "Shoe Bomber" was a Brit. Cat Stevens is a Brit. When the Special Forces eventually overran bin Laden's hideaway in Afghanistan, and ransacked the telephone numbers on his communications' system, almost half of them were in Great Britain.

And it may well be true that there were an excess of British Intelligence officials in Paris on the weekend of Diana's death. Certainly, we know from Mark Saunders and others that British Intelligence have engaged in some questionable surveillance activity with respect to the Royals. But again, this is a long way from suggesting that they were responsible for the death of Diana and Dodi.

The Gentlemen Officers of British Intelligence, at least before the Eighties, when they still knew about Gentlemen's Rules, always believed that they owed a duty first to the Crown. This was, rightly or wrongly, what was very much behind their scheming against the Socialist Government in the Seventies. They believed that they owed a higher duty to their Crown and to their Country than to the elected government.

Did this mean that some of them felt they had a duty to 'take out' what they perceived, again rightly or wrongly, to be a threat to that Royal Family? I don't have the first clue. But, I think that, if there were one or two, or more, even fairly senior officers, who felt antipathy towards Diana, then they might have been willing to 'open the door' and 'clear a path' for others; but I don't think they would have been the ones found to have been 'pulling the trigger.'

By the same token, even if the same officers were mega-pissed at al-Fayed for trampling all over the little earner they all had going for them with illicit arms sales, they would have let their merchant-thug friends do the actual 'dirty work,' rather than bloodying their own hands with the death of a Princess.

The bottom line is that al-Fayed has been very astute in fanning the flames of conspiracy theory, and pointing the finger in every direction, except at his own illegal arms-related activities, and his threats to expose ruthless arms middlemen . And why shouldn't al-Fayed have been on the ball? He has had one of the best publicists in the business crafting the campaign for him; our old anti-Tory friend, Max Clifford.

***

But, that may not have been the only help that al-Fayed was getting. The updated 2000 edition of Gordon Thomas's expose, *Gideon's Spies: The Secret History of the Mossad*, includes an extensive section, based on an interview with Ari.

Thomas also believes Ari is still active with Mossad, even if the relationship is conducted at arm's length, to allow Mossad deniability. Ari claims to have been fully aware of attempts by a chum of his, whom he calls

Geoffrey Gilson

"Maurice," to recruit Henri Paul as an informant for Mossad. The Israelis were, naturally, quite keen on knowing what illicit Arab arms deals were being transacted in the Ritz Hotel. There is one particularly let-it-all-hang-out passage:

> *"What part had his pressure played in the accident? Had Henri Paul lost control of the Mercedes, causing it to smash into the thirteenth concrete pillar of the underpass beneath the Place de l'Alama, because he could see no way of extricating himself from the clutches of Mossad? Was that pressure linked to the high level of prescribed drugs found in his bloodstream? When he had left the Ritz with his three passengers, had his mind continued to vacillate over what he should do about the pressure? Was he not only responsible for a terrible road accident but also the victim of a ruthless intelligence agency?"*

There has been some question raised as to the *bona fides* of Gordon Thomas. Apparently, if you write about the Mossad, and don't include all those scholarly things, like footnotes and references, then you must be a Mossad disinformation agent. Well. Guess that pigeon-holes me. When do I collect the paycheck?

But, let's follow this through. There are those who say that Thomas is not as unbiased as he would like us to believe. Then, we get to Ari. What can I say? I have every good reason to want to believe him; yet, I find it so difficult.

So, Ari and Gordon want to sell a few books. They jump on the Diana bandwagon, and claim that they know stuff we don't. It's all pretty harmless. We know Paul was on the take from someone. Maybe a lot of someone's. If it happens to include the Israelis, who cares?

Except that Thomas and Ari and Maurice go on and on and on, page after page, about how Henri Paul was sizzled morning, noon and night on pills and booze. This obviously becomes the whole point of the exercise. And yet, the point is so open to question. So, why do it?

If there is one thing I have learned over the past seventeen years, it is that people always write things for a reason, even when they genuinely think they are being objective. Just look to see who benefits, and you can pretty much work out the reason for yourself.

So, strip away all the pathos and angst. At the end of the day, where does this extensive section of Gordon's book leave us?

1. Gordon 'knows stuff.' Good for his publishing street-cred.

2. Ari is still at the center of things. As he always likes to have people think he is.

3. Israeli Intelligence comes off as ruthless, and pretty much capable of

doing anything nasty. They like that.

4. The official spin that Henri Paul was to blame is upheld. Hurrah for the French and the Royal Family.

5. And an Intelligence Agency was involved. So, al-Fayed is in the clear.

Now. Is the last point the real purpose of the updated version of the book? Namely, that Ari , continuing his deep-cover mission as a 'lone wolf' for Israeli Intelligence, steps up to bat for one of Israel's most secret assets?

***

"Were you there, Mark?" After days of trying, I had finally tracked down Mark Saunders. All of the immediate press reports stated that a bunch of paparazzi, who had been following Dodi and Diana's car the night of the fatal crash, had been arrested. I was concerned that Mark might have been among their number.

Mark had apparently come a long way since our last meeting in 1993. He had finally found a partner, Glenn Harvey, and the two of them had established themselves as the most 'successful' of Diana's tormentors.

In the days following the tragic crash, all of the television stations were devoted to the smallest minutiae concerning the accident itself, and the trials and tribulations of the one of the world's most favored glamour goddesses. And if the reports were true, Mark was one of her greatest trials.

His face and cocky voice were everywhere. On chat shows, on documentaries, and on one TV clip in particular, which was repeated night and day. It was the time that Diana had, somewhat unwisely, gone to Malaga, in southern Spain, on her own.

Once again, Mark, displaying uncanny prescience, had beaten the rest of the world's media to the chase, and was the only one with a camera as Diana walked through Malaga airport, without a bodyguard in sight.

There has never been anything shy about Mark. And there wasn't on this occasion either. As Diana walked along, trying her hardest to ignore him, he walked backwards, in front of her, his camera no more than a foot from her face, the only sound the continuous whirring of his motor drive, as the lightbulb mercilessly pounded away at her – perhaps a portend of her final tragedy?

"How could you do it, Mark?" I remonstrated.

"Oh Geoff," he gave me, putting on his worldly-wise voice, "she loved it. It was all an act. The minute we disappeared, she wanted to know where we were going. Why else do you think she had my cellphone number?"

Well, bearing in mind some of the more scurrilous stories about

Diana, and knowing Mark's reputation, I could think of all sorts of sordid reasons. To which I gave expression. Mark was surprisingly coy on the subject. What he would say is that he was on his way to America to sell the tape of the conversation he'd had with her on his cellphone, when she'd called to beg him not to publish his book. Which he'd done anyway, in 1996.

Mark wouldn't tell me on the telephone whether he'd been there or not. Ah ha, up for a little intrigue, was our Mark. I didn't really care, just so long as he was safe. "What I will say," he added, softly, "is that it was just an accident."

Oh yes? Well, I was all attention. I'd have expected a good conspiracy theory to be right up Mark's alley. And how do you know this? I asked him. Expecting him to have a juicy inside contact. "Because there were too many variables for it to have been anything else," he declared, deadpan.

Oh dear. So, I spent a few minutes introducing Mark to the concept of 'zones of opportunity.' There are always variables. One deals with them by narrowing them down to the minimum. Like making sure Kennedy drove through the Dealey Plaza. Like ensuring that Dodi and Diana drove through the underpass. Perhaps by bribing Henri Paul to do just that. Which may have been what the money was for. Without his knowing why.

Then, when the target is in a reduced 'zone of opportunity,' you throw everything and the kitchen sink at them. You have one gunman in the Depository building. And a couple of others, spaced around the Plaza. Unknown to each other. To keep it compartmentalized. With law enforcement prepped to keep innocent bystanders to a minimum.

Or you surround a Mercedes with a couple of slowing cars in front, a white Fiat Uno behind, and a few motorcycles darting about. You have noise, and horns blaring, and lightbulbs flashing. You have a driver who has, unknowingly, been drugged. You mix it all up, and hope for the best.

If it works, great. If not, you make your getaway. Perhaps in cars, with drivers supplied by a friendly Intelligence Service, like the British, who just happen to be in town. And then, you try again another day. Assassinations are very rarely the hyper-planned blueprints of Clint Eastwood movies.

But Mark was no more in the mood for one of my lectures in 1996 then than he had been in 1993. He just urged me to get my friends to buy his book. It turned out that he had the same publisher as Nick Davies, whom Mark knew vaguely. I asked Mark to quiz Nick as to whether or not Nick had known Hugh. And then Mark dashed off to catch his plane. I wondered, with a smile, if, with his own new-found fame, he would now find a paparazzi in his face as he ran through the airport.

Some months later, I read a press report that the US Government had admitted to being in possession of some 1,000 documents relating to the

Dead Men Don't Eat Lunch

Princess of Wales. I had attempted, without success, to find someone I could write to about the documents. I thought they might make interesting reading. Particularly, if they happened to include the Saunders' transcript.

***

In the meantime, I received in the post reading material of a different kind. A book I had ordered, and written by one of the names already mentioned in my story: Simon Regan. The book was primarily about Diana, but it contained information that would spark a whole new line of inquiry in my investigation. And, much to my surprise, all manner of interesting verification of the meat of Ari's claims about the Conservative Party, the Thatchers and Hugh.

Geoffrey Gilson

Chapter 27

AUTUMN WAS UPON US in Rabun County. The evenings were a little cooler. And yellow was creeping into the leaves; those that had not already started to fall. The air was crisper. And the dim sun cut through the diminishing leaf cover to carve sculptures of skipping light on the woodland floor around us. The chattering of insects was now replaced by that of birds, gathering to make their southward migration.

I had made a promise to myself to make a journey to the Cherokee Indian Reservation in North Carolina, when it was no longer warm enough to suntan, and I had the means to make the one hour journey to the north. That time had finally arrived.

The trip was uneventful. But the scenery became more lush, as the mountains became steeper, the further north I traveled into the Smoky Mountains. For these were no longer the Blue Ridge foothills. There were wildflowers of incredible variety, even this late in the season, with almost tropical masses of rhododendrons and other flowering shrubs. The original hardwood continental forest, untouched by the glaciers that scoured New England, still grew here, tall and majestic.

All of a sudden, I had a sense of *déjà vu*. It was not the slopes of Georgia or North Carolina that I saw, but rather the steep banks of the man-made valley through The Grove, at Hall Barn. The same tall trees, with even trunk, and high canopy of russet leaves. The undergrowth, a maze of tangled rhododendron. And at the base of the valley, a rushing stream, that raced and swirled, and then curled back on itself like some water serpent, alive and furious to breach the banks of its own entrapment.

None of this made any sense. And even less so when I turned a wide corner in the highway. The string of mountains that had, with graceful cantilever, traced the edge of the valley through which we passed, became, all at once, a series of craggy edges. I felt an enormous pain in my stomach, as if someone had hit me there with a huge bag of potatoes.

Dead Men Don't Eat Lunch

I almost lost control of the car. When I looked up, I was overwhelmed with the sense that I had been in this valley before. I knew the craggy edges. They were always a sign that home beckoned. By the small river below, would be my village. And sure enough, there were signs pointing to an ancient Cherokee village.

Without knowing what was guiding me, I drove into the Reservation. Past the new Casino, the tattoo parlors and the souvenir shops. Which, curiously, took relish in displaying the Battle Flag of the Confederacy. And then into the parking lot of the Museum.

I bought my ticket, and waited anxiously for the tour to begin. I tried to avoid the other tourists, who were happy to steer clear of the strange Englishman, who couldn't stop his tears. The Indian guide seemed preternaturally calm, and sent warm smiles in my direction, from time to time.

He took us through the halls of the display, with grace and charm, but I wasn't interested. Frantically I searched, without knowing for what. I saw the murals about the Cherokee Nation. How the Cherokee followed the white man's example, and became 'civilized.' How they took up agriculture, and created their own written language, the only Indian Nation to do so. But none of this satisfied me.

I didn't wait for the tour to end. I burst out into the hall, and saw before me a girl sitting behind the ticket counter. A girl I had not seen when I came in. Strange, because she was quite beautiful; the high cheekbones, and the long raven hair. I ran up to her, and ignoring the Dolly Parton accent, thrust aside her words of welcome, and asked her, please, to tell me if these were ancient Cherokee lands, or simply a later 'award' of the Government.

Like her friend, the Tour guide, she seemed infused with an eerie inner peace. She stopped, looked at me, and smiled. Yes, she confirmed, "these are our lands." She smiled again. And did not take her eyes off me, as, more settled now, I left the Museum, and made my way back to the car.

As I drove back through the valley, leading away from the reservation, I drove more slowly. The gut-wrenching feeling was no longer there. But in its place, a deep and residual sadness, which did not make any effort to explain itself to me. Then, a gust of wind blew over the trees, causing the carpet of multi-colored leaves to dance and tumble like a troupe of performing harlequins. And with that, even the feeling of sadness blew away.

Some time later, I described the trip to Maggi, who shared with me some matters that helped me to understand what might have happened. I had spent some 32 years of my life, up until 1988, believing I was 'safe' in my home town of Beaconsfield. Then, a life-changing event occurred, Hugh's death, which helped me, after some adventures, to realize that the 'safety' had been hollow.

Geoffrey Gilson

Maggi explained to me that my Cherokee experience was part of a process of my learning that my life was now a journey. Partly of geography, partly of investigation, and partly of spirituality. One where I was searching for a 'new' home. Perhaps a home that I had lived in before. But certainly one where I could find true 'safety,' both physical and spiritual. And in many ways, she added, my investigation was a metaphor for that search.

***

Scallywag was an independent investigative journal founded in the Nineties by one Simon Regan, a bit of an outcast journalist, who wrote for *The Guardian* from time to time. *Scallywag* liked to present itself as the scourge of the Establishment, but most of the flagellation seemed to be at the expense of Major's Conservative Government. A fact which most observers attributed to the rumor that it was financed, in the main, by Mohammed al-Fayed.

Both Regan and *Scallywag* had first come to public notice with their expose of activities at certain Boys' Homes in Wales. Regan alleged that there was a pedophile ring that operated out of these homes. And that the residents were taken to London, where they were 'provided' to a secret network of homosexuals, which apparently included the well-known lobbyist that had engineered the 'Cash-for-Questions' bribery for Mohammed al-Fayed. Which was, of itself, a rather delicious irony: Fayed's cash exposing Fayed's lobbyist. The suggestion, none too squeamishly advanced by Regan, was that, given the connections of the lobbyist, the 'clients' of the pedophile ring most probably extended to leading figures within the Conservative Party.

Regan's well-researched articles eventually forced an Inquiry, and several damning claims were upheld. But nothing much else happened, a paralysis that Regan felt was pre-ordained given the links to the Conservative Party, and the operation of what he described as insidious Freemason interference in the original Police investigations.

I was always on the lookout for possible assistance with my own investigation, and, notwithstanding the ghostly presence of al-Fayed in the background, I felt that it might be worth a shot having a closer look at Regan. What finally made up my mind was the news that Regan had written a 'stunning' book about the death of Diana.

I sent off for a copy. My first impression was that Regan had probably been the one to write his own review. The Diana allegations meandered and offered nothing new. What did catch my attention was the preamble about the death of his brother. The circumstances of which had been the trigger to his investigating Diana's death.

Actually, it wasn't Simon's brother, but rather his half-brother. But

Dead Men Don't Eat Lunch

he loved him none the less. And was just as angry at what he felt sure was a politically-inspired murder. In the run-up to the General Election of 1997, the half-brother had apparently come across someone with photographs allegedly showing two male Conservative Cabinet Ministers becoming very intimately acquainted.

Not even *Scallywag* was prepared to stoop this low, and so, for reasons best known to himself, the half-brother had traveled to the northern enclave of Turkish Cyprus, to get financial backing from the fugitive Asil Nadir, ostensibly to buy the photographs outright.

Why the half-brother thought that Nadir would help, God alone knows. Perhaps he thought that Nadir might want to embarrass the Conservative Government, as retribution for chasing him out of the British Isles, on what Nadir claimed were trumped up fraud charges? Or perhaps to use as blackmail, to negotiate his return?

Unfortunately, the half-brother was listening to the wrong grapevine. Mine told me that Nadir had, in all probability, fled to northern Cyprus, not to escape the Conservative Government, but to save it embarrassment.

Nadir had been, in his better days, a major donor to the Conservative Party. The press believed that a public trial of Nadir would expose links between those donations and the millions missing from the coffers of Polly Peck International, the company Nadir had headed, until his runner to northern Cyprus. My grapevine suggested that the real embarrassment lay in the connection to the *Savoy Mafia*, of which Nadir was reputed to have been a heavily-secret member, and to illegal arms profits, coming back through Nadir into the Conservative Party's coffers..

So. Nadir had disappeared to northern Cyprus. Which since its annexation by Turkey, had not been recognized by any Government, including the British Government, and therefore, conveniently, had no extradition treaty with any country, including Great Britain.

All in all, Nadir was sitting pretty, and, by all accounts, was living the grand life. He had no reason to want to negotiate with or blackmail anyone. Plus, northern Cyprus was pretty much lawless. Not a good place for a nice English boy to be. Plus, Nadir's new good friend and neighbor was one Brian Brendan Wright, acknowledged former kingpin of the UK cocaine trade, and someone who had not been too shy about making nuisances disappear in the past.

Talk about your wrong place, at the wrong time. Suffice it to say, the half-brother turned up dead, in a one-car road accident, on some godforsaken, isolated goat track in the boondocks of mountainous north Cyprus. Simon had been investigating ever since. I felt an immediate kinship. I wrote to him several times, and eventually had an excited response.

Geoffrey Gilson

***

I say 'excited.' Regan was also quite tentative. It became clear from our first e-mail exchanges that we were neither one of us convinced of the *bona fides* of the other. I was concerned at his links to al-Fayed. He was troubled by the fact that I might be an Intelligence stooge, writing to him so totally out of the blue.

Regan assured me that his connection to al-Fayed had been severed, that it had always been at arms length, and had only been about cash. Apparently, he became happier with me. We moved from e-mail to snail mail, neither one of us being particularly comfortable with computers.

He encouraged me, without much explanation, to read the back copies of *Scallywag*, which were available on the Internet. In the meantime, he waded through a 5,000-word briefing of mine, which I had originally prepared for Richard Norton-Taylor.

On Regan's web-site, I discovered a series of articles discussing the Conservatives' innovative fund-raising techniques in Eighties, and some $300 million sitting in secret offshore bank accounts, some under the personal control of Margaret Thatcher.

Regan went to some lengths to explain to me the distinction between 'Party' accounts, which were under Thatcher's control, in order to avoid the scrutiny of Party 'puritans,' and accounts that were under Thatcher's control, because they were for her personal use.

Regan was now very chipper about my investigation. He wanted the opportunity to fashion my briefing into a potential magazine article, then to assist me with the writing of my book. He sought nothing in return. He simply wanted to 'get' the people he felt had 'got' his half-brother.

I was not about recklessly to turn away any help. Particularly someone who knew the corridors of publishing in Great Britain. It didn't matter that Regan bore with him some doubts that had been raised about his credibility. Heck, here was I, was talking to Ari, when I wasn't talking to myself. I hardly stood out as a beacon of universal respectability. Besides, I warmed to Simon's genuine interest and concern. Plus, he was the first person, aside from Maggi and Geer, actually to gush about my findings.

We agreed that he would first meet with Maggi, in England, so that we could both add human faces and feelings to the paper and electronic bonds that had been formed. In the meantime, he urged me to contact a good friend of his, Kevin Cahill, who had also labored on the Tory 'fund-raising' issue.

***

Dead Men Don't Eat Lunch

Before I spoke with Cahill, I heard from one of the 'puritans' to whom Simon had made reference: John Strafford had been the Chairman of the Beaconsfield Conservative Association, when I had served as its Vice Chairman.

Hugh, Peter Smith, John and I, plus many others of a like mind, had worked long and hard to enable Beaconsfield to achieve its high-flying status as a fund-raising powerhouse for the Tories.

In case there is any confusion, I'm talking here about Beaconsfield's legitimate status as a Party fund-raiser; not the quite separate shenanigans, set out in this book, by which Hugh, and others in Beaconsfield, may have contributed substantially, yet illicitly, to the fortunes of the Conservative Party.

After Hugh's death, John had gone on to succeed Hugh as Treasurer of the Wessex Area of the Conservative Party. And that position, as with Hugh, had led to John's membership of the secretive Conservative National Board of Finance.

John not been the friendliest of souls towards me after the early revelations of Hugh's defalcation. But he had come across my own web-site, on which I had set out a summary of my information to date, particularly those allegations concerning the funneling of large amounts of 'secret' money into the coffers of the Tory Party in the Eighties. John's e-mails in 1998 were a deal sight friendlier than he had been in 1988.

John was a Chartered Accountant by profession, and his e-mails were a model of professionalism. He had things he wanted to say, but his loyalties still lay with the Party with which he had been involved his whole political life.

John would not directly answer my question as to whether or not he had come across any evidence of 'secret' offshore accounts while he was on the Conservative Board of Finance. All he would say is that, upon completion of his term as Treasurer, he had immediately set up his own organization calling for more democracy in the Conservative Party.

In particular, he wanted the National Accounts of the Conservative Party to be placed under the control of a National Treasurer – all the Accounts. And he stressed that the Treasurer should be elected by grass-roots Tory members, and that the Treasurer should make all of those Accounts fully open to the membership. Beyond that, John wished me well, asked me to keep in touch, and suggested that I draw my own conclusions.

***

Kevin Cahill was an independent journalist, who financed his own investigations by his research work for *The Sunday Times* Rich List; the annual list of the richest people in Great Britain. Apparently, he also used the contacts he made to gather information for those investigations of his own.

In 1993, Cahill had written a series of long articles detailing the full history of 'secret' Tory fund-raising, going all the way back to Winston Churchill. Originally, there were a number of what were called 'River Associations' (named after Britain's largest rivers), through which 'secret' donations were funneled. More often than not, these were donations from abroad, which might prove embarrassing to Party leaders.

In the Eighties, what had been a 'cottage industry' became serious business. This started under the Treasurership of Lord Boardman in the early Eighties, and continued in earnest with Alistair McAlpine. In his autobiography, *Bagman*, McAlpine (now Lord McAlpine) laid claim to having raised some $225 million for the Tories between 1979 and 1989. Barely a fraction of this appeared in any of the heavily-abbreviated National Accounts produced after the Audit each year by Peter Smith and his friends at Coopers & Lybrand.

Money was coming in from all over the place: from shipping tycoons in Hong Kong to banking overlords in Indonesia. The River Associations were dramatically expanded into a complex network of international money-laundering entities, all fronted by the Party's legitimate banking arrangements with the Royal Bank of Scotland.

I gently wondered where this money-laundering expertise might have been garnered. It wasn't just a case of opening a bank account in Switzerland. And McAlpine had no background to suggest that the planning was all his. A thought made all the more relevant by the suggestions that bank accounts under the control of McAlpine had themselves been used, not only for the Party's own money-laundering, but as a piggy-back vehicle for other peoples' funds as well. A mirror reflection of allegations made by the Law Society about Hugh's 'financial arrangements.' Who met with McAlpine, just down the hall in Conservative Central Office, for meetings of the Conservative National Board of Finance.

Kevin took Simon's explanation of 'personal' bank accounts a stage further. He stated that there was no such thing as 'The Conservative Party.' There were Conservative Constituency Associations, which were stand alone legal units. They then had their own umbrella group, the National Union of Conservative Associations.

These Constituency Associations chose their own Conservative Candidates, who were subsequently elected Members of Parliament. The latter, in turn, agreed to take a common Conservative Whip in Parliament. The same was true of the unelected Conservative peers in the House of Lords. These MPs then chose a Leader, who was recognized by the other component parts of the 'Party' as their Leader also. In recent years, the specific rules have changed, but the principle is the same.

However, in the Eighties, there was still no 'National Party.' Only the above loose arrangements, leading up to an acknowledged individual 'Leader.' That Leader had a support staff, which was collectively known as Conservative Central Office. That 'Office' had its headquarters on the edge of the 'Mayfair Square Mile,' a short distance from Parliament.

Central Office served all of the component parts of the 'Party,' but it was still the Leader's personal Office. She appointed the staff, and all of the Central Office and National Party bank accounts were in her name. So, if you were Jamshid Hashemi, you didn't make a check out to "The Conservative Party," you made a check out to "Margaret Thatcher, as Leader of the Conservative Party." And when she ceased to be Leader, it became "John Major, as Leader of the Conservative Party." And so on. And that's where the fun had begun.

***

Maggi met with Simon in a cozy pub in central London. Simon was in his fifties, and bore an uncanny resemblance to one of those seedy characters made famous by the British actor, Sir Michael Gambon. Lower middle-class; all worn blazer and comfy cardigan. Never without a tie. But equally, never without a glass of scotch in his right hand, and a cigarette dangling from his mouth. Maggi had taken to him instantly, and reported that he was thoroughly genuine and charming.

Simon's next letter to me was even more joyful than the first few had been. He had not initially picked up on the significance of my thoughts about illicit Tory arms dealing and the Mark Thatcher connection.

Simon said that it was well known that large amounts of the 'secret' monies, that had been raised by the Tories in the Eighties, had come from arms dealings. But no-one in the mainstream media had been able to find the money trail. Simon, on the other hand, had evidence that the trail led through Mark, and then back to the Conservatives and ultimately to Margaret Thatcher.

Apparently, Mark had been chosen as the money pipeline precisely because no-one 'sensible' would think that matters of such importance would be entrusted to such a 'clown.' And Simon, on the basis of his information, had become convinced that they hadn't. Simon knew that Mark had expert money-laundering advice – he just couldn't locate the individual; he was too 'well-hidden.' The more Simon learned about Hugh, his past, his skills, and his singular importance within the Conservative Party, and to Margaret Thatcher, the more Simon came to believe that the adviser was not now 'well-hidden;' he was dead. It was, and it always had been, Hugh.

Simon's information was the '2,' which, when added to Ari's '2,' became the '4' I had been looking for: Simon had evidence that Mark was the secret pipeline to Margaret Thatcher and the Conservative Party of illicit profits from international arms sales. Ari had evidence that Hugh was, in turn, the secret pipeline of those profits to Mark. I had discovered the missing money trail.

More to the point, I now had information that strongly suggested that Hugh had not been acting as a 'rogue' in his nefarious shenanigans. Rather, he was an essential link in the conduit of corrupt money to Margaret Thatcher and the Conservative Party. And, in all the circumstances related so far in this book, and unearthed during my investigation, it is inconceivable that Hugh was acting other than at the express request of the British Prime Minister of the day, namely Margaret Thatcher.

Two questions, more than any other, continued to bug me: why on earth would one of the most successful British Prime Ministers of all time risk her place in history for a few bucks; and why on earth would Hugh Simmonds risk his life to help her?

It was because of these questions that Simon became more anxious than ever to help me with further research for and then the writing of my book. Cahill, Simon, Kevin and I forged a three-way arrangement: Kevin would help with the research; I would provide Kevin with all of my information; and Simon would pull it all together, and do the bulk of the actual writing. Notwithstanding Simon's protestations, I always envisaged any ensuing credit as being shared three-ways.

Alas, this was not to be. I never heard from Simon again. In 2000, I discovered why. Simon had become very ill, and had then died. In the short time that I knew him, Simon was a good friend. He is sorely missed. And I hear him, even now, chuckling, as he reads this book. At least now, he knows for certain what happened to his half-brother.

***

A couple of years later, on November 25th, 2001, to be precise, there was an article in *The Sunday Times*, headlined: "Arms bribe police block £100 million ($150 million] fund)":

"More than £100 million hidden in a Jersey [semi-autonomous small island, part of Great Britain, and situated close to the northern coast of France] trust has been frozen by detectives investigating allegations that British arms companies paid financial sweeteners to help win lucrative defense contracts in the Middle East.

In what is believed to be Britain's biggest commercial bribery inquiry, police and legal officials have frozen assets in a trust fund controlled by a senior member of the ruling family in the Gulf State of Qatar [the base for joint US/UK operations in the Second Gulf War].

Judicial sources say the money is alleged to be the proceeds of commissions paid by arms firms to win contracts for military equipment worth hundreds of millions of pounds during the 1990's. British, German and Italian companies are all said to have made payments in the "cash-for-contracts" affair.

Yesterday, BAe [British Aerospace] Systems, Britain's biggest defense firm, confirmed it was co-operating with the inquiry. But Phil Soucy, its spokesman, insisted: "We are not the object of this inquiry and we would refute any allegations of corruption or any other wrongdoing."

The bank accounts belonging to the trust are now run by Standard Chartered Grindlays Trust Corporation.

Sources close to the investigation claim that payments were made into the trust in return for securing government contracts, including the purchase of military equipment such as aircraft. The money – which some sources suggest may be up to £230 million – was used to buy property around the world.

Britain has close ties with Qatar. The state's emir visited Tony Blair for talks at Downing Street two years ago.

Because of its excessive secrecy and tax-free status, Jersey has proved popular with wealthy individuals seeking to hide the source of their money.

Although its banking sector has been more strictly regulated in recent years, money laundering, tax dodgers and drug barons have all used offshore accounts in the Channel Islands to hide criminal profits.

Last March £100 million pounds linked to General Sani Abucha, the former Nigerian dictator, was uncovered by Jersey regulators. They found bank accounts used Abacha's associates at five island financial institutions."

The nice Press Officer from the Law Society was prepared to confirm to me that money associated with Hugh's bank accounts had been traced back to Nigeria.

Certainly in the Eighties, and while Hugh was with Wedlake Bell, the latter firm had maintained offices on the island of Jersey. I believe on Grenville Street, in St. Helier.

***

When next I spoke with Kevin, he confirmed what Simon had said about Mark Thatcher. Indeed, some of Simon's information had been unearthed during Kevin's research. Kevin suggested that I read a book called *Thatcher's Gold*, which was all about Mark's finances. And which, interestingly, had been co-authored by Paul Halloran. I wondered how much of Halloran's information had been obtained from his own personal involvement?

By the by, I raised with Kevin my own thoughts about alleged destabilization in Great Britain in the Eighties and Nineties, and any connection to the Leadership of the Conservative Party. Oh man. I opened the floodgates. The first thing that Kevin did was to fax me a whole bunch of information, including organization charts, to back up what he was about to tell me.

Then, Kevin began by recounting conversations he had had with Michael Heseltine, the former Conservative Deputy Prime Minister under Major, and Minister of Defense under Thatcher. Heseltine had described a serious plan by right-wing businessman and politician, Sir James Goldsmith, to take over the Conservative Party after the fall of Thatcher.

That plan had included the need to remove Major, and had further envisaged a possible transition period, during which there might be a Labour Government in power for a couple of General Elections – to allow the Conservative Party to re-group, and to 're-discover its true direction.'

Kevin considered Goldsmith to be a new 'breed' of 'parvenu' British businessmen, who easily slipped around the corridors of power in the City, in boardrooms, in Whitehall and in the Intelligence Services. Power was bought and wielded, not by adhering to the Rules and Conventions that had cemented the British Establishment in the past, but with money, lots of it. And very little of it from legitimate sources. In particular, Kevin was convinced that Goldsmith was heavily involved with Tory arms dealing.

Kevin suggested that I read a fictional novel by John Le Carre, called *The Night Manager*. The book described an unholy alliance between the head of Britain's Secret Service and a sleazy businessman, who could have been one of any number of real-life sleazy billionaires, operating in British business in the Eighties.

Kevin explained that Le Carre had originally written it as non-fiction, intending to expose the corruption that had overtaken MI6 in the Eighties, when Britain's Foreign Intelligence Service had decided to put aside 'service,' and go into business for itself. Primarily, the arms and money-laundering business.

MI6 had become overrun by people who were no longer 'Gentlemen,' and had no appreciation of 'Gentlemen's Rules,' or the concept of duty and loyalty. I wondered at the extent to which this new-found desire for money might have translated into 'greed,' and equally how new, 'parvenu,' no-Rules Intelligence Officers might have reacted to an unwelcome display of competing 'greed' in a fellow Intelligence Officer. How much had the Rules changed?

When John Major had been elected Thatcher's successor in 1990, everyone thought that they would be dealing with a Leader and Prime Minister of like mind. According to Kevin, Major had met with a delegation of the Grey Men of his Party the weekend before the succession became final. They shared with a stunned and decent John Major the full extent of the corruption in the Tory Party, the Intelligence Services and his new Government in general.

The Grey Men had not expected Major's reaction. In the space of a couple of years, he set up: the Scott Inquiry, which the Grey Men feared would expose all of their illicit arms dealing; the Nolan Commission into Standards in Public Life, which set as its first priority a thorough review of all party financing; and a further Government Commission, which sought to overhaul Corporate Governance, in particular the secrecy surrounding many of the financial decisions made in Board Meetings in Great Britain – the mandarins of Tory Finance saw the possibility that their donations would be decimated, since so many of those corporate donations were made only on the basis that they remained secret.

The next thing we knew: Goldsmith was planning to oust John Major, and take over the Conservative Party with his money; John Le Carre was planning to write in his non-fiction book that Goldsmith and others were in cahoots with the head of MI6; and I was seeing signs in Great Britain of a destabilization technique, in popular use by Intelligence Agencies, and potentially aimed at undermining the institutions of the British Establishment.

Kevin told me that, in Le Carre's final version of his book, the fictional character 'Roper' was Goldsmith, and 'Darker' was Braden Camp, reputed to be Chief of MI6 at that time. Kevin also said that, from his conversations with contacts in the City of London, 'everyone' knew what was going on. Heseltine, Major's newly-appointed Deputy, certainly knew.

After the publication of the first edition of this book, Michael (now Lord) Heseltine had his Executive Assistant write to me, to communicate the following message from him to me:

"I have seen the text of your book. You should know that the events and opinions relating to me are fiction. I cannot agree to any publication of such invented accounts."

I immediately responded. There is nothing in this book that is either invented or fictional. So, everything stays in. Not surprisingly, I have heard nothing further from Michael.

In the absence of substantive action from Michael, it is fair to say that his hollow protest is nothing more than the knee-jerk reaction one would expect from an accomplished political operator. I think it was Mandy Rice-Davies, a call girl involved in a previous Conservative sex scandal, who said: "Well, he would say that, wouldn't he?"

Essentially, Michael, by his inaction, and in contrast to his seemingly-unequivocal statement, is in fact doing the very thing he claims he won't do, namely, 'agreeing to…publication' of those events and opinions I attribute to him. Moreover, by direct connection, he is also confirming the truth of the primary thrust of this book, namely its expose of Tory Arms Corruption, in the Eighties and beyond.

One twist I was beginning to formulate in my mind was that any 'campaign' against Major may not have been so much about bringing Thatcher back to power, as it was about keeping secret what Thatcher had been doing in the Eighties.

Goldsmith had eventually been rebuffed by whatever powers-that-be, and had gone off to form the Referendum Party, along with McAlpine and one Paul Sykes, another rich, right-wing, British businessman.

The Referendum Party was formed nominally as a 'Eurosceptic' Party, and campaigned on a platform of wanting a referendum to allow the British people to decide on Britain's future in the European Union. Goldsmith made much of the fact that the Party was about Europe, and not about the Tory Party. He himself had been elected as a Member of the European Parliament for a French seat in 1994 – Goldsmith maintained joint British-French citizenship.

However, Sykes had been another potential major donor to the Conservative Party, whose overtures had also been rebuffed because he was too right-wing. He is currently a major backer of UKIP. Other Referendum candidates targeting Conservative seats included right-wing zoo owner John Aspinall, who had been active in the 'loony right' in the Seventies; right-wing businessman and yachtsman, Peter de Savary; former Thatcher economic guru, Sir Alan Walters (a founding patron of the Selsdon Group); and Sir George Gardiner, another leading light from the right of the Seventies, and a Tory MP who had defected to the Referendum Party, only to be deselected by his Conservative Constituency Association. A rose by any other name, the Referendum Party existed in a serious form long enough only to help to inflict defeat on the Conservative Party in 1997.

I didn't laugh at Kevin's suggestions. And he didn't laugh at mine. But then, he hadn't yet finished. He said that Goldsmith's plan, although binned by his ultimate rejection, bore an uncanny resemblance to what the new (and still unelected) Treasurer of the Conservative Party had been doing, since his appointment to that position in 1998.

***

Upon hearing news of his Party's electoral defeat in the 1997 General Election, John Major had graciously tendered his resignation, both as Prime Minister, and as Leader of the Conservative Party. He was succeeded in the first office by Tony Blair, of New Labour, and in the second, by a young, uncharismatic, compromise choice, William Hague, who had previously been the Secretary of State for Wales.

Dead Men Don't Eat Lunch

Although a compromise choice, Hague immediately made some moves which smacked of a new Thatcherite influence at the top of the Tory Party. He appointed Thatcher's favorite lieutenant, Cecil (then Lord) Parkinson, as the new Chairman of the Party, and the individual directly responsible for the operation of Conservative Central Office. Parkinson had previously held the same position between 1979 and 1983, in the run-up to the hugely successful 1983 General Election, which the Tories had won with a landslide majority of 100 MPs.

One of Parkinson's first moves had been to make the controversial Michael (later Lord) Ashcroft the new Treasurer of the Conservative Party. Ashcroft had his start in business with waste management companies, in southern England, in the Eighties. He had been very friendly with Denis Thatcher, and they had served on similar Boards.

There had never been any suggestion that Ashcroft was associated with the *Savoy Mafia*, but there were rumors that he had been instrumental in getting Mark Thatcher the job, which allowed him to move to Dallas, Texas, in the early Eighties.

Ashcroft had been wildly successful, and had ended up purchasing American home security giant, ADT. Then, in the Nineties, he had sold that company, coming close to, but not quite achieving, billionaire status.

The source of controversy surrounding Ashcroft and his connections to the Conservative Party lay not in his money, but rather in the fact that he was viewed as a foreigner, and a rather shady one at that.

He had been born in Central America, and always retained strong links to the former British Colony of Belize. In addition, Ashcroft maintained his primary residence in Miami, Florida.

Ashcroft banks and companies in the newly-independent country of Belize had been responsible for establishing its offshore banking industry and international shipping registry.

Ashcroft could move money and goods at will around the world. Any sort of goods. And there was considerable brou-ha-ha in the British press, a year after Ashcroft's appointment as Tory Treasurer, about US Government investigations into Ashcroft's alleged connections to drug-smuggling and attendant illegal money-laundering.

Unlike the majority of Britain's better-heeled media, I was able to obtain albeit heavily blacked-out documents from US Drug Enforcement Agency. A whole list of company and individual names, which I have not yet had time to investigate. But I will.

***

I came across an interesting epilogue to this particular episode in a 2003 article, posted on the www.Apostropher.com web-site:

Geoffrey Gilson

Irony Leaking Out All Over the Place

Except in a few highly egregious circumstances relating to national security information (espionage and atomic secrets), the US Congress has, in the past, never made it a crime to leak information to the news media. As a result, for over two hundred years, our government has operated without an "official secrets act."

Despite the free speech costs, President George W. Bush has created the equivalent of an official secrets act for America - and it is only growing stronger. Indeed, by cobbling together provisions from existing laws, Bush's Justice Department has effectively created one of the world's most encompassing, if not draconian, official secrets acts.

If Attorney General John Ashcroft has his way, we will see many more prosecutions of this ilk. Ashcroft has told Congress he wants a "comprehensive, coordinated, Government-wide, aggressive, properly resourced, and sustained effort" to deal with "the problem of unauthorized disclosures."

Attorney General John Ashcroft is making good on his word to aggressively prosecute leaks - or at least some leaks. Again, the target has been a low-level employee, a Morison for the new millennium. He is Jonathan Randal, an intelligence research specialist with a Ph.D. who had worked at the Atlanta office of the DEA.

Randal's alleged crime? Leaking negative information about one of the richest men in the UK, Lord Michael Ashcroft (no relation).

Still by John Dean (Former Nixon Counsel) writing for FindLaw:

"Lord Ashcroft, who makes his home in Florida and the former British colony of Belize, had been bankrolling the Conservative Party in Britain. His business empire is also based in Belize, an offshore tax haven. The London 'Times' reported that leaked information from the Foreign Office indicated that high officials in Belize viewed Lord Ashcroft with "deep suspicion." Then, a few days later, it reported that his name appeared in a number of DEA files relating to investigations into drug trafficking and money laundering in Belize.

The bad press forced Lord Ashcroft's resignation as the Conservative Party's treasurer. Soon, the US State Department issued a statement that it had no conclusive proof connecting Ashcroft to money laundering, or anything else. But the London 'Times' said that to the contrary, it had DEA documents showing that Ashcroft was index-numbered on the DEA files, a measure that, it said, is taken only when serious suspicions exist.

Dead Men Don't Eat Lunch

Lord Ashcroft filed a libel lawsuit against the 'Times', and soon traced the DEA documents back to Jonathan Randal. It turned out that Randal had leaked them to a freelance British journalist who was investigating Lord Ashcroft; the journalist, in turn, had sold them to the London 'Times.' According to Randal's attorney, Steve Sadow - who spoke to Robin McDonald of the Fulton (Georgia) County Daily Report and Felicity Barringer of the 'New York Times' - Randal himself received no payment for the information itself, no quid pro quo.

Lord Ashcroft settled his lawsuit with the London 'Times,' which agreed to a front-page apology and promised never again to investigate him. In addition, according to press accounts, he hired an Atlanta lawyer to encourage DEA and the Justice Department to prosecute Jon Randal.

The Case Against Randal

Randal was indicted by Bush's new US Attorney in Atlanta, William Duffey Jr. Duffey is a former Deputy Independent Counsel who worked for Ken Starr in Little Rock, Arkansas. (Starr, with Duffey's help, built a case against then-governor Jim Guy Tucker, sending him to jail on fraud and conspiracy charges.)

In February 2002, Duffey's office confronted Randal with a twenty-count indictment. The impact of the indictment was to criminalize Randal's leak. But to do so, prosecutors didn't bother to draw from an official secrets act - since they didn't have one. Instead, they twisted the existing law to issue an indictment to the same effect.

Count One is based on the general theft statute - with information, once again, alleged to be the "thing of value" stolen. Count Two relies on a statute adopted in 1994 designed to protect information in government computers, where most government information now resides. The government charged that Randal "knowingly and with an intent to defraud" the government, exceeded his authorized use of the DEA computer by pulling information about Lord Ashcroft.

Counts Three through Eighteen are based on the mail/wire fraud statutes; there are sixteen counts because Randal allegedly accessed DEA computers to obtain information about Lord Ashcroft sixteen times.

This pair of statutes is especially prone to misuse. As Chief Justice Warren Burger noted, "When a 'new' fraud develops - as constantly happens - the mail fraud statute becomes a stopgap device to deal on a temporary basis with the new phenomenon, until particularized legislation can be developed and passed to deal directly with the evil." The same is true of the wire fraud statute, as he also noted.

Counts Nineteen and Twenty are further fraud charges. They appear to address the reimbursement that Randal received from the London

Geoffrey Gilson

'Times' when he agreed to meet with them after they were sued by Lord Ashcroft.

Jon Randal decided to cooperate with the government, and to plead guilty to a violation of the theft statute. That's not surprising: If he had not, he could have faced a staggering statutory maximum of penalty of 580 years - or more realistically, life - in prison.

Randal's Sentencing: The Government Seeks a Long Sentence

For sentencing purposes, the government used expert testimony to claim the value of the information given the London 'Times' was up to $70,000 - an absurd contention. Still, Randal was given a year in jail; he will have to serve the entire year, followed by three years of supervised probation. He will also have to pay a $2000 fine.

US Attorney Duffey told the 'New York Times' that he was pleased with the sentence - and saw the prosecution of Randal as "a warning to other government workers."''

But what warning, exactly? The information was not classified. It did not compromise any investigator, investigation, or investigative method. Clearly, the warning is this: Keep your mouth shut at all costs, no matter how intensely a leak might be in the public interest, and no matter how integral leaking might be to the way a free press operates. In short, the message is: Never blow the whistle.

Meanwhile, there is still talk of prosecuting the London 'Times.' But I'll believe that only when it happens - which would doubtless only occur after November 2004, if ever.

I suspect the "fair and balanced" Mr. Murdoch, who owns the London 'Times', will be able to settle up with the Bush administration before then. If not, the American media, too, will get an ugly warning - for it may be the next victim of Bush's unofficial official secrets act."

Now, although it is true that it was a US Attorney that was conducting the prosecution, he would definitely have been receiving 'input' from the Attorney-General, in a 'political' case like this. Who, in turn, would have been getting his marching orders from his President.

Again, notwithstanding the close relationship between George Bush and Tony Blair, George's natural political soul-mates still reside in the British Conservative Party.

That said, my first question would still be: why on earth would Bush be interested in supporting a prosecution on behalf of an individual who no longer wielded influence in the Conservative Party? Unless he did still wield influence.

My next question would be: why on earth would Bush be interested in supporting a prosecution on behalf of a Party that was no longer in power, and over matters that were in the past? Unless those matters still had connection to the present, and to the future?

My final question would be: why on earth would Bush be interested in any of this, in any event, since it obviously had nothing to do with him? Unless it had loads to do with him.

***

Ashcroft did not first become associated with Conservative Party finances only in the Nineties. He was heavily, although not so openly, involved in the Eighties. Kevin had provided me with a wealth of information linking Lord Boardman to corrupt fund-raising by the Conservative Party in the Eighties, even after Boardman was succeeded as Treasurer by McAlpine. And Boardman, in turn, had intimate links with Ashcroft throughout the Eighties.

Lord Boardman, a long time member of the Law Society, was forced to resign his Chairmanship of National Westminster Bank after the scandal involving NatWest and Blue Arrow plc. Ashcroft was an 'adviser' to Blue Arrow in the Eighties, and as such, was questioned by the Department of Trade and Industry about suspicious loans made by Blue Arrow to Peter de Savary. Before his affiliation with the Referendum Party, de Savary, a maverick millionaire businessman, had been a leading Conservative Party donor.

All through the Eighties, Boardman served alongside McAlpine as a Director of the Bourne Association, one of the 'River Associations,' used by the Tory Party for channeling its 'dicky' donations. The 1985 Accounts of the Bourne Association record Boardman's other directorships as including Pritchard Services Group, which became part of Ashcroft's business empire later in the Eighties.

The primary similarity between the Goldsmith Plan, and Ashcroft's actions lay in the fact that, during his Treasurership, and maybe beyond, Ashcroft was virtually bankrolling the Conservative Party on his own. But, was it all his own money? Or was he a front for other money as well?

***

Ashcroft was one of the first to support Margaret Thatcher's City Technology Colleges initiative. Under this program, commercial enterprises could sponsor the establishment and administration of Technical Colleges in blighted urban areas. The terms were very clear: once you handed over the money, you had no say in the administration of the College. Clearly, no-one had fully explained those rules to Michael Ashcroft.

Geoffrey Gilson

A source has told me that, before 1996, she accidentally gained access to the heavily-secured top floor of the Technology College, in Wandsworth, London, that was sponsored by Adlearn, Ashcroft's personal charitable foundation.

The state-of-the-art computer was running. Idly curious, she had a nose around. She said that, while not stupid, she was nowhere near clever enough to understand all of the data in front of her, but she could clearly see that it involved money – a lot of money. And it involved Ashcroft. And there didn't appear to be a whole lot of distinction between money in the Caribbean; money in Belize; money in the UK; money that was Ashcroft's; money that was the College's – and money that was washing through the Conservative Party.

We know of Ashcroft's close personal and business relationship with Denis Thatcher in the Eighties. What if there was a second, and more secret, tier to the *Savoy Mafia*? What if it included the likes of Goldsmith, Nadir, de Savary and Ashcroft? Even the likes of al-Fayed? There was plenty of evidence associating al-Fayed with illicit arms dealing in general, but to be honest, I had found nothing concrete to link him to Tory arms dealing. But I did have an unholy itch on the subject.

What if Ashcroft had made his Belize operation available to the Conservative Party, to launder its own illicit money, and also the 'dirty money' of some of its 'friends'? Might that have made Ashcroft the indispensable 'Gatekeeper of the Treasure Chest,' to whom the Party would have had to go, cap-in-hand, when first so much of the Party's 'operating' illicit funds had gone 'missing' with Hugh's untimely death, and then, when its source for new illicit funds had taken a huge blow with Aitken's downfall?

***

Certainly it is the case that, since Thatcher's removal from power in 1990, there has been an almost continuous succession of Thatcherite Leaders of the Conservative Party. Indeed, an almost obscenely rapid succession of Leaders: a total of five in sixteen years.

We have seen the almost immediate moves by Hague, which would undoubtedly have had the effect of sending the 'right' signals to Thatcherites. Then, after the next Conservative defeat in 2001, he stood down, to make way for a more charismatic Leader. Most of the public and press were convinced this would be Michael Portillo. Until, on the weekend before the final tally of votes, amid all of Portillo's talk of reforming the Conservative Party, Lady Thatcher made it clear that she would not support Portillo.

Eventually, arch-rightwinger Iain Duncan-Smith was elected the new Leader. He was even more unassuming than Hague, his primary claim to fame being that he'd been one of the leading right-wing Euro-rebels, who had made life such hell for John Major in the early Nineties. Duncan-Smith was finally put out of his misery in 2003, when he was replaced with another Margaret favorite, Michael Howard.

Plus ca change, plus c'est la meme chose. Everything changes; yet everything is still the same.

In a further twist on my earlier twist, and bearing in mind that many years had passed since the Eighties had been in full swing, I found it difficult to believe that all of these musical chairs served the purpose simply of preserving the secrets of the Eighties. Nobody cared any more. Most people viewed the Conservatives as an irrelevance, and saw New Labour and Tony Blair as the new 'natural Party of Government.'

So why be so worried about preserving a Thatcherite leadership? Unless it was not the leadership that one was maintaining; so much as an ongoing arrangement for which a Thatcherite leadership was a necessary cover.

***

At this point, there was a regular exchange of information between Kevin and me. I was working on a list of names for Kevin. Anyone and anything I could remember being associated with Hugh, to give Kevin a starting database of leads for him to take his inquiries wherever they might go.

Then, one day, Kevin telephoned me to say that he'd been approached by a "person of credibility," who had told him, in no uncertain terms, to drop all interest in me and Hugh. Kevin seemed quite matter of fact about relaying the conversation to me. Not in the slightest bit worried. But I never heard from him again.

***

For my birthday, Maggi had sent me a copy of *In The Public Interest*, the book penned by Gerald James, setting out his experiences as the former Chairman of Astra. James was a Chartered Accountant by profession. In the early Eighties, he had become involved with Astra, a struggling company, which at that time, was best known for making fireworks.

James was brought on board to turn the company around. Yet, he wasn't terribly interested in fireworks. What he saw was the opportunity offered by the fact that a fireworks company already possessed most of the same work place conditions and licenses as an arms manufacturer. James was intent on fashioning Astra into one of Britain's leading defense

Geoffrey Gilson

contractors.

One of the first things I noticed about James was the similarity of his approach and Ari's in the writing of their books. They both told their stories in a disingenuous manner, which would have the reader constantly believe that the narrators were disinterested observers, standing by watching all this heavy stuff just happening around them. What they failed to share was the fact that, more often than not, they were the ones making it all happen.

I was aware of James' association with the active right in the Seventies; and, in particular, his membership of *The Monday Club*. He made no secret of his delight in Thatcher's accession to the Leadership of the Conservative Party, and then, to the office of Prime Minister. He seemed happy to be associated with all that he described as occurring within Astra. Until, it all started blowing up in his face. Excuse the pun. But, nevertheless, it gave me a fascinating perspective on the direction my thoughts were taking.

James built up Astra rapidly through the Eighties, by way of acquisition of existing defense companies. Between 1986 and 1989, Astra was transformed from a small group specializing in fireworks and military pyrotechnics, with assets of $2 million and an annual turnover of $8.3 million, to an international manufacturer of armaments and ammunition and other defense related products, with net assets at March 31st, 1989 of $78 million and an annual turnover of $142 million.

James focused particularly on explosives and ammunition companies, and that is why he bought the likes of PRB, the Belgian ammunition specialist, which was closely linked to Gerald Bull. Another company was BMARC, where he made Jonathan Aitken a director, at the latter's insistence. In his book, James is careful not to claim for himself all the credit for Astra's phenomenal growth. He had a lot of under-the-table help.

First, Thatcher's Government bent over backwards to supply him with all of the licenses and export credit guarantees that he needed. Even when the rules needed to be bent. Then, there was the active networking of the *Savoy Mafia*, rustling up contracts.

Finally, James found himself the newest member of another secretive arms network: *The Parlor Club*. This was a Europe-wide cabal of the heads of all of the major arms companies in Europe. They met on a regular basis to carve up arms deals around the world. No-one saw any reason to lose out on mindless competition when there were enough goodies for everyone in the global arms' 'gold rush' of the Eighties.

In return for all of this lucrative 'glad-handing' on behalf of Astra, all James had to do was play ball. And that meant, look the other way, as the Government used Astra to carry out its 'backdoor' arms deals.

Dead Men Don't Eat Lunch

Being a trained Accountant, when the dust finally settled, James did his sums. When Thatcher came to power, Britain ranked fairly low on the list of the world's exporters of arms. Thatcher was determined to see Britain move up that list. The two keys to this were continuity of supply and finance.

You sell the most arms to the people who use them, or who feel the most insecure. And those are generally dictators in the Third World, and the countries they have their eye on suppressing or invading. More often that not, since these entities are usually in a state of conflict, international arms' embargoes are in place, and the 'boy scout' countries have to withdraw from supplying them.

In the Eighties, under Thatcher, Britain sent out a message, loud and clear: we are open for business; all hours; whatever the conditions. If an embargo is in place, just use the backdoor. And Astra became the primary 'back door.'

James described in his book how Astra warehouses were regularly used as stopping off points for arms on their way to Iraq. He also confirmed the cross-Atlantic arrangement, whereby companies, on both sides of the ocean, got around their own domestic restrictions, on trading with the likes of Iraq and Iran, by using a subsidiary on the other side of the pond.

As for finance, and notwithstanding her much proclaimed disdain for public subsidy, Thatcher opened the Government check book (associated with the Export Credit Guarantee Program) for the newly-burgeoning arms industry. It was like a President Day's Sale, at the Pre-Owned Car Lot, gone wild.

Thatcher tramped the world, drumming up arms business. There was no state visit too grand or pompous that could not wait while she hawked some wares on the side. Bad credit rating? No matter. No money? No problem. Bad payment history? Who cares. Not likely to be in power long? Let's throw you in a nice villa in exile.

The shakiest of arms deals were done. On the basis of commercial letters of credit which everyone knew would never be honored. And all of which were underwritten by the Government's Export Credit Guarantee program. The reason? Because Thatcher took the view that the expense was worth the investment in building up Britain's arms manufacturing base, its sales network, and its list of recurring clients.

I mentioned that James had done his figures. In the Eighties, the revenues from the oil fields, discovered around Britain's shores in the Seventies, finally came on tap for the Government. To the tune of between $10 billion and $15 billion a year. James reckoned that, through the decade of the Eighties, almost all of this money, each and every year, went down the tubes, on fulfilling Export Credit Guarantees that had gone sour. Some President's Day Sale.

Clever man James. Knew a lot. Perhaps too much? By the end of the Eighties, Britain had secured its spot as the Number 2 arms exporter world-wide. Just behind the United States. The two major clients of the Eighties, Iran and Iraq, were no longer at war. It was time to 'clean house.'

That's when the deal to acquire PRB suddenly went sour for Astra. The next thing James knew, Astra was under investigation by the Department of Trade and Industry. The final report was so damning that Astra was closed down, and the component parts sold off.

Of course, being sold off didn't mean they stopped functioning; they just did it more quietly, under different ownership. But that was small comfort to James, because he was no longer the owner. He'd gone from practicing how to thank the Queen for his knighthood, to being an industry pariah. Over night.

He tried to talk to the media. But that did no good. James detailed in his book how one journalist, to whom he was feeding information, died in mysterious circumstances in a road accident.

Before cutting off contact with me, Kevin had passed on some of my information to Gerald James. We exchanged a few telephone calls and letters. Gerald always sounded kind of distracted.

Gerald immediately recalled Hugh, from *The Monday Club*, in the Seventies. Gerald was not a part of what he described as "the Simmonds' Set." These were a group of hyper-active fanatics, who included intense, right-wing political types and intense, right-wing Intelligence Officers.

Gerald told me that he had always assumed that Hugh was one of an increasing number of young activists, who straddled the fence between Intelligence and the Tory Party, because of his close friendship with Bee Carthew. Gerald also confirmed that he had, for the same reasons, naturally concluded that Hugh was himself an Intelligence Officer.

Gerald agreed with my feeling that I might best be able to track down what Hugh had been up to in the Eighties by tracing forward from his contacts in the Seventies. Gerald agreed to undertake some inquiries of his own, and then get back to me.

When he did, he was the most animated I recall him being. He confirmed that the trail from the Seventies was proving very fruitful. For starters, he had found definite connections, in respect of the matters interesting us, with: Tiny Rowland, Lonrho and sanctions-busting; Malcolm Rifkind; and a company called Anglo-Israeli Shipping.

Gerald said that he didn't have time to explain further. He had more leads to follow, and would be back in touch. He sounded quite energized, almost breathless. It was as if I had given him some sort of renewed hope for payback. But, this was much about the same time that Kevin stopped communicating with me. And, although I have tried from my end on a number of occasions since then, Gerald has never made contact with me again.

Dead Men Don't Eat Lunch

A flock of thoughts were once again swirling in my head. Among them: was this what the 'Thatcherite Succession' was supposed to be protecting? The shady arms build-up of the Eighties? But why go to all that trouble? The past was past. It was no secret any more – James' book was there for everyone to read. Besides, with the Tories no longer in power, why bother?

These thoughts, and many more, were only just beginning to coalesce in my mind, when I became totally distracted by another article in an English newspaper. With it, I believed I had discovered 'the lawyer,' with the shady Conservative connections, the mention of whom had caused Ari so much grief. And Haya to be so fearful. And it was very clear why Haya had been so scared.

Geoffrey Gilson

Chapter 28

Iₙ THE WINTER OF 1999, I was still walking to work in Clayton, since I had no car. I was working with Tom Slowen, an odd-job, country Attorney, from whom I'd originally sought some advice over a Landlord dispute.

Tom was a funny fish. He was born in Connecticut, and had gravitated to Rabun County, by way of the Emory School of Law, in Atlanta. He was New England to the core, and somewhat eccentric. The first made him stick out like a sore thumb, in redneck Rabun County; while the second made him right at home. He was a good man, and a fine lawyer; his only failing being that, on occasion, he was too good. To clients who had fine-tuned the art of taking advantage.

I am definitely getting old. Time was I never minded the cold. But now, I get cranky the moment it drops below 80 degrees. And, southern state or no, in the mountains of north Georgia, in the Winter, it got cold. I had never much been one for camouflage, but everyone who wore it seemed to be a lot happier than me, so I bought a camo jacket. But, not just any jacket; one of those big, fluffy numbers, that the hunters wear, while they're wait for six hours, to blow away a ferocious squirrel.

As chance would have it, one of my front crowns fell out that Winter, and it took me a couple of weeks before I had the money to replace it. Plus, on the weekends, I tended not to worry too much about washing and shaving. So it was that I was doing my regular jaunt down to the store, one crisp, Saturday morning, when I noticed that every one of the fat, female, mountain trolls that passed me would coo and wave.

Eventually, I tired of shuddering and hiding, and so I looked into a shop window, to try and work out what the heck the problem was. There, facing me, was every redneck, mountain troll's wet dream: an unwashed, unshaved scallywag; with a toothless grin, and a camo jacket. I never wore the camo jacket again.

Dead Men Don't Eat Lunch

What I did for Tom, in the main, was catch up on his backlog of personal injury cases, and then help with the land title searches. In England the title process is much easier. There is little 'new' land left. So, most of the land has become registered with the Land Registry. Proving ownership of land is simply a question of writing to the Registry, and asking who the last owner was. In the vast wilderness of Rabun County, almost every land transaction involves 'new' land. And so the title process requires creating a whole new proof of ownership.

It was while I was doing one of these 'proofs' on day, that I noticed that no 'proofs' pre-dated 1802. I asked one of the Attorneys whom I knew quite well, and who happened to be in the County Title Office that day, why this was so. He was quite shifty about it, and mumbled that there were no settlers before then.

But the plaque outside the Courthouse quite clearly stated that Georgia was one of the original 13 Colonies, and as such, had come into existence in the 18th Century. In my naïveté, I was confused. I left my book alone for a while, and engaged in some research. What I found should not have surprised me.

The Cherokee Indians used to inhabit a swathe of North America, taking in what today is parts of Kentucky, Tennessee, the western part of North Carolina, and most of North Georgia. The British had signed a Treaty with the Cherokee, allowing them to continue to occupy this region, as the 'Cherokee Nation.' The primary term of this Treaty was that the 'white man' was not permitted to settle in the Nation; nor to farm, nor to mine, nor to own land there.

When the Colonies became the United States, the new 'white nation' confirmed the existing Treaty with the Cherokee Nation. And everyone was happy. Until gold was discovered in the mountains of North Georgia. The southern gold rush was almost as massive – and as violent – as the later western gold rush.

The State of Georgia, in an early preview of the Civil War, made much play of State Rights, and declared that the Union's Treaty's did not apply to its internal affairs. Whereupon the Georgia 'white man' felt free to make merry hay in the Cherokee Nation, raping and plundering as he went.

The Cherokee took their case to the Supreme Court, and eventually won. But it was a hollow victory. The Union was not yet ready to fight a war, to enforce rights on behalf of the Natives; a war which it later proved more willing to support, in respect of the Slaves. Ultimately, the Cherokee packed their bags, and moved pretty much wholesale to Oklahoma, in what became known infamously as "The Trail of Tears." All that was left was the small Reservation that I had visited in North Carolina.

The newly-vacated lands of North Georgia, including Rabun County, were, at the beginning of the 19th Century, then parceled out by way

Geoffrey Gilson

of State Lottery. I looked around the shelves of the Rabun County Title Office, and finally found the old ledger, recording the Rabun Winners of that State Lottery. All around about 1802. Many of the family names in the book are still prevalent in Rabun County. Including that of the Attorney who had seemed so embarrassed by my question.

1999 was the year that Mexican immigration into Rabun County began in earnest. They received a mixed welcome. The male layabouts didn't much care for them. But the area's employers were overjoyed finally to have a labor market that wanted to work. On the whole, the Mexicans kept to themselves, in a couple of apartment blocks on the outskirts of Clayton.

Tom had kindly given me a key to his Office, which was in the center of Clayton. That way, I had somewhere to go at the weekends, to work on this book. That Christmas, I still hardly knew anyone, and so, decided to make a day of it in Tom's Office.

I set off from my own apartment early in the morning. I lived over a garage, about a mile from downtown Clayton. The air was chilly, but crisp; and as fresh as mint. The few wisps of high-flying cloud air-brushed the harsh blue sky. Rabun County was dead. It was Christmas morning after all. Everyone was either asleep, or hard at it, opening presents at home.

As I walked down the road, I noticed a lone hawk circling quite low overhead. Artfully, it made use of the relative heat rising from the road, to allow it to stay aloft by gliding alone, without having to exert energy to flap its huge wings. By the time I got to the bottom of the hill, and entered the outskirts of Clayton, there were dozens of hawks, doing lazy susan's in company, all over the deserted roads leading into town.

The streets themselves were empty. Save for a few Mexican women and their children, who viewed me warily, as they edged into the center of Clayton, and ogled the goods in the shop windows. Just before I entered Tom's Office, I looked around. The street had suddenly filled up with people. But every one of them was a Native, from the Land to the south of the United States.

Off in the distance, I caught sight of the hawks, confident and untroubled, still performing their carefree acrobatics in the air. I was overwhelmed by the sensation of how loose was the grip of the 'white man' on the lands he had so recklessly wrenched from those to whom it still properly belonged.

***

I came across an article on the Internet, which stated that a London solicitor, called Michael Rogers, had just been jailed for stealing a Client's money. The client was Dodi Fayed. But that is not what caused me to sit up.

The article went on to describe Rogers' plush offices in the

Dead Men Don't Eat Lunch

'Mayfair Square Mile;' his business dealings with Mohammed al-Fayed [who had a townhouse, around the corner, on Park Lane]; his services for Robert Maxwell; his representation of a number of senior Tories, including Sir Gordon Reece, Margaret Thatcher's close adviser; and the fact that Rogers had acted for Jamshid Hashemi.

Apparently Sir Gordon had instructed Rogers to post bond for Hashemi, when the latter had first been arrested and charged with selling arms illegally to Iran. Sir Gordon was essentially Thatcher's hairdresser, speech coach and 'walker.' He would not have dreamed of doing something like that unless it was at her specific direction.

Had I inadvertently uncovered Ari's 'lawyer,' and with him, discovered a major missing piece of the jigsaw puzzle?

***

Let's pause long enough to catch breath: we had a large number of the players, in the Eighties' 'Arms Game' we have been describing, all hanging around in the 'Mayfair Square Mile,' and all seemingly connected to each other through a lawyer. Surely this was all too much simply to be a co-incidence?

The one minor surprise, to be honest, was al-Fayed. I knew he had been involved with illicit arms dealing with Khashoggi, but I had not previously read of any direct link, either to the Iran arms deals of the Eighties, or to Margaret Thatcher. I had been forced to focus on more indirect connections. I checked a few sources, and elicited two articles through the trusty *Guardianlies.com* web-site:

"On 9th January 1986, three days before the publication of this article [following], the 10th January issue of satirical magazine "Private Eye" appeared on Britain's newsstands. It contained a leading article written by hard-Left "Daily Mirror" journalist Paul Foot [nephew of Michael Foot], reporting allegations that in October 1984 Prime Minister Margaret Thatcher's son, Mark, had accompanied Mohamed al-Fayed on a trip to see the Sultan of Brunei.

The article alleged that Mark was representing a construction company with ambitions of winning a contract to build a new university for the tiny Sultanate. It was suggested that Mark had with him a letter of introduction from the Minister of Finance of Oman, from whom in April 1981 the British construction company Cementation had won a similar university construction contract with Mark's help.

The article hinted that the company on whose behalf Mark had acted on the Brunei trip could have been the British conglomerate Trafalgar House, on whose behalf Mark was also said to have acted previously.

Geoffrey Gilson

The timing of the trip -- October 1994 -- is significant insofar as it was on 30 October 1984 that Trade Secretary Norman Tebbit inexplicably extended by another 90 days the Monopolies & Mergers Commission's investigation into Lonrho's bid for House of Fraser [Harrods].

As a consequence of the revelations in "Private Eye" Tiny Rowland supplied "The Observer"[owned by Tiny Rowland, whom, it has been suggested, bought the newspaper specifically to 'arm' himself with his own media vehicle to oppose al-Fayed – and "The Guardian" – in the battle between Rowland and al-Fayed over ownership of Harrods] with more information already in his possession, such as the dates of the flights to and from Brunei (24 & 26 Oct.), the route taken (via Singapore), and that the aircraft used was Fayed's own private Gulf Stream executive jet -- three bold statements of fact, which, if untrue, Fayed would easily have been able to disprove by reference to his diary and his Gulf Stream's flight log.

Armed with the information "Observer" editor Donald Trelford turned to his hard-Left political journalist David Leigh to write up an article. Leigh was the paper's resident 'expert' on Mark Thatcher, having been responsible for authoring some twelve articles between January and April 1984 on Mark's dealings in Oman. However Leigh, who had a burning antipathy towards Rowland, refused, claiming that the story was a "Rowland plant" -- though its original source, Paul Foot, was a personal friend and political soulmate of Leigh who had no connection with the Observer and no particular regard for Tiny Rowland either.

In the event Trelford wrote up the article himself, under the by-line 'staff reporter'. Following its publication Mohamed Fayed issued a denial (which he refused to sign), and which he failed to substantiate with documentary evidence such as his aircraft's flight log or appointment diary. Mark Thatcher, for his part, refused to deny the story, which remains the case up to the present time. Furthermore, the next issue of "Private Eye," published after "The Observer" article reproduced here [next], carried a follow-up piece implying that Mohamed Fayed's denial was untruthful:

The Observer
Sunday, 12 January 1986

Mark Thatcher's mystery trip to see Sultan
by a Staff Reporter

THE Prime Minister will be questioned closely when Parliament resumes this week about a remarkable sequence of events involving her son, Mark Thatcher, and his connection with the Sultan of Brunei, reputed to be

Dead Men Don't Eat Lunch

the world's richest man, and Mohammed Fayed, the mysterious Egyptian businessman who has obtained control of Harrods.

The questions will center on the extent to which Mrs. Thatcher's Government -- and her son -- may have been skillfully used by a foreign entrepreneur. They will relate to the following points: -

- Mark's unpublicized visit in October, 1984, with Mohammed Fayed to Brunei, the very small and very rich oil kingdom on the northern tip of Borneo which joined the Commonwealth last year;

- his involvement in a multi-million pound building contract in Brunei;

- his continuing commercial relationship with the Gulf state of Oman;

- a meeting at Downing Street early last year, attended by Fayed and the Sultan, after which five billion dollars were reported to have been transferred by Brunei from the United States to relieve the British sterling crisis;

- the circumstances in which Fayed, known to have access to the Sultan's funds, was given permission in March last year to bid for the House of Fraser without a reference to the Monopolies Commission;

- a hastily planned meeting in April last year in the Sultan's opulent palace in Brunei -- also attended by Fayed -- at which the Sultan officially presented the Prime Minister with a gold bracelet studded with diamonds and rubies, and which Fayed claims he arranged.

Mark Thatcher visited Brunei with Mohammed Fayed from 24-26 October 1984, traveling via Singapore on the Egyptian's private Gulf Stream jet. Their names appeared on the Royal Guest Immigration Register. The visit has also been confirmed to "The Observer" by a senior official of the Brunei Government.

According to a report last week, Mark Thatcher was introduced to the Sultan of Brunei by a letter from the Finance Minister of Oman. It is believed that he was representing a Gulf construction company with an interest in a £600 million university complex in Brunei.

Two years ago, "The Observer" revealed Mark Thatcher's involvement in a contract to build a university in Oman. He was representing the British company Cementation, a subsidiary of Trafalgar House, which won the contract after Mrs. Thatcher had urged the Omanis, on an official visit, to give the work to Britain.

Although the amount of Mark Thatcher's commission was never disclosed, a Cementation executive was quoted as saying: 'We did pay him -- and we used him because he is the Prime Minister's son.' Mrs. Thatcher said: 'I was batting for Britain.'

Geoffrey Gilson

Mark Thatcher announced that he had severed his links with Cementation in March, 1984, and went to the United States to represent the interests of Mr. David Wickins, of the Lotus car company and British Car Auctions, for an annual salary of £45,000 a year. He moved out of the Downing Street flat in which he had previously conducted some of his business.

His visit to Brunei, in the company of Mohammed Fayed, followed seven months later. It came just a week before the then Secretary for Trade and Industry, Mr. Norman Tebbit, unexpectedly extended an inquiry into a British public company's seven-year attempt to acquire House of Fraser, owner of Harrods, by an additional three months.

In March last year Mohammed Fayed sat next to Mark's sister, Carol Thatcher, at a Downing Street dinner to mark the State visit of President Mubarak of Egypt. Since the two Egyptians had never previously met, it was seen as an unusual piece of protocol for the British to invite Fayed to such an occasion.

Mark Thatcher is also reported to have seen Fayed a few weeks ago while staying at the Carlton Tower Hotel in London.

Two aspects of this matter may disturb MPs. One is that Mohammed Fayed and his two brothers were able to gain control of the House of Fraser within the remarkably short space of 10 days. The other is that, although the Monopolies Commission had by then given clearance, Mr. Tebbit did not release the British competitor, Lonrho, from its Department of Trade undertaking not to bid for the company until three days after the Fayeds had taken over.

Shortly before Christmas, 1985, Mr. R.W. Rowland, Chief Executive of Lonrho (and Chairman of "The Observer"), wrote to Mr. Tebbit's successor at Trade and Industry, Mr. Leon Brittan, saying:

'I have been told that on 24 and 25 October, 1984, Mr. Mark Thatcher visited Brunei, in company with Mohammed Fayed. A few days later the third House of Fraser inquiry and the Trade Department's embargo on a Lonrho bid for the company were extended for a further 90 days. Mohammed Fayed was also inexplicably enriched and before the end of October was offering me £100 million for my Lonrho shares, and £138 million cash for our embargoed House of Fraser shares. It wasn't long before Mohammed Fayed was able to boast: "and the British Government... they give me permission in ten days." Your letter to me of 3 December 1985, states that you are replying for the Prime Minister. I want it on record that you have had an opportunity to answer.'

Two days later, he wrote furiously to the Prime Minister:

Dead Men Don't Eat Lunch

'Why have you had anything whatsoever to do with Mohammed Fayed?... We have a natural right to know why,' he said, the House of Fraser decision was made. 'In contrast with Mohammed Fayed, Lonrho is a very large British company with 60,000 shareholders, against whose bid no good grounds of objection were ever made, but whose offer was put under restraints, which unbelievably were continued at the behest of your Minister, (Norman Tebbit), even after the clearance of the Monopolies Commission. The damage suffered by our company was devastating, when you gave this man, who boasted to me that he has never paid income tax anywhere in the world, what you denied to a long-established, internationally known, public company which employs 150,000 people world-wide, and which has annually published its accounts for 75 years.'

When Fayed made his £615 million bid for House of Fraser, it was unclear to many City observers who he was, or where he derived his funds. Fayed acted for the Sultan over the purchase of the Dorchester Hotel, which stands next to a Park Lane apartment block which Fayed owns, and where he lives.

He had wanted the hotel for himself, but conceded it, he says, because the Sultan expressed a strong personal wish to acquire the Dorchester directly, his parents having spent their honeymoon there. Mohammed Fayed inserted a 20-year management contract for his own company, which has been a subject of litigation.

The 38-year-old, Sandhurst-trained [Britain's premier military college] Sultan rules his 210,000 mainly Muslim, Malay subjects with the help of 2,000 Gurkhas [famous British Regiment, made up of Nepalese inductees] and without the benefit of political parties. He is currently staying with his family, including his two wives, at the Dorchester.

Fayed was introduced to the Sultan by his spiritual adviser, Shri Chandra Swami, who acts as a guru to several heads of state, including President Mobutu of Zaire and a number of Far Eastern leaders.

The Swami, contacted by "The Observer" in London last week, said: 'Fayed is not a spiritual man like the Sultan, who is a young leader with great potential in South-East Asia and who wants to be of assistance to Britain. But he has been subject to some manipulation and exploitation, as was your Prime Minister in this case.'

By the middle of 1984, Fayed had gained the ear of the young and inexperienced Sultan, eclipsing other court advisers to such an extent that he had a power of attorney which put funds of $1.5 billion under his control.

These monies allegedly reached Fayed in stages, through a maze of his own Liechtenstein companies to the Compagnie de Gestion et de Banque Gonet in Switzerland (COGEBA) in August and September 1984, in a classic pattern of concealment.

Geoffrey Gilson

When Lonrho was told by Mr. Tebbit in November 1984, that its application to bid for House of Fraser had been delayed for another three months, the company was warned by counsel to divest its near-30 per cent shareholding before it might be ordered to do so at a 'forced sale' price. This holding was acquired by Fayed, the only offeror for the block of shares.

Lonrho began to build a new holding by market purchase of 6 per cent, against the outcome of the Monopolies Commission.

Kleinwort Benson, merchant bankers retained to act for the Fayeds in this bid for control of House of Fraser, stated that the funds belonged to the family alone, and it was on this (largely unsupported) evidence that the Director-General of Fair Trading, Sir Gordon Borrie, recommended to the Department that the bid should be allowed to proceed.

"The Daily Telegraph," "The Financial Times" and "The Observer" have all carried articles casting doubt on the extent of the Fayeds' own fortunes.

Last April, the Sultan relieved Fayed of his power of attorney and relations between the two men were said subsequently by "Newsweek" to be 'strained.'

The publicity attaching to the Harrods deal has evidently embarrassed the position of the Sultan with his family and advisers in Brunei.

His embarrassment may be all the greater after the publication last Friday of an article in a New York paper, "Jewish Press," which accuses his associate, the new owner of Harrods, of being anti-Semitic.

Fayed is also quoted as claiming credit for introducing Mrs. Thatcher to the Sultan and arranging her visit to Brunei.

Fayed prides himself in the quoted conversation on the speed with which the Harrods deal was cleared -- 'they give me permission in ten days.' They did this, he says, 'because the British Government think Mohammed Fayed is up there, you know... up there inside Prime Minister...

'So three times we were with the British Government, myself and with the Prime Minister, are like that. Margaret Thatcher. He (the Sultan) know that I took him there. I made the Prime Minister go there, it was not in her program when she goes there in March, end of March, beginning of April. She put and went there. I arranged it.'

Last night, Mark Thatcher was said to be in the United States. The office of his employer, David Wickins, said they could not contact him. Mr. Fayed was not available for comment at his house in Park Lane, Mayfair."

***

"The article reproduced here [following] returns to a story first covered in "The Observer" five months earlier on 12th January 1986, which

Dead Men Don't Eat Lunch

itself had picked up from an article in "Private Eye" published on 10th January, and which the "Eye" had run a second time in its next issue of 24th January.

These three articles concerned an alleged trip taken by Prime Minister Margaret Thatcher's son Mark on 24 October 1984 to Brunei. The timing of the date was significant, because a week later on 30 October the Conservative Trade Secretary Norman Tebbit had unexpectedly extended by 90 days the Government's embargo on Lonrho's own long-standing bid for House of Fraser - the implication being that Thatcher's visit to Brunei and Tebbit's extension of the embargo were linked.

The hook for the article reproduced here, published five months later, was the Observer's recent possession of a certificate confirming the trip signed by Dato Ali, the Permanent Secretary of the Brunei Ministry of Home Affairs, the existence of which had been first aired in the second "Private Eye" article of 24 January. The article reports that the editor of local newspaper the "Borneo Bulletin," Han Ling, had also confirmed the trip:

The Observer
Sunday, 18 May 1986

Mark Thatcher and guru clues to Harrods deal
Exclusive: Staff Reporter

POWERFUL new evidence has emerged that Mark Thatcher visited Brunei with Mohamed Fayed at a crucial time in the Harrods takeover battle.

"The Observer" is in possession of a certificate, signed by the former Permanent Secretary in the Ministry of Home Affairs in Brunei, confirming the visit.

The two men flew in Fayed's private jet on 24 October 1984 and left two days later. That was just a week before the Monopolies Commission report into Lonrho's bid to buy the House of Fraser was delayed for three months. The Egyptian Fayed brothers used that time to acquire the group with the help of the Sultan's millions.

Mark Thatcher was representing a Gulf construction company with an interest in a £600 million university complex in Brunei. He was introduced by a letter from the Finance Minister of Oman, where he had previously earned an undisclosed commission on a building contract for the British firm Cementation.

Geoffrey Gilson

When the Brunei visit was first revealed in "The Observer" in January, Fayed denied that he had ever met the Prime Minister's son, and issued his denial as a press statement. "The Observer" refused to carry it unless Fayed agreed to sign it personally, which he declined to do. Mark Thatcher made no comment.

The visit has been independently confirmed by Han Ling, editor of the "Borneo Bulletin," which circulates in Brunei. 'I know for a fact Mark Thatcher was here,' he said.

Key figure

A rich and mysterious Indian guru is emerging as another key figure in the Harrods deal. It was he, Shri Chandra Swamiji Maharaj, who arranged the introduction of Mohammed Fayed to the Sultan of Brunei in 1984.

The Swami, a giant bearded figure in flowing white, claims to advise a number of leading political figures around the world, including King Hussein of Jordan, President Mobutu, Rajiv Gandhi and Richard Nixon. He is currently on his way to visit ex-President Marcos in Honolulu. He has met Mrs. Thatcher several times.

The Swami is always accompanied by his business adviser, Mamaji Kailash Nath Agar Vall, who relieves him of any unpleasant commercial transactions which may happily occur in the course of his spiritual interviews.

Fayed was asked for two million dollars for the introduction to the Sultan. Eventually Fayed paid the Swami half a million dollars plus a percentage of any future deals, which might result from the meeting. These turned out to be substantial.

By August 1984, Mohammed Fayed was established with a power of attorney to handle some of the Sultan's cash balances in Switzerland and Liechtenstein. Fayed acted for the Sultan over the purchase of the Dorchester Hotel, which stands close to two Park Lane apartment blocks which Fayed owns and in one of which he lives.

A sum of $86 million transferred from the account of Carl Hirschmann in Vaduz to Mohammed Fayed's bank account in Geneva, and a larger sum from the account of a Mr. Lavia with the Credit Suisse in Zurich.

Both these men were holding funds belonging to the Sultan. The rolled-up sums were held to the joint and separate order of the Sultan and Mohammed, and were very shortly used to guarantee the purchase of the House of Fraser in the form of certificates of deposit which were passed to Kleinwort Benson, the merchant bankers.

The Fayeds were finally given the go-ahead in ten days by the then Secretary of State for Trade and Industry, Norman Tebbit, who decided *against a Monopolies Commission reference. He was influenced in this decision by assurances from Kleinwort Benson that the Fayeds owned substantial assets. In fact, their net worth was then between £15-£25 million. Since the Harrods deal, they are now worth several billions.*

In January 1985, the Sultan and Mohammed Fayed met Mrs. Thatcher at Downing Street. Brunei then transferred five billion dollars from the US to relieve the British Sterling crisis.

In April Fayed arranged for Mrs. Thatcher to meet the Sultan at his sumptuous palace in Brunei. He presented her with a gold bracelet studded with diamonds and rubies.

Another Thatcher-Fayed connection is through Sir Gordon Reece, the Prime Minister's close adviser, who also acts for Fayed and has a flat in one of his apartment blocks.

MPs are likely to re-open the Harrods affair in Parliament this week."

***

So, all at once, we find al-Fayed in bed, not only with Mrs. Thatcher, but also with her son. Who was heavily engaged in both the *Savoy Mafia*, and all sorts of illicit arms dealing in the Eighties. With countries including the likes of Iraq. Plus, we have al-Fayed, through his lawyer, connected to many of the other players involved with arms sales to Iran in the early Eighties. And with his main London townhouse conveniently located just round the corner in Park Lane.

Is it safe to conclude that we now have a better understanding of how al-Fayed and Ari were able to know so much about what the Tories were up to in the Eighties? And perhaps, more to the point, a clearer perception of how Ari knew what Hugh was doing? I found myself drifting off into one of those moods, where I saw new patterns emerging in the bigger scenario.

***

It's the beginning of the Eighties. Everyone's in town, and in much the same place: the 'Mayfair Square Mile.' Rogers is slap bang in the middle. The American Embassy is off to one side. Various US mercenaries, plus Les Aspin, and a bunch of others connected to SSG/CPPG or 'The Enterprise,' are staying a few streets along, in the Portman Hotel. Al-Fayed is down the road, on Park Lane. Where you'll also find the main London branch of BCCI. And across the street is the Iranian Bank Melli.

A block or so away, all in a line, are London's famous Gentlemen's Clubs. Including the Reform Club. These Clubs are not to be confused with the American version of 'Gentlemen's Club:' there's just Old Boys in the London Clubs; not dirty-minded Good 'Ol Boys. Over on the Thames is Tory Headquarters. And just a tad downstream is the "Best Gentleman's Club in London," also known as Parliament. Meanwhile, we have Ari, Hugh, Maxwell, Oliver North, the Hashemi's and a few others popping in and out of the 'Mayfair Square Mile,' all through this period.

It's all very cozy. Everyone knows everyone else. And everyone's in Swinging London City to play 'The Biggest Arms Game in Town.' Namely, Iran. Heck. 'The Biggest Arms Game in the World,' at least, in the early part of the Eighties. And everyone's on the same team. Everyone's goal is identical: to sell as much military hardware as possible to Iran, and to make pot-loads of money.

First, it's the Israelis. Then, the Americans want to do their big 'thank you' number to the Iranians, for the *October Surprise*. The Yanks get bitten by the money bug, and decide to get more permanently involved. Then, it's all about releasing hostages, cuddling up to Iran, and helping the Contras. It's all good stuff. No-one minds. So long as the money remains good. Until 1984, and the first ripples of discord appear.

The Americans are getting a bit itchy about the Israelis. The Iranians don't mind the Israelis too much, until they started beating up on their Shiite Muslim brothers in Hezbollah, in Lebanon. And then, the Americans start having their own problems in Lebanon with Muslims; what with hostages and exploding Marine Barracks, and all. So, the Americans decide to back off using the Israelis as partners – just for a while.

The Israelis are a little miffed. But they shrug their shoulders. They're going to do their own thing anyway. But then, the Americans develop even more problems. Congress is getting antsy. Enforcing oversight. Wants to know what's going on. Oh no. The Seventies all over again. So, the Yanks need a surrogate to pick up the slack. Hello. Enter the British.

Now, Margaret and company have been doing their own thing, getting the British economy back in order, and trying to expand their domestic military machine. They had a wonderful six-month Arms Fair in 1982, known to the rest of the world as "The Falklands War." But they are now looking for other opportunities. Why? Ah. Good question.

***

The Socialists had pretty much left the UK bankrupt at the end of the Seventies. Industry had been destroyed by nationalization and by giving the trades unions too much power. Those companies that were still in private hands had been crippled by taxation and over-subsidy, which left them unproductive and uncompetitive.

The economy had stalled. Income from taxation was way down.

Dead Men Don't Eat Lunch

Public expenditure, particularly that for dramatically increasing unemployment, was off the meter. So too was inflation. The deficit was so large, no commercial bank would lend the Government any more money. The Labour Chancellor of the Exchequer had had to stand, cap in hand, behind Third World countries, to get loans from the International Monetary Fund.

Everything and everyone in Great Britain had run out of money. The country, the people, the trades unions, the economy, the Government, the military and the Intelligence Services. Maggie and her troupe were doing what they could. They were cutting public spending; getting inflation under control; de-regulating left, right and center; and removing the unhealthy support structure for British industry. In due course, the deficit would disappear; taxes would be cut; and the new 'enterprise economy' would be in place. But in the meantime, what little was left of the manufacturing base was collapsing.

British Industry had been so weakened by the Socialists that, when the support structures were removed, it wasn't strong enough to step up to the plate, and compete with the rest of the world. That is why Maggie was hell bent on building up the arms industry. To have something to replace the lost manufacturing base. And the Falklands War had allowed Great Britain to showcase the full range of weaponry and military technology it had to sell. But, Britain needed ongoing showcases, and it needed money for its own military. Plus, the Intelligence Services need money. And the Tory Party wouldn't mind a bob or two, either.

So. Maggie Thatcher hit on the idea of pimping out Great Britain Ltd. to America. Or more specifically, to her best mate, Ronald Reagan, his Vice President George Bush, and his SSG/CPPG. Lock, stock and barrel. In the Eighties, Britain became the global surrogate for America's military and intelligence adventures. Wherever and whenever the price was right.

All of a sudden, Bush and his SSG/CPPG were being forced by Congressional oversight to be a little more circumspect about their covert, and often illicit, global activities. So, they asked the British to step in, wherever, and whenever. And the British were happy to comply. Provided the price was right. Whether it was arms deals, military action, intelligence gathering, or a bit of covert operation, it didn't matter. Whatever was needed, the British were there. Provided the price was right. And assuming there was a little something for the Tory Party to put in its own back pocket.

John Loftus and Mark Aarons, in their book, *The Secret War Against The Jews*, describe how Britain, its Special Forces and its Intelligence Services, were much more involved in Lebanon, Central America and Iran than anyone had previously known. And slap bang in the middle of all the plotting, we find out old friend, Les Aspin.

Another problem that the Americans had was with assassination.

Geoffrey Gilson

There had been, since the purges of the Seventies, a Presidential Prohibition on American-sponsored assassination. Simple, the British did it instead. In Lebanon and in Afghanistan, among other places.

For centuries, Afghanistan, and its fabled Khyber Pass, had been seen as 'The Gateway' between the Middle East and the rest of Asia. Wielding influence in that country had become all important in power struggles in the region, a struggle which had been given the gloried title of "The Great Game." The British, the Russians, the Turks had all fought over this stretch of land in the centuries leading up to the First World War. The struggle had become the stuff of romance and legend, memorably captured in the writings of British author, Rudyard Kipling.

In the 20th Century, and into the 21st Century, Afghanistan once again became a focal point for military conflict. In 1979, the Soviet Union invaded Afghanistan, and placed a 100,000 man Army of Occupation within its borders. Carter and then Reagan were none too happy, but were prevented by Congress from direct interference in Afghanistan itself. The CIA had to comfort itself with setting up training bases for the anti-Soviet Muslim mujahideen in Pakistan. Eventually, the Soviets had had enough, and in 1989, they withdrew, leaving the country to the Muslim mujahideen, who established their own Taliban Government.

Post 9-11, most of us have become aware of the sorry fact that the very Muslim mujahideen, whom the CIA were training in techniques of assassination and sabotage, and who included Osama bin Laden and Al Qaeda, would one day turn their new-found skills on the United States and other western countries. This time, causing the United States itself to enter "The Great Game" with its own invasion of Afghanistan, in order to root out bin Laden and the Muslim mujahideen.

What was not generally known was the extent of the hands-on British role in the anti-Soviet effort; a role which played no small part in eventually persuading the Soviets to withdraw from Afghanistan. In his book, *Charlie Wilson's War*, George Crile continues the tradition of romantic writing about the ongoing military struggles in Afghanistan, with his lush descriptions of the heroic exploits of Texan Congressman Charles Wilson, in aiding the Muslim mujahideen. Wilson was a major factor in ensuring that the program of support for the Muslim mujahideen became the single largest military support operation ever undertaken by the CIA.

Crile describes the extraordinary spectacle of the CIA, joining forces with the Israelis, to provide weaponry to both Muslim Pakistan and the Muslim mujahideen. Pakistan was presented with Israeli-designed military technology for its own use, and in recompense for providing shelter for the Muslim mujahideen. And the Muslim mujahideen were armed with modern rifles and rocket-propelled grenades, in order to take on the Communist Soviets. Whom the CIA and the Israelis clearly regarded, at that

Dead Men Don't Eat Lunch

time, as a greater threat than Islamic radicals.

As part of the effort to arm the Muslim mujahideen, both the CIA and the Israelis were buying surplus Soviet weapons in Eastern Europe, so that if the weapons were captured by the Soviets in Afghanistan, there would be no immediate link back to either the CIA or the Israelis.

I wondered if this 'support' for Communist Eastern European regimes might not have conflicted with the goals of the Fraternal Orders of the Priory of Sion, who were working so hard to depose those very regimes? And whether this 'conflict' might have formed the basis for the 'grey' scenario that Reggie had described to me all those years ago?

However, due to the restrictions imposed by Congressional oversight, the US effort was limited only to support. They could not assist the Muslim mujahideen within the borders of Afghanistan. But the British, with their long tradition of involvement in this area, most certainly could. And did. For the right price.

As a first move, Britain stepped in with its own efforts to provide the Muslim mujahideen with arms and ammunition. The British arms pipeline began with deals in Marbella, and a supply line that meandered back through Palestinian quartermasters in Yugoslavia and Czechoslovakia. Again, raising in my mind visions of a possibly unhealthy competition with the CIA and the Israelis, notwithstanding the fact that the British were supposed to be acting as surrogates for America.

More important than mere support, British Special Forces and their Intelligence counterparts were able to run amok in the mountains of Afghanistan. Something the Americans and the Israelis could not do. And run amok, the British most certainly did.

They secured supply lines deep into Soviet-held territory. They lent invaluable assistance to the Muslim mujahideen in the efforts of the latter to harry the Soviets with bombings and rocket attacks. And, there being no British Prohibition on assassination, they proved themselves none too squeamish about taking out the odd dozen Soviets or so while they happened to be on the scene.

In addition to the 'official' Government interventions of the Americans and the British, a plethora of private "aid" agencies, think tanks and other odd-bod outfits joined the fray, with the ostensible aim of helping the Afghans to liberate their nation from the clutches of the Soviet invaders.

It was the usual story: nice looking humanitarian organization up front; donations going to buy weapons and ammunition by the backdoor, when no-one was looking. It's not just Hamas, Al Qaeda and the IRA who know how to play that game. Afghan Aid (UK), together with Radio Free Kabul of London, were the two most important co-coordinators of Muslim mujahideen aid efforts in the conflict with the Soviets in Afghanistan.

Afghan Aid was set up by Romy Fullerton in Peshawar, Pakistan, where the main Muslim mujahideen camps were located. Romy was the wife of a British journalist, John Fullerton, who wrote extensively on Afghanistan during the Soviet Occupation. The main sponsor and funder of the group was Viscount Cranbourne, who was Conservative Lord Privy Seal, Leader of the House of Lords and a Cabinet Minister under John Major.

Viscount Cranbourne is a member of the Cecil family, one of the oldest of the noble families in Great Britain. One ancestor was Lord Privy Seal and Lord Treasurer to Queen Elizabeth I, in the 16th Century. Viscount Cranbourne is the son and heir to the current Sixth Marquis of Salisbury. His grandfather, the Fifth Marquis, had been Colonial Secretary in the Second World War, and a post-War Foreign Minister, as well as having been Lord Privy Seal and Leader of the House of Lords. His great-great-grandfather, the famous Third Marquis of Salisbury, had been the British Prime Minister and Foreign Minister between 1878 and 1887, and again between 1900 and 1902.

The Viscount Cranbourne of the Eighties also represented a UK Parliamentary Constituency in the same Wessex Area of which Hugh was the Conservative Party Treasurer.

Radio Free Kabul was formed almost immediately after the Soviet invasion of Afghanistan by Lord Nicholas Bethell, a former Lord-in-Waiting to Queen Elizabeth II. A career British Intelligence official, with a specialization in Iranian and Arab affairs, Lord Bethell had served in the Middle East and Soviet sections of MI6. Lord Bethell had been a decades-long friend and colleague of MI6 operative Kim Philby, who 'defected' to the Soviet Union in 1963.

Lord Bethell also served, in the early Eighties, as the Leader of the Conservative Members of the European Parliament. Much as with their division over the Royal Family, British Intelligence was not of one mind over the issue of the European Union. Many of the older, more-'Gentlemanly' set found themselves in favor of greater European Union. Perhaps, it was their experience of the two great European conflicts of the early part of the Twentieth Century? Or maybe, it had something to do with the fact that so many of their number, like Reggie, found themselves members of those fraternal organizations, which were themselves allied with the Priory of Sion, and its spiritual and 'royal' aims for Europe?

Radio Free Kabul, which was formed virtually single-handedly by Lord Bethell, was run out of Coutts and Co., the private banker to Queen Elizabeth II. In 1981, Lord Bethell accompanied Margaret Thatcher on a tour of the United States, dedicated to drumming up support for the Muslim mujahideen. Thatcher and Lord Bethell met over 60 Congressmen and Senators, and aided in organizing the Committee for a Free Afghanistan, the *de facto* US arm of Radio Free Kabul.

In 1983, Radio Free Kabul sponsored the formation of Resistance

Dead Men Don't Eat Lunch

International, which pulled together various "freedom movements" set up by the Thatcher and Reagan-Bush Administrations, including the Muslim mujahideen of Afghanistan, the Nicaraguan Contras, anti-Castro Cubans, and various anti-Communist Eastern European and African movements.

One of the members of the Board of Radio Free Kabul was Ray Whitney, OBE. Ray was a former British Intelligence official, who had for years run the disinformation operations unit of the Foreign Office, the Information Research Department. I had served on the campaign to get Ray elected as Conservative MP for High Wycombe in the important By-Election of 1977. So had Hugh. No wonder the two of them had been so friendly. Notwithstanding the fact that Ray was avidly pro-Europe. Mind you, one of his saving graces was his wife, Sheila, who was another corker.

[Much of the preceding information about Afghanistan was obtained from the American journal *Executive Intelligence Review*, which was established by sometime Presidential Candidate Lyndon LaRouche, who believes that the British Royal Family, aided by British Intelligence, are the primary movers and shakers of the New World Order. Bless his heart, but anyone, who has paid close attention to the antics of the British Royal Family over the past couple of decades, would realize they have trouble moving and shaking their own household, let alone the rest of the world.

That said, the fact remains that, nutjobs or no, LaRouche and the *Executive Intelligence Review* are fed useful information by intelligence agencies, precisely because they lack credibility. Reggie told me that intelligence agencies will often use nutjobs as distractions, when there is information the agencies know will get out sooner or later. The agencies deliberately feed the legitimate information to the nutjobs, hoping that no-one will believe it, when it eventually makes the mainstream press. Bottom line: like Tommy Jones says in the movie, *Men In Black*, sometimes the tabloids are the best source for accurate 'disinformation.']

This new role of Great Britain Ltd, as global surrogate for the Great Satan, became pretty much fixed in stone during the decade of the Eighties. The money was simply too good. One unfortunate consequence of this corruption was that Britain became firmly established, not only as a troubleshooter for American 'state terror,' but also as an unofficial Offshore Trading Haven for all Global Terror, both state and factional.

Great Britain was still an open society, with ease of entry and exit; ease of movement; relative freedom of speech and political assembly; and the ability to raise and move funds easily. London, in particular, had, over the years, become a 'safe haven' for political refugees. However, as we have seen, with the political often came the paramilitary.

Whereas in the past, the British Security Services might have sought to crack down on any nascent paramilitary activity and its proponents, now they either turned a blind eye, or even worse, actively encouraged it.

On the one hand, there was money to be made acting as a trading exchange for all the needs of the modern terrorist. On the other hand, with its own nefarious activities around the world, on behalf of the Americans, the British Security Services sometimes needed their own 'surrogates.' And a readily available cesspool of fully-equipped 'pirates,' made for a useful pool of talent.

Beyond this, since London already had the commodities and financial expertise to be one of the world's leading exchange centers for everything from oil to foreign exchange to stocks and shares, why not for terror also? This was the Eighties. Money was 'King.' Nothing else mattered.

The upshot was that the very country the Tories were entrusted with protecting was transformed into a Global Quartermaster to all manner of wider terror networks, countries and factions: from the likes of 'The Enterprise' and 'InTerNet,' to Osama bin Laden, al Qaeda and Saddam Hussein.

Another, and in many ways, sadder consequence was that, with the very best of intentions, namely saving the economy of Great Britain Ltd, and ostensibly to protect a society that had a glorious tradition of not needing the same Rules as other less secure nations, Margaret Thatcher made scrap-paper of the few Rules that did still apply in Great Britain.

She was so assiduous in behaving as if the normal Rules of Conduct did not apply to her and her Government, that she made a mockery of the very Rule of Law, which she so vocally championed. As a result, she has effectively turned Great Britain into a country which is lawless in its activities at the highest level.

***

Meanwhile, back in 1984, Britain was only just beginning its role as America's new global surrogate. And the Israelis, who were feeling a tad the jilted lover, were none too happy. But, they pretty much keep it under their hat, and got on with their own arms-supplying and money-making ventures. Sometimes in competition with the British, and sometimes not.

'The Team,' in the 'Mayfair Square Mile,' was essentially still working together helping Iran, because Iraq continued to have the upper hand in its fight with Iran, and because everyone needed Iran's help to free their hostages in Lebanon.

True, one or two parties had begun the process of playing both sides, and were now supplying Iraq as well as Iran with military equipment and technology. But that was because the money was too good. Plus, the Israelis didn't seem to mind all that much – at least, not at that point.

Dead Men Don't Eat Lunch

Indeed, the Israelis appeared to be quite happy teaming up with the Christian Lebanese militias, in order to give a bloody nose to Hezbollah and the other Muslim Lebanese militias. And everyone knew that the other primary benefactor of the Lebanese Christians was none other than Iraq.

On the home front, it being 1984, Hugh was still smarting from his temporary political setback, and was starting to hurt for money. It was at this time, according to John Simmonds, that Karen George says that Hugh became involved in complex arms dealing for Margaret Thatcher.

So, there was a slight ripple in the water, but overall, nothing too terrible. Until we got to 1987.

***

At that time, Iran was beginning to win its war with Iraq. Iran was hurling millions of its youngsters against the border with Iraq, in the hope that sheer numbers would overwhelm its mortal enemy. The fanatic Shiite Muslim leadership in Iran showed no signs of moderating its stance or its strategy, notwithstanding attempts to put a more secular face on its radicalism. The last thing the West wanted was that same leadership in control of Iraq's oil reserves. While, at the same time, sitting perched, ready to strike, on the border of yet more oil reserves in Saudi Arabia.

The latter were becoming ever more important to the West, in particular, to the United States, which had seen the percentage of its oil imports from Iraq increase from single digits in the early Eighties, to very nearly 25% by 1987. In addition, everyone had become terminally tired of the hostage-taking by Iran's surrogates in Lebanon. And Iraq was becoming a better customer than Iran for arms. Which translated into more money. Plus, Iraq was not making as much headway with its own domestic military industry as it would like, and so its hunger for military technology seemed to be insatiable. Plus, Iraq was just beginning to get serious about using its WMDs, to stop the Iranian Tide; and WMDs, not withstanding their illegality, were a definite money-spinner. Plus…well…any one of a dozen other inexcusable, but highly remunerative, reasons the arms industry in the West cared to come up with. And so began the famous US-UK 'tilt' towards Iraq.

At which point, the Israelis finally cracked. From their own experience over the decades, Iraq had always proven to be more of a threat to them than Iran. Plus, the Israelis weren't selling any weapons to Iraq, so a 'tilt' towards Iraq didn't do them any good. On this occasion, the Israelis did more than just blow off steam.

Ari, who was by now the Counter-Terrorism Adviser to Yitzhak Shamir, the Israeli Prime Minister, was instructed to do whatever was necessary to put a plug in the now-burgeoning Iraqi Arms Pipeline. As luck would have it, Ari was in the perfect position to plug the Iraq 'Game,' because he knew all the 'players,' and where to find them; what they were doing, and how to 'get' to them. After all, he'd spent the best part of the Eighties 'playing' the Iran 'Game' with them, in London's 'Mayfair Square Mile.'

Ari knew about Maxwell in Eastern Europe. He knew about the Tories. He knew about Hugh. And he had his secret weapon – al-Fayed. And Ari proceeded to use the latter, mercilessly, to help blunt the Tories. Which led to the transparent "Cash-for-Questions" bribery scheme. And to the period of time when Hugh, under pressure himself, very likely from Ari directly, began to steal money from his Clients' Account.

We already know that the Israelis had become agitated with the British for supplanting them as America's favorite surrogate. Did this encourage Ari and 'his friends' to set about their task with an extra degree of relish? And did this cause the British to retaliate? For the knowledge game works both ways. The British knew what the Israelis were up to as well. Remember how quickly Ari had reacted when he thought Oliver North had been stepping on his toes.

Did the British know about the Maxwell-monitored CIA and Likud Arms Funds in Eastern Europe? Did they know about them through Hugh? Had Hugh helped to set them up? Was Hugh using the same channels to funnel money to Bulgaria and Yugoslavia?

Was Maxwell 'asked' by British Intelligence to mess with those Funds in his care? Was he then double-crossed by the CIA? Or murdered by Mossad? Or, was Hugh instructed by British Intelligence to mess with the Funds? Was he told to steal the Funds, or some part of them? Did he, perhaps, just steal some part of them for himself?

Did this aggravate the Israelis even more? Or, the CIA? Was this why Reggie was so fearful of the CIA? Did this give rise to the somewhat esoteric 'alliances,' that Reggie had so cryptically referred to as operating in Eastern Europe, in the immediate aftermath of the collapse of Communism in that region?

Did Ari, the Israelis, the CIA, even the Knights of Malta, or, indeed, all four retaliate in kind against Hugh? Was that the cause of the increased pressure on Hugh in the summer of 1988? Or did British Intelligence discover that Hugh was two-timing them, and were they the ones applying the pressure to Hugh?

Whatever the case, the next important period was the summer of 1988. The Iranians and the Iraqis declared a ceasefire. The Arms Pipeline to the Iranians pretty much dried up overnight. But not so the Pipeline to the Iraqis. All of the arguments for its original 'expansion' in 1987 now held true for its 'continuation' past 1988.

This went beyond the pale for the Israelis, who raised the stakes to new heights. This was when Ari started sending assassination squads into Western Europe and Great Britain. And on the subject of killing, there was one thing on which the superiors of all of the former Iranian 'players' agreed – it was time to 'clean house.'

Senior 'players,' from the US, Israel and Britain died in mysterious circumstances, were imprisoned, or were discredited in other ways. Ari went to prison in America for a while. Oliver North and company were convicted and then pardoned. Gerald James lost his company and his knighthood. And Hugh turned up gassed, in a small car, in a beauty spot, near his and my home town.

Co-incidentally, Margaret Thatcher was herself deposed just a couple of years later in 1990. Or was it co-incidence? In any event, is it safe to say, now, that there were two reasons for the frantic attempts to retain a Thatcherite legacy at the head of the Conservative Party thereafter?

First, to keep a lid on the antics of the Tory Party under her leadership in the Eighties. And secondly, to ensure that Conservative Governments of the future (immediately, under Major, and later, when New Labour was eventually defeated) would be ready, willing and able to reap the benefits of the groundwork that she had laid? Maybe. But, as was so often the case, a question nagged at the back of my mind. And once again, it was, at first, too faint for me to hear.

In the meantime, my frontal lobes were burning with questions for Reggie and Ari. I didn't care if they didn't want to speak to me. I wanted some answers from them. Perhaps it was my anger that encouraged them? Or perhaps I was beginning to strike a little too close to home? In any event, on this occasion, they both had much more to contribute on what exactly had been Hugh's precise role in my scenario. And why that role had also sealed his fate.

Geoffrey Gilson

Chapter 29

EVERYONE DESERVES to fall in love. Even emotional train wrecks. And in 2001, I fell madly in love with Tami. She came into my local bar one evening, an explosion of raven hair, high cheekbone and sexy bare midriff. She was a good head smaller than me, but the way she danced up and down against me, her arms over her head, I felt like she was looking down into my eyes the whole night.

Tami was 29, with those dark, elfin looks, which, one way or another, have haunted me all my life. Needless to say, she was of Cherokee descent, and had never lost the Indian fire. At first, she moved in with me. We laughed. We loved. We fought. We loved. And then we loved some more. I was late for work the next day. And the next day. And the following week. And for most of the ensuing month. Until Tom, in exasperation, was left with no alternative but to fire me.

Which was a good thing, because I got to meet Tami's three glorious children: Michael, who hugged me, and made me cry, because I was so surprised; Brittney, who thought I was silly, and made me laugh; and Zachary, who thought I was a new toy, and curled up around me late one night, and made me cry all over again. When I discovered that Tami's ex was trying to take the kids away from her, I moved in with them. And together, we rescued the kids for her.

Tami had serious issues. Mainly involving a strong desire not to be controlled. I didn't do a very good job of understanding. But I did learn that I had a temper, and was filled with mindless anger, none of which was Tami's fault. We both agreed I should go to see an anger therapist.

In short order, I made two fascinating discoveries: that I 'enjoyed' being angry. It was another barrier that I could erect around myself to create a false haven of 'safety.' And secondly, that anger was regarded as an addiction. I had been so numb for so long, I hadn't realized I was angry. And I was now using it as a substitute for alcohol.

Dead Men Don't Eat Lunch

Unfortunately, I didn't come to all of this realization in time to save my relationship with Tami. She wanted to hear me say that I needed her, and I wasn't yet secure enough to let go of my false safety, and recognize the 'true' safety represented by the warm embrace of her and the kids.

A good friend told me that at least now I knew what I was looking for, and that I just had a tad more work to do, to be ready for it, when it came looking for me again. In the meantime, Tami and I have patched things up. She has a new husband. And I go and stay with the whole family from time to time. They really do provide me with a genuine feeling of 'safety.' And I am, at last, beginning to be 'grown up' enough to welcome that.

More than anything, I love to watch the interaction between Tami and her children. She is a great mother. Just like Ma. Neither one of them is perfect. But through all the chaos, and the shouting, and the general untidiness of life, what shines through is the fact that the kids know that their mother loves them, and that she cares for them deeply. And, at the end of the day, that's all that matters. Not whether or not they get to school on time.

***

What follows is an article provided by the web-site www.totse.com. It was originally written in the Eighties, when the events it describes were still happening. It is, therefore, written in the present tense:

"Fifty-year-old Alistair Beckham was a successful British aerospace-projects engineer. His specialty was designing computer software for sophisticated naval defense systems. Like hundreds of other British scientists, he was working on a pilot program for America's Strategic Defense Initiative – better known as Star Wars. And like at least 21 of his colleagues, he died a bizarre, violent death.

It was a lazy, sunny Sunday afternoon in August 1988. After driving his wife to work, Beckham walked through his garden to a musty backyard tool-shed and sat down on a box next to the door. He wrapped bare wires around his chest, attached the to an electrical outlet and put a handkerchief in his mouth. Then he pulled the switch.

With his death, Beckham's name was added to a growing list of British scientists who've died or disappeared under mysterious circumstances since 1982. Each was a skilled expert in computers, and each was working on a highly classified project for the American Star Wars program. None had any apparent motive for killing himself.

The British Government contends that the deaths are all a matter of coincidence. The British press blames stress. Others allude to an ongoing fraud investigation involving the nation's leading defense contractor. Relatives left behind don't know what to think.

Geoffrey Gilson

"There weren't any women involved. There weren't any men involved. We had a very good relationship," says Mary Beckham, Alistair's widow. "We don't know why he did it...if he did it. And I don't believe that he did do it. He wouldn't go out to the shed. There had to be something...."

The string of unexplained deaths can be traced back to March 1982, when Essex University computer scientist Dr. Keith Bowden died in a car wreck on his way home from a London social function. Authorities claim Bowden was drunk. His wife and friends say otherwise.

Bowden, 45, was a whiz with super-computers and computer-controlled aircraft. He was co-founder of the Department of Computer Sciences at Essex and had worked for one of the major Star Wars contractors in England.

One night Bowden's immaculately maintained Rover careened across a four-lane highway and plunged off a bridge, down an embankment, into an abandoned rail yard. Bowden was found dead at the scene.

During the inquest, police testified that Bowden's blood alcohol level had exceeded the legal limit and that he had been driving too fast. His death was ruled accidental.

Wife Hillary Bowden and her lawyer suspected a cover-up. Friends he'd supposedly spent the evening with denied that Bowden had been drinking. Then there was the condition of Bowden's car. "My solicitor instructed an accident specialist to examine the automobile," Mrs. Bowden explains. "Somebody had taken the wheels off and put others on that were old and worn. At the inquest this was not allowed to be brought up. Someone asked if the car was in a sound condition, and the answer was yes."

Hillary, in a state of shock, never protested the published verdict. Yet, she remains convinced that someone tampered with her husband's car. "It certainly looked like foul play," Hillary maintains.

Four years later the British press finally added Bowden's case to its growing dossier. First, there appeared to be two interconnected deaths, then six, then 12 – suddenly there were 22. Take 37-year-old David Sands, a senior scientist at Easams, working on a highly sensitive computer-controlled satellite radar system. In March 1987, Sands made a U-turn on his way to work and rammed his car into the brick wall of a vacant restaurant. His trunk was loaded with full gasoline cans. The car exploded on impact.

Given the incongruities of the accident and the lack of a suicide motive, the coroner refused to rule out the possibility of foul play. Meanwhile, information leaked to the press suggested that Sands had been under a tremendous emotional strain. Margaret Worth, Sand's mother-in-law, claims these stories are totally inaccurate. "When David died, it was a great mystery to us," she admits. "He was very successful. He was very confident. He had just pulled off a great coup for his company, and he was about to be greatly rewarded. He had a very bright future ahead of him. He was perfectly happy the week before this happened."

Like many of the bereaved, Worth is still at a loss for answers. "One week we think he must have been got at. The next week we think it couldn't be anything like that," she says.

This wave of suspicious fatalities in the ultra secret world of sophisticated weaponry has not gone unnoticed by the United States Government. Late last fall, the American Embassy in London publicly requested a full investigation by the British Ministry of Defense (MoD).

Members of British Parliament, such as Labour MP Doug Hoyle, co-president of the Manufacturing, Science & Finance Union, had been making similar requests for more than two years. The Thatcher Government had refused to launch any sort of inquiry. "How many more deaths before we get the Government to give the answers?" Hoyle asks. "From a security point of view, surely both ourselves and the Americans ought to be looking into it." The Pentagon refuses comment on the deaths. However, according to Reagan Administration sources, "We cannot ignore it anymore."

Actually, British and American intelligence agencies are on the situation. When *The Sunday Times* in London published the details of 12 mysterious deaths last September, sources at the American Embassy admitted being aware of at least ten additional victims whose names had already been sent to Washington. The sources added that the Embassy had been monitoring reports of "the mysterious deaths" for two years.

English Intelligence has suffered several damaging spy scandals in the 20th Century. The CIA may suspect the deaths are an indication of security leaks, that Star Wars secrets are being sold to the Russians. Perhaps these scientists had been blackmailed into supplying classified data to Moscow and could no longer live with themselves. One or more may have stumbled onto an espionage ring and been silenced.

As NBC News London correspondent Henry Champ puts it, "In the world of espionage, there is a saying: Twice is coincidence, but three times is enemy action."

Where SDI is concerned, a tremendous amount is at stake. In return for the Thatcher Government's early support of the Star Wars program, the Reagan Administration promised a number of extremely lucrative SDI contracts to the British defense industry – hundreds of millions of U.S. dollars the struggling British economy can little afford to lose.

Britain traditionally has one of the finest defense industries in the world. Their annual overseas weapons sales amount to almost $250 billion. The publicity from a Star Wars spy scandal could seriously cut into the profits.

It would appear that only initial promises made to Prime Minister Thatcher hold the U.S. from cutting its losses and pulling out. A high-

Geoffrey Gilson

ranking American source was quoted in *The Sunday Times* saying, "If this had happened in Greece, Brazil, Spain, or Argentina, we'd be all over them like a glove!"

The Thatcher Government's PR problem is that the scandal centers around Marconi Company Ltd., Britain's largest electronics-defense contractor. Seven Marconi scientists are among the dead. Marconi, which employs 50,000 workers worldwide, is a subsidiary of Britain's General Electric Company (GEC (UK)). GEC managing director Lord Weinstock recently launched his own internal investigation.

Yet, GEC and the Ministry of Defense still contend that the 22 deaths are coincidental. A Ministry of Defense spokesman claims to have found "no evidence of any sinister links between them."

However, an article in the British publication *The Independent* claims the incidence of suicide among Marconi scientists is twice the national average of mentally healthy individuals. Either Marconi is hiring abnormally unstable scientists or something is very wrong.

Two deaths brought the issue to light in the fall of 1986. Within weeks of each other, two London-based Marconi scientists were found dead 100 miles away, in Bristol. Both were involved in creating the software for a huge, computerized Star Wars simulator, the hub of Marconi's SDI program. Both had been working on the simulator just hours before their death. Like the others, neither had any apparent reason to kill himself.

Vimal Dajibhai was a 24-year-old electronics graduate who worked at Marconi Underwater Systems in Croxley Green. In August 1986, his crumpled body was found lying on the pavement 240 feet below the Clifton Suspension Bridge in Bristol.

An inquest was unable to determine whether Dajibhai had been pushed off the bridge or whether he had jumped. There had been no witnesses. The verdict was left open. Yet, authorities did their best to pin his death on suicide.

Police testified that Dajibhai had been suffering from depression, something his family and friends flatly denied. Dajibhai had absolutely no history of personal or emotional problems.

Police also claimed that the deceased had been drinking with a friend, Heyat Shah, shortly before his death, and that a bottle of wine and two used paper cups had been found in his car. Yet, forensic tests were never done on the auto, and those who knew Vimal, including Shah, say that he had never taken a drink of alcohol in his life.

Investigating journalists found discrepancies in other evidence. "A police report noted a puncture mark on Dajibhai's left buttock after his fall from the bridge," explains Tony Collins, who covered the story for Britain's *Computer News* magazine. "Apparently, this was the reason his funeral was halted seconds before the cremation was to take place.

Dead Men Don't Eat Lunch

"Members of the family were told that the body was to be taken away for a second postmortem, to be done by a top Home Office pathologist. That's not normal. Then, a few months later, police held a press conference and announced that it hadn't been a puncture mark after all, that it was a wound caused by a bone fragment.

"I find it very difficult to reconcile the initial coroner's report with what the Police were saying a few months later," Collins contends.

Officials didn't fare any better with the second Bristol fatality. Police virtually tripped over themselves to come up with a motive for the apparent – and unusually violent – suicide of Ashaad Sharif.

Sharif was a 26-year-old computer analyst who worked at the Marconi Defense Systems headquarters in Stanmore, Middlesex. On October 28, 1986, he allegedly drove to a public park not far from where Dajibhai had died. He tied one end of a nylon cord around a tree and tied the other end around his neck. Then he got back into his Audi 80 automatic, stepped on the gas and sped off, decapitating himself.

Marconi initially claimed Sharif was only a junior employee, and that he had nothing to do with Star Wars. Co-workers stated otherwise. At the time of his death, Sharif was apparently about to be promoted. Also, Ashaad reportedly worked for a time in Vimal Dajibhai's section.

The inquest determined that Sharif's death was a suicide. Investigating officers maintained that the man had killed himself because he'd been jilted by an alleged lover. Ashaad hadn't seen the woman in three years.

"Sharif was said to have been depressed over a broken romance," Tony Collins explains. "But the woman police unofficially say was his lover contends that she was only his landlady when he was working for British Aerospace in Bristol. She's married, has three children, and she's deeply religious. The possibility of the two having an affair seems highly unlikely-- especially since Sharif had a fiancée in Pakistan. His family told me that he was genuinely in love with her."

Police suddenly switched stories. They began to say that Sharif had been deeply in love with the woman he was engaged to, and that he'd decapitated himself because another woman was pressuring him to call off the marriage.

Authorities claimed to have found a taped message in Sharif's car "tantamount" to a suicide note. On it, officers said, he'd admitted to having had an affair, thus bringing shame on his family. Family members who've heard the tape say that it actually gave no indication of why Sharif might want to kill himself. Sharif's family was told by the coroner that it was "not in their best interest" to attend the inquest.

"It's been almost impossible to get to information about deaths that should be in the public domain," Tony Collins laments. "I've been given false names or incorrect spellings, or I've not been told where inquests have taken place. It's made it very difficult for me to try to track down the details of these cases." In the Sharif case, two facts stand out: Ashaad had no history of depression, and there was absolutely no reason for him to be in Bristol.

Consider the peculiar death of Peter Peapell, found dead beneath his car in the garage of his Oxfordshire home. Peapell, 46, worked for the Royal Military College of Science, a world authority on communications technology, electronics surveillance and target detection. Peapell was an expert at using computers to process signals emitted by metals. His work reportedly included testing titanium for its resistance to explosives.

On the night of February 22nd, 1987, Peapell spent an enjoyable evening out with his wife, Maureen, and their friends. When they returned home, Maureen went straight to bed, leaving Peter to put the car away.

When Maureen woke up the next morning, she discovered that Peter had not come to bed. She went looking for him. When she reached the garage, she noticed that the door was closed. Yet she could hear the car's engine running. She found her husband lying on his back beneath the car, his mouth directly below the tail pipe. She pulled him into the open air, but he was already dead.

Initially, Maureen thought her husband's death an accident. She presumed he'd gotten under the car to investigate a knocking he'd heard driving home the night before, and that he'd gotten stuck. But the light fixture in the garage was broken, and Peter hadn't been carrying a flashlight.

Police had their own suspicions. A constable the same height and weight as Peter Peapell found it impossible to crawl under the car when the garage door was closed. He also found it impossible to close the door once he was under the car. Carbon deposits from the inside of the garage door showed that the engine had been running only a short time. Yet, Mrs. Peapell had found the body almost seven hours after she'd gone to bed. The coroner's inquest could not determine whether the death was a homicide, a suicide or an accident. According to Maureen Peapell, Peter had no reason to kill himself. They had no marital or financial problems. Peter loved his job. He'd just received a sizable raise, and according to colleagues, he'd exhibited "absolutely no signs of stress."

We may never know what is killing these scientists. Everyone has a theory.

The National Forum Foundation, a conservative Washington D.C., think tank, believes the deaths are the work of European-based, left-wing terrorists, such as those who took credit for gunning down a West German bureaucrat who'd negotiated Star Wars contracts. The group also claims the July 1986 bombing death of a research director from the Siemens Company – a high-tech, West German electronics firm. They have yet to take credit for any of the scientists.

Dead Men Don't Eat Lunch

A more outrageous theory suggests that the Russians have developed an electromagnetic 'death ray,' with which they're driving the British scientists to suicide. A supermarket tabloid contends the ultra thin waves emitted by the device interfere with a person's brain waves, causing violent mood shifts, including suicidal depression.

The genius of such a weapon is that the victim does all the dirty work and takes all the blame. Yet, if the Soviets have actually developed such a weapon, why waste it on 22 British defense workers?

Are the scientists victims of a corrupt defense industry? Have they been espionage pawns? Are the deaths nothing more than an extraordinary coincidence? Decide for yourselves:

DOSSIER OF DEATH

AUTO ACCIDENT--Professor Keith Bowden, 45, computer scientist, Essex University. In March 1982 Bowden's car plunged off a bridge, into an abandoned rail yard. His death was listed as an accident.

MISSING PERSON--Lieutenant Colonel Anthony Godley, 49, defense expert, head of work-study unit at the Royal Military College of Science. Godley disappeared in April 1983. His father bequeathed him more than $60,000, with the proviso that he claim it by 1987. He never showed up, and is presumed dead.

SHOTGUN BLAST--Roger Hill, 49, radar designer and draftsman, Marconi. In March 1985 Hill allegedly killed himself with a shotgun at the family home.

DEATH LEAP--Jonathan Walsh, 29, digital-communications expert assigned to British Telecom's secret Martlesham Health research facility (and to GEC, Marconi's parent firm). In November 1985, Walsh allegedly fell from his hotel room while working on a British Telecom project in Abidjan, Ivory Coast (Africa). He had expressed a fear for his life. Verdict: Still in question.

DEATH LEAP--Vimal Dajibhai, 24, computer-software engineer (worked on guidance system for Tigerfish torpedo), Marconi Underwater Systems. In August 1986 Dajibhai's crumpled remains were found 240 feet below the Clifton Suspension Bridge in Bristol. The death has not been listed as a suicide.

DECAPITATION--Ashaad Sharif, 26, computer analyst, Marconi Defense Systems. In October 1986, in Bristol, Sharif allegedly tied one end of a rope around a tree and the other end around his neck, then drove off in his car at high speed. Verdict: Suicide.

SUFFOCATION--Richard Pugh, computer consultant for the Ministry of Defense. In January 1987, Pugh was found dead, wrapped head-to- toe in rope that was tied four times around his neck. The coroner listed his death as an accident due to a sexual experiment gone awry.

ASPHYXIATION--John Brittan, Ministry of Defense tank batteries expert, Royal Military College of Science. In January 1987, Brittan was found dead in a parked car in his garage. The engine was still running. Verdict: Accidental death.

DRUG OVERDOSE--Victor Moore, 46, design engineer, Marconi Space Systems. In February 1987 Moore was found dead of a drug overdose. His death is listed as a suicide.

ASPHYXIATION--Peter Peapell, 46, scientist, Royal Military College of Science. In February 1987, Peapell was found dead beneath his car, his face near the tail pipe, in the garage of his Oxfordshire home. Death was due to carbon-monoxide poisoning, although tests showed that the engine had been running only a short time. Foul play has not been ruled out.

ASPHYXIATION--Edwin Skeels, 43, engineer, Marconi. In February 1987 Skeels was found dead in his car, a victim of carbon-monoxide poisoning. A hose led from the exhaust pipe. His death is listed as a suicide.

AUTO ACCIDENT--David Sands, satellite projects manager, Easams (a Marconi sister company). Although up for a promotion, in March 1987, Sands drove a car filled with gasoline cans into the brick wall of an abandoned cafe. He was killed instantly. Foul play has not been ruled out.

AUTO ACCIDENT—Stuart Gooding, 23, postgraduate research student, Royal Military College of Science. In April 1987, Gooding died in a mysterious car wreck in Cyprus while the College was holding military exercises on the island. Verdict: Accidental death.

AUTO ACCIDENT--George Kountis, experienced systems analyst at British Polytechnic. In April 1987, Kountis drowned after his BMW plunged into the Mersey River in Liverpool. His death is listed as a misadventure.

SUFFOCATION--Mark Wisner, 24, software engineer at Ministry of Defense experimental station for combat aircraft. In April 1987, Wisner was found dead in his home with a plastic bag over his head. At the inquest, his death was ruled an accident due to a sexual experiment gone awry.

AUTO ACCIDENT--Michael Baker, 22, digital-communications expert, Plessey Defense Systems. In May 1987, Baker's BMW crashed through a road barrier, killing the driver. Verdict: Misadventure.

HEART ATTACK--Frank Jennings, 60, electronic-weapons engineer for Plessey. In June 1987, Jennings allegedly dropped dead of a heart attack. No inquest was held.

DEATH LEAP--Russell Smith, 23, lab technician at the Atomic Energy Research Establishment. In January 1988, Smith's mangled body was found halfway down a cliff in Cornwall. Verdict: Suicide.

Dead Men Don't Eat Lunch

ASPHYXIATION--Trevor Knight, 52, computer engineer, Marconi Space and Defense Systems. In March 1988, Knight was found dead in his car, asphyxiated by fumes from a hose attached to the tail pipe. The death was ruled a suicide.

ELECTROCUTION--John Ferry, 60, assistant marketing director for Marconi. In August 1988 Ferry was found dead in a company-owned apartment, the stripped leads of an electrical cord in his mouth. Foul play has not been ruled out.

ELECTROCUTION--Alistair Beckham, 50, software engineer, Plessey. In August 1988 Beckham's lifeless body was found in the garden shed behind his house. Bare wires, which ran to a live main, were wrapped around his chest. No suicide note was found, and police have not ruled out foul play.

ASPHYXIATION--Andrew Hall, 33, engineering manager, British Aerospace. In September 1988 Hall was found dead in his car, asphyxiated by fumes from a hose that was attached to the tail pipe. Friends said he was well liked, had everything to live for. Verdict: Suicide."

***

Tony Collins went on to write his own book on these strange deaths, called *Open Verdict*. I bought a copy in 1991, and what I read sent chills down my spine.

Collins had a further twist to the odd scenario: he included mysterious 'suicides' that occurred within the same timeframe, and all involving employees of defense contractors. But the 'victims' were not scientists. They were lowly administrative staff.

Collins came up with an hypothesis, which I have slightly adapted. What if the CIA or others had defense-related projects that they wished to keep 'invisible' from Congressional Oversight? What if the British Government, in pursuit of its new-found role as global surrogate-for-hire to America, agreed to piggy-back these 'black' projects onto legitimate and 'visible' British Star Wars projects?

The scientists working on the 'black' projects, and the administrative staff rendering them support, would be unaware of anything untoward. Indeed, perhaps to lend even greater 'cover' to the projects' 'invisibility,' maybe the British Government dispensed with the need for staff working on the 'black' projects to sign the Official Secrets Act?

The only problem was that you couldn't tell the staff not to talk about what they'd been handling. At the same time, however, you couldn't have them wandering down to the local pub and gabbing, because you didn't know what media or foreign intelligence services might be staked out there, to pick up precisely those sorts of morsels. So, you needed to 'clean house,' without it looking like 'house-cleaning.' And you needed someone to do the 'cleaning.'

That thought began the shivers down my spine. Then I re-read the episodes concerning Bristol. And I remembered that, in 1986, Hugh and I had traveled to Bristol, ostensibly to attend some esoteric, regional Conservative Conference. The thing was that we'd never attended regional Conferences before. They were a waste of time. But we did spend a lot of time on Clifton Suspension Bridge. And Hugh had sent me back to the office a day early.

The shivers became icier. Finally, I read the following passages:

"In the case of the 'lady in the lake,' as it became known, the shortfall of forensic evidence was not only conspicuous, it was embarrassing. The search for the woman's murderer seemed to get little further than a dispute between the family and the authorities over whether indeed she was murdered.

Her death occurred on the night of Good Friday, April 17th, 1987. It was an Easter bank holiday weekend and, for Thames Valley Police, the beginning of what had seemed at first to be a routine murder investigation. It was an inquiry which would end inconclusively six months later, leaving behind a series of unanswered questions over not only the death but the direction of the subsequent investigation.

Early on the evening of Saturday, April 18th, 1987, physiotherapist Marjorie Arnold, out walking her Alsatian dog, saw the body of a woman lying near the edge of Taplow Lake, a popular sailing and fishing spot close to the homes of celebrities such as Terry Wogan, Michael Parkinson, Ernie Wise and Frank Bough [and about an hour's drive from Hugh's home]. It was also 150 yards from a manned police checkpoint on the A4.

Mrs. Arnold stopped a motorist and together they pulled the body ashore. The dead woman seemed about 20 years old and was wearing blue jeans, a red T-shirt and a quilted, sleeveless jacket. She had been gagged with a blue scarf, a noose was tied around her neck, her ankles were secured with a tow rope and her wrists were tied behind her back. She had been face down in eighteen inches of water for an indeterminate period.

Shani Warren's seemingly immaculate black Vauxhall Cavalier car was found parked in the lay-by adjoining the lake. It was later found to have a faulty gearbox which prevented it being driven away in first or second gear. Some of the car's contents were strewn around the grass, as if someone had been looking for something. Her handbag and some keys were missing.

Within a day of the body's discovery a high-ranking police officer spoke of suicide. Six months later that view was officially confirmed. A pathologist employed by the Home Office declared that Shani had tried to strangle herself, gagged herself, bound her ankles, tied her hands behind her back and hopped in stiletto heels into the shallow water where she drowned...

Against a background of the family's vociferous rejections of the suicide theory, a noticeable lack of evidence, and a growing disbelief among the public that Shani had killed herself, the police went on the BBC television program "Crimewatch" and announced that they were treating the case as murder and to make an appeal for witnesses...

The police's attitude to the whole investigation was curious. It did not take a person of exceptional perception to notice that they had no overwhelming desire to find a murderer. For example as soon as "Crimewatch" had finished, a reporter rang one of the numbers given and asked for further details of Shani's car. The reporter did not identify himself and, as far as the police were concerned, could have been an eyewitness.

A policewoman answered the telephone politely, listened to the question, went away to find the answer and returned within two minutes with the information. After this there was an embarrassing silence while the reporter waited for the policewoman to ask why the information was being sought, who was seeking it and whether the caller had information about the murder...

The BBC said that after its "Crimewatch" program 100 viewers rang with possible leads. One was certain she saw Shani in the lay-by and also remembered seeing a well-dressed man and another car, possibly green, perhaps a BMW...

But Mrs. Elsie Warren told the South Buckinghamshire coroner, John Roberts [who also acted as coroner for Hugh's death, the following year], that Shani had never shown any sign of contemplating death...

The only person believed to have seen a woman resembling Shani's description at the lakeside on Good Friday evening was nursing sister Mrs. Sandra Organ from Kettering, Northamptonshire, who had responded to the police appeal on "Crimewatch." She said her daughter had called 'hello' to a woman carrying dustbin liners. She said the woman turned, smiled and waved to them.

Mrs. Organ noticed a well-dressed man about 200 yards away. 'There was a man standing looking on, wearing a smart suit,' she said. 'He was in his late 30's or early 40's.' She said the man had been driving an expensive dark green car – probably a BMW. Police have been unable to trace the man or the car.'

Geoffrey Gilson

The shivers had stopped. My spine had turned into a block of ice.

***

After reading this book, I went down to a very large BMW distributor in Slough. I saw a standard BMW 6 series sedan – about the only model of BMW which, at that time, a passing onlooker would have reasonably described as "expensive," as in possibly large and "expensive." The sedans were painted a rather dusty green color. Hardly a color that would stand out.

I then asked to see photographs of the 6 Series Mark M. This was the limited edition sports coupe version of the 6 series, sufficiently 'limited' that they did not have a model hanging around in their showroom. As I recalled, the coupe had severely more distinctive lines, and was painted a much darker, and more noticeable, green than the sedan.

The salesman confirmed that the limited edition coupe had come out only in the middle of the Eighties. And that only a handful had been sold each year in the whole of southern England. Which conformed with my memory of Hugh having bought one in 1985, because he was a show-off, and wanted to have one of the first of a model that few other people would be driving.

It occurred to me that my 'detective' work had not taken all that much effort. And that if the police had been truly interested in finding 'the car' back in 1987, then it should not have taken them long to link the "expensive dark green…BMW" to a very limited ownership of "expensive dark green…BMW" 6 Series Mark M's.

And that showing photographs of the limited number of owners to the likes of nursing sister Mrs. Sandra Organ would probably have elicited the information that the "well-dressed" man "wearing a smart suit," and "in his late 30's or early 40's," was indeed Hugh Simmonds, former Mayor of a town just seven miles away, who was rarely seen in other than a tailored three-piece suit, and who celebrated his 40th birthday the following year, the same year in which he himself died in mysterious circumstances.

***

I hadn't forgotten that Reggie had told me that he didn't want to talk about Hugh's clandestine activities any more, but I needed some answers to this one. Reggie was all charm as he answered the telephone. He had a new girlfriend. He'd also had his own problems because the girlfriend's previous boyfriend had got a little jealous, setting fire to

Dead Men Don't Eat Lunch

Reggie's car, and causing the whole affair to make the front pages of the nation's tabloids.

Reggie's gurgling and gushing came to an abrupt halt as I read to him the above passages. After some moments of silence, he sighed deeply, and in a very quiet voice just said, "Geoff, you mate was trained to kill. That's what he did."

Fortunately, Reggie succeeded in lightening the mood, a hair's breadth, a few more seconds of silence later, when he added, "Of course, the bugger would never listen to me when I told him that he had to be inconspicuous. Not everyone, I told him, not everyone wears bloody three-piece suits when they do this sort of thing. It will be your downfall. I did warn him…"

Had it been Hugh's downfall? Had he been inconspicuous just once too often for his 'masters' any longer to entertain?

Reggie then reminded me of an episode that I had told him about when we had been together at the RAC Club in Glasgow. I had completely forgotten the incident. It had been in about 1978, when I was living on my own in a ground-floor apartment in Beaconsfield.

Hugh had come banging on the door at about 3 o'clock in the morning. He had looked awful: pale, ashen and shaking. This was not your usual Hugh. He made straight for the Scotch bottle; I can't remember that he even bothered with a glass. I asked him what was wrong. He didn't reply until he'd had a hefty swig or two of the amber.

Then, he looked at me a moment before speaking. His eyes were watery and out of focus. "There is no James Bond," he had said very quietly, with a voice as dead as I'd ever heard, "there's no-one fancy out there, wandering around, with a license to do whatever the hell he wants. It's all very bureaucratic. Very British. Something goes wrong, and someone has to be bumped off, then there's someone 'senior' on the scene to give the 'ok.' That's my job. Except this evening it all went wrong. And I had to do it myself. That's now my job, too." And then he'd got up, and gone home.

I hadn't thought much about the episode at the time. Just put it down to Hugh's overactive hyperbole. In fact, I'd felt embarrassed even telling Reggie about it in Glasgow. Particularly, when his only reaction then had been to look embarrassed. The reason for that embarrassment was now much more clear.

Was it the case that, while Thatcher was pimping out Great Britain Ltd to America as its military and intelligence Whore, in the Eighties, Hugh had acted as Whore for the Whore?

Was that the role for which he had been enrolled be back in 1984? Someone with a desperate desire to get somewhere fast; someone at loose ends; someone with all the right contacts and background; someone who could be trusted to stay quiet; someone who could straddle all the interfaces, and act as both a political and intelligence troubleshooter? And most important of all, someone who, at the end of the day, was eminently deniable and expendable?

Was it, indeed, the case that Hugh had not been acting on his own, as any kind of 'rogue' operative'? That, in fact, he was very much the 'insider'? One of the most closely-held secrets? A 'Dirty Tricks Meister,' acting for and available to anyone of the entities then building the 'new' Great Britain Ltd? To do the 'Dirty Work' that no-one else wanted to do?

Acting for the Conservative Party. And its Government? For the military? For defense contractors? For the Intelligence Services? For the *Savoy Mafia*? Whatever 'Dirty Little Job' needed doing? Arranging a highly secret arms deal? The one that led to Margaret Thatcher's very private bank account? Her very own 'retirement fund'? The one deal, the one money trail no-one could ever find? A little money-laundering here? Looking after the boy Mark there? Taking care of Tory kickbacks here? Or Maxwell's slush funds? In Eastern Europe? Yugoslavia? And Bulgaria?

The final twist was that, before he went 'off-line,' Kevin had remarked, in a moment that re-defined 'co-incidence,' that he knew Tony Collins personally. He, Kevin, had been the Deputy Editor of *Computer News* back in the Eighties, when it had first commissioned Tony Collins to pursue the strange deaths' story. The last thing Kevin had done was to promise me that he would put Tony in touch with me. And then, Kevin had gone 'off the air.'

And, in the context of *Open Verdict*, I couldn't help wondering whether Hugh's 'Dirty Tricks' in the Eighties might not have included 'cleaning house,' not so much to protect national security any more, as much as to protect other peoples' 'Dirty Little Secrets'? And that maybe, in a final twist of irony, Hugh himself had simply been 'cleaned' away? In which regard, it was difficult not to notice that the last scientist had died in September of 1988. Two months before Hugh was found dead. And in almost identical circumstances.

I ran all of this by Ari. Whom I managed to speak to, without being headed off by the now vigilant Haya. But not before I came across another article on the Internet. The title to this article had caught my attention because Reggie, Kevin and Gerald had all mentioned the organization in passing, in the context of 'Dirty Tricks' groups associated with British Intelligence:

Group 13
www.deepblacklies.com
David Guyatt

Dead Men Don't Eat Lunch

It is the number that carries the most occult significance. Throughout Europe it has historically been regarded as an ill omen. In Norse mythology, the number 13 often signifies death. Today, in the United Kingdom, there exists a paramilitary unit called Group 13. The sole purpose of this ultra secretive unit is deniable assassination and it operates in the world of shadows. So little is known about them, that it is exceptionally hard to document its activities with any certainty.

One individual - a former civilian undercover agent for the security services, recounted his story of an encounter with Group 13. Gary Murray, author of "Enemies of the State" had decided to research Group 13 to write a book on them. He soon changed his mind. One day during his research phase he was forcibly dragged into the back of a Transit van and had a gun stuck to his head. A voice told him it would be unwise to continue his project. Sensibly, he decided to abandon the project and instead write a book on an altogether different subject.

Group 13 is generally believed to have evolved from former SAS soldiers and Security and Intelligence operatives who were once active in Northern Ireland during the mid to late nineteen seventies when a Labour Government was still in power. Fred Holroyd, a Captain in British Army Intelligence, served in Northern Ireland during this period. Holroyd was tasked with developing informers and other human intelligence sources connected to the IRA. It was inherently dangerous work, made a lot worse by a vicious turf battle between MI5 and MI6 for control of the Northern Ireland "patch."

Matters grew increasingly nasty as "assets" for each of the two contending groups were tossed to the wolves. Holroyd, when interviewed, outlined some details of this dirty war, recalled incidents where bombs were placed by one of these factions and then roundly blamed on the IRA. Holroyd's story and later disgraceful treatment at the hands of the British Army are recounted in his book "War without Dishonour." Holroyd's account sheds light on the so-called "Shoot to Kill" policy in Northern Ireland that resulted in the dysfunctional investigation of former senior police officer, John Stalker. This investigation ultimately resulted in the gripping feature film: "Hidden Agenda.".

The Special Air Service was formed during WW11 by David Stirling with the intention to operate behind enemy lines and to perform acts of sabotage and assassination. By 1969, the SAS had been sent to Northern Ireland to perform covert operations against the IRA - which included assassination. To cover their deployment to this politically sensitive area they chose the guise of "training teams." A succession of cover names was used over the next few years; these included the Military Reconnaissance Force (MRF), the 14th Intelligence Unit, and the Four Field Survey Troop, Royal Engineers. Fred Holroyd states that the latter was very definitely a

Geoffrey Gilson

SAS undercover unit stationed at the Royal Engineers base at Castile Dillon, Armagh.

1974 was a critical year in British politics. It saw the election victory of the Labour Party in February and was soon followed by rumours of an impending coup d'etat. Right wing groups operating in the shadows of power began to form themselves. These groups saw Premier Harold Wilson, and certain members of his Cabinet, as no-holds-barred communists taking orders from Moscow. The idea that Wilson was a communist mole is, even by today's paranoid delusions, a farcical belief. At that time, however, planning for a right wing coup was seen by these extremists as the only alternative to keeping Britain from the wily grasp of Moscow. One of these groups was named GB75, and was organised by David Stirling, founder of the SAS. Significantly, GB75 and the other groups had close contacts to the British Security and Intelligence community, from which they probably received some form of unofficial succour.

Founded in 1970 was another mysterious group which called itself Resistance and Psychological Operations Committee (RPOC). RPOC was established in line with the Reserve Forces Association and was said to be a reflection of the Special Operations Executive (SOE) - a WWII dirty tricks operation. According to one former member, RPOC had a clandestine section which formed an underground resistance movement in the event Russia invaded the United Kingdom. With a nod and a wink of the Conservative Government of the day, it forged close links to the British Security and Intelligence apparatus, and "...formed close links with the SAS's...own secret intelligence network."

Little is known of the SAS's secret intelligence network, apart from one enlightening publication. Ranulph Fiennes, the Arctic trekker, was a one-time member of the SAS. In his book, "The Feather Men," he reveals the existence of an unofficial group of former SAS officers and soldiers who, amongst other activities, are tasked with protecting members of the SAS whose lives are under threat as a result of their activities. According to his book, Fiennes learned a contract had been put out on him, only after this SAS secretive group had more or less mopped up a freelance assassination team sent to kill Fiennes. In this case, "mopping up" meant killing members of the assassination team. Fiennes further alleged that this group had been founded by David Stirling.

It is not possible to say with any certainty that this group - or elements within it - evolved to become Group 13. However, the associations are clearly similar. Both are highly unofficial but desirable to certain factions within Government. Both are said to be responsible for political assassinations both in Northern Ireland and elsewhere. Both appear to lean towards right wing agenda's.

Perhaps the best known incident that involved the SAS in a "wet

Dead Men Don't Eat Lunch

operation" was the assassination of an IRA unit in Gibraltar on March 6th, 1988; an episode which subsequently led to the explosive TV documentary "Death on the Rock." The controversy surrounding this event raged for years, with the "Sunday Times" Insight Team leading the attack on the credibility of eye-witnesses who claimed the three members of the IRA unit were gunned down in cold blood. Placed in context against the numerous SAS assassinations which took place in Ireland during this same period, it is hard to lend much credence to the official story of cock-up.

Of some interest is the statement of former CIA operative and former member of an American-based, international assassination team, Gene "Chip" Tatum. The team, Tatum says, is called 'Pegasus' and operates around the world. Targets are normally influential politicians and financiers. Over a period of several months, Tatum has revealed a number of the operations he claims he was involved in, as well as revealing names of those at senior level he alleges are behind Pegasus activities. In recent correspondence, he alleges that the British end of Pegasus was operated during the mid-Eighties by a high-ranking British Government official.

Another operation that carries SAS hallmarks was the murder of WPC Yvonne Fletcher outside the Libyan Peoples' Bureau in London in 1984. This killing caused immense public outrage and quickly led to the ousting of the Libyan Diplomatic Corp. In a courageous piece of television, Channel Four broadcast a Dispatches programme in 1996 that suggested WPC Fletcher was murdered by elements inside British and American intelligence. Amongst other startling facts, the programme makers stated that the shot that killed the police officer may have been a "terminal velocity" round. This technique both reduces the sound of the gunshot as a result of its sub-sonic speed, and creates the impression that the shot was fired from considerable distance. It is a known technique of SAS snipers.

There may also be other connections between Group 13 and the United States intelligence community. J. Orlin Grabbe, an American Professor who runs his own financial advisory service, has in recent years earned a reputation within internet "conspiracy" circles as being well informed about a number of illegal intelligence operations. One of these focuses on the alleged assassination of Vincent Foster, a close associate and legal adviser to President Clinton.

Grabbe, a former professor at Wharton Business School, in one of his internet posts alluded to the existence of a highly secret US assassination team that operates out of the National Security Agency (NSA). The unit, Grabbe claims, is called "I-3." In a recent communication he added that the information on this unit was provided by a "former CIA agent with the CIA's highest security clearance." It may just be a coincidence that this NSA unit shares a common name with Group 13 and just happens also to be in the same line of business. However, in the closed world of the intelligence community such 'coincidences' should be viewed carefully.

Despite the stiff secrecy and widespread smoke and mirrors that surround the activities of Group 13, some significant additional information came to light following the Scott Inquiry into the Arms to Iraq affair. Gerald James, the former Chairman of Astra Holdings Plc - a leading British munitions manufacturer - has written of his knowledge surrounding Group 13 in his explosive book "In the Public Interest," which blows the lid on British Government involvement in arming Iraq's Saddam Hussein.

During a lengthy interview, James outlined how he had been ousted from the Board of Astra. He believes his removal was orchestrated by non-executive director Stephan Kock, a self-acknowledged former Security and Intelligence Officer in the employ of Midland Bank Plc. James, thereafter, undertook to learn more about the mysterious Kock

In written evidence presented to the House of Commons' Trade and Industry Select Committee looking into Exports to Iraq, on February 5th 1992, James stated that he was told, in an unguarded moment, that Kock was "... a former head of Group 13. This curious organisation is apparently a hit or contract squad for the Foreign Office and Security Services."

James adds, "The Foreign Office is said to draw Group 13 operatives from the SAS as well as from private security firms," and that "its duties involve 'service to the nation.'" James also makes clear that Kock had exceptionally high level contacts inside the Intelligence community, and that he boasted of his ready access to the highest levels of the British Government, including 10 Downing Street.

The Foreign Office reference clearly indicates an MI6 connection. Known also as the Secret Intelligence Service - a name well known by lovers of Bond movies - MI6 activities come under the control of the Foreign Office. Perhaps the now infamous "007" License to Kill pedigree has moved from those fictional men in black bow ties and tuxedoes, to those all too secretive men in camouflage smocks and shoulder patches inscribed "Death from Above.""

***

Ari's initial reaction was the same as Reggie's. He went very quiet for some moments. Then, his old sing-song voice was back. But slower, and more deliberate than usual. Almost as if Ari were choosing his words carefully. For the benefit of someone leaning over his shoulder. Listening. Figuratively speaking. Of course.

"Ah, the Eighties," Ari exhaled gently, "you know, when you get to the end of a period like that, you often have 'Dirty Laundry,' that you need to clean up. I was 'Dirty Laundry' for a while. That's why I was in jail. But then, I had some friends..."

Dead Men Don't Eat Lunch

He paused for a moment. As if looking for the right word. "Your friend," Ari continued at last, "had run out of 'friends.' He'd pissed off too many people. He was trying to please too many people at the same time. Plus, he'd got greedy. And he knew too much. It doesn't serve any purpose to talk about who might have wanted him dead. Or, did he die this way, or that way. He was simply on too many peoples' 'Dirty Laundry' lists. He was going to have to go, sooner or later. One way or another."

And that was the last word Ari had on Hugh. Save to repeat his promise that he would provide all of the necessary verification to a publisher, once I had one. And I made promises to myself about the various body parts of mine that I would be willing to lose, in the highly unlikely event that Ari ever kept his promise.

After that, Ari regaled me for a few moments with his exploits advising the then President of Azerbaijan on his national security. Azerbaijan was one of the Caucasian Republics that was loosened from the Soviet Union, after the collapse of Russian Communism.

It was situated on the western shore of the Caspian Sea, where vast reserves of oil had recently been discovered. Reserves, apparently, that rivaled those of the Middle East. I couldn't think for the life of me what Ari could possibly have to offer that country's President. Until I read about pipelines, and re-cast my thinking, so that Ari stopped being the 'rogue' he affected, and became a deep-cover 'Dirty Work' guy for Israeli Intelligence. Perhaps, along the lines of Hugh?

There was much debate about whether pipelines from the Caspian Sea, and Azerbaijan, in particular, should be routed south, through the Middle East, to the Mediterranean; or north, through Russia, and to the Black Sea. It didn't take a genius to work out that the southern route would leave another vast spread of oil in the monopolistic clutches of the Arab World. And that Israel would prefer to break that monopolistic grasp.

Of course, no President of a Muslim nation, especially one in a region becoming notorious for its radical Islamic movements, could be seen talking to 'official' Israel. But that shouldn't stop Israel planting someone 'unofficial' near the President, to be on hand when the all-important decisions needed to be made.

I didn't have enough information to raise any of this with Ari at the time. And this, as it turned out, would be our last conversation. But I did have one trinket to throw at him before we finished. All of the information available to me suggested that he, and perhaps a few others, had spent the Eighties administering a Likud arms' fund in Eastern Europe, which, at times, topped some $600 million.

So I asked Ari what one did with all of the money? All of the people in the Eighties, and, by all accounts, into the Nineties and the 21st Century. All of the people who were bribed, commissioned, stole, collected, 'earned' vast amounts of illegal money. Holes in banks. Holes in companies. Drug profits. Arms profits. Hundreds and thousands of millions of dollars. What did they do with all of the money?

It wasn't as if they could parade the money around. People would start to wonder if Margaret Thatcher went out and bought half a dozen supersonic jets. So, what did they do? Meet up in Switzerland on Tuesday, and the Grand Caymans on Friday, and sit around and count the shekels together?

Ari's answer was a model of simplicity. What? He exclaimed. You think the international Stock Market took off in the Nineties because little old women suddenly found money under their mattresses? Trillions of dollars found their way into legitimate investments. But the bulk of that money started off being anything but legitimate. And that was the beginning and end of another lesson according to Ari. This one on international economics.

***

So, at the conclusion of the Nineties, facing the onset of a new millennium, I was looking back at the closing stages of the Eighties, and this was where I appeared to be:

Margaret Thatcher and the Tories had inherited a country that was bankrupt. Their solution had been to turn the country into Great Britain Ltd., transforming its industrial base into an export-driven military-technology powerhouse.

Continuity of export sales required an illegitimate but officially-sanctioned 'back-door,' which, in turn, needed money to keep the hinges greased, and a 'doorman' to arrange that money, clear away any human problems, and generally be responsible for keeping that 'back-door' open.

We weren't just talking about the odd grand or two, every couple of years. The 'back-door' would only stay open, over a period of time, and through changes in Government administration, if both the civil service and the political establishment were being systemically, hugely and regularly corrupted.

It was appreciated that arms commissions and profits, on their own, might not going be sufficient to maintain that systemic corruption. So, the Tories set up 'piggy banks,' in a variety of offshore accounts, which could be dipped into by senior and trusted individuals, during 'dry periods,' when the arms business was slow. Both the setting-up and the maintenance of those 'piggy banks' were a part of the job description of that same 'doorman.'

That 'doorman,' or 'doormen,' needed to have the proper skills, the right political and intelligence connections, and the right attitude – let's not get squeamish now, I mean a 'killer' instinct. But more than this, the individuals needed to be utterly trustworthy, and eminently expendable. Enter Hugh: the Dirty Tricks Meister. The guy who kept the arms 'back-door' open for Margaret Thatcher. Her very own 'doorman.'

But it wasn't just the arms 'back-door' that needed looking after. An unfortunate consequence of the systemic corruption was that Great Britain Ltd. also became the Offshore Trading Haven for the world's terror activity. It was inevitable. You could hardly ask the forces of law enforcement to interfere because, for the most part, they would have been attempting to stop the terror activities of their own Government. But there had to be some measure of control, and so, it fell to the 'doormen' to keep some semblance of order.

Now, for sure, much of this corruption was just about buying Rolls-Royces, and having a vacation villa in the Caribbean. But I believe that Reggie was not wholly in denial when he spoke of a "higher purpose." I do believe that Margaret Thatcher may genuinely have convinced herself that institutional corruption was needed to keep open a 'back-door,' which was itself crucial to sustaining what had now become the life-blood of her country's new industrial base, namely arms sales.

As for Hugh, something went wrong. Maybe he got too greedy? Maybe he was double-crossed? Maybe he had too many fingers in too many pies? Or maybe it was just time to 'clean house'? What I can say is that I believe that, as with Margaret Thatcher, Hugh became involved, not just for the money, but because he too believed his activities were for a "higher purpose."

In any event, Thatcher was toppled, and various entities, both within the Conservative Party, and on the outside, conspired to retain a 'Thatcherite' Succession. Both to keep secret the tragic shenanigans of the Eighties, and to be ready to resurrect that 'tragedy,' its seeming "higher purpose," – and its considerable financial advantages – as and when the Tory Party returns to power.

Which brought me to the question, or rather to the questions, that were nagging me at the end of Chapter 28. They had suddenly come into focus. What would happen, the little voices were asking, now loud enough for me to hear quite clearly, what would happen when Tony Blair and New Labour came to power in 1997?

Would the whole corrupt edifice just get put on hold? Or would Tony Blair finally blow the whistle? Surely he knew, or was going to discover, what had been going on before he assumed office? The answers were not long in coming. But the story still had a little ways to go before reaching that water shed in 1997.

Geoffrey Gilson

Chapter 30

HOWARD IS A WARM and fuzzy, little Jewish gnome of a guy. When I first met him in Tom's office, he told me he could see my aura. I liked him immediately. And so we had lunch together. I was in the middle of regaling him with my stories of psychics, on both sides of the Atlantic, when he let out a yelp.

I asked him what was wrong. He told me, with an astonished smile on his face, that when I had mentioned the word 'wizard,' my aura had exploded into a huge, incandescent flame of gold. I was worried that this might be a problem. "Oh no," he explained, "it means you come from a very ancient soul. Possibly Merlin's." Alright. Toss the Toyota. Nothing less than a Ferrari for me now.

Next up was a Methodist preacher. Kirk was born to be a hell-raising, fast-living, trash-talking son of a… But he got the call, and became a preacher instead. He struggled every day with choosing the higher path. And bless him, it showed.

I was instinctively drawn to the rogue in him; but I also admired the courage of the preacher. Kirk fought against the sense that his life was a glass only half full; and I think I represented for him the other half of that glass.

He was stocky, but still good-looking. He just happened to like Chinese food more than he worried about the consequences. He was a brilliant musical actor, and could have made for himself a useful living on Broadway. We had a healthy, but friendly, competitiveness going between us, based in the main on the theatrical stage. Which is where we had met.

I had made the mistake of agreeing to accompany a friend, to give her moral support in an audition. She was trying out for the musical *Camelot*, the second production of a new theater group that Kirk, and a couple of his parishioners from the Clayton Methodist Church, had cobbled together. Next thing I knew, I was playing the role of the evil "Mordred."

Dead Men Don't Eat Lunch

My first instinct was to play my old manipulation game, and go in and 'mould' this new world; thereby converting its strangeness into a 'safe haven' for me. But, I caught myself. Took a deep breath. And went in, and just…was. At first, this was probably one of the scariest experiences of my entire life.

I introduced myself as 'me.' Without preamble, explanation or decoration. I accepted those around me at face value. Without judging them, or compartmentalizing them, or working out how to score any kind of brownie points. And it soon became one of the most rewarding experiences of my life.

I found that it was ok simply to be 'me.' That people liked me. And respected what I was attempting to do. I mean, I'd wanted to be an actor ever since I had worked out that my kid sister's Godfather, Lionel Jeffries, of *Chitty Chitty Bang Bang* fame, was one. But, I'd been too scared to try it out. Now, without having to worry about the impression I was making, I could concentrate solely on doing a good job. And I loved it. And I scared the shit out of Kirk

We were doing the scene where his "King Arthur" first met his illegitimate son, "Mordred." I was playing my role 'angry,' and apparently I was doing a good job of it. Too good. Kirk called a time out, and asked me what the heck the problem was. Why? Because you seem to be angry with me, came Kirk's response. I told him that was for the role. Kirk's demeanor immediately changed. He congratulated me on being so lifelike, wondered gently where on earth I was drawing it from, thought better of waiting for an answer, and we continued.

The fact was that I found it easy to call upon a whole range of emotions, because I had them all. Bottled up, deep inside me, just waiting for an opportunity to explode onto a waiting world. Or audience. The theater literally presented me with a stage on which to act out.

At the same time, as the rehearsals progressed, I became aware that I would never have been able to act with such confidence if I had tried to take up acting beforehand. I would have been incapable of investing any role with real humanity, because my own humanity would have been too firmly reined in, under lock and key.

And it was no co-incidence that, with each role that I came to play, I found myself taking the simplest of characters and turning them into dark and angry young men.

There was an intriguing irony to the whole experience: I had been putting on an act all my life, and now I was compelled to drop the act, in order to succeed in my desire to mount a stage and put on a different sort of act. I was forced to remove the façade of pretence in order to replace it with another made up of cosmetic cream and eyeliner. Fully and honestly to explore the depths of my own emerging emotions, so that an audience might be fooled by my charade of emotion.

Another theme which co-incidence threw my way with this introduction to acting was that of estranged relationships between father and son. I had played 'angry' opposite Kirk, because I was 'angry' that "Arthur" had caused me to be conceived, and had then abandoned me.

In the play, I found it hypocritical that "Arthur" could create a court culture, based upon purity of motive, while so casually turning a blind eye to his own lack of morality, and the loose morals of those who were supposed to represent the lynchpins of that moral court culture.

Art was not so far removed from my own life, where I found my father quick to perceive the mote in other peoples' eyes, but none too ready to see the handful of timbers in his own. I have tried to forgive, forget and move on, but my father prefers to maintain a stoic, if somewhat distorted distance.

And yet, this does not mean that I do not still love him. This fact was brought home to me most dramatically during the audition process for our next production, *The Sound of Music*.

This was a musical that evoked deep emotional ripples in my soul. As one of six young children, who tramped around the campsites of Europe, entertaining the gathered masses with a combination of American folk songs and musical numbers, some of the first songs that we learned from our first Danish *au pair* girl were the classic children's numbers from *The Sound of Music*.

I auditioned initially for "Captain Von Trapp." The auditioning committee was desperate to give me the role of "Uncle Max." Something to do with my sense of comedic timing. I've never quite worked out whether recognizing that apparent comic attitude from my role as an evil wizard-in-training was a compliment or an implied criticism of my first performance.

In any event, Lim Forgey, the President of the theater company, asked me why I wanted to audition for a role, for which, with the greatest of respect, they were quick to add, I was clearly wholly unsuited physically. Because, I replied, I wanted the opportunity, at least in the audition, to play my father.

This had them intrigued. Tell us more, came the response. Well, I said, I don't see the Captain as an ornery cur, simply waiting to be charmed by "Maria's" wiles. I see him as a gentle soul, hardened by the cares of authority and war, and withdrawn, after the loss of his first wife. It is not so much that Maria releases him, as he releases himself, when he sees that he has a second opportunity to discover his own humanity.

My father had that second chance when his second wife left him. I know because I spent five hours in a lonely restaurant with him, desperately trying to help him start down the road of re-discovering his humanity. But something held him back. Something stopped him from understanding what was meant by unconditional love. I wanted in my audition for *The Sound of Music* to have a moment of pretence. To play the person I believed my father could have become if the scales had been allowed to fall from both his eyes and his heart.

Lim told me afterwards of the estranged relationship between his father and himself. The difference, he had told me, with a misty look in his eye, was that he could sense that I still loved my father. And Lim was right. I only hope that my father works that out before he dies. Because he won't let me close enough to tell him.

But acting was not all about the serious. The days were filled with moments of lightness, and sometimes, outright high comedy. I enjoyed the moment in my audition for *The Sound of Music* when everyone watching my audition as the Captain was certain that I was going to kiss Kirk's wife, Carole, who was playing "Marie."

The script called for it, and notwithstanding the fact that she was another corker, I had no intention of carrying through. But you could have cut the suspense with a chain saw. Mind you, Carole was herself a highly professional actress in her own right. As were her two daughters. Both of whom will also be corkers. Although, I wouldn't dare say that to Kirk's face. Preacher, or no preacher.

Then there was the fact that, take away my glasses, I'm as blind as a bat. Of course, they didn't have spectacles in the days of *Camelot*, and my eyes are too far-gone for contacts. So, I had to do the role 'blind' – in more than one sense.

This wasn't a problem, except for my song and dance number. Kirk and I had worked out a hugely entertaining series of moves, all of which required nano-precision when it came to my picking things up, swinging them around and putting them down again.

The thing of it was that I could only find my props by counting the steps. And the children, bless their hearts, kept moving the props. So, I'd be swinging around masterfully, to lean up against something that was no longer there, only to end up crashing flat on my face. Much to the amusement of the same, said children.

The only downfall of the whole theatrical experience was that, at one of the administration meetings, I made another mistake, opened my mouth, and apparently said something sensible. Next thing I knew, I had yet another 'role,' this time as Chairman of the Board of Trustees.

Well, I guess I must have been too swayed by my recurring role as the 'dark and angry young man,' because I pretty much pissed everyone off, and that was the end of that chapter in my life.

***

Geoffrey Gilson

In the meantime, I found myself, there in Clayton, Georgia, at the conclusion of the Nineties, looking back at the closing stages of the Eighties, where, on the face of it at least, all of the 'acting out' by the Iran and Iraq 'players' appeared to be all but over. The Iran-Iraq War had concluded. Ari was on his way to jail. Oliver North almost joined him. Gerald and Astra were finished. Margaret Thatcher was toast. And, one way or another, Hugh had been 'cleaned away.'

But, in fact, the story continued. With gusto. The players, the networks and the money simply picked themselves up, and moved onto new stages. Yet, before that could happen, there was one last 'old' actor still to be removed: Saddam Hussein of Iraq – along with his WMDs.

In 1990, the world was aware that Saddam still had WMDs, in threatening abundance. Long and well-researched tomes had been written, describing Saddam's intense campaign of acquisition in the Seventies and the Eighties. Books such as Kenneth Timmerman's *Death Lobby* and Alan Friedman's *Spider's Web* gave lurid details of the supply processes, and included maps of each plant, factory, and chemical dump.

Whether or not removal of Saddam's WMDs was the overt purpose of the First Gulf War, it was a US Diplomatic Officer, April Gillespie, who, casually or otherwise, gave Saddam the 'nod and wink' in April 1990; and the next thing we knew, Saddam was enjoying the nightlife in Kuwait, as of August 1990.

This allowed Bush Senior to put together the largest international coalition since the Second World War. Then, with the full backing of the UN, and with new UK Prime Minister, John Major, as his chief Cheerleader, 'Poppy' Bush drove Saddam's forces back out of Kuwait.

There has been much discussion about whether or not Bush Senior wanted to fight all the way to Baghdad, and remove Saddam. The debate is moot. Gut-wrenching photographs of the awesome destruction wrought upon Saddam's army caused a worldwide outcry, and Bush called on the road to Baghdad.

It was the view of most senior policy advisers in the US and the UK that Saddam had, in any event, already been rendered harmless, because the massive bombing campaign, which had caused Maggi and others such delight on prime time television, had pretty much wiped out Saddam's WMD capability.

However, it also quickly became apparent that this conclusion was erroneous. The bombing campaign was found to have been virtually useless. Partly this was the result of bad pre-war intelligence – something that would come to plague Bush Junior also. And partly because of the extensive precautions that Saddam had taken while building his WMD machine.

For example, in the case of the former, Intelligence Officials had been saying before the First Gulf War that Saddam had only 50 SCUD-B missiles. After the War, however, it was leaked that, even after Saddam had lobbed a few of the SCUD-B's at Israel and the US forces in Saudi Arabia, and a few more had been taken out by the bombing campaign, he still had some 819 operational SCUD-B's littered around Iraq.

As far as the latter was concerned, Saddam had encased almost all of the more sensitive aspects of his WMD projects in bunkers, that had, for the most part, been unscathed by the Allied bombing campaign. That was why the US spent the next ten years developing larger and more powerful 'Bunker Blasters.'

In addition, ammunition, chemicals, spare machinery, and all manner of other component elements of the vast WMD machine, were stored in carefully crafted and compartmentalized 'dumps,' that spread over many square miles of the Iraqi desert. Each 'compartment' of a 'dump' was separated from its neighboring 'compartments' by sufficient space that it required a different 'Bunker Blaster' to take out each and every 'compartment.' The Allied Forces had not been fully aware of this fact. As a consequence, vast tracts of these 'dumps' remained untouched and fully functional after the First Gulf War.

So, first item on the agenda after the War were UN Inspections to track down and destroy Saddam's huge, remaining WMD machine. First UNSCOM (United Nations Special Commission) and then, its successor, UNMOVIC (United Nations Monitoring Verification and Inspection Commission) were given the job of sending multi-national inspection teams into Iraq, to confront Saddam's military bullies, and remove Saddam's WMD capability.

By general agreement, the inspection teams were none too successful with the 'destruction' part of their remit. Way too much interference from Saddam and his thugs. But they were surprisingly successful when it came to monitoring. Up until 1999, when Saddam finally threw out the UN, UNSCOM produced 28 thick reports, giving full and grim details of Saddam's WMD procurement triumph.

Indeed, one of Saddam's gripes, that led to the UN expulsion in 1998, was the fact that UNSCOM had been too successful with its monitoring. Perhaps, in ways that even the UN might have regarded as less than legitimate.

According to one of the more controversial inspectors, Scott Ritter, who was a former Major in the US Marines, US intelligence agencies 'offered' the UN inspection teams, support capability with their own intelligence efforts.

Ritter argued that, at the time, the UN realized that, to be fully effective, it would need to engage in some clandestine surveillance. And, to this end, secret monitoring cameras were installed at certain sites throughout Iraq.

More than this, Ritter said that the UN engaged in active covert operations to stifle Saddam's continuing efforts to expand his weapons' program. Ritter has described a sting operation, run by the US and the UN in Romania, which prevented Saddam's scientists from getting their hands on all-important nuclear triggers.

However, Ritter has since stated that, as the years passed, the US took over more and more 'responsibility' for the UN's intelligence effort, such that, by the end of the Nineties, it was, in effect, a US program, designed to give primarily the US Government the fullest information on the extent of and the location of Saddam's weaponry.

There have been rumors that Ritter might himself have been a 'deep-cover' agent for US intelligence, much like Ari Ben-Menashe and Victor Ostrovsky, for the Israelis. And, that, among other efforts, he might have been acting as a 'disinformation' plant when, in the run-up to the Second Gulf War, he appeared all over television chat shows, surprisingly stating that Saddam no longer had any WMDs.

In the Nineties, Saddam was ignored by the world community when he complained that the whole inspection effort was merely a front for US intelligence. But, maybe he had a point. After the Second Gulf War, Bush Junior formed the Iraq Survey Group, the stated remit of which was to locate the so-called 'remnants' of Saddam's WMDs. The first head of this Group was one David McKay, an acknowledged CIA Officer. No admission as to his membership of the CIA had been declared when he had served as one of the early chiefs of UNSCOM back in the Nineties.

In 1999, after UNSCOM had been thrown out of Iraq, and was then replaced by UNMOVIC, the UN Secretary-General commissioned one final report on the status of the 'destruction; efforts, and the extent of Saddam's remaining WMD capability.

The task was considered to be such a huge undertaking that the project was divided into three component elements, each dealing separately with either nuclear, biological or chemical weapons. One of the leaders of the biological team was a senior British Government scientist, by the name of Dr. David Kelly, who had gained considerable experience over the previous decade, confronting Saddam's military machine, and documenting the extent of its biological program.

The final report described hundreds upon hundreds of sites that had not been properly visited, and programs that had not been effectively destroyed or ended. The upshot was that, in 1999, UNSCOM took the view that Saddam remained a serious threat to world peace because of his vast, remaining WMD machine, and his continuing efforts to build on that capability.

***

Dead Men Don't Eat Lunch

In 1997, Tony Blair became Prime Minister of Great Britain, at the head of his New Labour Government. And eventually, I received a response from a civil servant in Blair's New Labour Foreign Office.

It was signed by a "Mr. D. Walters," which brought with it many flashbacks of my days at a British boarding school, where no one had a first name, just an initial. It was "D's" opinion that, in respect of my enquiries about illegal arms sales to Iraq, and the alleged attendant kickbacks, the new British Government had "nothing to add to your correspondence with [the] previous Prime Minister."

Plus ca change...

But there was more to this response than immediately meets the eye. Thatcher and her gang may have trampled rough shod over many of the Rules and Conventions previously governing the British Establishment, but one, for certain, remained. I know this, because I still see reference to it all the time in the British media.

When a new Administration takes power, there is a Convention that they do not rummage through the 'dirty laundry' of the previous Government, exposing all their 'dirty' little secrets. The reasoning is that, if this Convention did not exist, no one at a senior level in Government would engage in open debate, and in the sometimes unseemly, but equally necessary, functioning's of executive power, for fear of being ratted on by the next Administration.

A corollary to this Convention is another, which states that, if a Minister of one Administration wishes to make reference to correspondence of a predecessor Minister, either himself or through one of his civil servants, then that civil servant, must through his own Minister, gain the express permission of that Minister's predecessor.

Put more simply, "D" had to go to his Minister to get permission to refer to the previous Administration's correspondence with me. That New Labour Minister, upon seeing that the previous correspondence had been with the former Prime Minister's PPS, would have known that the previous correspondence would have, in fact, been issued at the specific request of the previous Prime Minister, namely John Major.

Therefore, the New Labour Minister would have passed on my request to the new Prime Minister, namely Tony Blair, and his PPS. Tony Blair would then have had formally to request of John Major his permission to refer to Major's PPS's correspondence with me. Once obtained, that permission would then have made its way from Tony Blair, through his PPS, to the New Labour Minister, to "D," allowing "D" to refer to "your correspondence with [the] previous Prime Minister."

That is the Convention. That is the only way that it could have worked. And it raised, once again, in my mind, all those questions about what it could have been that Hugh had been involved in that required, not only that his own political party keep it quiet, but also the opposing political party, who, in every other respect, had shown themselves only too willing to expose all manner of corruption associated with arms sales, and, in particular, those which had been illegal and had involved Iraq.

Was there some truth at the heart of what Hugh had been doing that was so 'awful' that even New Labour realized that, to expose it, would undermine the entirety of the British body politic? Could that something be the fact that Margaret Thatcher herself had succumbed to corruption. And that Hugh's GEC deal was that trail of corruption?

Was it the fact that New Labour realized that exposure would underline the fact that they had not done a proper job of 'opposition,' and that the public would form the view that they were complicit by their silence? Much as we now believe that the Democrats never really properly castigated Reagan for Iran-Contra, because they had been complicit in covering up many of the attendant operations themselves?

The Democrats had been happy to see neo-Communism opposed on the American mainland. But, by the time they understood that the entirety of the process also included massive corruption in Lebanon and Iran, it was too late to make a noise.

Or was there something else to the somersaults that New Labour were performing, in order not to have to answer my questions? Did they have some newfound 'investment' of their own in those matters, which I had yet to discover? And which, indeed, I was about to discover.

***

Before I could formulate the proper thoughts in my mind, I received a further letter from another civil servant in New Labour's Ministry of Defense. This one stated, without shame, that it was the policy of the New Labour Government to deny that the UK had ever engaged in illegal arms sales to Iraq.

I made a special trip to the Library in Clayton that day. I waited patiently in line until a computer was free. And I then spent three hours writing down the full names of each and every one of the some 160, out of some 350, New Labour Members of Parliament, I calculated would have a screaming fit if they knew that 'their' Government was now pretending that there had never been any illegal UK arms sales to Iraq.

Was this a slip? An over-eager civil servant? Someone who still regretted the passing of the Tories, who, after all, may first have been the only 'masters' he'd ever known? Remember, by 1997, the Conservatives had been in power for 18 very long years.

Or again, did this correspondence represent something more? Were

Dead Men Don't Eat Lunch

New Labour doing some 'house-cleaning' of their own? Did they have a secret agenda, to which we mere mortals were not privy? Was 'clearing me out of the way' part of the preparation for something new and large, on a horizon the rest of us could not yet see or define? Bottom line: what the heck was going on? What was the deal?

***

One of the most colorful of Tony Blair's new team was undoubtedly the controversial figure of Peter Mandelson. He had already won for himself a place in the history books as the man who, along with Tony Blair and Gordon Brown, had transformed the Labour Party, from a socialist footnote of the Seventies, into a powerhouse of politics, beginning in the Nineties, and lasting into the 21st century.

That, in itself, was a pretty formidable record. Unfortunately, the tactics he used – a mixture of spin, bullying and manipulation – won him as many enemies as friends, both within the Labour Party and the media. On an aside, I would say that there are some, who know me, who say, none too kindly, that, in this letter respect, Mandelson and I share more than the same first name. But back to Mandelson: even his greatest pal, Tony Blair, accepted that his friend was so widely disliked within the Party, that he once declared that his job would only be done when New Labour had 'learned to love Peter.'

That may have been a lost cause, and even Mandelson has since admitted that he probably made too many enemies at that time. But what truly astonished even those who despised him were the scandals with which he would become associated. No one expected him to be that careless or un-disciplined in his personal dealings. But what became more sinister was the alacrity with which Tony Blair allowed him to bounce back. Every time.

***

First up, in 1998, was the scandal of 'The Loan.' At the time, Mandelson was the Secretary of State for Trade, in Blair's New Labour Cabinet. Mandelson's Department was the one responsible for overseeing the Government's Export Credit Guarantee Program.

On December 23rd of that year, *The Guardian* newspaper, an unlikely left-wing source for an expose against a nominally left-wing Government, printed details, from a book by one Paul Routledge, of a secret loan of £373,000 ($580,000), to Mandelson from his Ministerial colleague Geoffrey Robinson. The money had been used to buy an expensive house in Notting Hill, London.

Geoffrey Robinson was the man who, as Paymaster General was

literally in charge of the nation's checkbook with the Bank of England. It is, perhaps, an unfortunate irony that money was also the cause of Robinson's own personal, political minefield. But then Robinson's wealth had proven to be a double-edged sword for more within New Labour, than the accident-prone Mandelson.

Senior officials of the Party, among them Tony Blair, had been able to enjoy lavish favors at Robinson's expense, including holidays at his homes in Tuscany and the South of France, and meetings at his penthouse flat in London's Park Lane, on the border of the 'Mayfair Square Mile, just a sheep's nibble away from Robert Maxwell's lawyer, Michael Rogers, who was the attorney with all the 'right' connections.

However, many of the headlines were to become much less welcome – the Mandelson home loan, undeclared interests in offshore trusts, corporate misgovernance, and an alleged financial deal with disgraced tycoon Robert Maxwell, to name but a few.

After national service in the intelligence corps, Robinson was recruited by the then Labour Prime Minister Harold Wilson as a researcher at Labour headquarters. In the days of Labour's fondness for nationalizing British industry, Robinson soon became involved in state-run industries, rising to become the financial controller of British Leyland and, at the age of 34, the chief executive of Jaguar Cars.

In 1976, Robinson entered the House of Commons, representing Coventry North West. His interests also took in ownership of the left-leaning *New Statesman* magazine, and a place on the board of Coventry City soccer club.

Throughout the Eighties, while Labour was in opposition, Robinson was seen as an asset to a Party that severely lacked business backers of any profile. He held frontbench positions, speaking for the Labour Party on trade and industry, and science.

However, almost from the moment that Robinson was made Paymaster General, straight after the 1997 General Election, his financial affairs came under tough scrutiny from the Tories.

Eventually they proved his undoing as a Minister when details of the home loan deal he struck with Mandelson became public. Despite being small change to a man whose personal wealth, at the time, was estimated at around £30 million ($45 million), Robinson's £373,000 ($560,000) informal mortgage triggered both men's resignations in December 1998.

***

Much about this time, *The Sunday Times* leaked a report from the Department of Trade and Industry that was highly critical of the improper role of Coopers & Lybrand (before it became PricewaterhouseCoopers) in the management of The Mirror Group by Robert Maxwell, and the disappearance of the pension funds into Maxwell's back pockets.

The article made clear that Coopers & Lybrand had already been fined £3 million ($4.5 million), and had made civil settlement of some £67 million ($100 million).

A little later, there was publicity of an equally damaging nature about the failure of Price Waterhouse properly to give warning of the shaky nature of BCCI's finances to, among others, the Bank of England, which was, at that time, the body responsible for monitoring legal compliance by all banks within Great Britain.

As Senior Partner of the newly merged PricewaterhouseCoopers, and as the immediate past Chairman of Coopers & Lybrand, Peter Smith's name was all over the groveling press releases which accompanied these shameful exposures.

***

In a move that shocked many in Westminster, Tony Blair brought Mandelson back to his Cabinet on October 11th, 1999, as Secretary of State for Northern Ireland, where he was able to rub shoulders, on a daily basis, with the cream of Britain's Military and Intelligence services. While there, he was said to have been a highly successful Minister, even though, once again, he failed to dispel his reputation as an arch manipulator.

***

An "Insight" article in *The Sunday Times*, dated August 27th, 2000 highlighted the links between Alan Duncan, a Conservative Opposition Trade Minister, and Sheikh Ahmed Farid, a well-known London-based Arab arms dealer. There was speculation that Duncan was taking over Aitken's role as a bagman for the Saudi Royal Family in their arms deals:

"*One of Farid's key Westminster contacts is still Aitken, who was released from prison last January [1999], after his conviction for perjury in a 1997 High Court libel case.*

Soon after his release from jail, Aitken introduced Farid to Kevin Maxwell, the son of Robert Maxwell, the disgraced media tycoon. Duncan is a close friend of Aitken and supported him during his recent troubles."

Two thoughts crossed my mind: first, what on earth use was a convicted felon to the Saudi's as an ongoing 'bagman'? Secondly, what on earth use was any Conservative to the Saudi's as an ongoing 'bagman'? New Labour was in power. Unless these meetings represented a passing of the mantle: to the new arms 'bagman' of New Labour, and to the future arms 'bagman' of a future Conservative Government?

***

In 2001, Mandelson was hit by a flurry of scandals, which forced his second resignation from Tony Blair's Government.

First, there were allegations of his misconduct over a passport application by a couple of Indian brothers, the Hinduja's. These brothers were already the focus of some controversy, having been linked to charges of bribery in connection with an arms deal between the Indian Government and Bofors, a Swedish gun manufacturer.

The press were saying that Mandeslon fast-tracked a passport application for the Hinduja's, in return for their financial support of the Millennium Dome, the huge white elephant in East London, for which Mandelson had originally been responsible. I checked my conversation with Ari, and there, sure enough, was a reference linking Hugh to money laundering for a couple of billionaire Indian brothers.

An interesting side issue appeared in connection with this last scandal. Apparently, the Hinduja's had first applied for British passports back in 1990, much the same time as al-Fayed. And like the Egyptian, the Indian brothers had been refused. However, unlike al-Fayed, they bided their time, and struck it lucky with New Labour.

The rumors were that the brothers had been friendly with al-Fayed, and had counseled him to take their approach, namely to wait it out quietly. Which advice al-Fayed had clearly ignored, to his considerable cost.

Next up, there was some suggestion that Mandelson had improperly used his influence to assist with gaining planning permission for a chum of his, by the name of Wafic Said. Wait a minute. Could this be the same Wafic Said, who, as partner to Jonathan Aitken, had been the mastermind behind the *Savoy Mafia*, and the *Al Yamamah* arms deals with Saudi Arabia? Hello. One and the same.

We were also told that Wafic was now very chummy with Charles Powell, former Foreign Policy Adviser to Margaret Thatcher; brother of Blair's very own Chief of Staff, Jonathan Powell; and a gentleman who was made a life peer by Tony Blair himself, in 2000. In fact, the friendship between Said and Powell extended to the former making the latter the new head of his asset management company, the position previously occupied by Aitken.

It was also in 2001 that Geoffrey Robinson faced another controversy of his own, surrounding an alleged £200,000 ($300,000) deal, done with Robert Maxwell. Robinson claimed he never received the money, but as with so many figures surrounding Maxwell in the Eighties, there have

Dead Men Don't Eat Lunch

been regular questions as to how Robinson made all of his money.

***

The fact is that, for reasons which have more to do with Britain's draconian libel laws rather than the truth, Geoffrey Robinson was much more closely associated with Robert Maxwell than the mainstream media has been willing to admit. He was essentially seen by many as being Maxwell's 'bagman,' and the person who, after Maxwell's death, knew where most of the skeletons were hidden, which may be another reason for so little being exposed about him.

Maxwell was a mighty financial supporter of the Labour Party, not least in the Eighties, and again, Robinson most probably knew the ins and outs of how that support operated. Certainly, he still seemed to be engaged in some form of active 'support' even in the Nineties, when he helped out a senior Government Minister like Mandelson with a house loan.

There were rumors, going back to the Eighties, that Maxwell performed some highly secret role for Margaret Thatcher. Certainly, Maxwell harbored a surprising affection and respect for the Lady who should have been his political opposite.

We've already seen that Maxwell had connections, through his solicitor, Michael Rogers, with many of the players involved in the British end of the Iranian arms pipeline in the early Eighties. Perhaps Maxwell did more than just help Ari and the Israelis with their arms sales. Maybe Maxwell had a finger in the British pie, also? Either with the arm's deals themselves, or with the money laundering?

Maybe Hugh helped Maxwell in his British endeavors? Maybe Robinson also? Maybe this is where some of the financial support for the Labour Party came from? Maybe the Labour Party knew? And maybe Robinson was the conduit? And maybe this continued into the Nineties? With Robinson acting in many ways like Ashcroft, as a 'front man' for 'dirty' money? Maybe some of it from 'funds' that Maxwell left behind, and which were never discovered by law enforcement agencies? And maybe Mandelson, the unscrupulous manipulator, became a part of this conduit operation?

Then, the Tories were out; and New Labour was in. The British arms industry had, by that time, achieved second place in world arms exports. Leaving aside all questions of political affiliation, everyone in that private industry wanted the exporting to continue. At full tilt. The capitalists and the unions. After all, one in every five people employed in the UK is now associated, in some way, with the burgeoning arms industry.

That required that the same 'front door'/'back door' approach to continuity of service had to be maintained. Meanwhile, the *Al Yamamah* series of arms deals with Saudi Arabia was still up and running. And hundreds of millions of pounds of illegal commissions were still piling into secret bank accounts with the Bank of England. So, would New Labour have continued to support the arms industry, in every way, just like the Tories? And if they did, who would get the commissions and the other financial advantages going forward?

What if Tony Blair was painfully aware of the decisions that needed to be made? What if he knew that there was simply too much to lose if anything were exposed about the arms shenanigans of the Eighties? That revelation would undermine the whole British body politic? What if he knew that his own Party had, to some extent, shared in the illicit largesse?

What if Tony Blair had been approached by his own group of 'Grey Men,' and like Major, was told the 'awful truth'? What if he was given an ultimatum: if you want to achieve any success with your Government, you leave defense, the military and intelligence matters well alone; in return, the Civil Service will bend over backwards to fast-track any other legislation and initiatives that you care to bring forward?

Did Blair reflect upon the Wilson years, and recall what had happened when Wilson took on the defense establishment – and lost? Did Blair do a 'Dirty Deal' with those Grey Men, to save his fledgling Government? Did Blair look out at the nation, and realize that the arms industry was now a major fact of life in its affairs, and that there was no purpose in fighting it?

Certainly, Blair has had uncanny success in negotiating the wiles of the Civil Service. Undoubtedly, his Government has drawn heavy criticism from many of its own left-wing supporters, for its stance on matters relating to intelligence. Blair actively sought the prosecution of both of the intelligence whistleblowers, Tomlinson and Shayler, to furious outcries from those in his own Party, who declared that Blair was betraying the Party's long fight against the innate and dangerous secrecy of the British Establishment.

And Blair's Government has continued the tradition of the Tories in the Eighties, of pursuing controversial arms deals with countries of dubious legitimacy. Perhaps most notorious have been the series of arms sales negotiated with the Indonesian Government, at the same time as that Government was using the equipment violently to suppress the legitimate aspirations of the East Timorese.

What if it is the case that the whole seedy arms network that Margaret Thatcher put together in the Eighties simply picked itself up, by its rather soiled petticoat, tiptoed gently around the 1997 General Election, and deposited itself, ever so gracefully, in the beckoning arms of the New Labour Party?

What if Tony Blair, resigned to this 'Dirty Deal,' but wishing to

Dead Men Don't Eat Lunch

make sure that his own hands never became muddied by direct contact, turned the whole matter over to his good buddies Mandelson and Robinson; the one who just happened now to be in charge of all Export Credit Guarantees, and the other, in charge of the Bank of England check book?

What if these two, who may already have had some contact with the *Savoy Mafia* of the Eighties, merely re-cast the whole seedy arms network in a New Labour mould? What if this included supplanting Aitken and Ashcroft with operators and bagmen of a more New Labour pedigree – a pedigree that also extended back in to the Eighties – say, themselves, along with Wafic, the Powell brothers and Kevin Maxwell?

And what if the 'Dirty Deal' included some realization on everyone's part that, in order to send the strongest message to the world about the certainty of Britain's offer of continuity of arms service to its clients, it was necessary to have some sort of under-the-table, cross-party co-operation on the secret aspects of the arms industry? Would this account for the passing of the mantle from Aitken to Duncan? Would this explain the apparent friendly dealings between Aitken, Charles Powell, Duncan and Wafic Said with Mandelson, Robinson and Kevin Maxwell?

Did this require of the Conservative Party that it also keep its mouth shut, the door firmly shut on its archive of secrets, and a power structure in place that would be seen to be one that could continue the 'dirty' arms dealings, as and when the Tories returned to power?

Would this, in turn, explain the almost unseemly haste with which the two Conservative Leadership 'failures,' William Hague and Iain Duncan-Smith, were dispatched, and Portillo was headed off, all with the open interference of Lady Thatcher herself? Would it account for one of the Thatcher 'old guard,' Michael Howard, eventually assuming the mantle of Leadership in 2003? And does it help us to understand the rather surprising return to the Conservative Front Bench, at that time, of the Hon. Nicholas Soames, as Shadow Minister of Defense?

If you were looking for a genuinely 'safe' pair of hands to inherit responsibility for overseeing Britain's corrupt arms industry, as and when the Conservatives return to power, then Soames is the gentleman with the model resume. He has a 'portfolio' that touches all the bases of the elements which once made up the *Savoy Mafia* – the City, intelligence, the military, defense, the Tory Party and the British Establishment generally.

Nicholas Soames was first elected to the House of Commons in 1983. In becoming a Member of Parliament, he was following in extremely distinguished family footsteps. He is the grandson of Sir Winston Churchill; and his father, Christopher (Lord) Soames, was the last British Governor of Rhodesia, and then Leader of the House of Lords, under Margaret Thatcher.

An Old Etonian, Soames is a hunting, shooting and fishing country gentlemen, who served as a Royal Equerry to the Prince of Wales, and is a strong constitutional-conservative. Soames has long been interested in military matters, as a former officer in the Royal Hussars (with rumored links to British Military Intelligence), and as a Minister for the Armed Forces for three years under John Major.

When not serving in Conservative Governments or on their Opposition Front Benches, Soames, who was born in the same year as Hugh, has pursued a successful career in the City of London as a broker. Currently, he is Chairman of The Framlington Second Dual Trust Plc, and of the Property Merchant Group. Soames is also a Director of Wiltons Restaurant (in St. James's, on the edge of the 'Mayfair Square Mile'), which is just down the road from the Asprey and Garrards, two Gentlemen's Clubs, of which Soames is a member.

***

Continuing the theme that this story never seems to end, in August 2004, Peter Mandelson sealed his reputation as the 'comeback king' of British politics, with his appointment to one of the most powerful jobs in the European Union. As the European Union's Trade Commissioner, Mandelson represents all 25 EU nations in important trade negotiations around the world, a crucial role in the continuing moves towards globalization.

More remarkable even than Mandelson's staying power is the fact that it is reported that Tony Blair was even planning to bring his old friend back into the Cabinet, but was forced to drop the idea after stronger than expected opposition from Gordon Brown, the Chancellor of the Exchequer, and Deputy Prime Minister, John Prescott.

Does Mandelson redefine the term 'Teflon' because of his insidious connections to the British arms network, and his role in assisting the pipeline for New Labour's 'dirty money'? Or did Mandelson get the new job simply because, as even his sternest critics accept, he is a slick political operator and a good networker – both skills that come in useful in the smoke-filled rooms of Brussels?

One could argue that being based now in Europe, Mandelson is too far removed from the whole arms and 'dirty' finance equation in the UK to be of any further use. And yet, one is reminded of James' talk of the European *Parlor Club*. Perhaps Mandelson will be of more use to the British arms industry, and to the financial advantage New Labour gains from it, exerting influence over that wider arms cabal in Europe?

Plus, as Mandelson was quick to point out upon his appointment, even in Europe he will be only a two-hour train ride away from the Prime Minister's official residence in Downing Street.

***

Dead Men Don't Eat Lunch

So, *plus ca change*... Same game, but different team. And even some of the same players. Yet, Hugh's death was not just a marker to signal the departure of the first team; it was an important requirement for the beginning of the next phase of the game.

The Conservative arms network of the Eighties had its strategists, its tacticians, its operators and its bagmen. And it had at least one 'Dirty Tricks Meister': Hugh. Before it was possible to move on 'cleanly' to new pastures, the old 'dirt' needed to be removed, so that it would not return to 'haunt.' Hugh's 'exit' was necessary to allow for the new incarnation in the Nineties, and beyond, of the Eighties' arms network.

In this past Chapter, I have tried to identify who might be the strategists, the tacticians, the operators and the bagmen of the New Labour arms network. What I have not been able to do is finger the New Labour 'Dirty Tricks Meister.' But you can be sure there is one. If not more than one. Follow the players, follow the money and you will find him. Or her.

Meanwhile, much of the rest of what Thatcher wittingly or unwittingly set in motion has also carried itself forward into the reign of Tony Blair and New Labour. Notwithstanding some half-hearted attempts at legislation, aimed at controlling the activities of terrorist organizations within Great Britain, the country still operates, under New Labour, as the primary Offshore Trading Haven for Global Terror. But why, you might very well ask? The answer is both simple and sad:

***

A fully-fledged and successful arms industry requires an ongoing 'back-door' for illegal arms deals. That, in turn, necessitates that there be a network of 'underground' services, on immediate tap: warehouses, false papers, personnel – and security.

Beginning with Thatcher's Government, and continuing through Major's, into Blair's (and beyond), that need has been met with classic British efficiency, at all levels: from the corridors of power in Whitehall, to the oak-paneled offices of the City of London, to the darkest of back-alleys in Soho and Leicester Square.

Add to this the further climate of corruption that has accompanied Britain's continuing role as covert surrogate for America's agenda of state terror. And London has become a full-service marketplace for all the accoutrements of the modern 'metro-terrorist': arms, explosives, mercenaries, money-laundering, and terrorist contacts.

Whether you are the CIA, MI6 or Mossad; InTerNet, the 'Enterprise' or Donald Rumsfeld's new "off-the-books" operation; al-Qaeda, Islamic Jihad or the Knights of some faction of the Priory of Sion. Whatever

Geoffrey Gilson

your name, whatever your need, you can obtain service from Great Britain Ltd. – the world's finest Offshore Trading Haven for Global Terror. They are open for business, to anyone and everyone – provided the price is right.

Of course, this is made all the easier by the fact that the UK is still a remarkably open society, that encourages full expression of political thought. The borders are open: not only to people, but also to the unfettered import and export of cash. London is the financial capital of the world. And Britain is an island, which sits within sight of the northern coast of France – an absolute dream for anyone wishing to bypass Customs and Immigration controls.

Is it any wonder that there are so many British connections to the worldwide bin Laden network; or that so much of 9-11 had its genesis in the UK? Are we truly surprised that second generation Pakistani immigrants, who, for all intents and purposes, should have been model products of Thatcher's 'British Dream,' and Blair's 'Enterprise Society,' were so easily able to manufacture and then to explode five bombs, with such devastating effect, on London's transport system, on 7-7?

Why then, doesn't Tony Blair do something to stop the corrupt arms trade, and all of its insidious offshoots and nefarious consequences? The answer is that he can't. It's too late. And it's too lucrative.

Ok. But couldn't Blair at least clean up some of the act, by refusing any longer to act as America's surrogate operative, in the export of its state terror? Not so fast. What makes anyone think Blair would be allowed so casually to abandon that role? Again, it was – and still is – way too remunerative.

In addition, Blair has too much to lose by coming clean: he knew what was going on under Thatcher and Major, and yet he stayed quiet – he wanted power too badly. Once New Labour was in office, it continued, at best, to turn a blind eye to the ongoing shenanigans, because it wanted to stay in power.

Blair now wants a legacy. He doesn't want to become a martyr. Which is what would happen if he were to blow the whistle. Because he'd be blowing the whistle on himself. One of the many issues that would come under the media microscope would be whether or not Blair benefited personally – and that is not the sort of scrutiny that Blair could survive. Even as I write, the tightly wound web is coming unraveled, with the furor surrounding Blair's personal role in New Labour's 'Cash-for-Peerages' scandal.

However, this is all moot. The fact is that Bush Junior never had any intention of allowing Blair to abandon Britain's role as America's surrogate. That is why the world has witnessed the curious courtship between what it perceives, on the one hand, to be a gung-ho, right-wing, imperial President, and, on the other, a seemingly articulate, intelligent, left-

Dead Men Don't Eat Lunch

wing Prime Minister.

So, what did Bush have in store for Blair? The world now thinks it has the full answer: Iraq. And indeed, the answer, which presented itself in fairly short order, has had much to do with the continuing saga of Iraq's WMDs. However, the true role that Blair played, with respect to those WMDs, and with regards to the Second Gulf War generally, was not the one the world has been led to believe. And which, indeed, it still believes.

Geoffrey Gilson

Chapter 31

R<small>ABUN</small> COUNTY was an icebox with empty shelves. Trees, that were no more than grey husks, stood silent sentinel on the lifeless slopes. And the waters of the lakes danced livid under wind-whipped whitecaps. The woodland wildlife had returned to its burrows in order to hibernate. While the wilder life of the woods had likewise taken leave, either for the central heating of Atlanta, or for the warmer climes of Florida. The abundance of sights, sounds and smells, so much the soul of summer, had been rendered frozen and locked in memory, until the dawn of a new year.

I stumbled stiffly through the cold, my trembling lips leaving a defiant trail of vapor in my wake. I had no reason to be out and about this bitter Saturday afternoon, save for my promise to Lim and Kirk to take part in the weekly rehearsal with their Methodist Church choir. I had not been converted, mind you. I merely sought the opportunity to improve my stage singing. But that didn't stop Lim and Kirk tag-teaming in their efforts to save my soul.

They were both quite charming, and surprisingly gentle, in their ministrations. And I was equally forthright in my denial of their advances. Yes, I believed in God. For I did, and do. And yes, I believed in Jesus Christ. But no, I did not want to take him for my Lord and Savior. And no, I did not believe that his teachings – whichever version you happened to subscribe to – were the only pathway to heaven.

My own spirituality was still very much a work in progress – a reflection perhaps of my life, and even this book…? But I didn't see God as some kindly grandfather figure, sitting Zeus-like on a throne, casting down judgment like so many bolts of lightening. I saw God as a more beneficent entity, with the emphasis on 'entity.'

I believe that the spiritual 'cement' of all life, both in its material form and in its spiritual 'alter ego,' is a form of intelligent 'electricity,' We know that the building block of material life, the atom, is held together by electricity, whether that material life is animate or inanimate.

Anyone who has seen a dead body knows, with certainty, of the existence of something that has clearly left the lifeless hunk of humanity before them. I am perfectly happy to call that a 'soul.' And I believe that also is a demonstration of 'electrical' intelligence.

I believe that this intelligent 'electricity' binds everything living and dead, soulful and soulless, animate and inanimate, God-fearing and Godless. All is connected. Indeed, and this is nothing original, I believe that the intelligent 'electricity' is God. And that God is in all of us.

I believe that the purpose of our 'material' life, the reason for our time on this mortal coil, is to gain a better understanding of God. And that as we, through our various incarnations, draw closer to God, we become of God. And I am happy to believe that Jesus was an individual who became so close to God that he was, indeed, a Son of God.

I keep stressing the 'intelligent' aspect of the 'electricity of life' for a couple of reasons. First, I believe that it helps, at least me, to understand the possibility of 'spiritual communication.' I'm not sure I believe in co-incidence so much as I believe that the 'electricity of life' offers an etheric information super-highway, along which our thoughts and desires travel. Someone or something picks up on the transmissions, perhaps even subconsciously, and bingo, the 'co-incidence' occurs.

Secondly, I believe that the argument between creationism and evolution is a hollow distinction. I do not believe that God is an accident, nor is anything that he created. Neither do I believe that God is static. That some 3,000 and some years ago, he waved a wand, created the world, and sat back, saying, well that's that then.

I believe that the whole of creation is guided by God's hand via this 'electricity of life' that is him. Or, indeed, her. I believe that we can, by becoming closer to God…who is in all of us… that we too can exert some sway over the direction this ongoing 'crevolution' takes. 'Crevolution'? Ok, it is more notoriously known as 'intelligent design;' but I prefer my moniker. In its very simplest form, I believe that every single moment we take the time to stop and take in the beauty around us, our very concentration helps to add to that beauty. Of both the physical that we see, and the spiritual that is inherent within it. Be it animate or inanimate.

Ok. Kirk and Lim would say. So, you're an animist. We've had to convert worse. And so the cycle would continue. But I did give them some cause for hope. I told them of my belief in my spiritual guides, and I also told them that I was perfectly happy to accept that one of them might well be Jesus Christ. He just hadn't yet introduced himself to me using that name. At least this got a chuckle.

At which point, my theatrical director, Jeanne, who is also a Native American storyteller, stepped in and wondered why I was talking to my spiritual guides so much. It was Jeanne who introduced me to the writings of Deepak Chopra. I'm still working my way through his teachings about the *Way of the Wizard*. As far as I can understand, Chopra refers to the part of God that is within us as our inner Wizard. One who sees and knows everything. Provided we believe that there is more to life than the mere material. And provided we accept that everything is one, and is bound by love. Ok. I'm not having too much difficulty to date incorporating this within my belief system.

And yet Jeanne wanted to know why I was talking to my spiritual guides, and not to God. She knew me well. She got me with the intellectual argument. If I was so hell bent against intermediaries between 'authority' and me, why did I allow my spiritual guides to get in the way of my personal relationship with God? I'm bound to say that, since I have been chatting to God direct, I have been experiencing way more satisfying fulfillment in my life. You should try it some time.

In the days after 9-11, in particular as the United States and Great Britain found themselves, once again, mired in the mountains of Afghanistan, repeating history, this time to rid themselves of the Islamic 'devil' they had helped to create, Kirk and I found ourselves in animated discussion about Islam.

The discussion groups within his Church firmly took the view that Allah was not God, and that there was little compatibility between the teachings of Christ and those of the Koran. I attempted to counter that Islam had been a peaceful religion, until the West had taken regularly and violently to invading and raping the lands of its birth. Beginning with the first Crusades. Continuing over the centuries, with agendas governed by geopolitics and oil. And finding their latest incarnation in the so-called "War on Terror," which many in the Middle East merely saw as the latest of so many ugly Crusades.

Bless him, Kirk seemed genuinely perplexed when I wondered if those in the West really believed that Lebanese farmers or Saudi Bedouin truly wished for their children to grow up to be suicide bombers. They made this choice because they had come to believe that the only way to stop the infidel raping their land, their women and their ways, and to convince him to leave, was to return the favor, in the infidel's own land.

For his part, Kirk wondered if I actually believed the letter I had written to the local newspaper hoping that, when the military action, which had been initiated to track down and capture the perpetrators of the New York attack, had finally succeeded in its mission, the West would then take the time to begin a serious dialogue in the Middle East. One that would take into account that definition of 'civilization' that was understood by those who had always occupied the lands that we so readily recognize as the 'cradle of civilization. Or if the West would merely impose its own 'burger and fries' version.

I guess I must have become quite animated in my response, because the next thing I knew we were talking about this book, my investigation, and the likelihood of the existence of the Priory of Sion. I really like Kirk, and I treasure all of our discussions. But even he surprised me with the interest that he espoused in these subjects.

It was either he, or indeed it might have been Lim's fun-loving wife, Chavaleh, who introduced me to the Charismatic Movement, a secretive brand of pseudo-Evangelical Christianity, that hovers around the edge of mainstream Christianity, waiting to snap up the slippers and the sliders.

Apparently, its members do not openly proclaim their affiliation. Rather, they join a congregation, establish themselves as active worshippers, and then go to work on their newfound friends, singly, or in small groups. According to Kirk or Chavaleh, it begins with a seemingly innocent conversation about Jesus being, not so much the Son of God, but rather 'the Eternal Light.' Next thing you know, the discussions are full-blown revivals, openly advocating what even I could recognize as an agenda of the New Age.

I was fascinated. I had not come across anything which so strongly resembled an active movement by what seemed to be another 'legion of footsoldiers' for the belief system held dear by the Freemasons and the adherents of the Priory of Sion. Like Reggie, back in Scotland, it put a human face for me on an otherwise often invisible 'conspiracy.' Coincidence, or connection? Kirk and Chavaleh, for their part, were equally fascinated to find someone they regarded as a 'New Ager' so ready to accept that they genuinely believed their Church to be under attack. It was all we could do not to dance around in a circle together.

And as I continue with the journey of discovery into my own spirituality, that is an apocryphal picture I hold clear in my mind. Three people of intelligence, with distinctively different beliefs, finding common cause and shared humanity in a joyous acceptance of their own spiritual differences. As 'Hallmark' as it is to say it, how nice it would be if everyone of different religious and spiritual persuasion could celebrate their similarities and their differences with such good humor.

***

Although the Knights Templar individually swore an oath of poverty, that did not stop the Order itself from amassing great wealth. Much of that wealth came from the Knights themselves, along with generous contributions from donors wishing to curry favor with the increasingly powerful Chivalric Order, in the Middle Ages.

Geoffrey Gilson

The Templars stored their wealth in heavily fortified castles, spread throughout Europe, on the roads leading to Jerusalem. They soon developed a tradition of protecting the wealth of monarchs and nobles in the lands around them, and so was born the modern tradition of banking.

Having little need of money for themselves, the Templars were also in a position to lend money to those same nobles and monarchs. And so they did. Increasingly using the loans as levers in pursuit of their own clandestine agendas.

Since the Middle Ages, the Templars, the Priory of Sion, and their associates and successors, have always had close connections with high finance, and have continued the practice of using the same towards their own ends. It is for this reason that your average redneck, on a mountain in Georgia, links the New World Order to the likes of the US Federal Reserve, the World Bank, The International Monetary Fund and the Rothschilds.

To be fair, it is not only secret societies that use money and high finance as a tool in engineering both overt and covert political agendas. Otherwise, Third World debt wouldn't be such a button issue at international gatherings. But those attending such meetings probably find little time to discuss the illegal money-laundering, which is the 'back door' cousin to legitimate high finance.

No covert undertaking can exist without a source of illicit finance, illegally laundered or piggybacked through the legitimate financial system. Sometimes the process is through offshore tax havens, and sometimes it makes use of piggyback mechanisms, covertly introduced into banking system computer software.

What is of interest to me is that it is possible to get some indication of where this is happening by paying attention to the havens, taking note of the unexplained banking collapses and the holes in corporate accounts. Follow the money trail, find the players, and there you will find the next budding scandal. All is connected. History repeats itself. *Plus ca change…*

Players never leave the game. Look at the likes of Ari. The money is too good, and the excitement too much of a buzz. They just move onto new scandals and new sources of income.

Bush's SSG/CPPG, 'the Enterprise,' InTerNet, the *Savoy Mafia*, the *Parlor Club*, and all of the other illicit networks of the Eighties and before, did not simply disappear at the end of the Eighties. They became big business. They became self-generating monsters.

And so long as there are covert agendas in the world, as long as an American Defense Secretary continues to talk of "off-the-books" military operations, there will be illicit networks to service his needs. And they will need players. And the players will need banks.

***

Dead Men Don't Eat Lunch

The world grieved after the heinous murder of so many innocent victims in New York on September 11th, 2001. And rightly so. Two ancillary issues, however, got missed among the necessary outpouring of sympathy and condolences.

The first is that the targets housed fully one-quarter of Manhattan's total office space, including some of the most important financial processing centers of both American and international monetary organizations. The third largest business center in the United States was destroyed by the attack, along with the head offices of 23 of its largest businesses.

The first attack on New York's World Trade Center occurred in 1993. Fortunately, on that occasion, the bomb had much less effect. Yet a few days earlier, the Center's equivalent in London, England – the NatWest Tower – was bombed by the IRA, causing sufficient damage to interrupt financial processing in London for several days.

Were the targets of these three attacks merely 'co-incidence'? Is it 'co-incidence' that freedom fighters, terrorists, criminals, however one cares to describe them, choose high finance as their target? Do they merely associate those targets with 'the West,' or is it that they link them to more clandestine efforts to introduce order into the globe's affairs? An 'order' which knows no room for 'rogues,' the 'little man,' or national independence and expression?

Without necessarily suggesting any formal connection, are the intentions behind such attacks not similar to the emotions felt by those who regularly demonstrate at international trade and finance meetings against moves towards 'globalization,' the buzz word which is, perhaps, increasingly interchangeable with the expression, 'New World Order'?

Certainly it is the case that banks in the United States were quite concerned that Bush Junior ordered the cessation of air traffic for several days. Why? Because those same banks lost millions of dollars while the checks they were processing sat idle on airport runways all over America.

Ok. Back up. What on earth am I talking about? Until 2004, the check processing system used to work as follows: you take a check into your bank and deposit it. Somebody processes it, along with all the others. The checks are bundled up, and are then trucked to operating centers, where they are separated, and sent to the banks which issued them, so that the amounts can be withdrawn from the accounts of the people who wrote them. Accompanying the checks is what is literally a glorified adding-roll strip that itemizes all of the checks bundled in that strip.

You may think this is arcane. I did. I told my brother so when I arrived in America in 1992 to help him market his company, which specialized in writing and supporting software that helped banks to process their checks. I was under the impression that banks, with all of their money, would be at the cutting edge of software development. Not so. As my brother pointed out, look at your average ATM screen. It's essentially still living in the days of black and white television. Banks are very conservative about spending their own money.

Anyway, all of the processing and trucking takes time. A couple of days. Which is why you and I have to wait those days before our checks clear. And while those checks are in the possession of the banks, or, as they put it, are 'on float,' they can literally earn interest on those checks. But only if they know where they are, and they can get their hands on them. When checks were sitting abandoned on airport runways immediately after 9-11, banks couldn't earn money on them, and the banks lost millions of dollars in interest.

And so, they got their buddy, Bush Junior, to pass the Check 21 Act in 2004. This now allows banks to do away with physically transporting all those checks. Instead, when your check is deposited, it can now be photographed, and the image is then transferred electronically, over the wire. This way there is no interruption to the processing function. Of course, it follows that the process will now be almost instantaneous. But don't expect your checks to clear any more quickly. The banks still need to earn their interest.

You may already have started to see the consequence of this process, which was being introduced slowly by some of the larger banks, over the years before 2004, in anticipation of an eventual change in the law. You may now receive with your monthly bank statement a photocopy of your checks, rather than the original returned checks.

The immediate consequence for my brother was that he and his partners became a hot property overnight, as large computer software companies up and down the country rapidly expanded their check processing divisions, to take advantage of the new legislation.

Another long-term effect may be the greater opportunity all of this new electronic processing offers to those wishing to piggy-back illicit transfers of money through the legitimate banking system. But surely that end result is merely another 'co-incidence'? Remember, keep checking the banks to start your own process of finding the next budding scandal. All puns intended.

***

I was doing my laundry one day in 2001, and happened to buy a cheap edition of *The Outlaw Bank*, one of the more authoritative accounts of the collapse of BCCI. While my underwear was drying, I came across a section on our George "W" (P. 227-30):

Dead Men Don't Eat Lunch

"*White suspected that Mahfouz, or other BCCI players, must have had a hand in steering the oil-drilling concession to the President's [George Bush Senior's] son. He thought it was part of a pattern, since Bath [James Bath, Houston businessman; big in real estate and aircraft sales; represented some of the richest Arab sheikhs] – who made his fortune by investing money for Mahfouz and another BCCI-connected Saudi, Sheikh [Osama] bin-Laden – had once confided that he was an original investor in George Bush, Jr.'s oil exploration company.*"

Well. I know I'm not the first to claim that bin Laden has his own sophisticated financial operation. He was, after all, a rich Saudi Sheikh long before he became the darling of the world's Islamic radicals. But, it's a point worth remembering when we talk about the role finance plays in clandestine agendas. It's not just the money trails of the West that are worth following.

And I know I'm not the first to suggest that, politics aside, bin Laden and Bush Junior had shared interests in oil and finance, and often used the same financial networks. All is connected. I know it's a little *Readers' Digest*. But tell that to the grieving families of the victims of 9-11, and to the families of those soldiers returning dead or crippled from the various conflicts resulting from Bush's "War on Terror." All of the 'soldiers,' whatever their nationality or political persuasion.

***

After several years, and not a few rainforests of letter paper, I finally achieved some results in my endless enquiries of the US Government under their Freedom of Information Act. My primary goal had been to obtain documentation relating to the Letter of Credit issued by BNL in Atlanta with respect to Hugh's arms deal with Iraq.

However, there were a few interesting 'train stops' along the way. The CIA had responded to me, after a little game playing, to say that they could not comment on Hugh Simmonds and matters relating to Iraq, for reasons of national security. And like the Prime Ministers of Great Britain, they were not prepared to expand on that point.

I did get something from US Customs. Two reports. One on Hugh. And one on me. Both of which had sections that were blacked out. I found it fascinating that there could be anything associated with me that required blacking out. Unless it had to do with my investigation of Hugh's activities.

But, after these sideshows, we came to the main attraction. I had become quite well acquainted, at least on paper, with one Richard Huff, who was, at the time – that is between 1996 and 2003 – the Co-Director of the Freedom of Information Unit of the US Department of Justice.

Richard had had to handle about six or seven Appeals of mine, that

Geoffrey Gilson

I had been faithfully registering with his Unit, over the failure of the Department reasonably to deal with my repeated requests for the Letter of Credit. Of course, they had it, because they were the Department, which oversaw the FBI, which, by its own admission, had taken the documentation, relating to the Letter of Credit, out of Drogoul's office, in Atlanta, in 1989.

Richard was always very proper and polite. And I even detected a slight wry sense of humor. But that might just have been my imagination. After all, how on earth can one detect a raised eyebrow and a quizzical smile from a piece of paper?

In any event, late in 2001, Richard finally wrote to me to tell me that my enquiries could no longer be entertained because all of the documentation had now been returned to the parent company of BNL, in Italy.

Well darn it. I guess that was me stumped? As if. I wrote back asking for copies of all of the internal Department documentation that my repeated requests had generated. I took the view that someone, somewhere, might have said the wrong thing, or that someone somewhere might have produced an index of the returned documents. A fishing expedition? Yes. But this whole exercise continued to be one vast (eighteen years and counting) rollercoaster of a fishing expedition. What reason was there to stop?

Well, we went though a couple of years of ding-dong about what could and could not be released. What had already been released. What I was entitled to. What times the movies were showing at the local cinema. Until, one day, in 2002, a package of papers arrived unannounced.

Most of them were overly stamped internal Department toilet paper. But then I came across a gem. It was a totally clean piece of paper. No Department heading. No memo heading. No stamps. No signature. No date. It was from one individual to another. Names which meant nothing to me. And simply stated that someone had spoken to the un-named Special FBI Agent, in charge of the BNL documentation, about my Request, and that the Agent could recall no Letter of Credit for GEC (UK).

This piece of paper screamed 'fake.' I engaged in a carefully crafted process of correspondence with Richard. I began by respectfully asking if someone would be willing to allow the Agent to talk to me. No.

I asked if there was any documentation to verify that a search had been conducted, rather than someone just making a wild declaration, off the top of their head. Couldn't comment.

I ever so gently posited my opinion that the piece of paper bore all the hallmarks of being a 'fake,' and wondered whether anyone would care to produce affidavits verifying the authenticity of the piece of paper. Didn't have to.

I then demanded authenticity. Silence. I stated baldly that silence would mean that Richard was agreeing that the 'memo' was indeed a fake. Three times, in three separate letters, I stated this. Like the famous 'count to ten' in *All The President's Men*. And Richard responded. With silence. Three times. I have never heard from Richard again.

In the middle of this elongated exercise, in the early summer of 2002, in some exasperation, I decided to initiate yet another contact with yet another 'horse's mouth.' Iraq was going through the motions, at the time, of pretending to comply with the UN's demands to furnish it with information about Iraq's WMDs program.

The Iraqi Ambassador to the UN apparently presented Kofi Annan with a complete chronological history of what had been the program, its sources of supply, and a detailed description of its destruction. Oh good, I thought, maybe the Iraqi report includes details of the GEC (UK) transaction. And so I wrote to the Iraqi Ambassador, asking if I could have a copy of the report.

I never did hear back from him. But I did get a telephone call from a well-spoken New England gentleman, wanting all sorts of details about the International Center for Public Policy and Social Studies. This organization existed only as the letterhead that I used, from time to time, when making some of my more esoteric requests in pursuit of my investigation. I had found that official bodies are more likely to respond to a similar-sounding 'official' body, rather than some individual in the boonies.

It was a fascinating, but useless conversation. All I could do was repeat my contention that the organization was nothing more than an alias. The gentleman was very charming when I called into question his *bona fides*. He gave me a 1-800 number that I could call to verify his connection to Dunn and Bradstreet. When the telephone call was over, I immediately called the number, and was not overly surprised to discover that it did not exist.

So, lots of furious activity with regards to my governmental requests, in 2001 (NB 9-11), 2002 (NB US and UK Intelligence Reports on WMD potential in Iraq), and 2003 (NB Second Gulf War). All to do with my requests for information about a possibly highly sensitive and illicit arms deal concerning equipment that could have been used to deliver Iraq's WMDs. Hmm. 'Co-incidence' or connection?

Could it have been that, after five years of being gently paddled around, like everyone's favorite ping-pong ball, I had finally become a dangerous nuisance? That my enquiries were no longer about an irritating past (Iraq's arms build-up before the First Gulf War). But, instead, were related to something that was about to become very much the present? And a very sensitive present at that; namely, the ostensible reason for the Second Gulf War – Saddam's WMDs?

Was I getting in the way of plans, because I was getting too close to a truth it was now time to make disappear; namely, the extent of British and American involvement in the development of Saddam's WMDs? Was it the case that honest answers to my questions might pose something more than a passing embarrassment?

And while we're in the mood for rhetorical questions, what about asking whether I was being monitored? And yet, the interesting thing about this 'surveillance' was that it appeared to be particularly benign; and no one seemed to be doing anything about hiding it, or following up on it. I mean, if you're going to be surreptitious, then be surreptitious. But if you're going to be threatening, then kindly do me a favor, and threaten me. So what was it all about?

It was while I was having this quite nonsensical wobbly that I received the strangest package of all. Again, completely out of the blue. At the time, it meant nothing to me. It was from the CIA, and seemed to be full of quite innocent internal memos, most of them referring to international press articles. But I re-visited the package when writing the final stages of this book. It was only then that I realized that the memos provided me with information, of which I had not previously been aware, and which apparently supported some of my more exotic contentions.

How to explain this more clearly? None of the content of the memos was all that secret, and none of it directly related to any of my specific requests. Rather, it was helpful in 'evidencing' some of my more 'left-field' theories. Thoughts and views that I had never shared on paper with the CIA. So, the CIA could only have known that the memos would be helpful if they knew what I was doing. Intimately. That said, the memos were helpful. Which was surprising. I mean, why would someone from the CIA want to help me?

I set out below one of the articles contained in those memos. Judge for yourself its usefulness to this book. Alongside your own knowledge as to whether or not you were previously aware of any of the contents. And perhaps set it in context with my conversation with Mark Saunders, and the brou-ha-ha that began brewing in 2005, over the allegations that Bush Junior was wire-tapping US citizens without proper authorization. All is connected:

"Article [in "The Sunday Times"] by Nick Fielding and Duncan Campbell [who was one of the many so-called investigative journalists in the UK, who turned their nose up at me]: "Spy Agencies Listened in on Diana; Global Eavesdroppers: Calls by Diana were Intercepted by a Worldwide Monitoring Network said to Include Menwith Hill in Yorkshire, England. The Consortium Building Tornado Fighter Planes [UK's next generation fighter plane; the one that took out all the runways in Iraq] and Mark Thatcher were also targeted in the operation."

FBIS Transcribed Text: Spy agencies in Britain and America

Dead Men Don't Eat Lunch

eavesdropped on Diana, Princess of Wales and Mark Thatcher, son of the former prime minister, as part of a global system of monitoring communications, according to former intelligence officials.

Calls by Diana were picked up because of her international charity work; Thatcher's calls surfaced in the monitoring of British arms deals with Saudi Arabia.

The officials also revealed that charities such as Amnesty international, Christian Aid and Greenpeace were secretly spied on. Overseas targets have even included the Vatican: messages sent by the Pope and the late Mother Teresa of Calcutta have been intercepted, read and passed on to Whitehall intelligence officers, the sources say.

Codenamed "Echelon," the monitoring system is part of a worldwide network of listening stations capable of processing millions of messages in an hour. At least 10 "Echelon" stations operate around the world. Canada, Australia and New Zealand participate, as well as Britain and the United States.

Former intelligence officials have spoken out after a decision by the European Parliament to launch an inquiry into "Echelon's" operations. Officially, the British and American governments continue to deny the network's existence.

Wayne Madsen, who worked for 20 years at America's National Security Agency (NSA) and other agencies, said last week: "Anybody who is politically active will eventually end up on the NSA's radar screen." [Oops, does that include me? And oops, was that one of the points of sending me this article? Or am I just getting paranoid in my old age?]

Charities operating overseas are monitored because they often have access to details about controversial regimes. Amnesty was a particular target in the late 1980s, sources said. According to Madsen, "undisclosed material held in US government files on Princess Diana was collected because of her work with the international campaign to ban landmines." [Hello, I think I hear al-Fayed calling, 'is this US disinformation'? Isn't this game fun?]

The NSA, a former insider has revealed, has also targeted communications concerning British military sales to Saudi Arabia in the 1980s.

Its monitoring intercepted communications sent by Thatcher, who was then involved in the giant "Al Yamamah" arms contract between Britain and Saudi Arabia. The NSA also eavesdropped on the Panavia consortium, which builds the Tornado fighter aircraft. British Aerospace is one of the main partners in the consortium.

"I just think of "Echelon" as a great vacuum cleaner in the sky which sucks everything up," said Mike Frost, a former Canadian intelligence officer. "We just get to look at the goodies."

Geoffrey Gilson

Frost, who retired in 1992 after 20 years' service, has also revealed that Canada's equivalent of GCHQ was used by Margaret Thatcher to monitor two Cabinet colleagues. "She wanted to find out not what they were saying," Frost said, "but what they were thinking."

The ultra-secret operation was conducted from an office at Macdonald House in Grosvenor Square, central London, which houses the Canadian Commission [and is across the Square from the American Embassy, situated in the heart of the 'Mayfair Square Mile']. According to Frost, Canadian spies were asked by GCHQ to undertake the operation because it was too politically sensitive for GCHQ to do itself. After spending three weeks tapping the Ministers' communications, the Canadian officer who led the operation drove to GCHQ and handed over the tapes.

Margaret Newsham, an American computer software manager who worked during the 1980s at the giant listening station at Menwith Hill in Yorkshire, confirmed last week: "I was aware that massive security violations were taking place. If these systems were for combating drugs or terrorism, that would be fine. But not for use in spying on individuals."

Newsham says she was invited to listen in on an American senator's intercepted phone call at Menwith Hill. Later she informed Congress about her experiences. "It was evident American constitutional laws had been broken," she said."

By the by, it is interesting to note the confirmation that this article purports to offer of my contention that the US and the UK 'contra' each other's domestic electronic spying operations, in order to get around their own domestic oversight obligations. It is also interesting to wonder how it was that two such well-known and very left-wing UK investigative journalists came across such juicy info, unless they were, in fact, covertly 'in bed' with their intelligence sources.

But a more important thought passed through my mind. Ok, the net effect of my communication with US Government entities from 2001 to 2003 was that I did not get a copy of the documentation relating to the Letter of Credit. Ok, I was made aware that I was, in all probability, being quite closely monitored.

But. No harm had befallen me. I was simply made aware. In a fashion that was so obvious that maybe that was the primary intention. Just to make me aware. And then useful information came my way. From the CIA. And then Richard Huff stood to one side as an obvious fake was produced by someone in what could only have been a rather hack-handed attempt to stifle further enquiries about the Letter of Credit.

Was that the primary point of the exchanges from that time? Were there individuals in the US Government, who, on the one hand, were following orders and 'removing' me as a nuisance, while on the other hand, were sending my not so subtly coded messages that they were unhappy about what was happening, and that I had friends on the inside? A definite case for a double hmm.

***

Meanwhile, we were all becoming accustomed to the fact that the Old Bush Gang was back in town. Like father, like son. History repeating itself. *Plus ca change*, and all that good stuff. Colin Powell (Daddy Bush's Chairman of the Joint Chiefs during the First Gulf War) was Secretary of State. Dick Cheney (Defense Secretary during the First Gulf War) was now the Vice President, and not so much a heartbeat, as a heart flutter, away from the Presidency. And Donald Rumsfeld, who had done service as the youngest-ever Defense Secretary, for Gerald Ford, back in the Seventies, was now back as the oldest-ever Defense Secretary.

After a quick detour into the old battleground of Afghanistan, to root out bin Laden and his cronies, the Americans, with their British puppies in tow, were now headed for the main action in Iraq. Was Bush Junior about to finish 'cleaning some laundry' that Poppy had left behind?

Whoa. Not so fast. I do a disservice to the political equivalent of the hellraising B-Boys from *The Blues Brothers*. Jake Bush, that reformed drink-druggie from the Seventies, and his erstwhile companion, former rock-guitarist, Elwood Blair, did go through a carefully choreographed ballet, before they set about imposing their 21st Century Crusade on a hapless Middle East. So, let's give the 'ballet' its full due.

As we know, Saddam threw out UNSCOM in 1998. Little was done to make Saddam adhere to his promises to destroy his WMD capability beyond a spot of carpet bombing by saxophone-blowing Willie 'Too Big' Clinton. Which owed a lot more to distracting us all from his dalliance with a 21-year old (we should all be so lucky as the Leader of the Free World), than any genuine desire to see Iraq's WMDs reduced. Frankly, I'd have been a lot more successfully distracted if Willie had simply paraded Monica in front of the cameras, with her offending dress on. Or off.

Soon after the successful frat party in Afghanistan, Jake Bush started up his whine about Al Qaeda and Saddam being linked. One of the more intriguing newspaper articles in support of Jake's contention was that filed on August 25th, 2002, by a senior journalist for the London *Daily Telegraph*, one Con Coughlin:

> *"Abu Nidal, the Palestinian terrorist, was murdered on the orders of Saddam Hussein after refusing to train al-Qaeda fighters based in Iraq, The Telegraph can reveal.*
>
> *Despite claims by Iraqi officials that Abu Nidal committed suicide*

after being implicated in a plot to overthrow Saddam, Western diplomats now believe that he was killed for refusing to reactivate his international terrorist network.

While in Baghdad, Abu Nidal, whose real name was Sabri al-Banna, came under pressure from Saddam to help train groups of al-Qaeda fighters who moved to northern Iraq after fleeing Afghanistan. Saddam also wanted Abu Nidal to carry out attacks against the US and its allies.

When Abu Nidal refused, Saddam ordered his intelligence chiefs to assassinate him. He was shot dead last weekend when Iraqi security forces burst into his apartment in central Baghdad. The body was taken to the hospital where he had had cancer treatment.

The Iraqi authorities later claimed that Abu Nidal had killed himself when confronted with evidence that he was involved in a plot to overthrow Saddam.

"There is no doubt that Abu Nidal was murdered on Saddam's orders," said a US official who has studied the reports. "He paid the price for not co-operating with Saddam's wishes."

Last week, American intelligence officials revealed that several high-ranking al-Qaeda members had moved to northern Iraq where they had linked up with Iraqi intelligence officials.

It now transpires that Saddam was hoping to take advantage of Abu Nidal's presence in Baghdad to persuade him to use his considerable expertise in terrorist techniques to train al-Qaeda fighters.

Abu Nidal worked closely with Saddam during the late 1970s and early 1980s to carry out a number of terrorist outrages in the Middle East and Europe, including the attempted assassination of the Israeli ambassador to London in 1982.

In recent years, Abu Nidal, who has been ill for many years, had scaled down his terror operations.

With the prospect increasing of the US launching a military campaign to overthrow Saddam, however, the Iraqi dictator was keen to combine Abu Nidal's expertise with the enthusiasm of al-Qaeda's fanatical fighters to launch a fresh wave of terror attacks. In this way, Saddam hoped to disrupt Washington's plans to overthrow him.

The presence of al-Qaeda fighters in Iraq has become a source of great concern in Washington.

US Defense Department officials said that a number of very senior al-Qaeda members was now based in northern Iraq close to the Iranian border at Halabja.

Although Iraqi officials have denied any knowledge of the al-Qaeda fighters' presence, Donald Rumsfeld, the US Defense Secretary, said last week that it was highly unlikely that they could have entered Iraq without Saddam's knowledge.

Dead Men Don't Eat Lunch

> *"There are al-Qaeda in a number of locations in Iraq," he said. "In a vicious, repressive dictatorship that exercises near total control over its population, it's very hard to imagine that the government is not aware of what is taking place in the country.""*

The problem was that the *Daily Telegraph*, with its Israeli-supporting owner, and its traditional rubber-stamping of all things right wing and Thatcherite, was not seen as the most 'independent' source of information on Iraq, during a period which would eventually become the run-up to the Second Gulf War.

Plus, Con Coughlin had some difficulty with his own *bona fides*: he was the author of a series of sensational pieces during that summer of 2002. All of which made a case against Saddam, and in favor of Jake Bush. And yet no other mainstream journalist seemed able to confirm either Coughlin's sources, nor his conclusions. The whole charade stank of a disinformation campaign. But, oops, there I go spoiling the flow of a good story with irritating facts. Wash my mouth.

In any event, this line of attack by Jake Bush, suggesting that Saddam presented a valid target because of his alleged links to Al Qaeda, produced zero response from anyone. Except for Elwood Blair, who applauded loudly from the balcony.

So, Jake gave the old PR machine another big crank, and tried a different approach: Saddam's WMDs were still a threat. And the world community ought to remove both. Immediately. Warnings that were met by that same world community with a deafening silence and a roar of yawns. After all, Saddam had had those same offending weapons for some four years, without anyone trying to rein him in, and he'd proven to be about as intimidating as a Dan Quayle spelling test.

And so began the Jake and Elwood Ballet. In earnest. Or would that be: *Ernest Goes to War*? First Jake and then Elwood produced intelligence reports, declaring Saddam's WMDs to be an 'immediate' threat to world peace. Huh? You what? Where did all this suddenly come from? Ah ha. US Intelligence had it on good authority that Saddam had been trying to buy Uranium from Niger. And British Intelligence had it on good authority that Saddam's WMDs could be launched within 45 minutes.

Now, while the rest of us were trying to find Niger on a map, or were attempting calmly to point out that the WMDs would likely only be launched against US and UK forces that had no business in the Middle East anyway, Jake sent 'Cab Calloway' Powell to the UN to argue for an appropriately harsh Resolution.

Well, Cab put on a pretty good dog and pony show. Jake didn't get quite the tough Resolution that he wanted, but it did demand that Saddam let the Inspectors back in, and it did threaten action if he did not. The point is that this sort of Resolution is like passing a Council Motion in support of the Girl Scouts, and threatening 'action' if you don't buy their cookies. No one meant anything by it. They just wanted Cab and Jake to go away.

But Cab and Jake and Elwood had learned their lesson from the masters – and mistresses – of the Eighties. Margaret Thatcher showed how to play the UN with the Falklands War.

In 1982, Argentina had invaded the Falklands, a small group of islands off its eastern coast, and to which both Great Britain and Argentina laid claim. Thatcher grabbed her handbag, and headed off to the UN. There she screamed at the assembled diplomats until they passed a Resolution.

Of course the Resolution condemned the invasion. We all condemn burglary, too. And, of course, the same Resolution called for 'action.' By which the UN meant, 'come back and talk to us about that action at a later date.'

But that wasn't what the Resolution explicitly stated. And so, without ever returning to the UN, Thatcher used the first Resolution as validity for her unilateral action to take back the Falklands for Great Britain. And Reagan and Poppy Bush used the same precedent for their own, um, 'bush wars' – damn, I'm a scream, eh? And now, their successors, Jake Bush and Elwood Blair would use the same rationale to invade Iraq.

For reasons best known to himself, if, indeed he had no more WMD war machine, Saddam stayed mum, refused to let the Inspectors back in, and Jake and Elwood prepared for unilateral war. I'm sorry. I misspoke. They were joined in their coalition by the massed ranks of the 3rd Artillery Regiment of the Duchy of Liechtenstein, and the 7th Catering Corps of the former Soviet Republic of Kickthekhan.

Blair made much of the fact that, even as a New Labour politician, he felt compelled to join with a US President, whose politics made Genghis Khan look like a Field Researcher for the National Geographic Society, because the world would be a safer place without Saddam as Iraq Leader. It would also be a safer place with Barney the Dinosaur as UN Secretary-General, but I wouldn't find myself supporting such a nomination.

I couldn't help but feel pity for a man I was sure was nothing more than a creature of his own military and intelligence services. A man who had danced with the devil of his own arms industry. And a man who could do no less now than kow-tow to a US President, who through his father, knew where all of the British skeletons from the Eighties and the Nineties were hidden.

And yet, the pity was short-lived. Blair had done nothing to expose those skeletons. Nor to stop the corruption behind them. Rather he had done his own 'dirty deal,' allowing the corruption to continue, in order to appease his own ambition, and write his own ticket to a place in the British history books. The price for which would be the continuing two-step with his

Dead Men Don't Eat Lunch

Transatlantic partner. Besides, the First Gulf War had taken place over a decade before. Britain needed another meaty war to showcase its military hardware.

Credit should be given where credit is due. Neither Jake nor Elwood, nor even Cab, nor Dick 'The Colonel' Cheney, nor Donald 'Duck' Rumsfeld, ever claimed that the intelligence reports that Jake and Elwood paraded before the media in the summer of 2002, were the last word on Saddam's WMD capability. Which, of course, they were not. And this was something of which all those who had been paying attention were well aware.

But the world's media suffers from perennial ADD, and so they did take those intelligence reports as the first and the last word. As may well have been the precise intention of Jake and Elwood. Blind the children with lights and fireworks. Or was that with 'shock and awe'?

Iraq was occupied in a military campaign, the speed and mastery of which had not been seen since the likes of the Six-Day War in 1967. The Americans were in Baghdad. Saddam was on the run. And I was sharpening my pencil, ready to rattle off letters to the appropriate military officer, asking for photographs of the SCUD-B missiles, with their GEC (UK) Royal Appointment logo's shining brightly, for all to see. Hallelujah. Pass the bread rolls. It's a brand new day.

But what was this? Jake and Elwood needed to set up something called the 'Iraq Survey Group.' Made up of about 1,600 intelligence agents. To scour the countryside to find the offending WMD Machine. To find...to scour...you what? What on earth needed 'looking for'? Everyone knew where the WMDs were. Didn't they?

US Intelligence had had monitoring cameras in place for a decade. What they hadn't been able to see on land cameras, they'd been able to find with all those spy satellites cluttering outer space.

If that didn't satisfy them, they could grab a couple of the UNSCOM reports. Or one or two of those books from the Eighties. And get to reading them. I wanted to write to the new Chairman of the Survey Group and offer to let him borrow my copies. They were the Deluxe Editions. With the colored maps. Freely available on Amazon.com.

Hang on, I thought, don't go anywhere. Look, I said to no-one in particular, I have here in my hand a copy of an e-mail from Jonathan Powell, Elwood's Chief of Staff, that clearly mentions one of the sites that needs to be destroyed. He seems to know where to find the WMDs. Put him in charge of the Survey Group. What gives?

What gave was that 20 months later, the Iraq Survey Group reported that, um, there were no WMDs. Oh come on. I was waiting for the world's media to fall about laughing. I expected press conferences where journalists, rendered weak from hysteria, would struggle to hold up placards saying, 'then prove it to us by showing us the empty sites.'

The irony was that Jonathan Powell had raised in his e-mail the very possibility that Saddam might have pulled a fast one, along just those lines, precisely to thwart America and Britain's military intentions.

Powell had warned Elwood to beware Saddam quickly destroying one of the 'known' sites, and then inviting the world's media to take photographs, in a charade to convince the UN that he had no WMDs.

So why didn't Powell advise Elwood to ask the international press to do just that now? If indeed it was the case that Saddam had destroyed all of his WMDs before the invasion?

I didn't have the answer to that question. But, what I did know was that there were no media visits. And no photographs. Nothing. Not one photograph of one site. Not one photograph of one former laboratory. Not one photograph of one destroyed chemical dump. Not one single solitary dickey bird. Zip. Zero. Zilch.

As with Iran-Contra in 1986, the international press simply rolled over and allowed the US and the UK very firmly to embed rather sharp instruments in the small places of their bodies where the sun didn't care to shine.

Jake and Elwood used the 20 months to make the WMDs disappear. Why? Because they had read the books. They had read the UNSCOM reports. And they knew of the extent to which those same WMDs were constructed from western content. A fact that Jake and Elwood knew they would not have been able to hide, and which they deemed to be too embarrassing to have revealed. So, they made the WMDs disappear, instead.

And the world's press stood aside and let them do it, without a murmur. The sad thing is the media did worse than simply act the patsy. They openly connived in the ensuing disinformation game played by Jake and Elwood, and helped along by the likes of Scott Ritter.

The Blues Brothers had gone to great pains to parade those intelligence reports the previous summer, and to highlight the more extreme of the claims they contained. That PR job would now pay off. For the world's media 'suddenly' discovered that those claims were, in fact, erroneous. Which had been the whole point. They had been deliberate plants.

Jake and Elwood had known that the world would need a show to distract it from the fact that the WMDs had mysteriously disappeared. There are no greater manipulators of the press than Jake and Elwood. They understood that newspapers needed headlines, and if they didn't want the headlines to be about the WMDs, then they knew the headlines would have to be about erroneous intelligence. And also knowing the press to be a bit stupid, they would have to make the 'errors' obvious.

The problem was that there were two individuals, one on either side of the Atlantic, who would not play ball. The ridiculous Niger claim was, at

Dead Men Don't Eat Lunch

first, attributed to a roving US Ambassador. Until the Ambassador broke ranks, and declared that he'd never said any such thing about Niger.

Oops, can't have the ruse exposed. So Jake hit back at the Ambassador by threatening his wife. Which was easily done, because she was a senior and active CIA officer, and Jake simply had one of his staff slip her name to a tame right-wing journalist with CNN. Big mistake. Exposing a CIA officer is a crime. That's going to hurt someone.

Of course, at the time of writing this book, we're not sure who it's going to hurt. Because we're still not clear who did the 'slipping.' Whether it was, in fact, a staff member. One, by the name of Libby, has already bit the bullet, hit the dust, taken one for the Gipper. In any event, done something that is the Washington equivalent of going on a duck-shoot in Texas with 'The Colonel.'

However, we the channel surfing, blog-reading public are not convinced by this self-serving sacrifice of Libby's. The trail appears to lead beyond him, possibly to 'the Colonel,' Karl the Roving Gay, or even to Jake himself. The investigation is still in progress as I write.

But while we watch and wait, it's the Nixon Musical Chairs Game, all over again. Whoever is still standing, when the media music stops, will get the big KO. Or some party-time with Big Bull Bubba, down at the Maryland State Pen.

In the meantime, a charade of much the same nature was unfolding in Great Britain. But this time, with more tragic consequences. The Senior British Government scientist, David Kelly, who had been requested to co-author the Final UNSCOM Report on Iraq's Biological Weapons Program, back in 1999, was well aware that Iraq still remained a threat.

His writings and speeches of the time made it quite clear that he was strongly in favor of removing Saddam, in this very regard. Although, unlike his political masters, Kelly restricted himself to warning that Saddam would continue to be a threat, more because of his desire actively to pursue his Biological agenda, rather than any trumped-up 45 minute launching capability.

What happened after that is a little hazy. And remains confused, even after a year long Judicial Inquiry, headed up by respected Judge, Lord Hutton. What is known is that Kelly spoke to a BBC reporter called Gilligan. That reporter then revealed that he had a source who said that Elwood's intelligence report, the one with the 45 minute warning, had been "sexed up.' And, shortly afterwards, Kelly turned up dead, in a beauty spot, near his home in the English countryside.

The death was particularly shocking for me because it bore so many similarities to Hugh's alleged suicide. Not least because I believe that the underlying issue behind both men's deaths was their knowledge of the western content of WMDs in Iraq.

As with the death of the Princess of Wales, I know nothing other than what I have read, but I can posit. And I do so. On this occasion with especial care. For, I have some experience of a family grieving a loss, grief made all the more poignant, because, as with Kelly, that family remains clueless as to why their loved one turned up dead.

What is now generally acknowledged is that, as with Jake, Elwood and his advisers were pretty much immediately aware of the source of Gilligan's story. And as with the American Ambassador and his wife, Kelly was hung out to dry. His name was slipped to the media.

With Kelly, however, there was one big difference. Having signed the Official Secrets Act, he had to be careful what he said, because he could be prosecuted by the Government for revealing anything they cared to define as a state secret. The American Ambassador and his wife, on the other hand, could not be prosecuted. Indeed, they were in the fortunate position of being the ones able to threaten prosecution.

As I say, I do not know exactly what happened with Kelly. No one does. But I wonder. Kelly knew that Iraq had a viable Biological Weapons program. He knew it was extremely unlikely that Saddam had destroyed it on his own. Perhaps, like me, Kelly was merely waiting for the Iraq Survey Group to reveal either the component parts of the remaining program, or evidence of their destruction. Then, nothing happened. And he smelled a rat. He may well have guessed, like me, that the reason behind the silence was the attempt to hide the western content of Iraq's WMDs.

Having signed the Official Secrets Act, Kelly couldn't do anything overt. But maybe he felt strongly enough to try to do something clandestine? Maybe he thought Gilligan, unlike his American Television namesake, had the smarts to understand a subtle approach. If Kelly made any mistake, it was assuming that Gilligan had smarts. He didn't. He was simply another tabloid bottom-feeder, dressed up in the fancy glad rags of the BBC.

I'm guessing that Kelly may have recognized the manner in which Jake and Elwood had deliberately seeded their respective intelligence reports with disinformation so obvious that even the media would pick it up, and run with it once the WMDs were not forthcoming.

Perhaps this is what Kelly meant when he pointed out to Gilligan that Elwood's report was "sexed up"? Perhaps he was overstating the case, with highly colorful language, in the hope that Gilligan would take it that one step further, and ask himself if there was a reason for the report to be so sexed up in this fashion. As in, it was a deliberate plant.

I was reminded of my own session in Florida, with Mark, when I had begged him to see beyond the immediate and obvious sensational 'value' of what he possessed, and start asking himself why he was in possession of such inflammatory documentation. I'm guessing that Gilligan displayed as much subtlety as Mark, bless his heart. As a result, Gilligan missed the point, and merely ran with the "sexed up" language.

Once Elwood had caused Kelly's name to be released to the press, Kelly was in an impossible situation. He had already been told by his supervisors that he would be neither reprimanded nor prosecuted for his initial meeting with Gilligan, even though it breached the Official Secrets Act. But the unspoken threat was that, unless he now toed the line, he would face disciplinary action, of one sort or another. That much became clear during the Hutton Inquiry.

The problem was that this was not simply an intellectual or ethical test of loyalty for Kelly. He did not have the option of lying low, and keeping his mouth shut. As a consequence of Elwood exposing him, Kelly had been sub-poenaed to appear before several Parliamentary Committees, where he would have to give evidence under oath. And there was the inescapable conundrum. Did he opt for prosecution, under the Official Secrets Act, for telling the truth; or face possible prosecution for lying under oath?

Everything that we have learned of Kelly tells us that he was a man of conviction and conscience. He was also a man of incredible but quiet courage. Those who claim that Kelly committed suicide out of shame should themselves feel deeply ashamed. This was a man who had faced down the trained thugs of a murderous dictator. With nothing more offensive than his disheveled British charm.

I believe that Kelly was a man who did not worry for himself about the prospect of a trial or prison, but who wished, at all costs, to save his family this embarrassment and ignominy. I have no reason to believe other than that he died at his own hand. But that he did so, in silence and with honor, to protect the good name of his family.

I do not for one moment pretend that Hugh's life was a model of decency and good works alone. Clearly, Hugh was involved with something unseemly. And he may have made his own predicament worse by his less than honorable conduct while still alive.

Yet, at the end, I believe that Hugh perceived that things had become so bad that his families had come under threat. And in that regard, I believe that, in his final moments, Hugh re-discovered his honor, and chose death, in silence, in order to protect his family from those threats.

And in those regards, I draw a parallel between the deaths of David Kelly and Hugh Simmonds. If nothing else, their deaths highlight for ordinary people the very human face of scandal.

I don't pretend to make any great claims for this book. I do believe that Margaret Thatcher suborned British society. She turned her country into one vast military-industrial complex, and made it a whipping boy for all the forces of terror in the world. Thatcher may well have done this feeling it was the only way to save a bankrupt nation. She may have done it to achieve

Reggie's "higher purpose." But at what price did she sell a nation's soul?

I believe that John Major tried to turn back the tide, but was overthrown in what was, to all intents and purposes, a very modern and very British coup d'etat. Tony Blair, on the other hand, couldn't wait to strip down and wade out into the trough of corruption, so great was his desire to become, and then to remain, Prime Minister of Great Britain.

I believe that Hugh, whether for selfish reasons, or for his own "higher purpose," made available his 'special' talents, to ensure that the notion of Great Britain Ltd., the military-industrial complex, became firmly embedded in the Establishment of his homeland, before he too was 'cleaned away.'

I have set out in this book my reasons for believing all of this. But, I do not necessarily pretend that I have set out all of the proof. I do not claim that this book is the definitive expose of all of the issues that it addresses. And I have not attempted to make it so.

Rather, I have limited myself to chronicling my adventures, and to sharing my personal experiences. Others may have more momentous things to say about the matters touched on in this book. I am more interested in touching the heart with the human story that lies behind a newspaper headline; to show the human face of what I believe will become Great Britain's defining scandal.

I wish David Kelly's family well. I hope that they may find the justice that I seek for the Simmonds Family with this book. And I hope that my 'friends' in Government, who may have revealed themselves to me, however briefly and subtly, will use their best endeavors to ensure that the truth that both gentlemen bore to their graves will eventually come out.

Even better, I would hope that, one day, the British and American Governments might themselves develop sufficient of a conscience to 'come clean.' However, that is highly unlikely. Not so much because they are wholly without morals. But rather because I believe that they may genuinely feel that they have a secret to hide that overrides in importance all other considerations, including the truth about Saddam's WMDs, and concerns over the death of two individuals linked, in their different ways, with those WMDs.

I believe that history will show that Bush and Blair did not go to war in the Middle East simply to depose a dictator, or to preserve a pipeline of oil, or even to hide the fact that their countries were the ones which supplied Saddam with his WMDs in the first place. No. I believe that Reggie was right when he spoke of a "higher purpose." And I believe that purpose is what ultimately will connect this story to the Priory of Sion. Speaking of which, what of the Priory of Sion?

Dead Men Don't Eat Lunch

Chapter 32

I NO LONGER believed in 'co-incidence.' I believed in God and destiny. And I was destined to find myself on the Louisiana Delta, in the middle of that cold and forbidding winter's night.

For a variety of unconnected reasons, I had decided to up sticks from North Georgia, and make the 1000-mile journey to Dallas, Texas. I had grown tired of mile after mile of piney woods and swamp as my companion scenery, and on a 'whim' had veered south towards the Gulf Coast.

Almost as soon as I hit the Delta, I was overwhelmed by a feeling of peace, that warmed the entirety of my body and soul. I have always been a friend of the night, the shadows my comfort and my support. The velvet darkness always helps to smooth the tortured contours within me. But I sensed it was more than that.

I sped along the flat highway, aware only vaguely of the grotesque shapes of the Bayou trees whipping past. The dripping moss lit up like a Mummy's ghostly rags, in the bright glow of the huge full moon.

Far off in the distance, I spied the spectral outline of oil refineries, their towers and turrets giving the impression of so many mystical castles, standing guard over the landscape; dragon's breath spewing skywards in warning to all who would bring danger.

I stopped at a much less ancient Wal-Mart to rest for the remainder of the night. In the morning, I awoke to find that, without any input from me, life had taken on a slower pace. The sun rose gently in the crisp morning air. A flock of large birds swept gracefully southwards. While a slightly putrid but not unpleasant smell hung static in the barely-moving air.

A rusty iron bridge rose before me on the highway, and within moments, I had my first glimpse of the mighty Mississippi. Huge, slow and graceful, its majesty dominated the landscape. It was easy to see how the Delta drew its life force and lifestyle from the enormous, meandering inevitability that was the 'Father of all Rivers.'

I glanced down at the small wharf, with its battered shrimping boats, and the grand, clapboard historic district behind. All was graceful decadence. As if man realized there were more important things than trying to stem the onward march of time. Houses, roads, even the Bayou trees, had their pre-ordained lifespan, and when the time came, they gently toppled over. To be replaced. When nature found the time.

A nod and a wink later, and I was on Esplanade Street, just off the French Quarter in New Orleans. All was hustle and bustle, in preparation for the festivities. It was All Hallow's Eve.

I parked the car and went for a stroll. Aimlessly. The streets were narrower than I had pictured them. Uneven, and twisting, the modern asphalt barely able to contain the old cobbles beneath. And the memories they held of all those footsteps. Of pirates and swashbucklers; voodoo queens, and hot, sultry evenings of spicy rum, and endless love. Of magic and romance. And mystery and intrigue. From the early days of Jean Lafitte and Lafayette, to the more recent exploits described by Oliver Stone in his controversial epic, *JFK*.

Tiny, dark courtyards, with shuttered windows. The occasional skeletal tree framing the famous wrought iron balconies. Peeling paint, and ancient stucco. Dust motes dancing above sun-dappled pavements. Shouting and laughing. The tangy aroma of garlic mixing with the sweet smoke of incense. Until I found myself gazing at the trinkets and souvenirs in the voodoo gift shop I had entered without noticing. I was face to face with yet another, but this time more exotic, example of Christian ritual superimposed on Pagan theology.

***

Santeria, for that is the proper name for voodoo, was brought over with the first black slaves, from West Africa. They believed in the existence of one supreme God, below which there were Spirits or Loa, who ruled over the world's affairs in matter of family, love, happiness, justice, health, wealth, work, the harvest and the hunt. The Loa also manifested through elements of nature such as the wind and rain, lightning and thunder; the river, the ocean, springs and lakes, the sky, the sun, certain animals, trees and stones.

Upon their arrival in the West Indies and the New World, the slaves found themselves unable to continue the practice of their ancestral rites, sometimes under penalty of death. But they quickly understood the essential similarities between their beliefs and those of the Catholics; the Catholics praying to their Saints to intercede to a higher God in their favor.

Dead Men Don't Eat Lunch

The slaves saw that criterion used to "make a Saint" was the ability to obtain miracles. And so, a substitution took place: the Loa often taking the name and some of the attributes of the Saints. The elaborate ceremonies and costumes of the church also had great appeal for the West Africans. The slaves and their descendants may not have seen it so much as a direct substitution, than as an added path of expression for their deep-seated faith and beliefs. [Many thanks to neworleansvoodoocrossroads.com.]

Which got me thinking. Once again. The adherents of Santeria, which at its base is now merely another 'version' of Christianity, mean no harm to anyone. Forget all the Hollywood nonsense about evil charms, and voodoo dolls. It is a simple nature-based Pagan religion, with Christian overlay. Its followers are more interested in preserving the delicate environment of the Delta than they are in bringing fire and brimstone into anyone's future.

The beliefs of the Priory of Sion are, at their root, also another 'version' of Christianity. Reggie made no secret of the fact that he was deeply spiritual, and held to the concept of religious beliefs requiring an element of witness through good works. So why the big fuss over *The Da Vinci Code*?

If the theology is actually 'wrong,' or the interpretation of this Gnostic Gospel, or that tract of ancient Aramaic text, then let the scholars sort that out. None of it changes the fact that the Priory itself is a very real entity, which is as ancient as the Roman Church itself. And it's pretty much here to stay.

So the '1,000 year war'? I can not seriously believe that there is any 'version' of Christianity which seriously propounds the view today that any God or any prophet supports violence of killing. And all 'versions' of Christianity, from the Roman to the Protestant to that of the Priory of Sion, have in their past enough history of horrors perpetrated in their name to keep their leaders in the confessional for the best part of the next two centuries. None is without shame.

I don't get it. And while we're on the subject, I don't understand why any religion, and in particular, Christianity, in all its 'version,' feels that it can proclaim to have the monopoly on the pathway to heaven.

Isn't it enough that 'good people,' of any religious persuasion, strive to have a higher vision for themselves? And a higher opinion of others? That they want to treat the world in which they live, and the other people living in it, with dignity? To want to fill a part of each day with good works? If that requires an organized religion to guide them, then fine? But is it right for this religion constantly to knock that belief system, to prove what?

A belief system is created when someone wants to understand, and they devise for themselves (or adopt someone else's) structure of viewpoint that helps them to find the answer to the question: why? Most of that belief boils down to 'faith' and 'trust.' And some of it is evidenced by the performance of 'miracles,' however minor or major.

For myself, I believe that these miracles come from within each of us. That by communing through our 'inner wizard' with the greater God that is all around us, we 'will' the miracles to occur. But you don't have to agree with me, to make the decision not to disrespect my views.

I am minded of a bumper sticker that I saw after the contentious US Presidential Election of 2004, one in which the theme of religion rang clear, if somewhat distorted, from the opening bell, to the last vote cast. It said: "God is too big for any one country or religion or Party."

For myself, I am content to respect anyone with deeply held views, who strives to use them to a good end. I have little interest in the origins of this theology or that belief system. I am much more fascinated by the psychology of conspiracy that infuses the creation and continued existence of bodies as ancient and as secretive as, say, the Roman Catholic Church, or, more to the immediate point, the Priory of Sion. Which neatly brings me full circle.

***

I didn't set out on November 15th, 1988 to discover the conspiracy to end all conspiracies. I just wanted to find out what had happened to my friend, so that his children might know. The irony is that I may have stumbled across the mother of all interconnected conspiracies: the proverbial riddle within the puzzle.

And yet, with all that I have unearthed, I still do not appear to have straightforward answers to the seemingly-simple questions that began my quest: why did Hugh take his Clients' money; why did he then turn up dead; and did he or did he not take his own life?

Are there lessons to be learned? While I have a natural aversion for adventure stories, which tend towards the pompous at their conclusion, with trite homilies of moral intent, I would say there a re a couple of lessons to bear in mind for the future.

First, the answer to finding a scandal that hasn't yet been revealed is to follow the money trail from one that has already been exposed. Players and networks do not wither away: they just find new 'games' to play.

Secondly, you should never accept things at face value; you should never believe what you are told second-hand. You can only trust what you have experienced first-hand. And if something doesn't make sense, then it probably isn't true. If that bothers you, then ask questions, until it does make sense. If it doesn't bother you, then just enjoy the sunshine. I am.

So, should you believe everything I've told you? That's for you to

Dead Men Don't Eat Lunch

decide. I will tell you this much: I have deliberately not connected all the clues in this story. I've left you to do that. So, go back and re-read what you have missed. And check it out for yourself. Remember, there is still anything between $45 million and $150 million sitting out there, waiting to be recovered. Follow the trail. The leads are there. Do I know where the money is? Now, why should I? After all I'm just an ordinary guy. Aren't I?

Do I believe everything I've been told? Same principle. Take the Priory of Sion, as a case in point. What do I believe? Well, I too was taught to be cautious. And therefore, I will say only this – at least, for the present: *The Da Vinci Code* is a fictional story. *Holy Blood, Holy Grail* is a conspiracy theory. But the Priory of Sion is real. I crossed swords with them. And I have good reason to believe that they have good reason to believe what they believe. Beyond that...?

Reggie told me that Hugh missed the Big Picture because he didn't know about Freemasonry. Yet, I know, from first-hand experience, that Hugh was intimately familiar with the various handshakes of some very senior Fraternal Orders of Freemasonry. And on the day Hugh died, Maggi discovered in Hugh's desk a crystal ball, and two very worn packs of Tarot Cards.

Maybe Hugh knew more than he let on? Maybe he let on more than he knew? Maybe I know more than I'm letting on? Then again, maybe not? After all. I'm just an ordinary guy. Or, am I...?

Geoffrey Gilson

Epilogue I

IT IS NOW November of 2005, exactly 17 years after the mysterious death of Hugh John Simmonds, CBE. David Cameron has been elected to the Leadership of the British Conservative Party. All the talk is of his far-reaching plans to 'modernize' the Party. Already, the Tories are slipping ahead of Tony Blair in the opinion polls. The good money is on the Boy David to beat Gordon Brown in the General Election of 2009, ending 12 years of electoral wilderness for the oldest political organization in the world.

Cameron, who, in an odd twist of irony, looks a lot like Hugh, but without spectacles, has just finished making the new appointments to his Shadow Cabinet and to the top ranks of the Conservative political organization. Those appointments do not speak well for the future of the Tories, or for the United Kingdom.

Lord Ashcroft is back as Deputy Chairman of the Party. I still believe him to be the 'keeper of the key' to the money illegally raised from arms deals and the like in the Eighties and the Nineties.

Alan Duncan, successor to Jonathan Aitken as the Saudi Royal Family's arms bagman in the UK, is in line to become the new Trade and Industry Secretary. In that position, Duncan will oversee the Export Credit Guarantee Program, which was plundered so heavily by the Tories last time round, in order to finance the illicit arms deals that transformed Great Britain into the world's Number 2 arms exporter.

Two of the future junior Ministers at the Ministry of Defense are a couple of old hands from the extreme right-wing of the Party, which was responsible for so much of the UK's illegal arms shenanigans in the Eighties and Nineties.

First, we find our old friend Gerald Howarth, now parading as the 'respectable' Member of Parliament for Aldershot, home to one of England's most prestigious army bases. He is accompanied by Dr. Julian Lewis, who used to be the Party's PsyOps expert in its Research Department, in which capacity he regularly fenced with my friend, the late Simon Regan. Lewis is a particularly nasty piece of work, who led the efforts to dish the dirt on opposition politicians in the Eighties, while using his considerable skills also to deflect media attention away from the illegal money-laundering activities transpiring within Conservative Central Office.

Zac Goldsmith, playboy Editor of *The Ecologist*, and multi-millionaire scion of deceased billionaire arms dealer and would-be Conservative Party 'proprietor,' Sir James Goldsmith, has apparently been seduced sufficiently by the Boy David's charms, that he has agreed to become the Tory Party's new high-profile Adviser on all matters Environmental. Or do I have that seduction the wrong way round?

The Sunday Times is reporting that another old friend of ours, Wafic Said, arms commission pimp for the Tories, is once again helping to fund the Conservative Party. Said has found a way around restrictions on donations by foreigners. He's getting his wife to make enormous bids at Conservative auctions. In this way, Said has already managed to slip the Tories about £500,000 since 2004, including £100,000 since David Cameron became Leader (just leaping ahead for a second, into the year 2006).

The bottom line is this: whatever else the Boy David may be claiming to 'modernize,' it is obvious that it has been made clear to him that he will not be interfering with the long-held Tory plans to revive the illicit arms-dealing and associated fund-raising activities from the Eighties and Nineties.

The next General Election (2009) will see a new generation of voters born after Margaret Thatcher's departure from power in 1990. David Cameron can insist that he is not "the prisoner of an ideological past," but the evidence suggests that, however good his intentions may be, he will continue to be the prisoner of a corrupt past. And now, of a mortgaged future.

The Boy David met his Goliath. And Goliath won. The return of Conservative Government will be a reprise of "Back to the Future." The *Savoy Mafia* will live again. It would seem that the Goldsmith/Ashcroft Plan for the Conservative Party, revealed to me by Kevin Cahill in Chapter 27, is still very much alive and on track.

Plus ca change...always, *plus ca change*...

On which subject, I wonder who will be the Boy David's new dirty tricks 'doorman'...?

Geoffrey Gilson

Epilogue II

JUST WHEN I think I may be over-reaching myself – heaven forbid the thought – I come across the following article in *The Sunday Times* of November 19th, 2006:

The Sunday Times
Sunday, 19 November 2006

Blair hit by Saudi 'bribery' threat
David Leppard

SAUDI ARABIA is threatening to suspend diplomatic ties with Britain unless Downing Street intervenes to block an investigation into a £60m "slush fund" allegedly set up for some members of its royal family.

A senior Saudi diplomat in London has delivered an ultimatum to Tony Blair that unless the inquiry into an allegedly corrupt defence deal is dropped, diplomatic links between Britain and Saudi Arabia will be severed, a defence source has disclosed.

The Saudis, key allies in the Middle East, have also threatened to cut intelligence co-operation with Britain over Al-Qaeda.

They have repeated their threat that they will terminate payments on a defence contract that could be worth £40 billion and safeguard at least 10,000 British jobs.

The Saudis are furious about the criminal investigation by the Serious Fraud Office (SFO) into allegations that BAE Systems, Britain's biggest defence company, set up the "slush fund" to support the extravagant lifestyle of members of the Saudi royal family.

The payments, in the form of lavish holidays, a fleet of luxury cars including a gold Rolls-Royce, rented apartments and other perks, are

Dead Men Don't Eat Lunch

alleged
to have been paid to ensure the Saudis continued to buy from BAE under the so-called 'Al-Yamamah' deal, rather than going to another country. 'Al-Yamamah' is the biggest defence contract in British history and has kept BAE in business for 20 years.

At least five people have been arrested in the probe. They include Peter Wilson, BAe's managing director of international programmes, and Tony Winship, a former company official who oversaw two travel and service firms that are alleged to have been conduits for the payments. Both deny any wrongdoing.

The Saudi threat was made in September after the royal family became alarmed at the latest turn in the fraud inquiry. Sources close to the investigation say the Saudis "hit the roof" after discovering that SFO lawyers had persuaded a magistrate in Switzerland to force disclosure about a series of confidential Swiss bank accounts.

The sources said the accounts relate to substantial payments between "third party" offshore companies that may have received large sums in previously undisclosed "commissions". Fraud office sources say they are now trying to get more documents that will tell them who benefited from the accounts. The trail is said to lead to the Saudi capital Riyadh.

The Saudis learnt of this development only when they were contacted by the Swiss banks in the late summer. "They hit the roof," said a source close to the investigation.

The Saudi royal family, which effectively controls the government, instructed a senior diplomat, said to be Prince Mohammed bin Nawaf, its London ambassador, to visit Downing Street. He held a meeting with Jonathan Powell, Blair's chief of staff, according to the sources.

The diplomat is said to have delivered a 12-page letter drawn up by a Saudi law firm demanding a detailed explanation of why the investigation was still continuing.

The Saudis had been given the impression during a meeting with Blair in July last year that the inquiry would be stopped, say the sources.

"The Saudis are claiming in this letter that the British government has broken its undertaking to keep details of the 'Al-Yamamah' deal confidential," said a source who has read the document.

"It regards the disclosure of these documents to the SFO from Switzerland, and from the Ministry of Defence, as a totally unacceptable breach of that undertaking. They are claiming the deal is protected by sovereign national immunity and that the British have no right to poke around in their private financial affairs.

"It is a really infuriated letter demanding a full and open explanation, pending which the 'Al-Yamamah' contract is suspended and all payments would stop."

Geoffrey Gilson

A defence official said that the preliminary contract, signed last August, to sell the first 24 of 72 promised Typhoons, better known as Eurofighters, was then temporarily suspended. That contract alone is said to be worth £11 billion and would safeguard 9,000 jobs at the Eurofighter's UK headquarters in Warton, Lancashire, for the next decade.

Downing Street is said to have persuaded the Saudis to reverse for the time being their decision to suspend the Typhoon payments. However, the Saudis made clear they would carry out their threats unless the demands in their letter were met.

During the meeting with Powell the Saudi diplomat is said to have issued a threat to sever all diplomatic and intelligence ties. Such a move would be damaging for Britain's strategic interests in the volatile region.

It would involve the Saudis withdrawing their ambassador to London, and the British ambassador in Riyadh would be sent home. Direct communications between the two countries on political, economic and security issues would have to be conducted through a third country.

"It was the Swiss stuff that sent the Saudis over the top. The threat to cut off diplomatic and intelligence ties was a very real one," said the defence official.

The row will put renewed pressure on Lord Goldsmith, the attorney general, to intervene. Earlier this year Goldsmith, who is the "superintending" minister for the SFO, was ongoing investigations."

'Al-Yamamah,' meaning "the Dove" in Arabic, has kept BAE in business for 20 years. It was signed in 1985 when Britain agreed to sell 72 asked to determine whether its inquiry was "in the public interest". That request followed earlier Saudi pressure on the Ministry of Defence.

A spokesman for Goldsmith said: "We do not comment on Tornados and 30 Hawks to Saudi Arabia.

The deal was renewed in 1993 when the Saudis agreed to buy another 48 Tornado warplanes. In a third stage of the contract signed last year, Britain is selling up to 72 more planes, the Typhoons.

A Downing Street spokesman said: "We don't speak about ongoing investigations and we don't speak about discussions with other countries."

***

Now, there is a mischievous part of me that says that this article is too obvious to require comment. But hey, let me earn my keep. And so...

There can be no doubt now that all of the corrupt slush activity that accompanied *Al Yamamah* under Tory rule has continued under New Labour. Since the Tory slush activity involved the Conservative Party itself and senior Conservative politicians receiving substantial kickbacks, there can be little reason to believe that the same has not been true with New

Labour. And this, in turn, only increases the possibility that the whole sorry mess will be revived by The Boy David when he returns to power with Michael, Alan, Gerald and Julian in tow.

At the same time, it is interesting to note that the Saudi Royal Family has become no less sensitive when it comes to having people expose the manner in which they amass wealth from their questionable arms activities. You will remember that the last time someone threatened to expose those same activities, their son turned up dead – along with the son's girlfriend, the Princess of Wales.

For more information about ongoing revelations about Tory Arms Corruption – and New Labour Arms Corruption – begin with the following:

http://www.timesonline.co.uk/article/0,,2092-2483551.html
http://news.bbc.co.uk/2/hi/business/3712770.stm
http://www.bbc.co.uk/pressoffice/pressreleases/stories/2004/10_october/04/money.shtml
http://www.bbc.co.uk/pressoffice/pressreleases/stories/2006/06_june/16/saudi.shtml

Oh, and by the way, I sent a letter to The Boy David before his first turn as Leader of the Conservative Party at the Annual Conservative Conference in October 2006. The letter called on David to take responsibility for past Tory Arms Corruption; come clean about the allegations in this book; and promise to prevent future Tory Arms Corruption, not least by sacking the aforementioned Michael, Alan, Gerald and Julian.

Lo and behold, David posted my letter on his new videoblog, *Webcameron* (http://www.webcameron.org.uk/blogs/377#comments). Hmm. Guilty conscience, or genuine call to arms? I think the answer to that question depends on how ultimately he responds to my challenges – be it in writing to me personally, or by the way he behaves once he becomes Prime Minister.

***

You know I could have left it right there. But, I'm really an even-handed guy. The brain got nagging again. Maybe, I'm being too hard on Tony? There's just a chance he didn't know that all this arms corruption was going on during his watch. He had so much other stuff on his plate: ruining a perfectly good country; starting a couple of wars…oops, wash my mouth. It's not as if his Government was responsible for negotiating *Al Yamamah*…right?

Wrong. New Labour may have had nothing to do with *Al Yamamah I* and *II*. But they are the ones who set up *Al Yamamah III*, the negotiations for which began in 2005 – that's what *The Sunday Times* article is all about.

Geoffrey Gilson

Ok. But we'll probably find that the New Labour Minister for Defence Procurement (remember, that means 'Arms Sales'), and the one responsible for establishing the structure of *Al Yamamah III*, was a charming, matronly, do-gooder from Nether-Wopping, who wouldn't know financial wrong-doing from a dropped stitch, bless her heart. So, let's have a look. And what do I find? Another *Sunday Times* article:

The Sunday Times
Sunday, 15 May 2005

Minister put millions in tax haven
Robert Winnett

A MULTI-MILLIONAIRE businessman who became a Labour minister last week has admitted holding part of his personal fortune in an offshore tax haven that experts say could have helped him avoid £3m in tax.

Lord Drayson, the new Minister for Defence Procurement, established offshore trusts and companies in the Isle of Man that handled £30m he raised from the sale of his pharmaceuticals business. Experts say such arrangements are normally set up to avoid tax.

His actions, disclosed after inquiries by The Sunday Times, will embarrass the government, which has repeatedly sought to stop wealthy Britons avoiding tax by moving fortunes offshore.

He closed his offshore companies on March 8 this year — the week before Gordon Brown, the chancellor, introduced new laws to restrict British residents' use of tax havens.

Last week financial experts said a scheme such as Drayson's could have saved millions in tax. His decision to put the companies into liquidation in March is described as "immaculate timing".

Yesterday, Drayson admitted holding "financial interests" offshore but said he brought his money back to Britain in the autumn.

Following an approach by The Sunday Times, his spokesman distributed a statement to left-leaning newspapers about the offshore trusts in the hope of diluting the political fallout for Labour.

Drayson was made a Labour peer by Tony Blair in May last year before being promoted to the defence team in last week's reshuffle.

He has been a prominent Labour supporter since 2001 and has donated more than £1.1m to the party.

The chancellor is known to take a dim view of wealthy individuals who employ leading accountants to devise sophisticated tax avoidance schemes.

Dead Men Don't Eat Lunch

The issue has become particularly sensitive because the middle classes have been hit by a series of tax rises — including a clampdown on schemes to avoid inheritance tax on family homes — to pay for Labour's spending on public services.

The Sunday Times can disclose that Drayson set up two offshore trusts — named Ventana and Amalfi — for him and his wife in 1997 shortly before PowderJect, the company he co-founded, was floated on the stock market.

Each trust, registered in Douglas, the capital of the Isle of Man, held 2.825m shares in PowderJect. Six months later the Draysons formed two offshore companies, Vardale and Sherdley, which were owned by the two trusts.

In 2003, PowderJect was bought by an American company that paid the Draysons' offshore companies more than £30m for their shares. The money was sent to the Isle of Man, beyond the grasp of the UK Inland Revenue.

Financial experts estimate that such an arrangement could have helped the Draysons to avoid at least £3m in capital-gains tax on the sale of the shares. There may also have been inheritance tax benefits.

They could also have added to their fortune, tax free, by investing in shares, property and boats via offshore trusts and companies.

Mike Warburton of accountants Grant Thornton said: "Although I cannot comment on the Draysons' circumstances, this type of offshore scheme was used to minimise British tax bills. However, the chancellor blocked this loophole in his March budget."

Labour was hit by a scandal in 1998 after it emerged that Geoffrey Robinson, then a Labour Treasury minister, benefited from an offshore trust.

Drayson's offshore links are the latest problem to beset his political career. He first rose to public prominence in 2002 for winning the contract to supply a smallpox vaccine to the government shortly after donating money to the Labour party.

The government has refused to release the minutes of a private meeting held between Drayson and the prime minister before the contract was awarded.

It has led to questions as to whether Drayson had any inside knowledge or influence.

However, he and the government were cleared of any wrongdoing by the National Audit Office and a parliamentary committee that investigated the matter.

Last year, Drayson was ennobled by Blair and donated £500,000 to the Labour party within weeks. He gave a further £500,000 last December and was appointed minister for defence procurement in last week's reshuffle.

Geoffrey Gilson

Yesterday a spokesman for Drayson said: "When Lord Drayson was an active businessman, some of his and his family's financial interests were held in trusts offshore.

"However, since entering public life Lord Drayson took steps to ensure the trusts came onshore and would be taxed accordingly.

"This move was completed last autumn. As a minister he abides by the ministerial code."

***

Well, so much for whiter than white. Tony put a crook in charge of the *Al Yamamah III* negotiations. And he wasn't put there to collect donations for Save The Children.

When it came time for New Labour to take their turn at the *Al Yamamah* trough, they made damn sure they were represented by someone who knew how to bargain, and who then knew how and where to hide the check book. And that is why Tony finally brought to a halt the SFO investigation into BAe's arms' slush fund. It had nothing to do with national security. And everything to do with the security of New Labour's political finances.

Why should the world have expected anything more from a man who, in the very same week that he spiked the SFO, became the first sitting British Prime Minister in history to be interviewed by the Police in connection with an ongoing criminal investigation? A Police inquiry, moreover, into another scam Tony used to raise money for New Labour: 'Cash-for-Peerages.' That along with 'Cash-from-Arms' will now be Tony's lasting legacy.

Plus ca change, indeed.

Dead Men Don't Eat Lunch

Bibliography

The Dirty War: Covert Strategies and Tactics Used in Political Conflicts
Martin Dillon (Routledge, 1999)

A Century of Spies: Intelligence in the Twentieth Century
Jeffery T. Richelson (Oxford University, 1995)

British Security Coordination: The Secret History of British Intelligence in the Americas, 1940-1945
Roald Dahl, William Stephenson, Nigel West (From, 1999)

Wild Bill and Intrepid: Donovan, Stephenson and the Origin of CIA
Thomas F. Troy (Yale University, 1996)

The CIA
Graham Yost (1989)

Allen Dulles: Master of Spies
James Strodes (Regnery, 1999)

Gentleman Spy: The Life of Allen Dulles
Peter Grose (University of Massachusetts, 1996)

Honorable Treachery: A History of US Intelligence, Espionage, and Covert Action, from the American Revolution to the CIA
George J. A. O'Toole (Atlantic, 1993, Reprint)

Presidents' Secret Wars: CIA and Pentagon Covert Operations from World War II through the Persian Gulf
John Prados (Dee, 1996, Revised)

Geoffrey Gilson

Reflections of a Cold Warrior: From Yalta to the Bay of Pigs
Richard M. Bissell (Yale University, 1996)

The Puzzle Palace: A Report on America's Most Secret Agency [NSA]
James Bamford (Viking, 1983)

Secrets: The CIA's War at Home
Angus MacKenzie (University of California, 1999)

Defrauding America: Encyclopedia of Secret Operations by the CIA, DEA and Other Covert Agencies
Rodney Stich (Diablo Western, 1998)

The Medusa File: Secret Crimes and Cover-ups of the US Government
Craig Roberts (Consolidated, 1997)

Warren Commission Report: Report of the President's Commission on the Assassination of President John F. Kennedy
(St. Martin's, 1992)

Deadly Secrets: The CIA-Mafia War against Castro and the Assassination of JFK
Warren Hinkle, William J. Turner (Thunder's Mouth, 1992)

The Kennedy Conspiracy
Anthony Summers (Warner, 1997)

Secret Team: The Conspiracy Behind the Assassination of JFK
L. Fletcher Prouty (Citadel, 1996)

Coup D'Etat in America: The CIA and the Assassination of John F. Kennedy
Michael Canfield, Alan J. Weberman (American Archives, 1992)

Plausible Denial: Was the CIA Involved in the Assassination of JFK?
Mark Lane (Thunder's Mouth, 1992, Reprint)

The Adamson Report: Zapruder/Bush & the CIA's Dallas Council on World Affairs (the George de Mohrenschildt Story)
Bruce Campbell Adamson (1999)

Live by the Sword: The Secret War Against Castro and the Death of JFK
Gus Russo (Bancroft, 1998)

Dead Men Don't Eat Lunch

Case Closed: Lee Harvey Oswald and the Assassination of JFK
Gerald L. Posner (Doubleday, 1994)

Appointment in Dallas: The Final Solution to the Assassination of JFK
Hugh C. McDonald, As Told to Geoffrey Bocca (Zebra, 1992)

The Assassination of Robert F. Kennedy: The Conspiracy and Cover-up
William W. Turner, John G. Christian (Thunder's Mouth, 1993)

Killing the Dream: James Earl Ray and the Assassination of Martin Luther King, Jr.
Gerald L. Posner (Harvest, 1999)

The Dark Side of Camelot
Seymour M. Hersh (Little Brown, 1997)

Rethinking Camelot: JFK, the Vietnam War, and US Political Culture
Noam Chomsky (South End, 1993)

The Secret War Against Hanoi: Kennedy and Johnson's Use of Spies, Saboteurs, and Covert Warriors in North Vietnam
Richard H. Schultz, Jr. (HarperCollins, 1999)

A Dereliction of Duty: Lyndon Johnson, Robert McNamara, the Joint Chiefs of Staff, and the Lies that led to Vietnam
H. R. McMaster (HarperCollins, 1997)

The Years of Lyndon Johnson
Robert A. Caro (Knopf, 1982)

Lost Crusade: America's Secret Cambodian Mercenaries
Peter Scott (U.S. Naval Institute, 1998)

Covert OPS: The CIA's Secret War in Laos
James E. Parker (St. Martin's, 1997)

RN: The Memoirs of Richard Nixon
Richard Milhous Nixon (Touchstone, 1990, Reprint)

The White House Years
Henry A. Kissinger (Little Brown, 1988)

Geoffrey Gilson

All the President's Men
Bob Woodward, Carl Bernstein (Touchstone, 1994)

Shadow: Five Presidents and the Legacy of Watergate, 1974-1999
Bob Woodward (Simon & Schuster, 1999)

Challenging the Secret Government: The Post-Watergate Investigation of the CIA and FBI
Kathryn S. Olmstead (University of North Carolina, 1996)

Born Again
Charles W. Colson (Revell, 1977)

Keeping Faith: Memoirs of a President
Jimmy Carter (Bantam, 1982)

Jimmy Carter: A Complementary Biography from Plains to Post-Presidency
Peter G. Bourne (Simon & Schuster, 1997)

October Surprise: America's Hostages in Iran and the Election of Ronald Reagan
Gary Sick (Times, 1992)

Honored and Betrayed: Irangate, Covert Affairs, and the Secret War in Laos
Richard Secord, Jay Wurts (Wiley, 1992)

A Very Thin Line: The Iran-Contra Affairs
Theodore Draper (Hill & Wang, 1991)

Lives, Lies and the Iran-Contra Affair
Anne Wroe (St. Martin's, 1992)

Charlie Wilson's War: the CIA and the Mujahideen in Afghanistan
George Crile (Grove, 2003)

The Politics of Heroin: CIA Complicity in the Global Drug Trade
Alfred W. McCoy (Hill, 1991)

Cocaine Politics: Drugs, Armies and the CIA in Central America
Peter Dale Scott, Jonathan Marshall (University of California, 1992)

Dark Alliance: The CIA, the Contras, and the Crack Cocaine Explosion
Gary Webb, Maxime Waten (Seven Stories, 1998)

Dead Men Don't Eat Lunch

Whiteout: The CIA, Drugs and The Press
Alexander Cockburn, Jeffrey St. Clair (Verso, 1999)

Veil: The Secret Wars of the CIA during the Reagan Administration
Bob Woodward (Buccaneer, 1994, Reprint)

A Spy for All Seasons: My Life in the CIA
Duane R. Clarridge, with Digby Diehl (Scribner, 1997)

The Master of Disguise: My Secret Life in the CIA
Antonio J. Mendez (Morrow, 1999)

Inside the Oval Office: The Secret White House Tapes from FDR to Clinton
William Doyle (Kodansha, 1999)

Compromised: Clinton, Bush, and the CIA
Terry Reed, John Cummings (Penmarin, 1995)

Confessions of a Spy: The Real Story of Aldrich Ames
Pete Earley (Putnam, 1997)

Victory: The Reagan Administration's Secret Strategy That Hastened the Collapse of the Soviet Union
Peter Schweizer (Atlantic, 1996)

At the Highest Levels: The Inside Story of the End of the Cold War
Michael R. Beschloss, Strobe Talbott (Back Bay, 1994)

The First Directorate: My 32 years in Intelligence and Espionage against the West
Oleg Kalugin, Fen Montaigne (St. Martin's, 1994)

Man Without A Face: The Autobiography of Communism's Greatest Spymaster
Markus Wolf, With Anne McElvoy (Mass Market, 1999)

The Sword and the Shield: The Mitrokhin Archive and the Secret History of the KGB
Christopher M. Andrew (Basic, 1999)

Contract on America: The Mafia Murder of John F. Kennedy
David E. Scheim (Kensington, 1991, Reprint)

Geoffrey Gilson

Crime Incorporated or Under the Clock: The Inside Story of the Mafia's First One Hundred Years
William Balsamo (Horizon, 1991)

Mafia Dynasty: The Rise and Fall of the Gambino Crime Family
John H. Davis (Mass Market, 1994, Reprint)

Wise Guy: Life in a Mafia Family
Nicholas Pileggi (Mass Market, 1990)

Bound by Honor: A Mafioso's Story
Bill Bonnano (St. Martin's, 1999)

The Pizza Connection: Lawyers, Money, Drugs, Mafia
Shana Alexander (Diane, 1999)

Latin America and the International Drug Trade (Institute of Latin American Studies)
Carlos Malamud (St. Martin's, 1997)

Whitewash: Pablo Escobar and the Cocaine Wars
Simon Strong (McClelland & Stewart, 1995, Second Edition)

Drug Politics: Dirty Money and Democracies
David C. Jordan (University of Oklahoma, 1999)

The Money Launderers: Lessons from the Drug Wars - How Billions of Illegal Dollars are Washed through Banks and Businesses
Robert E. Powis

The Laundrymen: Inside Money Laundering, the World's Third Largest Business
Jeffrey Robinson (Arcade, 1996)

Evil Money: The Inside Story of Money Laundering and Corruption in Government, Banks and Business
Rachel Ehrenfeld (Mass Market, 1994)

Safe as Houses: The Schemes and Scams behind some of the World's Greatest Financial Scandals
Sam Jaffa (Parkwest, 1997)

Dead Men Don't Eat Lunch

The Failure of the Franklin National Bank: Challenge to the International Banking System
Joan Edelman Spero (Beard, 1999)

Banking Scandals: The S&L's and BCCI
Robert Emmet Long (Wilson, 1993)

A Full Service Bank: How BCCI Stole Billions Around the World
James Ring Adams, Douglas Frantz (Pocket, 1993, Reprint)

False Profits: The Inside Story of BCCI, the World's Most Corrupt Financial Empire
Peter Truell, Larry Gurwin (Beard, 1999)

Barbarians at the Gate: The Fall of RJR Nabisco
Bryan Burrough, John Helyar (HarperCollins, 1991)

Vendetta: American Express and the Smearing of Edmond Safra
Bryan Burrough

Holy Blood, Holy Grail
Michael Baigent, Henry Lincoln, Richard Leigh (Mass Market, 1983)

The Messianic Legacy
Michael Baigent, Henry Lincoln, Richard Leigh (Mass Market, 1989)

Key to the Sacred Pattern: The Untold Story of Rennes-Le-Chateau
Henry Lincoln (St. Martin's, 1998)

The Templars' Secret Island
Erling Haagensen, Henry Lincoln (Windrush, 2000)

The Temple and The Lodge
Michael Baigent, Richard Leigh (Arcade, 1991, Reprint)

The Dead Sea Scrolls Deception
Michael Baigent, Richard Leigh (Cape, 1991)

The Secret Teachings of All Ages: An Encyclopedic Outline of Masonic, Hermetic, Qabbalistic, and Rosicrucian Symbolical Philosophy
Manly P. Hall (Philosophical Research Society, 1994)

Secret Societies: From the Ancient and Arcane to the Modern and

Geoffrey Gilson

Clandestine
David V. Barrett (Blandford, 1999)

Dungeon, Fire and Sword: The Knights Templar in the Crusades
John J. Robinson (Evans, 1992)

The Second Messiah: Templars, the Turin Shroud and the Great Secret of Freemasonry
Christopher Knight, Robert Lomas (Element, 1998)

Secrets of Jerusalem's Temple Mount
Kathleen Ritmeyer (Biblical Archaeology Society, 1998)

Jerusalem Betrayed: Ancient Prophecy and Modern Conspiracy Collide in the Holy City
Mike Evans (Word, 1997)

The Cathars and the Albigensian Crusade
Michael Costen (Manchester University, 1997)

Born in Blood: The Lost Secrets of Freemasonry
John J. Robinson (Evans, 1990)

Secret Ritual of the Thirty-Third and Last Degree Sovereign Grand Inspector General of the Ancient and Accepted Scottish Rite of Freemasonry
(Kessinger, 1997)

Emblematic Freemasonry
Arthur Edward Waite (Kessinger, 1992)

Masonry: Conspiracy against Christianity - Evidence that the Masonic Lodge has a Secret Agenda
A. Ralph Epperson (Publius, 1998)

The Secret Teachings of the Masonic Lodge: A Christian Perspective
John Ankerberg, John Weldon (Moody, 1990)

Fraternity of the Rosy Cross
Thomas Vaughan (Holmes, 1983)

The Illuminati Conspiracy
Richard Rees (1997)

Dead Men Don't Eat Lunch

Illuminati: New World Order
Steve Jackson (Castle, 1994)

Hidden Secrets of the Eastern Star: The Masonic Connection
Cathy Burns (Sharing, 1994)

The International Encyclopedia of Secret Societies and Fraternal Orders
Alan Axelrod (Checkmark, 1998)

New World Order: The Ancient Plan of Secret Societies
William T. Still (Vital, 1990)

The Occult Conspiracy: Secret Societies - Their Influence and Power in World History
Michael Howard (Inner, 1989)

The Occult: A History
Colin Wilson

The Outsider
Colin Wilson (Putnam, 1987)

The Celestine Prophecy: An Adventure
James Redfield (Warner, 1994)

The Celestine Insights: The Celestine Prophecy and the Tenth Insight
James Redfield (Warner, 1997)

The Pagan Information Pack
The Pagan Federation International (4th Edition, 1996)
HTML Version coded by Diana Aventina, NC – Belgium

The Secret Teachings of Jesus: Four Gnostic Gospels
Marvin W. Meyer (Vintage, 1986)

The First Messiah: Investigating the Savior Before Jesus
Michael O. Wise (Harper, 1999)

Vatican Council II
Xavier Rynne (Orbis, 1999)

Their Kingdom Come: Inside the Secret World of Opus Dei
Robert Hutchinson (St. Martin's, 1999)

Geoffrey Gilson

In God's Name: An Investigation into the Murder of John Paul I
David A. Yallop (Mass Market, 1997)

The Keys of This Blood: The Struggle for World Dominion between Pope Paul II, Mikhail Gorbachev and the Capitalist West
Malachi Martin, With Anne Kepler (Simon & Schuster, 1990)

How the Irish Saved Civilization: The Untold Story of Ireland's Role from the Fall of Rome to the Rise of Medieval Europe
Thomas Cahill (Doubleday, 1995)

The Gifts of the Jews: How a Tribe of Desert Nomads Changed the Way Everyone Thinks and Feels
Thomas Cahill (Doubleday, 1998)

The Secret War Against the Jews: How Western Espionage Betrayed the Jewish People
John Loftus, With Mark Aarons (St. Martin's, 1994)

Mein Kampf
Adolf Hitler (Mariner, 1999, Reissue)

The Occult Roots of Nazism: Secret Aryan Cults and Their Influences on Nazi Ideology - The Arisophists of Austria and Germany, 1890-1935
Nicholas Goodrick-Clarke (New York University, 1992)

The Spear of Destiny: The Occult Power Behind the Spear Which Pierced the Side of Christ, and its Significance in the Rise and Fall of Hitler
Trevor Ravenscroft (Weiser, 1987)

Blood in the Face: The Ku Klux Klan, Aryan Nations, Nazi Skinheads, and the Rise of a New White Culture
James Ridgeway (Thunder's Mouth, 1995)

Soldiers of God: White Supremacists and Their Holy War for America
Howard L. Bushart (Kensington, 1998)

Essential Law of Nature: The Creed of the White Church of God
Ben Kassem

Contract with America
Newt Gingrich, Dick Armey (Times, 1994)

Dead Men Don't Eat Lunch

To Renew America
Newt Gingrich (Mass Market, 1996)

The Silent Brotherhood: The Chilling Inside Story of America's Violent, Anti-Government Militia Movement
Kevin Flynn, Gary Gerhardt (Mass Market, 1995, Reprint)

The Ashes of Waco: An Investigation
Dick J. Reavis (Syracuse University, 1998, Reprint)

Others Unknown: The Oklahoma City Bombing Case and Conspiracy
Stephen Jones (Public Affairs, 1998)

None Dare Call It Conspiracy
Gary Allen (Amereon, 1976)

Hidden Agendas
John Pilger (New Press, 1999)

Secrets of the Temple: How the Federal Reserve Runs the Country
William Greider (Touchstone, 1989)

The House of Rothschild: Money's Prophets, 1798-1848
Niall Ferguson (Viking, 1998)

The House of Rothschild: The World's Bankers, 1849-1999
Niall Ferguson (Viking, 1999)

The House of Morgan: An American Banking Dynasty and the Rise of Modern Finance
Ron Chernow (Touchstone, 1991, Reprint)

The Warburgs: The Twentieth-Century Odyssey of a Remarkable Jewish Family
Ron Chernow (Vintage, 1994, Reprint)

Titan: The Life of John D. Rockefeller, Sr.
Ron Chernow (Random House, 1998)

A People's History of the United States: 1492 to the Present
Howard Zinn (Harperperennial, 1995, Revised and Updated)

Geoffrey Gilson

The Federalist Papers
Alexander Hamilton, James Madison, John Jay (Penguin, 1987, Reprint)

The Anti-Federalist Papers and the Constitutional Convention Debates
Ralph Ketcham (Mass Market, 1996)

The Debate on the Constitution: Federalist and Anti-Federalist Speeches, Articles, and Letters during the Struggle over Ratification
Bernard Bailyn (Library of America, 1993)

New Federalist Papers: Essays in Defense of the Constitution
Alan Brinkley, Nelson W. Polsby, Kathleen M. Sullivan (Norton, 1997)

Origins of the Bill of Rights
Leonard W. Levy (Yale University, 1999)

The Brethren: Inside the Supreme Court
Bob Woodward, Scott Armstrong

A History of the English-Speaking Peoples
Winston Churchill (Cassell, 1991)

The Oxford History of Medieval Europe
George Holmes (Oxford University, 1990, Reprint)

Early Modern Europe: An Oxford History
Euan Cameron (Oxford University, 1999)

The Oxford Illustrated History of Modern Europe
T. C. W. Blanning (Oxford University, 1998, Reprint)

The Story of Civilization
Will Durant, Ariel Durant (Simon & Schuster, 1983)

From Dawn to Decadence: 1500 to the Present; 500 years of Western Cultural Life
Jacques Barcun (Perennial, 2000)

A History of the Hapsburg Empire, 1273-1918
Jean Berenger (Longman, 1994)

The Great Game: The Struggle for Empire in Central Asia
Peter Hopkirk (Kodansha, 1994)

Dead Men Don't Eat Lunch

On Secret Service East of Constantinople
Peter Hopkirk (Oxford, 1995)

Like Hidden Fire: The Plot to Bring Down the British Empire
Peter Hopkirk (Kodansha, 1997)

Philby of Arabia
Elizabeth Monroe (Ithaca, 1998)

Sa'Udi Arabia
Harry St. J. B. Philby (Ayer, 1972)

Oil, God and Gold: The Story of Aramco and the Saudi Kings
Anthony Cave Brown (Houghton Mifflin, 1999)

The Rise, Corruption and Coming Fall of the House of Saud
Said K. Aburish (St. Martin's, 1996)

Abu Nidal: A Gun for Hire: The Secret Life of the World's Most Notorious Arab Terrorist
Patrick Seale (Diane, 1998)

Hizb'allah in Lebanon: The Politics of the Western Hostage Crisis
Magnus Ranstorp (St. Martin's, 1996)

Den of Lions: Memoirs of Seven Years as a Hostage
Terry A. Anderson (Mass Market, 1994, Reprint)

Taken on Trust
Terry Waite (Coronet, 1994)

Terry Waite and Ollie North: The Untold Story of the Kidnapping - and the Release
Gavin Hewitt (Diane, 1997)

Pan Am 103: The Lockerbie Crash and Cover-Up
William C. Chasey (Bridger House, 1995)

The Price of Terror: The Aftermath of Lockerbie
Allen Gerson, Jerry Adler (HarperCollins, 2001)

Terror in the Mind of God

Geoffrey Gilson

Mark Juergensmeyer (California, 2000)

Soldiers of God
Robert D. Kaplan (Vintage, 1990)

The Ends of the Earth
Robert D. Kaplan (Vintage, 1996)

Holy War, Inc: Inside the World of Osama bin Laden
Peter L. Bergen (Simon & Schuster, 2001)

Inside Al Qaeda: Global Network of Terror
Rohan Gunaratna (Columbia University Press, 2002)

Jihad -v- McWorld
Benjamin R. Barber (Random House, 1995)

Muslim Perceptions of Christianity
Elizabeth Gilson Aaron – Lecture (UNC-Chapel Hill, 2005)

Blowback: The Costs and Consequences of American Empire
Chalmers Johnson (Henry Holt, 2000)

Rogue State: A Guide to the World's Only Superpower
William Blum (Common Courage, 2000)

The War Against America: Saddam Hussein and the World Trade Center Attacks
Laurie Mylroie (Regan, 2000)

The 9/11 Commission Report: Final Report of the National Commission on Terrorist Attacks upon the United States
Thomas H. Kean, and Others (Norton, 2004)

Fateful Triangle: The United States, Israel and The Palestinians
Noam Chomsky (South End, 1999, Second Updated Edition)

Israel's Secret Wars: A History of Israel's Intelligence Services
Ian Black, Benny Morris (Grove, 1992, Reprint)

Gideon's Spies: The Secret History of the Mossad
Gordon Thomas (Diane, 1999)

Dead Men Don't Eat Lunch

By Way of Deception: The Making and Unmaking of a Mossad Officer
Victor Ostrovsky, Susan Hoy

The Other Side of Deception: A Rogue Agent Exposes the Mossad's Secret Agenda
Victor Ostrovsky

The Samson Option: Israel's Clandestine Nuclear Mission
Seymour M. Hersh (Vintage, 1993)

Profits of War: Inside the Secret US-Israeli Arms Network
Ari Ben-Menashe (Sheridan Square, 1992)

Maxwell: The Rise and Fall of Robert Maxwell and His Empire
Roy Greenslade (Birch Lane, 1992)

Death of a Tycoon: An Insider's Account of the Rise and Fall of Robert Maxwell
Nicholas Davies (St. Martin's, 1993)

The Enemy Within: MI5, Maxwell and the Scargill Affair
Seamus Milne (Verso, 1996)

Robert Maxwell – Israel's Superspy: The Life and Murder of a Media Mogul
Martin Dillon, Gordon Thomas (Carroll, 2002)

Foreign Body
Russell Davies (Bloomsbury, 1996)

The Arms Bazaar: The Companies, the Dealers, the Bribes
Anthony Sampson

Death Lobby: How the West Armed Iraq
Kenneth R. Timmerman

Arming Iraq: How the United States and Britain Secretly Built Saddam's War Machine
Mark Phythian, Nikos Passas (Northeastern University, 1996)

Spider's Web: Bush, Saddam, Thatcher and the Decade of Deceit
Alan Friedman (Diane, 1999)

The Shell Game: A True Story of Banking, Spies, Lies, Politics - and the

Geoffrey Gilson

Arming of Saddam Hussein
Peter Mantius (St. Martin's, 1995)

Arms and the Man: Dr. Gerald Bull, Iraq and the Supergun
William Lowther (Macmillan, 1991)

Guns, Lies and Spies: The Inside Story of the Supergun
Christopher Cowley (Hamish Hamilton, 1992)

The Unlikely Spy: Inside Matrix Churchill
Paul Henderson (Bloomsbury, 1993)

Betrayed: The Inside Story of the Matrix Churchill Trial
David Leigh (Bloomsbury, 1993)

The exchange of letters between the UN and Iraq – governing the rights of UNSCOM
May 1991

The Monitoring Plan [UNSCOM]
S/22871/Rev.1 of October 2nd, 1991

Notes on a meeting between Hussein Kamal and UNSCOM and IAEA
Ammam, Jordan – August 22nd 1995

The export/import monitoring mechanism
S/1995/1017 of December 7th, 1995

Twenty-six Reports of UNSCOM to UN Security Council
October 25th, 1991 through October 8th, 1999

Note on the establishment of the three panels
S/1999/100 of January 30th, 1999

The "Amorim Report" (panel concerning disarmament and future ongoing monitoring and verification issues)
S/1999/356 of March 27th, 1999

Draft Work Programme of UNMOVIC [successor to UNSCOM]
March 17th, 2003

Unresolved Disarmament Issues: Iraq's Proscribed Weapons Programmes
UNMOVIC Working Document – March 6th, 2003

Dead Men Don't Eat Lunch

Twenty-five Reports of UNMOVIC to UN Security Council
June 1st, 2000 through May 30th, 2006

Compendium Summary
UN document S/2006/420 of May 30th, 2006

Report of the Inquiry into the Export of Defense Equipment and Duel-Use Goods to Iraq and Related Prosecutions (including Appendices)
Richard Scott (HMSO, 1996)

Unclassified Report to Congress on the Acquisition of Technology Relating to Weapons of Mass Destruction and Advanced Conventional Munitions, January 1st Through June 30th, 2002
Central Intelligence Agency

Iraq's Weapons of Mass Destruction
British Government, September 2002

"A Decade of Deception and Defiance": White House Background Paper for President George W. Bush's September 12th, 2002 Speech to UN General Assembly on Saddam Hussein's Continuing WMD Program
US White House White Paper

Iraq's Weapons of Mass Destruction
Central Intelligence Agency, October 2002

The Decision to go to War in Iraq: Ninth Report of Session 2002-2003
UK Parliamentary Select Committee on Foreign Affairs, July 2003

Iraqi Weapons of Mass Destruction: Intelligence and Assessments
UK Parliamentary Intelligence and Security Committee, September 2003

Report of the Inquiry into the Circumstances Surrounding the Death of Dr. D. Kelly, CMG
The Right Honourable The Lord Hutton, January 2004

Review of Intelligence on Weapons of Mass Destruction
The Right Honourable The Lord Butler, July 2004

Comprehensive Report of the Special Advisor to the DCI on Iraq's Weapons of Mass Destruction
Iraq Survey Group, September 2004

Geoffrey Gilson

The Report of the Special Advisor to the DCI for Strategy Regarding Iraqi Weapons of Mass Destruction
US Senate Committee on Armed Services, 2005

Report to the President of the United States by the Commission on the Intelligence Capabilities of the United States Regarding Weapons of Mass Destruction
President's Commission on Intelligence Capabilities, March 2005

Knee Deep in Dishonour
Richard Norton-Taylor, Stephen Cook, Mark Lloyd (Orion, 1996)

In the Public Interest: An Account of the Thatcher Government's Involvement in the Covert Arms Trade
Gerald James (Warner, 1996)

Thatcher's Gold: The Shady Financial Dealings of Mark Thatcher
Paul Halloran, Mark Hollingsworth (Simon & Schuster, 1995)

Once a Jolly Bagman: The Memoirs of Margaret Thatcher's Fundraiser
Alistair McAlpine (Weidenfeld & Nicolson, 1997)

Dirty politics, Dirty times: My Fight with Wapping and New Labour
Michael A. Ashcroft (MAA Publishing, 2005)

In Defense of the Party: The Secret State, The Conservative Party and Dirty Tricks
Colin Challen, Mike Hughes (Medium, 1996)

The Price of Power: The Secret Funding of the Tory Party
Colin Challen (Vision/Satin, 1998)

The Path to Power
Margaret Thatcher (HarperCollins, 1996)

The Downing Street Years
Margaret Thatcher (HarperCollins, 1993)

One of Us: A Biography of Margaret Thatcher
Hugo Young (Pan, 1993)

The Conservative Party from Peel to Major

Dead Men Don't Eat Lunch

Robert Blake (Heinemann, 1997)

Disraeli
Robert Blake (Prion, 1998)

This Blessed Plot: Britain and Europe from Churchill to Blair
Hugo Young (Macmillan, 1998)

Conflict of Loyalty: The Memoirs of Margaret Thatcher's Foreign Secretary
Geoffrey Howe (Pan, 1995)

Mrs. Thatcher's Minister: The Private Diaries of Alan Clark, former Conservative Trade Minister
Alan Clark (Phoenix, 1994)

John Major: The Autobiography
John Roy Major (HarperCollins, 1997)

In Office
Norman Lamont (Little, Brown and Company, 1999)

The Liar: The Downfall of Jonathan Aitken, former Conservative Minister for Defense Procurement
Luke Harding, David Leigh, David Pallister (Fourth Estate, 1999)

Pride and Perjury
Jonathan Aitken (HarperCollins, 2000)

Open Verdict: Strange Deaths in Britain's Defense Electronics' Industry
Tony Collins

Smear!: Wilson and the Secret State
Stephen Dorril

The Silent Conspiracy
Stephen Dorril (Heinemann, 1993)

The Conspirators' Hierarchy: The Committee of Three Hundred
John Coleman (American West, 1992)

Enemies of the State
Gary Murray (Simon & Schuster, 1994)

Geoffrey Gilson

The Committee: Political Assassination in Northern Ireland
Sean McPhilemy (Rinehart, 1998)

Thatcher's Private War: The True Story of a Secret Agent and Hitman Working for Thatcher's Government
Nicholas Davies (Blake, 1998)

SAS, the Illustrated History
Barry Davies (London Bridge, 1997)

The Feathermen: Protectors of the SAS
Ranulph Fiennes (Bloomsbury, 1991)

A Web of Deception
Chapman Pincher (Sidgwick & Jackson, 1987)

Traitors
Chapman Pincher (Sidgwick & Jackson, 1987)

Faber Book of Espionage
Nigel West (Faber, 1994)

Faber Book of Treachery
Nigel West (Faber, 1997)

The Illegals
Nigel West (Hodder & Stoughton, 1993)

Counterfeit Spies
Nigel West (Warner, 1999)

The Cambridge Spies: The Untold Story of Maclean, Philby, Burgess in America
Verne W. Newton (Madison, 1991)

Spycatcher
Peter Wright

GCHQ: The Secret Wireless War, 1900-1986
Nigel West

MI5: British Security Service
Nigel West

Dead Men Don't Eat Lunch

Defending the Realm: MI5 and the Shayler Affair
Mark Hollingsworth, Nick Fielding (Deutsch, 1999)

Inside Intelligence: Memoirs of an MI6 Officer
Anthony Cavendish (HarperCollins, 1997)

MI6: Fifty Years of Special Operations
Stephen Dorril (Fourth Estate, 2000)

Diana: Her True Story
Andrew Morton (O'Mara, 1997)

Diana in Focus
Mark Saunders, Trevor Anthony Holt, Glenn Harvey (Blake, 1996)

Death of a Princess: The Investigation
Thomas Sancton, Scott Macleod (Weidenfeld & Nicolson, 1998)

Who Killed Diana?: An Investigation into the Various Conspiracy Theories concerning the Death of Princess Diana and Dodi Fayed
Simon Regan (Scallywag, 1998)

Diana, Queen of Hearts - CIA/MI6, the Princedom of Darkness
Dennis McDonough, Bruce Campbell Adamson (1998)

The Bodyguard's Story
Trevor Rees-Jones (Little, Brown and Company, 2000)

***

The Thirty-Nine Steps
John Buchan

Tinker Tailor Soldier Spy, Smiley's People, The Honourable Schoolboy, The Secret Pilgrim, The Russia House, A Perfect Spy, Our Game, The Night Manager
John Le Carre

Berlin Game, Mexico Set, London Match, Spy Hook, Spy Line, Spy Sinker
Len Deighton

The Day of the Jackal, The Odessa File, The Dogs of War, The Fourth

Geoffrey Gilson

Protocol, The Fist of God, The Devil's Alternative, The Negotiator, Icon
Frederick Forsyth

The Spy in Question, Spy Shadow, War Dance
Tim Sebastian

GBHP1
http://www.btinternet.com/~chief.gnome/gordon1.html

The Shoes of the Fisherman
Morris S. West

Black Lamb and Grey Falcon: A Journey through Yugoslavia
Rebecca West

Foucault's Pendulum
Umberto Eco

The Brotherhood of the Rose, The Fraternity of the Stone, The Covenant of the Flame, The Fifth Profession, The Totem, Double Image, Assumed Identity, Extreme Denial
David Morrell
The Once and Future King: The Legend of King Arthur and the Holy Grail
T. H. White

Dead Men Don't Eat Lunch

Geoffrey Gilson

Dead Men Don't Eat Lunch

The One remains, the many change and pass;
Heaven's light forever shines, Earth's shadows fly;
Life, like a dome of many-colored glass,
Stains the white radiance of Eternity.

Percy Bysshe Shelley

Geoffrey Gilson

Dead Men Don't Eat Lunch